ADVENTURES IN TEHUATL

Author: Tom Knauss

Additional Design: Tim Hitchcock and Rob Manning

Project Managers: Zach Glazar and Tom Knauss

Editor: Jeff Harkness

Art Direction: Casey Christofferson

Layout and Graphic Design: Charles A. Wright

Cover Design: Charle A. Wright

Cover Art: Adrian Landeros

Interior Art: Julio de Carvalho, Adrian Landeros, Santa Norvaisaite, Terry Pavlet, Thuan Pham, Hector Rodriguez, and Erica Willey

Cartography: Robert Altbauer

FROG GOD GAMES IS:

Bill Webb, Matthew J. Finch, Zach Glazar, Charles A. Wright, Edwin Nagy, Mike Badolato, John Barnhouse

ADVENTURES WORTH WINNING

FROG GOD GAMES

ISBN: 978-1-943067-43-5

TABLE OF CONTENTS

THE RE-EDUCATION OF COYOTL

BY TOM KNAUSS

"THE ROAD TO BECOMING AN ADULT IS BEST NOT CIRCUMVENTED BY SHORTCUTS."

— AN AZTLI PROVERB

The Re-education of Coyotl is an adventure for four Tier 2 characters and introduces them to the lands and people of Tehuatl. The opening foray into the world of Tehuatl takes the heroes into a local calmecac, where the teenage boys and their newly anointed leader Coyotl appear to have taken control of the boarding school and now run amok in the absence of any instructors or other authority figures. Bloodthirsty canines and other horrors seemingly under the children's control roam the grounds, apparently performing the bidding of their power mad adolescent master. Although the adventure may be run as a standalone product, it offers an ideal opportunity to gradually present the people and cultures of Tehuatl in an adventure setting.

ADVENTURE BACKGROUND

Whether consciously or by sheer accident, Coyotl, the second son of a prominent Aztli family, always emulated the traits of the canine hunter who shares his name. From an early age, the wily little brother demonstrated remarkable resourcefulness and an aptitude for outwitting or tricking his opponents during any contest or game. These traits served the youngster well, as he desperately lacked the physical size and strength bequeathed to his older brother Ezel, who seemed destined to become a great warrior. Although separated by only 18 months, the brawny Ezel towered over his wiry, younger sibling, giving him a decided advantage in sporting events and the martial arts. When push came to shove in Coyotl's family, Ezel received preferential treatment from his parents who admired his combat prowess and athleticism over Coyotl's intelligence and cunning.

As the sons of a noble family, Ezel and Coyotl spent most of their childhood away from home at the local calmecac, which operated under the guidance of the local temple of Nonotzali and its high priest Aloc. It was there that they received their formal education. Despite being the younger sibling, Coyotl always bested his older brother in academic pursuits, a harsh reality that greatly rankled the fiercely competitive Ezel. Indeed, Coyotl frequently gloated about his scholarly achievements to further antagonize his larger rival in the controlled setting of the calmecac. Yet the tables ignominiously turned on Coyotl when he turned 15 and began his military training. Now firmly in his brother's domain, the older Ezel pounded his younger and significantly smaller sibling into submission on an almost daily basis. In addition to routinely meting out decisive beatings to his younger brother, Ezel copycatted his rival's behavior by crowing over his fallen foe. Naturally, Coyotl seethed over losing the upper hand in his lifelong rivalry against his older brother. He vowed to reverse his newfound fortunes and defeat his sibling by any means necessary.

Coyotl recalled overhearing Aloc and his acolytes occasionally speak in hushed whispers about Ozhuma, a hermetic magician who lived in a secluded cave east of the school. Although his instructors feared the dangerous man who allegedly communed with the spirits of the netherworld, the desperate young man brushed their warnings aside and visited the reclusive spellcaster. When he told the wizened old man his name, Ozhuma's eyes sparkled.

"The coyote runs deep in your blood," the magician uttered while he raised his index finger above his eye. With a deliberate motion, he dragged his outstretched finger across the boy's forearm and drew blood with his sharpened cuticle. "Now, release the beast residing within you," he cryptically muttered. After this brief exchange, the old man dismissed his young counterpart. He refused to speak any further, leaving Coyotl at a loss to interpret the magician's enigmatic words and deeds. However, their hidden meaning became abundantly clear when the full moon appeared in the heavens the following evening.

A cold sweat inexplicably overcame the young man while hunger pangs wracked his empty belly. He instinctually curled into the fetal position, where he watched fur suddenly sprout from his arms and claws emerge from his paw-like hands. His jaw elongated, and fangs tore through his bloody gums. Much to his horror and delight, he became a coyote. Ozhuma's words and actions now made sense. He embraced what he had become and over the next few months, he learned to control the transformations, even under extreme duress including during his one-sided sparring sessions with Ezel. During his fleeting metamorphoses, the vile god Itzcuin, a shapeshifter in his own right, crept into his troubled mind and filled his thoughts with images of carnage and slaughter.

While Coyotl developed the ability to trigger or end his ability to change forms at will, he could no longer contain the primeval rage fuming inside of him. One night, the angry flames burned too bright for him to repress any longer. Consumed with bloodlust, he snuck into the acolytes' living quarters and savagely mauled them to death while they slept. The furious beast then confronted Aloc atop the temple of Nonotzali. In the ultimate act of sacrilege, he knocked the priest unconscious, placed him atop the sacred altar, and ripped his heart from his chest with his teeth. Coyotl then roused his brother from a deep sleep, poking his wet nose against his flesh while slowly slobbering onto his skin. The startled man awoke from a pleasant dream and slipped into a terrifying nightmare. After briefly taunting him, Coyotl leapt onto his brother, sank his teeth into his neck, and tore out his arteries, veins, and muscles in a single bite.

With their adult supervision and authority figures out of the way, Coyotl gave the remaining pupils an ultimatum: Obey him or perish. The menacing circle of coyotes surrounding the bewildered and frightened students bolstered the half-man/half-beast's threat. Within minutes, the vast majority of young people acquiesced to his demands. The handful who openly resisted his call soon met a gruesome end as Coyotl and his loyal underlings tore them apart within minutes. By the following morning, a new hierarchy emerged within the calmecac. Without any structure or authority, the children and their leader established a new pecking order. Under the accommodating gaze of their self-appointed headmaster, Coyotl's ardent supporters abandoned Nonotzali's teachings and devolved into an unruly, savage mob devoid of rules or morality, where the strong bully the weak into utter submission.

Although he exercises absolute authority over the calmecac and the temple, the impulsively violent Coyotl never formulated any strategy to keep Teohuacan at bay. While Itzcuin blessed him with newfound magical abilities, the cunning lycanthrope realizes he and his followers lack the military might to subjugate the neighboring town. However, he also knows that the settlement is unlikely to launch a full-scale assault against their own children, giving him some time to devise a scheme to even the odds against his adversaries. In furtherance of this end, he is in the midst of conducting a depraved experiment on his less enthusiastic followers. In an attempt to unleash their inner beasts, he mixes ground cacao beans with saliva from rabid dogs and gives this lethal concoction to some of the calmecac's students in a deliberate effort to transform them into savage beasts. Despite these efforts, the petulant teenager truly has no grand plan other than to indulge his impulsive, violent whims. Even without a cohesive strategy, Coyotl's reign of terror claims numerous lives and threatens to envelop the neighboring town of Teohuacan in mayhem as fathers may ultimately have to do battle against their sons solely for Itzcuin's and the werecoyote's amusement.

Adventure Synopsis

The characters begin the adventure roughly three weeks after Coyotl staged his coup in the calmecac adjacent to the settlement. If they are traveling to Teohuacan from another locale, they may explore the areas surrounding the town, including Ozhuma's cave on Teohuacan's outskirts. When the adventurers arrive in Teohuacan, residents and visitors alike appear in a jovial mood with the rain harvest festival just a few days away. However, the calmecac has largely fallen silent. The strange events greatly trouble the ruling hierarchy, who want to simultaneously get answers to these burning questions without unnecessarily bucking the temple of Nonotzali's autonomy. Several days earlier, a covert team of jaguar warriors sent to investigate the activities at the calmecac never returned, fueling speculation that something untoward is taking place on the school grounds. The adventurers present the perfect opportunity to infiltrate the calmecac without directly challenging the administrators' authority or ruffling the feathers of influential parents whose sons may be involved in scandalous activities. Unbeknownst to the town's adult residents, several of Coyotl's loyal minions anonymously walk among the townsfolk, where they relish any opportunity to eradicate potential threats to his burgeoning regime.

When the characters arrive at the calmecac at the behest of one or more concerned parties, they find the grounds in disarray. Wild coyotes and other beasts freely roam through the compound, while unruly teenagers indulge their cruelest whims and vilest fantasies without restraint. During their interactions with the undisciplined youth, the characters realize some are voluntarily acting out their darkest impulses. On the other hand, some youngsters suffer from the early stages of the deadly rabies virus (see **Appendix B**) that Coyotl deliberately transmitted to them through a contaminated cacao drink. During their investigation, the characters also discover that Coyotl is a werecoyote who butchered Aloc and his acolytes and then took control of the calmecac. His bestial nature and faith in Itzcuin captured the interest of several demonic minions who joined his ragtag band of followers. Despite Coyotl's absolute authority over the school, the characters meet a disorganized response as they make their way across its grounds and its residential structures.

After seizing control of the calmecac, Coyotl repurposed the temple of Nonotzali to serve as his command post, even though he has no coherent plan to combat Teohuacan's authorities. Nonetheless, the characters must wade through its bolstered defenses of loyal servants, demonic underlings, and insidious traps to reach its inner recesses where the horror and folly of Coyotl's scheme come into full view. The characters must bypass the formidable temple vault door to confront the teenager who perpetrated the calmecac's numerous atrocities. The wily lycanthrope hides behind his lackeys until he senses an ideal opportunity to ambush the unsuspecting adventurers, who must then vanquish him in this climactic battle to free the school from his and Itzcuin's baleful influence. If the characters defeat him, they and Teohuacan's authorities face the messy task of separating the guilty parties from the innocent children corrupted by Coyotl's tainted chocolate treat.

Starting the Adventure

For characters hailing from other locales within the Lost Lands, the adventure begins with a lengthy sea voyage from a distant port in Akados or Libynos. In this case, you must decide whether the heroes intentionally sailed for the shores of Tehuatl after perhaps hearing rumors about vast stores of gold or silver in these mysterious, unknown lands, or they got lost at sea and accidently landed on the large island's eastern beach. In either event, you may read or paraphrase the following description or recount their long days at sea with an original composition.

Characters indigenous to the lands of Tehuatl may omit the preceding sea voyage description and instead undertake an overland trek to the small town of Teohuacan for a specific purpose or on their way to another location.

Hooks

As the introductory adventure to the island of Tehuatl, the characters can become embroiled in the adventure in a multitude of ways. Characters originally from other areas of the Lost Lands, such as Akados, Libynos, or even the Razor Coast, must arrive here by sea. They can then stumble upon the town of Teohuacan by accident while wandering through the surrounding wilderness or receive some incentive to trek to the settlement, such as purchasing provisions in its marketplace or hearing a tale about its purported riches. Characters from Tehuatl may already live in Teohuacan or are traveling there from somewhere else to visit a relative, attend a ceremony, or participate in a local event. Alternatively, an individual residing in the town may summon the characters to the settlement for a different purpose. With the preceding ideas in mind, you may use one of the following hooks to draw the characters into the story or create a unique way to entice the heroes to make their way to Teohuacan.

Missing Dog

A hairless **dog** (use the **jackal** stat block and remove the Pack Tactics trait) with light tan skin digs its paw into the ground. Standing roughly two feet tall at the shoulder and weighing approximately 50 pounds, the obviously distressed canine with bat-like ears repeatedly barks at the characters and then turns in the opposite direction, as if beckoning them to follow. The animal wears a leather collar adorned with blue and red stones around its neck. Pictographs inscribed onto the collar indicate the dog's name is Zot. If the characters accept the dog's invitation to join him, he leads them to his hometown of Teohuacan and then to the calmecac where he lived until Coyotl killed his master Patil, one of the acolytes. If a character can communicate with Zot, the dog tells him that he found his owner's body drenched in a pool of blood, though he is unaware of the circumstance's surrounding Patil's untimely demise. Fearful of the coyotes now freely wandering the school's grounds, the clever animal slipped past the wild beasts during the night, though his circuitous route completely bypassed the town.

Religious Festival

Communities dependent upon agriculture rightly fear nature's unpredictable whims. Excessive heat or an early frost can severely damage crops, but these perils pale in comparison to the trepidation accompanying a long dry spell. Without water, plants eventually wither and die. Three times per year, Aztli communities gather to partake in the rain festival celebration, where they beseech the rain god Quiahuitl to call water down from the skies to nourish the maize and grasses. The nearby town of Teohuacan hosts one of the largest celebrations in the area, drawing visitors from the neighboring settlements to the sprawling community. In this circumstance, the characters may already reside in or be traveling to Teohuacan to partake in the celebration firsthand, or **Mintoch** (see **Teohuacan** heading below), the resident cleric of Quiahuitl, invited them to join him and his followers at the ceremony.

School Haze

In anticipation of the upcoming rain festival celebration, the temple of Quiahuitl usually dismisses its students to allow them to join their families for the revelry. However, the calmecac remains eerily quiet. Indeed, Aloc and his acolytes appear to have done nothing to prepare for the massive event. Meanwhile, the children attending the calmecac remain sequestered behind its walls, sparking concern from some worrisome parents. However, every time someone approaches the calmecac's entrance to inquire about their children, growling coyotes seemingly appear out of nowhere to block the way. While the temple stands silent, bloodcurdling screams periodically emanate from behind the school's impressive walls, prompting more cause for alarm. At the urging of the several concerned mothers, **Mintoch,** (see **Teohuacan**) the high priest of Quiahuitl, sent four jaguar warriors into the compound under the cover of darkness to investigate the strange occurrences at the calmecac. None of these accomplished soldiers returned to report their findings.

RUMORS

Characters spending at least several weeks at sea before arriving on Tehuatl's shores undoubtedly hear strange tales about the lands south of Akados and Libynos, if they were intentionally heading toward this foreign realm. Otherwise, adventurers who washed ashore by accident likely know nothing about this new world. Aztli heroes obviously have a far better lay of the land than a stranger. Therefore, they have advantage on Intelligence (History) checks and Intelligence (Religion) checks when attempting to recall information about local events and faiths. Conversely, characters from other lands who are unfamiliar with Tehuatl and its people suffer disadvantage on the preceding checks. Characters who succeed on Charisma checks regardless of their background may learn gossip and rumors from third-party sources if they can effectively communicate with the individual and if the person has some knowledge of the area.

A character who succeeds on a DC 10 Intelligence (History) check or Intelligence (Religion) check as noted below recalls or learns the following details about the area. Likewise, a character who succeeds on a DC 15 Charisma check and meets the preceding conditions for doing so may also discover any of the following facts about the area:

Three times per year, the temple of Quiahuitl in the town of Teohuacan holds the rain festival celebration. The next event takes place a few days from now. (Charisma, History, or Religion)

The Aztli people represent the largest human ethnic group in the region. They worship a large pantheon of deities with Nonotzali being the most important of them. Lesser populations of Tlotls and Tulita live among them. The latter group of humans venerate different gods than the Aztlis. (Charisma, History, or Religion)

Most inhabitants wield weapons crafted from bone, stone, and wood. The Tlotls tightly guard the secrets of forging iron and steel, though they sell some of their handiwork to those willing to pay their hefty prices. (Charisma or History)

Local residents have noticed an increase in coyote attacks and activity over the last few months. (Charisma check only)

A juvenile black dragon swims through the shallow channels and tributaries searching for a secluded spot to take up residence. (This is a false rumor.)

Gnolls have made a resurgence under a new chieftain they call Necapaluma. They plan to attack the small villages and towns in the near future. (Charisma or History. This rumor is partially true. Gnolls have reappeared in the area under their new leader, though a large-scale assault is not currently imminent.)

A character who succeeds on a DC 15 Intelligence (History) check or Intelligence (Religion) check as noted below recalls or learns the following details about the area. Likewise, a character who succeeds on a DC 20 Charisma check and meets the preceding conditions for doing so may also discover any of the following facts about the area:

The Tlotls originally descend from an Akadonian and his crew who came to Tehuatl centuries ago at the direction of a mysterious infernal being. Because countless generations have come and gone since their arrival, the Tlotls bear little resemblance to their forebears and appear more like the indigenous people than an Akadonian. (History and Religion)

An old hermit named Ozhuma lives on the outskirts of town. Many residents fear the recluse, claiming he made a pact with a foul being from the underworld in exchange for his powers of foresight. (Charisma, History, or Religion. This rumor is mostly true. Ozhuma is a warlock with exceptional powers of observation, but he cannot see into the future.)

A crotchety swamp troll the residents derogatorily call Fish Breath occasionally butchers a local fisherman or child who strays too far into the swamp. The townsfolk have undertaken several efforts to get rid of the oafish brute, but to no avail. (Charisma or History)

The Tulita gather in the swamp during the rain festival celebration to practice their bizarre rituals dedicated to their strange gods. (Charisma or Religion. This is a false rumor.)

TEOHUACAN REGIONAL MAP

The town of Teohuacan is the largest settlement in the sparsely populated and generally inhospitable Izmalli Swamp. It lies near the banks of the Elcomatl River and Lake Tlacuca, giving it access to a navigable waterway and bodies of water well stocked with fish. The water from the saline Elcomatl River is not potable. Therefore, the town's engineers built an aqueduct transporting freshwater from Lake Tlacuca into the community. Characters traveling to Tehuatl by sea arrive at the designated landing point on the map between the Elcomatl River and the path leading from shore to Teohuacan. If the adventurers are native to Tehuatl, they may begin their journey in one of the small settlements scattered throughout the area or at an intersection along a river or other landmark.

The following section describes the small towns and villages appearing on the local map. With a few exceptions, these settlements and geographical landmarks are generally too small to warrant extensive discussion in the *Tehuatl* sourcebook. Therefore, they are presented below for you to use if the characters hail from one of these locales or visit them during the course of the adventure.

AMEKA RIVER

Although the mangrove trees and hillocks encountered in the river's delta allow water to flow through these barriers, the tangle of branches, roots, and loose earth make it impossible to navigate a vessel larger than a canoe past this immovable obstacle. The strong current passing through its cataracts and rapids pose an even greater impediment to river travel. The Ameka River can be safely crossed only at a few points generally corresponding with the paths connecting the town of Milpachi to Ollitl and Teohuacan.

COMATL RIVER

The gentle current funnels saltwater from the neighboring ocean into the swamp until the waterway joins forces with an even larger river farther inland. The river measures 30 feet across in most spots with some fluctuations in width ranging from nine feet in a few isolated locations to 58 feet at its widest point. However, the slow-moving river is remarkably shallow, reaching a maximum depth of eight feet with most sections averaging approximately 3–1/2 feet, making it easy to ford. The challenge in getting across the Comatl River lies in avoiding the numerous crocodiles inhabiting its murky waters.

ELCOMATL RIVER

Few locals refer to this river by its proper name. Instead, they call it "The Little" as its official moniker literally translates to Little Comatl.

LAKE TLACUCA

Although found in a saltwater swamp, Lake Tlacuca displays features more typically found in a freshwater fen. The low-lying basin collects precipitation that falls in the immediate area, though groundwater seeping into the otherwise closed system mitigates the water's acidity.

LAKE ZUPIL

This vaguely bean-shaped saltwater lake reaches a maximum depth of 25 feet near its center, though the waters along its edges are only a few feet deep. Brine shrimp are the dominant form of marine life in this otherwise desolate ecosystem. Mangrove trees and shrubs grow in the shallow water covering the lake's banks. Some birds also feed and wade in these waters. The Aztlis swear the lake is cursed, which causes them to steer a wide berth around its condemned waters. Other human ethnicities and humanoid races scoff at this notion, though they rarely, if ever, venture to its bleak shores.

TEOHUACAN REGIONAL MAP
N
Izmalli Swamp
Xica
Elcomatl River
Comatl River
Teohuacan
Lake Tlacuca
Namatl River
Landing Site
Sacatl
Lake Zopil
Ameka River
Milpachi
1 Square – 2 Miles

Milpachi

Population: 464
Ruler: High Priest Ihcalzuma
Government: Aztli Confederation

Macabre images of dancing skeletons and festive corpses cover nearly every manmade surface in this small town. Despite the plethora of gruesome artwork bombarding the senses, the people paradoxically seem happy and lively, reveling in celebrating the lives of the dearly departed. Terraces cut into the face of a plateau house the mausoleums containing the earthly remains of the dead, while the temple of Micoateotl, the Aztli god of the dead, sits atop the elevated mound. Indeed, most wealthy Aztli families from other towns throughout the region make a pilgrimage here to bury their beloved family members, visit their graves on important religious holidays, or to commemorate a special day in the decedent's life such as the anniversary of their death or their birthday.

Milpachi's economy is built around its mausoleum and the steady influx of mourners that the tombs attract. Local florists design custom-made wreaths and other decorative items to adorn individual graves, while skilled artisans sculpt likenesses of the gods and the decedent onto monuments raised above their crypt or create funerary objects such as statuettes and jewelry to be interred with the body. Milpachi also offers the services of professional mourners known as chocas. Some specialize at carrying out hysterical displays of faux grief during the person's interment. Others offer to perform stirring eulogies at their graveside, while a small segment of this occupation engage in acts of self-mutilation or bloodletting as a sacrifice to the gods.

Namatl River

Rip currents scattered along the length of this narrow river make the waterway especially treacherous for swimmers and vessels alike. The swift yet unpredictable flow of water may impede humanoid travel, but it offers a boon to the shellfish and shrimp that live along the silty riverbed. Causeways placed at strategic locations allow travelers to safely cross the turbulent river.

Ollitl

Population: 386
Ruler: Jaguar Cuauhocelotl Imotica
Government: Aztli Confederation

Almost everyone in this community earns a living from the sea. Every morning, fishing boats set sail for the nearby ocean and return in the evening with the day's catch. Tulitas make up a significant percentage of the population, though Aztlis remain in the majority. Quell, the Tulitas' god of the sea, enjoys a widespread following in the community even among the Aztli who incorporated the deity into their pantheon of gods. The fusion of cultures is most evident in its unique cuisine, which blends maize-based dishes with seafood stews and gumbos. Despite sharing some aspects of their individual cultures, the village's leader, Jaguar Cuauhocelotl Imotica, strictly forbids Aztlis from marrying Tulitas. Although the prohibition does not explicitly preclude having a romantic relationship with a Tulita man or woman, a child produced from an unauthorized union between an Aztli and a Tulita never lives to see his or her first birthday. Under Imotica's supervision, the infant's young life ends as a sacrifice to Quiahuitl during the rain ceremony festival. Aztli mothers usually freely give up their newborns to appease their gods, deeming the infants' death as a small price to pay for engaging in taboo behavior. Conversely, Tulita mothers fervently cling to their illegitimate children. Some leave the village shortly after learning of their pregnancy to give birth in secret. Other common practices include entering into a sham marriage with a Tulita man to attempt to pass the infant off as their progeny and imbibing a malodorous cocktail known as moxtica to induce a miscarriage.

Sakatl

Population: 233
Ruler: High Priest Lacui
Government: Aztli Confederation

This small settlement benefits from the luxury of sitting atop an elevated parcel of land that allows its residents to plant crops without the incessant fear of losing them to flooding. The raised mound is also large enough to support the grazing needs of livestock animals, making Sakatl one of the few communities within the Izmalli Swamp to produce wool and milk. Because of the people's dependence upon rain to water their crops and nourish the grasses, humanoid sacrifices to Quiahuitl occur with frequent regularity. To satisfy the fickle deity's appetite for blood, his high priest Lacui offers cueyatls, gnolls, and orcs to his divine patron, though when supplies of these hated foes run low, the priest looks toward the villagers to make up the difference. Not surprisingly, Quiahuitl's followers give Lacui the least meritorious citizens for this dubious honor.

Traders from other neighboring towns and villages venture to Sakatl's farmers' market to barter for wool, milk, and maize. The merchants offer pelts, leather, and other commodities in exchange for Sakatl's rare items. Although they live in a remote community, the villagers are shrewd negotiators who rival any cosmopolitan peddler. They strike a hard bargain for their coveted wares. Sakatl's residents have no tolerance for an unscrupulous trader who tries to pull a fast one on their citizens, especially if the person is not of Aztli descent. On more than one occasion, an unsavory merchant got more than he bargained for when Lacui removed his still-beating heart from his chest while strapped to a sacrificial altar.

Xica

Population: 319
Ruler: Jaguar Cuauhocelotl Cipali
Government: Aztli Confederation

The people of Xica engage in a dangerous profession: crocodile hunting. Although they live far from a significant body of water, the aggressive reptiles thrive in the shallow streams and small tributaries surrounding their community. Some of these hungry beasts occasionally wander into Xica proper in search of a meal or for some other unknown purpose. Despite their expertise combating these creatures, fatalities still occur with alarming regularity. It is not uncommon to see a resident proudly displaying their battle scars from a disastrous encounter with a hungry croc or walking around the village with a missing hand or arm, which serves as a constant reminder of a rendezvous gone terribly wrong. However, the rewards gained from the perilous profession still outweigh the risks in the minds of most Xicans. The durable hide, meat, and other byproducts procured from the beasts fetch a handsome price from traders in neighboring communities, making their efforts worthwhile.

Although still predominately Aztli, many neighboring settlements equate Xicans with suicidal madmen. The Aztli warrior culture loathes fear, yet in their minds, combating an enemy warrior on the field of battle is a sacred duty. Wrestling a crocodile in a muddy stream seems like lunacy. Those engaging in this hazardous occupation have over time adopted a gruffer and less sophisticated demeanor than the townsfolk and villagers in neighboring settlements, giving the Xicans an undeserved reputation for being backward, even though they are just as well educated as their counterparts.

Conditions in the Izmalli Swamp

The Izmalli Swamp is a semitropical saltwater swamp supporting many small streams and ponds as well as several rivers and lakes. Although it is currently the dry season in Tehuatl, the earth remains spongy where grass grows and soggy in areas lacking any vegetation. In wilderness areas, the ground is treated as difficult terrain in all locations. Teohuacan's drainage system keeps soil within the town firm and reasonably dry, allowing characters to treat the area as normal terrain.

The Wilderness

Unless the characters begin the adventure in Teohuacan, they must spend some time trekking through the swamp surrounding the settlement before they reach their intended destination. When the adventurers enter the wetlands, read or paraphrase the following description of the area:

Saplings, shrubs, and other woody plants protrude from the damp earth partially covered by pools of standing water and tiny streams in some isolated sections. Mangrove trees and shrubs tower over the shorter vegetation, though the arboreal giants lack the height and density to create a true canopy over the swamp. A faint yet seemingly omnipresent buzzing sound lingers in the background with an occasional crescendo indicating a winged pest's impending arrival.

The villagers and townsfolk always stick to the downtrodden paths winding a route through the foliage. These makeshift roads predominately connect the settlements to one another and other points of interest in the region. Despite hosting more traffic than the unspoiled wilderness, these thoroughfares offer no guarantees of safety. Wild animals generally prefer avoiding contact with humanoids, but the same cannot always be said of men and monsters. For every hour spent trekking through the untracked wilderness around Teohuacan, there is a 50% chance of encountering one of the creatures appearing on **Table 1–1**. If the characters exclusively remain on the paths, the chance decreases to 25%, and they encounter only humanoids or monsters. A rendezvous with an animal is rerolled until the adventurers run into a humanoid or monster. When the characters approach within five miles of Teohuacan, the detailed map of the area surrounding the settlement determines whether they participate in a set encounter based upon the route they choose or deliberately venture to the predesignated location.

Table 1–1: Teohuacan Wilderness Random Encounters

1d10	Encounter
1	2d3 **Aztli hunters**
2	1d3+1 **Aztli jaguar warriors**
3	1d4+1 **beasts of Itzcuin**
4	1d4+1 **cadavers**
5	1d2 **cipatenhuas** plus a **cipatenhua disciple**
6	1d4 **crocodiles**
7	1d4 **gnolls**
8	1 **jaculus**
9	2d4 **orcs** plus an **orc sacrificial priest**
10	1d2 **swamp trolls**

Aztli Hunters

These **Aztli hunters** (LN male Aztli human **commoner**) from Teohuacan generally stay on the path until they spot prey from their vantage point on the road or deviate from the trail at a predesignated location where they have experienced past success. They give the appearance of nonchalantly going about their business, though they keep a very wary eye on outsiders. Despite their cavalier attitude, a character who succeeds on a DC 10 Wisdom (Insight) check senses their apprehension. The hunters never verbally acknowledge their nervousness. However, if the character allays their trepidation and earns their trust by succeeding on a DC 10 Charisma check (grant the character advantage on the check for an effective plea), the men tell the adventurers they must be constantly wary of the "fish-men" who roam the swamp. Otherwise, the hunters ignore the passersby and attend to their designated task at hand, while constantly glancing at strangers from another land.

Aztli Jaguar Warriors

Although the **Aztli jaguar warriors** (N male Aztli human **scout** armed with macuahuitls [see **Appendix C: New Equipment and Magic Items**] instead of shortswords) from Teohuacan pounce on the opportunity to kill game wandering too close to them, the attentive armed soldiers predominately look out for monstrous denizens trespassing in what they consider their territory. Unlike the hunters, these seasoned warriors display no signs of fear. Furthermore, they aggressively confront any non-Aztli they meet, vigorously questioning the interlopers in their native Aztli tongue while refusing to converse in any other language. If the characters give them a concise, plausible answer — such as mentioning the rain festival celebration or visiting the calmecac — the jaguar warriors back down and allow them to continue on their journey. The characters can appease the naturally suspicious jaguar warriors with a successful DC 10 Charisma check or Charisma (Deception) check, if the adventurer opts to tell the warriors a tall tale about their reason for infringing on their territory. In the absence of a satisfactory answer, the jaguar warriors attempt to detain the trespassers or attack the characters if they resist. Characters who satisfy the jaguar warriors' inquiries may in turn ask them questions about recent events in Teohuacan. Under these circumstances, the jaguar warriors sheepishly admit four of their fellow warriors never returned from their mission to infiltrate the calmecac several days earlier to investigate the inactivity at the temple of Nonotzali and the inability to contact the children residing within the school.

Beasts of Itzcuin

At first glance, these vicious canines appear to be mangy, oversized coyotes, but a closer examination reveals odd yet harmless deformities suggesting someone or something horribly altered these poor creatures. These mutations include grotesque underbites; elongated, flappy ears; mismatching eye colors; stubby tails; and other minor defects that solely affect its appearance and not its performance. Indeed, the vile god Itzcuin twisted these ordinary dogs into bestial abominations. Furthermore, their ability to verbally communicate among themselves and others immediately sets them apart from ordinary dogs. The **beasts of Itzcuin** (see **Appendix A: New Monsters**) dispense with pretenses and attack on sight, using their pack tactics to surround and maul one or more designated enemies. Although they speak Aztli, they refuse to converse with the characters unless compelled against their will. These beasts associate with the hermit Ozhuma and have no knowledge of the events at the temple of Nonotzali or the calmecac.

Cadavers

The wilderness claims many victims, and few of them go gently into that good night or receive a proper sendoff. These **cadavers** (see **Appendix A: New Monsters**) number among them. The Aztli teenagers who transformed into these shambling undead abominations foolishly ingested saline swamp water while frolicking in a deep pond. The salt content made them delirious and dehydrated. When one of them fell into the pond and started to drown, the others leapt into the water and vainly tried to rescue him. In the end, they all perished and began their existence as cadavers. The cadavers burn with hatred and anger for all living creatures, especially adult humans who remind them of the lives prematurely denied to them. Despite their shared loathing, they never act in concert with their fellow monsters. Instead, each wildly rushes their opponent in a mad attempt to slash and bite them to death.

Cipatenhuas

Cunning and clever, the predatory 2 **cipatenhuas** and the **cipatenhua disciple** (see **Appendix A: New Monsters** for both monsters) swim through the shallow, coastal waters searching for prey that blunder into their territory. Although they predominately hunt wayward vessels, the crocodilian, bipedal humanoids indiscriminately capture and kill any living creature unfortunate enough to enter their territory. They predominately stick to the rivers and streams bisecting their domain, though they occasionally take to land where their slippery, greenish skin blends into their surroundings remarkably well, giving them advantage on Dexterity (Stealth) checks made in this terrain. The vicious humanoids never flee or surrender.

Treasure: Each cipatenhua carries a greatclub and keeps a pouch containing 1d4 decorative mussel shells (worth 10 gp each) on a belt wrapped around their waists. The disciple has two pink pearls (worth 100 gp each) in a pouch affixed to his belt.

CROCODILES

These reptilian predators lurk in the shallow waters, waiting for prey to enter their territory. The **crocodiles** remain underwater, using their stealth to quietly approach their victims before lashing out with their massive jaws. Like most wild animals searching for a meal, the beasts flee when seriously threatened or injured. They retreat below the water's surface and swim to safety.

GNOLLS

As the rumors suggest, the **gnolls** in the region are stepping up their game, though the scope of their activities seems modestly exaggerated. The aggressive humanoids lack the vision to consciously expand their footprint in the area, but their inability to grasp the big picture fails to abate their bloodlust. They forego any efforts to sneak up on their quarry and instead madly charge one or two designated opponents. They always concentrate their attacks on as few opponents as possible to increase the odds of quickly dropping that foe. Gnolls who are badly overmatched escape if possible. Characters who attempt to follow their tracks back to a lair lose the trail when the monsters trudge through several streams and other small bodies of water. The gnolls have no knowledge of Teohuacan's inner workings.

Treasure: In addition to their listed equipment, each gnoll carries 2d10 gp and 1d3 obsidian stones (worth 10 gp each).

JACULUS

Although this small, light-brown dragon has feathered wings to propel it in flight, the creature is more adept at leaping than flying. The **jaculus** (see **Appendix A: New Monsters**) uses its powerful back legs to scale mangrove trees, where it makes its abode. While not brilliant by draconic standards, the monster exhibits tremendous cunning. When it spots a shiny object or other item that catches its fancy, the jaculus formulates its plan to steal the object from its unworthy owner. It may use its stealth and its darkvision to creep up during the night on a sleeping target and wrest the item from its possession while in a deep slumber. Alternatively, it can pretend to offer the characters assistance by relaying one or more of the prevalent rumors circulating throughout the region or fabricate a story the adventurers may want to hear. In this circumstance, the jaculus may provide the preceding information to acquire the object it covets as part of a bargain, or it may use the ruse to gain the characters' trust and make a bigger score after lulling them into a false sense of security. When forcibly confronted over its thievery, the jaculus stands and fights rather than making a futile attempt to outrun its adversaries or slowly fly to safety. The monster's bite and claws pack quite the punch for a creature of its small size. The naturally treacherous and suspicious jaculus never travels far from its arboreal lair carved into the trunk of a mangrove or other species of tree. Characters who search the surrounding area locate the jaculus' treetop abode from the ground with a successful DC 20 Wisdom (Perception) check.

Treasure: The jaculus keeps a *potion of healing* and a *bead of force* within an abscess inside the tree's trunk. It also stores three deep green jade stones (worth 100 gp each) and an amber brooch (worth 50 gp) in the same location.

ORCS

Orcs frequently imitate the bloody rituals conducted in other humanoid cultures. These cruel humanoids took to the practice of human sacrifice like ducks to water. The deadly rites performed by the Aztlis and other indigenous peoples carry an important religious significance, whereas the orcs seem to partake in this endeavor solely to satisfy their lust for violence. In furtherance of this end, an **orc sacrificial priest** (see **Appendix A: New Monsters**) accompanies his fellow **orcs** on their quest to find new victims to sacrifice. They gladly slaughter any sentient being as an offering to their gods, though they take fiendish delight disemboweling elves. Like most of their kind, these orcs retreat back into the swamp when seriously threatened by an obviously superior foe. They often target hunters and fishermen trekking through the wilderness to find game and a productive fishing hole, though they generally remain on the outskirts of town. Nonetheless, if compelled to speak, the orcs tell the characters that they noticed several strange beasts resembling filthy, oversized coyotes wandering through the swamp over the last few weeks.

Treasure: In addition to their listed armor and weaponry, the orc sacrificial priest carries two *scrolls* (*inflict wounds*, *spiritual weapon*) and a ceremonial obsidian dagger (worth 150 gp).

SWAMP TROLL

Despite its size, this **swamp troll** (see **Appendix A: New Monsters**), nicknamed Fish Breath by the locals, moves through the shallow water and soggy earth with surprising agility. The large, hulking brute uses its long, thick arms and legs to propel it through the water, while the sharp, filthy claws at the end of its appendages give it added traction when walking and serve as highly effective weapons. The moss and fungus covering its body, in addition to its dark brownish-green hair, allow it to blend into its surroundings, giving the remarkably nimble monster an opportunity to ambush opponents at a predetermined site or more likely to sneak up on them while they slog through the difficult terrain. The giant generally keeps a healthy distance between itself and the town of Teohuacan. Therefore, any confrontation with the swamp troll likely occurs in remote wilderness areas. However, the brute is clever enough to stalk the paths and roads leading to and from the settlements scattered throughout the region, where it exhibits no qualms killing and eating an inhabitant who wanders into its territory. Regardless of the encounter's circumstances, the swamp troll beats a hasty retreat if the characters seriously threaten its wretched existence. Because it can move through the swamp without impediment, the swamp troll stands a good chance of outrunning its pursuers. Following its tracks back to its lair through the waterlogged terrain proves virtually impossible, because the giant frequently swims atop the waterways crisscrossing the landscape. However, if the adventurers discover its hillock lair, they also locate the bulk of its treasure.

Treasure: The giant conceals an alderwood chest in its lair beneath a layer of silt and sediment on its hillock. Spotting the hidden container requires a successful DC 15 Wisdom (Perception) check. The unlocked device contains a *potion of resistance* and four *+1 arrows* as well as a bronze Aztli statue (worth 150 gp).

TEOHUACAN AREA SET ENCOUNTERS

The adventure focuses on the town of Teohuacan and its calmecac, but other residents have established permanent lairs in the surrounding area. The most noteworthy of these structures is the cipatenhua stronghold just north of the Elcomatl River. The location appears on the regional map, but it is detailed in the supplemental adventure *The Hidden Shrine of Tmocanotz*, as it is not central to this story. Other creatures have also established smaller footholds in the untamed wilderness outside of the Aztlis' influence. The following section details these areas.

AREA O: OZHUMA'S CAVE

The hermitic magician **Ozhuma** (see **Appendix A: New Monsters**) lives in a secluded cave 2-1/2 miles east of Teohuacan amid a dense tangle of mangrove shrubs and hillocks off the trail leading from Teohuacan to the coast. The devious warlock occasionally ventures to the island's shore to harvest food from the sea or to salvage treasure from the shipwrecks in the shallow depths near the beach. However, the infrequency of these jaunts and the conditions in the swamp make it extremely difficult to pick up the trail connecting his isolated cave to the path leading to the sea. The character must succeed on a DC 25 Wisdom (Survival) check to accomplish this nearly impossible task. The only other clue pointing toward Ozhuma's residence lies with the characters' knowledge of the area and their understanding of geology. A character who succeeds on a DC 15 Intelligence (Investigation) or (Nature) check recalls the location of an elevated rock formation ideally suited for an aboveground cave, if the character already reasoned that Ozhuma could not reside in a submerged cavern. Otherwise, adventurers seeking an audience with the reclusive man must bumble their way through the mass of shrubs, trees, and ponds surrounding his humble abode.

TEOHUACAN AND VICINITY
C
Elcomatl River
O
Teohuacan
N
Lake
Tlacuca
Namatl River
1 Square – 1/2 Mile

AREA 0
1 Square – 10 Feet
N

If the characters successfully locate Ozhuma's cave, you may read or paraphrase the following description:

Characters facing the cave's western side obviously see the entrance into the small chamber, while those viewing the mound from a different direction likely deduce where to find the opening by following the trail of smoke emanating from the cavity. The wily Ozhuma has a hawk familiar who always circles the area around his lair searching for prey and potential intruders. While awake, which is generally from noon until the early morning hours, Ozhuma intermittently telepathically communicates with his hawk familiar or views his surroundings through the bird's eyes. Alternatively, if he hears someone or something approaching, he may cast *clairvoyance* to monitor the trespasser's activities. If the creature poses an obvious threat, he casts *black tentacles* just outside the entrance to his cave to halt their progress while still allowing him to escape his abode without hindrance. The hermit exercises extreme caution when strangers draw near, though he may not necessarily attack intruders. If the visitor interests him, he may converse with the creature to gain knowledge about outside activities or simply to pique his curiosity. Before falling asleep, he performs *speak with animals* as a ritual to cajole a beast into keeping both eyes on the entrance to his lair and to alert him when any large creatures pass within 30 feet of the cave entrance.

If the adventurers peer into his cavern, read or paraphrase the following description:

Characters who approach Ozhuma's cave with weapons drawn and spells at the ready force the recluse to take defensive actions. If he has an available spell slot, he becomes invisible and telepathically communicates with the adventurers to gauge their intentions or, depending on the circumstances, he overtly threatens them. He is not keen on fighting the characters, though he does so if necessary, using his arsenal of cantrips and spells to fend off the intruders. Ozhuma only takes an interest in creatures with an affinity for animals, such as druids, rangers, and, of course, lycanthropes. He generally ignores everyone else and demands they leave his abode.

However, if the characters get his attention, the curmudgeon becomes surprisingly talkative, especially during discussions about animals. The normally reserved hermit divulges tales of mythical serpent warriors having no bearing on this adventure, though the rumor proves true in one of the later adventures in the series. If the subject veers onto Coyotl, the formerly gregarious Ozhuma returns to his aloof demeanor. He evasively responds to questions about the young man. Nonetheless, a character who persists may pry some information from Ozhuma with a successful opposed check. In this instance, the character who succeeds on a Charisma check, a Charisma (Intimidation) check, or a Charisma (Persuasion) check contested by Ozhuma's Charisma (Deception) check learns that the young man visited the hermit several months ago. He further reveals that the teenager suffered from lycanthropy, which gave him the power to transmute into a coyote and an enhanced affinity to interact with the roguish canines. Ozhuma has no additional information about Coyotl's actions or whereabouts after their meeting several months ago.

Treasure: The jars, beakers, and vials (worth 150 gp) on the bench contain an eclectic variety of animal byproducts such as hair, powdered bone, assorted organ tissues, and blood collected from several species. Ozhuma also has three *potions of healing* interspersed among the other items, as well as a packet of *dust of dryness*.

Teohuacan

Roughly 160 years ago, Aztli migrants founded Teohuacan atop the site of a drying lake bed. Local legends credit Teohuacan's birth to the visions of Caxto, an elderly priest of Quiahuitl. The tale claims the god directed his emissary to erect a temple in his honor on this site in his final, vivid dream before he passed on to the next world. Like many other Aztli communities, its ingenious builders used chinampas to lay the groundwork for their burgeoning settlement in a marginally hospitable land.

Today, Teohuacan is the hub of civilization in this section of the Izmalli Swamp. Situated near the Elcomatl and Namatl Rivers as well as Lake Tlacuca, the town of 1,102 residents is the largest settlement in the region. Aztlis make up a significant majority of the population, with a few pockets of elves, gnomes, and halflings living among their human counterparts. Most lead a frugal existence living off the land, harvesting maize, tomatoes, avocados, and squash in their gardens while supplementing their diets with fish harvested from the nearby lake and rivers as well as water fowl and other domesticated birds such as chickens and turkeys. Although not peasants in the typical medieval sense, the farmers who till the fields do so on property theoretically owned by the distant Aztli Confederation. Despite working and living on the same land for generations, the families who dwell in the community have no legal rights to the ground beneath their feet.

While Teohuacan and the surrounding communities fall under the dominion of the Aztli Confederation, the quartet of ruling city-states exerts little influence over the remote settlement in the heart of an overgrown wetland. Instead, jurisdiction over legal, economic, and military matters falls upon the local authorities, most notably **Mintoch**, the high priest of Quiahuitl who serves as the town's spiritual and political ruler. The temple of Quiahuitl is a three-level step pyramid decorated with seashells and iconography associated with its divine patron. Religious ceremonies take place atop its highest level, which includes a stone arch resembling the boundaries of a tidal wave and an altar where the high priest and his underlings offer feathers, maize, seashells, and an occasional animal sacrifice to their chosen deity. Mintoch is a lawful neutral male human Aztli who uses the **priest** stat block with the following changes:

He wears ichcahuipilli armor (see **Appendix C: New Equipment and Magic Items**) and has AC 11.

He is armed with a club instead of a mace, which deals 1d4 bludgeoning damage.

He speaks Aztli and Gnoll.

Mintoch leads a force of 26 **jaguar warriors** (N male Aztli human **scout** armed with macuahuitls [see **Appendix C: New Equipment and Magic Items**] instead of shortswords) complemented by a retinue of six priests (N male Aztli human **acolytes**) who reside in large residences just outside the temple grounds. They primarily function as temple guards who enforce the temple's edicts and moral code throughout Teohuacan rather than serving as the backbone for a professional army. Every adult male in Teohuacan has some martial combat training. Therefore, these citizen-soldiers make up the vast majority of Teohuacan's military forces, though the jaguar warriors associated with the temple typically lead the town's citizens into battle. These individuals use the **tribal warrior** stat block when called upon to defend their homeland against monsters or invaders.

Despite the looming rain festival celebration, the temple of Nonotzali located on the calmecac grounds has fallen silent, leaving Mintoch and his underlings to singlehandedly welcome citizens and visitors from other communities. This unexpected development sends the already irritable high priest into a grouchier mood than normal. The taciturn high priest appears at a loss for words about the situation, especially when the four jaguar warriors he dispatched to investigate the matter never returned. Although Mintoch has no verbal answers for the problems besetting Teohuacan, he has not sat still. He sent six jaguar warriors, whom he still awaits to return, into the surrounding wilderness to gather sacrifices for the festivities, including a jaguar. The high priest fervently believes that the offerings and freshly spilled blood will bring relief to the troubled settlement.

The temple currently serves as the town's seat of power, but most activity centers on the bustling marketplace. Business is usually brisk in Teohuacan's open-air shops. Local farmers, trappers, and hunters sell their products from makeshift stands, while professional traders dealing in exotic goods such as cacao, agave, and rare bird feathers occupy permanent stalls within the marketplace. The upcoming festival has the marketplace in a tizzy, as visitors and residents scour the shelves for the best deals. Shoppers with attentive ears can also overhear or solicit the town's juiciest gossip, especially as it pertains to events in the local calmecac.

Rumors

Characters who interact with the peddlers or their customers may learn the following information with a successful DC 15 Charisma check. Of course, the character must be able to effectively communicate with the person, and that individual must have some knowledge of current events within Teohuacan. Furthermore, a character who succeeds on a DC 15 Wisdom (Insight) check senses the person's apprehension and nervousness when discussing events at the neighboring calmecac:

No one has seen or heard from their children in the calmecac for the last several weeks. Although the teenagers usually remain sequestered behind its walls, visitors approaching the institution's walls have been met with snarling coyotes and mysterious beasts who block entry into the calmecac.

The temple of Nonotzali on the calmecac grounds also fell silent. Aloc, its high priest, has had no contact with the temple of Quiahuitl regarding the upcoming rain festival, leading many visitors and residents alike to wonder aloud about the reason for the unexpected schism between the normally cooperative priesthoods.

Mintoch dispatched several jaguar warriors to infiltrate the calmecac. These experienced soldiers never returned. Some claim to have heard bloodcurdling screams only a few minutes after they scaled the compound's walls.

Although no one has set foot on the calmecac's grounds since the strange events began, residents occasionally hear humanoid voices and other sounds from inside the complex's walls.

If you keep your eyes and ears open, you may be able to purchase peyote in the marketplace.

Dealers or No Dealers

Aztli society frowns upon public intoxication, especially among women and children. Despite these stigmas, some believe ingesting the hallucinogenic cactus opens a channel to the Miquito (the domain of the dead) or the gods themselves. Four **jaguar warriors** (see above) patrol the marketplace to deter thieves from stealing wares off the shelves as well as to protect the buying public from price gougers and unscrupulous peddlers. Transgressors face a merciless legal system renowned for its cruel and unusual punishments ranging from barbaric forms of execution for egregious crimes to a lengthy stint in the peticalli, the Aztlis' notoriously harsh penitentiary. Minor or petty offenses may require the perpetrator to pay restitution to the aggrieved party or to become that person's slave.

Despite these obvious hazards, four young men move through the marketplace subtly hinting that they may have peyote for sale. The four teenagers — Cuapac, Ichtli, Toltuma, and Yatli (NE male Aztli human **spies** armed with clubs and slings instead of shortswords and hand crossbows) — are students at the calmecac who serve as Coyotl's operatives within Teohuacan. The young men discreetly avoid friends and family while disguised as traveling merchants. Because they had ample time to prepare their disguises, they gain advantage on Charisma (Deception) checks made to keep their identity hidden. If the character has firsthand knowledge of the young men from living in the town or from spending a considerable amount of time in Teohuacan, he can see through their disguise with a successful DC 15 Wisdom (Perception) check. Otherwise, a successful DC 15 Wisdom (Insight) check detects something amiss about the teenagers' behavior and mannerisms, though it cannot precisely discern the exact cause.

The teenagers feign being peyote dealers because it gives them a pretense to lure a prospective buyer outside of town to conduct the illicit transaction. However, their main goal is to eavesdrop on conversations taking place within the marketplace to gauge the community's resolve regarding the mysterious events at the calmecac. When they overhear someone talking about the calmecac, the quartet subtly take interest in the conversation. Likewise, the sudden appearance of adventurers asking residents and visitors alike about the institution also attracts their full attention.

Toltuma, the oldest member of the group that ranges in age from 15 to 17, has a glib tongue and a shrewd mind. He suspects adventurers have no interest in buying peyote. Instead, he plays the role of double agent, claiming he has been secretly communicating with his brother who still resides within the calmecac. Naturally, Toltuma cannot discuss the intelligence he has gathered out in the open. If the characters want his intelligence, he insists on meeting them on the outskirts of town, where his cohorts wait to ambush them at a predetermined, overgrown swampy location. The site offers ample cover to the trio of spies who conceal themselves amid the dense vegetation surrounding a brackish, 40-foot-diameter pond of shallow water. Toltuma wades into the ankle-deep water that seems more like a nuisance than a hazard. However, the muddy water conceals numerous mangrove roots and branches. Any creature, including Toltuma, who moves into or within the pond must succeed on a DC 10 Dexterity saving throw to avoid getting snagged and falling prone into the water.

Characters who thwart Toltuma and his cronies may interrogate the teenagers. Despite their youth, Coyotl's loyalists bite their tongues at every turn. Because of their steadfastness, a character attempting to pry information from their lips using mundane methods must succeed on a DC 15 Charisma (Intimidation) check. On a success, the teenagers reveal that Coyotl, a shapeshifting coyote, murdered his upperclassman brother and then wrested control of the calmecac from the temple of Nonotzali's clergy. Students who pledged their loyalty to Coyotl and the institution's new divine master, Itzcuin, revel in their newfound liberation. Youngsters who openly defied Coyotl met a fitting end on the sacrificial altar, while those who seemed less than enthusiastic about the werecoyote's ascendance are supposedly going to be trained to be more bestial, though the quartet remain uncertain about the terminology's cryptic meaning.

Treasure: Toltuma and each of his associates carries a small leather bag filled with eagle feathers (worth 2d6 gp each) that they stole from the temple of Nonotzali within the calmecac compound. A character who succeeds on a DC 5 Intelligence (Religion) check identifies the objects as being associated with Nonotzali. Toltuma also has a *rope of climbing*, a magic item he uses to scale the calmecac walls when necessary.

Other Sites

While the temple and marketplace attract the most attention from residents and visitors alike, the town boasts several other noteworthy sites. The tzompantli may be the most gruesome of these locales, especially for characters unfamiliar with Aztli culture. This device resembles an upright, modern tennis racket with a rectangular frame. The strings sewn into the object's brackets hold skulls belonging to fallen enemies, sacrificial victims, and notorious criminals, with as many as 15 of these heads dangling on a single thread. However, most of these macabre display pieces came from the team who lost a match in the neighboring tlachtli, the court used to play ullamaloni, the Aztli ball sport. The field is a long, narrow chute surrounded by high sloped walls culminating in a broad platform where spectators watch the festivities. Two teams participate in a sport similar to modern racquetball or tennis, where each side lobs a rubber ball back and forth until the ball bounces twice on one team's section of the playing field. The contestants cannot strike the ball with any body part above their waist, though some variations of the game allow players to hit the ball with a rounded, wooden paddle or a long, wooden stick. The excitement and thrill of competition makes the sport a popular pastime among the populace, who venerate its most successful and beloved competitors. Gamblers frequently wager on the contest's outcome. The sport's governing body of several noblemen and acolytes added a wrinkle into the game to safeguard its integrity, with a randomly chosen member of their contingent drawing one of four tiles from a sealed bag at the end of each contest. Three of the ceramic tiles are blank, while the remaining tile bears the image of a skull. Whenever this tile is chosen, the temple of Quiahuitl sacrifices the members of the losing team to their god. The organizers believe this disincentive prevents bettors from bribing participants to intentionally lose a game.

<<INSERT TECOXO BALL GAME ART PIECE>>

Matches always begin at noon. The typical day's card features two contests, but with the impending rain festival ceremony, visiting teams from other communities have swelled the participants' ranks to allow for five individual contests. One of these includes a visiting team from neighboring Ollitl. Their entourage includes an amoral scoundrel named **Nezcapa** (CE male Aztli human **thug** armed with a club and shortbow instead of a mace and heavy crossbow). A **card shark** (see **Appendix A: New Monsters**) accompanies him. This strange, shapeshifting creature can take the form of any small object. Earlier in the day, the monster assumed the likeness of the death tile before being placed into the bag. Prior to the match featuring the Ollitl team, the card shark polymorphs into an ordinary tile, thereby eliminating any chance of selecting the death tile and removing the potentially dire consequences for intentionally throwing a match. With his scheme in place, Nezcapa bets heavily on the visiting team from Ollitl, whom he has bribed to intentionally lose their match in dramatic fashion to their presumably inferior opponents, giving the cagey gambler an even larger payoff.

Characters who observe the contest and succeed on a DC 15 Wisdom (Insight) check sense that Ollitl's participants oddly seem complacent and unafraid considering the high stakes. Furthermore, a character who observes

Nezcapa during the match and succeeds on a DC 15 Wisdom (Insight) check also notices that he exudes overconfidence in his response to the action unfolding on the ball court. His attitude would be logical if his hometown team were comfortably winning, yet he seems certain his team is going to lose despite their opponents' lesser abilities. Despite risking everything he owns on one game, Nezcapa acts too nonchalantly for the situation when considering he bet his entire fortune on the prohibitive underdogs.

Suspicious and clever adventurers may thwart Nezcapa's ruse in creative ways. For instance, a *detect thoughts* spell cast on the contents of the leather bag reveals the presence of a sentient mind among the inanimate objects. The character may also examine the tiles in the bag, though the intelligent card shark transforms into the death tile when it becomes aware of the characters' intentions by perhaps overhearing them discuss their plans or by emptying the bag's contents in an unexpected manner. Fighting is not the card shark's forte. When caught in a bind, the wily creature blames its unwitting host for the deception, implying that it is a mere pawn in its dubious game. Of course, it gladly offers its services to a potential new host. When faced with an unreceptive audience, the card shark flees at the first opportunity by leaping onto a passerby and disguising itself as an ordinary personal item.

With his scheme in tatters, Nezcapa feigns ignorance, claiming he had "inside knowledge" about the game's predetermined outcome, though he denies using the card shark to rig the contest. Unfortunately for him, the card shark happily throws its co-conspirator to the wolves to save itself. When weighing the evidence, the game's organizers focus on motive. The card shark gained no direct benefit from its role, while Nezcapa made a fortune on his wagers. In the end, Nezcapa faces swift and merciless Aztli justice for his crimes, along with the complicit team members.

THE CALMECAC

Teohuacan develops its future warriors, leaders, and artisans within the imposing walls of the community's premiere learning institution, which sits roughly one-quarter mile beyond the eastern edge of the town proper. The Aztlis built the calmecac on this sequestered piece of land surrounded by streams and rivers to reinforce the students' notions of independence from their friends and families outside the school. The stone walls surrounding the complex add to this ideal. The barriers are intended to prevent external teachings from influencing its students, which in turn allows its teachers to impart a uniform, uncorrupted curriculum regarding Aztli religious beliefs, ideals, and morality. The 10-foot-high outer walls surrounding the calmecac primarily serve a symbolic rather than a military purpose. When the characters approach the locale, read or paraphrase the following description:

> Nature reasserts its dominance as shrubs, bushes, and mangrove trees grow unchecked throughout the area surrounding a 10-foot-high brick and mortar wall partially covered by mud, greenery, and branches. Streams of brackish water carve meandering paths across the soggy, spongy earth and through the elongated woody roots of numerous plants. The upper levels of two stone buildings, one near the east wall and the other against the south wall are visible behind the imposing outer barrier. A wooden, latticed gate supported by hinges built into an entrance cut into the south wall offers a glimpse inside of the compound. The constant drone of buzzing insects drowns out most sounds, though an occasional bark or howl emanating from behind the compound's walls occasionally pierces the monotony.

Only a handful of trees and bushes surrounding the complex reach a height of more than 30 feet, but these woody giants provide ample cover for the 3 **mobats** (see **Appendix A: New Monsters**) concealed amid the tangle of twisted branches, leaves, and roots. The monstrosities occupy these perches

CALMECAC

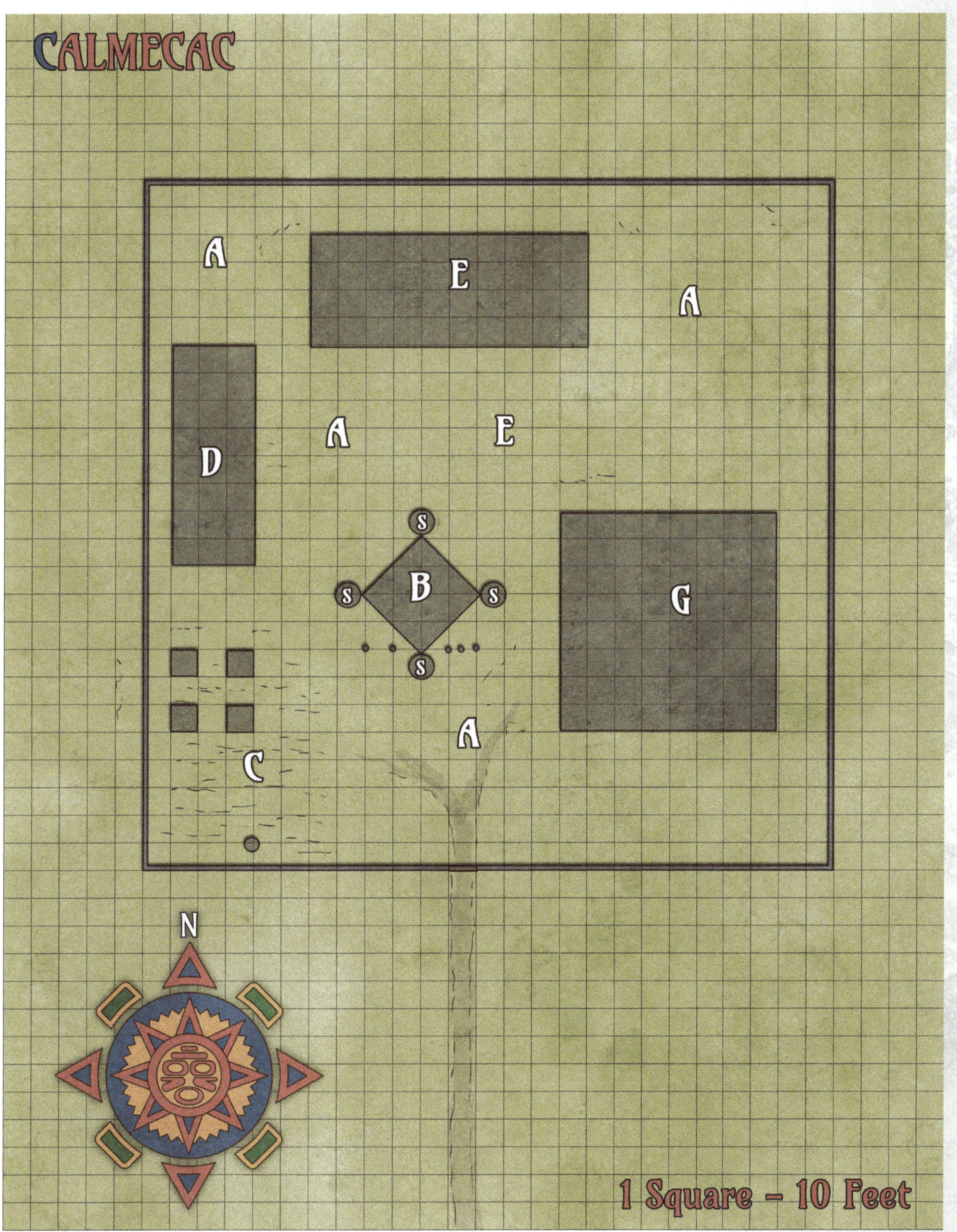

The characters' incursion onto the school grounds triggers multiple responses from the inhabitants who roam through the courtyard at various points during the day and night. The best way to adjudicate these reactions is to present them in waves. Although the numbers may initially seem overwhelming, some of the combatants are likely to flee at the first sign of adversity or pose very little real danger to seasoned adventurers. By staggering the encounters, the characters get an opportunity to recoup and regroup between battles rather than be inundated by seemingly endless horde of enemies to fight. This approach gives the characters an opportunity to explore their surroundings and learn more about the calmecac between engagements without any consequences for doing so.

only during daylight hours. Because they have ample time to hide, it takes a successful DC 17 Wisdom (Perception) check to spot the monsters even from close range. The mobats circle the skies around the calmecac at night. Because they rely upon echolocation rather than sight to detect prey, invisibility has no effect on the mobats. Characters spot the mobats overhead with a successful DC 12 Wisdom (Perception) check.

The swamp around the calmecac is treated as difficult terrain, which likely limits the characters' mobility in comparison to the airborne mobats. The monstrosities emit their piercing screech at the beginning of the encounter and then make flyby attacks for the balance of the engagement. The semi-intelligent mobats defend the calmecac at the behest of Coyotl and his divine patron Itzcuin. However, the creatures have no profound loyalty to either individual. If the battle turns against them, the winged beasts take to the skies and flee deeper into the swamp, likely never to return here again. Although the characters may perceive the mobats as guards, the calmecac's disorganized residents view them as creatures of opportunity. The commotion of a battle raging outside their walls fails to rouse the unorganized students from their self-imposed stupor.

After defeating or circumventing the mobats, the characters may approach the calmecac's outer walls. The 10-foot-high obstacles are more symbolic than practical lines of defense. A creature can scale the wall with a successful DC 10 Strength (Athletics) check. The wooden gate on its southern face is the only portal that grants passage through the wall. A character can climb over this impediment with a successful DC 5 Strength (Athletics) check or force it open with a successful DC 5 Strength check.

When the characters enter the compound or peek through the gate, read or paraphrase the following description:

> Three stone structures dominate the compound's interior. A roughly square, two-terraced stone pyramid decorated with painted images of feathered serpents stands near the eastern wall. A two-story rectangular building occupies the grounds adjacent to the north wall, while a similarly designed one-story wooden edifice stands adjacent to the west wall near a cultivated plot of land teeming with maize, squash, tomatoes, and pumpkins. Ducks and turkeys dwell within four pens near the irrigated tract of farmland. A diamond-shaped patch of bare earth littered with stone shards and wooden splinters is just inside the gate. Four crude wooden statues carved into the likenesses of men stand atop each of the dusty corners of beaten-down dirt. Five severed heads impaled on a spear in the center of the diamond-shaped area send an ominous warning to unwelcome guests.

While circumventing the barrier poses little problem for adventurers, the gates and walls are not wholly unattended. Two packs of 6 **coyotes** (use the **hyena** stat block) roam the grounds searching for intruders. When the animals detect an unfamiliar scent or see someone they do not recognize, the beasts loudly yip, bark, and howl. The canines attack the trespassers, though the coyotes hastily retreat after sustaining a wound. The ruckus attracts the attention of 3 **beasts of Itzcuin** (see **Appendix A: New Monsters**) that arrive on the scene within 1d4 rounds to investigate the disturbance. In addition

to the animals and beasts wandering around inside the compound's walls, 4 students (NE male human Aztli **bandits** armed with clubs and slings instead of scimitars and light crossbows) who submitted to Coyotl's will immediately after his takeover of the school haphazardly oversee the calmecac's defenses. The youngsters have some combat training, though they are not as adept as Coyotl's operatives in Teohuacan. The teenagers' most noticeable features are their disheveled, bestial appearances and the wild expressions on their faces. The outwardly feral children lurch and gallop around the area as if they were emulating the gait of the animals moving among them. Instead of summoning reinforcements, the students violently confront the characters, charging at them with greater abandon than the beasts of Itzcuin.

The four males — Ayohua, Cequi, Nayohua, and Palan — range in age from 11 to 14. Despite their noble upbringing, they behave more like crazed dogs than Aztli scions. They bark, growl, and yip like their canine counterparts, while interspersing some coherent speech amid their bestial sounds. During their brief moments of lucidity, they shout, "Bite the hands and necks that feed you!" Unlike their coyote counterparts, these youngsters never retreat even in the face of imminent death. If the characters capture any of the boys, they sit down and intentionally lapse into a near-catatonic state. They say absolutely nothing and are content to sit still for hours. However, a character who wins a Charisma (Intimidation) check contested by one of the boys' Wisdom (Insight) checks successfully pries information out of the reluctant child. (You may give the boys advantage on the preceding check to simulate their fanaticism and deviant behavior.)

On a success, the frightened teenager finally breaks down. He admits that Coyotl, whom he describes as a man-beast, murdered the acolytes and Aloc, the high priest of Nonotzali. They now worship Itzcuin, Nonotzali's younger, bestial brother. He also grudgingly admits that Coyotl's serves a cacao drink to his most reluctant followers in the belief that the liquid will instill bestial qualities in the young boys and men.

Characters who linger too long in the compound's courtyard unexpectedly meet one of the calmecac's latest terrors: a malevolent **wahuapa** (see **Appendix A: New Monsters**) that dwells among the ordinary maize plants. This bloodthirsty plant creature is a new addition to the calmecac, joining the compound's ranks after blood poured onto the soil around the maize plant triggered its transformation into a wahuapa. Itzcuin aided the strange creature's metamorphosis, ensuring its allegiance to the dark god. The sentient creature patiently watches and waits for an ideal time to strike, preferably while the characters are distracted investigating other areas of the courtyard or if they fortuitously wander into its territory. Alternately, the wahuapa may also cast *entangle* where the characters are standing to preoccupy them. Despite possessing some intelligence, the monster cannot effectively communicate with other creatures. It obeys simple commands, but it cannot converse with the characters.

The sounds of another combat are unlikely to evoke any coordinated response from Coyotl's subjects. They are either too lazy or disinterested to quickly investigate any disturbances in the courtyard. Nonetheless, 4d6 minutes after entering the compound, 4 teenage boys (NE male human Aztli **bandits** armed with clubs and slings instead of scimitars and light crossbows) finally emerge from the northern building, leisurely bouncing a rubber ball against the ground. These boys also charge headlong into the fray, though this time, they loudly call for aid from the **black skeleton** (see **Appendix A new Monsters**) standing atop the apex of the neighboring temple of Nonotzali. When summoned in this manner, the black skeleton abandons its station and rushes to engage the enemies without emitting an alarm. Azcatl, Cualne, Milice, and Zintli — the teenagers in this encounter — react in the same manner as their previous counterparts.

Calmecac Grounds

The calmecac's structures look intact absent some early signs of neglect and numerous empty jars and ceramic cups of pulque scattered around the area, but order has completely broken down. Schedules have been thrown out the window, and classes are no longer in session. None of the youngsters adheres to any of the school's previous rules. The children generally fall into two different camps — those who reject traditional Aztli beliefs and are now fiercely loyal to Coyotl's new order, and those children who begrudgingly went along with the werecoyote's unplanned revolution. The adolescents and teenagers belonging to the first camp behave like spoiled brats, unrestrained by social restrictions or norms. They often emulate canine mannerisms by barking, yipping, and exhibiting a pack mentality. The individuals in the latter group have been repeatedly exposed to the rabies virus through Coyotl's contaminated drink, making them either sick and lethargic or wild and unpredictable.

Area A: Outer Courtyard

This area refers to the open spaces between the major points of interest in the calmecac.

> Thick, vibrant green grass covers the lawn growing around the buildings scattered across the calmecac. Although not precisely manicured, the length of the grass remains fairly uniform across the grounds. Clusters of saplings grow near the structures' foundations and in the shadow of the outer wall.

During the school's heyday, the staff carefully attended to the grounds comprising its outer courtyard. Coyotl does not share their enthusiasm for the endeavor. Nonetheless, the residual fruits of their labors keep the vegetation in check with the exception of several bush and tree saplings making some headway in the outer courtyard. Creatures moving through the outer courtyard may do so without penalty or impediment.

Area B: Sparring Grounds

> Four badly splintered wooden statues of adult men stand at each corner of a diamond-shaped batch of bare earth littered with pieces of wood, chipped stones, and scraps of linen. Numerous footprints are still visible within its confines. Five severed heads sit atop spears embedded into the ground along the locale's southern edge. Only scraps of decaying flesh and hair still cling to the bones, making it impossible to recognize any individual faces.

The calmecac's teachers instructed their pupils in the arts of war atop this square patch of earth. Young men learned the art of wielding the club, spear, and other Aztli weapons, though Coyotl's unmotivated and largely directionless underlings spend little to no time honing their combat skills. A character searching through the debris littering the ground easily finds pieces of shattered obsidian and wood on the ground, though one who succeeds on a DC 15 Wisdom (Perception) check also locates chunks of copper just beneath a fine layer of dirt.

However, the characters' attention likely shifts toward the macabre displays facing the gate. A character who examines the decapitated heads and succeeds on a DC 10 Intelligence (Nature) check determines the heads were removed from the spinal column in an imprecise manner rather than with single, sharp cuts. Coyotl, in his coyote form, chewed through their necks and sliced through their vertebrae with his fangs rather than cutting or sawing through their spinal columns with a sharp instrument or weapon. The skulls belong to Aloc and the four jaguar warriors sent to investigate the events at the calmecac. However, the exposure to the elements, especially the high humidity, and the carrion-eating insects make it impossible to identify the individuals even though scraps of flesh still cling to their bones. However, a character who examines the bugs covering these decomposing faces and succeeds on a DC 15 Intelligence (Nature) check can confirm that the presence of maggots on four of the skulls indicates they have been here no more than a week. The remaining skull (Aloc's) has sat on display for at least two weeks.

Area C: Cultivated Field

> Maize stalks taller than the average man dominate a cultivated tract of land where squashes, tomatoes, and pumpkins flourish closer to the ground beneath them. Four large pens with wooden bars sit atop pedestals above the soil. The ducks and turkeys inside the enclosures frequently make clucking and cackling sounds. Bees frequently fly into and out of a honeycomb built into the cavity of a large wooden stump at the garden's southern edge.

The fruits and vegetables harvested in the calmecac's garden serve as a primary food source for the students, though a character who inspects the plants and succeeds on a DC 5 Intelligence (Nature) check notices that the edible parts of many plants are rotting on the vine or appear overripe. More importantly, characters who wander into the garden may run afoul of the resident **wahuapa** (see **Appendix A: New Monsters** and above). The maizefolk perfectly blends into its surroundings, granting it advantage on Dexterity (Stealth) checks made while concealed among the ordinary maize plants.

Despite its carnivorous nature, the wahuapa ignores the ducks and turkeys confined to the pens. The birds lack the coordination and digits to free themselves from their captivity, though a creature who can manipulate fine objects may easily spring them from their wooden pens with a successful DC 5 Dexterity check. A character who examines each pen and succeeds on a DC 5 Wisdom (Perception) check also discovers that each cage contains 1d3 unharvested eggs. The slaves from area **D** occasionally dump human and animal waste onto the soil as crude fertilizer. A creature walking through the area may avoid the decomposing matter without making a check. However, characters who encounter the wahuapa on its own turf are too distracted to pay attention to where they step. Under this circumstance, the creature must succeed on a DC 5 Dexterity saving throw each round to avoid stepping in the fetid material. A character who comes in contact with the feces suffers disadvantage on Dexterity (Stealth) checks for the next 1d4 hours. Creatures that already have advantage on Wisdom (Perception) checks relying upon smell automatically detect the creature. Removing any clothing stained by the waste eliminates the penalty, as does spending 10 minutes thoroughly washing it with clean water.

The honeybees at the southern edge of the field only attack visitors who disturb their honeycomb or who stray within five feet of their nest. The **swarm of insects** emerges from the hive's inner recesses to assault the unwelcome trespasser. The swarm pursues transgressors up to a distance of 100 feet from its abode, at which point, it ceases the assault and retreats back to its hive.

Area D: Food Production

> Adobe bricks form the foundation and walls of this one-story structure with a single door on its eastern face.

The typically impulsive Coyotl realized hunger can derail even the most idealistic revolt. He spared the lives of the compound's four Poqoza slaves who tend the gardens and prepare meals for the residents. The structure's walls and foundation are constructed from adobe bricks. Packed dirt makes up its floor, while the eight-foot-high pitched ceiling is made from wood and straw. The wooden door granting access into the mess hall is always kept ajar to allow light into the building and to let heat escape. The kitchen generally operates from dawn to dusk, though the servants toil for several hours before sunrise prepping for the next day's meals, and for an hour after sunset to clean. The staff leaves a few light snacks, such as uncontaminated cacao drinks, tortilla chips, and salsas, on a table during the overnight hours to accommodate stragglers looking for a quick meal.

D1: Kitchen and Dining Area

When a character peers into the room beyond the ajar door, read or paraphrase the following description.

> Stimulating aromas and warm air bombard the senses as various ingredients simmer and roast at several cooking stations. Hot coals and low flames beneath three clay disks resting atop three stones heat flattened dough and plant leaves. Chilis, tomatoes, and ground herbs fill numerous small bowls scattered around the room. Piles of wood and charcoal rest against the walls. Diners presumably sit on one of the four wooden stools near the entrance.

The 4 slaves Atexa, Cahuitl, Inexca, and Tahuauta, (N female Poqoza half-elf unarmed **commoners**) have no love lost for the Aztlis and certainly no fond feelings for Coyotl and his bratty cohorts. They never mourned for Aloc and his acolytes, but they fear the calmecac's cruel and unpredictable new master

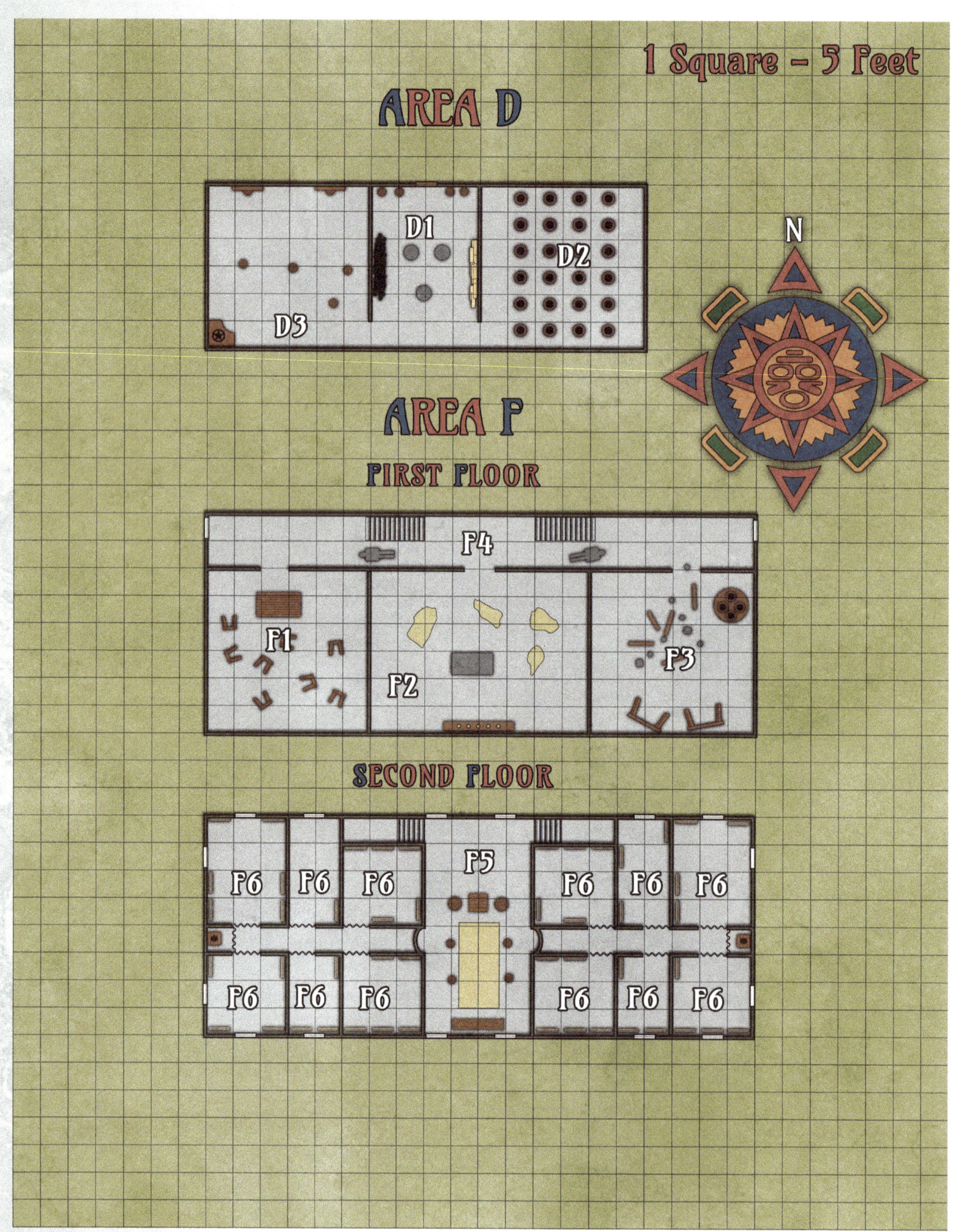

1 Square - 5 Feet
AREA D
D1
D2
D3
AREA F
FIRST FLOOR
F1
F2
F3
F4
SECOND FLOOR
F5
F6
F6
F6
F6
F6
F6
F6
F6
F6
F6
F6
F6
N

who revels in death and carnage far more than his predecessors. They bemoan the upstarts' obnoxious attitudes and disrespect toward them. A character who converses with the slaves and succeeds on a DC 10 Wisdom (Insight) check notices that Inexca appears sullen and upset while her counterparts vigorously bash Coyotl and the boys. If questioned, she sheepishly admits to having a clandestine romantic relationship with Coyotl for almost eight months. During her conversations with the teenager, he frequently spoke about his jealousy and hatred toward his older brother Ezel, who had bullied his physically weaker younger brother. Despite their age and size differentials, Coyotl vowed he would one day become the family's patriarch.

Inexca brushed his boasts aside, yet as their forbidden relationship grew stronger, Coyotl abruptly changed. He began ranting about learning the secrets of tapping into his inner beast. One night during an argument, the enraged Coyotl manifested into an upright coyote. His metamorphosis terrified her, especially considering she was now carrying his unborn child. The older and infinitely wiser young woman kept her pregnancy a secret from her fellow slaves and most importantly, from Coyotl, for as long as she could until she finally realized the truth. Eager to please Itzcuin, Coyotl forcibly extracted the unborn child from her womb and sacrificed the fetus to his divine patron in the ultimate display of fidelity to his ungodly master. Under the bestial deity's urging, Coyotl even devoured the girl's flesh and poured some of the child's spilt blood onto the maize plants, giving birth to the wahuapa now inhabiting area **C**. After relaying her tragic tale, Inexca and the other slaves fall silent until they slowly return to the tasks at hand.

The slaves use the cooking implements scattered around the kitchen to make tortillas from ground corn dough, tamales from peppers, pozoles, and warm cacao drinks to feed and nourish the boorish residents. They have no knowledge about the contaminated cacao drinks spiked with saliva harvested from rabid dogs. The comallis — the clay discs resting atop the stones — are used to heat the tortillas, while the stone bowls are used to grind, mix, and serve the soups, known as pozoles, as well as salsas and other cold dishes.

D2: Food Storage

The slaves store food inside the three-foot-tall clay pots. Eight clay pots emblazoned with images of maize are filled with dried kernels, while the four pots decorated by depictions of gourds contain squash and pumpkins. The remaining unadorned 12 clay pots hold an assortment of other fruits and vegetables, though two of these pots contain urine collected to dye and wash textiles. A character who drinks the urine must succeed on a DC 10 Constitution saving throw or be poisoned for 10 minutes. Alternatively, a character who succeeds on a DC 10 Wisdom (Perception) check can identify it through color and odor. To safeguard their food supply, 3 **cats** patrol the area. The friendly animals greet visitors with an enthusiastic meow and purr at the slightest provocation.

D3: Slaves' Quarters

In addition to feeding the calmecac's students, the slaves also use the looms to weave blankets and clothing, though most residents arrived with their own garments. The slaves sleep here during the overnight hours. A character who examines the plant fibers near the looms identifies them as maguey leaves with a successful DC 10 Intelligence (Nature) check. The wooden statue sitting atop the pedestal serves as a makeshift shrine to Tlatlcolli, the Poqozas' patron deity. It takes a successful DC 5 Intelligence (Religion) check to confirm the god as the statue's subject.

Area E: Well

Several underground canals connected to Teohuacan's main water system supply the calmecac with its life-giving liquid.

The water retrieved from the well is potable and safe to drink. However, over the last few hours, a **purple slime** (see **Appendix A: New Monsters**) has infiltrated the subterranean network of channels feeding the cistern. If a slave accompanies the characters to the well, the person tells them that the clay pot is usually stored upright on the ground rather than left bobbing in the water. This unusual change in protocol may alert the adventurers to potential danger. The unintelligent, yet cunning ooze has already claimed one victim, a student who tried to drink from the well, which explains the clay pot's strange location. The purple slime floats on the water's surface, granting it advantage on Dexterity (Stealth) checks. Therefore, it takes a successful DC 15 passive Wisdom (Perception) check to notice the creature. When it senses an approaching creature, it makes a spike attack against the trespasser. The mindless creature attacks until destroyed.

The water reaches a depth of 20 feet. The channels flowing into and out of the well are four feet wide yet narrow with a maximum height of only six inches. A character who can access such a tiny opening may travel westward back to Teohuacan or in a southeasterly direction into another cistern in area **G9**. To prevent accidental drownings, numerous handholds and footholds jut from the walls. A creature that falls into the well may scale the walls with a successful DC 5 Strength (Athletics) check. The youngsters occasionally use the well as a basket for their athletic competitions. They sometimes place the wooden board with a cutout hole on top of the well to make the game more challenging.

Area F: School Complex

The two-story brick and mortar building adjacent to the northern outer wall houses the calmecac's classrooms on the first floor and its dormitories on the second floor. The building is 20 feet high with a sharply sloped roof constructed from wood and plant fibers. The ceilings on each floor are nine feet high, while the internal doors are made from wood. Natural light trickles into the first-floor corridor through the doors, though the classrooms remain dark unless currently occupied. The two-foot-wide, roughly one-foot-high second-floor windows allow natural light into the dormitories during the day, yet dim light prevails on moonlit nights, with darkness enveloping the building on moonless or cloudy evenings. It takes a successful DC 10 Strength (Athletics) check to climb the wall, using the spaces between bricks as crude handholds and footholds. A character squeezing through the window must succeed on a DC 10 Dexterity (Acrobatics) check to shimmy through the tight opening without falling face first when it gets inside or getting stuck midway. Read or paraphrase the following description when the characters lay their eyes upon this edifice:

With no classes in session, Coyotl's underlings and his minions freely roam through the building at their leisure. The unsupervised children often remain awake well into the wee hours of the morning and sleep off their excesses until noon. Characters moving through the building have a 30% chance of encountering 1d4 adolescent boys (NE male human Aztli **bandits** armed with clubs and slings instead of scimitars and light crossbows) for every 10 minutes spent within the structure's confines. The youngsters carry a lantern when encountered in normally unlit areas within the building. There is a 50% chance that a **beast of Itzcuin** (see **Appendix A: New Monsters**) accompanies them.

F1: Social Studies Classroom

The artwork adorning the walls depicts several seminal events in Aztli history, including the building of the Great Canal, the formation of the Aztli Confederation, and the destruction of Xacota. A character who succeeds on a DC 10 Intelligence (History) check recognizes these major moments from Aztli history. Characters indigenous to Tehuatl have advantage on the preceding check, while those hailing from other lands suffer disadvantage on the check. Likewise, the codices on the desk include three history texts focusing on Xacota, while the remaining tome is a legal treatise on Aztli law. A character who can read Aztli may identify the texts' subjects without making an ability or skill check. Someone who examines the codices and cannot comprehend Aztli writing must succeed on a DC 10 Intelligence check to gain a basic understanding of the subject matter, though they cannot decipher specific details contained within the works. Only four wooden stools remain functional. The remaining eight are missing 1d4 legs.

Treasure: The three history codices (worth 150 gp each) are fairly rare. They describe several important yet obscure facts from this period of Aztli history. The codices were written on deer hide, making them relatively durable from a structural integrity standpoint, though they are still vulnerable to extreme humidity and temperature. The legal treatise (worth 50 gp) scribed onto plant fiber is more common and less sturdy, making it less valuable than its counterparts.

F2: Religious Studies

Aloc taught religion and, to a lesser extent, medicine within these walls. Students sat or kneeled on the colorful linens while the high priest and his acolytes imparted divine inspiration from the Aztli gods. However, Coyotl and his disciples smeared feces and dried blood from Aloc and his acolytes on the walls' painted images of Nonotzali and Quiahuitl. His minions also dug deep grooves onto the stony surfaces with rocks, stones, and bronze tools. The altar and the obsidian dagger also suffered the same fate. In an ultimate act of sacrilege, Itzcuin raised one of the acolyte's corpses as a **mummy**. The undead monstrosity lies atop the slab only to rise when a creature enters the room without uttering the password "Itzcuin." If the creature fails to say the word, it uses its deadly glare ability against the transgressor. Each round, the mummy switches targets, while focusing its melee weapon attack against a single target unaffected by its deadly glare. The mummy speaks Aztli and recalls portions of its past life, though it now venerates Itzcuin and refuses to converse with the characters unless they magically compel it. Under those circumstances, it reveals that Coyotl murdered him several weeks ago and that the teen can transform into a coyote.

Treasure: The vials on the shelf are three potions of healing, a potion of greater healing, and a potion of necrotic resistance. The medical codex is Cahuotl's Journal (see Appendix C: New Equipment and Magical Items).

F3: Artisan's Studio

The instructors used the raw materials and ingredients to teach students the arts of sculpting and painting as well as engineering. Not surprisingly, they used these newfound skills to adorn the walls with graphic depictions of Itzcuin. At the moment, 4 teenage students (NE male human Aztli **bandits** armed with clubs and slings instead of scimitars and light crossbows) are honing their craft, adding gory details to the earlier paintings. These older students obviously disavow Aztli traditions. They appear unkempt and exhibit a blatant disregard for the calmecac and its principles by further desecrating the building and the gods who supported it. The young men openly speak ill of Aloc, the acolytes, and Teohuacan as a whole. The fanatics never willingly speak to the characters. They do so only if magically compelled or if a character successfully intimidates one of them (see **The Calmecac** section for further details on forcibly intimidating the students).

A character who succeeds on a DC 15 Wisdom (Perception) check spots a codex underneath the overturned table against the far wall. If retrieved, the book contains numerous geometrical diagrams along with numerical values used for the study of engineering. It takes a successful DC 15 Intelligence check to correlate the geometric diagrams and mathematical formulas with the study of engineering.

Treasure: An Aztli architect and engineer named Quintin wrote the engineering codex (worth 200 gp) that was predominately used to build the neighboring temple of Quiahuitl as well as several other important sites in nearby Teohuacan. The room also contains two complete sets of carpenter's tools, three sets of mason's tools, and four complete sets of painter's supplies.

F4: Corridor

The rambunctious students defaced the artwork on the walls, replacing the scenes associated with Nonotzali's instructor with depraved images of Itzcuin's canine servants. Despite conveying their intention, the latter artwork appears primitive and juvenile in comparison to their predecessors. After overthrowing the calmecac's administration, the boys toppled the statues of Nonotzali, causing them to break apart. A successful DC 5 Intelligence (Religion) check determines that the decapitated statue and the other sculpture, which broke into three pieces as shown on the map, portrays Nonotzali.

F5: Common Room

A rug made from pelts and feathers covers a large portion of the stone floor in a spacious, common chamber. Four wooden stools and a long bench with a backrest surround the carpet. A small jar containing dozens of dried, red beans sits adjacent to a cross-shaped gaming board on a square table between two circular benches. Two colorful linen mats padded with feathers and plant fibers rest against the near walls. Bundles of thin sticks sit in four sconces built into the east and west walls.

During the day, light filters into the room from the windows on the north and south walls. The 4 adolescent boys (NE male human Aztli **bandits** armed with clubs and slings instead of scimitars and light crossbows) who occupy the common room spend their free time playing patolli, a game played on the cross-shaped board resting atop the table. The dried, red beans function as the game's playing pieces. Like the other residents, these boys behave in an unruly manner, display no interest in maintaining their personal appearance, and immediately attack intruders. They repeatedly refer to the trespassers as "blasphemers" amid other crude insults about the characters' appearances and characteristics. Under questioning, they react in the same manner as the children in area **F3**. In addition, an **elusa hound** (see **Appendix A: New Monsters**) reclines on the carpet alongside the boys. Coyotl uses the beast to sniff out spellcasters disguised as students. When the monstrosity detects a magical aura, it exclusively focuses its attacks against that target. In typical pack fashion, the elusa hound nonverbally encourages the boys to attack the same foe.

Obviously, the sounds of combat from area **F5** may evoke a response from the residents occupying areas **F6**. Under these circumstances, you may increase the chance of an encounter taking place from once every 10 minutes to once every minute while the characters are engaged in battle. When the commotion ends, the chances of a random encounter return to normal.

Treasure: The furnishings in the room are sturdy yet ordinary. The carpet (worth 10 gp) consists of plant fibers, deer skins, and feathers from birds of prey. Students use the mats (worth 5 gp each) near the entrance for short naps or brief relaxation.

F6: Dormitory

Each of the dormitory rooms houses between three and six students. Upperclassmen traditionally occupy the larger corner rooms, while the underclassmen dwell in the small and more crowded interior rooms. During the day, natural light filters through the windows into the rooms with an exterior wall. Students use bundles of sticks to illuminate the interior areas and during the overnight hours on moonless or cloudy nights. When the characters enter one of the dormitories, you may read or paraphrase the following description, adjusting it as necessary for the room's unique circumstances.

A blue, red, and green curtain hanging from a rod suspended in the doorway serves as a makeshift door. Heaping mounds of soiled clothing, food scraps, and torn pages from codices litter the floor. Colorful, linen mats are rolled up onto a bar against the wall. Niches built into the near walls display religious iconography, though most of the images are now covered by writing, dirt, and other materials.

When Aloc and his acolytes held sway over the calmecac, the student dormitories resembled military barracks in terms of order and cleanliness. In the absence of any formal discipline, the students wallow in sloth and filth. They rarely, if ever, wash the piles of dirty linens strewn about the floor, pick up leftover food, or read from their codices. As previously discussed, the youngsters usually stay awake until the wee hours of the morning and do not stir until at least noon. When exploring these rooms, you may consult the follow table to determine whether an individual room is occupied, and if so, what the occupants are doing at the time.

1d6	Early Morning to Noon	Noon to Sunset	Overnight Hours
1	Occupied, sleeping	Occupied, awake	Occupied, awake
2	Occupied, sleeping	Occupied, awake	Occupied, sleeping
3	Occupied, sleeping	Occupied, sleeping	Occupied, awake
4	Occupied, awake	Unoccupied	Unoccupied
5–6	Unoccupied	Unoccupied	Unoccupied

If the room is occupied, the residents' reactions depend upon whether they are Coyotl's loyal followers, who enjoy more privileges, or if they belong to the camp of indifferent followers succumbing to the ravages of rabies (see **Appendix B**) from Coyotl's tainted cacao drink. Fanatical devotees immediately attack intruders, while infected students behave in accordance with the effects of the disease. In general, the number of students in the room is equal to or less than the number of beds. As previously mentioned, the upperclassmen (NE male human Aztli **scouts** armed with macuahuitls [see **Appendix C: New Equipment and Magic Items**] instead of shortswords) occupy the corner bedrooms, while the underclassmen (NE male human Aztli **bandits** armed with clubs and slings instead of scimitars and light crossbows) reside in the interior rooms and smaller exterior dormitory rooms. Upperclassmen have a 75% chance of belonging to Coyotl's loyal henchmen. His loyal devotees respond to questions in the same manner as their fanatical counterparts. The underclassmen, on the other hand, have a 75% chance of suffering from rabies. If the characters encounter infected students, searching their quarters and succeeding on a DC 10 Wisdom (Perception) check locates a clay cup containing a foul-smelling cacao residue. Interrogating Coyotl's less-enthusiastic residents yields better results, especially if the characters cure the disease ravaging their bodies. Otherwise, all attempts to gather information from infected students automatically fail as their diseased minds are incapable of recalling any details. When cured, the students reveal that Coyotl forced them to regularly imbibe a presumably doctored cacao drink to "unleash their inner beast." He brewed and administered the concoction to them within Nonotzali's converted sanctum within the temple. They also tell the characters that Coyotl killed the students who initially resisted him and that a few of their classmates almost immediately took ill after ingesting the cacao drink and have not been seen since they exhibited signs of sickness.

To prevent the characters from monotonously going through one identical room after another, consult the following table to add random details or treasures to each different area in area **F6**. Do not give the characters the same discovery more than once, with the exception of the tlachtli ball that the characters may receive more than once. If die roll generates the same result a second time, reroll the die only one more time and give them that discovery instead. If they already unearthed the next discovery, they receive nothing.

1d8	Discovery
1	Cacao beans
2	Eagle feathers
3	Golden idol
4	Macuahuitl
5	Mysterious drawing
6	Pulque
7	Silvery earrings
8	Tlachtli ball (can be generated more than once)

Cacao Beans

A calmecac resident hid 16 cacao beans (worth 1d4 gp each) in a pouch concealed among the clothing. It takes a successful DC 15 Wisdom (Perception) check to spot the pods inside the gigantic mess.

Eagle Feathers

Four eagle feathers (worth 1d3 gp each) are rolled inside one of the linen mats. It is impossible to locate the feathers without unfurling the mat.

Golden Idol

This golden statue of a pouncing jaguar (worth 300 gp) is four inches high, six inches long, and weighs roughly two pounds. Its owner stuffed the valuable object inside of a shirt, yet an observant character can spot the object's outline among the linens with a successful DC 15 Wisdom (Perception) check. If the characters are from Teohuacan or are very familiar with the settlement, they may attempt a DC 15 Intelligence check. On a success, they recall hearing about this golden idol being stolen from Nonotzali's temple in the neighboring town roughly one year earlier, well before the current events that befell the calmecac.

Macuahuitl

This fearsome club laced with obsidian shards hangs from a bracket embedded in the wall. The *+1 macuahuitl* is wrapped inside of a linen cover to prevent accidental lacerations from anyone touching its keen edges.

Mysterious Drawing

Before Coyotl's ascendancy, a student devoted to Nonotzali doodled a cryptic drawing onto a ceiling's whitewashed surface. The image depicts a feathered serpent wrapping its coils around a wild-eyed coyote. Surprisingly, none of Itzcuin's followers defaced nor erased the remarkably well-done piece of artwork.

Pulque

A sealed jar contains roughly one gallon of pulque (worth 10 gp). The alcoholic beverage fermented from the sap of the maguey plant is a popular drink among the Aztli.

Silver Earrings

Before his transformation into a werecoyote, Coyotl planned to give this exquisite pair of silver earrings (worth 150 gp) to Inexca (see area **D1**). After this plan fell by the wayside, the irate young man tossed the earrings into the well, where one of the students later retrieved them.

Tlachtli Ball

This round, leather ball rests in the far corner of the room. The students use it to play the ball game in the courtyard (area **A**), using the well (area **E**) as the goal.

Area G: Temple of Nonotzali

Pictographs of geometric shapes and colorful paintings of feathered serpents adorn the step pyramid's adobe brick walls. A 10-foot-wide staircase with one-foot-high and one-foot-deep steps built into the structure's southern face ascends 40 feet onto a square shrine atop the temple of Nonotzali, which grants access to the temple complex within the pyramid. Perfectly symmetrical 10-foot adobe brick cubes form the foundation and building blocks of the temple. Creatures who forego the staircase and attempt to scale the walls must succeed on a DC 15 Strength (Athletics) check to climb up each 10-foot section of the exterior's vertical surface to reach the next level. Therefore, an attempt to breach the pyramid itself would require the trespasser to burrow through roughly 10 feet of brick and mortar. In addition to repelling intruders, the dense material also prevents light from entering into the temple's interior sections, which feature eight-foot-high ceilings and smooth walls decorated with carvings and paintings depicting storm clouds and the harvest. When the characters approach the temple, read or paraphrase the following description:

> Vibrant pictographs of geometric shapes with tick marks and paintings of feathered serpents adorn the step pyramid's exterior and culminate in a limestone shrine at the building's apex, just beneath a staircase that ascends along the structure's southern face. An altar chiseled from speckled red and gray stone stands outside the shrine enclosure atop the step pyramid. Several chunks of broken stone and loose scraps of maguey paper litter the base of the steps.

The objects and artwork adorning the pyramid's exterior are commonly associated with Nonotzali, who is depicted in several paintings of the feathered serpent. Six of these drawings adorn the pyramid's walls. The characters confirm Nonotzali as the subject of these artworks with a successful DC 10 Intelligence (Religion) check as well as associating the other images concerning the study of geometry with the Aztli deity. Characters who examine the broken stones and scraps of maguey paper must succeed on a DC 15 Intelligence check to confirm that they were once small limestone statues depicting serpentine creatures. The pieces of paper contain bits and pieces of mathematical ratios associated with geometric objects. Nonotzali's priests would have offered items associated with learning to their deity as a sacrifice.

G1: Apex Level

> Two wooden statues of coiled feathered serpents flank a stone slab carved from speckled red and gray stone. A black dagger crafted from stone rests atop the altar, which occupies the space in front of an enclosure dominated by a meticulously detailed bronze statue of an odd humanoid figure.

Unless previously summoned, a **black skeleton** (see **Appendix A: New Monsters**) stands vigil behind the altar. Before taking its post, the undead monstrosity wandered the surrounding wilderness until it sensed Itzcuin's presence in the former temple of Nonotzali. The evil guardian, who frequently sparred against Nonotzali's worshippers during his wicked mortal existence, freely offered his services to Coyotl's fledgling regime. The black skeleton immediately attacks any creature who fails to recite its safe word, "Itzcuin." If someone utters the passcode, the monster allows that person and their allies to proceed without hindrance. Otherwise, the creature hacks at its enemies with merciless precision. Although the serpent statues adjacent to the altar are also carved from wood, these objects keep their silent vigil without stirring to life.

During the temple's heyday, Aloc sacrificed objects and an occasional animal to his divine patron atop the granite altar. With the exception of Aloc who perished atop the sacrificial altar, Coyotl and his minions have refrained

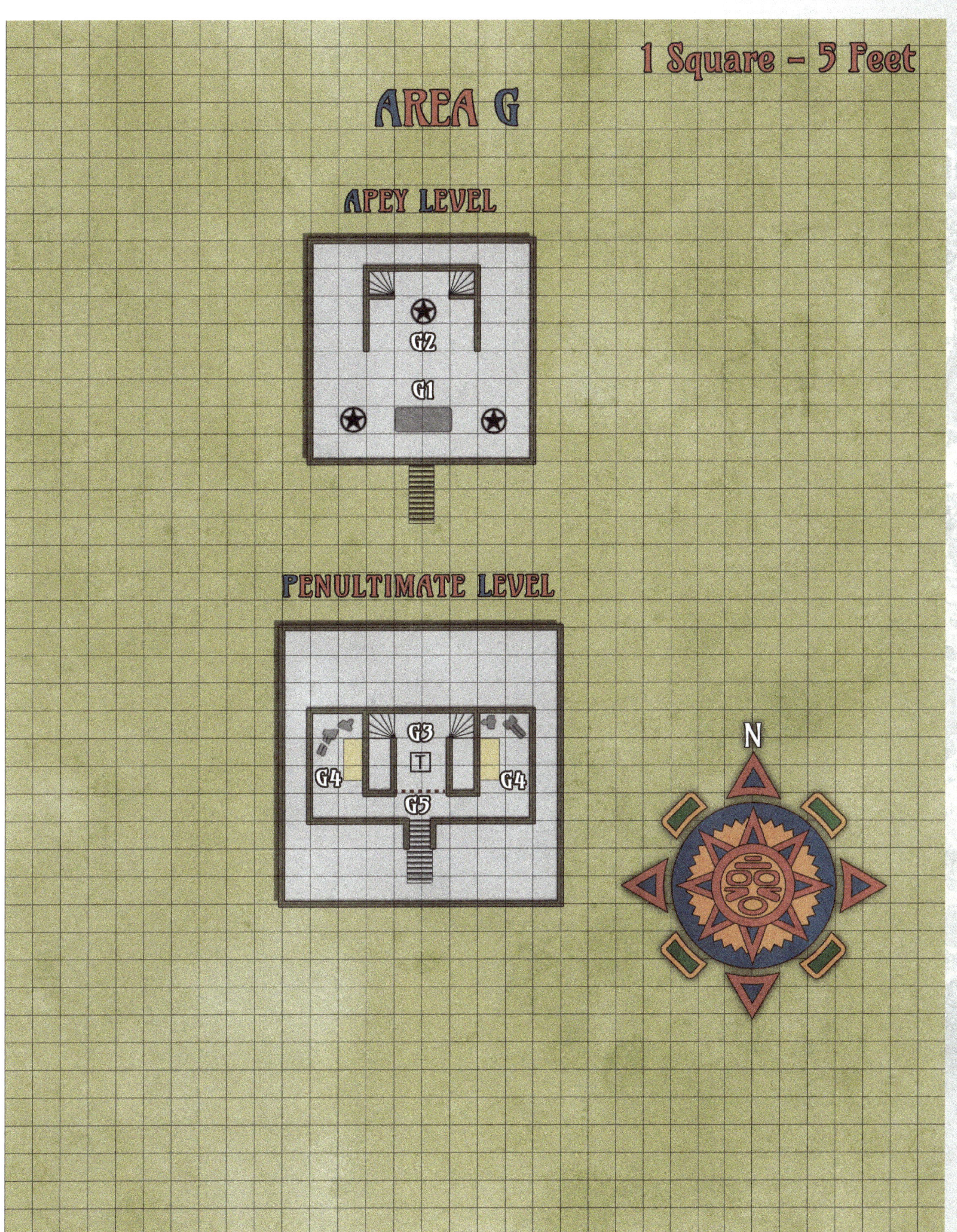

1 Square – 5 Feet
AREA G
APEX LEVEL
G2
G1
PENULTIMATE LEVEL
G3
T
G4
G4
G5
N

from butchering animals on the hardened stone, though mercy plays no part in their decision. The impulsive young man and his followers lack the discipline to adhere to the ceremonial killing's rigid protocols and instead prefer to immediately indulge their bloodlust rather than prolong the misery. It is impossible to distinguish the high priest's dried blood from previous animal victims slaughtered atop the altar.

Treasure: The serpent statues (worth 100 gp each) are carved out of oak. They stand 2–1/2 feet tall and weigh 40 pounds. The obsidian dagger (worth 500 gp) on the altar is extremely sharp and wondrously decorated with unique carvings. While it cuts through flesh with ease, it is too brittle and fragile to be an effective weapon. If wielded in combat, the dagger shatters into pieces when the wielder rolls a natural 1 on a melee or ranged attack made with the weapon.

G2: Shrine of Nonotzali

The statue dates back to the temple's founding more than a century ago. Forged from bronze, it depicts Nonotzali in meticulous yet interpretive detail during the war of liberation against Tlatoani. When Aloc presided over the temple, visitors and students would leave offerings at the statue's feet to beseech the god to acknowledge their intellectual breakthroughs and curiosity. In his aftermath, Coyotl encouraged his supporters to deface the statue with vulgarities; draw disgusting, juvenile images of extra genitalia; urinate on its base; and smear human and animal feces onto its formerly smooth, polished surface. A character with a sense of smell immediately identifies the malodorous substances covering it with a successful DC 5 Wisdom (Perception) check.

The seashells dangling from strings attached to the wooden beams in the thatched ceiling belong to a variety of marine species. A creature who examines them and succeeds on a DC 10 Intelligence (Nature) check identifies them as clam, scallop, and oyster shells. The staircases leading down are steep and narrow yet structurally sound and safe. They lead into area **G3**.

Treasure: Sixty-eight strands of seashells (worth 1 gp each) are affixed to the ceiling. It takes an action to carefully remove one strand without damaging them. A character who attempts to remove more than one strand at a time must succeed on a DC 5 Dexterity saving throw to avoid dropping the strands on the floor where they break into pieces rendering them worthless. A creature who tries to simultaneously remove at least five strands suffers disadvantage on the preceding saving throw. It is impossible to remove more than 10 at once. A *pearl of power* glued onto an oyster shell is hidden among the ordinary shells. It takes a successful DC 20 Wisdom (Perception) check to spot it from afar, though a character who takes the time to examine the individual strands notices the magical gem with a successful DC 10 Wisdom (Perception) check. Likewise, a *detect magic* spell or similar magic successfully locates the concealed magical pearl.

G3: Penultimate Level Landing

The stairs against the far wall connect this level to the apex level, specifically in area **G3**. The artwork adorning the walls dates back to the temple's creation roughly 160 years earlier and are obviously fading, chipping, and peeling away from the surface. Worshippers seeking counsel from Nonotzali's priests would wait in this vestibule before discussing their current field of study or debating the merits of a formative hypothesis. After slaying Aloc, Coyotl repurposed an alarm formerly used to alert the priests to the arrival of visitors into a juvenile yet potentially harmful trap.

Pressure Plate Trap

The pyramid's builders added a pressure plate to the floor covering the entire space between the dotted lines. When a creature weighing 50 pounds or more steps onto the plate, two bronze plates imbedded into the space beneath the floor emit low chimes that lasts for six seconds before ending. Fortunately for the characters, the alarm functions more as a courtesy rather than a loud, general alert. There is a 50% chance at least one occupant in area **G4** hears the noise, though they do not necessarily respond to the chime as an immediate call to arms. A successful DC 15 Intelligence (Investigation) check made when examining the floor discovers the trap and its operating mechanism. Because of its original intentions, it only takes a successful DC 10 Dexterity check made with thieves' tools to deactivate it.

However, the chime's purpose is now twofold. The sound now alerts the occupant to deactivate the second portion of the trap contained in the ceiling within 12 seconds. Coyotl thought it would be funny to conceal the shutoff switch in an obscene manner by requiring the trespasser to press a switch hidden in the painting of a priest's backside. A character who examines the paintings on the wall spots the switch with a successful DC 10 Wisdom (Perception) check, while one who inspects the ceiling detects a trapdoor with a successful DC 15 Wisdom (Perception) check. A successful DC 10 Intelligence (Investigation) check determines that pressing the switch deactivates the trap. If no one presses the switch within the allotted timeframe, the trapdoor opens, dropping roughly 20 pounds of moldy refuse and excrement into the center of the room. Creatures within five feet of the trapdoor must succeed on a DC 12 Dexterity saving throw or be covered in the debris. The garbage deals no damage, but an affected creature suffers disadvantage on Dexterity (Stealth) checks made to avoid being detected if the opposing creature has a sense of smell. This penalty lasts for 1d4 hours or until the creature removes its clothing and equipment and spends 1d4 minutes washing or cleaning off the garments and gear. In addition to this penalty, the character also contracts sewer plague if it fails a DC 11 Constitution saving throw.

In more pressing matters, the occupants of area **G4** arrive on the scene to presumably mock whom they believe to be one of their fellow associates who activated the trap. Their jest soon turns to anger when they realize trespassers entered their domain.

G4: Acolytes' Quarters

Nonotzali's acolytes occupied these humble quarters during their stay at the temple. While intact, the oak statue of Nonotzali stood four feet high. However, Itzcuin's worshippers hacked the limbs from the torso and decapitated the sculpture's head, leaving it in sundered pieces across the floor. Even in this state, a character who succeeds on a DC 15 Intelligence (Religion) check identifies Nonotzali as the statue's subject. Unlike the artwork, the acolytes' linen mats, which served as their beds, survived Coyotl's onslaught, though the textiles conceal a gruesome discovery. Moving the mats from their current position reveals a thick pool of dried blood, the grisly aftermath of Coyotl's bloodthirsty assault against Aloc's assistants. Although the characters cannot identify the blood's source, it is obvious that the congealed substance is blood. The acolytes kept the sloughed snakeskins as religious objects supposedly harvested from one of the first snakes in the region. The veracity of this claim is dubious at best, but a character who succeeds at a DC 15 Intelligence (Religion) check recognizes the braiding as being associated with these purported sacred artifacts.

A **coyote warrior** (see **Appendix A: New Monsters**) and a **beast of Itzcuin** (see **Appendix A: New Monsters**) now occupy each of these quarters (for a total of 2 coyote warriors and 2 beasts of Itzcuin). These young adult males are fanatical devotees of Itzcuin. They excelled in the sparring ring during their tenure at the calmecac, prompting Coyotl to reward them with their new lofty positions and a disgusting pet. Each coyote warrior and their beast focus their attacks against one opponent, which maximizes their combat abilities by granting them advantage against the chosen target and additional sneak attack damage. Like their counterparts, the coyote warriors fiercely resist any attempts to force their surrender or divulge information about the complex. See area **F3** for details regarding such efforts. If they crack under the pressure, the coyote warriors reveal that Coyotl plans to release a virulent contagion upon Teohuacan in the coming days. Although they cannot relay how he intends to set this scheme into motion, they believe dogs somehow play a role in his devious plans.

Treasure: Each coyote warrior has two *potions of healing*. One of the warriors carries a pouch containing 19 cacao beans (worth 10 gp each), while the other carries a *pumpkin seed* (see **Appendix C: New Equipment and Magic Items**).

G5: VESTIBULE

The vestibule connects the penultimate level to the third level via a staircase connecting area **G5** to area **G6** in addition to linking areas **G3** and **G4** together.

G6: OBSERVATORY

The pyramid's initial blueprints only planned for creating three levels, which would have placed the Aztli calendar and observatory outside as originally intended. However, Nonotzali's arrogant high priest Mocentini later decided to add two more levels to the pyramid in a deliberate effort to outshine the temple of Quiahuitl in neighboring Teohuacan. This amendment accomplished its desired goal, though it also relegated the calendar to the structure's interior sections. A character who examines the etching and succeeds on a DC 5 Intelligence check quickly confirms the diagram represents the Aztli calendar. The undecorated, one-foot-diameter pillars' exact purpose is less obvious. They bear no obvious clues, yet the paintings covering the walls, which were also a later addition after the level was enclosed, provide some insight. The boreholes carved midway through the six-foot-high obelisks descend at a sharp angle instead of being level, while the panorama on the walls depicts the changing of the seasons. A character who examines the calendar, the pillars, and the paintings and succeeds on a DC 15 Intelligence check determines that the pillars coincide with the seasonal equinoxes. Sunlight passes through the borehole and illuminates the corresponding point on the calendar associated with the season shown in the neighboring paintings.

Nonetheless, Coyotl remains convinced that the calendar harbors some additional meaning or secrets he is yet to unravel. In furtherance of his theory, three of his devotees, Ciuatl, Pachoa, and Tzona (CE male Aztli human **cult fanatics** armed with clubs instead of daggers), carefully study the objects. Although they are in earshot of any combat taking place in areas **G3**, **G4**, or **G5**, the determined students attribute any commotion to their fellow residents getting too rowdy rather than participating in a life-and-death struggle. The trio jots hand-drawn diagrams and notes about the calendar onto a leather-bound tome containing pages made from maguey leaves. When they spot the intruding characters, they drop the journal and try to quickly neutralize as many adventurers as possible using their *command* and *hold person* spells before dealing damage to their enemies. Like their counterparts in area **G4**, the trio never surrenders and actively resists any attempts to extract information from them. If forcibly compelled to speak, the trio discusses their research on the calendar, divulging that they have found no hidden meanings or purpose to the

etchings on the floor or the paintings on the wall. When pressed about details regarding Coyotl's activities or plans, they confirm he currently occupies the chambers one level below this one where he ruminates about ways to spread Itzcuin's influence to the neighboring towns and villages. His latest scheme uses dogs, though they are short on any specific details.

Treasure: The book (worth 50 gp) contains a surprisingly in-depth analysis of the Aztli calendar as well as the paintings adorning the walls. One also carries two *spell scrolls* (*floral bouquet*, *strength in numbers* [see **Appendix D: New Spells**]), while another has one spell scroll (*clairvoyance*).

G7: ALOC'S QUARTERS

A thick, gray curtain made from linens hangs from a rod imbedded in the doorframe. It takes a successful DC 5 Strength check to fully push the curtain aside. A character can walk through the curtain without a check, but is blinded until the character moves more than five feet from the entrance or uses an action to brush the curtain aside.

After desecrating Nonotzali's temple, the deranged Coyotl became obsessed with others embracing the inner beast. To that end, he became fascinated with the canine disease the Aztlis refer to as the "Drooling Sickness," which he associated with Itzcuin. The almost always fatal illness, commonly known as rabies (see **Appendix B**), also infects humans with equally deadly precision, a fact lost upon Coyotl. The preserved corpse of his first test subject now occupies Aloc's former chambers. A character who examines the dog and succeeds on a DC 15 Wisdom (Medicine) check confirms that the canine suffered from rabies.

Coyotl sawed the hands off of the oak statue depicting Aloc in his youth and inserted the thumbs into two of the statue's orifices. The crudely carved sculpture bears only a faint resemblance to its subject. A character familiar with Aloc must succeed on a DC 15 Wisdom (Perception) check to recognize him. A character unfamiliar with him may attempt the same check, though he does so with disadvantage. Wracked by his lycanthropy, Coyotl rarely uses the linen mat Aloc slept on during his stay in the temple. Instead, 3 **geruzous** (see **Appendix A: New Monsters**) now dwell here. Read or paraphrase the following description of these fiendish beings:

At the first sign of intruders, the demons spit slime and then rush forward to attack with their claws. The monsters telepathically communicate with characters, urging them to indulge their bestial natures and revel in carnage. Conversation is a one-way street for the demons, who never respond to the characters' inquiries nor reveal any details beyond "Itzcuin sent them here." They have no knowledge of what lies at the bottom of the staircase nor of Coyotl's ultimate intentions.

G8: SCRIPTORIUM

A thick, gray curtain made from linens hangs from a rod imbedded in the doorframe. It takes a successful DC 5 Strength check to fully push the curtain aside. A character can walk through the curtain without a check, but is blinded until the character moves more than five feet from the entrance or uses an action to brush the curtain aside. Furthermore, a character who succeeds on

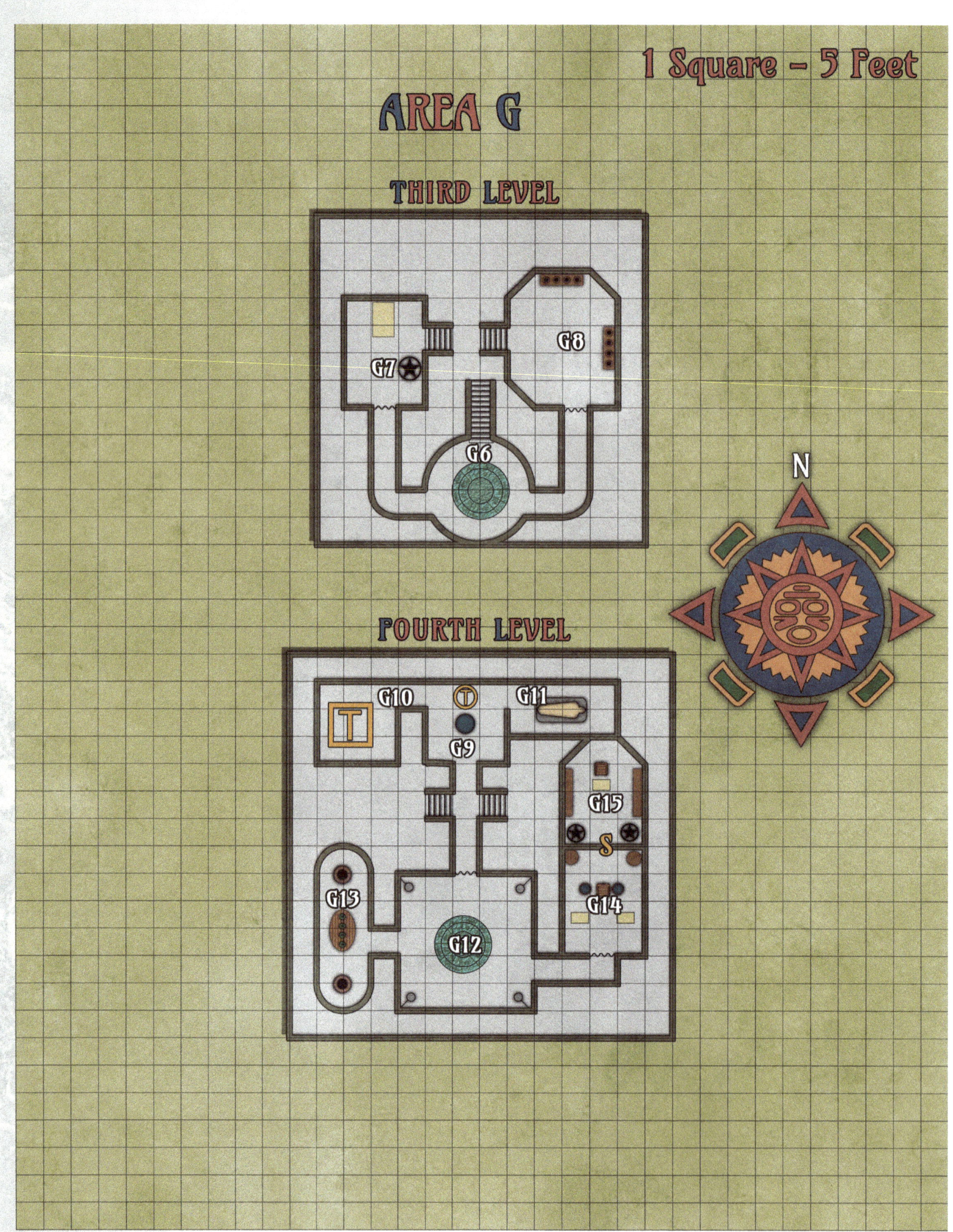

1 Square - 5 Feet
AREA G
THIRD LEVEL
G7
G8
G6
N
FOURTH LEVEL
G10
G11
G9
T
G15
S
G13
G14
G12

a DC 5 Wisdom (Perception) check hears intermittent snarls, yelps, and other animal sounds behind the curtain in addition to smelling a rancid stench.

Coyotl deliberately infected these unfortunate dogs with the deadly rabies virus (see **Appendix B**). He uses the bowls to collect their contaminated saliva, which he adds to the calmecac's cold cacao drinks to unleash the beasts inside his remaining followers. For their part, the tragic canines horrifically suffer from the final stages of the lethal virus. Although it appears to fit in with its diseased counterparts, a **retch hound** (see **Appendix A**) freely roams about the chamber, waiting for its inhabitants to expire so it can feast on their diseased flesh. However, the surly beast truly savors the taste of humanoid meat, prompting it to immediately exhale acidic bile at its potential prey before sinking its teeth into the tender morsels. The animal works in concert with 2 **beasts of Itzcuin** (see **Appendix A**) also wandering around the converted scriptorium. The trio coordinate their attacks to give the retch hound advantage while it waits for its retch ability to recharge.

Six codices sit atop the tables. Five of them are vestiges from the temple's former masters, but one codex details Coyotl's experiments on his captive hounds. A character may flip through the work of crude sketches and contemporaneous notes. A character who spends 10 minutes on this activity and succeeds on a DC 10 Intelligence check realizes Coyotl adds the infected saliva to the cacao drinks he serves his subordinates to whip them into an animalistic frenzy. His studies indicate that the dogs eventually died from the contagion. The misinformed Coyotl initially seemed to believe the disease would turn his human subjects into wild beasts without killing them. His research appears to end at this point.

Treasure: The five codices (worth 100 gp each) are rare works of Aztli poetry and song praising Nonotzali.

G9: Ceremonial Font

Shortly after consecrating the temple, Nonotzali's priests and worshippers collected ink and deposited the liquid within this turquoise receptacle. Despite the passage of 160 years, the stone basin remains half-full and the ink remains viable. During the Summer Solstice, Nonotzali's clergy used a few drops of the precious to chronicle local events that occurred in the prior year.

The trapdoor built into the floor adjacent to the north wall connects to the underground tunnels supplying water to area **E** outside. The wooden door opens with nominal effort, requiring only a successful DC 5 Strength check to lift it. The temple's architects attached a 25-foot-long rope tethered to a bronze pail to the inside of the trapdoor, allowing the user to retrieve water through a two-foot-diameter shaft below the trapdoor that descends 20 feet into a small cistern.

Cursed Ink Trap

When a creature removes the font from this chamber or more than two vials of ink from the receptacle per day, all creatures within five feet of the font must succeed on a DC 12 Wisdom saving throw or be cursed for one hour. While cursed, the creature takes 5 (2d4) radiant damage when it uses an action to eat or drink, including imbibing potions and magical elixirs. A *remove curse* spell or similar magic ends the effect. A character who examines the font and succeeds on a DC 15 Intelligence (Arcana) check locates the trap and discovers its triggering mechanism. Only a *dispel magic* spell or similar magic can disable the trap. Destroying the font permanently removes the trap.

Treasure: The turquoise font (worth 1,000 gp) rests atop a limestone pedestal. It weighs 200 pounds, though removing it from the temple is considered a sacrilege in the eyes of Nonotzali's devout followers.

G10: Pit of Bones

After rare animal sacrifices, Nonotzali's priests dumped the remains into the pit beneath the trapdoor. It takes a successful DC 10 Dexterity check with thieves' tools to open the lock or a successful DC 20 Strength check to pry the locked door open through brute force. If the characters bypass the trapdoor, read or paraphrase the following description:

The skulls, long bones, and vertebrae contain a mixture of humanoid and animal bones sacrificed to Nonotzali over the last 160 years, as well as Coyotl's recent additions to the pit. The students who resisted the vicious lycanthropy as well as Aloc's torso and the missing acolyte were dumped into the pit after he and his minions savagely butchered them. From the surface, it is impossible to discern the type, age, or number of skeletons in the pit, though the bones are roughly one to three feet deep in most spots. It takes a successful DC 15 Strength (Athletics) check to climb up or down the walls made from loose granular earth without falling. The characters may circumvent this obstacle by using a rope to raise or lower adventurers into or out of the pit. A character who examines the recent skeletons and succeeds on a DC 15 Intelligence (Nature) check confirms that they are almost all adolescent and teenage human males with the exceptions of Aloc and his acolyte who are both middle-aged human males. A character who explores the bottom of the pit and succeeds on a DC 10 Intelligence (Nature) check finds serpent bones accounting for a significant percentage of the animal skeletons.

While many of the skeletons are decades old, the uppermost layer are relatively recent additions almost completely stripped of their skin and muscles. The heat and humidity partially explain the rapid skeletonization of these earthly remains, yet the **ghast** and 3 **ghouls** picking through the bones are mostly responsible for the rapidly vanishing flesh.

The undead scavengers are recent additions to the complex. They are typically content to remain in the pit where they can freely pick the meat from the bones of the recently departed. However, the prospect of a fresh kill proves too irresistible to ignore. The cunning monsters know the best route to use when climbing out of the pit. Therefore, they gain advantage on Strength (Athletics) checks made to scale the walls. They have no information about Coyotl, as their attention is squarely focused on their next meal.

G11: Priest's Tomb

Nonotzali's priests laid the temple's founder Caxto to rest near the heart of the pyramid he designed and built. They wrapped his mummified body inside the preserved jaguar skin that serves as his crude coffin, using vines to seal it shut on both ends. It is impossible to unravel the skin without severing or removing the vines that bind the skin.

SUMMON CELESTIAL TRAP

Dealing at least one point of slashing damage to a vine instantly severs the magical bond keeping the makeshift sarcophagus intact. However, doing so immediately summons a **couatl** solely charged with the task of defending Caxto's corpse from defilement and theft. The couatl demands an explanation for the transgression, using *detect thoughts* to sense the characters' true motives for severing the magical bond. If the characters apologize for their actions and agree to leave the body undisturbed, the guardian allows them to leave unharmed, though the couatl casts *scrying* to keep a watchful eye on the characters' future actions to ensure they keep their word. Otherwise, the couatl attacks.

A *detect magic* spell cast on the coffin detects the presence of conjuration magic on the vines. It takes a successful DC 20 Intelligence (Arcana) check to spot the magical trap and then a second successful DC 15 Intelligence (Investigation) check to neutralize the trap. Alternatively, the characters may bypass triggering the trap by untying or carefully removing the bonds without severing them. It takes a successful DC 20 Dexterity check to manipulate the delicate bonds without breaking them. On a failed check, the character inadvertently snaps the vine, triggering the trap.

Character who successfully bypass the trap and unravel the coffin discover the withering, decomposed corpse of an elderly man. The decedent still wears a gold ring on each hand and a lapis lazuli necklace around his neck. He holds a dried husk of maize in his clenched fingers.

Treasure: The corpse wears a gold ring (worth 500 gp) on his right hand, and another gold ring (worth 250 gp) on his left hand. The gold rings bear no symbols or images, which makes them unique. However, the lapis lazuli necklace (worth 700 gp) bears a striking resemblance to a snake wrapped around a giant eagle, making it easy to associate the piece of jewelry with a priest of Nonotzali.

G12: KENNEL

A thick, white curtain made from linens and decorated with an embroidered depiction of a feathered serpent hangs from a rod imbedded in the doorframe. It takes a successful DC 5 Strength check to fully push the curtain aside. A character can walk through the curtain without a check, but is blinded until the character moves more than five feet from the entrance or uses an action to brush the curtain aside. Furthermore, a character who succeeds on a DC 5 Wisdom (Perception) check hears intermittent snarls, yelps, and other animal sounds behind the curtain in addition to smelling a foul odor.

> Urine, animal excrement, and vomit almost completely obscure a magnificent mosaic adorning the floor. Ropes tethered through a stone hook in each corner are attached to a leather, restraining harness.

Open wounds perforate the skin and fur of 3 **dogs** (use the **jackal** stat block), each outfitted with a harness that is attached to a rope affixed to one of the stone hooks. These animals suffer from the early stages of rabies, which leaves them feverish, lethargic, and obviously sick. They suffer from one level of exhaustion, but have not yet felt the full wrath of the virus. In this condition, they barely react to the unexpected intrusion. The characters can release the dogs from the harnesses with a successful DC 5 Dexterity check made to undo the straps keeping the harness in place. These animals are eventually slated to replace those in area **G8**, when those tragic creatures finally succumb to rabies.

Coyotl leaves the animals' bodily waste on the mosaic floor out of pure laziness and his crass need to debase Nonotzali and his worshippers. If the characters remove the excrement and vomit from the floor, they discover a magnificent tile mosaic. The grand artwork depicts Nonotzali in his humanoid form striking a serpent-headed humanoid with a lightning bolt. It takes a successful DC 5 Intelligence (Religion) check to identify Nonotzali as its subject.

The occupants in neighboring area **G13** expect some noise from the dogs, though any sounds with obvious humanoid origins, such as voices or a concerted effort to clean off the mosaic prompt these individuals to investigate the activity in the adjoining area.

G13: CACAO STORAGE AND BREWING

> Brown, oval beans fill two small clay pots stored near the edges of the walls. Some of these beans rest atop a rounded table with a pronounced lip along its borders. Heavy, flat implements presumably used to grind the beans into a powder also rest on the table, while small, clay cups sit on shelves built into its side.

Aloc stored dried maize and other nonperishable goods in this repository. Coyotl unceremoniously disposed of those foodstuffs with the exception of the cacao beans, which became an integral part of his fiendish plan to unleash the inner beast in his surviving charges. To that end, Cuxta and Quezatl (CE male Aztli human **cult fanatics** armed with clubs instead of daggers) grind cacao beans into a fine powder to be mixed into their deadly concoction. Two teen boys named Elzatl and Teuatal (N male Aztli human **bandits** armed with clubs and slings instead of scimitars and light crossbows) sit on the floor holding a clay drinking vessel in their outstretched hands. If the characters create a commotion in area **G12**, Cuxta and Quezatl temporarily abandon their post to look into the matter. Each carries a cup containing cacao powder as well as their weapon. Regardless of where they encounter the characters, they use an action to throw the ground material from the cup into the characters' faces to blind them. Treat this attack as an improvised thrown weapon with a range of 10 feet. There is only enough powder for one attack. A creature hit by the powder must succeed on a DC 10 Dexterity saving throw or be blinded. At the end of each of its turns, the target can make another Dexterity saving throw. On a success, the effect ends. Like their fellow fanatics in area **G4**, the duo remains tight-lipped about Coyotl's plans.

The younger boys surprisingly watch the battle unfold without interfering. So far, they are fortunate enough to have avoided contracting rabies from the contaminated cacao drink, which proves to be an imperfect method of quickly transmitting the virus. The duo, who have been best friends since childhood, have no knowledge of Coyotl's plans. They admit they did not speak out against Coyotl after his coup, but they never supported his violent takeover either. Since then, his ardent followers have forced them to come to the temple for their daily serving of his cacao drink. They believe the concoction is designed to make them more obedient, though they are concerned that several of their friends exhibit symptoms of a virulent illness or seem to have lost their minds.

Treasure: The two clay pots hold a substantial quantity of cacao beans (worth 400 gp). Cuxta wears a turquoise ring (worth 100 gp), while Quezatl carries three *potions of healing* and a *war paint, blue* (see **Appendix C: New Equipment and Magic Items**).

G14: AUDIENCE HALL

A thick, gray curtain made from linens hangs from a rod imbedded in the doorframe. It takes a successful DC 5 Strength check to fully push the curtain aside. A character can walk through the curtain without a check, but is blinded until the character moves more than five feet from the entrance or uses an action to brush the curtain aside.

> Two linen mats lie on the floor before an ornately carved oak chair decorated with etchings of feathered beasts. Two small clay basins containing water sit on each side of the chair. A small round table is in each of the far corners. An ornate painting of a grand library runs across the entire wall. Pictographs cover the face of a stone door against the far wall.

Aloc and his acolytes entertained visitors and guests in this understated audience chamber. The high priest sat in the oak chair, which bears carvings of feathered beasts along its back and legs. The water in the clay pots appears stagnant and cloudy. Aloc would normally sprinkle the water onto guests and visitors as a blessing or to wash their hands between morsels. The priests served food on the lightweight tables that they moved from the far corners and placed next to the chair and linen mats.

The pictographs on the stone door granting access to area **G15** are

arranged into five vertical rows. (The horizontal rows are obviously off-center.) Going left to right, each carving depicts the same feathered serpent. The first row contains four carvings, the second row has three, the third row has one, the fourth row has five, and the fifth row has two. Scrolled across the top of the carvings is another depiction of the feathered serpent followed by a horizontal line and two dots. Although the carvings look the same, a character who carefully examines the carvings and succeeds on a DC 20 Wisdom (Perception) check notices that the top carving in each vertical row has a slightly raised indentation that functions as a crude button near the base of the creature's tail.

The code is a mathematical formula. The horizontal bar represents the number five, and the two dots represent the number two. Therefore, the correct sequence is to push the top button in the fourth vertical row, which has five carved serpents, followed by the top button in the fifth vertical row, which has two. A character recognizes the horizontal line and dots as numerals with a successful DC 15 Intelligence check. Alternatively, the door can be forced open, though it takes a herculean effort to bypass this formidable barrier. However, a character who succeeds on a DC 25 Strength check can push the door open.

Vault Trap

When a character presses a button in an incorrect sequence or forces the door open without using the correct code, the images of the suns on the door's face emit a blinding flash of light in a 20-foot cone. Each creature in the cone must succeed on a DC 13 Dexterity saving throw. On a failed saving throw, the creature takes 28 (8d6) radiant damage and is blinded. At the end of each of its turns, it may attempt another Dexterity saving throw. If it succeeds, the blindness effect ends. A creature who succeeds on its initial Dexterity saving throw takes half as much damage and is not blinded. Once triggered, the trap is rendered inert until it resets 1d4 rounds later.

It takes a successful DC 20 Intelligence (Arcana) check to confirm a magical trap on the door. If the characters already discovered the concealed buttons, the preceding check also determines that pressing a button out of sequence or forcing the door open without entering the correct code triggers the trap. The trap can be disarmed with a successful DC 20 Intelligence (Investigation) check, though it still resets itself 1d4 rounds after being disarmed.

G15: Vault

Hardly renowned for his bravery, **Coyotl** (see **Appendix A**), has taken up residence in the vault housing the temple's treasury, the complex's most secure locale. The uprising's cowardly leader broods in his quarters, disappointed in his plan's lack of visible and obvious progress. Two adolescent boys (N male Aztli human unarmed **commoner**) bound by heavy ropes foam at the mouth while they helplessly twitch and convulse. The rabies virus quickly overwhelmed these two young boys. They rapidly progressed through the disease's initial stages without transforming into the killing machines Coyotl desired. Instead, they quickly cycled into deathly ill children who now suffer through rabies' horrific death throes. When Coyotl and his loyal minions saw the disease's effects firsthand, they removed these two individuals from the populace and kept them hidden to keep Coyotl's failure private and to prevent panic from spreading through the calmecac.

Behind the claws and fangs, Coyotl is a selfish young man obsessed with his sense of self-importance and resolving old scores. Despite his formidable combat abilities, he shies away from fighting an opponent who poses a realistic threat to his safety. If the characters' actions in area **G14** gave Coyotl any warning of their arrival, such as triggering the vault trap or pounding on the vault door, Coyotl sits on the oak chair and casts *minor illusion* to conjure ropes around his arms and chest to make it appear as if he is being restrained. A character who physically interacts with the ropes discovers it to be an illusion. A character

who uses an action to examine the ropes and succeeds on a DC 12 Intelligence (Investigation) check also determines the ropes to be illusory. Coyotl assumes a catatonic appearance to blend in with the other victims of the virus. In this case, Coyotl cautiously watches from his seat while the 3 **beasts of Itzcuin** (see **Appendix A: New Monsters**) fight the intruders. Coytol unexpectedly rises from his seat and joins the fray when the beasts hit more than one character or render a character unconscious. He transforms into his hybrid form and attacks the unsuspecting adventurer with his claws and bite. Alternatively, he may grab a club from the nearby shelf in lieu of his claw attacks. Coyotl prefers using his sneak attack ability to maximum effect while he still has allies rather than immediately turning to his limited repertoire of spells.

If the beasts fare poorly, Coyotl pretends to be in an irreversible stupor. An astute character who examines him and succeeds on a DC 15 Wisdom (Insight) check believes the young man is faking his current condition. Of course, if the characters attempt to restrain him, touch him, or say anything remotely threatening, Coyotl immediately snaps out of his catatonia and goes on the offensive. Surrender is not an option for the werecoyote. Left to the whims of Aztli justice, he would assuredly die a horrifically gruesome death on a sacrificial altar or a prolonged incarceration in the notoriously brutal prison system. While he cannot undo the murders he already committed, the cagey werecoyote blames his corruption on Itzcuin and Ozhuma who unleashed his lycanthropy. He offers permanent exile as the only alternative punishment for his crimes. He rejects any other option, knowing full well that any other choice gives him no hope for the future. If negotiations break down, Coyotl still has some tricks up his sleeve. Depending on the circumstances, he may cast *expeditious retreat* or *misty step* to slip past the characters and potentially outrun them into the wilderness. If flight does not appear to be a viable option, Coyotl casts *mirror image* and attempts to slug it out with the characters using his melee attacks or offensive cantrips.

Treasure: The shelf along the southern wall holds a *+1 itztopilli* (see **Appendix C: New Equipment and Magic Items**), a spell scroll (*divination*), and a *death whistle* (see **Appendix C: New Equipment and Magic Items**), in addition to ordinary objects including a bronze statuette of a pouncing cat (worth 150 gp), a collection of seashells (worth 75 gp), and 23 bloodstones (worth 10 gp each). The shelf on the northern wall holds 2,534 sp and 1,002 gp in open leather bags. The two bronze statues (worth 250 gp each) stand 5–1/2 feet high. Each statue weighs roughly 1,000 pounds. Eagle feathers and tufts of jaguar fur adorn the linen mat (worth 100 gp).

Concluding the Adventure

With Coyotl dead or otherwise neutralized, the characters face the dilemmas of what to do with the calmecac's infected residents, many of whom remain symptom-free. The *lesser restoration* spell offers a cure, but those left untreated face a tragic descent into delirium and ultimately death. However, Coyotl did not act alone. The characters and local authorities must also decide the fates of the young boys and men who willingly joined Coyotl's cause and helped put his diabolical plan into motion. Aztli justice often lacks mercy, but the notion of summarily executing the town's potential next generation of leaders and warriors generates political ramifications for Mintoch and the ruling nobility. In the end, the town likely punishes only a small handful of ringleaders as an ominous warning to the more malleable calmecac residents who fell prey to Itzcuin's empty promises.

Meanwhile, Quiahuitl's priest presides over the critical rain harvest festival that takes place in the outer courtyard of the temple of Quiahuitl within Teohuacan. The townsfolk naturally invite the heroes as honored guests, as some families express their gratitude by offering them a host of gifts ranging from the mundane (maize, squashes, trinkets, and similar baubles) to the extravagant (family heirlooms, tracts of arable land, and even marriage proposals from family patriarchs). If the characters did not explore the cipatenhua stronghold earlier in the adventure, Mintoch may ask the adventurers to investigate several recent kidnappings or ambushes involving the cunning monsters. From here, the characters may also travel to the neighboring Tepepan Mountains to begin *Gargoyle Pet Sematary*, the next adventure in the series.

Gargoyle Pet Semetary

By Rob Manning

"Tepetzin towers over us all! Hail to the stairway of the hero-gods!"

— A Mountain Dweller Saying

"The silver of a sprig of chachacomo is worth more than real silver to me."

— Aztli boast heard throughout the lands

"Miquiztli icuhea or Death comes quickly."

— The motto in the mountains

Gargoyle Pet Sematary is an adventure for four Tier 2 characters that introduces the heroes to the Tepepan Mountains in central Tehuatl where Aztli and dwarven cultures partially merge. When the characters arrive at the village of Alataq, they soon discover something is amiss within the settlement as several of its steadfastly loyal gargoyle servants appear to have gone rogue. What feels like an isolated incident turns out to be far more sinister as the architects behind the insidious plot have grander designs and greater horrors to unleash upon an unprepared world unless the adventurers stop them.

Adventure Background

There are no coincidences for the Aztlis. While fate may not be preordained, omens and signs frequently portend what the future holds. On this occasion, a chance meeting between a debonair demon named Chupura and a cunning night hag named Aytasina led to love at first sight for the smitten pair. The devious and alluring Aytasina had previously spent her lonely, forlorn existence wandering through the Tepepan Mountains perpetrating isolated murders and minor corruptions while dabbling in the pseudoscience of altering living creatures and studying arcane magic. At first, Chupura tried to convince his beloved hag to leave the small island for greener pastures and greater conquests. However, when the demon learned about the Aztli god Itzcuin's interest in canines and gnolls, he too came to believe that their encounter represented part of a divine destiny in Tehuatl.

Despite the demon's sincere belief in the couple's newfound destiny, the apathetic Itzcuin felt the need to test the fidelity of his neophyte disciples. To prove their worth, he appeared to the pair in cryptic visions, beseeching them to find the Lost Temple of the Twins hidden within the Tepepan Mountains. With nowhere else to turn for information or even hints about its whereabouts, Aytasina consulted her divination magic. Her spells and research led her to an obscure man named Hiuaui who lived in the village Alataq. The ambiguous clues pointed toward the secret being linked to a mysterious object in his possession associated with the settlement's unusual tukkuru gargoyles who serve and obey their humanoid masters as pet animals.

The connection between the item and the creature remained elusive, but the malevolent duo came upon a brilliant idea. They saw an opportunity to maximize their investment by exploiting the citizens' dependence and absolute trust in their generally benevolent and loyal servants. With these wicked thoughts in mind, they located and ventured into the tukkuru gargoyle graveyard within the mountain range where they began the process of corrupting these faithful creatures into conniving, evil, killing machines masquerading as stalwart friends. After several fits and starts, Aytasina sent prototypes to Hiuaui's home to spy on the old man and to discover where he hid the object of their mutual desire. To their chagrin, Hiuaui remained tightlipped about the item despite the monsters' cajoling and coaxing.

Frustrated by the lack of progress toward achieving their objective, the impatient demon and his lover ordered their minions to murder the old man and then torture his old gargoyle pets to reveal the location where he hid the object. Hours of agony and excruciating pain could not break Hiuaui's devoted gargoyle pets. Although they failed to accomplish their intended goal of retrieving their target, they wildly succeeded in their endeavor to build legions of deadly, innocent-looking creatures to wreak havoc throughout the Tepepan Mountain and beyond. They now stand on the precipice of unleashing mayhem upon the Aztlis and dwarves unless someone intervenes to stop them.

Adventure Synopsis

The adventurers' travels take them into the unruly Tepepan Mountains where Aztli and dwarven cultures collide in bizarre manners. During the initial foray into this rugged terrain, the characters are free to explore the region where they may engage in several random encounters with its indigenous denizens or become embroiled in the activities at the Obsidian Vault or the machinations brewing inside the quirky town of Aruapa. From there, the trail leads to the village of Alataq, where the adventurers arrive during a funeral for an elderly resident who died under very mysterious circumstances. After some inquiries, Calcata, the man's son approaches the characters and asks them to retrieve several items from his deceased father's house. Although this appears to be a curious request for such a minor task, Calcata tells them that he fears going to his father's residence because of recent unsettling events in the home.

When the characters arrive, they find the scene in disarray. With the evil gargoyles gone, the vile monstrous allies of Chupura and Aytasina torture Hiuaui's loyal servants to learn where he hid the object the demon and his lover desire. Fortunately, the characters appear in the nick of time to spare the tukkuru gargoyles any further suffering and retrieve the objects his son requested. After inspecting one of the items, they realize a maguey paper concealed inside Hiuaui's scepter leads them to the gargoyle graveyard where Chupura and Aytasina are ramping up production of their evil tukkuru assassins.

During this segment of the adventure, a benevolent tukkuru gargoyle may accompany the characters on its way to join its fellow gargoyles in the afterlife. When the characters arrive, they see troubling signs of the evil duo's recent insidious activities. The adventurers' investigation reveals that the two parties plan to extend their influence even further by courting potential discontent among the Firebrand dwarves. Their exploration first leads them to an encounter with the charming Chupura who attempts to procrastinate while trying to telepathically summon aid from his lover. If the distraction fails, he fights the characters until forced to flee. The characters then delve deeper into the complex where they encounter a crude alteration center for the modified tukkuru gargoyles as well as the ancient gargoyle graveyard itself. After navigating through these hazards, the characters meet the plot's mastermind within her secure vault where she and potentially her healed lover wait to deal with the trespassers infringing on their plans. The characters must defeat the pair to halt their production of the devious pet gargoyles and to restore solemnity to the somber gargoyle cemetery.

With the immediate threat neutralized, the characters return to the village where they learn the original message also contained an encoded map directing them to the hidden temple within the Tepepan Mountains. Although the malevolent locale poses no imminent danger to the region, its mere presence warrants taking action to prevent others from finding and using its power to spread Itzcuin's baleful influence across the land at a later date.

STARTING THE ADVENTURE

By Lost Lands standards, the island of Tehuatl and the Tepepan Mountains are a mere fraction of the size of most kingdoms in Akados and Libynos. The characters may begin the adventure along the southern edge of the mountain range that dominates the island's interior. The characters are free to be on their way to a location within the mountains such as the village of Aruapa or to travel directly to the settlement of Alataq, which is the main jumping-off point for this story. Because the distances between these points are relatively short, you can determine how far you want the characters to venture to reach their destinations. The following sections contains adventure hooks and random encounters you can throw at the adventurers during their trek through the mountains, as well as several fixed site encounters.

ADVENTURE HOOKS

You have several options to entice the characters to partake in this tale. You may use one of the following hooks or create one of your own. If you are using this adventure as a continuation of *The Re-education of Coyotl*, their discretion and valor in handling that situation may lead Kharu Amayana and Jark'iri from the town of Aruapa to request the characters' assistance in dealing with their bedeviled, small outpost.

THE SCRIPT

The Library of Alataq is renowned for its repository of knowledge and for offering sagacious advice to those seeking it. The characters recently acquired a curiosity that defies magical insight even though it appears completely nonmagical. The object is an ancient, weathered scrap of maguey paper containing faint drops of ink made from an unknown substance that form strange symbols and pictographs. The item is a coded message written in a cipher system that functioned as a precursor to the Aztli alphabet. Although the piece has no intrinsic value, the library's sages fawn over the rare piece, as they believe it was written by Nonotzali himself during his mortal lifetime. They appraise the item as being worth 500 gp for its value as a religious relic. The characters' journey to the mountain settlement then embroils them in the plot centering around Hiuaui.

THE GARGOYLE MESSENGER

Although the character has not seen him in years, a distant relative named Hiuaui (see **Alataq**) has one of his tukkuru gargoyles (see **Appendix A: New Monsters**) deliver a message to the character expressing his concerns about strange events taking place in his home. He asks the character to visit him to investigate his suspicions. The message conveys no specific details regarding his misgivings other than to vaguely allude to his lack of trust in others, and enemies murmuring behind his back. The dispatch seems coherent in parts and rambling in others, but the character recalls Hiuaui to be a remarkably sharp man before his advanced age apparently took its toll on him. If the characters respond to the summons, the gargoyle leads them back to its master's home, which is now a crime scene in utter disarray.

FIREBRAND AGENTS

If one of the characters is a dwarf of the Firebrand Clan, the influential and powerful Garunt Firebrand (LG male dwarf **knight**) approaches the characters to investigate a rumor about an evil entity attempting to make contact with disloyal members of the clan. Details about the plot are scant, but the source believes answers may be found in the mountain town of Alataq, where they believe some of the group's agents are currently active. Under questioning, Garunt reveals that he has no further information other than what he fortuitously overheard two patrons of unknown origin discussing in a tavern within Alataq. He never saw the parties before, and he has not seen them since, though he believes they were really otherworldly creatures in disguise. He also swears he heard one of the individuals mumble the name Itzcuin in an otherwise indecipherable language.

THE TEPEPAN MOUNTAINS

Through it all, the Tepepan Mountains survived. The cataclysm that laid waste to nearly all of the southern continent spared the northern tip that ultimately became the Tepepan Mountains. For generations, the humanoid populations crammed into this small corner of the world. When the island expanded and the waters ebbed, the Aztli people left the rugged peaks for the reborn grasslands and forest growing in the stony giants' shadows. While the Aztlis maintained some presence in the Tepepan range, the lonely peaks came under the Firebrand dwarves' dominion, giving the region a unique character that combines elements from both cultures. While the dwarves enjoy a great deal of autonomy, the Aztli Confederation still demands their literal and figurative pounds of flesh from the dwarves to keep their mighty armies at bay.

Despite the tropical conditions on the island, the mountains are a climate all their own. The elevation and comparatively dry air keep the temperatures mild and the humidity low during the daytime hours. When the sun sets, the air rapidly chills, dropping below freezing at the higher altitudes. Indeed, permanent snowcaps coat the tops of the tallest mountains, though nearly the entire area experiences some frozen precipitation over the course of the year. The onshore flow of air also pushes fierce winds through the peaks and valley, which makes the cool temperatures feel even colder.

The harsh environment and rugged terrain conspire to keep settlement populations low in comparison to communities with more accommodating weather and soil. With the exception of Balandrur, there are no major cities in the Tepepan Mountains. The hardscrabble people who make a go of life under these challenging circumstances tend to dwell in small, self-sufficient communities that are easier to clothe and feed than giant metropolises reliant upon trade. The Tepepan Mountains map appears on page 65.

MOUNTAIN ENCOUNTERS

The rugged, unforgiving terrain gives adventurers little respite from the natural and unnatural dangers that abound here. In the absence of any clearly discernable paths or trails, the characters must trek through trackless areas for much of their journey into the foreboding peaks. The extreme altitude in some spots makes travel difficult and harrowing to say the least. For every hour spent trekking through the untamed wilderness, the adventurers have a 25% chance of participating in one of the encounters found on **Table 2–1**. The encounters include a mix of combat and opportunities to explore the characters' surroundings in greater detail. These short encounters are also easily dropped in when you need a mountainous encounter in any campaign.

TABLE 2–1: TEPEPAN MOUNTAINS RANDOM ENCOUNTERS

1d12	Encounter
1	The Faeries and the Footman
2	Mummy Dearest
3	The Wyrmlings
4	Devilish Flames
5	The Church of Seeping Death
6	The Squid and the Whale
7	Rash Decisions
8	Wolves in the Distance
9	Hair of the Dog
10	Lightning Crashes
11	Orc Vision Quest
12	Drunken Dwarf Avalanche

The Faeries and the Footman

Once, a small coterie of elves under the orders of a high-level wizard made a home and observatory in the Tepepan Mountains. Only the first floor of the stargazing tower and one outbuilding remain. The wizard built two constructs to protect her library, and they are the only remnants of the expedition, save for a single book written in Elvish in the library. When the characters come within visual range of the mostly razed structure, read or paraphrase the following description:

When the characters move close to the observatory tower, 2 **phookas** (see **Appendix A: New Monsters**) hiding in the ruins of the roofless outer building attempt to ambush them. The duo discovered the library in the tower some time ago and their mischievous nature wouldn't allow them to leave without gathering the seemingly burning book resting atop the floor. The footman drove them back and now they wait, nearly invisible in the ruins of the other building, where a large tree now grows. After surprising the characters, they try to lure or steer the combat toward the library and the 2 **monolith footmen** (see **Appendix A: New Monsters**) that guard the entrance. Charged with the sole task of preventing intruders from entering the tower, the constructs attack only when a living creature moves within 10 feet of the tower's perimeter.

A character who peeks through the crack can see the book with a successful DC 10 Wisdom (Perception) check. If the combat or another ruse distracts the constructs, they can slip into the library uncontested through the crack and steal the book from its place on the floor. If the monolith footmen become occupied with attacking the characters, one or both phookas step into a nearby tree to stride into a tree close to the building and then run through the crack and into the tower to retrieve the book and escape with their prize.

Treasure: One phooka holds an onyx figurine of a wolf worth 200 gp in a small pouch. If the characters recover the book and succeed on a DC 10 Intelligence (Arcana) check, they confirm the book's cover has been enchanted by a *continual flame* spell. The book is a diary containing personal accounts of the wizard's life in excruciatingly dry, boring detail. However, the book also conceals two *spell scrolls* (*slither*, *wall of smoke* [see **Appendix D: New Spells**]).

Mummy Dearest

Many tribes of gnolls thrive in the high mountains. The humanoids preserve the bodies of their deceased for the afterlife by removing all the major internal organs, wrapping the bodies in a huddled position with shellacked hides, and burying them in narrow crevasses high on the mountainsides. The Anu Khunu were one of the most devout tribes, and some of their dead still wander the area above the timberline. At the beginning of this encounter, read or paraphrase the following description:

Visibility, deep snow, and the 3 **mummies'** Dreadful Glare likely give the mummies enough leeway for the pair in front to close in to attack. A third mummy delays its attack for a round or two before approaching the adventurers from behind. The three mummies have no regard for their personal wellbeing. They just want to kill any living creatures that cross their path.

Treasure: If the characters find the crevasse where these gnolls were once entombed, they discover a *ring of jumping* entirely carved from a large opal secreted among the paltry treasures left in the preservation jars. It takes a successful DC 20 Wisdom (Perception) check to locate the crevasse if the characters traverse up to the bare patches of rock ahead of them. Otherwise, a character who succeeds on a DC 20 Wisdom (Survival) check may detect faint tracks leading up to the hidden location.

THE WYRMLINGS

Some species of dragons in the Tepepan Mountains are nearly flightless. Their wings are underdeveloped, and their bodies are longer, more lupine, and sinewy. Their altered physiques help them to swiftly move through the narrow caverns beneath them. These youngsters usually set their sights on dwarves, but as this trio of immature beasts has learned, food comes in all shapes and sizes. At the beginning of the encounter, read or paraphrase the following description:

> A slight skittering across the crumbling rock surface is the only sound above the wind before a swift shadow blots out the sun.

The 3 **white dragon wyrmlings** attack in concert. One wyrmling tumbles into the largest group of enemies to bite, while the other two wyrmlings blast the characters from afar with their cold breath attack as they jump around the melee. Their mother, an adult white dragon, lumbers through the subterranean caverns hunting dwarves. She is too far away from her offspring to hear their cries or help them. However, if the characters kill her progenies, they earn an eternal enemy.

Treasure: The skin and teeth of the trio are worth 50 gp per dragon if the characters take the time and effort to remove these items from the corpses. Their lair is also nearby but difficult to find as several pillars of ice camouflage the opening at the base of an ancient, ice-covered waterfall. Discovering the cavern requires a successful DC 25 Wisdom (Perception) check if the adventurers look in the right place.

The dragons have amassed only a small cache of silver and gems worth 450 gp and a gold-filigreed breastplate worth 550 gp. If the mother dragon learns of the characters' identity through whatever means, she exacts her revenge later when the characters have the wherewithal to defeat or at least survive an encounter with the irate mother dragon. You may use the dragon to remind them of their time in the Tepepan Mountains, even if they are in a different climate.

DEVILISH FLAMES

This encounter occurs either aboveground or below. When it begins, read or paraphrase the following description:

> What seemed a trick of the mind soon becomes evident that this is no illusion. The air is getting warmer. Actual permeable soil supporting succulent plants covers the ground. An apple tree, a group of irises, and lush grass dazzle the senses with thoughts of eternal spring. Ahead, a cracked vent made of basalt sports an intense yellow flame that shoots three feet into the air.

This vent has burned for centuries. Natural gas and the right combination of elements created this small oasis in the mountains where it continues to thrive to this day. Any snowfall here quickly turns to mist or rain. Just below the surface, **8 magmin** gloomily sulk in the eternal flame. They rarely rise above the vent's lip but do so if the characters have any magical light source or if they camp here for any length of time. Magmin who leave their subterranean refuge attack trespassers with unbridled fury.

Treasure: Nestled among the topiary are some rare spices (cinnamon, cardamom, and mustard). If harvested, they are worth 150 gp.

THE CHURCH OF SEEPING DEATH

This encounter occurs underground in a shrine to the star spawn that brought forth chaos in centuries past. The shrine's power associated with the outer planes has weakened over time, though the imagery still evokes the fear of the Nights of Sillu and Claw. Gnoll cults used to worship here, offering blood and bone to the uncaring star spawn. If the characters happen upon this locale, read or paraphrase the following description:

Before the Aztli Confederation rose to power, the Aztli city-state of Xacota dominated the island. After its spectacular downfall in the wake of its crushing defeat at the hands of the Poqozas and their elf allies, chaos reigned in many parts of Tehuatl. The opportunistic gnoll tribes and their newfound patron deity Itzcuin capitalized on the situation. They quickly expanded portions of their territory within the Caya and Caxcalli grasslands. Whether of their own accord or at Itzcuin's urging, the gnolls' priests attempted to forge alliances with otherworldly beings and demons as they waged a proxy war against the lucrative city of Ixtla, which would open a gateway into the Tepepan Mountains. To prove their worth, the gnolls' bloodlust went into overdrive as they slaughtered and sacrificed thousands of displaced Aztlis in the wake of Xacota's collapse. Despite causing mass casualties, the gnolls' dreams of conquest slowly died when the rejuvenating Aztlis re-established their dominance. Further details on these events can be found in the accompanying sourcebook.

> The heat is oppressive in the tunnel as it widens to form a large cavern. The walls appear segmented and chitinous. Many pillars formed of insectoid skulls with mandibles form sconces of unlit torches. Everything has a sheen of oily water. The far end of the large room holds an elaborate shrine of human bones and skulls covered with the slick, shiny veneer that coats the entire chapel.

This shrine once held high ceremonies to summon creatures from other dimensions. Most have moved on to wreak havoc in the mountains or to spread even farther across Tehuatl. The characters swear they can still hear the chattering of the insects in their minds as they observe the intricate carvings dedicated to the ancient evil overlords.

However, the chapel is not abandoned, as **8 gray oozes** remain here to this day. They appear as moist patches of stone, with some clinging to the 50-foot-high ceiling, some near the shrine, and some just inside the door. They swarm the intruding characters and attack from all sides with no plan other than to kill. If one adventurer falls, the surviving ooze moves to another combatant. Each hit from a melee weapon causes an ooze to pop with an audible sound and causes pustules of jellied, infected fluids to spray out.

The shrine radiates evil and chaos. A cleric or other good-aligned character who destroys the shrine by casting a *hallow* spell in the area or who smashes the altar (AC 17, 60 hp) into pieces gains a 400 XP story bonus.

Treasure: A *+1 tecpatl* (see **Appendix C: New Equipment and Magic Items**) lies near the altar — also covered with the sickly sheen of the endless travels of the oozes across the surface of the entire chapel.

THE SQUID AND THE WHALE

Shortly after the great cataclysm, this comparatively low-lying area was completely underwater. In a remote area high in the mountains, a strange remnant of those primordial times still exists. If the characters begin this encounter, read or paraphrase the following description:

> Cresting the peak is within reach! This small crag offers respite from the near-constant wind. Icy fingers claw at the sky up the next bit of trail, large and bony. Upon closer examinations, these fingers reveal themselves to be ribs. The skeleton of a gargantuan, seemingly aquatic beast stretches up the mountainside. The enormous skull from this 150-foot-long creature points skyward at an unnatural angle with a massive two-handed sword piercing one eye hole.

Centuries ago, this site hosted a great battle. A massive mysticeti whale swallowed a large squid whole. Unwilling to cede dominance to its rival, the

Non-Combat Encounters

The following set of encounters are designed to give you an opportunity to throw something different at the players to keep them on their toes and engage their paranoia. You do not want the players to automatically start saying things like, "I cast *detect magic*," or something similar every time you roll dice. The Tepepan Mountains are a dangerous place, but not every encounter is a life-or-death struggle. Feel free to add monsters or intriguing non-player characters to beef up the combat encounters or use treasure found during one of these encounters to get a group back on track to help them refocus on the story you want to tell.

squid forced its tentacles back out of the gullet through the mouth, and the two beasts killed each other simultaneously. Their remains, which were once deep below the sea, now lie atop this peak. The only evidence of the squid to survive is the beak, buried under the snow midway between the whale's skull and its tail.

This locale is now the lair of Achila, a **spirit naga**. She remains invisible as she cunningly sifts through the minds of her adversaries. She thoroughly evaluates their strengths and weaknesses before launching her assault. The sword buried in the eyehole is a *minor illusion* the naga previously cast. Achila attempts to mentally dominate any heavily armored or equipped character first. If successful, she commands the enthralled victim to quickly run back down the mountain, taking a chance that the character falls hundreds of feet to their doom off the steep, icy cliff near her lair. It takes a successful DC 15 Dexterity (Acrobatics) or Strength (Athletics) check (character's choice) to avoid such an ignominious fate. If this attempt fails, she may then command her subject to throw their gear, including a weapon or shield, over the cliff. Magic-wielding characters are her second choice. She tries to get them to cast their most potent spell against a fellow adventurer after telepathically running through their abilities. She saves her *lightning bolt* until two or more enemies are in a line in front of her.

If the characters struggle with this encounter, you may have the whale's long dead spirit momentarily appear to distract Achila to allow the characters an opportunity to flee the area or disrupt one of her spells. After she dies, Achila rejuvenates three days later, unless magically compelled to not reappear.

Treasure: One of the smallest whale bones, located under the massive skull, functions as a *+1 wand of the war mage*.

Rash Decisions

This encounter may reoccur several times over the course of the adventurers' travels. In addition, you may add the effects of this encounter to any others below the timberline. While venturing across the Tepepan Mountains, the characters run across chachacomotzil (see **Appendix B**), a flowering herb that closely resembles its non-poisonous relative, chachacomo (see **Appendix B**), which vaunted mountain climbers and explorers greatly covet. The poisonous version is an irritant that grows more abundantly at a lower altitude.

Wolves in the Distance

To set the mood for this scene, read or paraphrase the following description:

> Rubble partially obstructs the valley ahead. A rockslide sprayed stones and gravel across the ground to choke off the level terrain. The slopes to the side are not covered in snow and there seems to be a natural trail up the eastern side of the scree. A small ground squirrel surveys his surroundings and then disappears among the larger rocks.

Animals and humanoids use this valley to traverse the area. The slide happened a long time ago and poses no immediate danger. As the characters start to move through the area, a pack of wolves intermittently howls in the distance. It is best to keep the number of wolves in the group indeterminate as well as concealing their exact location. While the encounter lasts, the animals neither draw closer to the characters nor move farther away. Furthermore, the beasts' verbal exchanges periodically occur in noisy but brief spurts between long periods of silence.

Hair of the Dog

Read or paraphrase the following description to set the action into motion:

> A long, low hall made of cut stones laid in a herringbone pattern butts up against the rise of a nearby cliff. The hall has a stone roof and appears to still be habitable. The wooden doors on either end are shut against the weather, but a painted sign depicts a hairless dog and a deer. Written in the Aztli, Dwarvish, Gnoll, and Orc languages is the legend: "Welcome to the Chichi auh Mazatl."

This was once a small inn called Chichi auh Mazatl. It used to be a wooden, two-story structure that catered to travelers seeking shelter in the rugged mountains. The building is long gone, with only a few stones left to mark where it stood. The remaining hall served as the inn's kitchen and dining room. A small pile of chopped wood and pine needles lies near a recently used fire pit. A great fire consumed the inn several decades ago, but many travelers still recount strange tales of mysterious events taking place during an overnight stay in the rough-and-tumble lodge owned by an eccentric Tlotl who allegedly scoured the nearby mountains looking for something.

Lightning Crashes

Mountain weather is frequently unpredictable and subject to change at a moment's notice. Read or paraphrase the following description when the storm clouds suddenly gather overhead:

> Ominous gray clouds coalesce in the skies surrounding the peaks, building against the upper ridge of mountains. Without warning, lightning crashes to the ground, and thunder resonates against the rigid stone. The light show is blinding, and the peals are almost deafening at this close distance. Yet not a drop of rain nor a single snowflake falls from the darkening sky. Chilly breezes whistle as they move across and through the intervening mountains.

Storms form quickly in the highlands. Most blow over in a matter of minutes, but some pack a significant wallop from rapid drops in temperature, fierce winds, and torrential downpours or snow squalls in freezing conditions. The precipitation and swirling winds often wash or blow away any evidence or tracks, making it difficult to pursue prey in this challenging environment. While such weather events are likely not deadly, they may force the characters to use resources to cope with the horrific conditions.

Orc Vision Quest

Read or paraphrase the following description of this locale:

> This shallow oubliette faces east. Graffiti covers the walls, with most of the scrawls written in Orcish. Caricatures of brave warriors doing battle with the fiery sun adorn the walls amid the scribble. Some are quick stick figures, but a few images display real talent.

In a rite of passage, young orcs must spend a week in this cave to further strengthen their resolve to conquer the sun-drenched lands. Every initiate must be awake before the sun breaks over the horizon, shouting to their god for the sun not to rise. The devotee partakes in the consumption of special fungi to aid them as they begin to understand the universe and their place in it. No brave warriors are here when the characters arrive, though a shaman and a daring orc youth may appear at any time.

Drunken Dwarf Avalanche

Dwarves continuously mine the mountains, looking for silver and gems. Sometimes, they dig a little too close to the surface and the resulting avalanche has a lasting effect. Some of these mishaps can be catastrophic, and they create a new tunnel leading to the dwarven lands below the surface.

A group of 11 drunken miners (CG male dwarf **commoners** armed with picks instead of clubs) are responsible for the rockslide. The men harbor no ill will and are truly sorry for the havoc their negligence caused. The avalanche poses no threat to the characters who are close enough to see, but are not in its direct path. If the adventurers move toward the avalanche, they must succeed on a DC 15 Dexterity saving throw or take 17 (5d6) bludgeoning damage, get knocked prone, and be buried beneath the debris. On a success, they evade the avalanche's effects in its entirety. A buried creature may use an action to make a successful DC 20 Strength (Athletics) to escape.

Regardless of whether the characters avoid the avalanche, the dwarves leave a silver ingot worth 30 gp and a *potion of healing* on the path ahead as recompense for their negligence. If forced to fight, they try to run back to the depths and rile the guards on duty or a patrol of dwarven soldiers from outposts connected to the Firebrand Clan as soon as possible.

This section presents two side treks the characters can partake in while exploring the Tepepan Mountains. The first is a short encounter involving events around an obsidian mine, while the second takes place in the unusual town of Aruapa.

Side Trek 1: The Obsidian Vault

This vault is in a small cavern system just below the surface of one of the mountains. Recently exposed due to seismic shifts, an enterprising gnoll named Anuqara discovered the crevasse and has been harvesting obsidian to bring back to Aruapa, a village a few miles away. Anuqara and her pack of minions are oblivious to any outside intruders. Luckily for them, a gang of plaresh demons roam around with them and should help the pack realize they are under attack before it is too late.

Area ST1-A: The Maws and the Bats

The strange worms are 2 **plaresh demons** (see **Appendix A: New Monsters**) who eat from the seemingly endless parade of bats for four rounds before returning inside the cave as the stream of bats tapers off. If the characters attack the monsters, they summon two more of their kind from **Area ST1-B**.

Area ST1-B: Vented Maw

The stench of bat guano fills the air. The remaining 2 **plaresh demons** (see **Appendix A: New Monsters**) feast while thrashing about in the 14-inch-deep guano pile. The decomposing waste emits methane gas that explodes when exposed to an open flame, spark, or any suitable ignition source. Creatures and objects within the chamber must make a DC 10 Dexterity saving throw, taking 17 (5d6) fire damage on a failure, or half as much damage on a success.

The demons are mostly mindless, but they do chant "wilanchana" (bloody ritual) as they attack.

Anuqara tasked a **gnoll** to retrieve these demons, and he is approaching from the other direction when the characters enter this area. His name is Lakin and though he is not extremely vigilant, the sounds of combat or an explosion immediately notify him to the presence of intruders. Lakin thought he was on a foolish errand. When alerted to the presence of intruders, he waits one round and then retreats to the vault to warn his mistress.

Area ST1-C: The Vault

Long ago, an ancient eruption deposited this formation of snowflake obsidian (speckled with flecks of white star shapes in the caramel-colored obsidian through cristobalite clusters). Anuqara only recently discovered the vault. She now endeavors to retrieve the stone and bring it to Aruapa. If Anuqara returns with this load, her queen promised her a promotion and a village of her own for her pack.

Obsidian Vault

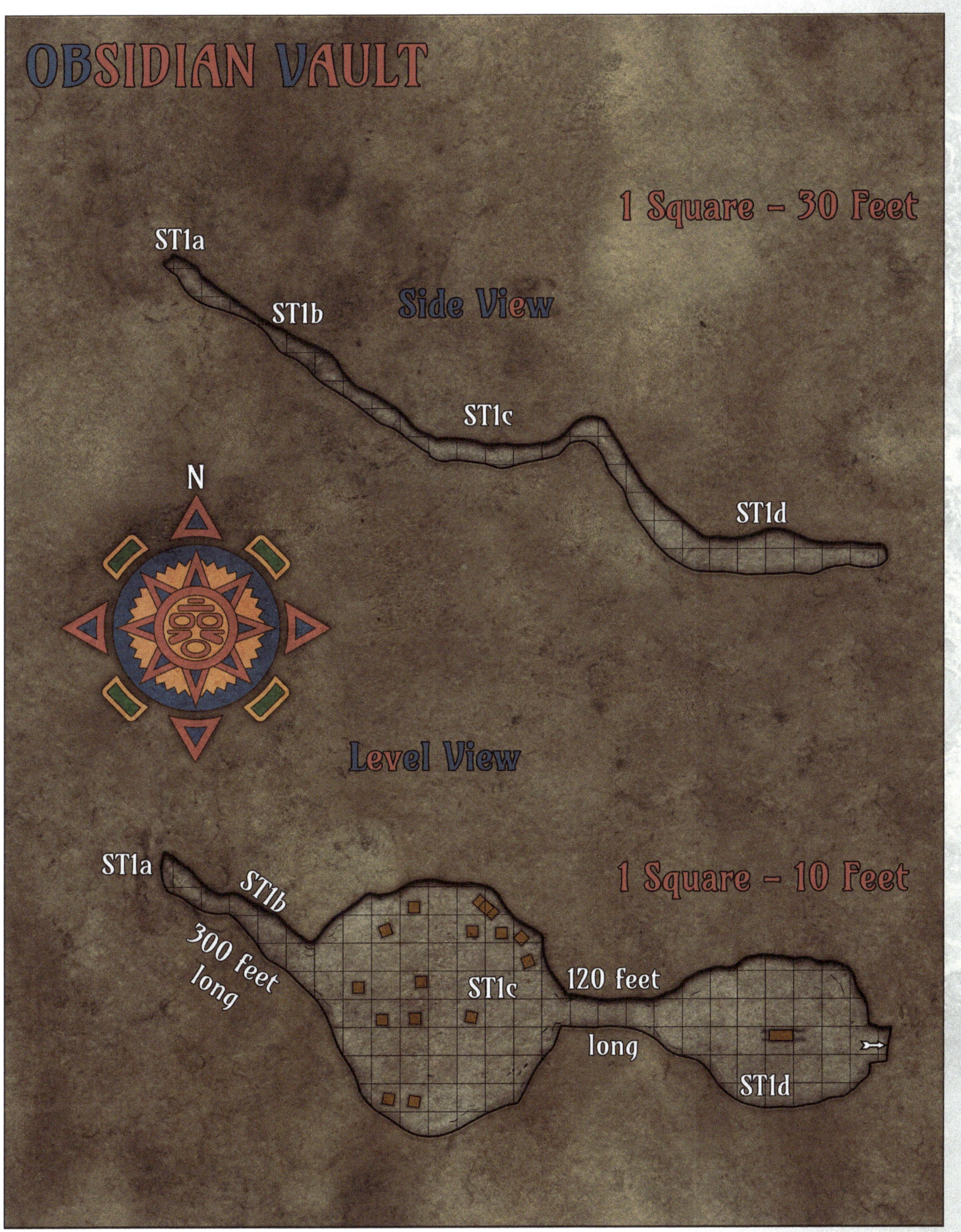

The vault itself is almost a hundred yards from the bats' room. There are no major splits in the cave and no dangerous drops, though the trail is continually going downhill as it delves deeper into the mountain. The following description assumes the characters have a light source, as Anuqara and her gang work without light, using their darkvision to complete their tasks. The loading process takes nearly three hours before the gnolls are ready to travel to the river to send the obsidian on the next leg of its journey.

> The now familiar satisfied grunting, lip-smacking sound echoes down the hall as the cavern widens in the distance. The room slopes upward and to the left 30 feet, where another of the monstrosities gnaws on the remains of a humanoid corpse. Wooden boxes lie scattered all around. Some lie open, their lids leaning against the edge. Some are stacked against the wall with their lids nailed shut. All have shards of obsidian in them. More of the black stone grows from the far wall, glinting in the light.

If the characters surprise the gnolls, you may add or paraphrase the following description. Change the number to three humanoids if the characters somehow killed Lakin, the gnoll from **Area ST1-B**, before they approach this room.

> Four tall humanoids are working in pairs, bent over the boxes. They load obsidian into them as fast as they efficiently can.

In addition to the **plaresh demon** (see **Appendix A: New Monsters**), there are 2 (or 3 if Lakin is with them) **gnolls** working under the cruel eye of Anuqara, a **gnoll slaver** (see **Appendix A: New Monsters**). If caught unaware, the gnolls fight with their pair of spears. They throw one of their spears and then rush into melee combat. The demon uses its Infest Corpse ability to spectacularly consume the dead gnoll in a burst of slime and offal, bringing forth a new **plaresh demon** in the bloody remains as the gnoll's soul goes to its next destination. The pair wades into melee as soon as the gnolls attack. Anuqara fires her longbow from cover at the other exit from the room. She concentrates all her attacks on a single intruder, while the gnolls throw and attack in pairs. If Lakin made it here, all three warriors arm themselves with bows, and they cling to the piles of boxes to use as partial cover.

All of Anuqara's gnolls sport brands on nearly every inch of exposed flesh. She enjoys the branding process and keeps many metal tools in a pouch to create her "art." If Anuqara is reduced to less than half her maximum hit points or if any three of her pack falls, she flees. She quaffs up to two *potions of healing* during her escape. If the character capture her and compel her to speak through magical means or a successful Charisma (Intimidation) check contested by her Charisma (Intimidation) check, she reveals that the obsidian is bound for the town of Aruapa to be delivered to its queen.

Treasure: The obsidian collected here is worth 1,000 gp. In addition to the gnolls' equipment, Anuqara also carries two *potions of healing*, if she did not already consume them while attempting to flee.

Area ST1-D: Burrows and Barks

The narrow, winding corridor connecting the vault to this cavern slopes down until it widens again into a level loading area. Scratches and footprints tell the tale of the gnolls' use of the passage. Anuqara directed her pack to load the boxes of obsidian onto a waiting sledge device pulled by a team of 4 hairless dogs (use the **hyena** stat block). If she passes through here, the dogs are riled and wandering aimlessly. If she has not fled, they stand staged and harnessed to the nearly full sledge.

Blood covers two of the four excessively branded dogs. Another gnoll corpse lies nearby. The reason for the dead gnoll and the current bloody dogs is the unexpected arrival of an oafish **hill giant** that stumbled upon the fresh meat and treasure. The brutish humanoid is an opportunist who surprised the gnoll and is not sure whether to eat the dogs or use them to pull the sledge back to his lair. When he spots the characters, the giant swings its massive greatclub to batter his opponents into submission. The giant is not bright, but he knows well enough to retreat if his life is seriously threatened.

Treasure: The piled boxes of obsidian are worth 2,000 gp. The hill giant carries a leather sack containing 429 gp.

The trail of the previous sledges leads away from the cavern and directly to a fast-moving river about a mile away. Anuqara follows her shipment downstream and rejoins her final pair of gnolls. They are stationed at an ox-bow in the river almost eight miles from the point of entry. They fish the boxes of obsidian from the stream and have them packed and ready for Anuqara's return. The characters can catch up to her at some point solo or at the ox-bow with her minions if she is swift enough. If the characters confiscate any of the uniquely patterned obsidian and try to sell it in the area, Kharu finds out and sends a small task force to track down the thieves.

Side Trek 2: Gaunt Whispers in Aruapa

You can run this side trek separate from the others or in conjunction with the previous excursion. If the characters encounter the town of Aruapa first, they hear of Anuqara the slaver, but not necessarily of her mission.

Aruapa is a settlement of misfits, made up of outcasts from communities across the island. They fled their homes and resettled here for various reasons. Some out of fear, some out of guilt, and some out of desperation. Here at Aruapa and other remote mountain villages, people can reinvent themselves. Aruapa boasts humanoids of Tosca descent, Tlotls from various cultures in Akados and Libynos, as well as other people displaced from communities in Tehuatl. Half-orcs, gnolls, gnomes, and elves make up nearly half of the population, and half-bloods of all combinations thrive in the settlement. Aruapa welcomes new arrivals (sometimes pressing new recruits into "freedom" from caravans that pass too close to their village). Loyalty to The Queen curtails racial animosity quickly here. Old enemies such as orcs and dwarves live peacefully in the same dwelling.

Aruapa is fairly civilized but harbors a deep distrust of Chacuina, another nearby outpost with a similar background. This distrust stems from an incident where warriors from Chacuina crept into Aruapa's holy place and stole a figurine of the hero-god Zipe-Toteque, also known as Xotite among the dwarves. Ithapina, the outpost's leader at the time, credited the statue for Aruapa's luck in the growing season. When it was stolen, it created the lasting rivalry with the Chacuina villagers.

The main reason for the current extended stretch of harmony in Aruapa is Kharu Amayana and Jark'iri. These two elf women rule the settlement and root out dissension before it has a chance to fester. Kharu is "The Queen" and Jark'iri, a couatl, acts as her counselor. Jark'iri took elf form to be closer to the object of her desire. Tattoos of moths decorating their bodies from neck to calf symbolize their loyalty to each other. Anuqara (see **Area ST1-C**) serves as Kharu's enforcers. When Jark'iri warns her Queen of treacherous thoughts among the villagers, Kharu sets her gnoll slaver to work. Sometimes, Anuqara presses the unruly citizen into her war band, and sometimes the unfortunate soul "accidentally" falls off a cliff. Jark'iri warns Kharu only if she detects murderous thoughts. She numbs herself to most other thoughts, including Kharu's. The couatl knows hers is an unrequited devotion, but her heart tells her she cannot live without the elf.

Fortunately for the couatl's potential redemption, Kharu rarely abuses her power. She spreads the wealth of their outpost's acquisitions among her people almost evenly, and she keeps Anuqara on a short leash. Nonetheless, she realizes she is losing control over her gnoll slaver and is growing wary of her rough manner. She has promised Anuqara her own tribe and her blessing to move on after she makes her final delivery of obsidian.

One of Aruapa's main exports is silk gathered from a colony of moths brought here and cultivated by a Tlotl family whose ancestors escaped their homeland in distant Libynos generations ago. Most villagers work in some way to further the silk trade here. Some tend the lichen surfaces and mulberry orchards where the moths feed, while others boil the cocoons and harvest the silk. Specialists dye and weave the product, and a few transport and sell it to neighboring Aztli villages that covet the unusually strong and luxurious material.

Unfortunately, when the characters first arrive here, Aruapa is in a state of panic. Ch'usuyana, a spökvatten, recently gave birth to Ikanp'akiri, her ice maiden daughter. Although the fey would normally stay on the outskirts of town, she and her ghastly child decided to use the villagers' suspicions about the neighboring settlement of Chacuina against them. The evil fey used her to guile and charm to plant stories about Chacuina spies infiltrating the village to kill its normally trustworthy citizens. After she and her daughter killed their first victims under this pretense, the terrified citizens' imaginations took hold. They saw traitors in their midst as mass hysteria swept through the village. Meanwhile, the alluring Ikanp'akiri quickly enthralled two vagabonds of Aruapa. One man's true love chased her beau through the driving snow and dragged him back to civilization with a determined kiss and saved his soul. The other thrall is still with Ikanp'akiri in a nearby hovel on the outskirts of Aruapa. For now, Ch'usuyana watches the spectacle of violence and suspicion unfold from the safety of the town's tavern as she tries to ensnare others into her devious web of lies and false accusations.

Imata, the gate guard (N male elf **scout** armed with a spear instead of a shortsword) used to be praised for his bravery and keen sight. He served as a guard for nearly his entire adult life. Ch'usuyana triggered childhood fears in him, and he sees the approaching strangers as otherworldly terrors from his youthful nightmares. If the characters allow him to fully retreat, he finds his way to the tavern, where he tells his tale to the frightened throng.

The outpost of Aruapa consists of 18 small homes and the large warehouse built into the side of the mountain. Up to six people occupy each house at this time, though some homes are abandoned while others are cramped. Terror grips most villagers as they cling to improvised weapons in the vain hope that the evil that has descended upon their community might move elsewhere. They never willingly open their doors. The warehouse has a tavern attached to the front where 11 people chug pulque from clay containers. Only Kharu and Jark'iri sit on the large work floor of the warehouse. They are preoccupied with trying to figure out what has happened to their village and are trying to devise a means to stop it.

Encounter ST2-A:
The Hovels of Aruapa

Each two-story building measures 10 feet by 20 feet and has a steeply sloped roof. Small, shuttered windows keep the chilly breezes out, and villagers bolt the sturdy front doors from the inside against intruders. Most of the villagers avoid any conversation with the characters. Trespassers hear a few snarled threats when they get too close to a house containing scared villagers. Some villagers left their homes to stay with others as evidenced by seven abandoned homes. Only a simple latch secures those doors. Even within the occupied homes, distress and rancor rule over the huddled villagers, as they rediscover how to trust no one. Ch'usuyana's plot has torn at the façade of camaraderie in Aruapa.

Within 30 minutes of the characters' arrival, two of the homes experiencing suspicion turn to bloodshed and murder as one frightened occupant turns on another terrified villager. When this occurs, six villagers (N male and female humans and elf **commoners**) approach the characters and beg for them to end the terror. Most of the remaining 66 villagers are commoners as well, though there are 11 more experienced warriors (N male humans and elf **tribal warrior**) and two civil authorities (N male dwarf **nobles** armed with warhammers instead of rapiers). This oasis of hope teeters on the edge of anarchy unless the characters restore their faith in others.

Encounter ST2-B: The Tavern Uana

If Imata successfully left the characters behind at the guardhouse, he points a shaking finger at them when they enter. Read or paraphrase the following response:

Although it seems as if everything is back to normal, the patrons watch the characters with great interest. Iquina, the barman (CN male orc **berserker**) oversees the activities of 7 patrons (various alignments, four male Aztli humans, one male orc, and two male dwarf **commoners**) and 2 druids (N male Aztli human and dwarf **druids**). There are 7 more patrons (four male Aztli humans, one male orc, and two female tiefling **commoners**), and 1 soldier (NG male dwarf **veteran**) outside Iquina's supervision. A female Aztli jaguar cuauhocelotl oddly accompanies the soldier, though this woman is really Ch'usuyana, the **spökvatten** (see **Appendix A: New Monsters**) polymorphed into an Aztli woman. She used her powers of persuasion to convince the soldier of her love for him. Although not magically charmed, he swears to defend his new acquaintance at any cost.

Meanwhile, several conversations take place around the tavern. The orc, an Aztli, and the dwarf pair tell bawdy tales as they try to outperform each other with their lies. One of the Aztli commoners sits alone, reading a thin tome and smoking a pipe. The soldier and jaguar cuauhocelotl appear well into their cups judging from the empties on their table as they smile at each other. The two druids give the characters a peace gesture before discussing their travels above and below the ground. The remaining patrons play a dice game in which a shooter rolls two six-sided dice, and then they bet on whether a third die's result will fall between the other two numbers shown. The characters are free to join in any of the discussions, though the participants are initially reluctant to accept the strangers into their midst, especially the polymorphed Ch'usuyana.

The conversations continue for almost 30 minutes before the chaos from outside crashes into the tavern. (If the characters leave beforehand, the following parties burst into the tavern as they prepare to leave.) A tumult accompanies 3 elves (CG male elf **scouts**) and 3 **gnolls** who enter the tavern, shouting at each other as they approach the characters. The elves approach the characters and irrationally demand the strangers prove they are not in league with the other community, while the gnolls dispute the characters' need to prove anything. A character can attempt to force one or both parties to back down with a successful Charisma (Intimidation) check contested by the elves' Charisma (Intimidation) check or the gnolls' Strength (Intimidation) check.

When this confrontation diffuses or reaches a crescendo, someone outside screams, "Murder!" Ch'usuyana uses this distraction to move to the rear exit where she uses her icy fog attack in the tavern and then reveals her true form to Imata, who acknowledges her presence. She then grabs a torch from the wall and ignites the wood supply in the back room to set the tavern ablaze. In the main room, the dwarf soldier attacks the remaining patrons, and the enthralled Imata charges the characters. No one else within the tavern attempts to attack the characters. Iquina desperately tries to restore order within the tavern without harming any paying customers, though the confusion and panic from the growing fire and the slippery floor make for tough sledding within the tavern, which is now difficult terrain.

Although spökvattens normally lie in wait for their prey in lonely ponds, rivers, or streams, the birth of her ungodly child has spurred her to grander ambitions. She and her daughter now see the humanoids as their bountiful playthings whom they can devour at their leisure. However, the adventurers' unexpected arrival leaves her in a quandary. Until she can assess their abilities, her present goal is to return to her shack on the outskirts of town. Ch'usuyana jumps into a frigid stream and swims back to her residence as her pursuers likely struggle to pursue her on the ice and snow. Nonetheless, her footsteps leave a trail on the solid, yet yielding packed powder. In her haste to leave, Ch'usuyana makes no attempt to conceal her tracks. A character can pick up her trail by succeeding on a Wisdom (Survival) check contested by her Dexterity (Stealth) check made with disadvantage.

If the spökvatten escapes without being followed, she hides in the shack while Ikanp'akiri, her **ice maiden** (see **Appendix A: New Monsters**) daughter remains holed up inside with her hostage (LE male elf **commoner**). The fey's ice maiden daughter attacks anyone who approaches the shack. Meanwhile, Ch'usuyana holds her hostage in one arm and attacks using her cold touch with her other free hand. Because she is using her hostage as cover, she gains a +2 bonus to AC and Dexterity saving throws. The cornered spökvatten and her ice maiden daughter flee if an opportunity to do so presents itself. Despite their familial bond, neither is willing to risk life and limb for the others. On the other hand, if Ch'usuyana eludes pursuit altogether, she returns to the village after a few days in a new guise to continue to spread fear.

Treasure: If the characters find the pair's shack, they discover the following items hidden throughout the building: *oil of sharpness*, a *potion of giant strength* (frost), and a pouch containing six amethysts worth 100 gp each. It takes a successful DC 10 Wisdom (Perception) check to find each object.

If the characters defeat the fey and her maiden — and keep the hostage alive (or raise him from the dead) — the citizenry of Aruapa treat the characters to a drink or two before letting their queen lavish praise and gifts upon them.

ENCOUNTER ST2-C:

THE QUEEN AND HER MAGE

Kharu Amayana and Jark'iri refuse to grant the characters an audience until they either deliver a sledge of obsidian to the village or defeat Ch'usuyana and Ikanp'akiri. If the characters attempt to barge their way in, the citizens unite to protect their rulers from the strangers, especially during these uncertain times. The mismatched duo appears as different as night and day. Kharu (NG female half-elf **berserker**) is tall and heavy for an elf, evidence of the human genes in her background. Jark'iri is a **couatl** disguised as an elf and is small and slight with pale charcoal skin contrasting her companion's ruddy tan. While Kharu is curt during an initial meeting, Jark'iri goes out of her way to make everyone feel welcome. Several loyal villagers (N male and female Aztli human **commoners**) are in the room when the adventurers finally meet the two rulers of Aruapa.

After perfunctory greetings, the conversation varies depending on if they beat her gnoll slaver and brought pilfered obsidian into her village or if they defeat the duplicitous fey and exposed her devious plot to turn the villagers against each other. Kharu keeps the discussion light but pointed, never losing track of the direction of the questions. She outwardly flatters any obvious warriors. On the second round, Jark'iri begins to *detect thoughts* and eventually focuses on either the one with greatest brawn (hoping to capitalize on a lower intelligence) or the one with the most boastful thoughts of their adventures.

If the characters have the obsidian, Jark'iri tries to find out what happened to Anuqara by sifting through the characters' thoughts. Kharu starts the negotiations to repurchase the obsidian at a low price but ultimately settles on something almost equivalent to what she promised Anuqara. The price of

the lost slaver is worth the removal of her most stress-inducing villager under her protection. In the next few days, Kharu makes Iquina her new "muscle," and he splits his time as War-chief of Aruapa and tending the bar at his tavern.

If the adventurers defeated the fey and her minion, the elvish pair speak freely with the adventurers, though Jark'iri still *detects thoughts* to unmask anyone with murderous designs on her queen. The pair offer their guests pulque to drink.

Treasure: With either conclusion, Kharu bestows the deed to the obsidian vault to the character she deems most worthy. The characters can use the vault as a launching point for other adventures in the Tepepan Mountains.

If they defeated the hag and the maiden, she also gives an obsidian *+1 tecpatl* (see **Appendix C: New Equipment and Magic Items**) to the bravest fighter. Kharu Amayana grants the characters a week's stay as guests of the village for free as well (to rest and recuperate from their battles). The village presents each adventurer with fine silk clothing tailored to fit them perfectly (worth 20 gp each).

THE VILLAGE OF ALATAQ

When the characters arrive at Alataq, the village is the midst of a celebration. A day before their arrival, a resident died a peaceful death, and within hours of his earthly demise, Manq'awi Aicha, a **priest** of Micoateotl, arrived as if summoned. Everyone took this as a sign of a good death, and the living kin of Alataq began their revelries.

Because there are very few places to bury loved ones high in the Tepepan Mountains and precious little firewood and flammable oil to help dispose of the body, the priests who serve the Lord of the Dead engage in ritual cannibalism to avoid having to inter the corpse. This simultaneously passes on the decedent's good traits to the survivors who feast on the flesh. After consuming the meal, the priest arranges the bones in an ossuary box, and honors the deceased with chants and other rituals to help grant a speedy journey through Miquito. In most cases, the box is then placed under the floor in the decedent's home.

Only the wealthy and powerful are laid to rest in splendor in a multiroomed vault elaborately decorated with pyramids of skulls and candelabrums made of femurs and fibulae. Some villages keep only the skulls on labeled shelves. Slotted boxes near the entrance collect small offerings to pay for the shrine's maintenance or to serve as tributes for the dead. On the rare occasion when a priest of Micoateotl arrives in a community with no recent dead, the superstitious Aztli residents see it as a bad portent indicating that someone's journey on earth is nearing an unexpected end. The next few hours are tense as the villagers watch their infants and infirmed with an agonized eye. A pack of 2d4 **giant vultures** usually accompanies the priest. In this case, Manq'awi Aicha has four such scavenger birds in tow when the characters meet him. The vultures stay in the upper reaches of the village's landscape and drop in only if Manq'awi engages in melee. The vultures' appetites help with the ritual to come.

The death ritual celebration is only one of the many festivals Alataq's citizens witness on a regular basis. The village of nearly 400 people (66% Aztli, 20% dwarf, 10% Tlotl, 4% other) has a fete about every 13 days in accordance with the Aztlis' Tonalpohualli religious calendar, in addition to family activities celebrating weddings, births, and other momentous events. Alataq is renowned within the Tepepan Mountains and regions beyond for its unusual architecture, which combines elements of Aztli, Dwarfish, and Tlotl designs. Originally constructed underground during the Nights of Sillu and Claw, the oldest tunnels are now mostly used as catacombs and storage in case of siege. Early settlers carved out the underground area with fortification in mind, and the passages are easily defended, with strategically placed arrow slits stocked with ammunition carved into the bunkers, along with tight passageways to facilitate a fighting retreat.

Aboveground, a family of Tlotl artisans imported their style of mysterious grotesques in the design of their buildings. The village of Alataq includes 50 structures. They are universally tall and narrow, with slate roofs and artful dwarven wrought-iron worked into the windows, doors, and guttering, though rust has taken a toll on some of the ancient metalwork. The masonry also defies conventional expectations. Fortified by enchantments, the stonework appears otherworldly, as the impossibly angled pinnacle designs could not withstand the structural forces without magical enhancements.

Alataq's other noteworthy marvel is the tremendous number of gargoyles incorporated into its architecture. Creatures carved from stone and clay appear everywhere. Some squat over drainage openings, fishing for coins or mice. Others spout water from rooftops. A few decorate the spindly towers around town. Their most wondrous feature is that almost all of the gargoyles move.

These sentient beings, known as the tukkuru gargoyles (see **Appendix A: New Monsters**), go about their daily lives among the humanoids of Alataq. Elders do not know where they came from or why they even coexist with the villagers. They display no malevolence like most of their kin, and some even adopt families or individuals for whom they perform basic tasks such as guarding their homes, washing their clothes, digging, and tending a garden. If someone is lucky enough to garner the affection of a gargoyle, that person has made a companion for life. Like pets, these gargoyles usually have a shorter lifespan than the humans they befriend.

Most tukkuru gargoyles live about as long as a domesticated dog (2d6 + 2 years). They neither eat, drink, nor breathe. Given their limited requirements, no one can explain their short longevity, though no one has ever researched them in great detail. When a gargoyle in Alataq senses death is near, it treks up into the mountains during the night to rejoin its brethren in the gargoyle graveyard, from where it never returns. Although their companion's passing saddens them, no one from Alataq has ever gone looking for the graveyard or an explanation as to why the gargoyle left them.

A council of nine individuals rules the village of Alataq: five Aztlis, two dwarves, one Tlotl, and a dour half-orc. The Aztli Confederation rarely sends a delegation to visit the remote locale as long as the annual tribute of stone and rare metal pours into the alliance's coffers. Alataq features many of the amenities of any large village, including dwarven metalworkers and jewelers, a moneychanger and lender who loans and converts currency minted by the Aztli Confederation and the Firebrand Clan to prospective clients. Many visitors spend their fresh coins in one of three taverns with homebrewed beers, distilled pulque, a few hallucinogens, and beds to sleep off the stupor (even by the hour). A library with a pair of sages staggers over the upper end of the main road, and several shrines honoring the Aztlis' hero-gods — most notably Quiahuitl, Atoyatl, and Contlati — dot the landscape. Alataq is ensconced in a light fog 350 days of the year. Many tunnels lead underground, and heated, moist air billows forth from them. The slightly smoky tang emerging through these vents mixes with the chilled environment to create a hazy soup.

CHAPTER ONE: DEAD MAN'S PARTY AT ALATQ

When the characters first arrive in Alataq, read or paraphrase the following description:

Three main paths lead to the village of Alataq — two aboveground and one below. The underground one eventually leads to the dwarven community of Balandrur, though many chambers and thoroughfares branch off to more remote destinations. Some of the caverns are not well traveled, and due to volcanism and earthquake activity, some of the neglected paths are prone to collapse. The two paths that meet in Alataq both head south to lower altitudes. One goes directly south through the grassland and forest before ending at the edge of the Great Canal. This trail, Malcu Aztana, once traversed the entire island from the northwestern beaches to the southern tip of the swamplands. Time, nature, and progress ravaged Tehuatl's thoroughfare, though the section from Alataq to the canal can still be followed with some extrapolation around the island's waterways. The other trail winds south and west and ends at Qana, a small fishing village on the coast.

The characters are not expected to join in today's festivities. Most shops closed their doors, but the tavern stayed open, and one of the smiths is hammering away on a piece of iron. The adventurers can visit with the few villagers not reveling in the death ritual or interact with the gargoyles on the street. Three of the creatures eventually notice the characters and approach. They are chubby and almost cube-shaped — 12 inches on a side. Their small legs and arms make them wobble, and they look up at the characters with inquisitive eyes. If given a metal coin, they jump and tumble about with glee. One consumes the coin with an audible metal-on-stone clanking noise.

The festival for the deceased takes place in Alataq's park and lasts for nearly an hour. Dancing and loud singing conveys the revelers' joy rather than their sadness over the loss. Manq'awi Aicha (LN male Aztli human **priest**) leads the throng as he escorts the elder's body up the mountain to the far end of the park, where it is laid to rest atop a simple, unadorned table surrounded by a curtain. The festival winds down after an hour of song and speeches. When its ends, the family of the deceased thanks every attendee whether they be friend or stranger. Manq'awi Aicha and his pack of giant vultures surround the table at the far end of the park, where he draws the curtain to separate the town from the next phase of the ritual. Etiquette and decorum prohibit anyone from observing the consumption of the body. Manq'awi Aicha eventually sends his birds into the sky with a flourish as the priest blows into a wooden whistle to signal the ceremony's conclusion and the beginning of the decedent's journey into Miquito. The man's skull remains on the table until the next time Manq'awi Aicha or another priest of Micoateotl visits the village. At that time, the priest and the family will inter the skull beneath their home. If the characters attend the ritual and act reverently, award them a story bonus of 50 XP.

The family of the man who passed fears returning to his home now that he is no longer there. Hiuaui lived in one of the houses built underground some distance away from the main village. He thought himself a guard of sorts. His family moves from the celebration of his death to the nearest tavern to help steel their nerves to go to Hiuaui's house. The characters can find them there or on their way to the house after drinking. The pair of men carry a lantern and wield a dagger. The smaller one seems to be braver and is leading the taller one. Eventually, the mourners summon the courage to engage the strangers in their town. When they do so, read or paraphrase the following description:

he would tell us strange tales about something stirring within his house. We thought he was kidding.”

He stops to take a drink of water as he ponders how to say the rest. He is obviously sad and distressed about his father’s mental state, but he finally continues his tale.

“He previously told stories of other noises near his home. It turned out to be his own gargoyles completing his monotonous tasks. He was at our last feast just a few days ago. He did not have a scratch on him. This morning though …”

The man trails off, his eyes blurry from drink and fear. He says he hoped the priest would accompany the family to the house, but the priest made excuses, claiming that another village was about to have another death tonight, and he needed to be there in the morning.

Calcata (CG male Aztli human **noble** wearing tlahuiztli armor [see **Appendix C: New Equipment and Magic Items**] instead of breastplate) is now the patriarch of his family after his father’s death. He and his partner Aqallor (NG male Aztli human **scout**) fostered several orphans they consider blood relatives, but they have no children of their own. Calcata is bald and bespectacled with a chubby countenance. Aqallor is also beefy from his previous military service but appears to take care of himself a bit more. He attends to Calcata as he discusses what they want to retrieve from Hiuaui’s house.

They ask the characters to retrieve a ceramic scepter and a book of family history from the home. They have a nicer home in Alataq and have no interest in what happens to Calcata’s father’s property. Indeed, they offer to gift the home to the characters if they retrieve the two items from the building. Read or paraphrase Calcata’s general description of the home:

> “Carved from the living rock of the cavern, my father’s house has three arrow slits. A locked door is the only entrance. My father created the small fortress with only the help of the gargoyles he took under his command. Hiuaui had a military mind and defended the caves from threats both real and imaginary.”

If asked, Calcata and Aqallor are unsure how many gargoyles occupy the abode, but he had four the last time they visited. Aqallor gives the characters the key to the front door and says they will wait in the house in Alataq, praying for their safe return.

CHAPTER TWO: CLEARING HOUSE

This chapter takes the characters into Hiuaui’s home to discover the circumstances surrounding his death.

AREA A2-A: ENTRYWAY

The nearly hourlong trek to Hiuaui’s house is uneventful. When the characters arrive, they find the narrow doorway to the house ajar. The lock and handle are shattered nearby.

> A deep hiss echoes through the cavern. It sounds like something a cat might make, but deeper and more guttural. Another deep voice intones from near the house, “This is not the way. Go back while you still can. Death to all who enter. Only the grave awaits you.”

Over the years, Hiuaui taught the gargoyles some Aztli phrases. They looked out over the caves nearby and gave him an early warning about intruders. Unfortunately for Hiuaui, a pair of unknown enemies sought something from him. They dispatched a squad of three demons and their diabolical leader to find what the old man was hiding. Hiuaui was mortally wounded by their minions and stumbled his way to Alataq to die.

The 3 **tukkuru gargoyles** (see **Appendix A: New Monsters**) here are feline-themed in design. They are severely damaged (reduced to 1 hp) and are afraid to fight. The demons tortured the stone beasts and broke pieces off them. The gargoyles ironically comply with Hiuaui’s training, as they now warn the geruzou demons inside about the trespassers. If the gargoyles fail to warn the current occupants, the characters may slip by unnoticed by succeeding on Dexterity (Stealth) checks contested by the geruzou demons’ Wisdom (Perception) checks.

The 3 **geruzou demons** (see **Appendix A: New Monsters**) slink to the front of the house while the gargoyles hiss and screech. One demon spits slime from the open doorway. The rest wait inside the door to bite and claw anyone who enters the front room. The front room is a mess of splintered wood and smashed ceramics. A large cabinet and pile of debris block the doorway to the chambers beyond the entryway. The room is considered difficult terrain because of the clutter.

Treasure: Hiuaui collected figurines and only one delicate obsidian panther worth 50 gp remains in the mess.

AREA A2-B: LIVING QUARTERS

> The rest of the living area is in chaos compared to the front room. A large fissure opens the floor wide, dividing this room in half. The floor caved away, revealing a lower level. Cold air and fog obscure the area below. Grunts and giggles — as well as a prolonged hissing sound — drift from the next chamber on this level.

The furniture that once decorated this room (including the bed) dropped through the fissure and into the lower level. A character attempting to traverse the chasm without falling in must succeed on a DC 10 Dexterity (Acrobatics) check. On a failure, the creature tumbles into the lower level, taking 3 (1d6) bludgeoning damage from the fall and getting knocked prone. A character attempting to climb down to the lower level must succeed on a DC 10 Strength (Athletics) check or suffer the same fate. The **geruzou demons** (see **Appendix A: New Monsters**) in **Area A2-C** beyond are too enraptured in their torture to notice anything short of an extremely loud commotion here.

Treasure: A large case lies unopened on a ledge, hidden among some other debris. It takes a successful DC 15 Wisdom (Perception) to locate it. Within lies the ceramic scepter as well as a half dozen books. Close examination shows that at least one of the manuscripts has to do with local history and may be the genealogy Calcata and Aqallor require. The case also holds a silver whistle with a trio of emerald chips embedded in its length inside worth 40 gp.

AREA A2-C: THE MESS HALL

This was Hiuaui’s dining area. He prepared meals at a cooking station and ate at a rather luxurious table setting. He even fed his pet gargoyles, though they needed no sustenance. The geruzou demons are now torturing one of

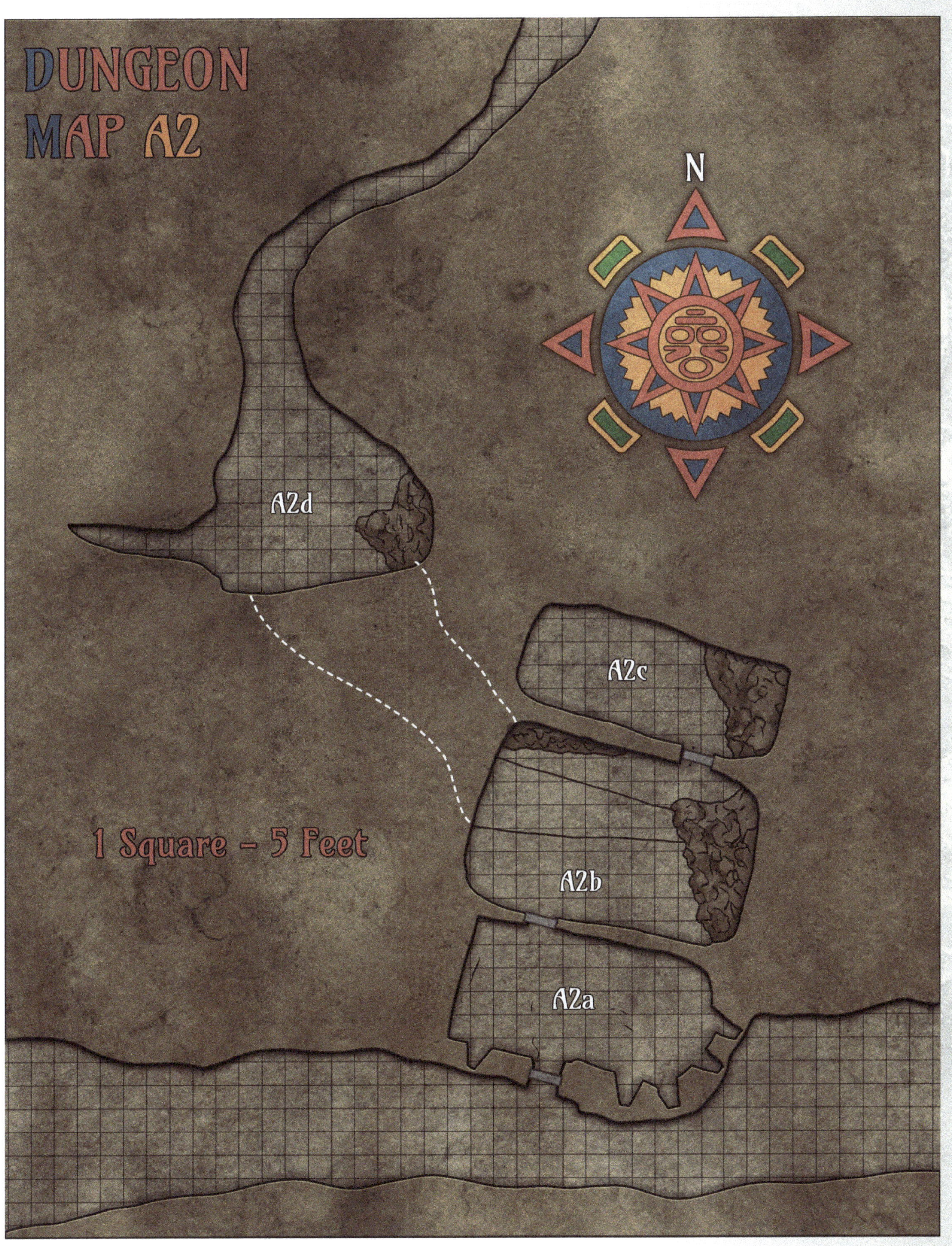

DUNGEON MAP A2
N
A2d
A2c
A2b
A2a
1 Square – 5 Feet

Hiuaui's gargoyles in the oven. They heated the loyal servant to a temperature that cracked both its arms and one half of its face.

These 4 **geruzou demons** (see **Appendix A: New Monsters**) rush forward to engage characters intruding on their fun. One of the fiends throws an *oil of slipperiness* into the melee area. The home once had a "safe room" beyond this mess hall, but the collapse that brought the demons from below also crushed the small oubliette and the supplies stored within the room. The **tukkuru gargoyle** (see **Appendix A: New Monsters**) suffers from severe burns. If the characters rescue it from the demons' clutches, it thanks them profusely. Characters who can converse with the gargoyle discover that the demons kept asking it about finding the "twins," though Hiuaui's pet has no idea what they were referencing. The creature also swears they kept repeating the name "Itzcuin" throughout their interrogation, though the gargoyle once again cannot explain the correlation between the devious Aztli god and the demons' inquiries.

Treasure: A wizard imbued the stove with magic, and it can generate flames to produce varying levels of heat by adjusting a lever on the front. Hiuaui inherited this item from his godfather. Despite its magical properties, its weight (100 pounds) makes it worth only 100 gp.

CHAPTER THREE: BACK TO THE VILLAGE

Any gargoyles who survive the geruzou demon attack croak and stutter their way through a conversation in broken Aztli with the characters. They tell their rescuers, "We must go home." All of the tukkuru gargoyles can sense their time on Tehuatl is nearly over, and when they are close to the end of that allotted time, they must make a pilgrimage back down to the heart of the mountains to the tukkuru graveyard. The characters can persuade the gargoyles to wait until they deliver the scepter and books to Hiuaui's family.

The citizens of Alataq stare at the damaged gargoyles with horror. Many adults approach, cooing and trying to crowd in close to pet the small creatures, offering support. A traffic jam forms around the characters, and one of the gargoyles gets to use its old warning voice to tell the gathered villagers to "back away." The villagers ultimately disperse with sympathetic smiles on their faces.

Calcata and Aqallor's house is near their bookshop. They usher the characters in, frowning at the state of their father's pets. Once settled, the couple accepts the case filled with genealogical materials and the scepter.

The couple explain that Hiuaui didn't have the heart to break the scepter, as he collected ceramic pieces almost religiously. When Calcata's father

AREA A2-D: BASEMENT

The geruzou demons collected a big bruiser to help spread mayhem. K'ullarana, a **hill giant**, is separated from his "chanaki" (little brothers) down here. He followed a **tukkuru gargoyle** (see **Appendix A: New Monsters**) back into the chasm below the house and is trying to chase it down and crush it with its huge hands. The gargoyle now hides in a narrow crevasse. Although the giant has extraordinary reach with its extended arms, it cannot grab the tiny gargoyle trying to elude its grasp. The gargoyle hisses and tells the giant, "Go away!" as loudly as it can.

The giant prefers pulverizing its foes with its fearsome greatclub. Despite its low intelligence, the giant may try to hurl rocks at the gargoyle if its attempts to reach it fail.

Treasure: If the characters search through the debris scattered here from the house above, they uncover *adamantine armor* (chain mail) of obvious dwarven craftsmanship.

The tunnel leading away from Hiuaui's house travels deep into the Tepepan Mountains. A small pocket of geruzou demons lives in a small, dirty community almost 11 miles from this breach, though this is accessible only through many forks and divisions and chasms.

MAP

If the characters did not rescue any gargoyles in the preceding encounter or were uninterested in visiting the tukkuru gargoyle graveyard, you can use this map leading to the location to spur their interest in doing so. Use the paper as a correction device if needed. Alternatively, it could also reveal the location of the obsidian vault detailed earlier in this adventure. If used this way, allow the characters to visit Quriana and Achtata, the elders in the library at the top of Alataq, in the morning to decipher the runes and legend to find where the characters travel next. If the characters are already committed to helping the gargoyles, the parchment refers to events in **Chapter Six**.

told them how he obtained the scepter, he warned them of what was inside. "It leads to great treasure and great danger." A traveler left it behind after disappearing mysteriously one night in a tavern Hiuaui used to frequent. The traveler regaled the tavern with outlandish tales of his journeys beyond the realms of men. He claimed that otherworldly beings — attracted to the silver thread with which he wove his life — followed him. The other tavern patrons thought him mad, but Hiuaui fed him leading questions, and they talked about other worlds until daybreak. When the traveler went to relieve himself, he never came back.

If any gargoyles are present, they nuzzle the characters and reiterate their need to "go home." Calcata and Aqallor understand and do not think themselves adventurous enough to try to find the treasure described on the paper, but they will talk to Quriana and Achtata, the elders in the library up the street while the characters are away. If the characters reach the destination appearing in the map and spirit away some of its riches, the pair tries to negotiate receiving a part of the treasure, but they make no concrete demands.

Chapter Four: The Tukkuru Gargoyl Graveyard

The gargoyles instinctually sense where they must travel and have only a limited vocabulary to describe the urge driving them forward, though they gladly accept any shoulder to perch on during the journey. These feline-shaped creatures weigh a few pounds and can just as easily rest in a backpack or cradled in someone's arms.

The trip takes several days. Feel free to use any of the random encounters from the previous sections to liven up the overland trek. When the characters make camp, the gargoyles harmonize great battle songs of previous generations. Some of the songs are ridiculously obscure. However, they gladly teach the words and melodies to a bard, wizard, or anyone interested in ancient history. After the third day, the gargoyles nudge the characters toward a gaping maw in one of the mountains. This great cavern was once the lair of a huge skeletal dragon queen and her undead horde, but heroes vanquished her majesty and looted the caves long ago. After traveling a full day belowground, the characters find their first casualty.

Graveyard, Upper Section

The graveyard's upper section allows the characters opportunities to rest and recuperate between encounters as the adventure's main antagonists rarely, if ever, venture here. Unless otherwise noted, the surfaces are all carved from stone. Ceilings reach a height of 2d6 + 10 feet.

Area A4-A: The Outer Regions

Ahead, the characters spot a number of gargoyles, at least 30, that did not make it to their ancestral home without assistance. Furthermore, without magic, the characters cannot carry them all. They can placate Hiuaui's pets by promising to deliver these statues to their final resting place after they are sure the way is clear. The gargoyles get nervous and jumpy whenever they get closer to their "home." They urge the characters to march faster. They even harmonize a batch of inspirational songs about adventurous exploits to encourage them to pick up the pace.

Area A4-B: Symbolic Entry

Hundreds of years ago, a strange wizard decided to modify this cavern to his own twisted vision. After spending a month fabricating this aperture with multiple uses of *stone shape*, the wizard spent another three months casting 300 versions of protective spells in this gaping maw until he believed he got it right. The light comes from three *continual flame* spells cast onto the walls.

Explosive Trap

The eccentric wizard scattered six magical traps around this chamber in random spots. Whenever a creature other than an elemental enters this area for the first time or ends its turn in this room, it has a 50% chance of encountering one of these traps, which is triggered by stepping onto an enchanted five-foot square. When a trap is triggered, it explodes. Creatures within 20 feet of the destination point must make a DC 12 Dexterity saving throw, taking 13 (3d8) fire damage on a failure or half as much damage on a success. Once triggered, a detonated trap becomes inert for one minute until it fully recharges. It takes a successful DC 15 Intelligence (Arcana) check to find one of these traps and a successful DC 15 Intelligence (Investigation) check to permanently disarm it.

Another way into the graveyard exists, but it is one mile out of the way to the south of this main entrance. The gargoyles know about the second entrance, but their pride never allows them to enter through that gateway. If the characters need to enter through the alternate passage, the gargoyles promise to meet them inside. The gargoyles practically beg to be let down and walk this final way into the graveyard. They offer the characters their sincere thanks for bringing them this far before gleefully taking the final steps through the open maw.

Area A4-C: Esophageal Lobby

A small ledge just a few inches wide rises up on the left wall about a foot above the flow. The gargoyles hop up and traverse the ledge relatively easily. Characters must succeed on a DC 10 Dexterity (Acrobatics) check to do the same. If a creature fails, it must succeed on a second DC 10 Strength (Athletics) check to catch itself or suffer 7 (2d6) fire damage as one of its feet comes into contact with the lava beneath the surface. A creature that catches itself does not fall in, but it must still succeed on another Dexterity (Acrobatics) check to walk along the ledge. The lava flow covers about 10 feet of hallway floor.

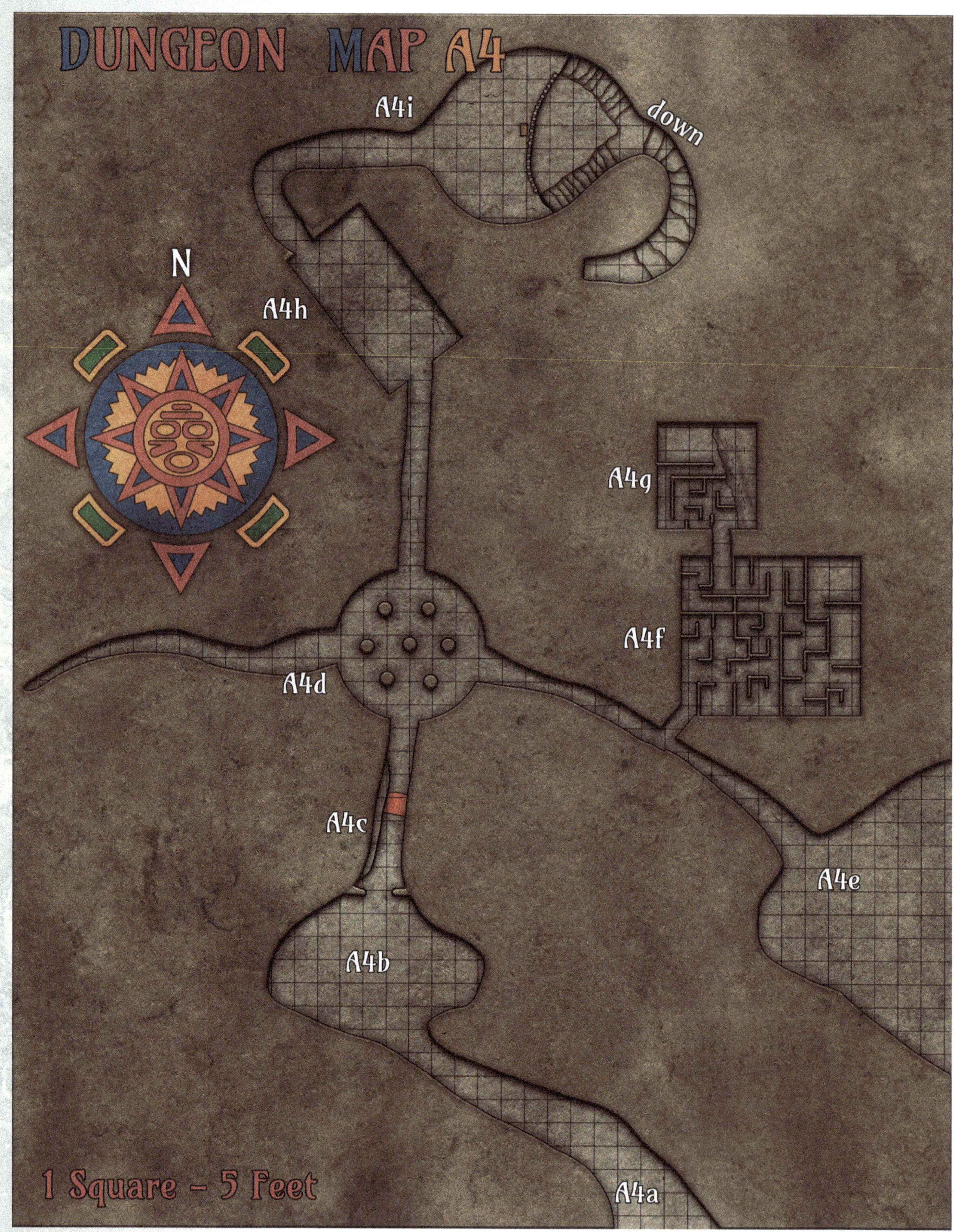

DUNGEON MAP A4
A4i
down
N
A4h
A4g
A4f
A4d
A4c
A4e
A4b
A4a
1 Square – 5 Feet

Area A4-D: Front Hall

The only area not covered with cobwebs is an area about 18 inches off the floor where gargoyles go through the area to the caverns deeper in this complex. As the characters disturb the webbing and move through the room, a **ghost** manifests near the ceiling. It is the apparition of a gnoll priest who used to preside over this area when the gargoyles first appeared. The ghost just wants all humanoids to leave and tries to horrify or possess interlopers into leaving through any of the doors. The ghost does not chase creatures outside of this room nor will it leave here if compelled by a turn undead effect. Unfortunately, it has been a long time since the ghost manifested and, in its absence, 2 **swarms of insects** infested the area. Frightened into near-paralysis by the ghost, the characters suffer the wrath of the newest occupants of this hall. The chittering horde of insects overruns one of the ghost's victims and burrows their mandibles and pincers into his or her flesh. A flood of chitinous pests flows under an intruders' protective armor and bites the vulnerable underbelly of those who try to pass. The ghost and the insects ignore the gargoyles, if present.

If constrained by a cleric powerful enough to sway it through faith and a holy symbol, the ghost retreats to its own remains. A small shelf near the floor in the central pillar holds a gnoll skull and a few bones resistant to time's decay.

Treasure: Nestled among the bones is a one-foot-long ivory tusk with scrimshaw along its length in the style of sharks. This device acts as a *wand of magic missiles*.

Area A4-E: Second Entrance

The 10-foot-wide trench completely divides the outer passage from the graveyard. The area is illuminated by three *continual flame* spells. If the characters approach from the graveyard side, they may trigger the trap before they can investigate the pit. If they approach from the outside, they can see the visible pit is 10-feet deep. A second pit located one foot farther into the graveyard beyond the trench awaits new victims. The idea is for trespassers to leap over the first pit, only to land on the hidden trapdoor just beyond it.

Locking Pit Trap

The hidden trapdoor covering the pit is spring-loaded. A successful DC 20 Wisdom (Perception) check detects the hidden cover of the locking pit. Whenever a creature or object weighing more than 70 pounds rests on its door (marked with an X on the map), the trap triggers. After a creature falls into the 30-foot-deep pit, the cover snaps shut to trap its victim inside. A creature falling in this manner takes 10 (3d6) bludgeoning damage. Two humanoid skeletons lie at the bottom of the locking pit. Their weapons and armor are rusted, and their other equipment is rotted and useless. One of the corpses is a halfling, and the other is a gnoll. It takes a successful DC 10 Intelligence (Nature) check to correctly identify their race.

For characters who fall into the locking pit trap, it takes a successful DC 20 Strength check to force the trapdoor open from inside the pit. Rescuers above can push open the trapdoor with a successful DC 7 Strength check or by placing at least 70 pounds on the trapdoor. A character in the pit can also attempt to open the door by disabling the spring mechanism from the inside with a successful DC 15 Dexterity check made with thieves' tools, provided the character can reach the mechanism. Those trapped in the pit can locate the locking mechanism hidden behind a secret panel with a successful DC 10 Wisdom (Perception) check. The secret panel is nine feet above the floor on the west wall.

Area A4-F: Irontooth's Realm

Long before the Aztli retreated into the depths of the earth, the Tepepan Mountains served as the home of a moon princess minotaur and her minions. The priestess led her progeny through her interpretation of the celestial bodies, especially the moon and all its phases. This civilization thrived for many centuries but died of a waterborne plague. In her hubris, she misread a premonition warning her of a melt, which came to pass. The event killed the entire minotaur population and collapsed their short passageway to the surface. However, four of her minions reanimated after death as skeletons. Irontooth assumed leadership by taking the priestess' silver axe and demanded fealty among the other undead. They follow Irontooth until he falls, then they scatter from this place, trying to go to their Great Beyond. Hiuaui's gargoyles know nothing of this area and, though they would rather have the adventurers carry them, they can walk through the maze underwater and out of sight.

This flooded labyrinth holds between three and four feet of chilly water. Debris makes the floor uneven below the surface. The short cul-de-sacs are easily distinguished with a cursory glance. The hidden tunnel leading to Irontooth's lair is in the floor, under the water, at the square marked by an X. A successful DC 20 Wisdom (Perception) check is required to find the entrance. It is fairly easy to get to the northeast corner of the maze. In that corner, a trio of iron levers jut out from a plaque on the east wall about two feet above the water level. The middle one is set to the uppermost position (designated with a full circle). The outer-left one is set to the lowest position (by a semicircle arc outline raised from the plaque). The rightmost one is slightly above level (just above a filled-in half circle on the plaque). A successful DC 20 Intelligence (Investigation) or Intelligence (Nature) check reveals that the symbols stand for different phases of the moon. It also tells the character the current phase of the moon. It takes a successful DC 10 Strength check to shift a lever. Moving the lever also changes the layout of the labyrinth. As the walls shift, the movement alerts the remains of the minotaurs to the intruders.

The 4 **minotaur skeletons** approach underwater and then burst from the muck to rush toward the characters to gore them. They try to surround the characters or isolate one or more adventurers. If Irontooth falls, the other three flee if possible.

Area A4-G: Irontooth's Lair

The tunnel connecting **Area A4-F** to **Area A4-G** is completely flooded and requires the characters to hold their breaths. It takes a successful DC 10 Strength (Athletics) check to swim or walk through roughly 12 feet of submerged tunnel to get from the labyrinth to the lair. Characters who cannot hold their breaths any longer while in the submerged tunnel ultimately suffocate if they cannot escape.

This area is only half the size of the previous maze. Once, the labyrinthine tunnels were a way to pass the time during the reign of the moon princess, but now the layout is a shadow of its former glory. There were many entrances and exits, but the flood caved in the other passages, leaving only this small area intact. The northwest corner has a wide area with a raised dais supporting a throne. Tapestries decorate the walls behind the throne, but time has left them in worthless tatters. A few silks and pillows lie about, hinting at the opulence once heralded here. A large ornate box behind the throne is all that remains of the place's treasures.

Treasure: A crystal ewer of aromatic oil and a jug of ambergris worth a total of 300 gp are in an unlocked iron box behind the throne. The silks and pillows scattered around are worth 100 gp.

Crumbled stonework chokes passageways leading away from the labyrinth, but it would take a herculean effort to excavate the collapsed tunnels to explore the minotaurs' former glory.

Area A4-H: Historical Hall

Gargoyles of importance entombed themselves here. The plaques, written in Terran, reveal the name, birth date, and date of death for those laid to rest here. A few have a note of accomplishment, though there are only about 15 of the 200 plaques lauded in this manner. The caretaker of this room died long ago, and no new burials have transpired in this room since his death. The caretaker's niche is near the front, and a plaque identifies the gargoyle in charge of this room and reveals that he died 1,129 years ago. The flashing patterns are the work of the mad wizard who created the entryways to this place. He enchanted the braziers with *continual flame* spells. These flames were once controllable by visiting gargoyles or other mourners, but the means of doing so have been lost as no one from the village has traveled to the graveyard for at least several generations. A visitor had to remember the gargoyle they wanted to visit and the lights would pulse and change colors to direct the bereaved to the final resting place. The light show is just that — a show. They pose no danger. If escorting any of Hiuaui's gargoyles through this area, they make reverent harmonies and quietly sing mournful dirges.

Area A4-I: The Grand Stair

If the characters wait at the balcony's edge for more than a few seconds, they hear the familiar hopping sounds of many small gargoyles coming up the stairs.

Phiskhuri the Dustman has kept this area nearly spotless for centuries. He is a fastidious **gargoyle** and defends the Lower Section from intruders. The book is a visitor's sign-in book. A mourner can record their name in the book and also describe whom they are here to grieve or visit. No entries are recorded on the previous pages. The book is magical. Each time Phiskhuri removes a page, a new one appears in the back of the book. A character who examines the book and succeeds on a DC 15 Wisdom (Perception) check can see the outline of the last entry in the book; a character could copy that previous name in the book to avoid a confrontation with Phiskhuri.

If anyone attempts to descend the Grand Stair without writing a proper entry on the page, Phiskhuri attacks. He watches and listens from a small alcove 30 steps down the Grand Stair. A character who peers down the Grand Stair must succeed on a Wisdom (Perception) check contested by his Dexterity (Stealth) check to see him. As Phiskhuri flies up to attack, the characters notice the 13 **tukkuru gargoyles** (see **Appendix A: New Monsters**) in this area are not the same as Hiuaui's pets. These little creatures have been re-carved with sadistic expressions etched onto their faces along with sharp, menacing teeth. The monsters aid Phiskhuri's attack by ganging up on the characters. All of the creatures here ignore Hiuaui's gargoyles.

If the characters inspect the tukkuru gargoyles after the attack, they notice that the thicker creatures are of the same species but are not as amiable as the ones all around Alataq. The gargoyles the characters are escorting find these creatures disgusting and remark that they do not know how these beasts came to be.

Treasure: The gold-leafed book is worth 200 gp.

Designer's Note

This staircase is the last encounter of the Upper Section of the graveyard. The encounters below might overlap and threaten to overwhelm the characters. The adventurers can retreat and regroup if they want. It is up to you if you wish to gently remind them of this option. If they opt to leave and come back later, the monsters of the upper section revert to their old patterns. The ones in the lower section gather more reinforcements. Feel free to add one or two monsters to each encounter.

Graveyard, Lower Section

The following entries describes the graveyard's lower and more difficult section.

Area A4-J: Mass Grave Ward 1

Another wave of 12 evil **tukkuru gargoyles** (see **Appendix A: New Monsters**) are here, moving toward the surface. Cavorting in the deeper part of the muddy floor, which is difficult terrain, are 3 **mudbog oozes** (see **Appendix A: New Monsters**). These monsters try to engulf the characters if they attack the gargoyles; otherwise, they impassively watch the combat unfold. A character trying to traverse a crevasse must succeed on a DC 15 Dexterity (Acrobatics) check. On a failure, the creature tumbles 25 feet to the bottom of the crevasse, taking 7 (2d6) bludgeoning damage and falling prone. It takes a successful DC 15 Strength (Athletics) check to climb out again.

Treasure: At the bottom of the crevasse is a silver *+1 trident* embedded into the skull of a gnoll. The entire weapon is made from a single piece of metal. An inscription on the shaft of the trident written in Common reads, "Tartarus." A character who reads the inscription and succeeds on a DC 25 Intelligence (History) check recognizes the name as an ancient great hero from a distant land lost to history.

Area A4-K: Common Graves Ward 2

This section and the next are vertically aligned. The characters must climb down the face of a cliff riddled with small shelves that hold tukkuru gargoyle husks (and some enemies). It takes a successful DC 5 Strength (Athletics) check to scale this surface. However, when attacked, the character must succeed on a DC 10 Strength (Athletics) check simply to hold onto the handholds and footholds while moving down. Furthermore, the character can attack only with one hand while holding onto the wall. If the character attempts to use both hands to attack or to perform an activity other than climbing, the character makes the preceding check with disadvantage. The adventurers can take other precautions to avoid falling, such as securing themselves with ropes or by using other climbing implements. The entire cliff face is 80 feet tall from the lip to ground level. One small ledge juts out at 50 feet from the floor and has a small chance to break a fall, though doing so requires a successful DC 25 Strength (Athletics) check.

This is where Hiuaui's pets leave the group. They vociferously thank the helpful characters and move over the edge to make their way to the nearest empty compartment. They confirm that they feel like they are about to rejoin the mountain as their ancestors did before them.

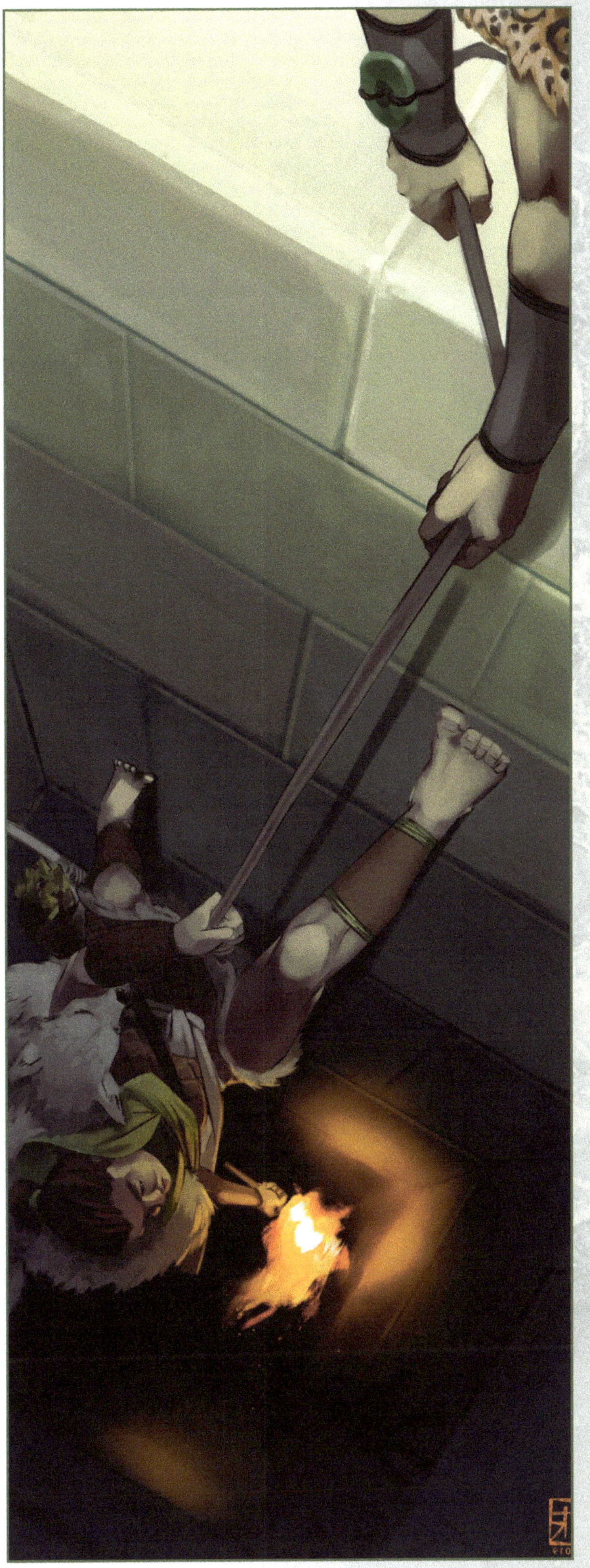

DUNGEON MAP A4

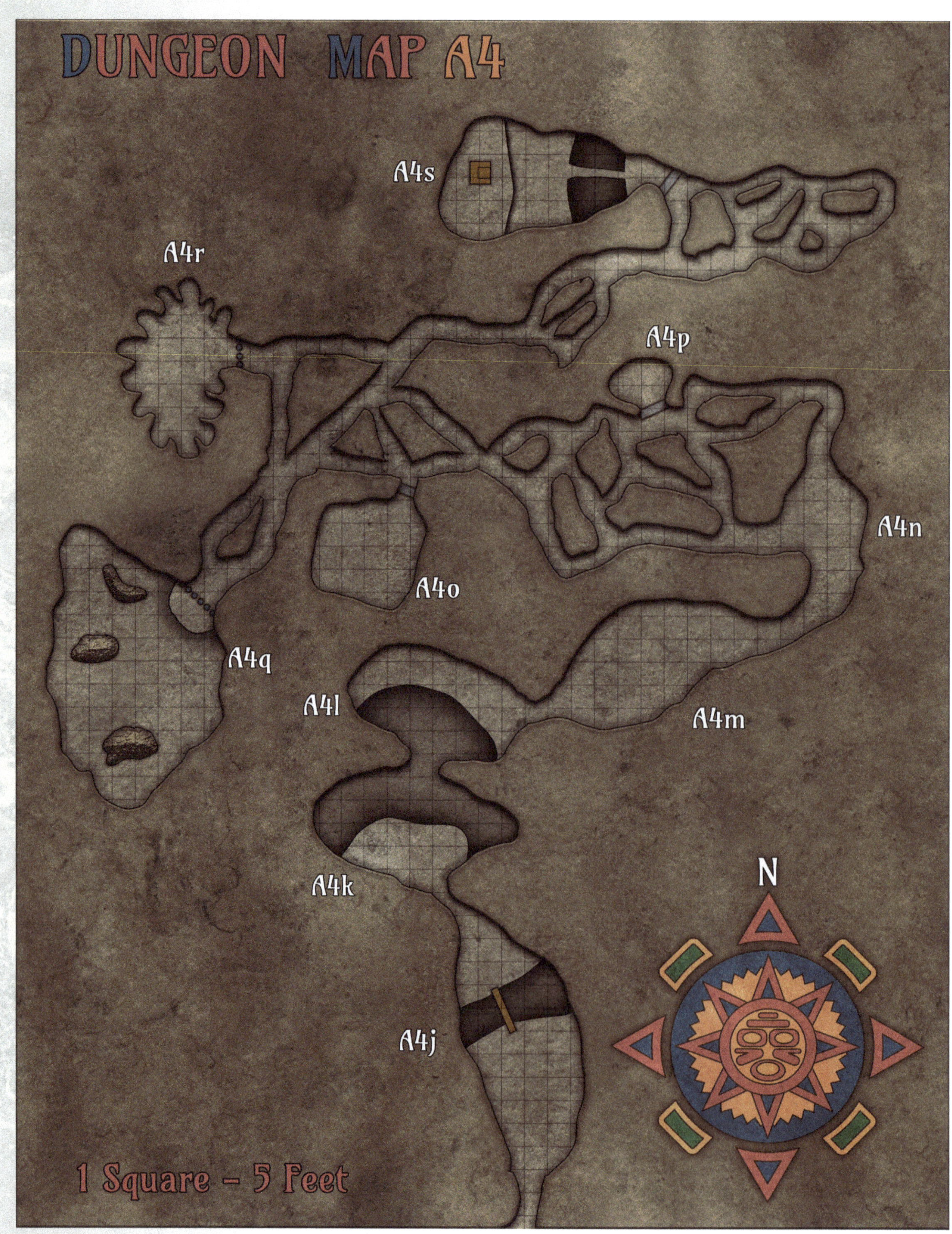

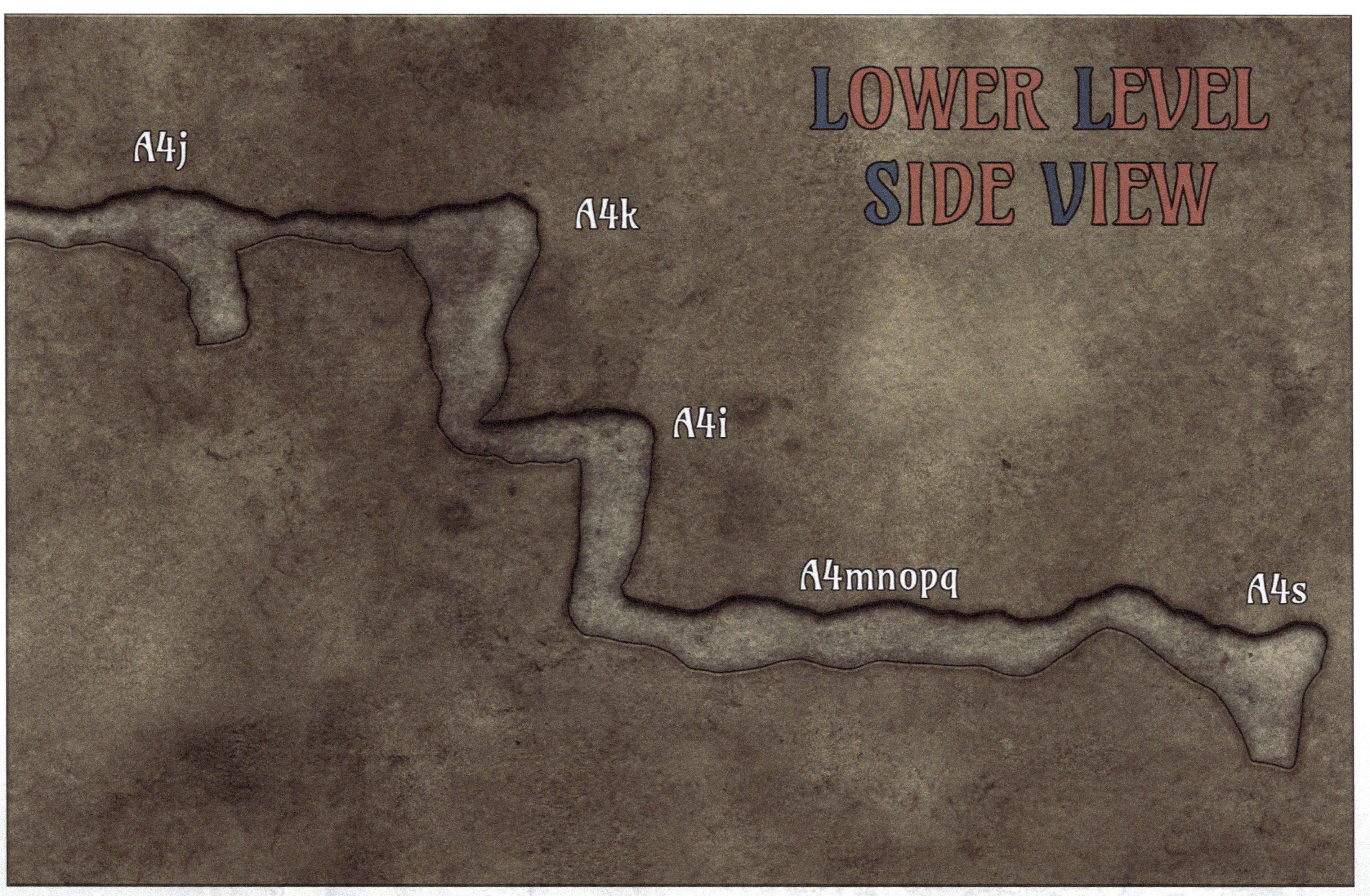

LOWER LEVEL
SIDE VIEW
A4j
A4k
A4i
A4mnopq
A4s

Hot air billows from below, and a character who succeeds on a DC 10 Wisdom (Perception) check hears a cackling echoing up from somewhere down in the darkness. Although the characters escorted the gargoyles to their final resting place as they requested, the sight of their evil counterparts greatly disturbs the gargoyle pets, and likely the characters as well who hopefully sense that something is amiss here. Nonetheless, the characters can turn back if they wish, though if they do so, Aytasina completes her ritual. The first wave of evil gargoyles makes its way out of the graveyard several days later, where they spread mayhem in neighboring areas. If the characters leave the region altogether, Aytasina discovers their identities by torturing Hiuaui's gargoyle pets. She publicly uses the characters as a scapegoat and blames them for unleashing the ensuing evil upon the world. With their reputations potentially ruined, the characters may ultimately have to decide to join her or defeat her.

The skin forming the gargoyles' final cocoon is malleable, created by the mountain itself in some sort of magical reclamation process. Creatures can use the shelves to climb up or down this cliff face as previously discussed. This section of graves, Ward 2, does not have any traps or enemies for the characters to fight. No treasure is located here either. If the players are trying to decide whether to climb down, have another 12 evil **tukkuru gargoyles** (see **Appendix A: New Monsters**) appear in a pool of light and start their climb.

AREA A4-L:
COMMON GRAVES WARD 3

This was the first area where the tukkuru gargoyles were "born" and then returned to be absorbed by the mountain. No one knows how the birthing began or the origin of the magic creating the stone beasts, but Aytasina warped and polluted the design during her time exploring this graveyard. When the gargoyles now emerge from the walls, they bear her hatred for the Aztlis and all other humanoids with them.

The dimensions of this area are nearly identical to the description of **Area A4-K**, though there is no jutting ledge for falling characters to land on or grab to break their fall. It is just an 80-foot-tall shaft from lip to floor. The entire area feels unsettling, though not in a distinctly tangible sense. However, the presence of 2 **purple slimes** (see **Appendix A: New Monsters**) gives some credence to the uneasiness. These monsters root around this area, feeding on the amniotic fluids and whatever detritus is left behind in the hollows after the mountain gives birth to a tukkuru gargoyle. The first **tukkuru gargoyle** (see **Appendix A: New Monsters**) loiters around the top 20 feet of the vertical surface, nearly invisible as it flattens itself into a hollow. A second **tukkuru gargoyle** languishes in the drainage pool at the base of the cliff. They are devouring the husks left behind by the newest gargoyles. In addition, 6 recently birthed evil **tukkuru gargoyles** sit in their individual hollows at various points along the cliff face. The gargoyles attack if the characters begin their descent; the slime on the wall attacks adventurers already engaged with the gargoyles. The slime at the base of the cliff attacks any creature, including a gargoyle, if it is unfortunate enough to fall into the 18-inch-deep lagoon of waste at the bottom of the cliff.

Characters traversing from here into **Area A4-M** must trudge through this waste. The roof of the tunnel is only another 18 inches above the surface of the disgusting, slimy water. Taller creatures will need to crawl to get through to the next area. Wading through the sickening muck without consequence requires a successful DC 10 Constitution saving throw. On a failure, the creature is poisoned for one minute as it heaves and retches from exposure to the malodorous water.

AREA A4-M: THE WHEEL

When Aytasina arrived here, luminescent fungi covered the walls of this tranquil cavern, and the large wooden waterwheel centerpiece rotated from the runoff dripping down from an underground spring near the ceiling. The paddles of the wheel delicately delivered nutrients over a large area of colorful lichens. After her takeover, Aytasina quickly plugged the ceiling, shoving early prototypes of her gargoyles' bodies into the opening and softening them with *stone shape* to seal the opening to the spring. Some of the gargoyles embedded into the ceiling move their appendages in feeble attempts to escape their hell. She completely repurposed the wheel, knocking it off its axis and setting up bindings to strap down newborn tukkuru gargoyles to spin them faster than humanly possible to teach the beasts to embrace their fear and follow her every command. As she perfected her training, she stopped using the wheel and unleashed a more direct psychological torture on the creatures before they are "buried." They now come out of their hollows as chaotic and evil as she is. After large patches of the ground cover died horribly from the fires and filth she caused, the lichens and fungi retreated below the surface. They hibernate until the raucous energies dissipate, at which time they can flourish again. There are no light sources in this area.

If the characters have a light source, read or paraphrase the following:

This is Aytasina's lover, Charphu, who is also a **kishi demon** (with a *+1 vicious spear*, see **Appendix A: New Monsters**). He set the dinner table to celebrate his mistress' successes so far in her bid to expand her influence over the Tepepan Mountains. He had been on a diplomatic mission to meet with dwarven representatives from Balandrur. The meeting quickly went sour when the dwarves discovered his true identity. The setback forced him to kill nine dwarves before escaping to safety. However, an Aztli warlock posing as a dwarven priest of Xotite (the dwarven version of the Aztli god Zipe-Toteque) contacted him telepathically and sought to establish an alliance. The warlock secretly worships Itzcuin. He is a member of a secret cabal seeking to infiltrate Balandrur's upper echelon. He explained to Charphu that he had magically observed the initial meeting from afar and would welcome cooperation between their two factions to remove the Firebrand dwarves — the clan that serves as the Tepepan Mountains' de facto ruler — from their position of power.

Charphu was sitting in the dark, thinking of the proper way to tell Aytasina this good news while preparing a dinner of seared, blackened dwarf hearts and dark blood wine. Unfortunately, he must now deal with the unexpected intruders in a slightly weakened state after his encounter with the hostile dwarves. He thinks he can use his abundant charm and suave demeanor to persuade the trespassers to join their cause. Just as his lover turned her misfortune of being shunted to this plane into an opportunity to gather forces for her eventual return to the underworld, he operates under the impression that he can do the same with his unexpected guests. Charphu masquerades as a charming gnoll draped in luxurious silk scarves and gold jewelry. The scarves cover his second face, which he believes is a blessing Itzcuin conferred upon him.

Fortunately for the characters, he used all three of his *glibness* spells and his *dominate person* spell during his earlier encounter with the Balandrur dwarves. He uses his divination magic to gauge the characters' intentions and mystical powers when they emerge from the flooded tunnel into this room.

Charphu speaks at length, emphasizing his interest in what any female characters have to offer. He does not ignore male opinions, but deflects their ideas in favor of any females' plans. If women do not speak up, he still steals glances at them as he converses with the males. He tests the group by suggesting it is time for the gargoyles to return to the surface in the form they were meant to have.

"Surely," he says, "you have never seen such abominations as … this?" He produces a husk of a tukkuru gargoyle as he talks of how unnatural those gargoyles are. He wants to bring them back to the way they have always been. He tells them his research is nearing its conclusion, and the exhausted adventurers are welcome to partake of the meal he provides. Afterward, they could return to the surface to gather any stray beasts and send them down here to their home to integrate them into the new plan. Despite his outward friendliness, he is secretly trying to delay the characters for as long as possible until Aytasina joins him.

During their meeting, Charphu weaves his *suggestion* spells into the conversation by telling individual characters to leave their weapons down in the mud or to take off their armor and stay awhile. A character who drops an item into the mud must then succeed on a DC 10 Wisdom (Perception) check to find it again. Because he expended his most potent resources, the demon lacks his usual confidence. He loves fighting alongside his paramour, as the pair finds battle to be an aphrodisiac for both of them.

When Charphu finally attacks, he throws spears until the characters engage him in hand-to-hand combat. If there are no dwarf characters, he wields his magical weapon with both hands, and attacks with his spear and bite. If a dwarf is present, he taunts the characters with the scalps of his dwarven kin that are attached to his trophy shield. His pouch of 12 throwing spears lies near his feet by the table. He fights with his main weapon *Chuymani-Ari* (see **Treasure**, below), which has taken many lives during his existence.

Aytasina is very busy at this time. If Charphu successfully delays the characters for two minutes, she finally comes within range of the demon's telepathic pleas for aid. Aytasina (see **Area A4-S**) arrives on the scene 1d3 + 2 rounds later, using her ability to become incorporeal to pass through intervening objects. If Charphu is reduced to less than half his maximum hit points, he flees, leaving himself vulnerable to opportunity attacks. He works his way to **Area A4-P**, where he uses his copy of the key and hides. He drinks as many *potions of healing* as he can in the interim. When fully healed, he tries to summon his uncle, Acwa Anchhicha who is also a **kishi demon** (with *+1 longsword*, see **Appendix A: New Monsters**).

Treasure: *Chuymani-Ari*, Charphu's weapon, is a *+1 vicious spear*. His mass of gold links and rings adorned with rubies and emeralds is worth 1,200 gp. A fine scarab made of yellow gold and six-pointed star-shaped rubies of the deepest crimson are woven into his headdress and is worth 600 gp.

AREA A4-N: CROSSROADS

This wide crossroads in the tunnels is now used as a staging ground as Aytasina sends her minions, the altered tukkuru gargoyles, to the surface or to other destinations farther abroad. She has sent very few of them underground toward Balandrur while her lover attempts to negotiate with the Firebrand dwarves. This area is naturally unlit, but if the characters can see, read or paraphrase the following description:

Aytasina could potentially run into the characters here on her way to her dinner with Charphu, but more than likely, this is an area for the characters to take a short rest before trying to defeat the demonic influence corrupting this once consecrated graveyard. This area is the first room without niches carved into the walls as it was only recently constructed.

AREA A4-O: THE LABORATORY

This is another encounter where Aytasina could interact with the characters, but is set as another reason for her final encounter to be fully buffed and ready for attack. She discovers the aftermath of this lab's destruction and then hunts down the defilers in her throne room.

The 6 servants (CE male Aztli human and gnome **acolytes**) are working on different projects for Aytasina's gargoyles. They follow her blueprints to design the next upgrade to make them tougher and more durable. If one of them notices the intrusion by succeeding on a Wisdom (Perception) check made with disadvantage contested by the character's Dexterity (Stealth) check, the servant assigns that person a mundane task to perform. The servant shows the character the task once and then expects him or her to complete the repetitive job of chopping, cutting, pouring, lifting, or mixing until the character creates a refined pile of ingredients. The chemicals are caustic and dangerous. A character who spends one minute performing any of the tasks must succeed on a DC 5 Dexterity saving throw or take 2 (1d4) acid damage from an accidental spill.

The servants are accustomed to temporary slaves popping in unannounced. Therefore, they likely do not notice the characters' weapons at first. The servant eventually declares the weapon to be a safety hazard and demands the transgressor put it away and get to work. The servants do not initiate an attack against the characters, even if they openly defy their directions. Instead, they vow to report the incident to their superiors, whom they never name, and continue about their business. On the other hand, if the characters attack them, they fight back, using their repertoire of spells to bolster their defenses and bombard their foes with *sacred flame* spells.

Treasure: The lab holds several labeled potions ready for transport. There are two *potions of resistance* (acid) and a *potion of resistance* (necrotic). A vial labeled as a potion of necrotic resistance instead contains pale tincture poison. Another rack contains a *potion of speed* and two *potions of giant strength* (hill). The other philters are empty or just have partially completed recipes in them. Aytasina hopes to incorporate potions into a batch of gargoyles in the future. She has not fused the newer advancements she and her team have made into her growing army yet. She plans to experiment on new strength enhancements into a clutch of gargoyles hatching in 14 days.

AREA A4-P: THE SAFE ROOM

Only Aytasina and Charphu have the keys for this door. Otherwise, it takes a successful DC 26 Strength check to bash the door open or a successful DC 20 Dexterity check made with thieves' tools to pick the lock. Charphu hides here if he can retreat from the characters in **Area A4-M**. If possible, he locks the door from the inside and summons his uncle. If successful in this endeavor, his uncle scoffs at Charphu, smacks him upside the head disdainfully, and moves out into the corridors to find the characters who brought shame upon their demonic family. The door was a patch from a *robe of useful items* that Charphu wore during the construction of this part of the catacombs. The same robe produced the ladder.

Treasure: The small room beyond the door holds potable water (60 gallons), dried fruits and meats (16 meals worth of rations), eight blankets, three heavy coats of ermine worth 20 gp each, a six-foot-tall ladder, a light crossbow with 11 bolts, a drum, a lyre (nonmagical), four *potions of healing*, and one *potion of greater healing*.

Area A4-Q: The Kennel

Aytasina houses another experimental creation in this area. A latched iron gate blocks the cavern, keeping her pets from wandering around. She used them in the excavation of this part of the catacombs, and she is breeding them as a gift to the Firebrand dwarves or the cabal they hope to be working with soon. This is where Aytasina starts when the characters encounter Charphu in **Area A4-M**.

> A wrought-iron gate, its frame wedged into the rock walls of this passage, blocks the way ahead.

After opening the gate, read or paraphrase the following description:

> A cliff edge drops away about 20 feet past the gate, looking over a sea of apparently freshly cut small rocks 10 feet below the ledge that are meticulously scattered around a 50-foot-radius expanse. Dust settles over the area. A few bigger rocks scattered about the area disrupt the conformity of an otherwise well-maintained rock garden.

This cavern is 300 feet below the surface and serves as a repository for all the excess stone excavated while constructing the complex's network of tunnels. Aytasina uses 7 **t'shanns** (see **Appendix A: New Monsters**) to maintain this area. She plans to mutate these creatures when she gets more time after her gargoyle project becomes self-sustaining. The creatures adhere to their normal protocol, burrowing about five feet below the surface while they wait for an opportunity to play with Aytasina. They recognize the sound of the grating iron in the tunnel above that signals her arrival. The creature nearest the entry relays the message of imminent excitement to its cohorts, causing them to all lay in wait for their master to arrive. Aytasina never brings anyone else into this room. Therefore, they immediately attack if they sense more than one creature moving around the sea of stones.

Treasure: A successful DC 16 Wisdom (Perception) check reveals a cache of deep-green tourmaline worth 400 gp inside a cracked geode.

Area A4-R: The Cell

Aytasina trusts few beings on this plane. She must work with some who have skills she requires, but she never truly understands them. These include the acolytes in her laboratory, the t'shann excavators, and possibly the Balandrur dwarves. During her outbursts, Aytasina sometimes kills those who disappoint or frustrate her without a moment's hesitation. She binds and holds those who survive her violent fits in this dungeon until they prove their worth again.

> A wrought-iron gate, its frame wedged into the rock walls of this passage, blocks the way ahead. Heavy iron chains reinforce the gate and weave through the bars to diminish the open areas, culminating in a complex metal lock near the center of the barricade.

The locked barrier has three keyholes. Each key — and by extension, keyhole — is slightly different in shape and thickness. Only Aytasina carries the keys to unlock this device. A creature can force the door open with a successful DC 27 Strength check or alternatively bypass an individual lock with a successful DC 20 Dexterity check made with thieves' tools.

She keeps her slaves in individual cells, but only two cells are occupied at the moment. The cells are minimalist at best — no bed, no chamber pot, and no food bowl. Simply put, she expects her captives to die rather than redeem themselves. Most of the individual cells have a hook embedded into the ceiling where she can string up a poor soul and flog them. Almost every cell has copious bloodstains on the walls and floor. There are 11 cells in all.

At the moment, Cell 4 holds Avvisana, a **unicorn**. Tehuatl has no horses,

making unicorns an even greater oddity. Tragically, Aytasina found, captured, and painfully removed the noble beast's horn. His beard has grown scraggly, large patches of his once-luxurious coat have grown matted or fallen out, and he has only 7 hit points. He has been here for months and strangely only remembers how to converse in Elvish, though he can do so only using his telepathy. If an elvish woman is among the adventurers, Avvisana swears fealty to her if she can return his horn from "that usuchana," an insulting word he uses to describe Aytasina. The beleaguered unicorn apologizes for using such harsh language. He solemnly says that if that task is too great, the characters are welcome to put him out of his misery. If the characters heal Avvisana back to fighting condition, the unicorn relishes the chance to vanquish Aytasina from this world either on his own or alongside the adventurers. He has no knowledge of her lover or their plans regarding the gargoyles.

You are free to determine the exact means of reattaching or regenerating Avvisana's missing horn without using likely unavailable potent magic such as *regenerate*, *wish*, and the like. At your discretion, you can make this a side quest requiring consultation with the elders of Alataq's library or with another suitable party to uncover a nonmagical method of restoring his horn. Aytasina carries the detached horn and uses it as a component of her spellcasting, even though it is not necessary to do so.

Cell 11, the one the farthest from the gate, holds a **giant ant** (see **Appendix A: New Monsters**). Captured from an invading swarm, Aytasina hopes to use the creature as a nourishing host for invasive egg-laying. She is learning how to "impregnate" a living host to feed freshly hatched larva housed within them. All of these experiments have been fatal missteps so far. Aytasina used acid to drill holes through its exoskeleton, leaving open wounds in its wake. Leather straps restrain the ant to the floor. Its mandible is still intact.

Area A4-S: Throne Room

> Across a gaping moat of lava, a beautiful throne dominates a raised dais. Gouts of flame erupt from the liquid stone surrounding the island of solid rock. Heat waves disrupt the view of the empty throne, warping the details of the island's contents. A small chest appears to peak out from behind the seat. The temperature in this area is sweltering. A single iron beam traverses the gap between the hall and the island where the throne sits. The beam is one foot wide and stretches 15 feet to the island.

This is where Aytasina likely encounters the characters after she finds her lover's corpse, the dead acolytes, her slaughtered pets, or her prisoners freed. If she is aware of the characters' impending arrival, she uses the magic at her disposal to fortify her defenses and tries to summon her paramour to her side, provided he still lives. Enraged by the damage they have done, Aytasina strives solely to destroy the trespassers who may have foiled her intricate plans. Her location is her first line of defense, as the lava surrounding the island is an imposing natural obstacle. It takes a successful DC 15 Dexterity (Acrobatics) check to traverse the narrow beam connecting the hall to the island. A creature who falls into the lava for the first time or starts its turn in the lava takes 21 (6d6) fire damage. If she has enough warning, Aytasina casts *grease* on the beam to make it slippery.

If she is prepared for her showdown with the characters, she uses the most advantageous magical gear among her treasure. She drinks a *potion of giant strength* (fire) from her stores to boost her physical might, and she assumes her incorporeal form to hide inside of her trapped chest where she waits for the allure of treasure to compel a character to approach and open the container. If the characters trigger the trap or occupy their time squabbling over the chest's contents, the incorporeal Aytasina moves away from the chest and uses her bonus action to reassume her corporeal form.

Poison Needle Trap

The lock built into the chest conceals a poison needle. Opening the chest without the key causes the needle to spring out and deliver a dose of poison. Triggering the trap extends the needle three inches straight out from the lock. A creature within range takes 1 piercing damage and 11 (2d10) poison damage and must succeed on a DC 15 Constitution saving throw or become poisoned for one hour. A successful DC 20 Intelligence (Investigation) check allows a character to deduce the trap's presence from alterations made to the lock to accommodate the needle. A successful DC 15 Dexterity check using thieves' tools disarms the trap, removing the needle from the lock. Unsuccessfully attempting to pick the lock triggers the trap.

A stunningly tall and beautiful fiend, Aytasina is a **night hag** with the following changes to increase her challenge rating to 6 (2,300 XP):

Spellcasting. Aytasina is a 10th-level spellcaster. Her spellcasting ability is Intelligence (spell save DC 14, +6 to hit with spell attacks). She has the following wizard spells prepared:

Cantrips (at will): *bumble*, fire bolt, message, ray of frost, stumble**
1st level (4 slots): *charm person, grease, protection from evil and good, witch bolt*
2nd level (3 slots): *alter self, invisibility, web*
3rd level (3 slots): *fireball, triplicate*, vampiric touch*
4th level (3 slots): *dimension door, stoneskin, wall of fire*
5th level (2 slots): *contact other plane, wall of stone*
* These spells appear in **Appendix D: New   Spells**.

Aytasina appears as a blue-skinned, black-haired fiend wearing a sweeping cloak. The look of absolute hatred she aims toward her enemies seems permanently etched onto her chiseled features. Aytasina bolsters her defenses when an opportunity presents itself, casting *invisibility* and *stoneskin* on herself or Charphu. If her lover accompanies her, they coordinate their attacks on one or two individuals rather than spreading them out over the characters. She may use one of her magical walls to separate the party into smaller groups or to encase a corner in sticky fibers. When one of the paramours falls in battle, the other surprisingly disregards their personal wellbeing and uses their movement to race to their fallen lover's side and use that turn's action to exchange their final farewells.

If defeated, Aytasina disappears in a flash of painfully bright light. She leaves no trace of her existence behind other than the objects she carried on her person. After her defeat, the characters sense a sea change in the overall mood filling the graveyard. The ominous feeling of sin and corruption gives way to a reverent solemnity for the gargoyles laid to rest here. Furthermore, with Aytasina's scheme foiled, the scourge of evil gargoyles plaguing the land comes to an end.

Treasure: The chest contains 4,520 sp and a jeweled tiara made of silver and emeralds worth 1,500 gp. The paranoid Aytasina built a false bottom into the chest to confound thieves in addition to wasting their time searching for it. It takes a successful DC 15 Intelligence (Investigation) check to locate the concealed compartment. Beneath it are five rings. Four of them emit magical auras. One silver band with a turquoise gem is a *ring of water walking*. Another ring, carved from a single opal, is a *ring of warmth*. A matching pair of thin gold bands worth 100 gp each with runes etched into them have had *arcanist's magic aura* cast upon them. The last ring is a thick palladium band carved from the metal of a meteorite that is worth 400 gp.

Aytasina herself carries a unicorn horn taken from Avvisana in **Area A4-R**, the keys to every lock in the complex, her *heartstone*, two *spell scrolls* (*goodberry, locate animals or plants*), *sandals of the mitote* (see **Appendix C: New Equipment and Magic Items**), and her soul bag, which contains the soul of a wicked sorcerer who served Itztliteotl.

CHAPTER FIVE: BACK TO THE VILLAGE, PART II

The characters return to Alataq on a clear, warm day to find the citizens once again in the midst of another celebration — the feast of the maize harvest honoring Tonacayotl, the Aztli god of maize. Tiny booths have popped up all over the village, with most concentrated in the park. Seventy-five different dishes containing at least some maize capture the grain's remarkable diversity, while masks, woven mats, and a large maize-*mâché* dragon puppet crafted from husks, leaves, and even eaten cobs adorn many of the awnings outside these stands. Several people maneuver a green dragon puppet from booth to booth, sampling the food in a grandiose ritual to give thanks to Tonacayotl for the bountiful harvest. Songs of praise resonate throughout the settlement, but the joyous voices grind to a screeching halt when the characters come into view.

The Aztlis intently listen to the characters' tales about the gargoyle graveyard with rapt attention, asking questions and delighting in the harrowing story. They tell the characters that no one has seen any of the evil tukkuru gargoyles. They also have contacts with different shop owners who may be interested in purchasing some of the treasures the adventurers found. If the characters mention it, they also have ideas on how to aid the unicorn missing its horn. They claim to know a druid in the lowlands who performs miracles. "If anyone knows how to make this fine creature whole, it is her."

Eventually, they begin their story of the research they made on the map their father left them.

The raucous celebration abruptly ceases as everyone stares in unison. Children race out to greet the heroes who ended the scourge of evil gargoyles. The elders smile, nod assertively, and display non-verbal gestures signaling approval. Everyone wants to touch the people they call the "Ahillita." Shouts of congratulations and adoring smiles flow through the crowd. The Aztlis bring food and ask about Calcata and Aqallor, while pushing through the mob and toward the quaint house where the excursion began. The couple are waiting there, waving from the front door, and gesture for them to step inside. They shut the door behind you to give you a moment's peace.

"We have found out part of what the document in the scepter means ... Oh, wait. Welcome back to Alataq, friends!" With that, Aqallor finds a decanter of pulque and pours a glass. They salute you with raised glasses and ask if you need a bath and a bed.

"It took a long time to establish this was not a map, by itself," Calcata begins, producing the document. "The beautiful rendering of the mountains is a gorgeous depiction, but neither we nor the elders of the library could discern a specific location." Aqallor lays the paper on their table and anchors the corners with the art side facing down.

"Look here," Calcata says, pointing to a series of dots on the back of the document. "These splashes of ink tell a tale." He explains the seemingly innocent ink marks and imperfections in the page itself on the back of the document correspond to a cipher system the ancient Aztlis developed thousands of years ago that ultimately fell out of favor.

"The elders had a series of scrolls that helped decipher the code. The basics, anyway. There was some extrapolation to gather what we have." Aqallor produces a second folded piece of weathered maguey paper from his pocket. "This is what those marks say. 'Look to the rise of our blessed night orb from the top of the tallest peak. After she changes from umber to pale white, removing colors from your sight, you will know. Ome guide you. Monk is key.”

“Ome means duo or two in that language, so we think it has to do with Chachacua Cahxatana, known as the mountain between men.”

The reference to the tallest peak refers to the mountain that gave rise to Tehuatl itself, the stratovolcano Tepetzin. Chachacua Cahxatana is an otherwise unremarkable, 7,000-foot-tall mountain renowned for only one thing — being the reputed site of the Lost Temple of the Twins, Itziuhqui and Tlahuizcal. Because it has no features that distinguish it from the other surrounding peaks, the mountain's precise location has also fallen into the realm of speculation. Calcata advises the characters that they must scale the range's tallest mountain to find the presumably long-abandoned religious site. The cryptic portion afterward indicates that Chachacua Cahxatana's hidden location can be revealed only by observing the moon's change in color while it travels across the night sky.

The trip into the mountains in search of Chachacua Cahxatana follows the script for the characters' previous excursions into the wilderness. You may challenge them with some of the random encounters presented earlier in this adventure or allow them to pass through the untamed landscape without

hindrance. Trekking to the top of a perilous mountain is not an easy task. At various points along the way, the characters must succeed on DC 10 Wisdom (Survival) checks to avoid losing their bearings and finding the best route to climb up the mountain. If the characters fail any of the preceding checks, add several hours to their trip. In addition, at several critical points the adventurers must succeed on DC 10 Strength (Athletics) check to climb up challenging vertical surfaces without falling. Failing one of these checks causes the climber to fall 1d6 x 10 feet onto a hard surface. A falling character takes 1d6 bludgeoning damage for each 10 feet fallen. Alternatively, a character who succeeds on a DC 10 Charisma check can locate a suitable guide to navigate the adventurers up the mountain for a 50-gp fee. While traveling with the guide, the characters know the best route to the summit, do not get lost, and have advantage on Strength (Athletics) checks made to climb vertical surfaces.

CHAPTER SIX: WHERE EAGLES DARE

This section begins after the characters scale Tepetzin, which allows them to set their sights toward their destination.

The breathtaking vista from the top of Tepetzin awes even the most cynical observer. Endless fields of moss-coated lava, sweeping plains of black sand, jagged peaks, and vast craters stretch out in every direction. A few peaks belch puffs of smoke into the heavens or weakly grumble while the ground beneath them tepidly shakes. The mountains themselves seem to move and stretch as they reach their stony fingers into the sky.

The moon rises peacefully in the east. It initially emits a rusty red hue as it crests over the horizon, then it transforms into a hazy tan for a few minutes before finally morphing into a piercing bone-white color when it breaks through a bank of low clouds roughly around midnight.

At that moment, a small flash illuminates from an unknown source as a large, oblong stone inexplicably levitates several feet off the ground. Presumably, the strange occurrence represents a marker leading to Chachacua Cahxatana. The lightshow lasts until the sunrise before it dims into a faint glow followed by nothing. The dazzling display appears in the crook of a deep, V-shaped surface facing Tepetzin that is angled in such a way that you believe it would not have been visible from the ground or even an adjacent mountain. With the location in sight, the descent into Chachacua Cahxatana begins in earnest.

orbiting the planet, the object crashed into the sea shortly after the cataclysm devastated the entire continent. The meteor longs to return home. Therefore, every time the moon is within sight of the stone carved from its remnants, it strains to rejoin its former partner. Of course, gravity wins this contest, though the boulder nonetheless rises five feet and stays there while the moon remains visible in the night sky. It takes roughly four hours to conventionally traverse from the summit of Tepetzin to the opening. If the characters can fly to the site or travel there by another means, it takes significantly less time to get there. When the moon finally disappears, the stone falls back to the ground, essentially sealing the temple's entrance and crushing anything underfoot. According to legend, one night in the future, when the moon rises blue and stays that shade during its entire nightly passage, the statue will break free of its earthy bonds and rocket back up into the heavens to rejoin the moon, free from its isolation on this world.

The flash of light comes from the mouth of the temple of Itziuhqui and Tlahuizcal. Built roughly halfway up the mountainside at a height of about 4,200 feet, a giant-sized moonstone inexplicably levitates with every moonrise. Carved from a single meteor originally from the satellite currently

TWIN GODS' TEMPLE
A6f
A6g
A6h
A6e
A6d
A6c
N
A6b
A6a
1 Square - 10 Feet

Area A6-A: Temple Entrance

A giant-sized moonstone with a vague resemblance to a humanoid creates a virtually airtight seal around an entrance into an illuminated tunnel bored into the mountain. The crushed skeleton of a humanoid lies beneath the stone, while a mangled hooded lantern and a shattered axe litter the ground close to the nearly pulverized bones.

At one time, the moonstone was carved into the likeness of an Aztli priest, but time eroded the statue into an indistinguishable, upright oblong stone. While the stone floats above the ground, the entrance is accessible. When it descends back to the earth, it is virtually impossible to move it or squeeze past it. It takes a successful DC 35 Strength check to move the stone out of the entrance and an equally difficult DC 35 Dexterity check to wriggle a way into the temple. The light illuminating the hallway comes from six *continual flame* spells cast in niches cut into the wall at roughly eye level. This was the source of light that the characters saw from the top of Tepetzin.

The decedent is a poor soul who could not escape the falling stone. If a character suffers the same fate of being beneath the stone when it descends to the ground, that person must succeed on a DC 20 Dexterity saving throw to get out of the way or take 70 (20d6) bludgeoning damage and be buried underneath the stone. A buried creature takes 17 (5d6) bludgeoning damage each round it remains buried. It or another creature can use an action and succeed on a DC 35 Strength check to escape or free the trapped creature.

Area A6-B: The Nave

The walls and ceiling bear numerous chips and gouges, as if something was removed from the abscesses left in these surfaces. The floor descends into a shallow pool filled with clear water. Steam rises from the water. The floor ascends beyond the pool, leading into an adjoining chamber.

During the temple's brief heyday, worshippers cleansed themselves in the pool, which has remained remarkably pristine. Fed by the waters from an underground, volcanic spring, the warm water emits steam. The twins' priests would routinely consecrate this sacred water, but the magic of this place is long gone just like the gems and flecks of precious metals that the worshippers tore out of the recesses in the walls and ceiling before abandoning this place forever.

Area A6-C: The Chapel

Overturned pews are stacked like firewood, while pieces of the demolished pulpit lie scattered across the floor. A stone plinth altar majestically rests upon a stone dais. The bare altars' accoutrements are also missing. Bas-relief sculptures of predatory birds, cats, and a lone monkey adorn the walls along with painted images of Aztli warriors.

One wall depicts numerous beasts bowing before the sun and moon, though decorative pieces that were attached to the painting are now missing. Numerous white dots set against a black background adorn the ceiling. The image of a ring and a triangle are also visible. A hastily drawn image on the wall behind the altar shows a pair of Aztli warriors hurling javelins from their atlatls at the rising sun. The artwork appears unfinished, as the painting's fine details were never completed. The painting fills the surface surrounding a detailed calendar, which has numerous charcoal markings along its edges.

A character who succeeds on a DC 5 Intelligence (Nature) check identifies the artwork decorating the ceiling as an image of the night sky, though the ringed planet and triangle are anomalous features in the heavens. The charcoal marks around the calendar's edges also bear images of the ringed object and the triangle. However, a detailed examination reveals no clues as to their meaning.

A character who examines the artwork surrounding the calendar and succeeds on a DC 15 Intelligence (Religion) check identifies the two figures hurling the javelins as Itziuhqui and Tlahuizcal. If the character learns their identities, the character also recalls the pair unsuccessfully challenged Notonatiuh for his position as the god of the sun. If the preceding check succeeds by 5 or more, the character remembers the complete Tale of the Twins from the earlier sidebar and also believes the triangle and ring represent the twins' positions in the night sky.

The animal bas-relief sculptures have no special significance, though rotating the monkey's tail in a clockwise direction causes the altar to swing in a counterclockwise direction to reveal a sloping passage leading into darkness. A character who examines the altar and succeeds on a DC 20 Wisdom (Perception) check detects the secret door. Opening the hidden portal without engaging the mechanism on the monkey's tail requires the character to succeed on a DC 30 Strength check to pivot the massive and heavy object into the opened position. A character who locates the secret door and then succeeds on a DC 15 Intelligence (Investigation) check believes there must be a device that opens the door. The riddle in Hiuaui's document about the "Monk is key" offers a clue. If a character asks to review the riddle or document again, give the player an opportunity to figure out the solution on their own. If the player does not recognize the significance, give the character a chance to succeed on a DC 10 Intelligence (Investigation) check. On a success, the character focuses on the riddle's play on words.

AREA A6-D: TILT-O-WHIRL

The artwork depicts the twin gods' transition from benevolent deities to gods corrupted by Itzcuin. They portray the deities interacting with their newfound Aztli worshippers before Itzcuin transformed them into malevolent beings, though the transformation is moderately exaggerated. The paintings were completed shortly after the twins' destruction as an effort to placate the angry hero-gods who vanquished them. It takes a successful DC 10 Intelligence (Religion) check to identify the hairless dog in the images as a representation of Itzcuin. Figuring out his corrupting influence is up to the characters.

A pressure plate is poorly concealed just inside the entrance. It is easily located with a successful DC 10 Wisdom (Perception) check and disabled with a successful DC 10 Dexterity check made with thieves' tools. The pressure plate activates nothing and is solely intended as a ruse to make thieves and trespassers think that they outsmarted the defenders. The real trap awaits ahead.

TILTING FLOOR

This insidious trap turns the floor into a steep ramp. The floor rests on a pivot at the midpoint in the hallway, much like a seesaw. The first portion of the floor rests on a solid stone foundation. The latter half of the hallway sits atop a 40-foot-deep pit lined with spikes. When the weight beyond the hall's midpoint exceeds the weight before the midpoint, the floor tilts on its pivot at a severe slope. A character on the floor at that time must succeed on a DC 15 Strength saving throw to grab hold of the floor or wall to avoid sliding down into the pit. Alternatively, the character may elect to succeed on a DC 15 Dexterity saving throw to maintain their balance on the tilting floor and not fall into the pit. A character who fails either saving throw slides down into the pit unless he or she can fly or otherwise avoid falling. The creature takes 10 (3d6) bludgeoning damage from the fall into the pit and 10 (3d6) piercing damage from the spikes lining the pit's bottom.

A character can climb out of the pit with a successful DC 10 Strength (Athletics) check provided that the floor is still tilted at an angle that allows the trapped creature to escape. It takes a successful DC 15 Wisdom (Perception) check to notice faint grooves marring the wall's surfaces at the near end of the hallway. Figuring out their relationship to the trap and the trap's inner workings requires a successful DC 15 Intelligence (Investigation) check. The trap can be circumvented by keeping a sufficient counterweight on the near end of the corridor. A character can also disarm the trap with a successful DC 20 Dexterity check made with thieves' tools to prevent the hallway from tilting. The twin gods' priests and worshippers used the former method to circumvent the trap and avoid falling prey to it.

AREA A6-E: THE TWINS' CAVERN

The twins' worshippers and priests almost unanimously abandoned the destroyed gods, but two of the acolytes refused to leave. They painted the images on the cavern walls to commemorate their patron deities in bleak fashion. To punish them for their insolence, Yaocteotl transformed them into 2 **wraiths**. The hateful monstrosities attack any creature who trespasses on their sacred grounds. If a character serves an Aztli god other than Itzcuin, they focus their attention on that individual. They curse and hiss at them throughout the combat. Despite their sad condition, they remain steadfastly loyal to their former masters, proclaiming that Itziuhqui and Tlahuizcal deserved the greatness Yaocteotl denied them. The artwork on the walls are the final depictions of the fallen twin gods becoming feebler and sicklier just before Yaocteotl utterly destroyed them.

AREA A6-F: COLLAPSED CREMATORIUM

A crematorium operated at this site while the temple was active. However, neglect and seismic activity caused shifting earth to bury the entrance to the crematorium's chute and gas flame. The deceased were lowered into the chute buried beneath the rubble and then incinerated by the gas flame. Loved ones retrieved the ashes from the grated chute and interred them here in the room's mausoleum section or spread them at another location significant to the decedent or the surviving family members.

Continual flame spells cast onto the walls illuminate this area. When the characters reach the upper landing, read or paraphrase the following description:

The lock and chain are merely for show. The lock opens with the press of a button, which releases the chain. The twin gods' connection to the sun prompted their worshippers to incinerate most of their dead in this crematorium using natural gases from fissures beneath the crematorium for fuel. Of course, with the flame extinguished and the colorless, odorless gas still seeping into the room, it makes for a volatile combination. If a character spends at least one minute in this room, the character must succeed on a DC 12 Constitution saving throw or take 7 (2d6) poison damage and be poisoned for 10 minutes. The character must repeat this saving throw for each additional minute spent in the room. To make matters worse, the gas is flammable. If an open flame, spark, or any other plausible ignition source comes into contact with the gas, it explodes in a 40-foot radius centered on the ignition source. Creatures within the blast radius must make a DC 15 Dexterity saving throw, taking 28 (8d6) fire damage on a failure or half as much damage on a success.

Treasure: The silver rails are worth 300 gp each but are nearly 15 feet long. The silver lock and chain are worth 400 gp.

Area A6-G: Vault's Interior

The coffin bears no images and appears cracked and warped in spots. Despite its obvious state of decay, it takes a successful DC 10 Strength check to pry off the coffin's lid. Inside, the characters find strips of moldy linens. More importantly, the characters see that the floor beneath the coffin opens into a passage from which the horrible smell originates.

Area A6-H: Dead Mass

The shaft beneath the coffin descends 20 feet at a 60-degree angle until it opens into this area. It is impossible for any creature larger than Tiny to stand upright in the shaft. All other creatures must crawl. The shaft is too tight to accommodate any creature larger than Medium. Even while crawling, the creature must succeed on a DC 10 Dexterity (Acrobatics) check to safely drop from the shaft and land on the ground eight feet beneath it. On a failed check, the creature falls prone on the ground but takes no damage.

When the characters see the room, read or paraphrase the following description:

The creature is a **derghodemon** (see **Appendix A: New Monsters**), otherwise known as a cockroach demon, that the two priests from **Area A6-E** summoned thousands of years earlier. The dimwitted monster has tried to escape on numerous occasions to no avail. After centuries of boredom, the prospect of killing living creatures invigorates the diabolical monster. The demon casts *confusion* against its foes then wades into combat with its savage claws and ferocious bite. The monster fights until destroyed. The bodies it feasts on are those disloyal worshippers who turned their backs on the twins after their demise. The two stalwart priests who never renounced the twins deemed those who abandoned them as traitors. They consigned these unfortunate souls to a certain death in the cavern beneath the crematorium.

The two priests were unaware that the high priest interred in **Area A6-G** took a vital secret to the grave with him. Like his two counterparts, a priest named Iaqito never renounced the twins. He stepped into the coffin, wrapped his body in fine linens, and then swallowed a lethal dose of poison. Iaqito, a contemporary of Itzcuin and his twin brother Nonotzali, scrawled a scandalous, firsthand pictograph account of Nonotzali sleeping with his sister Quetzalpetlatl during a drunken stupor onto a stone tablet buried with him. If the characters search through the bones and other debris, they find the faded stone with a successful DC 15 Wisdom (Perception) check. Figuring out the stone's significance requires a successful DC 20 Intelligence (Religion) check. While the stone has no monetary value, the ancient drawing corroborates the rumors surrounding the event, which were largely dismissed as Tlatoani's handiwork or Poqoza propaganda at the time. Iaqito believed the drawing along with his eyewitness testimony could force Nonotzali to intervene on the twins' behalf, but his uneasiness cooperating with Itzcuin and his minions led him to rethink his plan. He opted instead to take his secret with him to the grave. While its revelation would have been a bombshell after the hero-gods' victory, the vulgar images have lost their impact on the god's status within the Aztli pantheon.

Treasure: The derghodemon had no interest searching the dead for any valuables, which gives the characters an opportunity to search through these items themselves. There are 16 pearls worth 100 gp each, a *figurine of wondrous power*, a *bronze griffon*, a *green war paint**, a suit of *+1 ollixalli armor**, and a *giant slayer tepoztopilli**. Iaqito's stone tablet is worth 1,500 gp.

* See **Appendix C: New Equipment and Magic Items**

Wrapping Up The Mountains

It is almost eerie returning to Alataq without a festival or jubilee in full swing, but the town is quiet save for a few of the villagers who smile and nod at the characters' fresh wounds and new equipment. Calcata and Aqallor greet the characters at their door with open arms, escorting them inside to hear the tales. The couple congratulate the characters on their good fortune and expertly weave the conversation to those less fortunate. They tell of them of the Bloodmoon's imminent appearance and the harbingers it foretells. If you are continuing along the adventure arc, you may segue the conclusion of this adventure into the next one, *Seven Year Harvest*.

Seven Year Harvest

By Tim Hitchcock

Seven Year Harvest is an epic adventure designed for four Tier 2 characters who must enter the Great Void bordering the Realm of the Dead to retrieve the soul of a young boy and undo a terrible curse that has fallen upon his small village.

Adventure Background

This adventure takes place in the village of Cintlipetl within the Cuahtla Forest region of Tehuatl. The events occur at the end of the Seven Year Harvest Season a few days before the rise of the Bloodmoon. The Bloodmoon is an auspicious holiday whose coming is predicted by the Xiuhpohualli, a calendar that runs tandem to the Tonalpohualli used to count the passing of days and years.

Character Options

This adventure contains a few character options to help instill the players with a deeper sense of immersion. You or the players can tie one or more of these choices to the characters' backgrounds or create similar options to help them feel invested in the village, its people, or the situations that befall them.

The Local

This character either hails from the village or has family in the village.

Icnoyotl the Herdsman. Icnoyotl is either your brother or brother-in-law, as well as the uncle or aunt of his young son Itoxo. He always has a warm bed and food for you for as long as you stay in the village.

Xotaxtl the Sorcerer-Priest. Xotaxtl was either a close friend or cousin. He is something of a loner. He now serves as the headman's chief advisor and holds a fair amount of prestige in the town. Still, you know his real name is Citlalli, the girl's name his father gave him before he learned magic from Coaxoch.

Coaxoch the Medicine-Witch. The medicine-witch had no children but fortunately was gifted with the knowledge of magic from her grandmother. As a child, you may have studied magic or herbalism with her, or she may have been a family friend after treating them through a sickness.

Camaxtl the Headman. You are either the beloved grandchild of the headman or a warrior who earned his confidence and respect in some earlier trial. He trusts your word and respects your judgment, enough so that he feels entitled enough to ask you to fulfill certain obligations. Likewise, should he ask something of you, you would feel obliged to fulfill the request to uphold your name and honor.

The Outsider

The villagers distrust your intentions because you hail from a rival town or practice a religion that follows a set of ideals the villagers find distasteful or immoral. Alternately, you could simply be the black sheep of the town whose views and conjectures have always challenged the status quo.

Aluxes and the Forgotten Gods

Some of the creatures and gods appearing in the adventure **Seven Year Harvest** predate the ascendance of the hero-gods and even Tlatoani. The proto-humans known as the aluxes are the most prominent remnants of these bygone eras. The aluxes and their contemporaries speak Primordial Notoan, a distant ancestor of the current Aztli language. These beings and their deities — sometimes known as the Forgotten Gods — existed during the Age of Man and the Age of Strife as described in **The World of the Lost Lands** campaign setting book from **Frog God Games**. Displeased with the aluxes' progress and actions, the Forgotten Gods brought about the destruction of the Four Suns that all but wiped out the aluxes and their kin, leaving only a few, scattered survivors in their destructive wake. However, Aztli scholars and the hero-gods themselves dispute these accounts, believing the suns to be figurative expressions symbolizing the dawn of a new era rather than the literal recreation of a new sun. They counter that the Forgotten Gods directed their wrath solely at the aluxes and their counterparts rather than devastating the entire world. According to their argument, the northern continents of Akados and Libynos would have also seen the same wholesale devastation of their lands, yet the Tlotls cannot corroborate the aluxes' version of prehistory or even acknowledge the creatures' existence in their distant past.

Regardless of where the truth lies, it is impossible to refute that Tlatoani turned the tables on the Forgotten Gods during his rise to power. On the road to attaining utter supremacy, Tlatoani obliterated some of them outright, exiled others to distant worlds beyond the stars, and hurled the remainder of the Forgotten Gods into the Great Void, where they presumably waited to greet him when the gods of Boros subjected Tlatoani and his minions to the same fate.

Although the Forgotten Gods have long faded from Tehuatl's collective memory and have no known humanoid worshippers on the island, some vestiges of their existence remain as evidenced by their presence in the nether regions bordering Miquito, the Land of the Dead, and within pockets of the Great Void. The aluxes and their continued devotion to these Forgotten Gods likely play a significant role in preventing these fallen deities from completely slipping into oblivion and allowing them to affect the Material Plane. These deities include Auyinah, the goddess of dreams, Chalatihuatl, the goddess of sacrifice, and Iquixilli, the god of justice. While no longer present in the mortal world, their living or dead essence, depending upon your perspective, still endures in the ethereal realm.

Adventure Synopsis

The adventure begins in the village of Cintlipetl while the villagers scramble to prepare for the Seven Year Harvest festival correlating to the anticipated rise of the Bloodmoon. At the height of the ceremony, the villagers must sacrifice several peccaries to appease the hero-gods' demands for blood. However, the unanticipated and mysterious slaughter of the local herdsman's ritual offerings strikes panic throughout the village, prompting the town council to organize a small party of willing adventurers (the characters) to capture the peccary slayer, for fear that the harvest offerings will be ruined and the village will be cursed until the rising of the next Bloodmoon roughly seven years later.

The characters track down the peccary slayer to discover it is an alux, a supernatural human-like creature from the era before Tlatoani's downfall. Unsure of the implications of finding such a creature, the villagers confine it in a cell while the town council conducts a hearing to determine its fate. The characters may voice their opinion during this debate. Before its fate is determined, the sunrise brings ominous news. A chom has been sighted within the town, perched near the alux's prison hole. These mystical bird-like creatures are ancient bearers of ill-omen.

As if in response to the omen, the villagers discover the alux dead in its cell, apparently from eating a poisoned rat. A quick investigation determines the killer is the herdsman's young son who reacted to his father's distress. However, the son has fallen ill. The cause? A chom stole his soul as payment for the murder and is taking it to face judgment in Miquito, the Realm of the Dead.

After informing the council, the members blame the misfortune on the soured advice of Xotaxtl, the headman's chief advisor sorcerer-priest. They direct him to lead a party into Miquito to save the child's soul and determine proper payment for the death of the alux.

The characters venture through the Corpsewood, a small sliver of the Cuahtla Forest bordering the Tepepan Mountains, to seek passage to the Obsidian Spire at one of the gates of Miquito, which lies beyond the Great Void. There they must enter the sacred mines to procure the jadeite beads they need to pay passage into Miquito. Once they have the beads, they must find the place within the mountains' shadow where they can locate the first portal and perform a ritual that opens it so they can enter the Great Void. From there, they must then take the correct path to the Obsidian Spire, where they must then pass through several fabled challenges before confronting the judge who holds the child's soul. The judge demands the soul of the first individual who started the events as payment: the headman's advisor Xotaxtl. Unfortunately, Xotaxtl's soul has also been stolen after being consumed by a monstrously deformed giant alux during a brutal fight in the jadeite mines.

In the final section of the adventure, the characters return to the land of the living to confront the giant alux who, after consuming the sorcerer, gained access to his powers. The alux now calls himself Xotaxtl Nitlocati and uses his powers to lead a horde of aluxes against the village seeking to reclaim the world that humanity stole from them after the gods destroyed their world with the great cataclysms. The adventure ends when the characters defeat Xotaxtl Nitlocati, restore peace, and allow the people to restore the festival of the Seven Year Harvest.

Chapter One: On the Rise of the Bloodmoon

Starting the Adventure

The adventure begins during the last few days of the harvest season in the village of Cintlipetl. It is the year of the Bloodmoon, an auspicious time when the people of Cintlipetl hold a weeklong festival to honor the bounties bestowed upon them by the gods. Like everyone else in the village, the characters are slated to attend the festival. Skipping the festival is viewed as an insult to the gods and is likely to bring bad luck upon the village. Therefore, attendance is virtually mandatory.

The adventure gets underway when the village's Headman Camaxtl calls for a town gathering at the temple to discuss and ready the upcoming events. Read or paraphrase the following passage to describe the opening scene:

> You have been called to attend a meeting to discuss the upcoming Harvest Festival at the village temple, a large structure of neatly stepped stone located in the heart of the settlement. Here, the headman holds court. The people come to celebrate the rise of the sun and the moon, and the priests bless the harvest and give thanks and sacrifices to the gods who have individual shrines within the structure.
>
> You enter with a small crowd of villagers and find seats on the woven cloth mats laid across the floor. Slowly, more villagers drift in, quietly taking their places before the headman's great chair. Seated on the left of the headman is a man decorated with feathers and bones, the headman's sorcerer-priest and chief advisor. Next to the sorcerer-priest sits a woman dressed in a colorful cotton gown, a bald man wearing red paint and an ocelot skin sash, a man with dark skin and a complete set of gold teeth, and a woman dressed in a bright purple cloth gown embroidered with thousands of beads. On the right sits a man in a cloak with a feathered collar, a woman wearing a gold pendant and large golden ear spools, and an older warrior wearing a jaguar mask. At the far right sits a withered, gray-haired woman dressed in simple clothing, but wearing a collection of small cloth satchels indicating her power as a medicine woman. All of these people wear large jade lip plugs that identify them as members of the town council. The headman raises his hand and the crowd goes silent, waiting to hear him speak.
>
> Before the proceedings can even begin, a terrified man dressed in simple common clothing rushes into the temple waving about a wooden crook and shaking in terror. He begs to speak with the headman on a matter of utmost urgency. Before anyone has time to react, four warrior guards spring forth, seize the man, search and strip him to his loincloth, and have him crawl forward before the headman.

While to some this act might seem cruel, such humiliation and prostration ensure Camaxtl's safety in the event the man is an assassin. If the characters attempt to intervene, allow them first to attempt a DC 5 Wisdom (Insight) skill check to recall such procedures are normal and expected under such conditions. Once the characters are content to let the drama unfold, continue with the following scene.

> Camaxtl the headman looks down upon the fearful commoner and utters a single word,
>
> "Speak." He lets the full weight of his gaze bear upon the villager.
>
> The villager speaks in a fear-filled whisper.
>
> "Headman Camaxtl, my name is Icnoyotl. I am but a simple herdsman. I came here to warn you that I fear a terrible pox may fall upon our harvest. This morning

I found lying in the fields several of my peccaries, each brutally slaughtered with its throat torn out and its hide savagely stripped from its flesh. Surely this bears upon us an ill portent, for those were the same peccaries I had marked for the harvest sacrifice."

"And upon whom do you cast blame for this crime?" asks the headman.

"Of those within our village, none would commit such a crime. … Therefore I shall assume the burden and serve as an offering. I ask only that my son be cared for and taken under the tutelage at the telpochcalli to be trained as a warrior to help repay my family's debt."

Upon finishing his plea, Icnoyotl the herdsman falls quiet and lowers his eyes as he awaits the headman's judgment.

At this time, the characters can intervene or ask questions. However, their input is uninvited in the court and causes them to suffer the headman's disfavor.

The headman turns to the sorcerer-priest, his chief advisor, and nods. He informs the crowd that he is postponing the village meeting and tells them to return to their homes for the time being. Once all have cleared the room, he calls for his advisor, the herdsman, and the town council to remain to discuss matters. He then commands the warrior-guards to seal the entrance and prevent anyone else from entering.

The characters are also asked to remain, depending on their background. If they share a connection to members of the council, they are invited to stay as they may well be needed for their expertise. If they are related to the herdsman, he requests they stay for similar reasons. If they chose the outsider option, the sorcerer requests they stay as he suspects they may have something to do with the slaughter of the peccaries. Once the room is secure, the headman turns to the sorcerer and asks him for his thoughts.

The sorcerer tells all in attendance the following legend. Read or paraphrase the following section:

"Last night I saw the coming of the Bloodmoon, a deep red rime around Ihueltiuh. This is an auspicious sign, but one that can either bring us years of prosperous harvests or lay our fields fallow. We must make the proper sacrifices or our fields will wither and our people starve to death. However, whoever has done this must face the judgment of this council so we can make amends with the gods, or we shall be cursed for seven years until the coming of the next Bloodmoon."

Concluding the Introduction

The council quickly concludes that for the good of the entire village, whoever has slain the peccaries must be caught and brought to face their judgment. Of all those present, the characters are most qualified to hunt and capture the perpetrator. Allow the characters to prepare themselves, gather whatever equipment they need, and then meet with the herdsman to survey the crime scene.

Cintlipetl Map Key

During this portion of the adventure, the character may roam around the town to speak with villagers about what they may have seen or simply take in the local sites to get a better feel for the task at hand. Each numbered location on the accompanying map of Cintlipetl corresponds to the following legend.

1. Temple of The Sun. This temple is devoted to several gods, most notably Yaocteotl, the Aztli God of War and the Sun. The headman frequents the temple, and most of the time it is where he holds court. It is also used as the main communal temple for public assemblies and open town council meetings. The Temple of the Sun is the town's most important structure and the focal point of the settlement.

2. Temple of the Moon. The second-largest temple is primarily dedicated to Itztliteotl, the Aztli God of the Night, though small shrines to other gods can be found here. While the Temple of the Sun serves some secular purposes, this structure is solely devoted to housing the priesthood and conducting religious ceremonies. It is frequently used for more intimate or personal worship and rituals, as well as for special ceremonies to celebrate private events, such as weddings and funerals.

3. Sacred Courts. The council uses the courts to mete out swift and terrible justice. Death is a frequent punishment for those who defy the hero-gods' will. Individuals condemned to serve a prison sentence do so in the Aztli Confederation's brutal penitentiaries, which many believe to be a fate worse than death.

4. The Arena. These structures are used for outdoor performances, festivals, and sporting competitions, most notably the ball game.

5. Temple of the Harvest. This temple pays homage to Quiahuitl and the lesser gods and goddesses who provide the citizens rain, good harvests, abundant fishing, and healthy livestock. Those looking for meals can find them here provided they leave a donation or provide the temple with a sacrifice or service.

6. West Crossing. A packed earthen road wanders up the plateau and leads to a small section of modest homes facing toward the distant sea.

7. Lower Square. Several paths merge near this small square. Its buildings consist of several merchant shops and homes. People come here to trade for grain, pottery, cloth, soap, flowers, and other mundane items.

8. The Point. A series of larger communal homes make up the Point. Laborers, farmers, and other families not of noble birth pool their resources to reside in these spacious yet cramped residences.

9. The Clay Pits. This collection of caves provides the village with clay for pottery. Potters, other crafts folk, and laborers make up a large number of residents in this neighborhood.

10. Telpochcalli of the Ocelot. This martial school trains students in the arts of combat and strategy. Scholars live in the dorms and practice their trade almost nonstop.

11. East Ridge. A long switchback road runs the length of this ridge. At the end stand the broken ruins of several houses. They were torn down several years ago, and it remains taboo to build there. Some say this is because the people living there were dirty and carried the plague.

12. The Medicine-Witch's House. Coaxoch lives toward the west end of the north market community. She is an important member of the community and frequently gives them advice or represents them at the temple or court.

13. North Market. A tangle of small streets runs past modest homes and shops that sell wares such as wool, meat, pottery, cloth, and medicines. The area sits above the lower plateau with a view of the temples.

14. Herdsman's Home. The herdsman lives toward the upper edge of the plateau on the outskirts of town facing the woods and mountains to the west. The community here consists mostly of woodcarvers and hunters, along with other herdsmen who graze their animals in the fields along the woods.

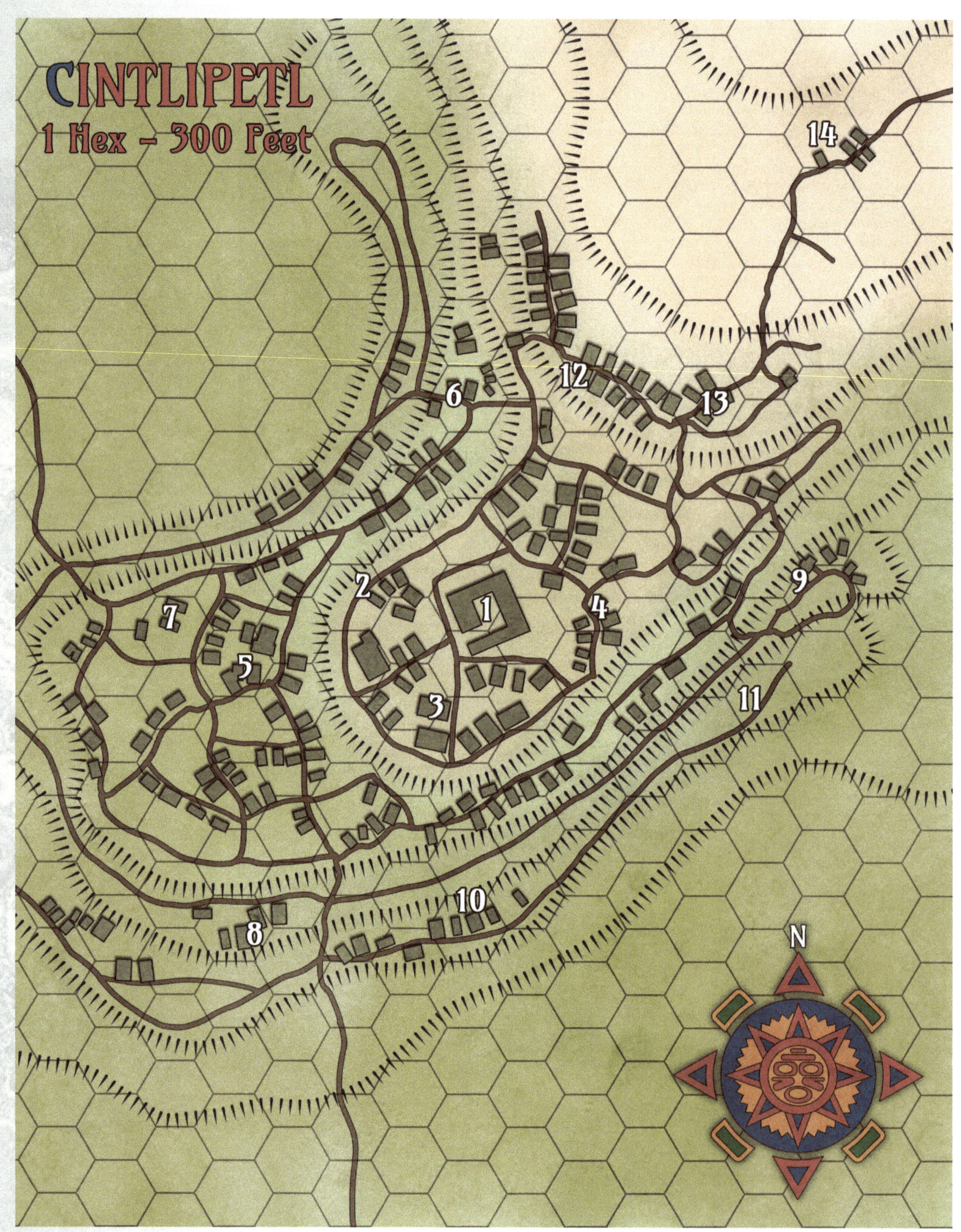
CINTLIPETL
1 Hex – 300 Feet
1
2
3
4
5
6
7
8
9
10
11
12
13
14
N

Cuahtla Forest
CENTRAL TEHUATL
Minnalin
Xacota
Caya
Grasslands
Teotlachco
Frowl
Onacatoya River
Hillamati
Quimichin
Ateztecatl
Darl
Tepepan Mountains
Citlitoch
Atinaquina
Hrawrg
Uolli
Tepetzin
Octli
Aliqtana
Kurn
Turew
Nepalta
Ixtla
Kulm
Domladur
Kulgan
Balandrur
Ipaconoytl
Cepual Desert
Node 226
Otimpo
Nochtli
Quannaqa River
Xalpit
Mactli
Ouatulli Lake
Omiex
Droomph
Teocua
N
Cuahtla Forest
Yoaltica Ilaquiloz
1 Square –
20 Miles
Necocyaotl
Amilotetl
The Great Canal
Quizaloa
Huitzineo
Azuato
Ixchicta
Zacatl
Good fortune
Ezhuacoza
Cotza
Toxana
Mimicapoli
Quitlacatl
Blibleblup
Ahuacua
Tolzolotli
Hilaya River
Ezhuitotl
Cuiateotl
Toctli Forest
The Spring
Mototoloa
Ixnenatl

Tracking the Peccary Slayer

When the characters secure their provisions and any additional equipment that they may need, they are ready venture over to the herdsman's small hovel so he can take them to the crime scene.

The Herdsman's Hovel

The herdsman lives with his young son in a small, single-room hovel just outside the village. He has just finished making a bowl of corn mash and beans for his son when the characters arrive. Upon seeing them, he quickly grabs his crook and a light cloak before leading them on the two-mile walk to the fields where he grazes his peccaries. The fields sit along a small rocky outcropping that stands near the edge of the Corpsewood, a transitory section of the Cuahtla Forest bordering the Cepual Desert, the Caya Grasslands, and the Tepepan Mountains roughly 35 miles due north of Teocua.

The herdsman directs the characters to the ghastly scene where the disemboweled bodies of more than a dozen peccaries stain the grass black. Massive wounds torn through their skins are plainly visible, and dried blood and rotting entrails litter the ground.

A character who examines the corpses and succeeds on a DC 10 Intelligence (Nature) or Wisdom (Medicine) check confirms that a sharp instrument or object created the gaping lacerations on the bodies of the peccaries. The character also finds evidence of blunt force trauma injuries.

If the same character succeeds on a DC 15 Intelligence (Nature) or Wisdom (Medicine) check, that individual discovers two additional details. The meat is shredded, pierced, and torn, yet very little of it is missing, indicating the perpetrator ate very little of it. In a more disturbing development, the peccaries are missing their hearts.

A character who searches the area for tracks and succeeds on a DC 12 Wisdom (Survival) check notices a pair of bloody footprints heading west. The trail disappears into the neighboring forest.

The bloody footprints lead a short way into the forest. There, a successful DC 15 Wisdom (Survival) check can track a path left by bent twigs and trampled underbrush to a small spying hutch used by the peccary slayer before it made its attack.

E1: The Spying Hutch

A successful DC 10 Wisdom (Perception) skill check locates telltale signs of peccary scraps, fur, and skin, along with a couple of small bones and some blood scattered about the encampment. The alux left the sack behind to ensnare the unwary. While the stains on the sack are peccary's blood, the creature placed several small stones of no value and an extremely venomous snake from the Land of the Dead inside the bag. The **Miquito adder** (see **Appendix A: New Monsters**) immediately bites anyone reaching into the bag to feel what might be inside. If a character opens the bag and looks into it, the snake gains advantage on its attack roll against that character. Conversely, if the character dumps the contents of the bag on the ground, the snake slithers out and attacks as normal. The sack is secured by a drawstring that requires an action to open or close.

A character who examines the odd carving and succeeds on a DC 13 Intelligence (Religion) skill check identifies the figure as a mythical creature known as the alux, a deformed humanoid creature said to be the last of the proto-humans slaughtered during a prehistoric cataclysm. Folktales describe the creature as an aggressive monster renowned for the savagery of its attacks. Nearly every recorded encounter with an alux took place deep within the

Using the Teoctlan Map

The map of the Corpsewood and the lands beyond it is unscaled. The lack of scale is deliberate, as the map is intended to serve as a general reference for you to give a basic idea of the locations of things, allowing the pacing of the game to account for distance rather than the precision of the map. Teoctlan is a Primordian Notoan name the aluxes gave to the vast section of the Tepepan Mountains west of Xalpit and south of Ipaconoytl and Balandrur. Although the preceding settlements came into being long after the aluxes' heyday, the location of the portal opening into the Great Void remained the same. The sites shown on the Teoctlan map may be placed anywhere in this region thus explaining why they are not detailed on the Central Tehuatl map from the *Tehuatl* sourcebook. Traveling across it to find the portal and enter the land of the dead is meant to be epic. As a general guideline, the locations in the **Tracking the Peccary Slayer** section are only a few miles apart, while later locations should be dozens of miles apart, requiring days of travel through rugged terrain. More general information about the distances between farther locations is noted in the descriptive text for specific locations.

forest, especially in the areas around Teocua, though it is said the creature occasionally wanders into human lands to feast on turkeys, dogs, and peccaries when its normal prey becomes scarce.

A character who succeeds on the preceding Intelligence (Religion) check by 5 or more acknowledge the previous tales but also questions their accuracy, as the aluxes were described as a race of proto-humans whom the Forgotten Gods destroyed during the ages of the Lost Lands before Tlatoani's ascendence. The more prevalent folklore derives from the latter revelation, but the more popular version better serves its intended purpose of scaring children from wandering into the forests.

Surveying the surrounding area and succeeding on a DC 8 Wisdom (Survival) skill check uncovers footprints belonging to a humanoid-like creature. The tracks head northeast to what appears to be a shallow hole dug into the ground. Anyone inspecting the hole immediately detects the distinct stench of dung. From this point, the tracks continue onward north toward the Corpsewood, a sallow land that most people deliberately avoid. Any character re-examining the area who succeeds on a DC 14 Wisdom (Survival) skills check notices another set of prints returning. Following these tracks east leads characters to **Area E2**.

E2: The Buried Shrine

A character who examines the stones and succeeds on a DC 12 Intelligence (Religion) skill check believes the buried stones to be a shrine or older temple dedicated to a prehistoric nature deity.

The flowers are unusual and rare. A character who succeeds on a DC 15 Intelligence (Arcana or Nature) check identifies them as zac nicte. Some practitioners of ancient magic and healing consider them sacred, but they have no special properties.

This site harbors the buried remains of an ancient shrine devoted to a goddess of dreams worshipped in the time before the hero-gods and even the emperor. Like most of the ancient structures, it was destroyed when the seas swallowed most of the land. Still, the alux refused to forget the goddess, prompting it to pay her tribute before journeying onward.

Despite the obvious neglect, the shrine is not unattended. A **fey drake** (see **Appendix A: New Monsters**) watches over the locale. When it hears trespassers approaching, it quickly *polymorphs* into a small field mouse and hides among the nearby tree roots to monitor their activities. The fey drake is shy and does not reveal its presence unless the characters attempt to take the goddess's tribute. If this happens, it returns to its normal form and confronts the thieves, accusing them of stealing the goddess's tribute.

Although it is a capable combatant, the drake is willing to listen to reason.

TEOCTLAN
The Eye of the World
Iztaccihuatl
Popocatepetl
Gate to the Great Void
Jadeite Mines
Corpsewood
Cuauhtenco
Crazing Fields
To Cintlipetl
N

Nonetheless, it dislikes people and is extremely wary of their intentions. It never initiates an attack, preferring to turn invisible again to avoid a confrontation. However, if pressed into a corner or if the characters destroy or otherwise desecrate the shrine, the fey drake defends itself and the sacred ground against defilers. If the characters manage to gain its trust by returning the tribute and possibly adding to it, the drake entertains some of their questions, though it remains as aloof and obscure in the details as possible.

The drake can tell them an alux passed by the shrine and left the tribute. It knows the alux is one of the beings of humanity whose race was destroyed by the Forgotten Gods during the prehistoric cataclysm and that it worshiped Auyinah, a peaceful goddess of dreams to whom this shrine was dedicated. She is one of the hundreds of gods these creatures once worshipped who are now lost to the annals of time. He knows the alux was returning home when it passed the shrine, and he wished the creature good fortune and fair omens before it departed. It knows only these few details but requests the humans not forget the goddess and attempts to get them to promise to one day return to pay her tribute.

E3: River's Edge

The second set of tracks leads to the edge of the Cuauhtenco River, a small, shallow waterway nearly 20 feet across that serves as the unofficial boundary between the Cuahtla Forest and the looming desolation of forbidden lands known as Corpsewood. The tracks run cold at the water's edge. However, a quick scan of the river followed by a successful DC 12 Wisdom (Perception) check reveals a small, crudely constructed raft beached on the opposing riverbank, about 100 feet downstream.

Characters who enter the Cuauhtenco River find it to be rather shallow, with a depth of five feet at the center with a gentle current. Being a minor tributary of the Quannaqa River, the waterway is inaccessible to vessels larger than a small canoe. Swimming through the lazy waters are 5 **swarms of quippers** that immediately respond to any noticeable disturbance and race to feast upon the unlucky trespasser. The bloodthirsty, aggressive fish never disperse. They attack until they either eat their fill or eat their last meal.

Sabotaged Raft Trap

The clever alux tampered with the raft after crossing the river. It loosened several of the knots on the raft's bindings so that if more than one Medium creature attempts to use it, the bindings slowly pull loose and cause the raft to come apart in the middle of the river. A character who examines the raft and succeeds on a DC 16 Intelligence (Investigation) check notices the sabotaged bindings. The raft can be repaired with a successful DC 12 Intelligence check. If the characters operate the raft without repairing it, there is a 50% chance each round that the bindings come undone, causing the raft to fall apart. The raft can hold three Medium creatures at a time without sinking into the river and capsizing, spilling its riders into the stream.

Along the eastern side of the river, characters who succeed on a DC 15 Wisdom (Survival) check near where the raft was beached find the alux's tracks. The trail leads up the shoreline and then eastward into the Corpsewood.

The Corpsewood

Across the Cuauhtenco River stretches a fallow and desolate land of dry, rocky soil and leafless trees whose dull gray bark constantly peels and flakes off, exposing an eerily flesh-colored wood beneath it. The Aztlis believe Yaocteotl fashioned these trees from the remains of warriors who fled during battle.

The Corpsewood stretches north and eastward, climbing into a series of low, rocky hills on the outskirts of the Tepepan Mountains.

Dozens of caverns bore into the surrounding hillsides. Those who have spiritually passed on but whose physical bodies still endure take refuge in these caverns. Within this dank land, they spend their final, lonely days contemplating the mysteries of the universe until their physical bodies eventually die. Some individuals succumb to natural causes, though many ultimately take their own lives rather than exist for another day in this dreary realm. Other times, aluxes that occasionally travel here eat them on their way to collect souls seeking passage to Miquito.

When the characters approach the Corpsewood for the first time, they spot a small copse of trees covered with ebon leaves. Moving closer to investigate, they soon realize that what first appeared to be leaves are really a flock of strange and silent black-feathered birds. If the characters approach within 300 feet of the 14 **choms** (see **Appendix A: New Monsters**), the birds quickly take wing and race off. The winged monstrosities have no interest in fighting the characters at this time. Therefore, their sole inclination is to flee unless the adventurers force them to fight.

A successful DC 15 Intelligence (Religion) check recalls stories of black-feathered birds called choms, whom the Forgotten Gods punished for their meddling and dishonesty by stripping away their bright plumage. It is believed that the gaze of a chom is an ill omen.

C1: The Canals

The characters enter a section of the Corpsewood that stands upon the ruins of an ancient aqueduct. The stone bricks once made up canals that led water to the fields and villages that existed here during the Third Sun, a prehistoric epoch before the ground shook and cracked them beyond recognition.

As the characters continue, the area slowly transforms into a wide and murky glade. Although traveling upon the bricks is safe, the mire covers nearly everything, thus hiding deep spots along the center of the canals or areas where the water flooded into the earth and turned it to quicksand. In this area, characters have a 10% chance of being able to move 30 feet across the bricks without impediment, and a 20% chance of being able to move 15 feet across the bricks without impediment. Otherwise, all movement is across difficult terrain. Once in the swampy glade, the characters lose all trace of the peccary slayer's tracks.

Despite the inhospitable conditions, 3 **black puddings** lurk in the canal searching for living prey to envelop. The instant they sense creatures moving through the murk, they slither forth to attack. They blend in perfectly with their dark, soupy background, giving them advantage on Dexterity (Stealth) checks and imposing disadvantage on Wisdom (Perception) checks made to notice them.

C2: The Alux

When the characters approach this section of the Corpsewood, characters who succeed on a DC 12 Wisdom (Perception) check hear a rough, guttural voice quietly chanting strange words in an unknown language. If they win a Dexterity (Stealth) check contested by the alux's passive Perception, they can draw close enough to see the creature speaking this seemingly alien tongue. If they fail the contested Dexterity (Stealth) check, their disturbance interrupts the creature.

At this sacred site, the **alux of the second sun** (see **Appendix A: New Monsters**) has once again stopped to make offerings and pay homage to the Forgotten Gods. If the characters confront the alux, it turns to them wild-eyed and full of rage for daring to interrupt the ceremony. The strange creature spits out a foul and guttural language unknown and unheard of by modern mortals, then it clenches its stony fists and grits its sharpened teeth.

The alux first attempts to intimidate the characters and scare them off. As the alux snarls, one of the black-feathered birds lands on its shoulder and chatters something directly into the creature's ear. The alux looks quickly at the chom (see **Appendix A: New Monsters**) as if to acknowledge the message and then makes a quick gesture, which causes the bird to rapidly fly east.

Characters who previously identified the black-feathered birds recognize the bird as a chom.

A character who succeeds on a DC 20 Intelligence (History or Religion) check notes the significance of the colored maize offerings as tributes made to the Forgotten Gods who watched over each of the four earthly kingdoms before Tlatoani's arrival.

The alux fights until subdued or killed. It begrudgingly surrenders if the characters reduce it to less than one-third of its maximum hit points. The creature is proud and angry but not stupid. It knows there will be dire consequences if the humans kill it, a fact it assumes they already know along with who it is and whom it serves. It does not understand why the characters interrupted his ceremony or attacked him. It thinks they are crazy to perform such an act.

The alux is not a difficult opponent, and the characters likely have little difficulty subduing and capturing it. Hopefully, they do not kill the creature in the process. It might even be helpful to remind the characters that the headman sent them to capture the peccary slayer and not to kill it. Similarly, if they can determine that the creature is the alux, you can allow them to succeed on a DC 15 Intelligence check to recall that killing such a creature can afflict them with very bad luck.

Chapter Two: The Feast and the Omen

After capturing the alux, the characters should return to the village with the creature to present it to the headman. It is reluctant to travel with them, perhaps even fearful, but willfully accepts its fate. Regardless, the alux refuses to speak except for occasionally calling upon the Forgotten Gods in a harsh primordial language. No attempt to translate the speech yields any reward, for no creature of this world recalls how to speak its guttural and vile forgotten tongue without the use of *tongues* or similar magic. Still, anyone attempting to decipher the creature's words determines they are loaded with anger and disdain by succeeding on a DC 7 Wisdom (Insight) check. Most certainly the creature feels its captors are somehow ignorant, thus its physical struggles against its captors convey its defiance and pride rather make a desperate escape attempt or revenge retributive attack. The alux acts almost as if it expects someone or something to free it.

The headman meets the adventurers outside his house, where he walks around the beast in a circle, carefully observing it. Staring widely, it seems as if he cannot believe his eyes. After his third circle, he stops, pauses for a moment and then calls to a nearby warrior guard, "Quick, go and get the sorcerer."

While waiting for the sorcerer, a crow flutters down to perch in a nearby tree to watch. The crow seems almost thoughtful. The alux glances at it and utters a raspy whisper-scream. *"N'gah-tah!"* Upon hearing the strange syllabic noise, the crow immediately launches from its perch and wings off.

Anyone checking the direction of its flight knows it headed northeast toward the Corpsewood.

The characters, the headman, and the sorcerer are all free to interrogate the alux. However, it glares defiantly and refuses to speak with any of them. Unable to determine a clear course of action, the sorcerer suggests they lock up the alux, at least until he can research it a bit. It most certainly is a powerful creature and killing it might bring the village even more bad luck. The characters are free to weigh in on this debate and may attempt to provide further information by making Intelligence (History or Religion) checks to recall any of the following tales concerning the alux with a successful check against the DC listed on **Table 3–1** below.

Table 3–1: Investigating the Alux

DC	Result
5	The alux comes every seven years with the rising of the Bloodmoon.
10	The alux can speak to the choms, once colorfully plumed birds cursed by an ancient deity who turned their feathers black and condemned them to eat only carrion.
13	Killing the alux would certainly bring bad luck, especially during the Bloodmoon (partially true).
14	The alux is a hideous, immortal creature and single survivor of the First Sun, the first cataclysm in which the Forgotten Gods summoned jaguars to feast upon the first men so that they might be built from their remains. The alux is the last of the first men, kept in Miquito as a model (partially true).
16	The alux is a cannibal that only consumes hearts of mortals (partially true)
20	The alux can carry souls to the gate of Miquito and tell them which path they must follow to live forever in the afterlife.

Running the Debate

There are only three choices for the alux's fate: The characters can execute the creature, set it free, or imprison it until more information about the creature and its intentions can be acquired.

Most of the meeting's participants lean toward prudence and want to keep the alux imprisoned, at least until they learn more about what happened.

Each NPC holds a certain number of votes, which they can exercise as three different verdicts: free, execute, or imprison. At the end of the trial, the votes are tallied and the council swiftly carries out the verdict to free the alux, execute him, or imprison him in a pit to delay his final judgment. At the start of the debate, each council member holds a specific position. Everyone has the opportunity to speak and persuade others to their position. After every member has spoken his or her piece on the matter, tabulate the final number of votes in each category. The most votes win, with any vote resulting in a tie resulting in the creature's imprisonment and retrial on the following day. Characters can also participate, but they have only a single vote.

The Characters

Each character gets a single vote, but more importantly, they also gain an attempt to sway the opinion of specific council members with a successful Charisma (Persuasion) check. A character can attempt to sway the opinion of only a single council member, though multiple characters can attempt to sway the opinion of the same council member.

The Headman. Camaxtl the Headman (LN male Aztli human **bandit captain** armed with a club instead of scimitar) holds five votes and places all of them on imprisonment. The headman feels he lacks the information to make a prudent decision at this time. He is greatly influenced by the sorcerer and if the sorcerer's opinion changes, the headman can be swayed toward the sorcerer's decision by his total number of votes. All other characters can sway him with a successful Charisma (Persuasion) check (DC 10 + number of votes he remains opposed to the speaker's position).

The Medicine-Witch. Coaxoch the Medicine-Witch (N female Aztli human **cult fanatic**) holds three votes and places all of them on immediate release. She cannot be convinced to kill the creature under any circumstances. Characters can sway her to imprison it with a successful Charisma (Persuasion) check (DC 10 + number of votes she remains opposed to the speaker's position)

The Sorcerer. Xotaxtl the Sorcerer (see **Appendix A: New Monsters**) seeks prudence and spends all three of his votes on keeping the creature imprisoned until the council can learn more about what happened. The sorcerer is a coward at heart. Therefore, he can be readily convinced to change his position in either

THE ANGRY HERDSMAN

If the council determines the alux is innocent of any real crime and decides to free it, Icnoyotl the herdsman becomes extremely angered and storms off to his hut to be alone. Instead of attending the festival, he takes up his hunting spear and pursues the alux into the woods, presumably to slay it. This can be confirmed by talking to either his wife or his son, to whom he complained bitterly before saying, "I'm going to get my vengeance." He stormed out of the hut, presumably to hunt down and kill the alux for what it did to his peccaries. As the characters have prior experience with the creature and the dangers of the Corpsewood, they know the herdsman is in way over his head. If this happens, the headman asks the characters to pursue Icnoyotl and bring him home safely. Have the characters catch up with Icnoyotl just as he is confronted by another alux while standing over the body of his slain quarry. The unknown alux is an alux of the third sun named Ohtli (see encounter **Ohtli**) who explains the true nature of how the events unfolded.

---

direction with a successful Charisma (Persuasion) check (DC 8 + number of votes he remains opposed to the speaker's position).

Although a rather competent sorcerer-priest, Xotaxtl failed miserably at recognizing the alux as a servant of the Forgotten Gods, and the religious significance of the fey eating the peccaries' hearts. Xotaxtl worships the hero-gods, yet he is still familiar with some of the older traditions, especially being from this neck of the Cuahtla Forest that borders the Corpsewood. If he had understood the alux's true nature and its purpose, he would have vociferously argued to free the creature at once and allow it to return to Miquito to appease the Forgotten Gods. Instead, he meekly acquiesces to the will of others, sealing the alux's fate and eventually his own in the process.

The Herdsman. Icnoyotl the herdsman (N male Aztli human **commoner**) holds a single vote that he places on killing the alux. His decision is unyielding and unreasonable, and he refuses to change it under any circumstance.

Town Council Members. The remaining council members consist of 6 nobles (various alignments, male and female Aztli human **nobles** wearing tlahuitztli [see **Appendix C: New Equipment and Magic Items**] instead of breastplate and armed with tecpatls [see **Appendix C: New Equipment and Magic Items**] instead of rapiers). Ignorant of the nature of the old gods and the alux itself, they perceive it as a bloodthirsty and vengeful monster (it does, after all, eat people and serve some bloodthirsty Forgotten Gods). Half of them are ready to vote to kill the creature while the others opt for imprisonment. Any of the council members can be convinced to change their position in either direction with a successful Charisma (Persuasion) check (DC 10 + number of votes he remains opposed to the speaker's position).

When all the votes are tallied, the council makes its decision. Most likely the alux is sentenced to either imprisonment or death. In either case, it is sent to a prison pit, either to serve a sentence or to await a ritual execution at dawn. In the unlikely event that the council decides to release the alux, then there is a slight change of events. See the **Angry Herdsman** sidebar.

CONCLUDING THE COUNCIL

After the council determines the alux's fate, Camaxtl the Headman draws the meeting to a close, then calls for the feast to commence. At this point, the council members disperse to prepare for the celebration. Give the characters 20 minutes of game time to prepare, finalize plans, organize themselves, and plot a course of action before the festival begins. If they seek the advice or counsel of anyone else in the village, they must succeed on a DC 15 Charisma (Persuasion) check to convince that individual to delay their preparations for the evening's festivities to speak with them. If the check succeeds, they get five minutes to converse with each person. When the allotted time expires, the person shoos them away to resume their preparations for the festival.

Most likely the members of the council determine that whatever fate the alux deserves, they should hold it captive until dawn before it faces it. They have no jail, as justice usually comes quickly and terribly, though the council remains undecided. Instead, several of the village warriors lead the alux to the Clay Pits, lower it into one of the pits and seal the opening with a wooden grate held fast with boulders. The village stations 2 guards (N male Aztli human **thugs** armed with a longbow instead of a heavy crossbow) to keep watch at the entrance and switch out with new guards every four hours. Lest a worse fate befalls the village, no one is to speak of the strange creature or utter a word about the trial proceedings until the council reaches a verdict.

THE FESTIVAL

Entering into the center of town, the square has been transformed by lanterns and torches and drenched in colorful decorations of feathers, beads, and paper. Along the perimeter, a great feast is laid out upon long wooden tables laden with roasted corn, baked squash, beans, corn tortillas, tamales, spat rabbit, several whole roasted peccaries with their skin blackened and crisp from the coal pits, plank-smoked fish, and roasted frogs along with dozens of other delights. In the center, a wide circle of stones forms a tremendous fire pit stuffed with wood for the celebration pyre, and the surrounding earth has been swept clean to provide a smooth surface for the dancers and musicians.

The crowd mingles together, exchanging greetings and gifts and offering praise and thanks. Characters are free to engage with each other or others at this time, though only the council know about the recent troubling events and would scorn them for attempting to discuss them with others during the celebration. After some time passes and the moon peeks over the horizon, the music begins. Read or paraphrase the following description:

As the drums pound beneath the sounds of bamboo pipes and trumpeters blowing conch shells on the hollowed thighbones of their ancestors, the chanting songs of the village storm the night as if to summon the very stars. The celebration swells as chains of elaborately costumed dancers wearing draped clay beads, feathers, bone, and precious metals weave themselves into triumphant flaying patterns that distort their figures in the flickering light.

Any characters with proficiency in Performance or entertainer as a background may partake. A successful DC 12 Charisma (Performance) skill check earns that individual an honorable performance, allowing them advantage in one social interaction with the king. The character must declare they are using this benefit before attempting the check.

When the dancing dies down, the characters and villagers take their places for the feast as wood is gathered for the Great Pyre.

As the moon rises, the fire is lit in an attempt to have the fire roaring by the time the Bloodmoon reaches its apex. A murder of black-feathered birds flutters wildly across a blood-red moon, their ebon wings dancing like shadows. The event passes quickly and quietly, almost as if it never occurred, as most fail to remember or even acknowledge it.

"Odd, birds don't fly at night, oh well …"
"Are you sure you saw birds, perhaps it was bats?"

Yet to those who know of the day's strange proceedings, the appearance of the black-feathered birds casts a strange and far more ominous omen. These individuals fall silent and deathly serious for a moment before trying to regain their composure to continue through the festival. The sighting is not something they want to see, or that they are going to speak of until the next day.

SIGHTING OPINIONS

If the characters have a background relationship with one of the following characters and question them about the birds, the character receives a single opinion from them before that individual goes silent and tells the character to wait until the morning to discuss the matter further.

Xotaxtl. This is not a good sign. I would like to read entrails or cast stones for advice.

Camaxtl. I am unsure of the meaning of what I witnessed. I must consult with the sorcerer.

Icnoyotl. I knew we should have killed that horrid beast. Now I see the omens of death descend upon us.

Coaxoch. I fear the worst for I know we have witnessed the casting of a most wicked omen.

The Morning After

At dawn, a murder of crows sits in the trees surrounding the village square, eerily watching all within their gaze. Yelling at them does little to scare them away. The villagers are afraid of the crows. They keep their distance and avoid meeting their gaze for fear of being cursed. If the characters approach the crows and physically attempt to shoo them off, the birds fly straight up into the sky, swirling together in a whirlwind formation, then head for the prison where the alux is being kept (see **The Clay Pits**).

The Clay Pits

About an hour after sunrise, a messenger seeks out the characters to inform them that they must hurry to the temple and speak with the headman's chief advisor. When they arrive, the sorcerer-priest quickly leads them inside. In a hushed and terrified whisper, he tells them that the alux is dead, poisoned in his pit during the night by an unknown assassin.

Upon inspecting the corpse, a successful DC 15 Wisdom (Medicine) check reveals that the creature died after eating a rat that was first gutted and then had its stomach cavity stuffed with poison. The potion is a mixture of several highly toxic roots known as Eternal Sleep. It is known that the medicine woman uses the poison to help the mortally wounded die without pain.

If the characters seek out the medicine-witch, they find her at home, frantically searching through her shelves and jars of reagents. Upon seeing the characters, a horrified look washes across her face as she reveals her fear to them that someone has stolen a powerful poison from her.

If the characters decide to search her home for clues, a successful DC 12 Intelligence (Investigation) skill check uncovers a knife with a peccary-bone handle and a chipped blade in the garden near the front door. The weapon likely was used to pry open the sealed stone jars holding the medicine. A successful DC 10 Intelligence (Nature) skill check recalls that herdsmen commonly use such knives.

The knife suggests the herdsman Icnoyotl might know something about the murder. At first, his demeanor makes him appear guilty, but upon further interrogation, a successful DC 8 Wisdom (Insight) skill check reveals no indications of guilt, but he may be hiding something from the characters. Characters searching the house who succeed on a DC 10 Intelligence (Investigation) skill check find a rat stick and pouch of poison hidden beneath the sleeping pallet of his young son, Itoxo. If asked as to the location of his son, the herdsman pleads ignorance. He claims that when he arrived home, he found the door open, and his wife and son gone.

Unfortunately, Icnoyotl's lament was as ignorant as his son's actions. Killing the alux brings bad luck upon the village. The boy is found deathly sick, lying in his parents' bed, his mother soaking him with water to cool his raging fever. A lone **chom** (see **Appendix A: New Monsters**) flutters into the window and perches upon the sill, surveying the room. All fearfully avert their gaze to prevent the bird from locking eyes with them, for they know the chom curses those who gaze into the death-bird's eyes with foul luck. Coaxoch the medicine-witch notices the chom and makes some crazed gestures, then throws a handful of black and red corn seeds at the creature. In response, it cackles madly and flies off.

When Coaxoch turns to face the people in the hut, her eyes are rimmed with tears.

"The chom," the medicine-witch utters somberly, "it has taken the boy's soul."

The boy is scared and willing to talk to the characters for he is now desperate to undo his actions, as are his mother and father who encourage him to speak the truth. Characters who wish to speak to the child get him to reveal the following information.

Itoxo readily admits his crime, exclaiming that he hates the alux and blames it for the recent whirlwind of trauma and emotional upheaval that plagues his family since the peccaries were found slain. He tells the characters that the day before, he overheard his father lamenting that he had caused a bad omen to befall the village and dark curses to sallow future harvests for the next seven years. In his rant, Icnoyotl blamed the alux for cursing his family and their fields and wished death upon the hideous and loathsome creature. Upon overhearing his father's lament, the child determined to do something to help him. During the excitement and commotion of the festival, he slipped away to the medicine woman's hut and snuck off with the poison. He then stuffed a significant quantity of the poison into the gut hole of a large rat and went to see the alux. He simply told the guards he was there to feed it (a festival gift!) and dropped the rat into the pit. The guards did not bother to question the child's intention, though they can easily testify to the fact that he showed up with a rat and dropped it into the alux's cell.

After speaking, Itoxo tires and soon passes out in a feverish sweat. Coaxoch attempts to cast several spells and applies her salves and potions to help the boy, but her attempts prove futile. As the moon rises, the child suddenly stirs and speaks in a voice no longer his own. In his feverish state, he utters a haunting prophecy.

At the end of the speech, the child collapses and falls still. Characters who make a successful DC 12 Wisdom (Medicine) check determine he is barely alive and will likely perish in a few short days if nothing is done to save him.

Conversely, upon hearing the blackbird's prophecy, Xotaxtl becomes enraged and horrified as the terror of being cursed flood his thoughts. He knows that the headman and his fellow villagers will rightfully blame him for misinterpreting or outright missing the omens and signs portending these events. In his defense, he rattles off numerous potential dooms and at some point has an "I told you so" moment in which he starts tossing around accusations of guilt at the characters for being outsiders (whether this is a truly accurate statement or not) and for being the only unexpected change to the otherwise perfect harvest celebration preparations. Regardless of his rants, he is easily silenced by anyone that reminds him that capturing the peccary slayer was in fact, his idea. At the accusation, he pauses, turns pale, and defiantly pleads that he never intended for the creature to be killed. Still, deep down, he knows that the alux's death is on his hands, not the child's.

With the village cursed and the herdsman's young son doomed, the council once more meets in the temple to discuss a solution. As the headman and council listen, Coaxoch takes the floor and does her best to interpret their situation.

The medicine-witch then reveals that the Oracle of Moons resides in a towering black mountain called the Obsidian Spire that lies within the Great Void and marks the third gate to Miquito.

At this juncture, the characters are free to ask questions of Coaxoch or any other council members.

Once the characters' voice their questions and all understand the gravity of the situation, the headman appeals to those in attendance for brave individuals to undertake the journey to the Land of the Dead.

Coaxoch shakes her head. "I am too old for this quest; it is not of my fate. If we leave this tragedy undone, the boy is doomed and the village shall be cursed."

Allow the characters to respond and offer their services. If they attempt to decline, the headman requests it of them as their sacrifice to the people.

After the characters accept the quest, the sorcerer-priest interjects. "But how will they approach the oracle? All know none may safely approach the oracle without the proper payment?"

All realize the sorcerer is correct. Common knowledge holds that upon death, a disk of sacred jadeite is placed upon the tongue of the deceased as tribute for safe passage.

The headman replies, "Thank you for reminding me of such. Your priests are responsible for these payments and make them from the jadeite you collect in the sacred mine, which you keep secret. As the only one among us who knows the location of the secret mines, I appoint you to accompany the group to their location and procure for them the payment they require."

Xotaxtl starts to protest, then realizes quickly that the headman has given him no choice in the matter. Upon finishing, he draws the council to a close.

At this point, the characters can gather their things and begin their journey. Xotaxtl asks when the characters intend on leaving and asks for at least one hour to gather the items he requires for the trip. Unfortunately, one of the items he decides to take is several fingers from the alux, which he threads through a cord and tosses into a belt pouch, believing he might need them later to help guide him in the mines. Characters are free to spy on him, rest, or gather their own supplies. When they are ready, they meet at the edge of the border and venture east toward the Corpsewood to get jadeite from the mines before seeking passage to The Land of the Dead.

Chapter Three: Return to Corpsewood

The characters can return to Corpsewood the way they came during their first excursion into this domain. In most likelihood, they used the raft to cross the waterway and beached it on the western shore. Assuming they safely cross the river, they are free to venture in whatever direction they prefer. If they seek jadeite to pay for an audience with the oracle, Xotaxtl readily informs them the Jadeite Mines lie somewhere to the northeast. If pressed further about their location, the sorcerer-priest admits he has never seen the mines but assures the characters he has memorized the sacred signs and markings that his sacred order uses to mark the path.

A few miles into the Corpsewood, the terrain climbs upward, the trees thin, and the plain rises into Teoctlan's low and rocky hills. Scores of caves and caverns crack through these hills where the sacred Jadeite Mines are hidden. Whenever the characters reach an X on the map, they arrive at a random cave site. Use **Table 3–2** to determine what is in the cave. If you generate the same roll twice, ignore it and roll again. You can also use the table to beef up the exploration with more encounters or as additional locations if the characters decide to explore the region more extensively.

Table 3–2: Corpsewood Caves

2d8	Results
2	**Pitfall.** The entrance to this cave is protected by a deep natural ravine concealed by sticks and leaves covered with soil. It takes a successful DC 15 Wisdom (Perception) check to spot the pit. A creature who falls into the pit takes 3 (1d6) bludgeoning damage from the 10-foot plunge.
3	**Shallow Cave.** This cave goes only about two feet into the earth and then narrows to a thin crack, offering the characters little shelter. If they thrust a stick or torch or some other kind of probing object into the cave, they rile up a **swarm of bats**. While the swarm of bats poses little threat if the characters accidentally drive them out of the cave mouth, the sudden disturbance draws the attention of others lurking in the forest. A patrol of 5 **gnolls** riding 5 **giant hyenas** spots the swarm of bats and the opportunistic raiders rush to investigate activities near the cave. They arrive in 1d6 + 4 minutes, approaching stealthily. If the characters left the area before they arrive, the gnolls search for tracks and attempt to purse them until they catch up, at which point they attack.
4	**Empty Cave.** Currently, nothing occupies this cave though it bears evidence that someone once lived here. Long ago someone stenciled a series of handprints on all the walls. *Treasure.* A successful DC 12 Intelligence (Investigation) check finds a small trinket made up of a feather, a snail shell, and three human finger bones strung together. The trinket is a set of *lucky fingers* (see **Appendix C: New Equipment and Magic Items**).
5	**Cave of Doom.** A hunched-over skeleton sits propped in front of a woven basket of dried corn in this cave. If the characters attempt to take the corn, the skeleton stands then topples into a pile of bones, animating as a **bone swarm** (see **Appendix A: New Monsters**). It rushes to attack the characters to defend its bounty.
6	**The Ghostly Boar.** This large cave serves as the home to a hermitic **boarfolk rager** (see **Appendix A: New Monsters**). Aluxes sometimes form alliances with these creatures that also originate from the Land of the Dead.

2d8	Results
7	**Nhatyol.** This small cave sits high along the ridgeline. An **alux of the second sun** (see **Appendix A: New Monsters**) named Nhatyol sits near the mouth of the cave having a conversation with 3 **choms** (see **Appendix A: New Monsters**). The small, black-feathered birds visit her to bring her messages and updates of recent developments. They just brought her news of tragic events at the nearby village. Still, she is not foolish enough to trust the choms. She waits for news from a more reliable source. Despite her curiosity, if she spots the characters approaching, she attempts to hide, fearing that if the humans find her, they might murder her.
8	**Abandoned.** A small round pit has been dug near the entrance of the cave. The bottom of the pit is caked with potash. Nestled deep in the back of the cave is a pallet of dried grass. A thick layer of spider's webs blankets the fire pit, the cave, and its contents. *Treasure.* Hidden in the pit beneath the webs is a small wooden box with a sunstone carved into its face that is worth 350 gp. The box holds six feathers and three small polished gemstones, each carved with a different image. A pale white moonstone with an image of the goddess Atoyatl (165 gp), a piece of polished lapis with the image of the goddess Cualliteotl (150 gp), and a piece of turquoise with the image of Contlati (175 gp). A successful DC 8 Intelligence (Nature) skills check determines the feathers are from a great heron and are worth 10 gp. A successful DC 16 Intelligence (Investigation) check spots a deeply faded image sketched into the stone that depicts two mountains.
9	**The Deep Cave.** This cave descends into the hillside for several dozen yards and eventually slopes downward into a small pool of foul-smelling, stagnant water. Characters who attempt to climb to the pool must succeed on a DC 15 Strength (Athletics) check to navigate the slippery rock. The pool is only five feet deep. Anyone drinking the water must make a successful DC 13 Constitution saving throw to avoid being poisoned for 10 minutes.
10	**Hermit Cave.** This cave shows signs of recent use. There is a sleeping pallet, a peccary skin blanket, and a wooden table holding three clay jars, two of which are filled with water while one holds cornmeal. A message written on the dirt floor with a stick says, "Leave Me Alone!" in Aztli. An old **tribal warrior** lives here and keeps a vigilant watch over what he considers his territory. If the characters approach, he quickly shuffles off to hide in the nearby brush and waits patiently for them to leave. If they spot him, he yells at them to go away and leave him to his contemplations. He is annoyed by their company but can give them one or two hints about what's nearby if they promise to leave his home and give him back his peace.
11	**Hyena Cave.** The cave floor is littered with dried dung, snapped bones, and pawprints. It reeks of wet dog. As one might expect, this cave is the home of a pack of 12 **hyenas.** The ravenous canines are currently hunting and drinking water, though if the characters wait long enough, they return in about two hours. The hyenas attack any creatures they encounter in their cave without hesitation.

12 — **The Stash.** The cave extends only about 10 feet before a pile of stones wall off the passage. Digging out the stones takes about 20 minutes and reveals a small alcove that contains a parcel wrapped in cornhusks.
Treasure. The parcel contains a set of four ancient obsidian knives worth 30 gp each and two ear spoons of polished bone inlaid with gold in the visage of a serpent worth 300 gp.

13 — **Mushrooms.** Anyone entering this cave is assaulted with a potent sour, earthy smell. Hundreds of tiny gray-brown mushrooms cover the cave floor. A successful DC 10 Intelligence (Nature) check determines the mushrooms are edible and can be used to brew six servings of foul-tasting liquid that ironically removes the effects of nausea. A successful DC 20 Intelligence (Religion) skills check recalls a folktale about the hero Temoaco who used such a potion to ward off hallucinations on his voyage to the Great Void. Gathering and preparing the liquid takes 30 minutes and a successful DC 15 Intelligence (Nature) check. The solution lasts only for three weeks, after which it turns rancid and has the opposite effect.

14 — **The Third Sun.** Loud slamming and hideous chomping sounds echo from this cave. Shortly after, a towering and obese ogre-like creature squeezes from the entrance, its mottled skin and mousy black hair spattered with gore. It clutches a still-beating heart in its fist, which the creature greedily pops into its mouth, after which it lets out a deafening belch. The creature is an **alux of the first sun** (see **Appendix A: New Monsters**) that has just finished devouring the heart of an old mystic to take it back to Miquito. Inside, the creature ransacked the man's meagerly furnished dwelling. His broken body lies crumpled amid his torn blankets and crushed wooden tools and utensils. If the characters capture the alux alive, they can attempt to interrogate it. Still, the stupid creature knows little, claiming it is here only to gather souls of those seeking to travel safely to the afterlife. If pressed for what kind of creature it is, the alux responds only that it is like its captors, though most modern humans have trouble seeing or believing this and view all such creatures as monsters.

15 — **The Ominous Bones.** A collection of bones litters the floor in this cave. The bones are human and are all oddly cracked with strange scratches on them. A successful DC 10 Intelligence (Nature) or Wisdom (Medicine) check finds the markings consistent with teeth marks, implying that the inhabitant was eaten.

16 — **Grave Cave.** The cave smells dry and is entirely empty except for dust. A successful DC 12 Intelligence (Investigation) skills check discovers a small crawlway in the back of the cave. Characters attempting to use the crawlway must lie prone and squeeze through it. The crawlway continues for about 20 feet before it opens into another cave about 15 feet in circumference that is lit by a small crack in the ceiling. Around the perimeter of the cave are the propped-up forms of five humanoids curled into the fetal position and wrapped with cloth strips. Each is sprinkled with petals of dried flowers. The small cave is a grave, and characters entering its sanctity are obligated to make a sacrifice to its occupants. Those who succeed on a DC 5 Intelligence (Religion) check recognize it as such along with their obligation to make an offering to the dead. Characters failing to pay tribute are cursed and suffer disadvantage on all saving throws until the next sunrise.

OHTLI

During their wanderings in the Corpsewood, the characters capture the attention of another alux named Ohtli, who is an **alux of the third sun** (see **Appendix A: New Monsters**) and of more recent origin than those the characters previously encountered. He was tasked with finding the alux the villagers unwittingly slew. When he spots humans wandering through the Corpsewood, his curiosity gets the better of him and prompts him to follow them to gather whatever intelligence he can. He stays out of sight for as long as possible. He remains hidden until the characters spot him or until he overhears them discussing the details of their doings, at which point he steps forth of his own accord.

Ohtli can speak broken Aztli at best, which requires a character to succeed on a DC 8 Intelligence check to understand. He explains in his best faltering Aztli that his name is Ohtli and that he has been looking for his kin, an alux of the second sun named Noycotl whom he believed inadvertently wandered into Cintlipetl seeking the seven year harvest sacrifice for the Forgotten Gods.

If the characters do not connect Ohtli's tale to recent events, give the characters an opportunity to succeed on a DC 15 Wisdom (Insight) check to correctly infer that he refers to the alux that died under the villagers' watch. If the characters share their story with Ohtli, he struggles to understand them but listens thoughtfully. Telling him the news greatly saddens him, and he grimly informs the characters that without the gifts, the Forgotten Gods will most certainly be angered and curse the village. He shudders as he recalls the cataclysm that the Forgotten Gods used to destroy his world and his people.

Ohtli then offers to help the characters, sharing his belief that since the child is made from the remains of his ancestors, he is also his kin. Ohtli believes that aiding the humans might help restore the balance of hostility and violence that has infested his people and help move them in a direction back toward achieving some measure of humanity.

Ohtli can serve as the characters' advisor or guide to the Gate to the Great Void. He explains as best as possible that mortals cannot travel into the next world as long as their bodies possess a soul. To pass through the gate, the characters must leave their souls behind in the land of the sun. Ohtli offers to care for them and promises to keep them safe until their return. However, he warns them that if they die in the Great Void or in Miquito, he must immediately surrender their life sparks to the gods. If they die in either locale, they cannot come back. Ohtli speaks the truth on this subject as confirmed by a successful DC 14 Intelligence (Religion) check, which recalls several scriptures forbidding the living from entering the Great Void or passing into the afterlife. Those who defy the word of the gods suffer all manner of violent tortures.

If the characters accept Ohtli's offer, he claims he can perform the ritual at any time, but further stresses that he needs them to understand that if he takes their souls, he must go into hiding to ensure their safekeeping. If he dies, the characters die as well. If the characters return to the village with Ohtli, the headman offers to hide and protect him. The medicine-witch makes it clear to him that should any ill-fate befall Ohtli, those whose souls are in his possession would instantly perish.

When the characters are prepared to journey into the afterlife, Ohtli provides them with verbal instructions on how to reach the Void Gate, a mystic portal opening to the Great Void from whence they can follow the causeways anywhere in the universe. The Void Gate lies hidden within the valley of two sacred mountains known as the lovers, which lie east of Corpsewood, near the center of the world. Ohtli is forbidden to write or draw instructions showing the path to the Void Gate, for it is only for the dead and he would be flayed alive and his flesh fed to the choms if it came to light that he had revealed it. Similarly, he requests they not record his instructions and reminds them that his fate is now theirs until the matter is resolved. He whispers the instructions in the form of a sacred verse (see **Ohtli's Sacred Verse** sidebar).

OHTLI'S SACRED VERSE

When the shadows where the mountain lovers cross, the location of the portal becomes clear.

To pass through the portal you must appease the divine guardians so that you may step into the Void before the Birth of Creation.

To awaken the Shadow Soul, we must hold back the First Sun

To awaken the Elemental Soul, we must hold back the Second Sun

To awaken the Spirit Soul, we must hold back the Third Sun

To awaken the Temporal Soul, we must hold back the Fourth Sun

C3: The Jadeite Mines

The location of the jadeite mines has been a long-kept secret passed on through whispers and secret chants from one generation to the next. Those blessed with this esoteric knowledge maintain the responsibility to care for the mines and the first humans who watch them — those made by the gods during the dawn of the world, which the gods then cast aside or destroyed as each coming age passed. Still, it is these creatures that hold the secrets to Miquito, the realm of the dead, and its safe passage. Jadeite, the most precious of stones, serves as a gift to those who dwell in the realms beyond. When the sacred stone is worked into beads or plates and placed into the mouths of the deceased, the dead are given passage and allowed to venture across the bridge of souls to face judgment. The damned dare not interfere with those bearing gifts and tribute to the lords of the dead. The Aztlis and their relatives believe it is taboo to venture into the mines. Stern warnings fill their ancient tales regarding those who would steal from them, for they consider jadeite as a tribute to Miquito. The sorcerer knows of the mines but holds many superstitions and fears about them.

Along the northeast border of the Corpsewood rises the tightly cramped, dry and rocky hills of Teoctlan. They seem to grow together to form a tightly bound cluster that creates a broad impasse. Little exists in the way of passage beyond; however, a successful DC 15 Wisdom (Survival) check discerns several paths of least resistance through the range. The rough, crudely formed trails are steep and covered with scree and other loose matter, making them difficult to traverse. Characters must succeed on a DC 10 Strength (Athletics) check roughly once per hour to safely navigate the path and scale the high hills. Those who fail to locate the best way through this terrain must instead succeed on a DC 15 Strength (Athletics) check to trek through this rugged terrain. Creatures that fail any of the preceding checks slip, fall prone, and must make a successful DC 12 Dexterity saving throw or slowly slide 10 + 1d10 feet down the mountain, taking 3 (1d6) bludgeoning damage in the process.

The hill reaches its crest at around 600 feet, where it empties onto a worn, wide plateau that runs for miles in either direction. On the opposite side, the plateau drops sharply into a wide chasm consisting of several levels of stepped cliffs that collapse into an open maze of wide gouges hacked into the earth.

Mine General Features

The mines consist of a series of open ravines, so technically one can enter them from any point. The ravines are leveled into two terraces, with the lowest about 30 feet below the ground level. Sunlight penetrates into portions of the mines, but the dim light makes the area lightly obscured. Atop the first step, a narrow walkway encircles the entire mine. Creatures on lower levels cannot see the activities of creatures on the levels above them. To the south, an upper tier surrounds areas **M6** and **M7**, completely blocking them from sight. When it rains, the mines collect water and sometimes flood, leaving the ground muddy.

M1: The Mine Entrance

Despite its appearance, the ladder is well built and sturdy. Still, it serves as the main entrance to the mine and therefore the aluxes have sought to protect the entrance against trespassers by boobytrapping several of the rungs. About halfway down, a 10-foot length of knotted hemp rope dangles from a metal spike pounded into the cliff face. The rope is within easy reach of the ladder. The knots make climbing the rope easy, requiring only a successful DC 5 Strength (Athletics) skills check. Using the rope allows the aluxes (or anyone else) to safely bypass the trap.

The trap is more difficult to detect while descending the ladder; thus, any Intelligence (Investigation) checks made to detect it suffer disadvantage.

Exploding Ladder Rung Traps

When a character of Small size or larger steps on one of these rungs, it immediately snaps, triggering an alchemical explosion that splits the ladder down the middle, causing it to collapse. Creatures and objects within the 20-foot-radius blast area take 10 (3d6) fire damage and 10 (3d6) thunder damage. The creature can grab hold of a handhold or ledge with a successful DC 25 Strength (Athletics) check. Otherwise, the creature falls to the bottom of the mine where it takes 1d6 bludgeoning damage for every 10 feet it fell. In addition to dealing thunder damage, the loud explosion alerts every alux in a quarter-mile radius.

The first to hear the alarm is an **alux of the second sun** (see **Appendix A: New Monsters**) that is hiding in the southeast corner. It waits to see which way the characters go when they reach the bottom. The characters must succeed on a Wisdom (Perception) check contested by the alux's Dexterity (Stealth) check to notice him. If the characters begin moving toward him it obvious they saw him, he suddenly breaks cover, screams out in strange tongue, and then rushes to **Area M2**. Anyone who succeeds on a DC 13 Wisdom (Insight) check knows he screamed out a warning to alert the other aluxes.

A wide, worn passage, trampled by years of priests and their secret allies who mined the hills for jadeite and other precious metals, is at the bottom of the ravine.

M2: Bridges in the Sky

If the characters did not catch the alux in **Area M1**, he waits here, hiding in the curved passage just a short dash from the knotted climbing ropes. He keeps a sharp eye out for the characters. The moment he spots intruders or otherwise learns of their presence, he lets loose another screech and then dashes for the climbing ropes as he attempts to ascend to the plateau as soon as possible. When he reaches the top, the foul creature teases and taunts the characters. Should the characters pursue the alux up the cliffs, the creature waits until they are a little more than halfway up and then calls for out for Xoctlzti. On the next round, Xoctlzti, an **alux of the first sun** (see **Appendix A: New Monsters**), rushes to the edge of the cliff and begins pounding on it, hoping to target climbers with his trigger rockslide feature. Xoctlzti waits with his second sun ally and attempts to kick invaders off the plateau.

M3: The Carcass

A character who succeeds on a DC 10 Wisdom (Nature) check determines the kill was recent, despite the large swarm of flies feasting on it. A successful DC 5 Wisdom (Survival) check reveals no signs that the animal was dragged here or that any tracks are around it. It almost appears as though it simply fell out of the sky.

Further inspection of the walls discovers a series of small alternating gouges ascending the rock wall that are likely used as climbing handholds. Characters can use the handholds to make the easy 15-foot climb up to the plateau to the north without having to succeed on a check. A rope bridge connects the plateau to the ledge that circles the perimeter of the mines.

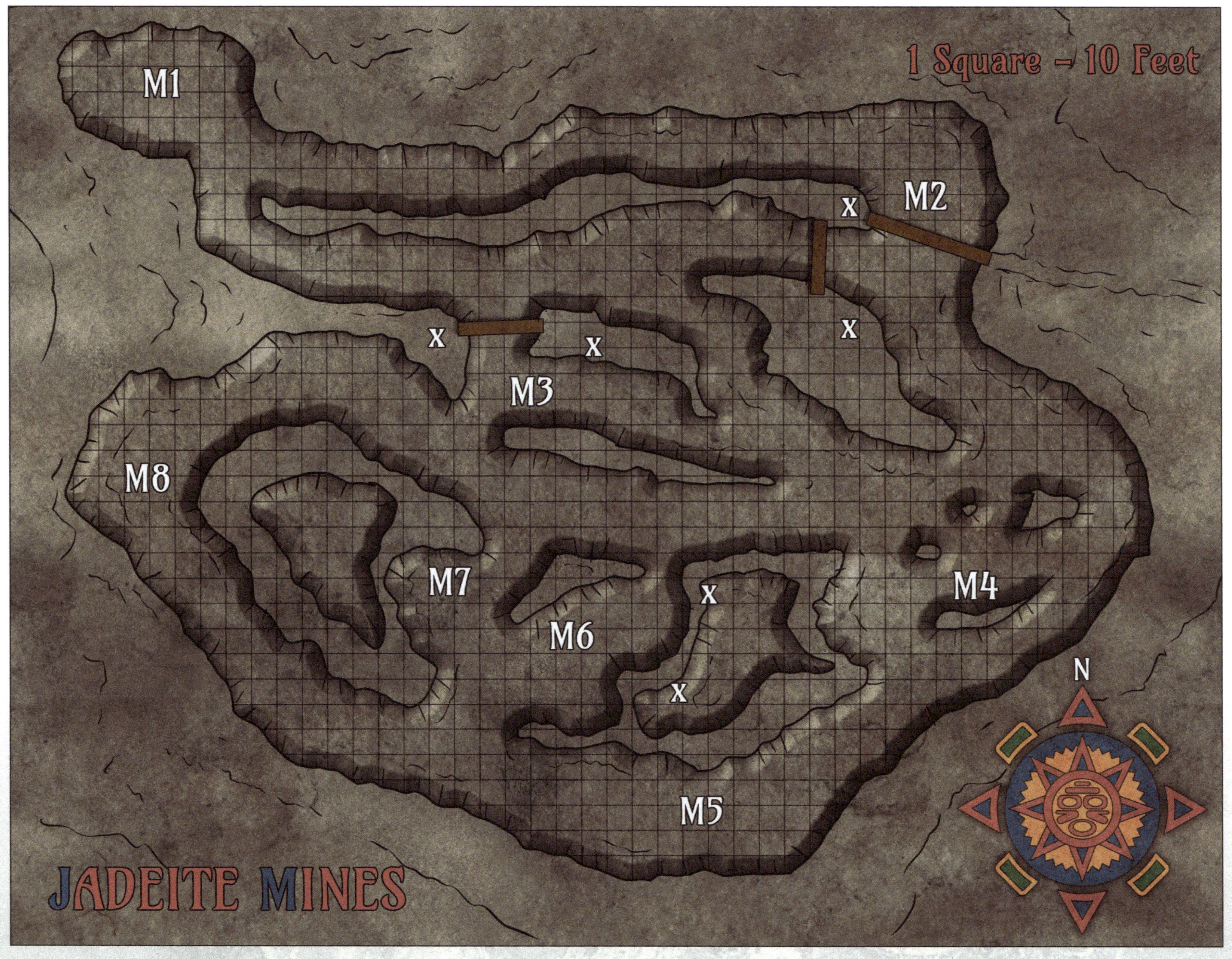

1 Square = 10 Feet
N
M1
M2
M3
M4
M5
M6
M7
M8
JADEITE MINES

M4: The Mounds

Extensive excavation created a tangle of interlocking rifts that weave through several pick-worn mounds of earth.

A character who succeeds on a DC 10 Intelligence (Investigation) skills check determines this area was heavily mined and then abandoned. A character familiar with mining operations has advantage on the preceding check.

A successful DC 15 (Wisdom) Survival check finds numerous footprints covering the area, all human size or slightly larger. The most heavily trafficked paths lead south.

M5. The South Passage

The passage widens at a point where it makes a slight curve that snakes between two towering steps that rise 30 feet on either side.

A band of 5 **aluxes of the second sun** (see **Appendix A: New Monsters**) and 2 **aluxes of the first sun** (see **Appendix A: New Monsters**) wander down this passage. The creatures are bold enough to attack intruders, but realize they lack the numbers to win the fight. During combat, they slowly retreat to the dead-end in area **M6** where their kin have prepared an ambush.

M6: The Ambushers

A gaping passage to the east reveals broad gouges ripped into the plateau that form a massive, cave-like hollow. In the north, a narrow pathway climbs between taller mounds, emptying into another partially exposed ravine.

Xotaxtl's True Colors

In this section of the adventure, the characters suffer a fearsome attack that reveals the sorcerer's true colors. Halfway through the encounter, his fears get the better of him and cause him to use his magical powers to transform into a peccary to flee. The peccary uses the **boar** statistics, with the following changes that decrease its challenge rating to 1/8 (25 XP). It does not have the Relentless features, its tusk deals an extra 1 (1d3) slashing damage on a charge, and its tusk deals 2 (1d3+1) slashing damage on a hit.

The sorcerer plays a very important role in the development of the plot of this adventure. Not only is Xotaxtl the cause of the curse, but he also serves as its solution. For events in the adventure to unfold as intended, an alux of the first sun must eat the sorcerer and assume his mantle of power.

If the characters somehow prevent the sorcerer from taking this course of action, there are other ways to assure the sorcerer gets eaten. The alux could pick him off with a trap, a sneak attack of some sort, or grab him during the night while the characters are resting. Alternatively, he could sneak off in the night after witnessing something horrific or after getting into an argument with the characters. However he meets his fate, make sure you give the alux an opportunity to eat his body. The two most difficult scenarios involve the characters taking the body with them (forcing the alux to steal the sorcerer's body from them) or burning the body. If the latter situation unfolds, the pyre stinks so profoundly that it threatens to draw attention to their actions, encouraging them to vacate the area to avoid detection. Once the characters leave, the alux returns to claim the scorched meat. Prepare to be creative to make sure events unfold as intended, but do your best to not make the situation feel forced. While the plot has some railroad tracks, in this case you are forcing the actions of an NPC and not those of a character.

A successful DC 10 (Wisdom) Perception check made while searching the ravine to the north, reveals a series of handholds cut into the stone allowing a character to easily climb to the top of the plateau without a check.

An ambush awaits the characters as 8 **aluxes of the second sun** (see **Appendix A: New Monsters**) and 2 **aluxes of the first sun** (see **Appendix A: New Monsters**) have taken up strategic positions. The aluxes of the first sun are above the characters on the top tier, where they use their abilities to create rockslides or to toss opponents from the hill. If the characters retreat, they advance to the first tier and try to hold the higher ground while continuing the fight. The aluxes of the second sun strategically maneuver themselves into spots where they can surround an enemy or gain advantage on their attack rolls, if possible. The monsters deliberately focus their attacks on the sorcerer.

If the sorcerer takes a few significant hits, his cowardice kicks into high gear. On his next turn, he magically shifts into the form of a peccary and flees up the steep rocky mine walls only to be plucked up at the last moment by a monstrous hulking primordial alux that snaps his spine, tears him to pieces, and gluttonously devours the entire animal in under a minute. After finishing his macabre feast, the creature wipes its gore-smeared face with a meaty arm, screams something unintelligible, belches, and then dashes off, vanishing down the opposite hillside.

M7: The Jadeite Boulder

A massive boulder sits propped up on its side between two large stumps. The rind is partially chiseled away to reveal the smooth greenish-blue mineral inside it.

The boulder has some monetary worth, but unfortunately, it weighs nearly 400 pounds. It is also sacred and therefore its handling should be left for the priests. A character who succeeds on a DC 10 Intelligence (Religion) check reaches the conclusion that stealing it or removing the jadeite without performing the proper rituals would bring one great dishonor and likely a potent curse.

Luckily several flecks of jadeite lie on the ground around the boulder. It takes a successful DC 10 Wisdom (Perception) check to spot the scattered beads.

Treasure: There are five detached chunks of jadeite worth 25 gp each. It takes a successful DC 15 Dexterity check made with jeweler's tools or a DC 20 Dexterity check made with thieves' tools or the mining tools in area **M8** to transform one chunk of jadeite into 1d4 beads or plates with the same value. Alternatively, a *stone shape* spell or similar magic automatically accomplishes the same feat on the jadeite without a successful ability check. The characters can use this jadeite to gain access to the Great Void and the realms that lie beyond it.

M8: Tool Stockpile

In the corner of this wide alcove, animal hide tarps cover a large unknown pile, tied down with rope strung through spikes hammered into the ground.

The tarp covers a stockpile of crude mining equipment fashioned from stone wood and iron. The tools are primitive but effective. There are also a few hemp ropes and coarse cloth blankets. Most of the equipment is covered in dust.

Treasure: Among the tools are a stoneworker's kit and a bundle of moldy cotton cloth containing a stash of raw gold nuggets worth 100 gp.

C4: Cave of the Old Master

The cave of the Old Master is the key to accessing the Eye of the World that leads the characters on the path to the Gate of the Void. It lies in the mountains a little more than a week's journey into the rugged terrain. As the characters proceed closer to the heart of the Tepepan Mountains, the altitude increases and it becomes colder. The jungles and lowlands often reach sweltering temperatures above 90° Fahrenheit by midday. For each day of travel deeper into the mountains, the increasing altitudes drop temperatures by 2d4 degrees. The steady decrease should serve as a warning for characters used to the warmer climates of the tropical forest to get ready for chillier days ahead. By the time the characters reach the foothills surrounding the Eye of the World, the temperature averages 50° Fahrenheit, which is chilly for anyone dressed in light robes or a loincloth.

The crevasse is steep and deceptively slippery as it is slicked with water, requiring the character to succeed on a difficult DC 25 Strength (Athletics) skills check to climb it. The hermit built the shaft to use as a climbing ladder, giving anyone attempting the climb advantage on their check.

The climb leads to a narrow ledge that is less than three feet deep and five feet wide. The crevasse continues upward. A successful DC 10 Wisdom (Perception) or Intelligence (Investigation) check spots a faded carving on the rock that depicts what appears to be a stylized eye and an arrow pointing up the crevasse. As with the first climb, it requires the character to succeed on a very difficult DC 25 Strength (Athletics) check, though using the shaft once again grants the climber advantage on the check. Sixty feet up, a small opening in the rock leads to a hollow shaft with handholds cut into the surrounding stone. These handholds ascend another few hundred feet to a wider ledge, about 20 feet across, that faces another footpath continuing farther up the mountain. The footpath winds for several hundred yards and then empties into a dark, deep cave face.

Environmental Factors

The temperature drops as the characters continue their ascent until it is 3d6 degrees colder by the time they reach the cave opening.

A successful DC 18 Intelligence (Religion) check identifies the X as having four stages, each representing the apocalypses, but possibly also interpreted in this context as meaning "The World."

Not long after the characters arrive, a single **chom** (see **Appendix A: New Monsters**) lands on the withered tree and curiously stares at them. In its beak, it clasps a small leather satchel. If approached, it tilts its head and stares, waiting to be engaged in some sort of conversation. However, if it succeeds on a Wisdom (Insight) check contested by the characters' Charisma (Deception) check, it senses hostility. In this case, it simply drops the satchel and wings off quickly. If any character attempts to communicate with the chom, it nods and drops the satchel, spilling the kernels inside on the ground. It then wings down, eats one of the kernels, and uses its beak to gesture to a character, pushing another kernel toward that individual as if suggesting they eat it too.

The satchel contains nine pieces of dried corn and a plate of jadeite carved with a grinning skull. The kernels are magical; the jadeite plate is not. Creatures ingesting a single kernel (or more) gain the ability to speak to others as if under the effects of a *tongues* spell. The effect lasts for 10 minutes.

Characters who eat the magic kernel can communicate with the chom (as can any character that speaks Primordial Notoan).

The chom tells them they have found the cave of the old master that holds the secrets to the Eye of the World. From its peak, one can interpret how to get to any location in the world. Despite its great height, it is not as much a lookout as it is a sort of compass for determining points and directions.

The chom does not know how to use it, but its dead master does. However, the chom assures the characters that its master can speak to them from beyond the grave if they place one of the kernels along with a bead of jade in his mouth.

If asked why he is helping them, he claims he is neutral in their affairs and curious as to what will happen if the characters actually get to Miquito. It knows of their affairs because all choms know. After all, they never hold their tongues and spread secrets like the wind. After giving them the corn and answering as few questions as possible, the chom excuses itself and flies off, wishing them good luck and telling them to keep the corn and the jade before departing.

Although they are legendary liars, this chom speaks the full truth, as it faithfully serves the old master. It chooses its words carefully and deliberately, but avoids going into detail. It is not lying, and the characters can follow its instructions to speak with the Old Master …

The Master

Anyone inspecting the wooden bowls notes that some contain traces of colored powder. A character identifies one of them with a successful DC 15 Intelligence (Arcana) check. The first bowl is empty; the second has an eagle feather; the third has traces of feline fur (likely jaguar); and the fourth has traces of marigold seeds. The bowls obviously held offerings, and any character who makes a successful DC 12 Intelligence (Religion) check recalls the following associations between deities and their preferred offerings: the eagle feather with Notonatiuh; jaguar with Itztliteotl; and marigolds with Quiahuitl.

The Old Master lies dead. If anyone takes the chom's advice and attempts to talk to him by placing the kernel and the jadeite into his mouth, they are in for a rude awakening … literally. Performing this act causes the creature to rise from the dead, transcending his bound corpse as an **unresurrected wraith** (see **Appendix A: New Monsters**), and while truthfully it can talk, it is furious. It accuses the characters of being blasphemous heathens who have disturbed its rest for taboo purposes.

Treasure: The mummified corpse in the back of the cave is the Old Master who is thoughtfully wrapped with the *blanket of daggers*. The blanket is magic and when wrapped around one's body like a shroud, the individual can safely pass through the **Wind of Daggers** (see **Chapter Five: Beyond the Pale Portal**) without a scratch. Otherwise, it has no magical properties.

The Empty Cave

The pitcher and cups are empty, while cornhusks and silks fill one of the baskets. Another holds a pile of dirty wool and eight spools of spun yarn. The third basket holds several bolts of wool cloth (about eight yards worth), and the last basket holds an arrow and a collection of sticks of various sizes easily identified as measuring sticks. One is a land-rod, the other is an arrow, and there are three hands and six hearts.

A thorough inspection of the rocks discovers that each one is painted with a name, a number, and a symbol. After investigating several of them, a few of them register as common names of various places in Tehuatl. A character who succeeds on a few Intelligence (History) checks of varying difficulty identifies many of them as contemporary, though some are older and less familiar. A small number of them bear names of places believed to have once existed in the ages before the cataclysms.

The character can use the rocks to solve the mystery of the Eye of the World as described in the **Eye of the World** section below. One of the stones bears the icon for Popocatepetl and another the icon for Iztaccihuatl. Popocatepetl is marked with the symbol for water and the number 8. Iztaccihuatl is marked with the symbol for Death and the number 9. Locating the specific stones takes 20 minutes for each successful DC 15 Intelligence (Investigation) check. You may even wish to have the characters find one of the mountains by "accident" if they seem stuck and you need to nudge them forward.

Characters searching the room find a concealed exit. Behind one of the baskets hides a cramped and unlit crawlway with a two-foot-square opening. To enter the crawlway, characters must lie prone and those of Medium size must also squeeze their way through it. If the characters go through the passage, read or paraphrase the following description:

Upon emerging here, the characters notice another drop in temperature. It gets 1d6 degrees colder at the base of the stairs, then another 1d6 degrees even chillier halfway, and finally 1d12 degrees colder at the summit.

Similarly, the wind also increases, which is already factored into the cooler temperatures. The winds start at light speed (13 mph) and increases by 1d6 mph at the halfway point and another 1d8 mph at the top. You may also want to determine the chance of precipitation along the way.

The stairs climb another 2,500 feet up the mountain until they reach the apex where the top of the mountain has been shorn off and transformed into the Eye of the World, an elaborate tool for determining every location in Tehuatl.

THE EYE OF THE WORLD

Perhaps even more intriguing than the view is the strange carvings set into the platform floor. They consist of a great disk from which protrude four lines in a cross, each marked with one of the cardinal directions. Four symbols run the length of each of the directions. A second circle runs the perimeter of the disk, similar in appearance to a sunstone. The perimeter circle is divided evenly into 20 numbered sections.

A small pile of stones, similar to those found in the caves below, is near the entrance. While all have similar markings, none of these contains the names of mountains the characters seek.

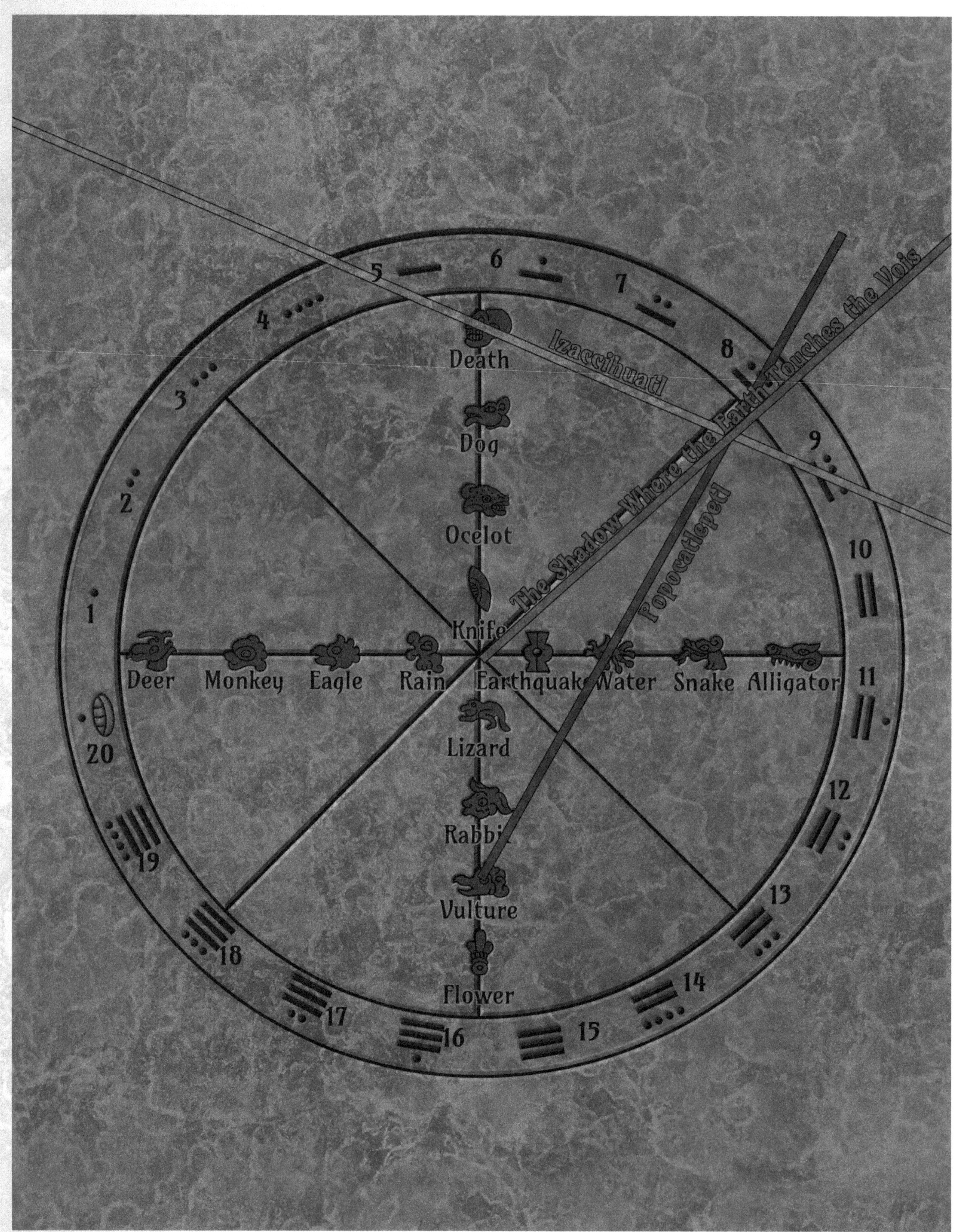

Death
Dog
Ocelot
Knife
Deer
Monkey
Eagle
Rain
Earthquake
Water
Snake
Alligator
Lizard
Rabbit
Vulture
Flower
Izaccihuatl
The Shadow Where the Earth Touches the Vois
Popocatlepetl
1 2 3 4 5 6 7 8 9 10 11 12 13 14 15 16 17 18 19 20

Solving the Eye

The Eye of the World can be used to determine the location of almost any location in all Tehuatl. To use the device, one stone must be placed upon the correct icon marking a specific point along one of the cardinal directions. The individual then rotates until they face the correct number along the perimeter. Following a straight line from the stone's location to the number gives the viewer a directional sighting point to the location they seek. If the path to the location is between two points (such as the location the characters seek), the individual reading the Eye of the World uses the intersection of the two points to make a new cross-section and uses that to determine the location by looking through that cross-section from the center of the Eye.

If characters correctly find the locations of both mountains, they can use them to make a new cross-section and then line it up with the center of the eye. This gives them the precise direction to travel to reach the location of the Shadow Where the Earth Touches the Void (aka the Gate to the Great Void).

Traveling to the Gate

The vale that hides the gate is a good distance east of the eye. The journey consists of approximately 50 miles of travel through rough, mountainous terrain. Unless the characters have some magical ways of transporting themselves, the trip takes at least several days, depending on events. At the start of the journey, the mountain weather is relatively cold, but temperatures quickly warm as they descend in the valleys. The west side of the mountains tends to get less rain, but no less wind. The rains and lush greenery return as the characters reach the valley. At first, the vale thrums with the sounds of life, but as they draw closer to the shadows of the Twin Mountains, things quiet down, and the number of animals and birds slowly dies out until, by the final day, they detect none. At this time, they see the mists ahead and know they have reached the site where the gate is hidden.

If you want to play out the journey, you can flesh it out by running any of the following encounters.

Travel Encounters

Upper Mountains: Amid the blue sky, characters see a dark form winging in the distance. Little by little, the creature approaches and soon its massive form blots the sun. It is a **roc**. The bare and barren slopes offer them few places to take refuge, and the loose scree and pitched landscape make movement difficult.

Lower Mountains: The characters cross paths with 2 **stone giants** on their way south to the hunting lands. They seek prey much large than the characters and do not want to be bothered with a confrontation. However, they are willing to trade items and three pieces of jadeite for water (at least 10 gallons per piece) or a common magic item. Characters can use the jadeite to make additional beads should they still require payment for the oracle of Miquito. Conversely, the giants threaten those who offend them and fight if attacked.

Into the Valley: While walking into the valley, randomly determine which one of the characters accidentally stumbles into a colony of flying, stinging insects, which constitutes 3 **swarms of stinging insect**. Allow the character an opportunity to succeed on a DC 15 Wisdom (Perception) check to spot the strange colony before stepping on it. If the individual fails, he or she must succeed on a DC 16 Dexterity (Acrobatics) check or their foot breaks the hive and the hive gets stuck on it, reducing the individual's speed by half. The swarms of insects viciously attack that individual as they try to free their foot. Each round, allow the character a new Dexterity check to try to shake the hive lose.

Early Valley: As evening falls, a herd of 3d6 **deer** suddenly rushes from the wood and scatters across the trail. Seconds later, a sacred jaguar (use the **panther** stat block) bounds out of the brush in pursuit. For a moment, it stops and stares at the characters and then bounds off. Have each character roll 1d20. The character who roll highest receives good luck for spotting it first. Award the character Inspiration. If the player instead decides to hunt and kill the creature, the sky opens up upon its death and a downpour immediately begins. The torrential rains last for the next three hours.

Later Valley: As the characters work their way deeper into the valley, they pass through a forest of strange trees, their thick trucks warped and gnarled. Hiding in the trees are 4 **shambling mounds** that drop from the branches to attack and devour any living creatures they encounter.

Edge of the Mists: Three creatures guard the edge of the Shadow Mists and know the location of the Gate to the Great Void. The **guardian naga** introduces herself as Imitlapia and the 2 **couatls** as Cuezali and Icoatzin. If characters convince them of their good intentions, the naga claims to know the location of the gate and offers to lead them directly to it, provided they prove themselves worthy. Imitlapia requests the seeds of the giant purple-blossomed cocoxochitl. The sacred flowers once grew here in great abundance, but her two evil sisters poisoned the flowerbeds and stole the last remaining seeds for themselves. Her two spirit naga sisters live 12 miles to the north, near a river that runs along the base of the mountain. If the characters recover the seeds for Imitlapia, she leads them to the gate. However, she doesn't know the secrets of opening it. Such knowledge is forbidden to her, as is helping the characters any further. Upon completing her promise, she immediately departs.

If characters complete this challenge, they can offer the names of any of the guardians to the couatls watching over Ohtli as partial proof of their intentions.

Conclusion

Completing this section of the adventure is a good time to award experience points or to use a story award to raise the characters to 8th level.

Chapter Four: The Gate to the Great Void

The entrance to the gate to the Great Void lies in the mist-drenched vale that hides between the two mountains known as the lovers Popocatepetl and Iztaccihuatl. The Gate of the Void is unguarded, for it does not exist in the earthly realm and the living must coax it from its slumber with sacred rituals. Only the dead (or an entity without a soul) can call forth the gate with impunity, for the Great Void serves as the entrance to the paradises of Ilhuicac and the land of the dead, Miquito. Mortals are forbidden from performing the ritual and just uttering the words to call the gate forth is punishable by eternal imprisonment under Micoateotl's direct supervision. If a mortal performs the ritual, they stand marked for judgment and must pay for the consequence of their action upon facing the Oracle of the Empty Moon.

The characters searching the valley will find the spot where the shadows of two mountains meet.

This phenomenon takes place only when the sun slips above the edge of the eastern horizon near dawn. The shadow marks a small spot upon the earth where an ancient sunstone nearly five feet in diameter is buried a few inches below the surface. To perform the ritual that opens the gate, the sunstone must first be cleared, which takes a few hours, though it can be completed before the sun is high. When they finish, they reveal a large stone disk carved with a snarling face sticking out a bladed tongue. A carving of twin serpents encircles the face, and numerous numbers and images representing animals, elements, flowers, and gods are inscribed into the circles. The characters easily recognize the disk as a massive sunstone, a device their people use to measure and record the cosmic motion of the universe. It is used to determine sacred days, lucky and unlucky signs, and to predict future events. This sunstone also functions as a portal to the afterlife.

Characters can use Ohtli's verses to perform the ritual that opens the portal. The ritual is difficult and requires intimate knowledge of prehistoric Tehuatl lore. While the aluxes of the second sun and third sun know the order and causes of the cataclysms, most Aztlis do not. It is suggested that any character with a religious background or intimate knowledge of religion, history, or arcana can use the verses to activate the portal. While you can allow the characters to make checks to solve the various hints and solutions, be advised that a roll of 1 might make it impossible for them to complete the ritual. If you decide to go this route and a character rolls a 1, allow them to make a sacrifice to try again. Similarly, you can also allow characters to make sacrifices to roll their checks at advantage. It takes a successful DC 20 Intelligence (Arcana or Religion) check to recall the circumstances and order of each cataclysm as well as determine the names of the goddesses and gods that keep them balanced and what they might require as a sacrifice. A successful DC 15 Intelligence (History) check accomplishes the same feat. The character must succeed on a check for each verse. Therefore, it takes four successful checks to decipher the verses in their entirety. Alternatively, spells such as *divination* and *legend lore* and similar magic may offer useful insight to the characters.

The characters have opened the portal to the Great Void, yet they have little time to enter before it closes again. They have only one minute to decide whether or not to step through it.

Into the Void

The characters stand at the center of the Great Causeway, a path that stretches between the four realms. While the characters are unable to determine the cardinal directions in the void, anyone studying the torches can make a successful DC 15 Intelligence (Investigation) check to determine slight differences in the colors of their flames.

The torches in one of the causeways flicker with dull orange flames that leak foul-smelling crimson haze. In another, the torch flames have a cold, purplish-green tint and leak a steady stream of black soot. In the third passage, the flames give off a faint, pale white glow and spit thin wisps of gray smoke. Along the last causeway, the torches crackle with bluish sparks that occasionally spit out and sizzle when they hit the water.

The colors possess great significance and allow each traveler to determine their correct path in the afterlife. Each color is associated with one of the cardinal directions and the four points that lead to the realms of the gods. A successful DC 10 Intelligence (Arcana, History, or Religion) check quickly interprets the colors corresponding to the cardinal points as follows:

1. The red flames mark the east, and its causeway leads to Tlahuizlampa.
2. The purple flames leaking black soot mark the north, and its causeway leads to Mictlampa.
3. The white flames mark the passage west to Cihuatlampa.
4. The blue flames mark the south and the passage to Huitzlampa.

Characters interpreting the signs and colors know that if they wish to find the Obsidian Spire, they must take the causeway that leads to the north.

The Void and Hallucinations

Journeying through the Great Void is long and timeless. Except for the characters and the seemingly eternal causeway, there is no sound, no depth, and no volume. Mortals exposed to the Great Void have an extremely difficult

Cracking the Code

1. **Hint:** Jaguars caused the first great cataclysm. When the provider of the shadow soul is Itztliteotl, the god quells the jaguar.

Solution: An offering to Itztliteotl must be placed upon the image of ocelotl (the jaguar) to appease him. The god accepts sacrifices of obsidian or precious metals and gemstones stolen from others.

2. **Hint:** Winds caused the second great cataclysm. When the provider of the elemental soul is Nonotzali, then the wind falls still.

Solution: An offering to Nonotzali must be placed upon the image of ehecatl (the wind) to appease it. The god accepts sacrifices of artwork and objects created by hand.

3. **Hint:** Fire caused the third great cataclysm. When the provider of the Spirit Soul is appeased, his fires birth life.

Solution: An offering to Contlati must be placed upon the number Ce (1). The god accepts offerings of seared meat or turquoise.

4. **Hint:** Floods caused the last great cataclysm. When the provider of the Temporal Soul is appeased, the waters subside.

Solution: An offering to Quiahuitl must be placed upon the image of Quiahuitl (the rain). The god can be appeased with marigolds or heron feathers.

Void Checks

After a character has been in the Great Void for more than 1 hour, they must begin making void checks every 1d6 x 10 minutes. To do so, the character must make a DC 10 Charisma saving throw. On a failure, the character hears faint sounds and voices and experiences feelings they cannot quite grasp. On a success, the character hears and experiences nothing.

The character must make a new void check when called upon, regardless of whether the character succeeded or failed on a previous void check. If a character fails a second void check, the sounds grow louder and start to resemble voices spoken in unknown languages or perhaps many languages. Alternatively, a character can voluntarily fail its void check to hear these sounds and experience the strange feelings. If they do so, the character adds +2 to the Voices in the Void roll for each void check intentionally failed.

After spending more time in the void, any character who failed two previous void checks must succeed on a third and final DC 10 Charisma saving throw. If the character fails, the sounds become clear. Determine the results of specific sounds using **Table 3–3: Voices in the Void**. If the character succeeds on the void check, the sounds do not escalate and the character hears what was heard in the previous stage.

time coping with its vastness and the number of unknown energies traveling through it at any given time. Energies, souls, lifesparks, and thoughts race freely through the void. When they strike mortals, they erupt within their minds, unleashing emotions and desires, words and ideas, revelation and epiphanies, none of which truly belong to the mortal. When a mortal first enters, they are barely perceptible, but over time they slowly increase. Distractions dissolve thoughts, voices call from worlds unknown, emotions of forgotten entities express their longing to connect, and loved ones and gods offer power, acceptance, and immortality. The effects of all this are sometimes mind-shattering. Use Void Checks to determine the extent of the void's effect on the characters.

Special: Characters who possess beverages brewed from the fleshy mushrooms growing in the cave in Corpsewood can consume them to gain advantage on void checks made to resist the mental effects caused by exposure to the Great Void.

Table 3–3: Voices in the Void

Roll 2d8 to determine what happens to a character who fails or forfeits three void checks.

2d8	Result
2	*Voices.* "Come into the void. Return my child, we await you. We are timelessness. We are one with eternity." The character responds by leaping into the void, traveling in a straight line at a speed of 60 feet per round.
3	*Voices.* "Feel your strength from within, do not burden yourself with the lies of materialism. You are greatness, release that which is not you." The character tosses a random magical item or weapon into the void. The item travels at a speed of 120 feet per round and vanishes at the end of the round with a loud pop.
4–6	*Voices.* "Offer yourself to the void, it is your flesh, heart, and blood. Bond with us and share our strength." Character deals 9 (2d8) points of slashing damage to themselves, spilling the blood into the void. The hit points cannot be healed until the character takes a long rest on the Material Plane.
7–9	*Voices.* "The knowledge of the void is infinite. You share all of this knowledge with us and we all with you." The character's thoughts fill rapidly, flooded with overwhelming amounts of vast knowledge. They find it difficult to think and suffer disadvantage on Charisma, Intelligence, and Wisdom checks and saving throws for as long as they remain in the void. When they leave the void, the character gains a new proficiency in either Arcana, History, Nature, or Religion (player's choice).
10–14	*Voices.* "The void is boundless; it is everywhere at all times. We see all. We see through forever." The character's eyes widen as they stare deeply into the void until their irises merge with their pupils, eclipsing into vacant black pools. Thereafter, until they leave the void, the character is blind. After leaving, their pupils turn starry and they gain the ability to cast *augury* as a ritual, once per day.
15	*Voices.* "We are the same. You cannot exist without us, and we cannot exist without you. We are forever merged." The character blurs for a few moments and then winks out of existence. The character becomes ethereal, and no one senses their existence for the duration they are in the void. Upon leaving the void, the character returns to normal and thereafter can cast *invisibility* as a ritual on themselves once per day.
16+	*Voices.* "All that has, is, and ever will be now fills you. You are the inevitable. You are the cataclysms." The character returns to normal. Nothing happens. Let the paranoia begin. At some point in the distant future, the character becomes certain that the void is telling them "Now is the Time," and they believe with all certainty that they are at the dawn of the next cataclysm, and that the gods have once again prepared to clear the slate of existence.

The City that Sleeps upon the Doorstep of the Evening Flame.

After traveling for some time in the Great Void, the causeway eventually leads the characters to an archipelago of four small floating islands, each populated by those wanderers denied passage into the Realms of the Dead. As the characters approach, read or paraphrase the following description:

Ahead in the distance, the causeway leads toward what appears to be several islands drifting across in the great starry void, sprawling like blackened clouds blotting the distant stars. Atop the colorless islands rise temples of unknown gray stone surrounded by fields of withered gray shafts of empty cornstalks. As you draw nearer, you spot people walking through the fields, yet they too are colorless, with gray flesh and gray clothing, silent, cold, and peering into the void with stone gray, nearly lifeless eyes. They watch your approach yet show no sense of enthusiasm or curiosity.

Unless they decide to turn back, wait, or jump from the causeway, the characters have little choice except to approach the strange city. The causeway appears to lead directly into a large area, dipping through a broad stone archway as if passing through a tunnel. Only when one draws close does it become apparent that the causeway ends several feet shy of the arch, and that what first appeared to be a shadow is a 10-foot gap between the causeway and an open drawbridge blocking the entrance.

The somber gray people appear to be of human descent, but from what age or ages one cannot tell. If the characters attempt to call out or otherwise communicate with the people, they offer no response and only stare.

VI. The Forgotten Ones

The drawbridge connects to a causeway on the other side that leads directly into a towering stepped temple. As with everything here, the temple and all that surrounds it appear dull gray and completely devoid of color.

THE GREAT VOID
1 Hex – 150 Feet
V1
V2
V3
V4
V5

Characters can either attempt to lower the bridge themselves using magic, by pulling it open with ropes and grappling hooks, or by convincing the gray people to lower the bridge. Any of these methods easily succeed (DC 5 check if needed), leaving characters to wonder if there is even a point to having a drawbridge.

THE FADED

As soon as the characters cross the bridge, droves of gray-fleshed people surround them. Their expressions appear sad and curious but always steeped in desperation. When the characters first arrive, the Faded slowly approach and huddle around them, reaching out to touch their bodies and begging for their warmth. All are lost souls, perhaps waiting to continue, but going mad. Some cannot afford the fare, others are too scared to continue, and many cannot even remember how long they have been here. For many, this time has been infinite.

These lost souls call themselves the Faded. They cannot remember their names, their truths, or their past. All of this has faded from them. They barely remember their memories and hunger for the memories of others who still possess them. They long to be told tales and rituals, long to hear of color and sun and the moon, the rain, and the gods they hope might one day return to save them from the endless void. They are cold to the touch, near lifeless, and cast no shadows. Their curiosity with the newcomers is short-lived, and swiftly the throng begins to swell with paranoia, fear, and panic. The Faded start pulling at the characters, frantically whispering things such as "We must leave now," "It's not safe," "*They* will be coming soon," "You must get to Teotlachimalli before the shadows fall," and "Quickly! Quietly."

The Faded do not converse or answer outside the temple, but promise to explain everything once everyone is safely inside.

If stats are necessary, treat any of Faded as **commoners**. If threatened or attacked, they take defensive postures and flee to the temple. They have no weapons and do not fight back.

THE TEMPLE OF THE GOD'S SHIELD

Teotlachimalli is what the Faded call the temple. The name means something like "god's shield." However, the temple is unadorned and washed clean of all colors and symbols, so it remains unclear which god the shield might belong to. The Faded mass in and around the temple where they feel safe. It consists of a single large room where the people either walk in circles around a wooden post muttering prayers and wards of protection or cower in small groups crowded against the walls and corners, shivering beneath colorless threadbare woolen blankets.

If characters attempt to speak with the Faded, it is readily apparent that they have little to offer. The Faded believe they worship a god of protection and fear leaving the temple for they "know what lies beyond." Unfortunately, they are not entirely clear on "what lies beyond" and only stress something is out there and that the "something" is to be feared.

If characters question the Faded about what lies beyond the next two causeways, they can glean some insight. They call one of the causeways the **Bridge of Hearts (GV3)** and the other causeway the **Bridge of Bone (GV2).**

BRIDGE OF HEARTS

"Across the Bridge of Hearts lies the island bearing another temple. It belongs to a goddess of death, though I cannot recall her name. Once she was powerful and held vast armies and all worshipped her, but I suppose even gods must fall. The cataclysm is the only power and the only truth. Its inhabitants rip out their hearts as offerings, but it serves no purpose. It has lost its power and mysticism. … The people remain, like us except none of them have hearts, just empty holes in their chest cavities. Many cry endlessly, but they cannot say why. I have watched people from this island venture across the bridge, determined to get to Miquito, determined to make their sacrifices as they stand atop the temple, cut out their hearts and throw them still beating into the Great Void. It is madness, you know. … It is all madness."

BRIDGE OF BONE

"Across the Bridge of Bones lies desolation. There is nothing, and any who go, disappear."

While characters have no problems entering the temple, should they attempt to leave, the crowd panics and blocks the exits, screaming and crying for them to stay, fearful for their deaths outside the temple. They grab and pull, grapple, and block the characters' movements to the best of their abilities. They clearly are not attacking and instead act out of extreme fear.

Anyone caught in the panicked throng or attempting to move through the throng is grappled and their vision is heavily obscured. Moving through the throng requires either a successful DC 12 Strength (Athletics) or Dexterity (Acrobatics) check. Characters crawling through the tunnel are prone and treat the area as if they were squeezing through a tight space. The shouts and screams of the Faded also make it nearly impossible for characters to communicate with each other by normal means. To escape, the characters must blindly force their way through the throng and out the main entrance. Once they leave, the throng pleads for them to return to safety, but they are too overcome with fear to stop them. Instead, they stand there weeping and sobbing uncontrollably.

THE CORNFIELDS

The perimeter of this island and most of the other is filled with sweeping fields of gray lifeless corn. Dried and withered upon the stalk, it stands as if forgotten. The Faded avoid the fields for venturing into them means oblivion. However, when the madness takes them, some walk into the fields of their own accord and never return. More eerily, the details of such actions are quickly forgotten, only to have the memories replaced by a constant unending sense of dread. Numerous walkways wind through the cornfields and allow characters to traverse them freely and without constraint. Traveling through the maize proves slightly more difficult, and those attempting to move through it must use their action to clear pathways through the plants while the area is considered to be lightly obscured. What the Faded do not know is that the cornfields are overrun with greater shadows patiently waiting to take the Faded when they fade completely. Those who lose their memories become prey after they forfeit their fear, walk into the fields, and disappear to the creatures lurking in the corn.

Characters might encounter several challenges when traveling through or around the cornfields.

THE WALKWAYS

The walkways consist of pathways cut through the corn. Corn shafts cover the floor of each walkway. The shadows take advantage of this when laying their traps to snare travelers. It is also worth noting that the shadows can use their Lair Ability to alter the shape of the walkways and the surrounding cornfields in a limited fashion.

PIT TRAPS

The shadows employ pit traps to capture their prey and place them strategically along the walkways, then rush from the surrounding fields and swarm victims trapped within them. While the pits are only simple traps, the Faded do not possess memories of the pits and simply remember that those who travel the walkways suddenly disappear.

When traveling the walkways, each time the characters enter a new hex, roll 1d6 to determine the location of the pit trap. A roll of a 1–2 means it's near where the characters entered the hex; a 3–4 means it's somewhere in the middle of the path; and 5–6 means it's near where the path exits the hex. The shadows use **hidden pit traps** covered with shafts of corn. Characters can discern something odd about the passages with a successful DC 15 Wisdom (Perception) check, and confirm the precise location of the pit trap with a DC 15 Intelligence (Investigation) check. If a character falls into a pit trap, 1d4 **greater shadows** (see **Appendix A: New Monsters**) rush to attack and use their Legendary actions to alter the structure of the surrounding cornfields to hide the location of the pit from any allies.

IN THE FIELDS

Soon after any living creature leaves a walkway and enters the fields, they attract the attention of a group of 1d4 **greater shadows** (see **Appendix A: New Monsters**). The creatures surround targets and attempt to isolate them by driving them into pit traps and confuse or entangle any stragglers.

Similarly, characters wandering through the fields attract the attention of 1d4 **greater shadows** (see **Appendix A: New Monsters**). To determine where the shadows strike, each time the characters enter a new hex, roll 1d6 with a roll of 1–2 indicating the ambush happens as they enter the hex; 3–4 in the middle of the hex; and 5–6 as they leave the hex.

V2. WELL OF EMPTY PROMISES

Characters crossing the causeway the Faded call the Bridge of Bones enter a massive cornfield growing upon the ruins of what appears to be an aqueduct. The cornfields are dense, as if no one has traveled here for countless eons.

The ground consists only of dry gray dust and broken bone that spills into the empty aqueduct's cracked stone channels. Determine the encounters in this region using the **In the Fields** section above. If you feel like you want to increase the challenges in this section, add 1d4 **shadows** to each encounter.

THE DESICCATION

In addition to the cornfields and shadows, the Well of Empty Promises saps water from the environment. Every time the characters travel a distance of one hex, all water (mundane or magical) is mysteriously reduced in volume. Living creatures whose bodies rely on water must succeed on a DC 14 Constitution saving throw or suffer 1 level of exhaustion. The saving throw is made with disadvantage if the character is wearing medium armor, heavy armor, or heavy clothing. Characters traveling at a fast pace instead of a normal or slow pace take a –5 penalty on their saving throws against desiccation. They can restore this damage by consuming one pint of water. However, any water they carry is also reduced by one pint per hex. Potions and other magical fluids are also subject to this effect. For each hex the characters enter, roll a 1d20 to determine if the item has lost enough water to become nonfunctional. A roll of 1 means the potion or item is desiccated and becomes useless.

V3. THE TEMPLE OF HEARTS

As the characters draw closer, they quickly confirm the gruesome rumors told to them by the people of Teotlachimalli. These people have gaping holes in their chest that expose where their hearts have been torn out.

Halfway across the causeway, a Faded woman calls out to the characters, "Have you brought us the jadeite!"

If the characters answer "no" or something similar that denies they have any jadeite, the Faded one responds, "We need jadeite to enter the Realm of the Dead. Do not return until you have brought the sacrifice."

If the characters respond by giving any indication that they have jadeite, the Faded responds extremely favorably. The crier again calls out, "Honored champions, we have waited for your coming since the dawn of eternity. Come! And let all the spoils of the Temple of Hearts be your blessing!" As the Faded finishes speaking, the others watching the causeway lower their arms and bow, throwing husks of corn into the pathway in celebration and to honor the characters.

DESIGNER'S NOTE

The Faded stuck on this island do not possess the jadeite they need to cross into Miquito. They are not asking for the jadeite to allow the characters proper passage, but seek to take the jadeite for themselves. If the characters give them their jadeite, they may not have enough to make an offering to the oracle.

At this point, the characters are free to cross the causeway and enter the island. The Faded who had been speaking rushes to meet them. She introduces herself as Cimoya and tells them that meeting them is her greatest honor.

If asked why, she responds with a broad smile and tells them, "Because you are our saviors, of course." She then attempts to usher them into the temple.

If the characters go to the temple, go to the **Incident at the Temple of Hearts** section below. If they refuse, go to the **A Moment of Truth** section.

THE INCIDENT AT THE TEMPLE OF HEARTS

If the characters enter the temple with Cimoya, she shows them their gift, a great pool of blood collected from the hearts of thousands of lost travelers who have made an offering to the God's Shield in a desperately misguided effort to summon his agents to bring them jadeite.

At this point, the characters likely realize that the Faded do not want the jadeite as their payment, but instead have some sort of need for it themselves. The gift that Cimoya offers the characters is the blood, for she believes they have come as representatives of the God's Shield who has finally come to accept their sacrifices in exchange for the jadeite they need to bring them to their final resting place. Should Cimoya discover this is not the case, she becomes angry and turns on them. Go to the **A Moment of Truth** below.

A MOMENT OF TRUTH

Cimoya at first becomes confused, asking the characters why they do not want to receive their blessings. When it becomes clear that the characters are not their saviors, she becomes angry and demands they hand over the jadeite they need to finish their journey. If the characters deny these people jadeite, the heartless people beg for jadeite. They weep and prostrate themselves before them, blocking their path as others slip behind to rummage through their possessions in a desperate attempt to steal anything resembling the precious sacred stone. As soon as they find anything resembling jadeite, they greedily grab it and flee toward the last causeway. Those denied jadeite or pushed back by the characters howl and curse them as demons and torturers.

Characters can flee Cimoya and her allies by exiting from whence they came or by taking **The Blood Baggers' Path** that appears below. They can also duck into the surrounding cornfields. While the Faded will not pursue them out of fear of the shadows, the shadows eagerly attack mortal trespassers. Again, determine their actions using the **In the Fields** section above and add 1d4 **shadows** if necessary

The Blood Baggers' Path

Consumed with their toil, the blood baggers pay no mind to the characters taking this route and do nothing to help or hinder their journey. Instead, they work tirelessly to appease their god, walking the long journey from the Temple of Hearts to the temple on the last island. They do not stop and refuse to be interrupted. If forcibly stopped, they attempt to push back and complete their efforts. However, if they drop their loads and spill any of the black fluids, they scream hellishly and run straight for the edge of the islands. If they do not disappear into the corn and reach the edge, they then jump off, flinging themselves into the Great Void to drift off into infinity. The black fluid is blood, though in the void it has changed its consistency, scent, and color to something duller and far less lifelike.

As the characters travel down the path, the final Void Island comes into view. To describe it, read or paraphrase the following text:

V4. Disciples of the Dying God

The temple holds a great hollow sarcophagus carved from the surrounding rock, in which his form has been reconstructed from cornstalks and clay, along with those parts they managed to recover, along with blood and other sacrifices taken from the Faded and other travelers who unwittingly passed through their domain. For centuries, the god's devoted followers have been trying to restore him by siphoning materials from other islands, the last little bit of life and hope to which they still cling.

The last island in this archipelago once served as a peaceful resting place for at least some of the Forgotten Gods that Tlatoani presumably hurled into the Great Void. Throughout the cornfields are the remnants of dozens of crumbling monuments, battered totems, defaced images, and ancient obelisks, all of which are toppled and smashed. These gods were captured and slain just centuries after their arrival. Logic suggests that Tlatoani is likely responsible for the carnage, but no vestiges of Notos' former divine ruler have ever been found in the Great Void. Whoever or whatever destroyed the Forgotten Gods and their faithful worshippers ultimately ground them into a sludge that now pollutes the River Miquiatoyatl.

The island also hides several pieces of the god of justice Iquixilli, whose body was dismembered and scattered through the void when the other Forgotten Gods met their unfortunate end. For thousands of years, his followers have searched the void, seeking these remains in hopes of restoring him. Upon discovering this location, they erected a great temple and seek to pump life back into them presumably to exact justice against the entity who destroyed him along with the other Forgotten Gods and their devout followers.

The followers of Iquixilli are strange, bluish-colored humans that the Faded refer to as sightless servants. These sightless servants keep their ever-bleeding eyes wrapped in bandages and believe that by restoring Iquixilli, their god will avenge his death and reveal to them the secrets of attaining godhood in reward for their actions and devotion.

A single **sightless servant** (see **Appendix A: New Monsters**) stands posted every 100 + 1d20 feet along the perimeter of Blood Bagger's Road. While they supposedly keep a sharp lookout for trespassers, they have grown lax in their duty, which causes them to suffer a –5 penalty to their Wisdom (Perception) checks. They remain in their lackluster state of attentiveness until they spot at least one intruder.

Entering the heavily guarded temple is near impossible. Nonetheless, stealthy characters able to ascend to the fourth level can see into it from several small openings. Far below, the god's great sarcophagus lies in the middle of the chamber as blood spills down from the pool above, soaking into the clay-and-cornstalk form. The runoff from this gory ritual flows out the back of the temple, traveling between two cleared cornfields and toward a strange opening surrounded by brambles. While the void continues beyond the opening, the opening appears to pierce the void, traveling into it, or through it, rather than across its expanse.

V5. The Miquiatoyatl

The next passage leading to Miquito is located where the brambles open. Here, the characters find the entrance to Miquiatoyatl, the Black River that marks the border between the Great Void and several of its adjacent planes. How the characters navigate the river falls upon them; however, the most likely means of transportation is a boat or raft.

Characters attempting to collect resources to make a boat must be industrious, as there is not much material available for them to use. Plenty of dried cornstalks can be used to make lashings and such, though they are not reliable or strong. Rope proves a far better option. Some characters might carry items such as blankets to help with the construction. The blood baggers' yokes are wood and can easily serve as planks, though if characters rob or slay more than 10 + 1d4 of the laborers, they can expect a group of 1d3 + 1 **sightless servants** (see **Appendix A: New Monsters**) to investigate their disappearances. The characters may also attempt to gather wood from other sources such as the drawbridge (or parts of it), weapons, buckets, or magic. Feel free to encourage and reward characters for being industrious.

When the characters figure out a way to travel the Miquiatoyatl, introduce the next section with the text below. Note, however, that although the black river hides within the strange living brambles, it is still another causeway within the Great Void. Any conditions characters acquired within the void remain active during this section.

Characters can avoid all contact with the thorny tendrils by keeping to the center of the river where the tendrils cannot reach them. The tendrils qualify more as a trap than as a monster. They cannot move except for their vine-like branches, which can be damaged and destroyed.

Tendril Vine Trap

The tendril vines are plainly visible, negating the need for characters to succeed on checks to notice them. If a character moves away from the center, the tendril vine lashes out at the creature. Treat the tendrils as if they were conjured by a *black tentacles* spell. The tendrils have a reach of 10 feet. Rather than affecting an entire area and for the purposes of adjudicating their effects, the tendrils have a spell save DC of 14.

Despite the thickness of the water, its current flows at a brisk speed approaching 15 mph.

While swimming through the river may be the characters' only option, living creatures in direct contact with the water take 2 (1d4) necrotic damage when they first enter the water on a turn or start their turn in the water. On occasion, the waters bubble and splash, spitting the caustic murk into the air. When this happens, they splatter onto one randomly determined creature. Characters can avoid taking 2 (1d4) necrotic damage by dodging the splatter with a successful DC 12 Dexterity saving throw.

If a character shines light upon the murk, it reflects off hundreds of pale broken branches floating in the mire which, on closer inspection, turn out to be hundreds of bones that churn like schools of fish in the hideous muck. Although the water's blackness prevents characters from visually determining the river's depth, they can estimate from the diameter of the tunnel that the center is near 30 feet deep.

More importantly, the waters are not uninhabited. An ancient and immortal guardian known only as the **beast from below the black** (see **Appendix A: New Monsters**) dwells in its depths. This tremendous crocodilian creature lurks below, waiting to suddenly surface and pound anyone foolish enough to trespass in its territory. It can easily crush the hull of any vessel bobbing atop the water's surface, which it does so if the characters travel aboard any type of watercraft during this leg of the journey. After ramming the vehicle, the crocodilian fiend lashes out to bite and then tail slap creatures knocked overboard by its attack on the boat.

Between their encounter with the preceding monster, the characters feel as if numerous hours have passed as they lazily glide forward on the slow, churning current. Whatever lies ahead in the darkness remains unknown.

CHILDREN OF QUAMAXOTZ

Descending on the characters, 6 **swarms of bats** viscously attack. They create so much noise and obscure the characters' vision that they steal their attention away from the much greater threat looming ahead. Characters caught in the swarm suffer disadvantage on Wisdom (Perception) check, including any made to notice the upcoming waterfall.

CHAPTER FIVE: BEYOND THE PALE PORTAL

<CH>Chapter Five: Beyond the Pale Portal

Characters who successfully make it across the chasm find themselves on a wide stone ledge suspended within a massive cavern. A pale glow shines in the distance. As the characters approach, they notice a path of small, glimmering white stones leading toward the circle.

A pair of divine sisters keep vigil before the Pale Portal. They are 2 **xoco tepeyollotl** (see **Appendix A: New Monsters**), the daughters of the Great Jaguar who watched the mountains during the age of the Forgotten Gods. These battle-scarred jaguar-headed priestesses paint their faces to resemble bestial skulls and wield huge macuahuitls whose jagged teeth tear at their foes with the biting coldness of death.

To pass through the portal, the characters must somehow win their favor or rush past them without getting stopped, for they hold the energies keeping the portal open. If they are slain, the Pale Portal immediately closes, forcing them to find some other means of traveling beyond it or to head back to the village

LEAP OF FAITH

A successful DC 13 Intelligence (Nature) check determines the line is caused by light reflecting off the edge of the water, which typically means the water ends, either at a shoreline or the edge of a cliff. Since the line is straight, it is likely a cliff.

At this point, the characters are 120 feet away from the edge of a sheer cliff into which the river empties. The waters begin to flow faster, and each round the craft gets 30 feet closer to the edge, which means the characters have only three rounds to act before their craft breaches the lip of the tunnel and plummets into oblivion.

Fortunately, just opposite the waterfall about 10 feet away stands a stone ledge, nearly 30 feet across, that sits atop a column occupying the center of the cavern. The pale glowing disk stands in the center of the ledge. Characters can use whatever means they have at their disposal to traverse the gap between the tunnel and the ledge. If they can fly, that likely serves as their best option. Turning gaseous or applying similar magics also work, as does simply leaping across, which can be accomplished with a successful DC 10 Strength (Athletics) check. Those who fail are in serious trouble as the drop descends thousands of feet deep into the lowest reaches of Miquito. Any character that falls into the chasm perishes.

unsuccessful in their attempt to reach the Judge of the Dead. The pair enjoy a great deal of autonomy in their decision-making, leaving them open to reason or granting passage to accomplish a noble purpose.

THE WIND OF DAGGERS

As the characters step through the Pale Portal, it contracts and collapses in upon itself, disappearing in a matter of seconds.

After passing through the portal, the characters exit the Great Void and now stand on the edge of one of the outermost layers of Miquito, the Realm of the Dead. Any afflictions they acquired from exposure to the void now fade and any post-Void effects now become active.

The characters detect a strange ringing sound in their ears that a successful DC 13 Wisdom (Perception) check translates as a message of some sort that says, "Pain beyond pain to the living is but nothing to the dead." Immediately, the characters experience a 15-degree drop in temperature.

Characters making a DC 10 (Wisdom) Survival check also note the coldness comes from a steady current of air that wafts up from the tunnel and escapes out of the portal. If a character succeeds on a DC 10 Wisdom (Perception) check, that individual notices that the howling winds seem to grow louder and that the temperature keeps dropping. Characters who took the *blanket of daggers* from the cave of the ancient holy man can wrap it around themselves to gain immunity to the wind's effects.

Allow any character who succeeds on a DC 13 Intelligence (History or Religion) check to infer that they have reached the fabled Wind of Daggers. Legend says that the dead suffer unimaginable pain from passing through the wind and that mortals are ripped to shreds. To pass safely, there is a shroud that protects those on their death journey. This is why the dead are cloaked in blankets, though only a priestess can imbue it with the power it needs to resist the wind, and the powers which she instills must come from the dreams and heart of the deceased individual making the journey.

If the characters possess the blanket, they can use it to pass safely through the Wind of Daggers.

Within the Wind of Daggers, creatures gain three-quarters cover, its space is difficult terrain, and the area is heavily obscured, even if the characters have a light source. When a creature enters the Wind of Daggers for the first time on a turn or starts its turn there, the creature must make a DC 14 Dexterity saving throw. On a failed save, the creature takes 33 (6d10) slashing damage. On a successful save, the creature takes half as much damage. The Wind of Daggers fills 120 feet of the tunnel.

The Wind of Daggers is a permanent magical effect of godlike power that can temporarily be suppressed or bypassed, but not dispelled. Characters could attempt to *teleport* to the other side, which is still a risky proposition, or increase their speed to quickly race through the Wind of Daggers even though they cannot tell how long the tunnel extends without additional magical insight. Furthermore, because the Wind of Daggers is a magical effect dealing slashing damage, resistance to slashing damage from nonmagical attacks does not benefit the characters in this situation.

Emerging from the Wind of Daggers, the characters enter a haze of crimson mist so thick that they can see only the faint shadows of their allies. The mist seems near-impenetrable and cannot be cleared beyond small, 10-foot areas that quickly refill with mist the moment an effect keeping them at bay ends. The passage continues for approximately a quarter of a mile, at which point anyone succeeding on a passive DC 10 Wisdom (Perception) check detects the unmistakable stench of rotting corpses filling the air. Characters who continue for another 100 feet emerge into Innetotcayan, a vast plane surrounding the Obsidian Spire that writhes with a sea of ravenous walking corpses.

Innetotcayan

Sitting upon the ledge overlooking the throng of the dead is a small howler monkey wearing various amulets: a skull icon carved from bone, a jade jaguar,

and a sharpened obsidian shard. He wears a cloak of colorful feathers and clutches a wooden staff hardened by flames and topped with the skull of a small animal. A deep firepit filled to the rim with white ash is near him. The monkey remains nearly silent when the characters enter, and if they do not immediately spot him, he shushes them away scornfully and tells them to keep it down lest the dead find out they arrived. If the characters introduce themselves, he politely replies and gives his name as **Mocayahua** (see **Appendix A: New Monsters**).

Anyone pondering the monkey's name who succeeds on a DC 5 Intelligence check determines that the name means, "He deceives, mocks, or makes fun of." Mocayahua's name provides an accurate description of his intent. His purpose is to watch over the entrance to Innetotcayan and dissuade the living from entering. Still, as an agent bound to maintain the cosmic balance, Mocayahua must remain somewhat neutral. This means he can barter with the characters and will not stop them from entering of their own free will nor prevent them from taking the ash. However, he does not readily help or aid them unless they attempt to barter or trade with him. While he may feign interest in several treasures or items, he is most interested in musical instruments, ancient poetry, games of chance, or riddles.

If the characters seek his counsel, he offers them the following riddle:

The answer, of course, is ash. Mocayahua has a pit full of ash — bone ash to be precise — that he created by burning the bones of the dead. As previously noted, characters can freely take the ash and use it as they wish. However, it is most effective if the characters cover their entire bodies with the ash to disguise themselves from the skeletons.

Micquinemi Horde

The number of undead in the Land of the Dead is incalculable. For every walking dead that gets destroyed, more rise up and fill the void. If the characters enter the Graveyard, the horde immediately senses them and rushes to devour their living flesh. While they can attempt to fight their way through (most likely a suicidal plan), they have another option. They can join the dead and pass through the horde unharmed by covering their bodies with lard or fat and rolling in the ashes of the first race of humans. In the event the characters must fight their way through the horde, refer to the **Fighting the Horde** sidebar.

As Mocayahua informed them, the characters can use the bone ashes to mask their mortality from the dead. Characters who paint themselves with bone ash can move through the horde without immediately attracting the zombies' attention. Characters moving through the horde must shove their way through the current of lumbering corpses. Treat them as if they are squeezing through a smaller space, but also grant them half-cover. Characters can increase their movement by hacking away at the horde. However, if they attack the horde, they risk revealing themselves and being attacked. Each five-foot square of the horde has an AC 6 and 30 hit points. If the characters clear away a square, they can move through it at normal speed.

In addition to contending with the dead roaming the ground, 4 **chomtzitzimitls** (see **Appendix A: New Monsters**) circle the skies above, using their somewhat limited *detect life* ability to scan the crowd. Although Mocayahua divulges clues as to how to use the ash to bypass the horde of undead, he holds off divulging anything to the characters about the chomtzitzimitls. Instead, the impish little trickster keeps their presence secret until the characters get about halfway to the spire then yells loudly, "Oh I forgot to warn you about the chomtzitzimitls. … They can sense you just fine. … You might want to hurry it up!"

The monkey's yelling also catches the chomtzitzimitls' attention, if the characters did not already do so on their own.

Mocayahua cannot resist one last taunt. When he spots the chomtzitzimitls closing in on the characters, he jeers loudly, "Stupid humans! Did you really think you out-vexed me by solving that obviously simple riddle?"

Once the chomtzitzimitls spot living creatures, they swoop down and mercilessly attack. Badly injured characters begin to bleed or wash off their ash disguises, allowing other dead to begin to recognize them. This awakens their hunger, at which point they too start attacking the characters and forcing them to focus on moving the remaining distance to the spire before the hordes and demons shred them.

When the characters near the spire, read or paraphrase the following description:

> As the spire looms closer, a break in the hordes of the dead comes into view. There appears to be a cliff or similar feature that opens into a great chasm spanning several yards, though the chaos of the throng of shoving corpses makes it difficult to be precise. The bodies closest to the edge simply topple over the side and disappear.

A character who makes a successful DC 15 Wisdom (Perception) check spots a jade bridge that spans the ravine, arching up to the great obsidian spire. Curiously, the bridge is clear and unoccupied by any dead.

The hordes are unable to occupy the bridge because none of them possesses the necessary fare to cross. They are damned without payment. At this time, the characters need to place the jadeite bead or plate beneath their tongues to pay the fare. Otherwise, when they reach the center of the bridge, they trigger the trap.

Fare Collection

If the characters have not defeated the chomtzitzimitls yet, the demons spot them the second they step onto the bridge and swoop in to make a final attempt to prevent them from crossing. If they defeated the demons and place the fare beneath their tongues, they are free to cross. However, if anyone did not first remove their soul before entering beyond this point, they immediately die unless they succeed on a DC 18 Dexterity saving throw to jump back at the last minute. Nonetheless, a successful saving throw deals necrotic damage equal to one-half their remaining hit points from the near-death experience.

The characters cannot speak during the final passage and must carry a jade bead or plate in their mouth. Each mortal must offer its jadeite bead or plate to the oracle as payment.

The Oracle of the Empty Moon

> The bridges arch upward toward the immense obsidian spire, climbing higher and higher until finally reaching a broad ledge more than 100 feet across. Its smooth surface gleams like polished glass. In the center, the spire continues to rise into the jagged slashes of the midnight-purple and crimson-orange sky filled with endless flocks of dark-feathered chom. The wind whips fast and erratic, howling against the echoing caws and the thrumming of wings.
>
> Cut into the spire, a great obsidian stair descends to the ledge from a towering throne. Atop the throne sits a huge woman, a cloak of black feathers draped across her shoulders, and an ornate tunic woven from the petals of black flowers spilling onto the ground. A swirling haze of black smoke chokes the air and in it stumble the hunched and crooked forms of dozens of misshapen humanoids. The misanthropic creatures mill around her, moaning softly as if unable to comprehend the reality in which they exist. They greedily crowd about the edges of the oracle's gown as if desperate for her affection or shelter.

The huge woman seated on the throne is a **Daughter of Chalatihuatl** (see **Appendix A: New Monsters**) one of the goddess's many daughters who in turn serve as the Oracle of the Empty Moon. The misanthropic humanoids are 20 **lemures**, failed reconstructions of humans fashioned from the remains of those fallen in each of the cataclysms.

Fighting the Horde

Running a combat between the horde of shuffling corpses and the characters may seem like a daunting task, though it is not quite as difficult as you may imagine. Remember, the horde is a flavor event, with the actual combat and greatest threat coming from the chomtzitzimitls.

If the characters' disguises start to fail, or if they insanely try to plow through the horde, only calculate the damage per round. Because the horde is so tightly packed, most of the undead cannot close ranks to attack. Essentially, the characters have (and will have because the supply of dead is endless) cover from most of the horde. If they stick together in some sort of formation (such as surrounding their weaker members or clumping together), they reduce the hordes' ability to surround an individual and cause them to suffer disadvantage on their attacks. Use the following table to calculate the damage the horde deals each round:

Table 3-4: Horde Damage Per Round

1d20	Damage
1–5	3
6–12	6
13–14	9
15–16	12
17–18	15
19	18
20	21

INNETOTCAYAN

If the characters agree to bring Xotaxtl to face her judgment, the Oracle of the Empty Moon offers to return them to the land of the living but warns that if the debt is not paid, all of them are obligated to assume it. If the characters accept, she marks all of them on the forehead with a single smeary line of black soot. Make the characters aware that they have until the calendar shifts to complete their task, a time equivalent to approximately six days. If they do not complete the task, she immediately slays all of them and takes their souls as payment.

When the characters settle on a course of action with the oracle, she summons a massive swarm of choms that descend upon the ledge. A small flock grabs each of the characters and wings them straight into the searing sky, hundreds of feet upward to where a single hole directly above the spire pierces the red mists. The light beyond is blinding. At this point, all of the surviving characters pass out, drawing this section of the adventure to a close.

When this section concludes, characters should be ready to advance a level before running the final section of the adventure.

GRAVE AWAKENINGS

Climbing from their grave-pits, the characters immediately note that they are decorated in funerary trappings and all have unusually pale, corpse-like complexions. The pallid skin is a secondary effect from their journey, and it does not return to normal until they retrieve their souls.

Checking their surroundings, they determine that they are back at the edge of the Corpsewood. The sun is just rising. They have no idea how long they have been gone, though it feels as if they are still within the Harvest Season.

Any character who makes a successful DC 15 Wisdom (Survival) check catches the last glimpse of the Bloodmoon dipping below the horizon, confirming that only a day or two has passed.

From here, a successful DC 10 Wisdom (Survival) check determines that the village lies about a day's walk to the west.

The characters now face overwhelming odds. However, they have been sent to speak with the oracle and hopefully know better than to fight her. If they resort to violence over reason, refer to the **This Means War!** sidebar below.

The oracle knows why the characters have come, though she believes them to be arrogant and foolish to have gone through the trouble, especially without having brought her a proper sacrifice. Throughout their interaction, she remains aloof, possibly amused and perfectly willing to let the mortals play out their dramas. In the end, she has the child's soul and is content to present that to her mother as their offering.

If the characters question her about the boy, she can tell them that much. She makes it clear that the herdsman offered her a sacrifice, and she is pleased with the boy he presented.

If told that the boy is not the sacrifice, she seems unfazed and perfectly willing to keep him anyway. Characters can continue to discuss the matter with her, as she is not toying with them and cares only that she has a suitable sacrifice to present to her mother at the start of the festival.

If the characters offer one of their own souls as a sacrifice, she accepts the exchange and hands them a small jade bead containing the boy's soul. If they return, they must place the soul beneath the child's tongue, wash him in the temple bath, and wait until his skin returns to a normal color. They must then crush the bead and spill its dust upon the gate to the Great Void. The sacrificed character remains in Miquito forever.

Alternately, if the characters question the oracle for other means of aiding the boy, she tells them they can undo the curse by delivering the soul of the sorcerer who failed to recognize the omens and the coming of the alux as a sign that the Forgotten Gods had accepted the herdsman's peccaries as a suitable sacrifice despite his intentions for the beasts. She looks at the characters sternly and emphasizes that Xotaxtl's failure alone created the current chain of events and that means he alone must pay the cost of recompense. The characters likely witnessed an alux devour Xotaxtl, which may lead them to believe his soul has already passed into the next world. However, the Oracle of the Empty Moon reassures them that Xotaxtl's soul still resides within the alux who ate him and thus can be brought to her for judgment.

CHAPTER SIX: FINAL FRONT

In this section of the adventure, the characters return to Cintlipetl to discover it is under siege by a horde of renegade aluxes whose leader **Xotaxtl Nitlocati** (see **Appendix A: New Monsters**) rallies his kin to take back the world from the human usurpers. He seeks to conquer the villagers and turn them into slaves for his new empire.

Events that Transpire During This Time: After a violent lumbering alux of the first sun killed and ate the sorcerer, its mind and body were flooded with innate and bloodborne arcane powers that transformed the creature into a higher version of itself that demands its followers call it Xotaxtl Nitlocati. Using its powers, Xotaxtl Nitlocati began seeking out other aluxes and preaching to them to help him carry out the prophecy it believes it was rebirthed to lead: the reclaiming of the Material Realms that the Forgotten Gods stole from its kind during the earlier cataclysms. In its first order of attack, it leads a horde of aluxes on a raid upon Cintlipetl in which its kin do what the Forgotten Gods did to them, by either slaughtering or enslaving everyone.

THE SIEGE OF CINTLIPETL

A plume of thick black smoke clots the sky as the winds smear it across the clouds and treetops. Pungent scents of wood, meat, and hair fill the valley. Beyond the tree line, flames rip through the small shacks surrounding the village, jumping nimbly across the thatched rooftops like a pack of wild dogs. On the ground, the villagers grapple with an assailing force of unyielding proto-humans with rough primordial features and wide, rage-filled eyes. The attackers seem to effortlessly lay waste to the villagers, bludgeoning them to the dirt with their heavy fists and smashing their skulls with rocks and clubs.

The characters have little time to stop the siege before the entire village is wiped out. Unfortunately, they are wildly outnumbered and a direct assault seems suicidal, especially without their souls.

Run the siege by allowing the characters to use strategies to stop the siege by addressing specific events individually. As they successfully handle each of the events, they gain points that help them in the final conflict against Xotaxtl Nitlocati.

CONTAIN AND QUELL FIRES

Many of the homes in the village have thatched roofs, particularly the smaller hovels of the common folk who live along the perimeter. The alux assailants began their attack by setting several of these homes on fire across the main roads leading into Cintlipetl. Winds now spread the conflagration across open ground as the arsonists attempt to direct it toward the center of the village.

When the characters first arrive, three separate bands of arsonists have set several rows of buildings ablaze in **Areas 6, 7, and 8**. They continue to set additional buildings on fire each round, and the combined power of the arsonists and the wind set an area of 30 square feet of flammable buildings or materials ablaze each round. Each band of arsonists defeated decreases the spread of fire by five square feet. The characters can also attempt to douse flames using magic or ingenuity, such as by smothering areas with water or soil. If the characters defeat all the arsonists, they save this section of town and allow several of the village's warriors to help them with the fighting. In this case, 4 Aztli fighters (LN male Aztli human **thugs** armed with longbows instead of heavy crossbows) join them. They can direct them to create distractions or fight forces in other sections of the village to help the characters complete further tasks. If the characters contain or extinguish the fire and successfully prevent it from spreading through the rest of the village, feel free to award one of the characters with Inspiration.

1	**Torchers. 5 aluxes of the second sun** (see **Appendix A: New Monsters**) and 3 **aluxes of the first sun** (see **Appendix A: New Monsters**) rush through the middle of the street hurling jars of alchemist's fire and lit torches.
2	**Bowyers. 2 aluxes of the second sun snipers** (see **Appendix A: New Monsters**) shoot lit arrows wrapped in oil-soaked rags at buildings while 2 **aluxes of the first sun** (see **Appendix A: New Monsters**) spur 2 agitated dogs (**mastiffs**) on a wild rampage up the streets with flaming stalks of corn tied to their tails. They attack any villagers in their way as they unwittingly create a wake of flames.
3	**Barrels. 5 aluxes of the first sun** (see **Appendix A: New Monsters**), each carrying a barrel of flaming coals, shuffle down the street. They take the coal barrels and roll them at houses or at characters attempting to stop them. When rolling, the barrels spill coals that deal 7 (2d6) fire damage and scatter the coals across the street to create difficult terrain for one minute before they burn out. It takes a successful DC 14 Dexterity saving throw to avoid taking damage from the coal. Rolling barrels travel in a straight line and move 60 feet per round for 1d6 rounds until they hit an object and shatter, dealing 9 (2d8) bludgeoning damage and 7 (2d6) fire damage from the coals. Any character who makes a successful DC 14 Dexterity saving throw avoids taking damage from the coals altogether.

FREE THE CAPTIVES

When the invaders first attacked, they snuck into homes and captured many of the villagers while they were resting or otherwise unprepared. Those captured, particularly warriors or others who might put up a fight, were brutally beaten and bound and then taken to nearby pits where they are now being held captive. The aluxes have scattered 14 prisoners throughout the Clay Pits (see **Area 9**). They paired or grouped some together, while others of greater threat are kept isolated.

To prevent any escapes or rescue attempts, 6 **choms** (see **Appendix A: New Monsters**) keep watch around the perimeter of the pits. When they spot intruders, they warn 3 **aluxes of the second sun** (see **Appendix A: New Monsters**) and an **alux of the first sun** (see **Appendix A: New Monsters**) that stand guard over the pits.

Pit 1: *Family Tied.* This pit holds a small family consisting of a man, a woman, and their two young children (N male and female Aztli human **commoners**). The man is bound and unconscious, and bleeding from a head injury. The woman is unbound, but her arm is broken. The mother desperately attempts to keep her two terrified children from crying.

Pit 2: *Naxutilli.* This pit holds two bodies, one recently slain from having his neck broken when the aluxes pushed him into the pit. The second is a muscular woman decorated with numerous ritual scars. She has two black eyes and a swollen nose from being struck in the face while sleeping. Her injuries have reduced her to 3 hit points. Her name is Naxutilli (CN female Aztli human **tribal warrior**). If healed, she eagerly joins the fight to save her village.

Pit 3: *Council Secrets.* This pit imprisons 3 middle-aged men (LN male Aztli human **nobles** who are unarmed and unarmored). All are bound and gagged. A successful DC 8 Wisdom (Insight) skills check notices that they are wearing fine clothing that denotes their status as either pochtecas or nobles. They were captured outside the temple by the first wave of aluxes that snuck into the village to clear the streets before the main attack. One of these men is Atlysis, the husband of Cothoti, one of the women serving on the town council. If the characters free him, Atlysis joins their fight and can direct them to where the headman and council members are holed up.

Pit 4: *Favored of Quiahuitl.* The aluxes took no chances with this warrior. They chopped off one of his legs, and he is now swiftly bleeding to death. Upon discovering him, the characters quickly realize he is unconscious and

Molyatl's Hut

The hut is located somewhere in the village not overrun by fire. You can have the characters discover it before saving Molyatl or even if they do not manage to find or rescue the warrior. Read or paraphrase the following description:

> The inside of this small hut shows signs of an intense struggle, with much of the furniture and other contents toppled over or smashed.

Any character who scans the contents and décor of this small hut and succeeds on a DC 10 Intelligence (Religion) check determines it is the residence of a powerful warrior blessed by the gods of the village to protect it. A successful DC 15 Intelligence (Investigation) check made while searching the hut uncovers some items wrapped in cloth that are stashed in a shallow dugout beneath the sleeping pallet.

Treasure: The cloth-wrapped items are a macuahuitl that turns out to be a *macuahuitl of Quiahuitl* (see **Appendix C: New Equipment and Magic Items**) and a wooden mask carved to resemble a jaguar covered with gold trim and jadeite inlays that is a *mask of Quiahuitl* (see **Appendix C: New Equipment and Magic Items**).

bleeding out. He must receive a treatment in the form of a successful DC 20 Wisdom (Medicine) skills check or magical healing. Otherwise, he dies. If characters save him and bring him back to consciousness, he tells them his name is Molyatl (CG male Aztli human **veteran** whose speed is reduced to 0 and he has no armor or weapons). He is one of the chief warriors from his village. He cannot fight in his condition. However, he tells the characters where he stashed his macuahuitl (see **Appendix C: New Equipment and Magic Items**) and helmet, both of which are blessed by the gods. If the characters go to Molyatl's hut, they find the items without succeeding on a skill check.

Pit 5: *The Scorpions.* Three villagers frantically cling to the pit walls, desperately attempting to remain as still and silent as death.

Scorpion Death Rig Trap

The sadistic aluxes rigged an insidious trap in which they tied a scorpion to the backs of all three prisoners, and then lashed the tails of the 3 **scorpions** together with three long strings. At present, the victims are positioned so that all the strings are just taut enough to prevent the scorpions from stinging them. If any of the strings break or if any of the villagers change their position and cause the strings to go slack, the scorpions can sting them with their tails. A successful DC 10 Wisdom (Insight) check reveals that the prisoners are too scared to move or speak, while a successful DC 12 Intelligence (Investigation) skills check spots the scorpions and the strings, deducing the nature of the trap. The secret to freeing the individuals is to simultaneously incapacitate or kill all three scorpions.

If the characters defeat the guards and help the individuals escape, one of them gives them a small carving hidden in their robes.

Treasure: The carving gifted to the players is a *figurine of wondrous power (onyx dog)*.

Pit 6: *The Warriors.* Two warriors anxiously pace the bottom of this pit. Both put up a good fight, and the aluxes barely managed to imprison them.

The aluxes had such difficulty capturing them that they were unable to bind them first. To remedy the situation, they called a **chomtzitzimitl** (see **Appendix A: New Monsters**) to keep watch at the mouth of the pit to prevent the warriors from getting out. The demon concentrates on teasing and harassing the victims in the pit. Therefore, until it is attacked or until someone creates a huge distraction, the sadistic creature has disadvantage on its Wisdom (Perception) checks and on its passive Perception.

The 2 warriors (CN male Aztli human **berserkers**) are only halfway through their hit points and, if freed, are eager to get back to fighting.

Rescue Camaxtl

After the first wave of attacks hit Cintlipetl, Camaxtl led Coaxoch, a few of the council members, and a small group of 6 warriors (CG male Aztli human thugs) to the courthouses to muster a quick defense. Unfortunately, the alux forces were too well organized and flooded into the city with such efficiency that Camaxtl and his allies became trapped in the building before they could lead a counterattack.

Xotaxtl Nitlocati believes Camaxtl the Headman is hiding Ohtli, whom he refers to as the Betrayer. He sent four alux warbands to surround the courthouse, seize Camaxtl, and drag him to the temple so he can torture him into revealing the location of the Betrayer and then destroy him and all his opponents in a single act. Each of the warbands lays siege to one of the sides of the courthouse as described below.

1. North Side. A row of five windows runs the length of this side of the courthouse, but there are no ground-level entrances. 1 **alux of the first sun** (see **Appendix A: New Monsters**) and 4 **alux of the second sun snipers** (see **Appendix A: New Monsters**) monitor this side, trying to sniff out any potential escapees and sniping at anyone nearing the windows. Additionally, 3 **choms** (see **Appendix A: New Monsters**) fly overhead. They issue an alert when anyone other than an alux approaches.

2. West Side. On the second floor, a narrow balcony frames a series of windows that overlook the plateau. Dug into the ground, a cellar door allows access to a basement. 5 **aluxes of the second sun snipers** (see **Appendix A: New Monsters**) watch the windows, while 2 **aluxes of the first sun** (see **Appendix A: New Monsters**) wait near the cellar door with their backs pressed against the building. 2 **choms** (see **Appendix A: New Monsters**) watch from the window balconies and squawk alarms if they spot anyone approaching

3. South Side. A loud rhythmic pounding comes from this side of the building where 6 **aluxes of the second sun** (see **Appendix A: New Monsters**) repeatedly slam against a reinforced wooden door with a large log they are using as a makeshift battering ram. A single round window is above the door on the second floor. Every so often, rocks and other debris fly out the window, pelting the creatures as they try to break down the door.

Special: When the characters become aware of this encounter, give the alux door bashers another two minutes (game time) before they break the door down and gain entrance to the courthouse and its occupants. In addition, 3 **choms** (see **Appendix A: New Monsters**) fly overhead, keeping watch and issuing an alert if they spot anyone other than aluxes approaching the area.

4. East Side. This is the main entrance to the courthouse. It has two reinforced doors and two large circular windows on the second floor. An encampment of aluxes holds a defensive formation in front of the building as a larger alux yells angrily at the courthouse as if making demands. Anyone capable of understanding Primordial Alux understands that the creatures are demanding the surrender of the individuals inside, one of them being the Camaxtl the Headman. The small encampment consists of 4 **aluxes of the second sun**, 2 **aluxes of the first sun**, 2 **aluxes of the second sun snipers**, and 1 **boarfolk rager** (see **Appendix A: New Monsters** for all monsters listed here). In addition, 4 **choms** fly overhead, keeping watch and calling an alert if they spot anyone other than aluxes approaching the area.

Reaching the headman and his allies is difficult. The characters can attempt to fight each of the warbands on their own by splitting them up and diverting their attention. Similarly, they might create a distraction using freed villagers and warriors to pin down the aluxes elsewhere, giving them an opportunity to enter the courthouse and free the headman.

Successfully rescuing Camaxtl provides the characters with two additional advantages in their fight against Xotaxtl Nitlocati. First, if Camaxtl accompanies the characters to get Ohtli, then they can readily bypass the couatl guardians (see **Recover their Souls**). Second, while Xotaxtl Nitlocati holds the Temple of the Sun, Camaxtl knows how to access a series of secret subterranean tunnels leading into the temple. Originally designed as an escape route, those entering them from the opposite direction can slip into the main room undetected, entering into a secret chamber hidden directly under the throne (see **The Final Confrontation**).

Recover their Souls

Characters likely recall that Ohtli still possesses their souls and until they recover them, they risk having their souls lost or destroyed if they fall in the final conflict. To recover their souls, the characters must find the alux. Achieving this course of action ensures that the characters do not permanently die if reduced to 0 hit points. The headman hid Ohtli in the grain cellars beneath the temple.

Coaxoch summoned 4 **couatls** to protect the alux. The spirit serpents stand guard over the entrance to his chamber and deny access to any who approach it without the medicine-witch. To reach Ohtli, the characters must convince the four couatls (named Iquiza, Nepantia, Onaqui, and Youal) to let them pass. The creatures are powerful and sworn to guard the alux with their lives.

If necessary, they are willing to fight to the death to keep him safe. If the characters contemplate slaying the creatures to free Ohtli, have the characters attempts an Intelligence (Religion) check. If a character succeeds on a DC 5 Intelligence (Religion) check, that person recalls that killing the sacred creatures brings extremely bad luck. If they fight and kill a couatl, whoever participates in performing such an act gains disadvantage to all attack rolls, skill checks, and saving throws until they perform the proper sacrifice ritual to undo the damage of their actions. The ritual should involve some sort of additional quest. However, the details of such penance are not covered in this adventure.

If the characters are in the company of Coaxoch or Camaxtl, all they must do to pass freely is to convince the couatls that the individuals they travel with are authentic. If not in the company of either of these individuals, gaining access to Ohtli is a little more challenging.

The characters must succeed on a near-impossible DC 30 Charisma (Persuasion) check to convince the spirit serpents that they require an audience with the alux to regain their souls. They can prove they do not have souls by providing evidence that they have been to Miquito (which one cannot do with a soul). There are numerous ways to convince the couatls, but a single piece of evidence alone is not enough to convince them (neither is the testimony of a chom). For each piece of evidence the characters provide, they gain a +5 bonus to convince the couatls of their intentions. Evidence may include (but is not limited to) items taken from Miquito, accurate descriptions of some of the encounters, the *blanket of daggers*, an accurate explanation of how to work the gates, or any lasting effects a character might have from being in the Great Void.

If the characters get stuck, you can opt to have the couatls test them by offering the characters a trial by combat. The characters should, of course, refuse the trial on the grounds that if they lose, death will immediately claim their souls. Characters contemplating the gravity of this loss in front of the couatl might also aid in convincing the serpents of the sincerity of their intentions.

Once the characters gain an audience with Ohtli, he returns their souls. Ohtli offers to aid them in their fight, and he can also help them turn some of the aluxes from enemies to allies by convincing them that Xotaxtl Nitlocati's actions are misguided and as angry and capricious as the treatment they received at the hands of the Forgotten Gods. He still holds the belief that for the aluxes to prove their humanity, they must show they are human and not capricious monsters.

Similarly, the couatls offer to aid the characters in defending their village. You should decide whether they fight alongside the characters or fight against some other threats while the characters confront Xotaxtl Nitlocati at the temple in the final scene.

THE FINAL CONFRONTATION

After completing some or all of the tasks, the characters can finally confront Xotaxtl Nitlocati.

The would-be emperor sits on the throne in the temple overlooking his allies as they deface the walls by hacking at the sacred images and using blood and mud to paint crude and gory depictions of their own gods over the holy artwork. Xotaxtl Nitlocati delights in gorging himself on the spoils of the sacrifices and offerings intended to appease the gods during the Seven Year Harvest Festival. He commands the aluxes to throw them into a large bonfire that burns in the center of the room. A ring of large wooden posts are driven into the earthy floor around the fire. A villager is lashed to each post, including three of the council members, the herdsman's son, and his mother. The herdsman is nowhere to be seen. Swarms of choms sit high in the rafters and ledges, gazing down in the flickering light as multiple aluxes rampage and dance, feast, and fight in a bestial frenzy of elation and gleeful violence.

As noted in the description, **Xotaxtl Nitlocati** (see **Appendix A: New Monsters**) sits upon the throne, giving him the higher ground. He uses 3 **choms** (see **Appendix A: New Monsters**) to keep watch and squawk warnings if they spot intruders. They then swoop down to attack. The rest of his entourage includes 6 **aluxes of the second sun** (see **Appendix A: New Monsters**) and 4 **aluxes of the first sun** (see **Appendix A: New Monsters**). As soon as they detect intruders, they rush to attack, allowing Xotaxtl Nitlocati to use spells from a distance.

Early in the fight, Xotaxtl Nitlocati targets either one of the council members or the most physically combative of his opponents with a *flesh to maize* spell (see **Appendix D: New Spells**). If the victim fails the spell save, as a free action the alux calls out to the chom and commands them to swoop down and devour the victim. As the fight drags out, Xotaxtl Nitlocati commands three of his alux allies to start beating on the captives and yells at the intruders to surrender before he has them killed. He is not bluffing. If his allies start to drop, Xotaxtl Nitlocati also commands one of the chom swarms to break off and get help. Each round thereafter, determine if reinforcements arrive by rolling 1d6, with a roll of 5–6 indicating they found 1d4 + 2 **aluxes** to aid in the melee.

As long as their leader remains strong enough to command them, the aluxes continue to actively participate in the fight. Conversely, if the characters fell Xotaxtl Nitlocati, the remainder of the aluxes panic, break from combat, and attempt to flee. If the characters defeat Xotaxtl Nitlocati, the fighting slowly subsides as word spreads of his defeat. Villagers drive off the remaining attackers while others readily surrender and beg for mercy. The choms ask for no quarter or forgiveness, but simply fly off chattering and laughing as if mocking the folly of the entire event.

CONCLUDING THE ADVENTURE

Xotaxtl Nitlocati's death frees Xotaxtl's soul from its earthly prison, sending it on its journey to the Oracle of the Moon for her judgment.

The Daughter of Chalatihuatl then appears to the characters in a vivid vision, where she accepts the sorcerer-priest's soul as recompense for the slain alux and the insult to the Forgotten Gods. The herdman's son regains his soul, and the characters have fulfilled their end of their bargain with the Oracle of the Moon.

In the wake of the attack, there is much to do to restore and rebuild the village, especially with the Harvest Festival looming. Characters are free to help rebuild the village and participate in the festival where they are lauded as heroes. Camaxtl thanks Ohtli for his bravery and understanding. The alux is extremely moved by his gesture and returns his thanks. That night by the fire, Ohtli spins epic and dramatic tales of the third cataclysm and moves the audience to tears. In the morning, he bids his goodbyes and heads off to the Corpsewood to seek to restore order to his people. Not all ends well though. Many are dead, including the herdsman. His orphaned son weeps inconsolably and blames himself for the tragic events. Thereafter, Coaxoch the medicine-witch offers to take him on as her apprentice. If the characters choose to stay, the headman offers them property and housing as well as seats upon the village council. If not, he gifts them with some treasure.

Treasure: The headman gives the characters 11 large disks of gold (200 gp each), a *+2 shield*, a *pearl of power*, and whatever mundane equipment they require. Coaxoch adds a few more gifts to their stash: 3 *potions of superior healing* and a *potion of invisibility*. Lastly, the herdsman's son gifts them with a small peccary's hoof whistle he carved for his father. "For when you are in trouble," the boy tells them. "This time I shall listen."

After their experiences, the characters are ready to progress to the next adventure in the series, ***Rider on the Storm***, which takes them out of the Aztlis' lands and into Poqoza territory across the Great Canal.

RIDER ON THE STORM

BY ROB MANNING

"YAHUITAMOTL IS HERE! DOOM UPON US!"

— COMMON SAYING DURING A THUNDERSTORM

SEASON OF THE QALLUCHA

Once the child is of the age, they must enter the Mulla Chanacu.
There, they will find their way. Embrace their true nature.
Fear not — revelation is at hand.
— The Way of the Quata Maque

Can't go over the grass. I'm not a toucan.
Can't go under the grass. I'm not a paca.
Must swim through the grass.
— Children's rhyme

Rider on the Storm is an adventure for four -12th-Tier 3 characters that takes them on an open-ended, whirlwind tour of the Caxcalli Grasslands in the heart of Poqoza territory. Here, they must face the dreaded Storm Rider and an otherworldly entity threatening to disrupt the Poqozas' way of life and bring them under its proverbial thumbs.

ADVENTURE BACKGROUND

Thousands of years ago, long before the hero-gods' ascendance, a meteorite streaked across the Tehuatl sky before it crashed into earth and created a massive crater in its wake. Although time largely healed the island's wound, the cosmic body brought a tiny organic hitchhiker along for the ride, a fungus known as shori huasca. Incredibly, the organism survived the harrowing trek across space and the devastating crash landing that followed. For countless centuries afterward, the fungus flourished in the depths of the earth, where it basked in the meteorite's residual cosmic energy that it needed to survive.

The fungus would have gone unnoticed if not for the ambitions of one Poqoza man — Elix Cucita. The bohemian explorer and his entourage found the strange plant and naturally began experimenting with its intoxicating properties. Much to their hedonistic delight, ingesting the fungus spawned wild hallucinations and transcendental experiences. Elix constructed a laboratory on the location's outskirts to further study the fungus. In time, Elix and his inner circle achieved the presumably impossible. Their consciousnesses escaped their physical bodies and entered the Great Beyond where they encountered a cabal of unexpected inhabitants — a small band of nihileth aboleths intrigued by their humanoid visitors. Much to the aboleths' horror, Elix and his associates resisted their mental powers, allowing them to reach a truce with the normally dominant monsters. At a standstill, the parties agreed to negotiate an agreement to share their knowledge. To ensure their mutual safety, one member of each delegation would reside in the others' home world until they completed the exchange. To conclude the bargain, one nihileth aboleth traveled to Tehuatl and remained hidden beneath the surface, dormant while it waited for its instructions.

The undead monstrosity waited there for centuries until it received a signal from its counterparts to reawaken. Meanwhile, word of the fungus's hallucinatory properties spread throughout the land. The Poqozas dubbed the site and its caverns as the Mulla Chanacu. In time, all adolescent Poqoza boys and girls traveled to the isolated locale as a rite of passage into adulthood. While the caverns of the Mulla Chanacu stayed active, Elix's research facility fell into neglect and disrepair until a new occupant arrived on the scene. Yahuitamotl, a bored and corrupted storm giant, entered the complex. He soon came to the realization that the location's unusual properties gave him an unnaturally long life. What seemed like a blessing soon became a burden as the isolation and ennui ate away at his soul and psyche. To amuse himself, the capricious giant summoned massive storms and foul weather to terrify the populace, earning him the moniker of the Storm Rider. Yahuitamotl remained directionless until a celestial occurrence set current events into motion.

Roughly once every 1,000 years, an enormous rogue gas giant planet passes through the solar system, creating a prolonged solar eclipse. After centuries of inaction, the nihileth aboleth took the event as its signal to reactivate. Over the next several weeks, the undead abomination began to enslave the unsuspecting teenagers venturing to the Mulla Chanacu, transforming the vibrant youngsters into a zombie horde. The monster then struck a bargain with the increasingly evil and destructive Yahuitamotl, who agreed to be his herald of the apocalypse and spread death and destruction across the Caxcalli Grasslands. The nihileth aboleth now gathers intelligence about the people and lands of Tehuatl to prepare an invasion force from the Great Beyond. Despite its efforts, the uneasy truce between Elix and the aboleth's kin devolved into a bitter conflict. Hurling terrible magic and frightening weapons, the combatants vanished into Oblivion, never to be seen nor heard from again. Although the aboleth has not received a response to any of its reconnaissance information, the monster proceeds full steam ahead on its dream of conquering the Poqozas with its undead army and adding the island to its vile race's inventory of conquered territories. That is unless characters intervene and stop these dire events from happening.

ADVENTURE SYNOPSIS

The characters arrive in the Caxcalli Grasslands where they embark on a series of encounters involving the Poqozas' social groups: the Thalus (farmers), the Thayanas (hunters), and the Alaxpachas (the craftspeople). During the course of these events, the characters increase their goodwill among these stratas within Poqoza society by saving lives, protecting property, and ridding their homes of evil. After winning the people's trust and admiration, an elder from the group asks the characters to assist them in a matter pertaining to their interests. After completing this task and again earning their gratitude, the characters learn of the Storm Rider who has been terrorizing Poqoza communities for many years. The weather activities in the area lead them to an ancient, largely abandoned laboratory where the bored Storm Rider laments the folly of existence and his self-proclaimed godhood. The Storm Rider's removal does not eradicate the threats looming over Tehuatl. The reawakened nihileth aboleth now poisons the land surrounding the Mulla Chanacu where young Poqozas experience visions to guide them into adulthood. Over the past several weeks, he has killed and raised many of them as zombie thralls under his command. Furthermore, the adults sent to check on their well-being also fell prey to the monster that now swims in the muck at the bottom of the Mulla Chanacu crater. The characters must destroy the malevolent creature to rid this wicked threat from the land once and for all.

OVERVIEW OF THE CAXCALLI GRASSLANDS

The grass is the lifeblood of the Caxcalli lands. It provides nourishment, clothing, shelter, and more for the people and beasts who call the grasslands home. The land is a sea of green and tan grasses, some reaching heights of five feet with stunted and twisted acacia trees dotting the landscape. The coarse blades are sharp, and the grains produced in the fields range from maize in the east (especially near Zacatl) to quinoa in the west (nearer to the Toctli Forest). Bamboo grows in abundance in the southeast, and the Thalu spread its use for construction and medicinal purposes across the countryside. Caxcalli experiences a wet and a dry season. Seven long months of minuscule rainfall strip the grasslands of most of its color, and nearly every year wildfires cleanse the land of brush and eliminate the weaker of the species. Five months of

Kurn Domladur
Turew
Octli
Ixtla
Tamazoli
Nepalta
Shassal
Balandrur
Ipaconoytl
Cepual Desert
Nochtli
Xalpit
Quannaqa River
Mactli
Omehual River
Hana'aloa
Ouatulli Lake
Omiex
Droomph
Teocua
Cuahtla Forest
Yoaltica Ilaquiloz
Necocyaotl
Quizaloa
Amilotetl
The Great Canal
Huitzineo
Azuato
Ixchicta
Zacatl
Ezhuacoza
Good fortune
Cotza
Toxana
Mimicapoli
Quitlacatl
Blibleblup
Ezhuitotl
Cuiateotl
Ahuacua
Hilaya River
The Spring
Mototoloa
Zinacan
Ixnenatl
Moyome
Atoyaxalli
Tlococua Marsh
Xoxoquetzpali
Hamachi
Temetzin River
Mauhque
Iachacina
Ixtama
Yolqui
Yoyoliton
Mulla Chanacu
Hualcitzen
Onacina
Xicotli
Cuanintli
Nezcatayotl
Eei
Rommpf
Caxcalli Grasslands
Yuri
Tlahapina
N
CAXCALLI GRASSLANDS
1 Square - 20 Miles

rejuvenating rains bring the grasslands back to a vibrant palate of green.

The Poqozas who inhabit the grasslands divide their society into social strata based upon their lifestyle. The three primary strata of this adventure are the Thalu, Thayana, and Alaxpacha. These strata are more akin to medieval guild membership. While everyone identifies as a Poqoza, they subdivide their society based upon their profession. Regardless of which strata they belong to, all submit to the wiles of Chuxuntana, "The Sea of Green."

The Thalu are the farmers. These sedentary people learned to grow and manipulate plants to meet their needs. The Thalu mostly dwell in small villages and towns across a wide swath of land bisecting the grasslands from east to west, starting at the edge of Lake Moyome. They build chinampas atop a large freshwater lake on the eastern edge of the grasslands where it butts against the trackless swamp farther east. Simple and honest, the Thalu are a humble people who pray for good crops and peace.

The Thayana are the hunters. They follow the deer herds and know nearly every watering hole in the entire grasslands. Familial and loyal, these Poqoza band together in small groups that are usually led by a powerful ranger or druid. These self-sufficient nomads carry their homes on their backs in their constant pursuit of prey. More primal than their domesticated cousins, the Thalu, the Thayana acknowledge some of the older nature spirits, though they still place Tlatlcolli at the top of their religious hierarchy.

The Alaxpacha are the stargazers, the artists, and scholars of the Caxcalli. Their minds never rest. Many become wizards and rogues who congregate in the city of Zacatl and other urban centers, though some seek solace in isolated places toward the southern shore where the sea's salty breezes tame the tallgrass. The hills grow a bit taller just north of the sandy beaches, allowing the Alaxpacha better opportunities to study the inky expanse of the night sky. The Alaxpacha believe they have a better understanding of the workings of the planes and worship knowledge over all else.

For many generations, these three groups have harmoniously coexisted in the Caxcalli Grasslands. Occasional squabbles break out from time to time, but the participants generally accept such disputes as part of the grand plan without holding grudges or bad blood. Each Poqoza tries to further their life's experience by contributing all they can to the betterment of their people.

When couples bring forth new life into the Chuxuntana, their children eventually reach the age where they must go into the Mulla Chanacu and find their way in the barbarous wastes. Caves riddle the landscape, and strange fungi grow in the steamy earth. Shamans of each tribe encourage the adventurous youngsters to imbibe a variety of these mushrooms to help unlock their inner spirit and embark on a transcendental experience. After a month or more, the young person leaves the wild Mulla Chanacu and travels to meet members of their new profession and social strata. A Thayana youth might emerge as a Thayana, or an Alaxpacha, or some other profession completely, depending on what the spirits told them. The Poqozas have other smaller subsets of social strata who are offshoots of the three major groups. A few youths have left Mulla Chanacu to completely forsake the grasslands and move to another territory entirely. All Poqozas born in the grasslands must face their fears and enter the caverns to complete their transition from childhood to adulthood. The visit happens at different times for different individuals, but most enter around age 13 to 15. There the adolescents must partake in the tradition of ingesting the shori huasca, the fungus that guides them on their journey from childhood to adulthood.

Hooks

You are free to use any of the following ideas to draw the characters into the story or create one of your own.

Canals and Contracts

A powerful group of Aztlis calling themselves the Achni contacts the characters to set up a meeting with them in a luxurious audience hall in a metropolis of your choice, though it most likely takes place in Zacatl. The gist of the meeting is to ask them to explore the Caxcalli Grasslands. The Achni have been speaking with several Poqozas interested in developing a secondary canal running north to south that would help facilitate trade between the former archenemies. Before they undertake such a massive undertaking, they want to ensure that tales of the savage grasslands are just that — stories borne from overactive imaginations. The group grants the characters an advance of 1,000 gp to purchase any provisions necessary for the exploratory expedition they expect could take several weeks or even months.

Skulls

Dangerous beasts roam the Caxcalli Grasslands. A wealthy, retired Aztli hunter regrets he never got the opportunity to hunt in Poqoza territory. Therefore, he contacts the adventurers and gives them a list of skulls he needs to complete his trophy collection. The list covers most of the basics: a rhinoceros, a caiman, a paleolithic specimen, and most notably at the bottom of his list a single word, "Achachila," which means the "one that got away." The hunter tracked his quarry up to the edge of the Tlacocua Marsh before he lost it. He never truly saw the creature other than catching glimpses of a vicious pair of eyes, a lone, clawed footprint, and a fleeting shadow. The beast strikes only at night and has legendary status among Aztli and Poqoza alike. Few have seen it and lived to tell the tale. Indeed, the descriptions of the beast vary from one person to the next. Although he desires to acquire all the missing skulls, he really cares only about one — that of the AchachilasanacaAchachila. Remember, the AchachilasanacaAchachila is not a specific creature, so feel free to use a suitable monster of your choice for this quest.

Medical Mission of Mercy

Hucksters come in all shapes and sizes. An evangelist who arrived on the southern edge of the Caxcalli Grasslands began a tyrannical conversion therapy camp to force the Poqozas and Aztlis he encountered to renounce their faith and accept his one true, foreign god. He placed those who refused to convert into a brutal, forced labor compound he built on the back of the Poqoza living there before his arrival. Within its stone walls, he and his acolytes indoctrinated the unwilling participants in his religion. In addition to breaking the will of the free Poqoza living there, they also spread a coughing disease among the locals. The evangelist and his retinue are allegedly immune to the pox, but the Poqoza they imprisoned are not. The cough transforms into a choking fever after a few days, followed shortly thereafter by exhaustion, incapacitation, and ultimately death unless properly treated. The characters hear of this outbreak and must travel to the southern edge of the Caxcalli Grasslands to fight the spreading sickness, even as it moves farther north from village to village, and tribe to tribe. The characters come equipped with the proper treatment, a sulfuric powder that when mixed with water and imbibed provides immunity against the contagion or cures an infected person of the ailment.

Settlements of the Caxcalli Grasslands

The Caxcalli Grasslands south of the Great Canal provide nearly ideal living conditions for most forms of life. Vast herds of deer and antelopes graze on the abundant grasses under the watchful gaze of predatory cats and canines alike. The biome is almost perfectly designed to support nearly every variety of flora and fauna, including maize, the lifeblood of the Aztlis and their offshoots, the Poqozas. Maize and other wild cereal grains thrive under these conditions, making this region ideal for agriculture and to maintain fertile hunting grounds. During the course of this adventure, the characters are likely to travel vast distances, potentially bringing them into contact with multiple settlements along the way. If you are using the *Tehuatl* sourcebook from **Frog God Games** along with this adventure compendium, you may use the settlements in that guide to aid you in populating the wilderness with suitable settlements. Nevertheless, the preceding work cannot detail every community within the grasslands, especially considering that some are only transient settlements established by nomadic people.

For each day of travel across this verdant landscape, you may consult **Table 4–1** to determine if the characters encounter a settlement during the course of their journey. We recommend you use these locations to give the adventurers an opportunity to rest, restock their provisions, and gather rumors or information from the inhabitants. Cities do not appear on this table as they appear on the Tehuatl main map and are not intended to be randomly generated. At your option, you may roll with advantage whenever the characters traverse an area near a large body of water or other strategic location. Conversely, you may roll with disadvantage when the characters enter an area without a readily available source of water.

1d20	Settlement Found
1–4	No settlement
5–7	Transient settlement
8–15	Village
16–18	Small town
19–20	Large town

As previously discussed, the Poqoza essentially divide their society in strata along the lines of city dwellers (Alaxpacha), sedentary rural inhabitants (Thalu), and nomads (Thayana). This section describes their populations within each of the following settlements:

Transient settlement: Lean-tos, huts, and other portable shelters comprise a transient settlement almost exclusively made up of Thayanas, with a few elves or even renegade Aztlis tagging along with them. These are a hardy people who live off the land and know nature's cycle like the backs of their hands, If they win their trust, characters who encounter these folks can expect to share a meal, and they are the best source of gossip for news throughout the area, including information about the Storm Rider. However, they are generally short on supplies and have little in the way of magic. Transient settlements have 2d8 x 10 residents (various alignments, male and female Poqoza half-elf **scouts** armed with spears instead of shortswords) with a leadership cadre of 2d4 elders (various alignments, male and female Poqoza half-elf **druids**) and 1 chieftain (various alignments, male or female Poqoza half-elf **veteran** armed with a sling, macuahuitl, and tecpatl [see **Appendix C: New Equipment and Magic Items**] instead of a heavy crossbow, longsword, and shortsword and wearing ollixalli armor [see **Appendix C: New Equipment and Magic Items**] instead of splint). For a fee of 2 gp per day, the characters can hire one of the residents to serve as a guide across the Caxcalli Grasslands. In the company of the guide, the characters have no chance of getting lost and have advantage on Wisdom (Survival) check made to hunt wild game and avoid natural hazards.

Village: This small community generally consists of several families living together in communal housing or in huts scattered across a wide area. Thalus make up the bulk of the population, though some Thayanas may use the village as a temporary base of operations between hunting expeditions. Most villagers spend their days working the land by either tending to the fields or minding the livestock, usually consisting of turkeys and occasionally goats. Poqozas make up the majority of the population, though some elves, gnomes, and halfling may cohabitate the village alongside these people. Characters who visit one of these settlements can expect temporary shelter from the accommodating residents as well as some provisions and news about the outside world. A village always has at least a minor temple dedicated to Tlatlcolli, where characters can find some magical healing as well as stores of alcohol and hallucinogenic agents including shori huasca. The typical village has 2d10 x 10 permanent residents (various alignments, male and female Poqoza half-elf **commoners**), 2d10 transient residents (various alignments, male and female Poqoza half-elf **scouts** armed with spears instead of shortswords), and a leadership council made up of 2d6 religious elders (various alignments, male and female Poqoza half-elf **priests**).

Small town: Individual homes, farms, and a town square are the hallmarks of this larger settlement. Although many people still work the land, some have the resources to hire transient laborers to harvest their crops and maintain their livestock, which usually consists of dogs, turkeys, and some goats. Thalus remain the most populous social strata within a small town, though Thayanas who may also double as traders, furriers, and merchants are frequent visitors. In addition, several Alaxpachas may take up residence in town to serve as sages, artisans, and skilled craftsmen. A small town is a good source of information about events in surrounding areas and has a well-stocked inventory of provisions for travelers, including commonly found magic items, some adventuring gear, weapons, armor, specialized equipment. Commerce is generally conducted in the town square. Furthermore, most small towns have a small military force to fend off incursions by their less hospitable humanoid neighbors. Poqozas are the dominant people in most small towns, with some elves, gnomes, halflings, and more exotic races scattered among the generally tolerant populace. Guest houses, inns, and other businesses accommodating travelers as well as a temple dedicated to Tlatlcolli can also be found in a small town. The temple always has ample supplies of intoxicating substances, including shori huasca, on hand for religious festivals. The typical small town has 10d10 x 10 permanent residents (various alignments, male and female Poqoza half-elf **commoners**), 8d10 transient residents (various alignments, male and female Poqoza half-elf **scouts** armed with spears instead of shortswords), a military force of 6d10 soldiers (various alignments, male and female Poqoza half-elf **thugs** armed with slings instead of heavy crossbows), and a leadership council made up of 2d6 religious elders (various alignments, male and female Poqoza half-elf **priests**).

Large town: Although not quite a city, a large town has almost every amenity found in a great metropolis. The town square dominates this community as fewer people earn their livelihoods directly from the land. The Thalus inhabit the arable land on the settlement's outskirts, while Alaxpachas earn their keep producing manufactured goods and engaging in a myriad of academic studies. Thayanas also sell some of their fresh kills in the bustling marketplace, which serves as central hub for all activities within the town. Otherwise, the large town has the same general features of a small town except in greater supplies along with a larger percentage of Alaxpacha inhabitants than a small town. It may also house several shrines devoted to the deities of its non-Poqoza inhabitants, most notably its elvish population. Poqozas are still the dominant people in most large towns, though elves, gnomes, halflings and more exotic races share the same space. It is also not unusual to find an insular Aztli neighborhood within a small town. Although they tolerate the humans' presence, the Poqozas strictly forbid them from establishing shrines and temples within their communities. Some Aztlis may go figuratively and literally underground to honor their deities, yet doing so risks expulsion from the dominant Poqozas if they learn of such activities. A large town has 10d10 x 50 (minimum 1,000) permanent residents (various alignments, male and female Poqoza half-elf **commoners**), 20d10 transient residents (various alignments, male and female Poqoza half-elf **scouts** armed with spears instead of shortswords), a military force of 20d10 soldiers (various alignments, male and female Poqoza half-elf **thugs** armed with slings instead of heavy crossbows) commanded by a retinue of 2d4 officers (various alignments, male and female Poqoza half-elf bandit **captains** armed with slings instead of scimitars), and a leadership council made up of 2d6 religious elders (various alignments, male and female Poqoza half-elf **priests**).

THE LEGEND OF YAHUITAMOTL

Every community in the Caxcalli Grasslands knows the legend of Yahuitamotl. No one has details on the appearance of the Storm Rider, but all have a connection to an encounter of some sort. Yahuitamotl appears only under a cloudy sky, sometimes in mist or dense rain. The Poqoza always encounter the Storm Rider at a distance. The legends say that his voice is commanding, but only at a whispering volume, even in the midst of a torrential downpour. Yahuitamotl is fickle, unpredictable, and temperamental. Most people leave offerings of food and other treasures for the being when it arrives, though many speculate that Yahuitamotl cares little about these tributes as he has sometimes taken them into their entirety and on other occasions left them untouched. When the characters ask Poqozas about the Storm Rider, you can provide them with any or all of the following rumors.

• "Our cousin in a nearby village saw the Storm Rider just after dawn the other day. As the mist of the morning rolled away, there Yahuitamotl stood, towering 25 feet tall. My cousin tried to run, but fear froze her to the spot. The Storm Rider asked how many Poqozas were in her village, and she responded quickly. She did not take into account the outliers and field workers, and now she is deathly afraid Yahuitamotl will return to beat her for her miscount. The village has left extra portions of food in their shrine to make up for her folly."

• "No one sees the Storm Rider. You only hear him as he rides the lightning down from the heavens above and strikes the ground with such force!"

• "Yahuitamotl made an entire village disappear! Where we used to set up camp, Yahuitamotl found us on ground we think was sacred to him. The world shook from his anger as he called down lightning to destroy our huts and scatter us to the winds. I have not seen any of the other hunters from that pack since."

• "Yahuitamotl warns us of a coming doom! All who live in the tallgrass fear this change. He whispers of the spirits of our ancestors rising from the very ground to strike us down. We must prepare, but how? Most Poqoza just live in fear and hope it doesn't come to pass."

• "The winds knocked me down. By the time I regained my feet, Yahuitamotl had already come and gone."

The tellers of these tales fully believe them to be true.

CHAPTER ONE: EVENT ENCOUNTERS

These encounters do not directly tie into the story of Yahuitamotl or the adventure's main protagonist. They are designed to give the characters an opportunity to explore the Caxcalli Grasslands and win the favor of one of the three strata within Poqoza society. The events can be run in any order. At the end of each event, the characters gain goodwill points for resolving these situations in a manner favorable to one of the three groups. If the characters accumulate four goodwill points for a particular group, the adventure proceeds to **Chapter Two: Social Business** and the corresponding strata's final encounter before moving onto the adventure's main storyline. Of course, news spreads swiftly in the grasslands as the characters' reputation grows with each triumph or sinks with every failure.

None of these events takes place in the Mulla Chanacu. The tallgrass hides the area well, and the priests who supply the shori huasca try not to reveal its true location. Of course, the characters might try to cajole, bribe, or threaten their way to the Mulla Chanacu, or someone else there. If the characters explore that area, proceed to **Chapter Four: The Nihileth Assault**.

EVENT ENCOUNTER 1:
THE LADY IN THE IRON COFFIN

> A small crowd gathers around a team of Poqozas shoveling mud out of a massive hole in the ground measuring almost eight feet on a side. Another team assembling a pulley system with hemp cables that dangle down into the cavity appears to be trying to overtake the digging team. Excited onlookers munch on snacks and give unsolicited advice.

These Poqoza are almost all Thalus. A farmer digging up a field near a crossroads stumbled upon some ancient religious relics, including wooden death whistles and small figurines of indiscernible identity. The chance discovery spurred him to keep digging to figure out what lies buried beneath his crops. After several hours of excavation, he discovered an iron sarcophagus four feet below the surface. Excited by the find, he summoned his family and friends to help him disinter the coffin. Almost everyone who sees the coffin feels an inexplicable desire to liberate it from the cold earth and reveal its contents. None can explain their rationale for this seemingly irrepressible feeling.

When the characters arrive, the farmer **Yacha Tol** (LN male Poqoza half-elf **commoner**) and his closest family explain their desire to remove the coffin from the ground to **Aqi Ciqana** (CG male Poqoza half-elf **priest**), an Alaxpacha priest from a neighboring village. Despite the priest's inexplicable curiosity, he warns the farmer about the dangers of meddling in affairs beyond his understanding. When Yacha sees the characters, he beckons them to join him and assist in the efforts.

The coffin houses the still living remains of Aukka Castigas, a female **black orc high priest of Orcus** (see **Appendix A: New Monsters**). Tlatoani's snake advisors attempted to negotiate an alliance with the treacherous priestess, but her unwillingness to abandon Orcus and accept the Immortal Sun as her divine patron sealed her fate. Fearful of angering another god by killing one of his steadfast servants, the cunning serpents deceived her into willingly allowing a wizard to cast a *sequester* spell on her. The spell placed her in a state of suspended animation that allowed them to seal her within the iron sarcophagus, which they buried deep beneath a crossroads to prevent someone from accidentally stumbling upon her burial site.

Over the last several thousand years, the ground shifted as weather events and seismic activity brought the coffin closer to the surface. Furthermore, an *arcane lock* spell cast on the coffin was accidentally dispelled during a magical duel between two sorcerers that took place on this very spot several hundred years earlier. Nonetheless, the iron coffin still radiates magic, though in this case, it amplifies the emotion of any creature within 20 feet of it who fails a DC 15 Wisdom saving throw. Those who fear it, become frightened of it. Curiosity- and treasure-seekers greatly desire to open it and discover its malevolent contents.

When the characters arrive, the coffin is nearly free of the mud. Yacha Tol approaches, pushing aside the wizard as he and the others in the crowd beg for someone to crack open the lid and bask in its treasures. The numerous voices sound like a mad cacophony as each individual begs them to hear their side of the story. Suspended about halfway out of its hole in the ground, the featureless iron sarcophagus dangles in a mass of ropes and scaffolding in the light rain.

Feel free to allow the interaction between the characters and the crowd to play out as much as you want. A few individuals, including the wizard and a village elder, demand that the villagers re-inter the coffin, while the farmer and the majority demand to see it opened.

With the coffin exposed to the elements, Orcus may sense the presence of a long-buried servant or a spiteful Aztli god such as Itztliteotl or Itzcuin may see an opportunity to spread mayhem among their former worshippers. Regardless of the cause, a wild, unanticipated lightning bolt strikes the ferrous object, awakening the long-buried servant of Orcus from her sleep. The suddenly rejuvenated black orc takes a round or two to cast defensive spells on herself before bursting forth from her coffin to rain death upon any who stand in her way.

Goodwill Points: Destroying the evil within the coffin earns the characters one goodwill point with each of the three groups — the Alaxpachas, the Thalus, and the Thayanas. If the mage survives the encounter, he tells the story to anyone willing to listen, giving the characters one more goodwill point for the Alaxpacha. If the characters keep the farmers alive and restore at least one slain farmer back to life, the Thalus praise the characters, earning them one more goodwill point with the Thalus. If the characters refuse to heal any injured Poqozas or raise at least one of the dead Poqozas, the characters lose one goodwill point.

EVENT ENCOUNTER 2:
THE PLAGUE OF TEETH

The characters catch up to a traveling band of Thayana to learn of the surrounding lands. One of the hunters warns the characters to step away. In the distance, the characters hear the wailing and pleading of the rest of the small group.

> You have been following the trail for a few days. You seem to be gaining ground on the Thayana ahead only to notice the telltale warning signs of a quarantine on the trail. A lone hunter stands behind the sign and gestures not to come any closer. He silently uses several hand signals to indicate that the way beyond is too dangerous, and all must turn back. He turns at the keening wail of another in the camp located ahead in the taller grass. He turns back, tears filling his eyes.

The hand signals are part of a regional sign language known as Hunter's Argot. The Thayana use the silent form of communication while hunting prey. The code contains only a handful of words and phrases pertaining to the hunt. Therefore, it takes only a successful DC 15 Intelligence check to get the gist of its meaning. The language has its roots in Thieves' Cant. Someone versed in that language has advantage on Intelligence checks made to understand Hunter's Argot.

The vague admonitions and warning can be attributed to the ancient curse the Alcati family stumbled upon in the high grass when traveling near Mulla Chanacu. They are growing an extraordinary number of teeth not just in their mouths, but on their fingers and toes, and more recently on their torsos. Several family members have died from the curse.

If the characters ignore the warning and investigate, they encounter a lone sentry (LN male Poqoza half-elf **scout** armed with a spear instead of a shortsword). The characters can slip past the concerned guard using their stealth or persuade him to let them pass. If the characters view the gathering, they see a tormented family huddled together in a tight circle. A man and a woman (N male and female Poqoza half-elf **druids**) equipped with a small chisel and hammer move from person to person. Using these implements, they chip the teeth loose from the skin in a sickening scene of blood and gore. They throw the extracted teeth into the fire with a plaintive prayer asking for relief from Tlatlcolli.

The characters find the family grateful for any assistance they can offer. Removing the teeth is a straightforward yet painful process requiring the character to succeed on a DC 10 Wisdom (Medicine) check. Any individual who has proficiency with the use of either tool gains advantage on the check. After extracting the teeth, the two healers tell the characters to throw them into the fire. Some family members have 100 extra teeth, while others have up to 600. Most are molars, though some incisors and canines also protrude from the raw skin. An extraction causes a popping sound that leaves a small pool of blood and a fading, throbbing pain until the next tooth pops through to add to the torture.

There is no monster to fight during this encounter. It takes time to calm the 41 remaining Alkatiri tribespeople (various alignments, male and female Poqoza half-elf **scouts** armed with spears instead of shortswords) as they work to help ease the suffering. Before the curse, the Alkatiri numbered a little over 300. Now they are a shadow of their former selves. The ones left behind offer tears, songs, and prayers to Tlatlcolli to end the misfortune. The healers tell the characters that anyone who grows more than 1,000 teeth dies an agonizingly horrific death. The teeth grow from the nails of the outer extremities first, then move to sprout out of the head and mouth. In the final stages, the canines and incisors mostly emerge from the torso around the belly.

The curse they suffer is from wandering too close to the baleful effects the nihileth produces in the Mulla Chanacu, but they think they have offended Tlatlcolli or even one of the older Aztli gods by slaying an albino deer. The Thayana elder Illa Qullqi (N male Poqoza half-elf **priest**, replace *spiritual weapon* with *augury* on his list of spells) still holds the skull and pelt of the beast in his pack. He is trying to commune with the gods to find the way to pay penance for their misdeed.

The characters can help Illa Qullqi and the two healers with the removal of the protruding teeth and alleviating the curse against their band. A character with the ability to cast *remove curse* or spells with similar effects can rid one person of the curse. Magical healing that cures hit points rids the person of a number of teeth equal to 10 times the number of hit points healed. If the spell rids the person of all their teeth, the curse is lifted. Spells that do not cure damage stop any new teeth from forming for a number of days equal to the level of the spell.

Illa Qullqi cast multiple *augury* spells, yet his stubbornness and insistence upon performing an atonement for the slain albino deer clouds his judgment. If the characters perform an *augury* spell or similar divination magic, they learn that the curse can be magically removed or by drinking a tea brewed from the stems of the totencaxihuitl plant, which the characters can locate with a successful DC 15 Intelligence (Nature) check. Despite the breakthrough, any magic short of a *wish* spell does not reveal the true source of the curse.

Goodwill Points: If the characters save more than half of the group, award them one goodwill point for the Thayana. If the characters rid the people of the curse in its entirety, award them an additional goodwill point for the Thayana

EVENT ENCOUNTER 3:
HERDING THE CAIMAN

The caimans live along the eastern edge of the grasslands where the marshes bleed over into the Sea of Green. Grassland residents use the scaly beasts for food and leather products. The characters become embroiled in a rigorous dispute over who has the right to the largest pelt any of them has ever seen.

A pair of representatives from each of the three societal strata of the grasslands all lay claim to the deathblow that felled the mighty caiman they are cooking. The beast was 37 feet long and had killed many humans and other humanoids during its long life. However, the crocodilian's luck finally ran out as it happened to be in the wrong place at the wrong time. Each pair of Poqozas has a legitimate claim on the skin.

The first pair are Alaxpachas (N male Poqoza half-elf **mages**, replace *ice storm* and *cone of cold* with *dimension door* and *teleport* on their spell list) who ventured to this location to kill the massive reptile to study its anatomy and use parts of it in their magical experiments. They portended the beast's appearance in this very spot by correctly interpreting the omens in the sky. They struck the beast down with a mighty *lightning bolt* that singed the high grass near the bank of a languid creek.

The second pair are Thalus. They normally would not venture into the grasslands to hunt caiman, but the father and son used the opportunity as a bonding experience. They used an old hunting technique the older man learned from his father when he was a boy. They cornered the caiman into a garrote they laid where they knew it had to go. The rope anchored the beast as they closed in with knives.

The third pair are Thayanas who have extensive experience capturing and killing these reptilian beasts. They know what these creatures are thinking before they do. They tracked the caiman to this spot and threw their javelins to strike the beast in one of its great yellow eyes, effectively blinding it.

The three factions cajole the characters to take their side in this dispute over the course of the evening. Each tells the tale from their perspective, treating the other individuals as if they were not there at all. The Thalus and Thayanas dismiss the lightning strike as a minor distraction and even claim that it was a natural event rather than a manmade occurrence. The Thayanas downplay the garrote as a mere nuisance that got in the way of their javelins. They also scoff at the notion that foolish novices had any chance in Miquito of killing the creature. The Thalus are still feeling the adrenaline surge from their first successful hunt.

The arguments drag on well into the night. The character may offer any commentary or judgment they want including presiding over the discussion as if it were a legal matter. Without the characters' intervention, the trio of groups ultimately agree to divide the skin into equal shares. Everyone partakes in the delicious meal, with the Thalus complementing the dish with maize flour tortillas, while the Alaxpachas add herbs and spices to the meat to further enhance its flavor. With the night and fire winding down, the Alaxpachas nonchalantly walk over to the skin to admire it. As soon as an opportunity presents itself, one casts *teleport* on the skin, while the other casts *teleport* on them to escape with their prize. The Alaxpacha pair live in a large town far from this location. The pair possess an associated item from their intended destination to ensure that they arrive on target.

The *teleport* spell requires only a verbal command, which makes it difficult to notice what the mages are up to by the skin. However, if a character readies an action to stop the mages from casting their spells, they can attempt it. While the mages can likely best the Thalus and Thayanas, the characters present a significant challenge. They attempt to weasel their way out of a sticky situation by claiming they were going to return the skin intact after showing it to their colleagues or by concocting another plausible yet false explanation. The Thalus and Thayanas naturally want to punish the treacherous pair by forcing them to relinquish their share of the skin or teach them a brutal lesson. Nonetheless, none of the participants believes the skin is more valuable than someone's life, forcing them to ultimately reach a mutually agreeable resolution to the situation.

Goodwill Points: If the characters prevent the mages from stealing the skin, award them one goodwill point for both the Thalus and Thayanas. The two groups then come to an agreement between themselves over who gets to take home the skin. Preventing the Alaxpacha from taking their prize causes the loss of one goodwill point for the Alaxpachas as they retreat. If the characters aid the Alaxpacha plan, they gain one goodwill point for the Alaxpachas. Of course, siding with the Alaxpachas causes the loss of one goodwill point with the Thalus and Thayanas unless the characters' intervention in the matter goes unnoticed by both or either party.

Treasure: If the characters end up with the caiman skin, it is worth 800 gp. The skull also completes part of the list for the earlier **Skulls** adventure hook.

EVENT ENCOUNTER 4: THE DEVIL OF THE MERCHANTS

Aitayna made a name for himself by robbing merchants. He and his growing band of gnoll underlings have taken down quite a few pochtecas in their time. Some traders go so far as to take out "Aitayna insurance" when shipping large quantities of grain from one place to another.

The Alaxpachan train is not the normal grain shipment he is used to, and Aitayna knows it. The defenders used powerful magic and killed a few of his gnolls before the devil killed the pochteca escorts with *chain lightning* from a scroll he had socked away for years. Aitayna is a **salt devil** (see **Appendix A: New Monsters**) and is becoming supremely confident with his efforts at building his small, portable empire. A foolish warlock summoned him to the "green place" a decade ago, and he has remained here ever since. Unwilling to share his loot or his power with his infernal kin, Aitayna never called for aid from other devils. He would rather die a prince than live as a commoner. In furtherance of his ambitions, Aitayna soon took over a gang of gnoll raiders that feast on travelers and merchants in the grasslands' numerous pockets of lawlessness.

In this case, the avaricious devil feels obliged to take everything of value from these merchants because they forced him to use a scroll he had been saving for a rainy day. For this score, Aitayna changed his routine and decided to rob this band of merchants traveling south from Zacatl on a rarely used trail through the grasslands. After discussing the situation with his **gnoll slaver** (see **Appendix A: New Monsters**) lieutenant, they agreed that a group trekking along such a backwater trail likely carried something of great value or illicit goods, which are likely one and the same. Along with the **8 gnolls** who now accompany them, they picked off several guards and now have the survivors surrounded. Aitayna is about to cast *darkness* on a stone and throw it into the middle of the defenders when the characters first arrive. With the gnolls' attention focused elsewhere, the characters have advantage on Dexterity (Stealth) checks made to take the gnolls in the rearguard by surprise. They are lying on the ground waiting for their salt devil leader to plunge the defenders into darkness.

Discipline keeps the gnolls from attacking until the devil's signal, but if the characters interfere, all bets are off. The gnolls currently have their longbows in hand, readying an attack for the moment they see a defender emerge from the darkness. The defenders include 2 Poqoza guards (NE male Poqoza half-elf **spies** armed with macuahuitls [see **Appendix C: New Equipment and Magic Items**] instead of shortswords) and a Poqoza druid (NE male Poqoza half-elf **druid**). The 8 laborers (N male Poqoza half-elf **commoners**) with the group are laden with goods, making them ineffective for combat. If the characters come to the group's rescue, the Poqozas fight alongside the characters. Characters who foolishly opt to assist the gnolls and salt devil encounter fleeting allies who turn on their benefactors the first chance they get, which is whenever the characters suggest getting any spoils from the raid.

Goodwill Points: Destroying Aitayna earns the characters one goodwill point for the Thalus. The characters soon discover the Alaxpacha druid and

spies are minions of a wealthy landowner to the south who belongs to a seedier criminal cartel in Zacatl that traffics in psychoactive plants, tobacco, and some deadly poisons. If the characters help the Poqozas escape this dicey situation, the characters gain one goodwill point for the Alaxpachas. If they help deliver the merchandise, they gain one more goodwill point for the Alaxpachas. However, the Poqozas in this encounter are inherently evil, which creates its own moral dilemma for good characters, especially exalted heroes and those in the service of a good deity.

Treasure: The goods include six jugs of pulque worth 100 gp each, eight jugs of honey wine worth 20 gp each, six crates of tobacco worth 100 gp each, three doses of assassin's blood, two doses of truth serum, and one dose of wyvern poison.

EVENT ENCOUNTER 5: FIRE IN THE DELL

A rare day without rain feels like a minor blessing, until the smell of black smoke chokes the air. A raid on a hunters' camp leads to animosity between two groups.

This is the site of a Thalu potato farm run by the Qinaya family. Hinayana Qinaya, the leader of this farm, captured and killed several hunting dogs of a Thayana hunting party that trespassed on his property and dug up his potatoes. Hinayana and his fieldworkers issued several warnings to the dogs' owners to stay away from potatoes and their prized rat terriers renowned for their ability to sniff out vermin and other pests. However, the untrained dogs and their owner refused to heed the warnings, which ultimately forced Hinayana's hand.

The hunters did not take the slight lightly. Instead of targeting Hinayana directly, they chose to attack his prized possession — his landmark villa. The two-story structure made from wood imported from the neighboring Toctli Forest is an architectural marvel. Indeed, the magnificent home attracts the interest of sightseers and architects alike. In an act of revenge, the Thayanas tossed a torch onto the back of the home in a deliberate attempt to burn it and its occupants to the ground.

The wood burns slowly, but the flames capture the attention of 2 **fire phantoms** (see **Appendix A: New Monsters**) who venture from the Plane of Fire to partake in the conflagration. The monsters immediately incinerate the stunned arsonists, while the remainder of their company flee for their lives. Meanwhile, Hinayana and his family members desperately try to douse the blaze before it destroys the home in its entirety. They feverishly lower a bucket into a well behind the property and are poised to splash its contents onto the timbers as quickly as possible. However, the fire phantoms stand in their way. The characters have 2 minutes to defeat the fire phantoms, which would give the firefighters enough time to save the home from certain destruction. Of course, if the characters have a means of extinguishing the conflagration, they may attempt to do so as well. In addition to saving the residence, two young, frightened children remain trapped in the building, unable to escape because of the blinding smoke starting to fill its hallways and rooms.

Goodwill Points: Defeating the fire phantoms earns the characters one goodwill point for the Thalus. If the characters save the home and the children, they gain one more goodwill point for the Thalus.

Treasure: If the characters succeed at these tasks, the family invites them to attend a victory feast. Before the celebration ends, Hinayana presents them with *+1 ollixalli* armor (see **Appendix C: New Equipment and Magic Items**). This armor functions as chain mail except it is made from hardened rubber rather than metal. It is a family heirloom that has been handed down for generations, much like the villa the characters saved.

ENCOUNTER 5
1 Square – 10 Feet
N

Event Encounter 6: The Lost Children of the Chuxuntana

The emaciated boys greet the characters with a distilled liquor made from fermented walnuts in tiny cups woven from the grass. The one pouring from the flask tells them his name is Cachana, and the other two are his cousins, Ziegler and Zemsky. They have lived their entire lives in the tall grass. They beg for information about the outside world, which they happily exchange for stories about this area. The boys have intimate knowledge of the region and its history, teasing the characters with the tale of a big cat that murders Poqozas in their sleep.

The boys tell the characters whatever they want to hear, moving from one tall tale to the next with the greatest of ease. Despite their propensity for telling fibs, the boys have no talent for making their stories sound true. However, they are so engrossed with the conversation that they make it uncomfortable for the characters to discreetly terminate the conversation and leave. While the characters talk to them, a successful DC 10 Wisdom (Perception) check notices tiny thorns growing out of the boys' chubby, cherubic faces. In addition, their eyes, which initially looked hazel, now resemble polished pieces of wood.

The boys are not menacing in any way, though they act right on the edge of disturbing. Ziegler plays with a small knife, stabbing in quick succession between his fingers splayed out wide on the dirt floor. However, he sheaths the knife when politely asked to do so. Zemsky keeps looking outside, giving the impression he knows exactly when and where the next lightning bolt will strike. Cachana smiles good-naturedly and continues to pour out small draughts of the intoxicating liquor — if only for himself.

Cachana is the most gregarious of the group. He truly wants to know about the outside world. He trades stories of his mother deeper in the tallgrass, and how she does not like strangers around here. He offers to lead the characters out of this area of tallgrass and away from his mother, though he refuses to elaborate on his offer or provide any details about his mother. He leads characters who unquestioningly accept his offer past his "Mother" in the upcoming **Encounter Event 7: Mother of the Tallgrass** to a safe location in the grasslands where he and his cousin harmlessly part ways with the characters. However, if the characters discuss any terms of his offer with him, he casually rescinds the bargain, telling the characters he was only joking as he is just a boy. During the course of the conversation, he eventually puts his foot into his mouth when he tells them about the dead tree where his father died, and how his mother loves the tree more than any of her children. He awkwardly smiles while he conveys that unpleasant detail.

While the boys tell stories, the characters notice more of the thin boys emerging from the tallgrass into the trampled clearing. They sit out in the rain with smiles on their faces, catching the falling raindrops on their tongues and drinking them. When there are 14 boys in the clearing, read or paraphrase the following description:

At this juncture, the characters now stare down 14 **children of the briar** (see **Appendix A: New Monsters**). During the combat, the boys click in a foreign tongue as they assess the characters' potential strengths and weaknesses. They then attempt to entangle the characters as soon as possible while spitting thorns at them.

Goodwill Points: The mischievous boys have attacked many of the surrounding farms and game animals. If the characters bring proof of the death of a child of the briar to any nearby Thalu farm or Thayana hunting party, award them one goodwill point for that group. The characters can gain a goodwill point from both groups. This encounter feeds directly into **Event Encounter 7: Mother of the Tallgrass**.

Treasure: The flask Cachana pours the liquor from is made using a rare and presumably lost technique. It is worth 100 gp.

Event Encounter 7: Mother of the Tallgrass

"Mother" is a **duskthorn dryad** (see **Appendix A: New Monsters**). The characters' natural instinct may be to rescue the woman being dragged into the dome. However, the vines are intended to drag her into a better defensive position within the area. To further the ruse, she may attempt to charm a character into saving her or suggest that a character follow her into the dome. Mother uses her magical abilities to remain out of sight by turning invisible or obscuring the characters' vision by filling the air with fog. She leaves the melee combat to her guardian, a **vine troll skeleton** (see **Appendix A: New Monsters**) that lies in wait just inside the grass curtain. It lashes out at the characters when they pass through the curtain.

If the characters present her with any evidence of the child of the briar's demise, she appears upset for a moment before quickly moving on from the tragedy.

Goodwill Points: If the characters tell anyone in the Caxcalli Grasslands that they defeated the Mother of the Tallgrass, they are welcomed into the person's home or business, where they receive food, drink, and a bed, if available. In addition, they gain one goodwill point with the individual's group. They can retell the tale to each of the three strata, though they never receive more than one goodwill point from a single strata.

The base of "Mother's" main tree, the one with origins of her creeper vines that infest the area, holds a locked, trapped chest.

Treasure: The chest contains gold ingots worth 2,400 gp and a set of jade and amber chess pieces. Each piece is two inches across at the base and nearly four inches tall. One bishop and one queen are missing. Each piece is worth 20 gp for a total of 600 gp. The two missing pieces and the board are in **Area 1-D**.

Event Encounter 8: Strange Weather

> Clouds gather in the east as the sun is about to set in the opposite direction. A storm appears to be brewing. As night falls across the land, the first raindrops hit the ground. Several minutes later, a subtle yet noticeable sizzling sound accompanies the precipitation. In an even more disturbing development, odd croaking sounds now drown out the rain.

The effects of the nihileth on the rain patterns in the southwest are unearthly. Acid rain falls nearly every time a storm develops in the lee of the Mulla Chanacu. The acid rain deals no damage to creatures, but 10 minutes of exposure to the caustic liquid deals 1 point of acid damage to nonmagical objects. The grass in this area has adapted to the change in weather. It is hardier and more resistant to the acid than typical grass species in the region. The fauna is also very limited, with burrowing animals making up the majority of its population.

This freakish storm also picked up some small travelers: 10 **swarms of poisonous frogs** (see **Appendix A: New Monsters**). The winds lifted the tiny amphibians roughly 40 feet in the air. The downdraft that pushed them back to earth deals 4d6 bludgeoning damage to the swarm. The roiling mass of poisonous frogs attacks anything in their path, biting living creatures with reckless fury. After 1d4 + 1 rounds, the creatures break off the assault and make their way to the closest puddle of standing water.

Goodwill Points: No goodwill points are available for this encounter.

Event Encounter 9: Strange Weather II – The Reckoning

Torrential rain sometimes spawns flash flooding in the grasslands. In this case, a sudden deluge combined with saturated ground and swollen rivers gives birth to a raging flash flood.

> Rain pounds the earth, drowning out all sound or so it would seem. A dull roar emanating somewhere in the distance rapidly draws closer. Moments later, a wave of four-foot-high water surges across the land as several panicked animals feebly try to outrun the onrushing water.

The raging waters are four feet high and measure 180 feet wide as the mindless body follows the path of least resistance across the intervening terrain. When the characters first notice the water, it is roughly 1d3 x 100 feet away and traveling at a speed of 100 feet per round, giving the characters potentially up to three rounds to evade the massive hazard. When a creature enters the floodwaters for the first time on a turn or starts its turn there, it must succeed on a DC 15 Strength saving throw or take 9 (2d8) bludgeoning damage, get knocked prone, and get pushed back 1d10 x 10 feet in the same direction as the current. On a successful saving throw, the creature remains upright in the same spot and takes no damage. A character swept away by the current takes 4 (1d8) bludgeoning damage at the start of each of its turns spent in the floodwaters. Furthermore, the creature must hold its breath while underwater. It can regain its footing with a successful DC 15 Strength (Athletics) check or Dexterity

(Acrobatics) check. If the creature regains its footing, it is not prone nor being swept away by the current that round.

If a character makes a successful Strength saving throw, it has advantage on all subsequent Strength saving throws against this hazard. The flash flood area is treated as difficult terrain. On its turn, a creature who succeeds on a DC 10 Strength check can move toward safety. On a failed check, the creature makes no progress. Creatures moving in the direction of the current have advantage on the preceding check, while those moving directly against the current suffer disadvantage. Creatures moving in neither direction make their checks normally. A creature with a swim speed can move through the water without making a check unless it swims against the current, which requires a successful DC 10 Strength (Athletics) check. On a failure, the floodwaters impede the creature's progress.

The floodwaters automatically sweep away any loose, unattended objects in their path. The deluge has carried off a frenzied **weasel**, a nest of 5 **scorpions**, and a **swarm of poisonous snakes** that attack any nearby creatures, including the characters.

Goodwill Points: No goodwill points are available for this encounter.

Event Encounter 10:
I am the Rat God

Capybara, nutria, cavies, and chinchilla roam the grasslands, destroying crops in civilized lands, but providing protein for creatures further up the food chain. These rodents usually gather in small groups of their own and feed on plants and grains they can find. One larger group follows and worships an ichneumon, a massive weasel who sometimes eats its followers, but mostly scares away larger predators to allow the ordinary rodents a near paradise in a warden of small burrows away from civilization.

The **ichneumon** (see **Appendix A: New Monsters**) disappears into one of the hundreds of burrows riddling this area. The large beast can only enter the honeycomb's larger tunnels, though these passages ultimately connect to the smaller one the rodents use during the course of their daily travels.

The monster and the 185 rodents under its sway (use the **rat** statistics) are not itching for a fight against the characters. It waits below, hoping to detect the presence of a dragon, its ancient blood enemy. In the interim, the creature relies upon its rodent spies to gather intelligence about the unexpected trespassers. The rodents periodically emerge from their holes to keep tabs on the characters. They use high pitched shrills and other sounds to communicate their findings to each other and the ichneumon. The racket is so disruptive that characters attempting to maintain their concentration do so with disadvantage. Furthermore, the characters suffer disadvantage on Wisdom (Perception) checks relying on hearing. If the characters attempt to explore any tunnel or attack a rodent, the reluctant ichneumon emerges from its hiding spot and attacks the aggressor. As previously mentioned, the creature does not relish a confrontation with the adventurers. If seriously wounded, it retreats into a tunnel, hoping the characters opt not to follow it.

Treasure: If chased underground and cornered, the ichneumon nonverbally offers the characters a green dragon egg to broker a truce. The egg is nearly ready to hatch. The ichneumon uses its rodent followers to incubate the egg until the wyrmling inside hatches. The ichneumon considers the tasty treat a rare delicacy. If the characters accept the ichneumon's offer, the egg is worth 2,000 gp.

Goodwill Points: If the characters defeat the ichneumon, the hunters of the grasslands soon find out about the death of one of their wily foes. Grant the characters one goodwill point for the Thayana.

Chapter Two:
Social Business

When the characters accumulate four goodwill points for a single group, a coterie of representatives from that group approaches them. If the characters complete all the event encounters without garnering four goodwill points, they are met by members of the group with the most goodwill points

The Poqozas taste samples of all the dishes to reassure the characters that they are not poisoned. The hosts reiterate that they are here to praise their honored visitors rather than harm them. The Poqozas refuse to sit at the table until the

characters do so first. The man who first introduced himself explains to them that his name is Oacce. He leads a small community in the area that has fallen on hard times. He and his people require the expertise of brave heroes to eradicate the blight plaguing their lands. The nature of the evil depends upon which strata the representatives belong — the Thalus, the Thayanas, or the Alaxpachas.

Alaxpacha Final Encounter:
Invaders! Within and Without

Characters partaking in the **Medical Mission of Mercy** hook may be surprised to learn that some of the rumors are true. A hobgoblin warship from distant Akados landed on these shores after their fellow goblinoids expelled them from their native homeland of Exor because of their heretical beliefs. To make matters worse, the Irpanuqana hobgoblins already met with the Achnis from the **Canals and Contracts** hook. The hobgoblins took their charge to explore the Caxcalli Grasslands as free rein to explore and conquer the region under their own banner. As they made their way inland, they used a combination of the Poqozas' proclivity for experimentation and an elixir of potent hobgoblin mead to sway some to their cause. The hobgoblins beat those Alaxpachas who refused to willingly forsake Tlatlcolli and embrace the invaders' newfangled religion. After several rounds of torture, they conscripted the resisters into forced labor camps where they toil day and night to build their fabled highway to riches outside the compound.

An unusually charismatic hobgoblin evangelist named Banc commands the military and religious expedition. The new faith he espouses is his belief in his own divinity, and he resorts to any means necessary to propagate his belief, including unspeakable acts of cruelty and barbarism. As proof of his godhood, he demonstrates his ability to cast powerful spells, an act he could not achieve without divine intervention. Of course, the arrogant Banc is a charlatan who cannot explain how he obtained his priestly powers. Unbeknownst to him, the Aztli god Itztliteotl took an interest in the conniving huckster. He grants the hobgoblin his magical powers to amuse himself and indirectly to spite the Poqozas and Tlatlcolli. Many Poqozas, including some of Tlatlcolli's priests, fell prey to his abundant charms and brutal tactics. As punishment for their lack of faith, the angry god condemned his former priests to an undead existence as huecuvas who are partly to blame for the illnesses afflicting the Poqozas.

The characters can get involved in this storyline in several ways. Characters who embarked on the **Medical Mission of Mercy** hook may actively be searching for victims and could even arrive here by canoe. Alternatively, the characters could run across sick Poqozas who either fled the evangelist's compound and its horrendous working conditions or were infected by the huecuvas' diseased claws. Despite their poor health, the infirmed Poqozas get squirrely discussing how and where they may have contracted the disease. None wants to tell their fellow half-elves about their dalliance with the hobgoblin's warped faith after they abandoned Tlatlcolli either willingly or through coercion. However, a character who succeeds on a Charisma (Persuasion) or Charisma (Intimidation) check contested by the individual's Wisdom (Insight) check may learn the truth about how that person contracted the illness. Because of their intense guilt and self-loathing, sick Poqozas have advantage on the proceeding check. Oacce may direct ask the characters to investigate or corroborate the stories coming from the hobgoblin compound. The characters could potentially encounter a hobgoblin patrol (see **Area E1-B** and use that opportunity to infiltrate the compound by claiming to be new converts or people who want to learn more about the evangelist and his burgeoning religion.

Regardless of how the characters get to the hobgoblin compound, read or paraphrase the following description when they arrive:

The 4 Poqozas laborers (various alignments, male Poqoza half-elf **commoners**) obviously seem underfed and overworked. A character who examines one of the workers and succeeds on a DC 10 Wisdom (Perception) check notices they conceal scorch marks and burns beneath their loose-fitting clothing. The men are terrified of the hobgoblins and their leader Banc. They refuse to converse with the characters unless compelled to do so through magic or a with successful DC 15 Charisma (Intimidation) check. Otherwise, they pontificate ad nauseum about the one true god — an individual they identify as Banc the Resplendent, Master of the Seas and Lord of the Lands. Other than prattling on about Banc's might and greatness, they cannot provide any details about the tenets of his religion. The grounds are currently quiet as the laborers in the field toil to construct the evangelist's roads and the patrols monitoring them search for fugitives and more converts.

AREA E1-A: THE BEACH

The Poqoza on the beach is the Alaxpacha who used to be in charge of the community. If the characters approach him, he tells of his deep sorrow.

Niya Qachana (N male Poqoza half-elf **mage**), the former Alaxpacha leader, sits on the beach every day lamenting his loss. The hobgoblins left him a broken man after their brazen pre-dawn raid, which caught him and his followers literally napping. The Irpanuqana hobgoblins led him to believe that they burned his spellbook and other possessions. However, the hobgoblins stole these objects along with the rest of his and the other Poqozas' possessions, which they now store in the compound's main building. The evangelist left him to wallow in his self-pity. The characters can rouse his spirits by succeeding on a Charisma (Persuasion) check contested by his Wisdom (Insight) check. If the characters already recovered his items, they have advantage on the preceding check. Otherwise, he seems content to take no actions other than to blubber about the loss of his people and his magical powers.

AREA E1-B: THE ROAD TO NOWHERE

After taking over the Alaxpacha compound, the evangelist immediately began constructing two roads. The first thoroughfare stretches north of the sand dunes on the southern beach and travels west toward the Toctli Forest, following an ancient, well-worn path. The trail is fairly flat with cobblestones marking its edges. The Poqoza laborers (various alignments, male Poqoza half-elf **commoners**) who toil on these endeavors use this first road to haul supplies and materials for the highway Banc believes is destined to lead him to fame and fortune. The evangelist took the Achnis' offer as described in the **Canals and Contracts** hook, yet he interpreted their offer to mean he had free rein not just to explore the Caxcalli Grasslands but to conquer it. Being an impulsive leader, the evangelist never bothered to survey his surroundings. Instead, he decided to build a path to Xicotli the instant he learned about the Poqoza city and its longstanding rivalry with his hobgoblin kin. Unfortunately for him, his path heads straight toward a vast swath of grass teeming with poison ivy. Despite the warnings from the Poqoza laborers familiar with the area, the evangelist dismissed their concerns out of hand as he declared that no patch of itchy weeds can stop him and his god. Those who express their opposition to his plans quickly vanish to an unknown fate.

The characters can intersect either of the six-foot-wide paths at any juncture along their route. At this point, the roads are merely earthen paths bordered by cobblestones. The laborers remove any debris, vegetation, and stones from the trail. The evangelist wants only to reach Xicotli to find more worshippers and exact his brand of hobgoblin revenge against the city's inhabitants. He cares not how he and his followers get there.

A team of 20 laborers languish at these miserable tasks. It is evident that they live in utter squalor, often sleeping on the dirt and eating meals unfit for livestock. To prevent them from escaping during the night, their captors bind their hands and feet. During the day, a patrol of 6 hobgoblin guards direct their activities while preventing any from escaping. These guards use the **veteran** statistics with the following changes:

• The hobgoblins are lawful evil.

• They are humanoid (goblinoids).

• Once per turn, the hobgoblin can deal an extra 7 (2d6) damage to a creature it hits with a weapon attack if that creature is within five feet of an ally of the hobgoblin that is not incapacitated.

• They have darkvision 60 ft.

• They have 1 level of exhaustion, giving them disadvantage on ability checks.

• The hobgoblins speak Common and Goblin.

In addition to monitoring the laborers under their command, they keep a watchful eye for fugitives, vandals, and potential new converts. A character who succeeds on a DC 10 Wisdom (Perception) check notices that the heat and humidity are taking a toll on the beleaguered guards, who wear heavy armor. If the characters attack them or attempt to free the laborers who are bound together by heavy ropes, the hobgoblins blow whistles attached to a leather strap dangling around their neck. When they sound the alarm, there is a 30% chance that another hobgoblin patrol of 6 guards arrives 1d4 minutes later to investigate the disturbance. In any event, the characters never encounter more

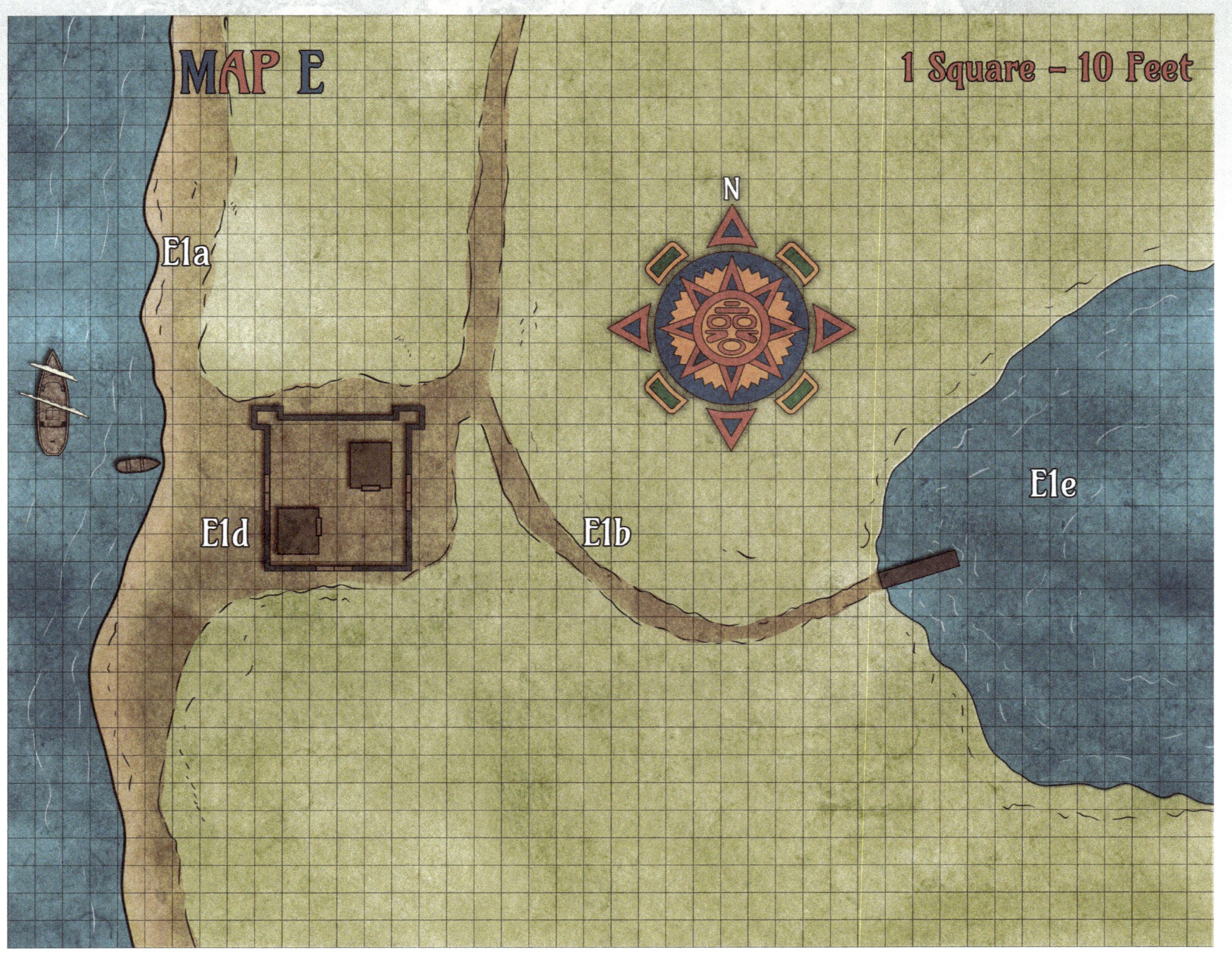

MAP E
1 Square = 10 Feet
N
E1a
E1d
E1b
E1e

than 18 hobgoblins in this manner. The patrols' leader is a brutal taskmaster named Achima. He uses the **gladiator** statistics with the following changes:

• Achima is lawful evil.
• He is a humanoid (goblinoid).
• Once per turn, he can deal an extra 7 (2d6) damage to a creature he hits with a weapon attack if that creature is within five feet of an ally of Achima that is not incapacitated.
• He has darkvision 60 ft.
• He speaks Common and Goblin.

Almost all of the Poqoza laborers and a handful of elves with them are malnourished, diseased, injured, or a combination of these conditions. When liberated, the emaciated laborers crowd around the adventurers as if they were Tlatlcolli himself, whom they credit for sending the adventurers to rescue them. Some suffer from the disease the huecuvas spread while others have fallen ill with influenza and several other contagions normally associated with filth, starvation, and fetid sanitary conditions. If the characters participated in the **Medical Mission of Mercy** hook, they may administer the powder they received at the beginning of the adventure to cure the Poqoza stricken by the disease spread by their former priests who fell under the evangelist's influence. Otherwise, the characters can use their magic, medical skills, and any supplies they have to tend to their wounds, feed them, and cure them of any ailments. If the characters do not have any powder on hand, residents of neighboring villages in the hobgoblins' future path provide them with a fresh supply of powder. In any case, you may award the characters a 500 XP story award for fulfilling their obligations to assist the sick and infirmed Poqozas.

AREA E1-C: THE ACOLYTES

Although labeled as an area, this encounter is intended to be a precursor to the characters' rendezvous with Banc. Therefore, its exact location depends upon the circumstances. If the characters explore the surrounding area, they encounter Ampeyo and Paysh, the acolytes, somewhere during their travels in the surrounding wilderness. If the characters proceed directly to **Area E1-D**, they meet them outside of the compound. Ampety and Paysh loyally serve Banc as his trusted lieutenants, but the pair secretly pray to Kakobovia while outwardly professing their faith in Banc as a self-proclaimed deity. They suspect

that Banc does the same, though they naturally fear raising the subject with him. Their doubts in Banc's divinity do nothing to lessen their enthusiasm and devotion to his grand plan and overall vision. The 2 **hobgoblin acolytes** (see **Appendix A: New Monsters**) carry out their orders with ruthless efficiency. At the moment, the pair is using their divination magic to discern what lies ahead for the hobgoblins in their adopted homeland. They seem concerned about the portents they recently witnessed, and the characters' arrival does nothing to temper their fears. A character who succeeds on a DC 20 Wisdom (Insight) check senses the acolytes' trepidation regarding the adventurers' unexpected appearance. When they notice the intrusion, the acolytes command the 6 **hobgoblins** accompanying them to attack the trespassers. The pair never surrenders, even in the face of superior opposition. The acolytes are intimately familiar with Banc's plans to build a road to Xicotli to facilitate its downfall. The characters may already be familiar with this plan too. On the other hand, they likely do not know that the hobgoblins plan to supplement their force with their hobgoblin kin already living on the island and are preparing to make overtures to the indigenous gnolls to join forces with them. Unfortunately for Banc and his hobgoblin allies, the gnolls would never willingly forsake Itzcuin for what they perceive to be an imaginary hobgoblin deity.

Treasure: The acolytes carry three jars of *restorative ointment* as insurance against contracting any disease, *black war paint* (see **Appendix C: New Equipment and Magic Items**), a pouch containing six pearls worth 100 gp each, and a small bag holding 18 pp.

AREA E1-D: THE EVANGELIST

The Irpanuqana hobgoblin evangelist **Banc** (see **Appendix A: New Monsters**) spreads death and controversy wherever he goes. Before his arrival in Tehuatl, Banc was a revered and respected priest of Kakobovia and served in Exor's armies in their endless battles against the dwarf clans in the Stoneheart Mountains. Banc grew weary of waging a repetitive war of attrition against these hated foes and lost faith in his god's narrowminded vision. Inspired by the warlord Grugdour and his ascendency, Banc took a page from his playbook and renounced his faith in Kakobovia. In his place, he declared himself to be a god.

Unlike Grugdour's ploy, Banc's fell flat on its face. He temporarily lost his ability to cast spells, and his heresy earned him the swift wrath of Exor's

traditionalist ruler, Teth Khan. In his haste to escape, Banc fled the city with his devoted entourage and headed for the coast, where he stole the moored vessel, *The Aviary*, and set sail on the open seas. He initially forced the ship's halfling crew to man the craft until he marooned them on a deserted island and took command himself. The novice navigator and his hobgoblin charges spent six months sailing *The Aviary* across the ocean with periodic stops along the way to "redistribute" supplies they found in far-flung ports of call before finally landing on Tehuatl's shores where they encountered the Achnis. By this time, Banc had regained his priestly powers thanks to Itztliteotl's intervention. Before departing for the southern coast of Tehuatl, he and his men burglarized a temple of Tlatlcolli and killed some of its clergymen in the process. The authorities used their magic to speak with those slain during the crime, giving them an accurate description of the perpetrators. Buoyed by the surprising restoration of his priestly powers, the deluded Banc now believes he can amass enough followers and coins to allow him to comfortably retire in the Caxcalli Grasslands, where he can lead a leisurely life of wanton excess.

When characters encounter him, Banc is dramatically preaching to a new batch of 17 followers (various alignments, male and female Poqoza half-elf **commoners**). These enthralled worshippers hang on Banc's every word, as they are unable to resist his persuasiveness and enchantment magic. Banc immediately responds to the intrusion by attempting to charm as many enemies as possible using his Proselytize ability. He uses his new thralls as human shields, imploring them to run interference for him, while 4 **hobgoblins** defend him against attacks. While survival is naturally first and foremost on Banc's mind, he secondarily wants to add more followers to his retinue rather than outright kill the characters. Nonetheless, if left with no other choice, Banc foregoes subdual and submission in favor of death. Although the hobgoblin evangelist believes himself to be a god, he is unwilling to find out for sure if he is reduced to less than 20 hit points. He pleads for mercy and offers to serve the characters if necessary. Unfortunately for the characters, Banc is a habitual liar who betrays them at the first opportunity. If the characters confront him about the rampant diseases spreading across the area, he admits the huecuvas are responsible for spreading some of the contagions while the others arose from the squalid conditions.

Treasure: Banc has a *staff of charming* in his arsenal along with two jars of *restorative ointment* he keeps on hand to ward off disease. His ship *The Aviary* is anchored 100 feet offshore. The vessel is barely seaworthy and would require extensive repairs and maintenance to bring it up to snuff. Nonetheless, it is worth 4,000 gp, though it is rightfully owned by a halfling family in Akados. It is currently defended by 6 **hobgoblins** who fight to the death. Banc keeps the spoils he burglarized from the temple of Tlatlcolli in a chest in his private quarters. The container holds 3,204 cacao beans worth 1 gp each, 602 gp, 1,923 sp, and a bronze figurine depicting Tlatlcolli worth 1,500 gp. A character who succeeds on a DC 5 Intelligence (Religion) check identifies the subject as the Poqozas' sole god. While there is no way to trace the cacao beans and coins back to the temple, selling the figurine south of the Great Canal is a dicey proposition that is likely to attract the interest of the god's worshippers looking for Banc and the pilfered loot.

Area E1-E: Staging Area

In one of the strangest and perhaps worst-planned plots, Banc and the hobgoblins plan to export the 8 **huecuvas** (see **Appendix A: New Monsters**) gathered here by sea to numerous areas throughout Tehuatl. So far, his scheme sounds plausible. However, with *The Aviary* on the brink of falling apart, Banc needed to find an alternative means of getting them to his targeted destinations. The hobgoblin evangelist thinks he can charm animals to do his dirty work, in this case 2 **killer whales**. Because the huecuvas are already dead and cannot drown, he plans to charm or train the killer whales into performing this task. So far, his efforts have proven unsuccessful. Meanwhile, Tlatlcolli's unfaithful undead priests attack the characters when they approach this area.

Thalu Final Encounter: Three Days of Darkness

Oacce tells the characters a tale of woe. He describes a rattling wail of unearthly origin that came from the tallgrass surrounding his village. His people thought it was the coming of Yahuitamotl. They set out offerings for the Storm Rider, hoping he would take them and move elsewhere. However, when the wailing moved toward the village and the destruction began, they knew Yahuitamotl had not paid them a visit. The costumed villagers ask the characters to rid them of the malevolence tormenting their community.

The village is a few days' travel from the feast, where Oacce and his fellow villagers wait until the adventurers expunge the evil from their lands.

> The morning after accepting Oacce's quest, the sun hides behind the clouds, refusing to appear as rain falls. Although it seems a normal occurrence, the sky seems darker and more ominous than a normal stormy morning. Rain continues to fall throughout the day as the weather turns unseasonably cold and dreary. Over the course of the day, the sun's absence duplicates the lighting conditions of twilight.
>
> The next morning, the sun continues to hide as the precipitation becomes viscous with syrupy drops clinging to every surface. A seemingly unnatural chill fills the air.
>
> The village Oacce described lies ahead, its fields of maize flattened, its huts in disarray, and scraps of detritus scattered throughout the farm. Nothing moves. Turkey and dog carcasses rot out in the open, and the corpses of several villagers lie on the bare earth. The rattling wail echoes throughout the farm, and the wind picks up as the jelly-like rain continues to fall.

Centuries ago, a doomsday Alaxpacha cult created a golem to exact their revenge against a village elder, now long deceased. They programmed the monster to attack when the sun disappeared from the sky, but the deranged cult's leader proved to be a better magician than an astronomer. The solar eclipse he predicted never came to pass before he and his quarry died. The sun's prolonged disappearance is attributable to a total solar eclipse caused by a massive gas giant that orbits the sun in a wide, elliptical path that causes this eclipse once every 345 to 1,235 years. The planet's enormous size completely blocks the sun and causes some gravitational shifts that alter weather patterns and plunge the land into darkness for three consecutive days.

While the predicted darkness has finally come to pass, the doomsday cult's **witch-doll golem** (see **Appendix A: New Monsters**) finds itself in the right place at the wrong time. With its intended target nowhere in sight, the construct attacks anyone and anything that gets in its way with its fists and needles. The monster appears doll-like with human skin stuffing, buttons for eyes, and crude stitching for a mouth. It wears rags and has a hangman's noose around its neck. Pins and needles protrude from its body where its vital organs would normally be found.

The Alaxpacha predicted the eclipse, calling it "Tucuchana Ithuithu." A character who recently interacted with an Alaxpacha may have learned of the impending eclipse with a successful DC 15 Charisma check. Otherwise, a character who succeeds on a DC 20 Intelligence (Nature) check recognizes the phenomenon as a solar eclipse. If the character succeeded on the previous check by 5 or more, that person identifies the enormous gas giant as the planet Nemini. That character also knows that its appearance is also sometimes associated with the coming of a new sun.

Treasure: The designers wove gold filaments into the golem's body. Harvesting the bands takes 30 minutes, but the materials are worth 1,000 gp.

Thayana Final Encounter: Ghost Dance

Oacce tells the characters about a malevolent spirit that possessed his family's ticitl, a practitioner of traditional Aztli medicine. The ticitl named Amacaina and Oacce's hunting party recently captured the leader of a rival hunting party that habitually trespassed on their lands and even tried to steal their kills on several occasions. Amacaina uses the **priest** statistics with the following changes:

She is chaotic evil.

She wears hide armor and is AC 12.

She is armed with a dagger.

She has *animate dead* instead of *spirit guardians* as one of her 3rd-level spells.

She speaks Aztli and Elvish.

Amacaina told the family she intended to terrify the captive leader by performing an ancient ritual her grandfather taught her decades ago that opened the gates to the realm of spirits, something Oacce and his counterparts greatly feared and warned against performing. Nonetheless, Amacaina proceeded with her idea despite the potentially dire consequences of doing so. Oacce now appeals to the characters to save their ticitl as well as their rival to avoid escalating the situation and unleashing something none of them can stop or control. While Oacce believes their rivals gravely offended his people and need to make reparations, he also thinks Amacaina is taking the feud too far.

Ixana, a **lamia**, has sporadically kept tabs on the ticitl for years. She has slowly converted Amacaina to embrace evil thoughts and vile inclinations. The transformation was subtle at first, but over time Ixana has charmed her way into exerting greater influence over Amacaina's actions, culminating in her first murder of a warrior from the rival hunting party. She lured the warrior into the wilderness with the promise of a tryst and then ambushed him with a garrote that she used to strangle him. Amacaina collected some blood and hair and tried to animate the dead body, but she lacked the skill to restore the slain warrior to an undead existence. Frustrated by her failure, she buried the corpse in a shallow grave near a creek bed. Fortunately for her and Oacce's family, a hungry jaguar smelled the fresh kill and partially devoured the unearthed body, which led to the hunting party blaming the big cat for the tragedy.

The rival Thayana parties have a long history of animosity from sparring over the same hunting grounds. The conflict has spurred minor raids and other petty acts of vengeance, yet neither group seems willing to cede the coveted territory to their foes and move into unknown lands elsewhere. Oacce almost convinced his group to leave once, but Amacaina talked them into staying. A week ago, their rivals finally crossed the point of no return when they accidentally killed Amacaina's son in a surprise attack while he was sleeping. When she saw her son's lifeless body, Amacaina swore to avenge his death. Ixana overheard her furious mutterings and blasphemous cries to the heavens and saw the perfect opportunity to convince her protégé to fully embrace her evil side.

This morning, Amacaina captured Amriuhu (N male Poqoza half-elf **scout**), the rival group's leader, and keeps him hogtied inside her abode. She spent the day sewing hides together and chanting over him as she sliced his flesh more than 200 times as part of a gory ritual long forbidden within her culture and by Tlatlcolli. When the sun set, she wrapped Amriuhu in her cinched hide bag and dragged him over a roaring fire so the heat could evaporate the moisture in the hides and crush the tortured person wrapped inside the bag.

The characters arrive on the scene as Amacaina calls down bolts of lightning from the clouds as she dances in a contorted manner to a melody only she can hear. The wounded Amriuhu struggles to breathe inside the bag, hastening the torturous ritual. Amacaina is also not alone, as 2 **greater shadows** (see **Appendix A**) who share her interest in spreading chaos and evil hover nearby in the shadows beyond the fiery light. Their malevolence seems to capture and suppress some of the radiance emanating from the flames as they seem to taste the victim's lifeforce ebbing from him. Although normally confined to the maizefields of Miquito (the Land of the Dead), Ixana's ritual inexplicably summoned them to this location.

Ixana also gleefully watches from the darkness. She feels her time with her ticitl is drawing to a close. She waits to say goodbye to Amacaina until after Amriuhu finally succumbs to the pressure of the shrinking hides and the heat. She swears she heard several bones snapping and faint, wracking wails over the crackling of the flames caressing the hide bag as it dips lower into the blaze.

When the characters arrive, the rest of the villagers are nowhere to be found. Amacaina's grisly ritual and her unearthly associates scared everyone away except for one young Poqoza woman who bizarrely smiles at the spectacle. She is Ixana, who is disguised as a female humanoid. The participants are so engrossed in their ritualistic killing that they suffer disadvantage on their Wisdom (Perception) checks. The characters can interrupt the ritual by physically preventing Amacaina from performing her frenetic dance. If they do so for more than three rounds, the lightning stops and the cloud dissipate. If the characters fail to stop the ritual in less than one minute after they first see Amacaina, Amriuhu dies and is reborn as a **cinder ghoul** (see **Appendix A: New Monsters**).

Naturally, the shadows, the lamia, and Amacaina do not take kindly to the intrusion. They immediately attack the characters. The greater shadows hide in the darkness then lash out at their foes to sap their strength from them. Ixana casts *mirror image* on herself and then rakes her adversaries with her claws and dagger. Amacaina is a less-formidable combatant than her counterparts. She tries to keep her distance from the characters while striking at them from afar with her ranged spells. Ixana's primary goal is self-preservation, though she is unlikely to outrun the characters. She may attempt to bargain with the adventurers for mercy. The greater shadows and the now-disgraced Amacaina fight to the bitter end.

If the characters save Amriuhu, they may attempt to finally resolve the long-standing dispute between the rival hunting parties. Characters who drive off the lamia, shadows, and Amacaina can find Oacce and tell him his home is now safe. Read or paraphrase the following description of this interaction:

Oacce smiles sadly as the characters tell him about the carnage in his village.

"At least the horror is over," he grimly says.

The other brightly decorated Poqoza hunters shuffle back to what remains of their homes with their masks in hand and their costumes in disarray. Any semblance of normalcy appears to bring them comfort.

Chapter Three: Telling the Tale of the Storm Rider

Oacce is pleased as he enthusiastically shakes the characters' hands. He gently bows while he profusely thanks the heroes for freeing his community and people from the menaces that threatened their lives. He is not a wealthy man by any means, though he does have a trick up his sleeve or — more accurately — tethered to his shoulder. He unstraps a leather case containing eight stoppered vials.

Treasure: The stoppered vials are a potion of clairvoyance, a potion of diminution, a potion of gaseous form, a potion of giant strength (hill), a potion of greater healing, a potion of superior healing, a potion of mind reading, and a potion of water breathing.

If a character searches the case itself and succeeds on a DC 19 Wisdom (Perception) check, that individual finds a hidden compartment within the case that contains an ornate ring of regeneration carved from bone in the likeness of an open-mouthed skull.

Before Oacce and the villagers depart, they have one more request. Read or paraphrase the following:

Oacce and the villagers must devote their energies to rebuilding their communities and cannot take a prolonged overland trip to the center of the Caxcalli Grasslands. However, they know how to get to the mysterious laboratory where the odd traveler found the leather case and claimed the storm activity was the greatest. They also convey a brief history about the Mulla Chanacu and its otherworldly origin. Every young Poqoza must venture there to transition from a boy into a man or a girl into a woman.

The trip to the laboratory goes uneventfully unless you want to spice up the journey with some early encounters that the characters previously missed. Although the monstrous activity seems low, the same cannot be said about the weather. The winds howl and the rain falls with greater intensity as the characters get closer to the laboratory.

The sun reappears after being gone for three full days. The rain thins to its normal consistency, and the ground warms with the first rays of light. A birdsong shatters the still and awakens the harmonious nature of the tallgrass. Soon, the pace of life resets, and life in the Grasslands returns to its normal tempo, balancing the violent nature of the food chain and the peaceful grandeur of untouched beauty of the savanna.

Area 1-A: Laboratory Entrance

The laboratory of Elix Cucita lies on the southwest corner of the Mulla Chanacu. Elix established the facility on the principle of sharing the shori huasca. He designed the structures and grounds asymmetrically, with scrolling curved themes and sculpted molding with theatrical pastel colors to create surprise and the illusion of motion. Very soft edges and natural curves, eroded over time, emphasize the childlike wonder of the compound.

Elix built the laboratory into the side of a hill. The exposed area outside covers about 1,600 square feet of gated courtyards where Poqozas under the influence of the hallucinogenic fungi sit and converse about esoteric subjects and transcendental thoughts while still protected from the elements. Colorful tents and refreshing fountains took up the courts Elix did not fashion into gardens. Isolated shreds of fabric and crumbled stonework represent all that is left of that earlier time. The courtyard is completely devoid of life, including the omnipresent insects. A small, roofless outbuilding in the southeast corner of one of the courts is empty. The doors leading into the laboratory are 15 feet tall and made of thick oak. They are flung open.

If the characters survey the surrounding landscape and succeed on a DC 21 Wisdom (Perception) check, they see a hidden cave located in another low hill roughly one-half mile away. Strange tracks make deep impressions along a muddy trail from a lagoon on the outskirts of the Mulla Chanacu into the laboratory's back entrance (Area 1-G). Yahuitamotl lets a small outpost of cueyatls live here to protect his lair and to worship and care for his mount.

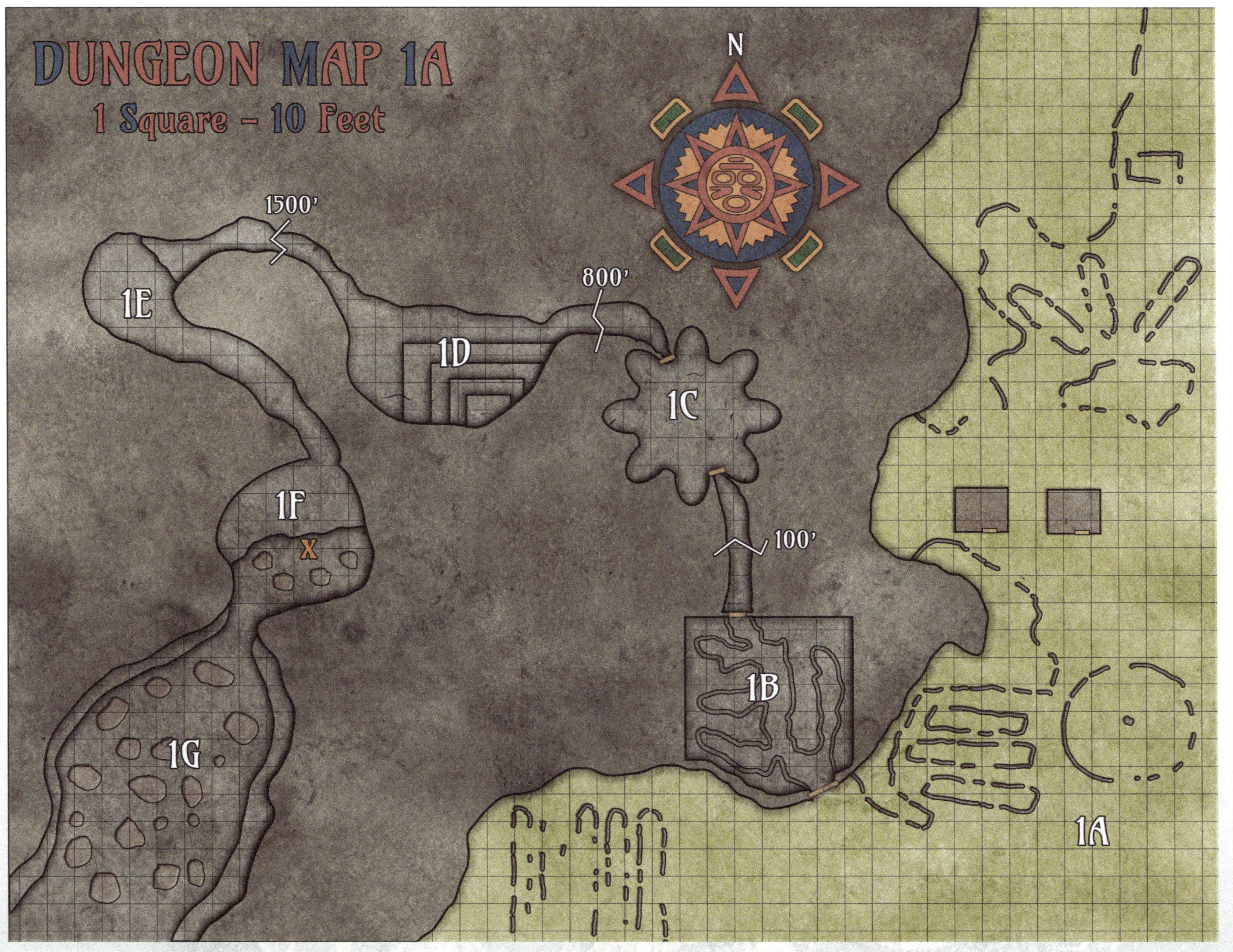

DUNGEON MAP 1A
1 Square = 10 Feet
N
1A
1B
1C
1D
1E
1F
1G
100'
800'
1500'
X

Area 1-B: Inner Lobby

> Low padded sofas and bland, background artworks decorate the space, which obviously served as a waiting room. Although presumably abandoned, flames burn in several braziers affixed to the walls, illuminating the room in a soothing yellowish hue that extends into the back of the large area. Clay and bamboo pots hold rows of renegade hostas and other plants that grow unchecked, spilling over the sides of their containers. What once appeared to be a comfortable and well-kept area now resembles a steamy jungle greenhouse.

Vegetation and warmth overrun this once-welcoming chamber that is still bathed in the light of *continual flame* spells cast on the braziers. The combination provides a perfect environment for the **8 violet fungi** now inhabiting the room. The mindless, purplish mushrooms slowly slither across the floor, attacking any living trespassers who enter the room. They ignore the **7** almost equally dimwitted **zombies** cohabitating the area alongside them. None of these monsters ever leaves the room.

Treasure: This room is where the mysterious stranger found the leather case containing the potions. The explorer he took the case from is still here as one of the zombies. This undead monstrosity still wears a belt pouch containing 70 sp and a silver locket worth 100 gp. A successful DC 15 Wisdom (Perception) check reveals a silvered short sword under a nearby potted plant's foliage.

A simple lock and a pile of heavy crates bar the door to **Area 1-C** from the other side. It takes a successful DC 10 Dexterity check made with thieves' tools to open the simple lock. A character must succeed on a DC 20 Strength check to push the heavy crates back from behind the door to gain entry into **Area 1-C**.

Area 1-C: The Laboratory

Elix and his inner circle of followers conducted controlled experiments on the users of the shori huasca within this laboratory as they sought to explore the depths of their own inner spaces rather than looking outward to the stars. They believed the fungi could potentially mutate ordinary people and unlock their hidden possibilities in a vein similar to the ascension of the hero-gods Micoateotl and Itztliteotl. They believed the legends about the Lord of the Dead making contact with temporal travelers and otherworldly beings as well as the God of Night tapping his inner potential for mystical energy. They wished to follow in their footsteps using the fungi to free their consciousness and transcend their mortal bodies. After years of experimentation, Elix and his inner circle succeeded, taking their knowledge and experience with them while their mortal bodies slowly withered into nothingness. Later generations attempted to duplicate their success but to no avail. Many believe Elix and several others currently wander another plane of existence, though no one has ever confirmed this controversial theory.

> Only a few tables remain intact along with a bank of shelves attached to the walls. Scrolls and glassware are scattered throughout the room. Twenty-two fiery vents brightly bathe the chamber in cool, white light. A massive painting on the domed ceiling exquisitely details the cosmos. Five stone statues stand evenly spaced along the outside edge of this room, apparently poised to cast a spell or incantation, while a sixth obsidian statue depicts a hulking man with a jaguar's head emitting pinpoints of blue light from its eyes. The same obsidian statue also stands at the due west compass point. The spot designated as true north holds a mirrored sphere roughly four feet in diameter that basks in blue light. A door is on the northern edge of the northwest quadrant.

The fiery vents and the blue lights are all the products of *continual flame* spells. Five of the six stone statues along the outer edges are artistic renditions

Designer's Note

At your option, you can include another message in the bone tube that might give the characters additional insight about a loose end they are having trouble closing.

of Micoateotl and Itztliteotl during their mortal existence. A character who views the statues and succeeds on a DC 15 Intelligence (Religion) check can identify them as such. A character who searches the Itztliteotl statue closest to the entrance and succeeds on a DC 17 Wisdom (Perception) check discovers a bone tube tucked into the stone. In addition to the magical writing inside of it, the tube also contains a scrap of weathered maguey paper. The medium contains the following message written in an archaic form of Aztli: "Here we come! Loving the trip! Elix." A character who reads the message and succeeds on a DC 25 Intelligence (History) check recalls hearing of Elix and his attempts to free his mind and consciousness from his mortal body.

While the stone statues are ordinary, inanimate sculptures, the obsidian statues are **2 obsidian minotaurs** (see **Appendix A: New Monsters**) with the slight alteration in their appearance. The monsters immediately respond to the intrusion by lowering their horns and charging toward trespassers. Elix and his followers programmed these two constructs to protect the laboratory in the event they decided to return here at a later time. Their sole task is to kill everyone not in the company of Elix. They have no regard for causing damage to the laboratory. Yahuitamotl attempted but failed to reprogram the two guardians. Therefore, he never visits this location and has not been here for years.

Treasure: The bone tube contains five *spell scrolls* (*continual flame*, *confusion*, *haste*, *passwall*, *war cry* [see **Appendix D: New Spells**]).

Area 1-D: Living Quarters

The Storm Rider Yahuitamotl waits here for a new challenge to alleviate his ennui. In apropos fashion, he is a neutral evil **storm giant** who also contacted the same mysterious, extraplanar entity that Micoateotl contacted long ago. The being granted Yahuitamotl the ability to stop aging while he remains here, but the loneliness and boredom that set in over the centuries since he acquired this "gift" changed his alignment from chaotic good to neutral evil. His longevity and the insight he gained from his discourses with the otherworldly entity convinced him that he is indeed a god in his own right. In the past, he used his time traveling outside the complex judiciously. Confident in his immortality, Yahuitamotl cares little about wasting any precious time and now endeavors to compel others to worship him as a capricious god. The whimsical giant uses the Poqozas' offerings as a tool to intimidate and frighten them into submission. He has no real interest or need for their sacrifices. Instead, he views his interactions with the terrified people as an amusing game, just like the chess board he keeps in his personal quarters. When the characters first encounter Yahuitamotl, read or paraphrase the following description:

> "You have come!" the purplish-skinned man excitedly proclaims.
>
> "I knew it would be you. Your deeds have reached my ears. Many in this miserable land grovel at your feet. How many followers do you have? How many worshippers? Would any of them give you their right arm? Their wife? Their last kernel of maize? I have gathered many to my fold. As you have seen, no doubt. Puny mortals, you are not gods like me!" He gestures to a frog-like humanoid resting on one of the cushions. "They give of themselves so freely."
>
> The man bids his guests to take their seats. There are many comfortable pillows scattered about, including a nest of plump cushions surrounded by gauzy veils. A library of scrolls and hardbound books illuminated by three lights spans the height of the wall. Trays of fresh fruits and breads are served at different stations throughout the cozy lounge, which features several pyramid-shaped tiered with six three-foot-high risers at each ascending level.

If the characters are not outwardly hostile, Yahuitamotl gauges their strength. If they came in through the front entrance, he gives them a low evaluation, whereas characters who slogged their way through the cueyatl side earn his respect and trepidation. In the former case, the storm giant seems at ease engaging them in conversation mostly about the futility of existence, the foolishness of mortals, and the vanity of the hero-gods to believe they are the only divine beings in Tehuatl. In the latter circumstance, Yahuitamotl errs on the side of caution with the characters, blasting them with a devastating lightning strike at the first sign of trouble. The **cueyatl warrior** (see **Appendix A: New Monsters**) joins in the fight alongside Yahuitamotl, but the storm giant shows no concern for the creature's wellbeing. If the cueyatl is in the line of fire from one of his spells or abilities, Yahuitamotl makes a matter-of-fact comment about the cueyatl being no great loss to the world.

When faced with imminent defeat, the storm giant accepts his fate with resignation. He laments the loss of such a wonderous individual, greater than any other who ever set foot in Tehuatl while he vows to defy death and return as an immortal deity. He never surrenders and refuses under any circumstances to give the characters any credit for their astounding victory.

Treasure: The storm giant's library holds many ancient, sacred texts worth 2,200 gp. The eight cards in the suit of clubs from a *deck of illusions* are in a small carrying case near the nest at the top of the pyramid. The liquors stored in the nest are mostly gallons of common peppery red wines or ordinary tequila worth 200 gp, but a delightfully potent pulque decanted in a crystal bottle contains 11 ounces of the beverage worth 30 gp per ounce. Stored here are the two missing chess pieces and the chess board worth 1,750 gp that Yahuitamotl confiscated from **Event Encounter 6: The Lost Children of the Chuxuntana**.

AREA 1-E: DRAGON ROOST

Several years ago, Yahuitamotl took an aspiring black dragon named Kullana under his wing. The storm giant uses the winged beast to perform aerial reconnaissance and underwater exploration before he leaves his compound to spread terror across the grasslands. The pair work well together, though the bombastic Yahuitamotl can sometimes be overwhelming. The partnership is not entirely altruistic, as Kullana covets coins and treasure more than his counterpart. He plans to amass a hoard worthy of winning the hand of an older and even more avaricious black dragon mate he has had his eyes on for the last two decades. Kullana has some measure of loyalty to the storm giant but would never compromise his safety to save Yahuitamotl in a pinch. He has a similar attitude toward the cueyatls, as he sees them as his playthings and fodder to help ensure his safety. Likewise, he enjoys spreading misery and suffering to the Poqoza communities that Yahuitamotl devastates. Although he stays in the background during the assault, the dragon mops up any stragglers who stumble across him in the chaos. Kullana now rests among the coins filling his lair.

Kullana, a **young black dragon**, naps most of the day away. He burrows beneath one of the mounds of coins, though portions of his tail and body can be seen beneath his metallic camouflage. Nonetheless, Kullana has advantage on his Dexterity (Stealth) check while he remains motionless and partially hidden. The young black dragon uses his blindsight and enhanced perception to detect intruders. When he senses trespassers in his lair, he pushes the coins aside and unleashes a line of acid in the most advantageous direction before engaging the characters with his claws and bite. Kullana ultimately prioritizes his life over his treasure. He reluctantly bribes the adventurers to leave his lair with some of his riches in exchange for sparing his wretched life. Kullana may alternatively barter information about Yahuitamotl if the characters broach the subject. In that case, he divulges details about the storm giant in the same manner as a shrewd merchant negotiating a suitable price for his wares.

Treasure: Although numerically impressive, Kullana's hoard contains a disproportionate number of copper and silver coins. He has 20,128 cp,

5,230 sp, and 902 gp. There is also a silver scepter worth 100 gp, a ceramic chihuahua statue worth 35 gp, an elaborately beaded headband worth 60 gp, and an expertly carved conch horn worth 150 gp. It takes a successful DC 15 Wisdom (Perception) check to spot these items amid the coin piles.

The passageway leading from this cavern to the living quarters of Yahuitamotl is partially concealed by a luminescent column of stalactites and stalagmites. It takes a successful DC 19 Wisdom (Perception) check (DC 19) to notice the hidden tunnel connecting the two rooms.

AREA 1-F: CUEYATL QUEEN

Chaxtata, the **cueyatl moon priest** (see **Appendix A: New Monsters**), thinks the characters are here to see their patron saint, the dragon Kullana. Even if they enter here from the dragon's room, she tries to usher them out of the cavern system while also demanding a monetary tribute for passing through the cueyatls' territory. She recognizes the characters as a serious threat to her and her people. She wants to avoid a fight with them while not appearing weak in the process. In sharp contrast, her 4 **cueyatl warriors** (see **Appendix A: New Monsters**) are itching for a fight and a chance to prove their worth. They bravely thrust out their chests in defiance and stamp their spear butts into the muck. Chaxtata can barely control the quartet, who react violently to the slightest provocation. She hopes to keep the characters away from her clutch of eggs that is poised to hatch into three dozen new cueyatl tadpoles near her nest on the western edge of this cavern.

The sounds of battle reverberate through the empty space, ensuring that the cueyatls in **Area 1-G** hear the ruckus. Half of their number respond to the noise, joining in the melee 1d4 + 1 rounds later. The swarm of quippers from **Area 1-G** follow shortly thereafter, though they must remain in the roughly two-foot-deep pools of standing water. They attack only if the characters get into the water at the point designated with an X.

If pressed into battle, Chaxtata orders her thralls to attack in groups. The cueyatls gang up on a single character, while a pair of warriors also try to isolate a lone combatant. She starts the combat using her Night's Chill action followed by conjuring *spirit guardians* to protect her. Despite her reservations about engaging in combat with the characters, she and her people give no quarter nor expect to receive any from the interlopers.

Treasure: Each cueyatl warrior carries a small pouch with 2d10 cacao beans worth 1 gp each. One also wears a silver ring worth 100 gp. Chaxtata has a small cache in her nest of 20 gp, a healer's kit, a leather collar with seashell sewn into its surface worth 30 gp, and a leather-bound maguey paper book gifted to her by Yahuitamotl. She cannot read it, though she leafed through it nightly. The book, which is written in Aztli, contains a detailed history of the laboratory that is worth 100 gp. Its pages contain the background information about Elix and his inner circle as described in **Areas 1-A** and **1-C**.

AREA 1-G: FROG ROOM

The characters are not the only new arrivals on the scene. Several days earlier, the cueyatls butchered a troupe of entertainers traveling across the grasslands to perform at a funeral. The men did not take the unanticipated cancellation of their performance lightly. Instead, they rose from the grave and now seek revenge on the creatures who cut their musical careers short.

The river emerging from this cavern floods the entire room. A rim of exposed limestone rings the cavern about three feet from the water's surface, connecting the mouth of the cave to a narrow passage leading deeper underground. A dozen huge boulders poke out from the surface as well, offering the option to traverse across them rather than wade or swim through the water. Most of the boulders have flat surfaces, but a few bear jagged shards of rock pointing toward the ceiling. Hundreds of bats flit from the rocky outcropping to stalactites throughout the room.

Roughly 10 frog-like humanoids cluster around the cave mouth. They hurl spears at a pair of shadowy figures inanely babbling at the cave mouth. The humanoid creatures seem disturbed by the intruders' tireless, nonsensical chatter.

This locale has several moving parts to it. The 7 **cueyatls** (see **Appendix A: New Monsters**) and 5 **cueyatl warriors** (see **Appendix A: New Monsters**) encountered here were fishing for quippers in the deeper end of this room. Of course, if they rushed to the aid of their priestess in **Area 1-F**, adjust the cueyatls' numbers accordingly. While the cueyatls were hunting individual fish, the school is actually a **swarm of quippers** that attacks any creature entering the water, which floods the uneven floor in this area to a depth of 1d8 + 4 feet at any given spot. If the cueyatls responded to the racket from **Area 1-F**, at least half remain here to fend off the 2 **allips** (see **Appendix A: New Monsters**) at their doorstep. The incorporeal, flying allips are unfazed by the water or any other physical obstacles in their way. The undead spirits exclusively attack the cueyatls until no cueyatls are left to fight. If that occurs, they turn their anger toward the adventurers. If you want to simplify the combat between these parties, you can designate that the allips deal 8 points of psychic damage to the cueyatls each round, while the cueyatls deal 5 points of piercing damage to the allips.

Treasure: Each cueyatl and cueyatl warrior carries a small pouch with 2d20 sp. The water conceals a *+1 shield*, though a character searching the water must succeed on a DC 15 Wisdom (Perception) check to find it. One of the cueyatl warriors also has a cylindrical tube containing 18 rubies worth 50 gp each and two *feather tokens* (bird and tree).

CHAPTER FOUR: THE NIHILETH ASSAULT

After the Storm Rider's defeat, the palpable sense of unease gripping the Caxcalli Grasslands subsides. The storms still come, but the overwhelming dread that once accompanied their appearance is gone. Yet the elation is short-lived. Within days, the rain regains its slimy, viscous coating and blood-like consistency that started with the eclipse. Yahuitamotl's destruction certainly caused a setback to the nihileth aboleth's plans. However, the monster's corruption of the Mulla Chanacu grows only stronger. Without its herald to spread the word of the coming of a new age, the nihileth is now concentrating on the next phase of its strategy to destroy the entire grasslands and usher in the Season of the Qallucha. While only farmers and scholars notice the contamination of the water supply on Mulla Chanacu's west side, the monster's corrupting effect on the tallgrass and the flora appears more obvious. The strange rain turns the soil into gooey muck in many places. Formerly healthy vegetation withers and rots in the fields, only to be supplemented by sickly weeds. The abomination's baleful influence spreads not just from above but also from below as the deconstructed earth supports only an invasive new species — the **caustic thistle** (see **Appendix B**). This invasive weed covers much of the ground at the Mulla Chanacu and spreads in an outward wave from that central crater, expanding primarily to the south and west where the conducive rains and soil are more prevalent. However, as the wind picks up its lightweight seeds, patches of caustic thistle are starting to appear in other locations as well.

The plants are the nihileth's advance guard, but the teenagers and rescuers who ventured to the Mulla Chanacu are its army. The young Poqozas who set off from their homes to partake in the spirit quests quickly fell prey to the nihileth, who killed them and reanimated their corpses as zombies under its command. The nihileth also stalked the tallgrass to slaughter bandits, fugitives, and hunters to supplement its band of recruits. With its ranks of nihileth zombies rapidly swelling, it gave the undead abominations standing orders to kill two other creatures and then go into hibernation beneath the damp earth. Over time, the plot has created the zombie equivalent of a modern minefield with dozens or perhaps even hundreds of these creatures in this near state of suspended animation. After the characters defeat Yahuitamotl, the nihileth set off a chain reaction by ordering the zombies closest to him to reawaken themselves and the other slumbering zombies near them. Now, they rise! Now, they kill!

The nihileth stored the ethereal undead roughly 20 feet underground. It concentrated them around the Mulla Chanacu, with a few outliers stationed up to 20 miles away from the crater. With Yahuitamotl gone, the nihileth fears the heroes who defeated Yahuitamotl would soon come after it. Rather than stay strictly on the defensive, the nihileth disperses its zombie hordes across the area to kill neighboring villagers and keep the characters' attention focused elsewhere.

EVENT ONE: LIGHTNING FLASHING ACROSS THE SKY

The hill is the site of the meteorite crash that created the Mulla Chanacu and currently serves as the nihileth aboleth's lair. Although they do not realize it yet, the nihileth has dispatched its minions, and the current storm provides the perfect cover for this action. Across the area, the nihileth's zombie servants attack with reckless abandon. Meanwhile, the rains and the mutated soil encourage the rapid proliferation of the caustic thistle. Anyone foolish enough to drink the standing water in this area is subjected to the regional effects from the **nihileth aboleth** (see **Appendix A: New Monsters**).

Naturally, a cluster of lightning bolts blasting a single location is sure to attract the characters' attention. The iron particles scattered throughout the crater account for the strange anomaly. With a prospective target in sight, the characters' approach to the nihileth's lair is treacherous. The rain and mud make the entire area into difficult terrain. Although the lightning poses no immediate danger to the characters, the caustic thistle and zombie hordes greatly impede the adventurers' progress toward their intended goal. The **caustic thistle** (see **Appendix B**) grows in wide rows 1d6 x 100 feet across and 1d4 x 10 feet thick. They almost appear as if their seeds were deliberately sown to create broad fences or palisades to protect a strategic location.

Amid the chaos, a Poqoza tribesman named Alaxa (CG male Poqoza half-elf **berserker** armed with a spear instead of a greataxe) sobs in a shallow ditch along the characters' path. He tried to singlehandedly defeat the nihileth to avenge what the monstrosity did to his son and daughter. Yet his fear and a small horde of 11 **nihilethic zombies** (see **Appendix A: New Monsters**) got the better of him. The undead creatures are closing in on the broken man when the characters arrive. The zombies know Alaxa is near, but the characters appear to be a greater threat to their master than a lone person crying in a hole. If the characters defeat the zombies, Alaxa regains his composure and peeks over the edge of the ditch to presumably confirm the characters' victory. When the last one falls, Alaxa cries out for them to listen.

EVENT TWO:
A FRIENDLY FACE IN THE CHAOS

When the final zombie sinks into the malodorous soil, a filthy Poqoza rises out of a ditch and desperately waves in an obvious attempt to attract attention.

"Wait!" he shouts, his words barely heard over the storm.

"If you go on to free our children," he shouts to you, "you must take these." He fumbles through his belongings to locate a leather pouch. He sets his spear down into the mud while bumbling through its items.

"Do this in the name of my children Ajama and Cahuri," he proclaims. He then unwraps a vial of red liquid and produces a black ring from the pouch.

"I do not know what is here, but it is evil, and you must stop it. Save the Caxcalli Grasslands. Stop the evil before it takes over Tehuatl."

He tells the characters that the village ticitl sent him here to investigate the disappearance of the settlement's teenagers who never returned after their expedition to the Mulla Chanacu. Along the way, he learned that the children from other small communities were also missing, though some witnesses also claimed to have seen them rise from the grave as grotesque shambling corpses. Although the creatures are clearly wicked, even the bravest warriors hesitate to strike down a beloved child when faced with such grim reality. Alaxa begged the ticitl to accompany him, but he needed to defend the village and steel the people's nerves against the approaching doom. However, to aid Alaxa in this dangerous endeavor, the ticitl gave him a potion and a ring. Alaxa freely offers the items to the characters to help them fulfill his mission to defeat the evil and rid the Mulla Chanacu of the cancer eating away at its soul.

Treasure: Alaxa gives the characters the *ring of resistance* (necrotic) and the *potion of giant strength* (fire) that the ticitl gave him. If they succeed at their given task, they are welcome to keep the items.

DESIGNER'S NOTE

There are no maps for this section of the adventure as the nihileth's lair can be of any size of your choosing. Although the nihileth can pass through earth and even stone to reach its abode, the characters must pass through the muddy channels descending into the earth unless they can reach the nihileth's lair by an alternative means such as a *teleport* spell or similar magic. If the characters must traverse through the channels and tunnels to reach their goal, you can make the journey as difficult or easy as you choose depending upon the characters' current condition and your style of play. For instance, if you want the characters to defeat the zombie horde aboveground and immediately thereafter take the fight to the nihileth belowground, use that idea. For a tougher descent, you can make them work their way past levels of nihilethic zombies stored in isolated oubliettes with rows of caustic thistles intermittently blocking their way. Also, the nihileth can use its major illusion ability

EVENT THREE: BUG HUNT

The sun still hides behind the billowing, charcoal-colored clouds, while the seemingly unnatural storm builds more energy, as if it were feeding off the energies of the netherworld. Lightning smashes the ground, while peals of thunder drown out all other sounds in the region. The acidic rain stirs up the yellowish mud, sending it out in rivulets to infect the surrounding area. The mud then washes away and exposes a huge crater.

Channels running away from the cavity transport the mud deeper into the earth. Amid the cacophony and dazzling light show, the storm suddenly ceases as a menacing, otherworldly clicking echoes through the crater, followed by a thick burbling laugh.

The sinister voice whispers, "You defeated my Storm Rider. Do you think it will be that easy to defeat me? He was merely my servant, and I was his master. Save your lives and flee this land. Let the land fester. If you refuse, only death awaits you."

The nihileth abruptly ends its telepathic communication with a disturbing chuckle. If a character attempts to re-establish telepathic communication with the nihileth, the adventurer suffers the effects of the monster's Infecting Telepathy.

The nihileth then dispatches another horde of 16 **nihilethic zombies** (see **Appendix A: New Monsters**) to the surface to attack the characters and drive them away from the crater. The concerned nihileth moves ethereally through solid stone to its lair 100 feet below the surface.

The channels leading to the nihileth's lair are large enough to accommodate an average-sized man, but the soggy ground makes the area into difficult terrain. Furthermore, although the passages corkscrew into the ground at a relatively modest angle, any creature walking down the tunnel must periodically succeed on a DC 10 Dexterity (Acrobatics) check to avoid slipping on the slick surface. On a failed check, the creature falls prone and slides 1d10 x 4 feet down the tunnel.

The nihileth left some areas under the Mulla Chanacu undisturbed. If you want to mix up the encounters on the way down to the nihileth's lair, you can allow them to explore a deserted, subterranean amphitheater infested by a group of 6 **black puddings** or lead them into an underground archway defended by a **clay golem** and 6 **flying swords** that leap off the walls to bar trespassers from proceeding through the archway. These interim conflicts give the ethereal nihileth an idea of the characters' strengths and weaknesses. Before facing the intruders in its lair, the ethereal nihileth observes the adventurers and uses its telepathy to gauge their mental fortitude. It then attempts to enslave the mentally weakest character. If the ploy succeeds, the character shows no outward signs of being under the monster's influence. However, during the showdown with the nihileth, it uses its legendary action to force its thrall to claw at its own face and shout, "Not safe! Not safe!" This action causes a psychic drain on the victim.

If the characters finally reach the nihileth's lair, read or paraphrase the following description:

EVENT FOUR:
FIGHT FOR YOUR LIVES!

Liquid drips from the ceiling and seeps from cracks in the walls to flood this chamber to a depth of eight feet. Ripples show that something large lies beneath the surface. Six tentacles writhe up from the murky depths, sloshing water ahead of the quick-striking limbs.

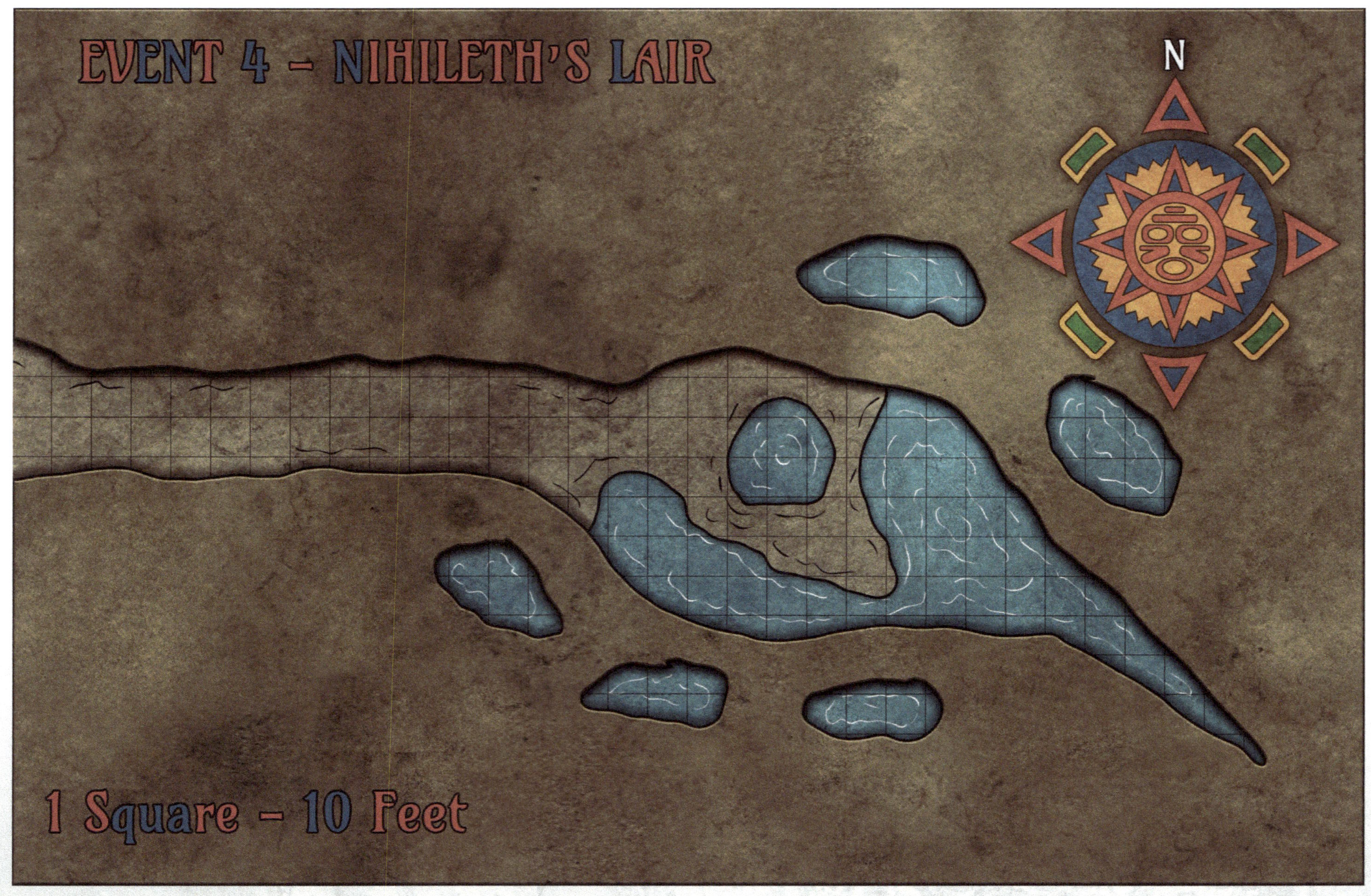

EVENT 4 – NIHILETH'S LAIR
N
1 Square = 10 Feet

This is the **nihileth aboleth**'s (see **Appendix A: New Monsters**) lair. It has spent a long time inconspicuously slumbering under the Mulla Chanacu, waiting for its time to come while transmitting intelligence reports back to its alien homeland. In this foreign land, it has a created a microcosm utopia for itself far below the surface. It seeks to make the landscape above its subterranean abode more habitable for its own kind as well after spending thousands of years confined to its underground realm.

While the rippling in the water is real, the tentacles protruding through the water are a *major image*. The nihileth hopes the characters direct some of their firepower at the tentacles. While physical objects pass through the illusion, magical attacks that do not deal physical damage may not uncover the illusion. The monster uses its lair action to pull opponents into the water when they realize the tentacles are not real. Unless the characters flee or have the ability to pommel it with effective ranged attacks, the nihileth remains submerged. If forced to leave the pool, it assumes its ethereal form. It also knows the location of 9 **nihilethic zombies** (see **Appendix A: New Monsters**) concealed within pockets outside its lair. It uses these unfortunate creatures as a hit point reservoir to heal its injuries and return to its lair to rid itself of the pesky adventurers instead of using them as reinforcements. The nihileth also uses a psychic drain on an enslaved character to regain lost hit points.

The nihileth believes it has already fulfilled the requirements of its reconnaissance mission to gather data for its kin and signal the beginning of their invasion force. It believes the storm and lightning strikes are a beacon to summon more of its vile kin to this world to conquer it. However, the storm is a fortuitous coincidence for the characters, as it is the dying vestiges of the Storm Rider's residual energies rather than something of the nihileth's creation as it believes. Firm in this conviction, the nihileth would rather fight to the death to attempt to slay the characters and prevent them from derailing the invasion than flee to save its wretched life. Throughout the combat, the arrogant monster telepathically boasts about its brethren's imminent arrival and humanity's weakness. The creature remains supremely confident in its inevitable victory regardless of the circumstances and the characters' successes against the nihileth. If the characters kill the nihileth, it releases a bellowing laugh and utters the words, "Doom is falling" before its lifeless corpse turns into mush.

Treasure: With the nihileth out of the way, the characters are free to explore its lair. Concealed within the muck at the bottom of its pool is an obsidian chest. Within the confines of the unlocked container, the characters find 4,230 gp, a *potion of giant strength* (storm), a *spell scroll* (*heal*), a *rod of rulership*, and a *helm of telepathy*.

WRAPPING UP

When the characters leave the nihileth's lair and return to the surface, the storm is abating. Although the soil still reeks, the rain now falling to the ground washes away the acidic liquid and makes the ground incapable of supporting the invasive caustic thistle. With the nihileth destroyed, the zombies under its command go dormant or mindlessly wreak havoc in Poqoza communities throughout the region.

Although this adventure implies that the nihileth failed to summon more of its kin to Tehuatl, you are free to adjust that conclusion if you wish. These creatures could also bring other alien invaders to the island.

Regardless of how you conclude the adventure, the disturbing thoughts swirling in the nihileth's mind torment the adventurers' during their sleep, filling them with horrific nightmares of strange worlds teeming with bizarre, vile creatures.

Poqoza communities throughout the region celebrate the characters. Feasts, games, and even marriage proposals from ambitious nobles follow them wherever they go. At your discretion, you may segue this adventure into the next and last one in the series — ***The Daughter of the Drowned Serpent***, where the Poqozas once again ask the characters for assistance or the characters learn about the attack on the Poqoza village near the Great Canal.

Daughter of the Drowned Serpent

By Tim Hitchcock

And the children, the little ones.
Those who barely walk, those who crawl.
Those still on the ground making little piles of earth and broken shards
*   of pottery*
The infants lashed to their boards and slats
All of them stare hollow-eyed.
Everyone knows anguish and affliction.
Everyone gazing upon torment; no one has been overlooked.
— Verse 18: The Commandments of The Serpent

Daughter of the Drowned Serpent is an adventure for four Tier 3 characters in which the characters must investigate the forces behind the recent sacking and looting of several Poqoza villages. The raiders brutally slew numerous villagers, including a son of the tlamacazqui, the supreme priest of the southern half of Tehuatl. The attacks appear to be orchestrated by an alliance of humanoids and warriors from the neighboring Aztli city-state of Mactli. The elders and priests of the Poqoza villages now demand that the rulers of Mactli mete out justice for the victims and pay full restitution for the damages. The northerners deny responsibility for the attacks. Tension escalates as the Aztli city-state and Poqoza people prepare for an all-out war unless the characters can unmask the real culprit behind the attacks.

ADVENTURE BACKGROUND

After Tlatoani's defeat and the cataclysm that followed, those servants who remained loyal to the fallen ruler embarked on a mass exodus. Hunted and pursued at every turn, many fled to other planes of existence to avoid capture and certain death. Those who successfully escaped went into exile. For centuries they kept hidden until the day they would once again re-emerge to spread the word and power of their faith.

When tensions between mortals escalate, egos clash and individual desires for power become all consuming. The crafty Tlatoani has always known this, and his servants count on such mortal weakness to usher in his return. Mortals have short memories. Time dulls the recollection of the sufferings and trials their ancient ancestors faced. It obscures the foundations they laid for the betterment of their descendants. Good and evil share a commonality — a thread of non-duality in which both rely on each other for their existence. Only time and forgetfulness allow one to supersede the other. The serpent waits for these conditions to take hold.

The Poqozas have little regard or use for political leaders. Temporal authority painfully reminds them of the Immortal Sun's oppressive yoke, who in his mortal form once dominated the land as its unquestioned emperor. Instead, they refuse any type of centralized government and choose to live in autonomous communities that rely on the guidance and counsel of their elders and priests. To ensure that no settlement exerts more authority than another, each priest serves only a single aspect of their god Tlatlcolli. All priests pledge loyalty to the tlamacazqui, who serves as the mortal representative of Tlatlcolli. The tlamacazqui has no dwelling and wanders the lands freely, staying within each of the villages for a few weeks before moving on. For this reason, many of the tlamacazqui's children live scattered throughout the Poqoza villages, each one serving as an act of solidarity and trust between their people.

The tlamacazqui's fifth and youngest son Metzpil resides in the small village of Atoyatetl, one of several settlements along the southern bank of the Acaotilihuei, (the waterway flowing through the Great Canal), where it serves as one of the main trade outposts for the rest of the Poqoza nation. Metzpil works on a trade barge and spends much of his time traveling and debauching himself in various ports. On a recent trip, he indulged in his first taste of a highly addictive mind-altering substance smoked by the violent warrior priests known as the Maldraht maht. Unbeknownst to Metzpil, he was deliberately given the substance by Tlatoani's demonic daughter to feed him dark dreams and manipulate him into seizing power. He became convinced that he would become Tlatoani's new host and through him would rule all of Tehuatl as its undisputed emperor.

In a few short months, Metzpil spiraled into a deep chasm of addiction and delusion where he believes himself to be the second coming of Tlatoani. To further his deranged ambitions, he began grooming a small group of disciples, all of whom share his addiction to Maldraht maht, which he refers to as the Serpent's Kiss. Seeking to create dissention among his people and incite them into a war against the Aztli people to the north, Metzpil and his disciples orchestrated several brutal attacks on Poqoza villages. He staged these attacks to appear as if Aztli jaguar warriors committed them. To carry out the attacks, Metzpil garnered the aid of a tribe of gnolls by promising them the raid's spoils in exchange for their help in the sacking and burning of the town. To further his ruse, he and his minions stole a black dragon's eggs, and he had his gnoll allies tell the furious beast that they saw the humans take them to their villages. Naturally, the conscientious gnolls offered to help the outraged beast exact its revenge on the human thieves to further solidify their alliance

Between the vengeful dragon, the gnolls, and Metzpil's depraved followers disguised as Aztli Jaguar Cuauhocelotls, the village of Atoyatetl stood little chance. The violence that fell upon the village tore it to shreds and sent its few survivors fleeing for their lives, taking with them horrific accounts of the devastation and murder.

ADVENTURE SYNOPSIS

Investigating the violent attacks of several villages along the Acaotilihuei, the waterway flowing through the Great Canal, the heroes must unravel a series of clues to figure out who perpetrated the murderous attacks. Several parties with their own motives committed the ghastly crimes, giving the heroes an opportunity to pursue each of these culprits to their base in a collection of sandbox style mini-adventures. These locales include three Poqoza villages, a riverside outpost occupied by hostile humanoids, a swamp hiding an outpost of ancient mummified warriors, a cavern complex that serves as a home to a brood of dragons, and a visit to a monstrous oracle living off the coast in an abandoned floating war-temple. After undertaking these related excursions, the characters likely have enough evidence to direct their investigation toward the southern human revolutionaries under the renegade son of the tlamacazqui, who has fallen under the baleful influence of an ancient evil. After defeating him, the heroes learn his puppeteer is none other than the demon daughter of the ancient serpent emperor Tlatoani who is seeking to restore her father onto Tehuatl's throne. In the final encounter, the adventurers square off against the demon-daughter in a heroic attempt to eradicate her and her diabolical parent from the world forever.

STARTING THE ADVENTURE

The adventure begins when the characters hear tales of the mysterious and violent destruction of a small Poqoza trading village known as Atoyatetl that rests along the southern shore of the Acaotilihuei, roughly halfway between the city of Zacatl and Azuato. Accounts tell of bodies burned by acid, villagers with their hearts torn out, and rumors of cryptic runes encircling the villages, all of which bear the hallmarks of the Aztli hero-gods Yaocteotl and Quiahuitl. Encourage the characters to travel to Atoyatetl to investigate the rumors. Make it clear to them that if the rumors prove true, such an act would sow the seeds of war between the Poqozas and Aztlis.

As a trading outpost, Atoyatetl is readily accessible via the Great Canal separating the Aztlis from the Poqozas. Additionally, four trails connect the village to surrounding Poqoza settlements. Two paths meander off to the south while the other two skirt along the edge of the canal in opposite directions.

As the characters approach the section of the canal where the village is located, they spot its precise location from the trail of thick black smoke rising up into the clear blue Tehuatl sky.

When the characters arrive at Atoyatetl, read or paraphrase the following description:

Walking the ruins are 12 **Poqoza warriors** (see **Appendix A: New Monsters**), each accompanied by a **war dog** (see **Appendix A: New Monsters**). As soon as any of the characters enter the town, one of the Poqoza warriors spots them and demands they halt and identify themselves, or die. The warriors are particularly suspicious if the characters are not Poqozas and appear to be outsiders. However, defending against the attack has left them exhausted and several of them bear ghastly-looking wounds. The warriors have only a third of their full hit points (28 hit points each). They are not willing to risk an all-out fight, which gives the characters advantage on Charisma (Persuasion or Intimidation) checks contested by the warriors' Wisdom (Insight) checks to convince the battered warriors to stand down and listen to reason rather than engage in a physical altercation with the heroes. Furthermore, characters who succeed on a DC 5 Wisdom (Insight) check notice that the warriors are obviously exhausted. Most sport significant injuries that inhibit their ability to fight.

Characters who heal the injured warriors or civilians earn the Poqozas' trust, giving them advantage on all Charisma checks involving social interactions with the villagers. Similarly, characters assisting in the village's reconstruction or who help fortify against another potential attack also gain the same benefits as those who tend to the wounded.

Once characters earn the warriors' respect and trust, the witnesses readily provide the characters with a detailed description of the attack.

After hearing the tale, the characters can attempt skill checks to try to discern more about the creatures or further question the warriors.

If asked what happened to the villagers, the warriors tell them that less than half of the people were able to escape. Some took to the roads, but others fled into the forest and grasslands.

A successful DC 10 Intelligence (Arcana) check discerns the winged serpent described by the warrior is in fact a black dragon. If the characters attempt to figure out what the dragon took from the house, a successful DC 12 Intelligence (Investigation) check infers that the objects sound like they might be dragon eggs.

A successful DC 5 Intelligence (Religion) check notes that the children of Itzcuin are in fact gnolls.

If the characters ask where the dragon came from, the warriors say the serpent came from and flew off toward the swamplands on the northern side of the canal known as the Yoaltica Ilaquiloz.

If the characters ask about the house with the eggs, the warriors explain that it belonged to the tlamacazqui's youngest son, Metzpil. They suspect Metzpil was killed during the attack, but they have yet to recover his remains.

Those inquiring further into the nature of the dragon or dragon-summoning rituals are told to speak to the village storyteller. She explains that dragons are the offspring of the Drowned Serpent, the Emperor-God Tlatoani, and they were driven off after the gods defeated him by drowning the world. Beyond that, she admits ignorance — as such knowledge is far older than mortals. She then adds that if they require more information, they should seek Nahualipazotic. Gifted with great longevity, Nahualipazotic is a witch-priestess said to be the sea bride of the hero-god Itztliteotl. Legends say that the sea bride lives off the eastern seacoast in a floating temple-barge (see **Chapter 2: A Tangled Fate**).

A successful DC 10 Intelligence (Religion) check identifies that the Jaguar Cuauhocelotls performed a ritual sacrifice often associated with Quiahuitl, a hero-god of the Aztlis often associated with the neighboring city-state of Mactli.

A successful DC 20 Intelligence (Religion) check instead reveals that while the ritual appears to honor Quiahuitl, it is inauthentic and was staged. Instead, the deception is an insult to Quiahuitl, and the rites are more reminiscent of those performed to honor Tlatoani rather than the Aztli hero-gods.

If asked which way the gnolls fled, the warriors tell them that the hyenamen took the paths to the west, then headed off through the woods.

If asked which way the Jaguar Cuauhocelotls fled, the Poqoza explain that the Aztlis paddled their boats back into the canal and headed north, likely toward the city-state of Mactli.

Wrapping Things Up

This section concludes when the players decide which course of action they want to pursue. If they choose to follow the gnolls, continue to **Chapter 1: Run Through the Jungle**. If they choose to seek the sea bride, go to **Chapter 2: A Tangled Fate.** If they choose to attempt to track down the dragon, proceed to **Chapter 3: Yoaltica Ilaquiloz**. If they attempt to follow the Jaguar Cuauhocelotls, go to **Chapter 4: The Secret of the Fallen Son**.

Chapter One: Run Through the Jungle

If the players choose to follow the gnolls, the characters can easily follow their tracks along the west road with a successful DC 5 Wisdom (Survival) check. The tracks continue for approximately one-half mile until they reach an intersection where the main road bends south and a smaller footpath runs northward through the jungle. The gnolls' tracks clearly follow the northbound trail, likely headed toward the canal. Although technically part of the Tlococua Marsh that dominates Tehuatl's southeastern coast, trees and woody shrubs thrive along the banks of the Great Canal, making this wetland region into a combination of swamp and marshland.

At this point, allow any characters tracking the gnolls to succeed on a DC 12 Wisdom (Survival) check to spot some curious tracks. If successful, the character notices that several sets of humanoid footprints break away from the road through the brush and into the forest, while the gnoll footprints continue along the road. If the characters pursue the gnolls, the tracks lead them to **The Children of Itzcuin**. If they instead break from the road to pursue the second set of prints, read or paraphrase the following description:

> The tracks haphazardly wind through the swamp, though they seem to be headed toward the northeast. The woods thicken quickly, and the path becomes more difficult to follow as the terrain transforms into tangles of knotted tree roots interlaced with swaths of moss, vines, and other small shrubs.

If the characters continue to follow the tracks, they soon encounter a quickly rigged trap set by the fleeing villagers to slow or deter anyone pursuing them.

Stinging Insect Trap

During their flight, the villagers found a wasp's nest and decided to set a small snare that might cause any pursuers to anger the stinging insects. A tripwire strung across the forest path triggers the trap. If touched or cut, the wire snaps, releasing a second cord holding a weighted log that swings into a nearby wasp nest, which causes the insects to erupt in a frenzied **swarm of insects** that viciously attack the nearest living creatures. Anyone actively

Accommodating Alternate Plans

If the characters insist on returning, use the following encounter with the wood apes to cause conflict on the return journey. You can also run an alternate encounter for the Children of Itzcuin in which a group of 10 **merrows** spots the gnolls loading their boats from the water. The sea ogres attack and devour most of the group, preventing the last few from leaving. In this event, the characters arrive to face the merrows who have the remaining 4 **gnolls** cornered up a tree. The gnolls attempt to flee once the merrows turn their attention to the characters.

searching the forest floor (such as an individual following tracks) who succeeds on a DC 15 Wisdom (Perception) check spots the wire. It then takes a successful DC 15 Intelligence (Investigation) check to associate the wire with the weighted log that crashes into the wasps' nest. The wire can be safely and easily disabled with a successful DC 5 Dexterity check with thieves' tools or a successful DC 10 Intelligence (Investigation) check to jury-rig a solution to disable it.

A band of 25 Poqoza escapees (various alignments, male and female Poqoza half-elf **commoners**) fled down this road, but they were forced to veer off into the jungle and hole up in the brush when they heard the gnolls chasing after them. Wounded and weary, they were forced to stop and tend to the injured. They hid themselves a short distance off the trail and set perimeter defenses around their makeshift camp. Scared and cornered, the Poqozas fight back against anyone pursuing them, attacking first and asking questions later. Nonetheless, they are weak and pose little threat to anyone, especially the adventurers. If the characters convince them they are here to help them, they quickly yield. Similar to the warriors in the village, offering assistance or healing gives the characters advantage on Charisma checks made to interact with the escapees.

While little remains of Atoyatetl, the villagers want to return home. The characters are free to continue in pursuit of the gnolls or to lead the villagers back to Atoyatetl. However, make sure the players are aware that time is of the essence if they hope to catch the fleeing assailants.

Kurn Domladur
Turew
Octli
Ixtla
Tamazoli
Nepalta
Shassal
Balandrur
Ipaconoytl
Cepual Desert
Nochtli
Quannaqa River
Xalpit
Hana'aloa
Mactli
Omehual River
Ouatulli Lake
Omiex
Droomph
Teocua
Cuahtla Forest
Yoaltica Ilaquiloz
Necocyaotl
Quizaloa
Amilotetl
The Great Canal
Huitzineo
Azuato
Ixchicta
Ezhuacoza
Zacatl
Good fortune
Cotza
Toxana
Mimicapoli
Quitlacatl
Blibleblup
Ahuacua
Ezhuitotl
Cuiateotl
Hilaya River
The Spring
Mototoloa
Zinacan
Ixnenatl
Moyome
Atoyaxalli
Xoxoquetzpali
Hamachi
Tlococua Marsh
Mauhque
Iachacina
Ixtama
Yolqui
Yoyoliton
Temetzin River
Mulla Chanacu
Hualcitzen
Onacina
Xicotli
Cuanintli
Nezcatayotl
Caxcalli Grasslands
Eei
Rommpf
Yuri
Tlahapina
N
CAXCALLI GRASSLANDS
1 Square - 20 Miles

The Woods Apes

If the characters have been wandering the jungle for a while, or if they decide to take an alternate path, they run across an angry patrol of 4 **woods apes** (see **Appendix A: New Monsters**) who have had their fill of trespassers wandering across and disturbing their lands. Although blessed with sentience, these irate beasts are tired of watching humanoids despoil their forest. They have no patience for chatting with the interlopers and instead violently attack them on sight. If the characters attempt to reason with the woods apes, they do so with disadvantage on their Charisma checks contested by the woods apes' Wisdom (Insight) checks. A character who converses with the beasts in Druidic instead has advantage on the preceding checks. In the event the characters successfully negotiate a peaceful resolution, the woods apes point the characters in the right direction in their pursuit of the gnolls.

The Children of Itzcuin

Before the characters break from the forest's edge, a character who succeeds on a DC 15 Wisdom (Perception) check hears the rough guttural barks of the gnolls shouting directions at each other as they rapidly load their boats to flee north, back across the canal.

When the characters reach the edge of the forest, read or paraphrase the following description:

> The forest breaks into a rocky plain that slopes down toward the bulkhead of the Acaotilihuei canal. Along the edge of the bulkhead, a large band of scraggly hyena-like humanoids scramble about packing sacks with loot, tying them into bundles, and lowering them over the seawall.

The tree line sits about 10 feet from the edge of the canal, exposing a small clearing that runs for 30 yards parallel to the water. The manmade bulkhead of piled logs and concrete rests 15 feet above the waterline.

Just beyond the tree line, 18 **gnolls** work feverishly, binding up packages and crates of loot with coarse ropes and then lowering them down the bulkhead.

Below the bulkhead and out of the characters' sight, another group of 6 **gnolls** stands waist-deep in the water to load the packages into the canoes. Once finished, they intend to head back across the canal.

Overly confident in their numerical superiority, the gnolls work loudly and clumsily. They exert no effort to keep an eye out for trouble, giving the characters advantage on their Dexterity (Stealth) checks contested by the gnolls' Wisdom (Perception) checks. Indeed, the gnolls are so distracted that the characters automatically succeed on their contested Dexterity (Stealth) checks made up to the edge of the tree line, provided the characters do not disclose their positions in a blatantly obvious manner. If the characters break cover, they surprise the gnolls if the monsters fail to notice them.

Ultimately, the craven hyena-men fear defeat. If the heroes reduce their numbers by half, the surviving gnolls break formation and attempt to flee. The gnolls are poor swimmers. If the characters corner them and force them over the bulkhead and into the canal, they wade along the water's edge until they find a safe location to climb up the bulkhead and flee into the forest.

If the characters prevent a gnoll from fleeing and call for its surrender, the monster drops its weapon and stops in its tracks if the character succeeds on a Charisma check made with advantage contested by the gnolls' Wisdom (Insight) check.

A character who forces a gnoll to surrender may interrogate it by succeeding on a Charisma (Intimidation or Persuasion) check contested by the gnoll's Wisdom (Insight) check. Each time the character succeeds, that individual can ask the gnoll 1d4 questions, which it answers to the best of its ability. If the character fails a check, the gnoll says nothing for the next 10 minutes, at which point another character can try again.

The gnolls convey the following bits of information if asked why they raided the village or if faced with a similar inquiry:

• A man calling himself Cuanmitztlactl bribed them into participating in the raid by promising them the spoils.

If pressed for a description of Cuanmitztlactl, they reveal he is a Poqoza with distinctive tattoos, which he covered with clay paint before the attack to presumably disguise his identity. Anyone who speaks Aztli knows that the name Cuanmitztlactl loosely translates to Jaguar Lord, suggesting it is likely an alias. If the characters convey the Poqoza's description to any resident of

Traveling the Canal

Characters traveling to the various locations in this adventure are likely to use the canal at some point to reach their intended destination.

Because it connects to the surrounding ocean, the water levels in the canal ebb and flow with the tides. The **Children of Itzcuin** encounter starts at low tide. At this time, the waters at the bulkhead sit at a shallow 3-1/2 feet deep with a three-mile-per-hour current moving east. The depth drops off moving toward the center of the canal, which is deeply dredged to accommodate safe passage for larger ships.

If the characters arrive at the canal at a later point in the adventure, determine the tide randomly by rolling 1d4 on **Table 5–1** below. Start the tide at the determined position but continue to mark the shifts as time passes.

TABLE 5–1: TIDES IN THE GREAT CANAL

1d4	Tide
1	Ebb tide (tide is going out). Determine tide speed in miles per hour by rolling 1d8.*
2	Slack tide (tide is switching from going out to going in). Tide speed is zero.**
3	Flood tide (tide is going in). Determine the speed in miles per hour by rolling 1d8.*
4	Slack tide (tide is switching from going in to going out). Tide speed is zero.**

* Both ebb and flood tides last approximately 10 hours.
** Slack tides last about two hours each.

Characters moving with the tide increase their speed by the speed of the tide. Characters going against the tide decrease their speed by the speed of the tide.

At least once during their travels, the characters attract the attention of the canal's most fearsome predators. A hunting party of 10 **merrow** spots their boat. If possible, they attempt to redirect the crafts by latching on underneath and swimming them off course. Once they isolate a boat, they flip or smash it and greedily attack the nearest target floundering in the water.

Atoyatetl, that person identifies Cuanmitztlactl as Metzpil. If the characters accurately describe the tattoo to the village priest, the skein witch, a similarly trained person, or any Poqoza, that individual identifies the man as the son of the tlamacazqui with a successful DC 10 Intelligence (Religion) check.

• If the characters raise questions about the dragon, the gnolls divulge that the dragon is not a true ally nor was it magically summoned. Instead, Cuanmitztlactl (Metzpil) manipulated the beast into leading the attack against the village to retrieve her stolen eggs. They also pin this plan on Cuanmitztlactl, explaining that he stole the eggs and then sent one of them to tell the dragon that they had witnessed the humans stealing the eggs. They told the beast where to find its missing eggs.

Wrapping Things Up

This section concludes if the characters defeat the gnolls. At this point, they can use any information they discovered to follow other leads or return to the village. The gnolls stole a number of tools, cloth, food, and other items from the village. The characters can travel on foot; however, they may also use the gnolls' dugout canoes to paddle along the canal. The dugouts have the same statistics as a rowboat.

The drop to the water is 15 feet. If the characters spot the ropes and grappling hooks with a successful DC 10 Wisdom (Perception) check, they infer the creatures used these tools to land their dugout canoes and scale the bulkhead. The gnolls set spikes into the face of the logs to create makeshift cleats to which they tied off the six large dugout canoes. If the characters decide to take the canal, use the **Traveling the Canal** sidebar as a reference.

Chapter Two: A Tangled Fate

The temple barge of Nahualipazotic floats 5,000 feet off the coast, just east of the mouth of the canal. The chillier northern winds hammer against the warm, sun-soaked coast to create a dense and almost unnatural fog infamous among sailors and mariners who ply these waters. These waters just offshore are particularly dangerous to large vessels, as what lies just beneath the surface was once the top of a large mountainous region before the gods sank Tehuatl under the sea. Dozens of jagged rocky spires patiently wait to rip ships' hulls into splinters. The notoriously desolate shoreline consists entirely of pebbles and stones that churn angrily in the rolling surf.

The dense fog prevents the characters from spotting the concealed barge from the mouth of the canal. The vapors lessen and ultimately dissipate when the characters move approximately 1,500 feet away from the shoreline. However, finding their way through the fog poses a challenge. A character must succeed on a DC 15 Wisdom (Survival) check to maintain a sense of direction and to avoid getting lost or running aground, though a character with a sailor or other nautical background has advantage on the check. When the characters exit the fog and scan the water for Nahualipazotic's barge, read or paraphrase the following description:

> Drifting in the foggy reaches off the coast, near the mouth of the Acaotilihuei, bobs the decrepit remains of an abandoned Maldract maht temple-barge. Its towering array of badly weathered volcanic bricks floats low in the water, with its now lower levels completely submerged. Desolate and bare, from the shore it appears as little more than a large rock jutting out of the sea like one of the numerous ancient peaks whose mountainous roots hide beneath the ocean waters.

Getting to the Temple

The temple drifts less than one mile off the coast. The characters may attempt to reach the barge in several different ways. A boat is probably the simplest option, though characters at this level are also likely to have some flight capabilities as well. While the current can be tricky due to the area's close proximity to the canal, a successful DC 10 Wisdom (Survival) check determines when the currents are optimal, particularly if the tide is going out. Swimming (while also an option) is slightly more difficult, particularly if the character is swimming against the tide (see **Traveling the Canal** sidebar).

When the adventurers near the temple barge, it becomes visibly obvious that the worn pumice blocks that hold it afloat have grown sodden with age. The temple barge floats low and at a slight angle and only the crest of the upper steps still struggles to stay above the gray water. A jungle of seaweed clings to the blocks and bobs slowly in the waves, sending it into a swirling hypnotic dance.

To get aboard and enter the barge by mundane means, a character must succeed on a DC 10 Strength (Athletic) check to climb up the steps. Once aboard, the character can search for the entrance. Because the water-slicked stone floors of the barge sit at a slightly uneven pitch, coupled with the constant rocking motion caused by the ocean waves, the barge counts as difficult terrain. While four main entrances are at the base of the temple, all of these are now submerged and overgrown with seaweed. The only exterior entrance sits at the top of the structure.

The sea bride has 4 **eel hounds** (see **Appendix A: New Monsters**) that actively keep watch over the barge, entering and leaving through the submerged entrances on the lowest floor. Within 1d4 minutes after the characters' arrival, the hounds pick up their scent and start howling ominously to alert their mistress that there are intruders. They swim a few times around the barge to see if they can spot the intruders before calling off their search. They try to remain hidden while alternating their howls to distract the characters. After circling the barge twice, the creatures enter through the submerged entrances and go to meet with Nahualipazotic. At this time, allow the characters to react and plan whatever actions they intend on taking. As they do so, Nahualipazotic allows her eel dogs to lead her to the intruders. When the characters finish their actions, she arrives to confront them as described in **Encounter T1** below.

Encounter T1: The Sea Bride

Nahualipazotic is a **marid** (see **Appendix A: New Monsters**) who served as the sea bride of the hero-god Quiahuitl. Before he ascended into godhood, the mortal Nahualipazotic gave her life to save her husband from drowning during a tidal wave spawned by Tlatoani. The forlorn Quiahuitl searched the outgoing tide but could not find her body. After several days, he presumed she died and was washed out to sea. However, her heroic act of self-sacrifice caused her lifeless body to fuse with the Plane of Water, giving her a new existence as a genie. The marid initially remembered nothing about her former existence, though faint glimpses and memories of her past slowly crept back into her mind over the centuries. Meanwhile, the widower Quiahuitl later married Atoyatl, who still bristled at the mention of her husband's first great love and the woman who sacrificed herself to save him. Now thousands of years old, the venerable genie largely keeps out of sight to avoid attracting Atoyatl's jealous glare, which rears its ugly head every few centuries. She secrets herself away in the decrepit remains of a half-sunken Maldraht maht temple-barge, where she simmers with anger toward the humans who forgot about the sacrifices of her husband, and more importantly, those she made, to liberate them from the oppressive Tlatloani.

When she meets the characters, the haughty genie berates them for dishonoring her husband and warns them that if they do not leave immediately, she will order her 4 **eel hounds** (see **Appendix A: New Monsters**) to feast on their flesh. The characters have one round to act before she makes good on her promise. If the characters do not flee, agree to leave, or adequately convince her to listen to them, she commands her eel hounds to rip out the characters' throats. The eel hounds then rush to attack as she pelts the characters with her spells and trident.

To gain the sea bride's assistance, the characters must convince her of their integrity. They can accomplish this in several different ways. The characters could take non-hostile actions on their turn, such as the Dodge action or throwing their weapons to the ground in an obvious sign of their willingness to negotiate with her. Next, they must promise an offering, sacrifice, or some other suitable tribute to her husband. The gift must be worthy of a deity, though if the characters are stumped in this regard, they may plead ignorance as to an appropriate sacrifice, leaving her to decide what they must offer her. In her temperamental mind, a gift of blood, such as a powerful enemy's heart, or precious objects, preferably with a connection to the sea or the rain, worth at least 1,000 gp, will suffice. However, if the characters killed any of her eel dogs before beginning the negotiations, she demands additional compensation for her losses.

Alternately, any character who explains they came to seek her assistance to slay a black dragon that lives in the swamps immediately gets her attention. Nahualipazotic despises the black dragon Aaq'eq' because as a serpent, she considers her one of Tlatoani's daughters and by extension a sworn enemy of her mortal husband.

Once told about the dragon, clever characters can easily convince Nahualipazotic to aid them by vowing to seek out and kill the creature. If they do so, the sea bride asks them to wait for a moment and then disappears into the inner chambers of her temple. When she returns, read or paraphrase the following description:

> Nahualipazotic returns several minutes later carrying a single arrow of blacked wood, ebon fletching, and an obsidian head carved in the shape of a dragon's open maw.
>
> "This," she croaks, "this arrow was carved by the hero-warrior Yaocteotl. He had several others like it, all for laying low the foul spawn of the Serpent God, whose name I shall not speak.
>
> I fear however that its powers have waned over these many centuries and at present it is useless. That said, I may be able to restore some of its strength with the right components. Bring me a flawless black pearl from the sacred pearl beds, and I shall make you a weapon to kill the dragon Aaq'eq'."

If the characters agree to retrieve the black pearl, Nahualipazotic gives them further instructions on how to find the pearls.

At this point, allow the players to discuss and determine how they intend to get to the pearl beds as well as to ask further questions of Nahualipazotic if they deem it necessary. If the characters swam to the temple, Nahualipazotic offers them the use of several small pontoon canoes, ghastly crafts crafted from human skin and bone left behind by the Maldraht maht. If the characters ask Nahualipazotic about the wraith of Quiahuitl, she tells them that the sacrificial victims of the god of storms guard the sacred pearl beds and warns them to steer clear of their sodden corpses.

Once the characters are ready to depart, read or paraphrase the following description:

Upon seeing the corpses, the eel dogs stop and begin snarling. They refuse to go closer.

The floating corpses are 4 **drowned maidens** (see **Appendix A: New Monsters**), women sacrificed to the gods to protect the sacred pearl beds.

If characters approach, the creatures attempt to stealthily use their kelp hair to entangle the vessel in an attempt to capsize the vessel so they can attack opponents floundering in the water.

If the characters defeat the drowned maidens, they are free to explore the sacred pearl beds.

The oyster reef is eight feet below the water's surface. Finding an oyster with a black pearl in it proves slightly more difficult, but can be achieved with a successful DC 25 Wisdom (Survival) check or by spending two hours harvesting and shucking oysters. The pearl they eventually find is flawless.

Treasure: The pearl is worth 500 gp.

Wrapping Things Up

This section concludes if the characters return to the sea bride with a black pearl. Nahualipazotic uses the material component to recharge the *arrow of slaying* (black dragon). The process takes her the entire evening. The characters are free to spend the night in the temple, though she cannot offer them much in the way of formal accommodations beyond a hard floor to sleep on, cold fish, and rainwater. After Nahualipazotic presents them with the arrow, the characters may depart for the saltwater swamp known as Yoaltica Ilaquiloz. When they depart, the sea bride makes them a final offer, which you may deliver by reading or paraphrasing the following dialogue:

If the adventurers kill Aaq'eq' and later return to Nahualipazotic with proof of the dragon's death, she offers them a small stone bearing a carving of a face set inside a sun. The characters can use the small medallion to contact her to seek her advice. They may use it to contact her three times, after which it turns to dust.

While her powers of insight are not unlimited, Nahualipazotic possesses a substantial amount of information about demons, Tlatoani, the creation of Tehuatl, and numerous other details that might help them defeat the Drowned Serpent's Daughter in the final chapter. Characters must choose their word carefully. Treat any questions posed to the sea bride as if the characters had cast a *wish* spell.

Chapter Three: Yoaltica Ilaquiloz

Yoaltica Ilaquiloz is a saltwater swamp along Tehuatl's eastern shore that consists of almost 4,000 square miles of flooded lowlands. It stretches northward from the canal to an elevated plateau of eroded hills that forms a natural barrier preventing it from spreading farther north. The swamp is an ecological, manmade newcomer to the island. It formed 75 years earlier, after the Flood of Quiahuitl's Tears brutally battered the coastline, causing the partial collapse of nearly 20 miles of the canal wall bordering the northern part of the island.

The harsh and desolate saltwater swamp makes traveling on foot difficult. Those who need to travel through the swamp typically do so by poling flat-bottomed rafts through mazes of shallow channels that weave through small islands of mud and silt. These small islands hold little aside from clumps of shaggy reeds and stout stocky mangrove shrubs with long, broad leaves. The soft mush forms small hummocks, though these are barely stable enough to support more than a few pounds of weight. Any creature larger than a cat walking on them slowly sinks into the muck and finds it impossible to move more than 20 feet before sinking into a few feet of mud. The mud affects characters in the same manner as quicksand, although it is just four feet deep. If a character gets stuck in the mud, it takes a successful DC 15 Strength (Athletics) check to swim back to the surface or pull someone out of the gooey material. The mud poses no immediate danger unless the character is not tall enough to keep his or her head above water, in which case the character may drown without outside intervention. The water in the channels is 1d4 feet deep, resting above three feet of soft silt that covers the bottom. The channels are 2d4 feet wide, meandering in a web throughout the swamp, where they occasionally form larger pools that are 1d4 + 6 feet deep.

Vermin thoroughly infest the tropical saltwater swamp. Swarms of mosquitos, large toxic-skinned salamanders, stinging mudfish, frogs, and serpents fly and slither through the muck. While undoubtedly annoying, few of these creatures pose any serious threat to the characters if they took the proper precautions. On occasion, travelers might also encounter larger predators such as crocodiles or some of the more hostile reptilian humanoid tribes that inhabit the region, such as the lizardfolk and tsathars.

The dragon's lair is at the northern edge of the swamp near the edge of the plateau, about 60 miles due north of Azuato on the regional map. If the characters travel at normal speed through the difficult terrain, the journey takes approximately five days. During their travels, you can occasionally slow the pace and add further description with the following obstacles and encounters. Consider one or more of the encounters from about the midway point (about the second day or so into the journey) to the black dragon's lair, before you run **The Temple of Necocyaotl** encounter. You may also want to consider adding your own encounters to the list, as well as saving one or more of them for the return trip.

Swamp Encounters

Insect Attack: Near midday, the burning sun breaks through the haze, hot enough to pierce the dense tangles of the swamp thickets. Clouds of insects shoot into the sky, enticed by the heat to seek out warm-blooded creatures bold enough to violate their secret abodes.

The small stinging insects swarm the characters. Those exposed to the swarm are bitten and exposed to sewer plague. Characters can easily drive the swarm off with fire or smoke. Those who thought ahead and slathered themselves with herbal poultices or swamp mud repel the irritating insects and avoid contracting the disease.

Shambling Mounds: At this location, something triggered the swamp's foul alchemy, releasing an overwhelming stench of decay and decomposition. Suddenly, the reeds bend as 3 **shambling mounds** emerge from the vegetation and attack.

Reeds: The channel empties into a wide pool filled with dense, spiny swamp reeds. The pool fills a 1,000-square-foot area surrounded by stumpy clots of tiny mud islands. The reeds' abrasive shafts slash and tear any creatures attempting to move through them. A creature must succeed on a DC 15 Dexterity saving throw or take 1 hit point of piercing damage for every five feet of movement through the reeds. A creature moving through the area at half speed does not need to make the save. Of course, you are free to add sound effects and other overt signs of trouble to hasten their movement through the tangled vegetation.

Wispy Clouds: The day drags as a low fog rolls ashore, followed by scattered light rain showers. The weather conditions drive away the insects, but it also reduces visibility and lightly obscures the area. After one hour, clothing and equipment becomes sodden and clings to the skin. Those wearing armor or carrying heavier equipment and poling or wading begin to tire and chafe from the exertion, heat, and humidity. Anyone performing moderate activity for longer than one hour succeed on a DC 10 Constitution saving throw or gain 1 level of exhaustion.

After a while, it almost appears as if the fog is breaking, and the characters spot flickers of light ahead. The flickering light is an effect created by a gang of 1d4 + 8 **will-o'-wisps**. The mysterious creatures surround the characters and attempt to drain away their life energy.

Orange Lotus: This intersection opens into a wide channel that seems to offer easy passage through the swamp. An enticingly sweet scent drifts from large clusters of water lotuses that line the edges of this waterway. Their bright orange petals are in full bloom, but the cloying honey and mint scent of their nectar belies their toxicity. Anyone exposed to the blossoms or nectar of the orange lotus (see **Appendix B**) is exposed to its poison.

Downpour: While crossing a wide pond, the sky suddenly opens and a loud thundercrack ushers in a torrential downpour. Characters who wish to avoid getting thoroughly soaked can seek shelter beneath a nearby outcrop of mangroves that line the shore. If the characters travel in a craft that can take on water, the rains begin to fill their craft at a rate of one inch per minute. The swift downpour lasts only for 3d10 minutes, after which the weather shifts into a glum mixture of intermittent fog and drizzle.

The Temple of Necocyaotl

The swamp waters become shallower, and a dense thicket of vegetation claws up from the murk to block your passage several hundred feet ahead. The channel splits at the edge of the thicket and circles around the mass, forming a small island. Great square blocks of stone are visible through the tangles of vines and swamp plants. Cracked and weathered, the stones no longer bear any runes or carvings, though they could not possibly have arrived here by natural means.

A large temple to the lesser-known hero-god Necocyaotl — the enemy of both sides — once stood at this location. The priest-warriors who occupied this temple remained neutral during the conflict between the Poqozas and the Aztlis. Their territory served as a buffer zone between the two sides, earning them the enmity of both. They vigorously defended their territory against trespassers belonging to either faction. When the canal walls that created the Yoaltica Ilaquiloz flooded the region, the temple tumbled and sank into the mire. The warrior-priests, unable to escape the destruction, sacrificed themselves to Necocyaotl using sacred potions to mummify their remains so they could continue to serve their god in death.

They are known as Necocyaotl's Chosen and appear as shriveled bodies wrapped in rotted leaves and sealed with mud. Their faces are covered with obsidian masks stylistically carved with hideous expressions with a single stripe of gold inlayed down the center. There are 10 **mummies** with the following changes:

Swamp Walker. The mummy does not treat swamps as difficult terrain and has advantage on Dexterity (Stealth) checks made to hide in swamp terrain.

Rotten Mudball. *Ranged Weapon Attack:* +5 to hit, reach 20 ft., one target. *Hit:* 6 (1d6 + 3) bludgeoning damage plus 7 (2d6) necrotic damage. If

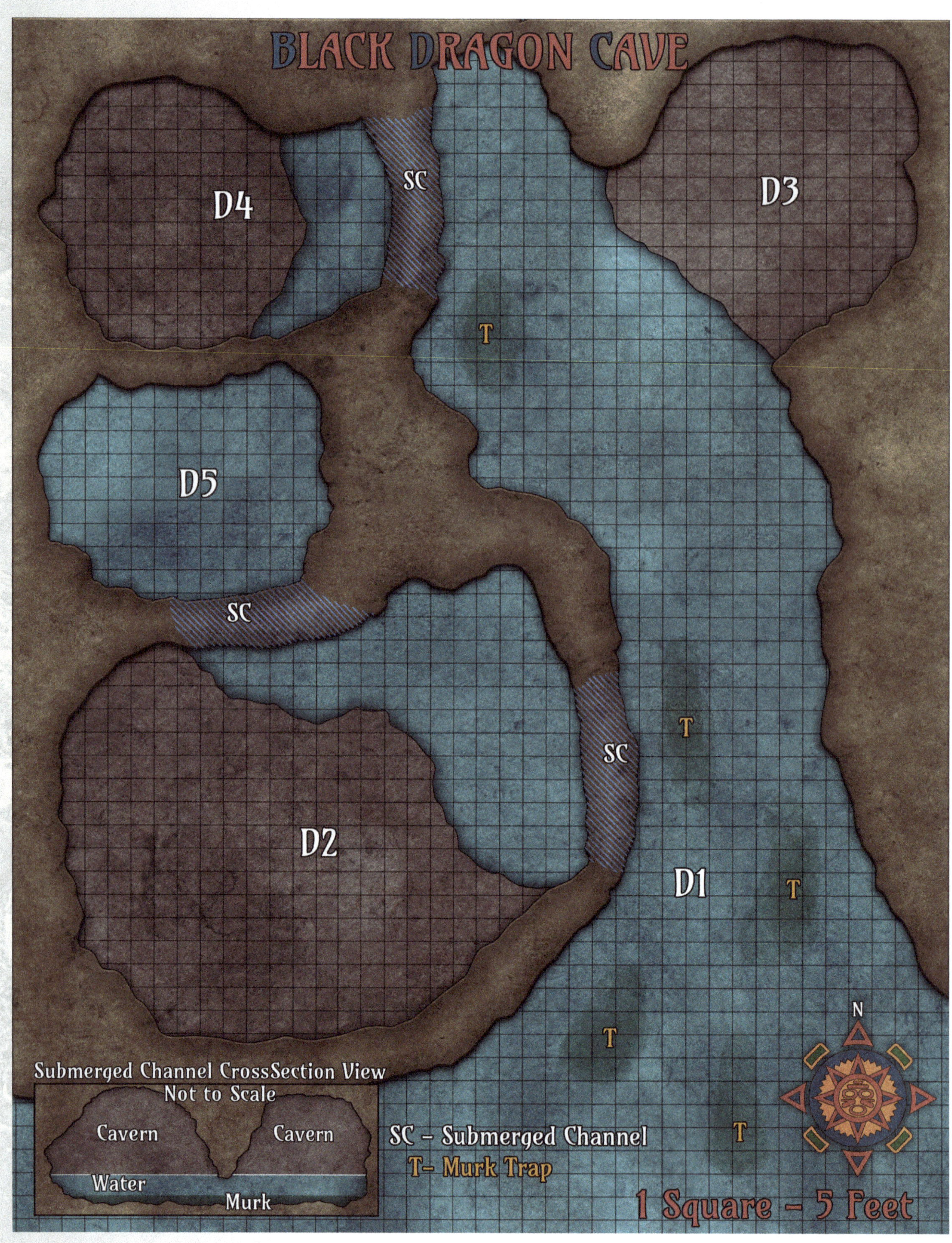

BLACK DRAGON CAVE
D4
D3
SC
T
D5
SC
T
SC
D2
D1
T
T
N
T
Submerged Channel CrossSection View
Not to Scale
Cavern
Cavern
Water
Murk
SC – Submerged Channel
T- Murk Trap
1 Square - 5 Feet

the target is a creature, it must make a DC 12 Constitution saving throw or be cursed with mummy rot on a failure. The cursed target can't regain hit points, and its hit point maximum decreases by 7 (2d6) for every 24 hours that elapse. If the curse reduces the target's hit point maximum to 0, the target dies, and its body turns to dust. The curse lasts until removed by the *remove curse* spell or other magic.

Treasure: Six of the masks are badly chipped and damaged and worth 1d10 gp each. Three are in average condition and worth 55 gp, 40 gp, and 25 gp. One is in superb condition and is worth 350 gp.

THE BLACK DRAGON'S LAIR

The dragon's lair is found where the swamp meets the plateau, in a series of flooded caves that carve their way into the elevated ground. If the characters approach, they notice that the grassy clumps and mud islands that block the outer swamp thin, giving way to freshwater flora such as floating lilies, cattails, and rushes that favor the improving conditions. Near the entrance of the caves, the swamp waters deepen, pooling against the stony barricade. Before the characters enter the black dragon's lair, you should make note of the following general cavern features.

GENERAL FEATURES

The dragon Aaq'eq' and her brood inhabit a series of caves that consist of several large chambers formed of natural stone. The caverns have extremely high, natural ceilings that (unless otherwise noted) climb between 30 to 40 feet from the chamber floor. A series of partially submerged channels connects the individual caverns using entrances hidden below the water line (see map). This means that a soupy morass of four-foot-deep water floods the majority of the cavern floors. The water rests atop another few feet of goopy murk. If the characters enter, the murk has settled on the bottom. However, when turbulence disturbs the murk, it mixes with the water and causes it to turn cloudy, reducing visibility in the water to 0 feet. The dragons use this knowledge to their advantage when they swim, deliberately stirring up the murk to mask their movements and locations. The murk also obscures the submerged tunnels that lead to the lair's outer caverns.

The caves are unlit, except for any daylight that happens to filter in from the main entrance. The caves reverberate sound easily, creating echoes from the constant lapping of water against the walls and condensation dripping from the ceilings. Inside, the air feels thick and still, unbearably humid, and carries a rank, fetid stench.

The caverns are inhabited by three dragons: Aaq'eq', an **adult black dragon**, and her children, 2 **young black dragons**. This section assumes that each of these dragons is in a specific location when the characters arrive; however, the dragons move freely about the caves and respond accordingly to the actions of the characters and to each other.

The dragons are intelligent creatures and have specific strategies for protecting their lair as noted throughout this section. You are advised to familiarize yourself with their tactics and motivations before running the encounter.

Lastly, Aaq'eq' and her brood have little interest in the affairs of humans. Having completed her assault on Atoyatetl, the dragon has little interest or motivation to attack other human settlements (as she exacted her retribution and recovered her precious eggs). Still, she does not take kindly to trespassers and believes any humans entering her domain seek to abscond with her eggs or steal her riches. If the characters find a way of presenting her with the truth about the individuals who stole her eggs, she furiously seeks out the gnolls and reaps all manner of vengeance against those who "set her up."

D1: LAIR ENTRANCE

To defend the territory surrounding their lair's entrance, the dragons dug out several deep spots that hide unseen beneath the murky sludge. Those traveling on foot and unaware of their presence can easily stumble into them, making them extremely vulnerable to swimming dragon attacks.

SWAMP MURK TRAPS

Those unwary or dimwitted enough to stumble into these hidden traps quickly sink into the mire as the dark waters force their way into their gasping lungs. Anyone stepping into a deep spot triggers the trap and risks becoming engulfed and suffocating in the mire. The triggering creature must succeed on a DC 15 Dexterity saving throw to avoid sinking. A successful save indicates the creature splashed its way back to shallower ground before sinking into the muck. On a failed saving throw, the target sinks into the mud and is restrained. The murk is 1d3 + 3 feet deep. If the creature cannot keep its head above the water, it must hold its breath to avoid drowning. Creatures submerged in the murk are blinded for as long as they remain underwater. The thick, soup-like water makes swimming difficult. Creatures smaller than Medium have disadvantage on Strength (Athletics) checks made to swim through the water. The creature can use an action on its turn to escape the murk trap by succeeding on a DC 15 Strength check. Another creature can use its action to help the trapped creature, giving it advantage on the proceeding Strength check. It takes a successful DC 15 Wisdom (Survival) check to notice the slight disturbance in the murky water, suggesting the presence of a deep spot.

If a character falls into a murk trap, the vibrations in the water immediately alert the nearest dragon, prompting the beast to swim forward and (if possible) try to surprise the character by swimming through the cloudy water and attacking the creature from below the surface.

When the characters enter the first cave, read or paraphrase the following description:

The western wall of the main entrance hides a submerged channel leading to the largest of the caverns. It serves as the inner sanctum for Aaq'eq', the adult female dragon that sired the entire brood inhabiting these caves. Characters actively searching the wall detect the submerged channel with a successful DC 15 Intelligence (Investigation) check. While the submerged channel appears only as deep as the rest of the caverns, it is carved slightly deeper and hides beneath another 15 feet of silt and murk. The 40-foot-wide, 10-foot-long channel empties into a broad pool that floods the northwestern portion of **Area D2**.

The passage continues for about 100 feet before intersecting with **Area D3**. There, it continues for almost another 100 feet at which point it appears to hit a dead-end. Here, a second submerged channel conceals **Area D4**. The channel is not as wide as the first one, but has otherwise identical properties. If the characters disturb the water, make loud noises, or otherwise perform actions that might alert the dragon of their presence, allow each of the dragons to attempt Wisdom (Perception) checks contested by the characters' Dexterity (Stealth) checks to sense them.

If Aaq'eq' senses intruders, she waits for them to enter deeper into the cavern and then tries to slip behind them. She readies her breath weapon for when the characters confront either of her children.

D2: AAQ'EQ'S SANCTUM

The submerged channel provides the only physical entrance to this cavern. If Aaq'eq' has not left the cavern, characters attempting to swim through the submerged channel risk disturbing the murk and alerting her to their approach. If this occurs, the dragon plunges into the water and uses her Legendary

Action (see below) to make an underwater wing buffet attack that creates a powerful current to sweep any characters caught in the passage back into the main entrance and toward the nearest murk trap.

The cavern that serves as Aaq'eq's sanctum is pitch black; thus, individuals who cannot see in darkness must procure a light source. Cut off from the outside, the overwhelming reek of her foul stench permeates the entire cavern, and the air is twice as humid and stifling as the outer passages.

If the characters enter Aaq'eq's sanctum, read or paraphrase the following description:

While the boulder platform poses no difficulty for the larger feet of dragons, smaller creatures find it difficult to walk across the slippery surfaces without slipping or twisting an ankle. In addition to being difficult terrain, any creature of Medium or smaller size that attempts to cross the terrain at normal speed must succeed on a DC 12 Dexterity (Acrobatics) check to avoid slipping and falling prone. Anyone who rolls a natural 1 on this check gets a foot stuck in a hole between the rocks. It takes an action to free the foot from the crevasse without taking damage. Alternatively, the creature can continue its movement without expending an action, but doing so deals 1d4 points of slashing damage.

If the characters have not yet alerted Aaq'eq' to their presence, she rests atop the stony platform feigning sleep. She waits for the intruders to get closer, then blasts them with acid hoping to force them to retreat back into the water. Aaq'eq' is an **adult black dragon** with the following additional Legendary Action:

Underwater Wing Buffet. While submerged, Aaq'eq' can flap her wings to create a turbulent current of water. The current churns a 50-foot cone of water with such force that all creatures standing or swimming in the area must succeed on a DC 25 Strength saving throw to avoid being knocked prone (if standing) and pushed back by the current. On a failed check, the current sucks characters underwater and pushes them 3d10 feet away from their previous location. Additionally, the powerful turbulence violently forces water into the creature's lungs and forces a creature who failed the preceding Strength saving throw to also succeed on a DC 15 Constitution saving throw. A creature who fails the saving throw gasps for air and cannot speak. In this state, the creature has disadvantage on ability checks, attack rolls, and saving throws, and its speed is halved. At the end of each of its turns, the creature can attempt another Constitution saving throw to expel the water. On a success, the creature forces the water out and no longer suffers any harmful effects from this attack. Creatures who cannot expel the water in a reasonable amount of time risk drowning.

D3: MAIN CAVERN

Medium and smaller characters treat the bloodstained boulder field as difficult terrain. Anyone who makes a successful DC 8 Intelligence (Nature) check readily identifies the bones as a combination of livestock and humanoids. The rocky incline rises at a fairly steep angle but can be ascended with a successful DC 10 Strength (Athletics) check. A section of loose scree halfway up the cliff can be spotted with a successful DC 10 Wisdom (Survival) check. Once spotted, it is easily avoided; however, characters attempting to climb over it jar some of the loose stones free, requiring them to succeed on a new DC 18 Strength (Athletics) to reacquire their grip and avoid sliding back down the incline, which deals no damage but forces the creature to start its climbing attempt anew.

A **young black dragon** hides in the far corner of the overlook. The eldest of Aaq'eq's spawn, the dragon uses this perch to watch over the cavern entrance.

As soon as he senses intruders, he swoops down to attack, ushering a wailing screech that quickly alerts the other dragons within the lair. Upon hearing the screech, the others rush to his aid at maximum speed.

D4: THE EGGS

The nest stands about five feet tall and is 10 feet in diameter with an open top. Anyone peering over the top observes that it is hollow and filled with mud. Floating in the mud are three large ebony colored eggs. They are of course black dragon eggs, which a successful DC 8 Intelligence (Arcana) absolutely confirms.

Another of Aaq'eq's spawn usually dwells here to protect her eggs. If prior events have not drawn her from her duties (such as being called to battle by her brood-mate or her mother, or being drawn out by the actions of the characters), then an **young black dragon** lurks here.

If any harm comes to these eggs or if anyone absconds with one or more of them, any surviving dragons swear a vendetta to tirelessly and mercilessly hunt down and slay whomever they believe to be the perpetrators of this act. They are singularly focused while hunting and use every available resource at their disposal. They refuse to be thwarted by any distance or opposing foe.

D5: DRAGON'S HOARD

The water in this cavern is five feet deep and floats above a thick stew of mud. A character who pokes around in the mud and succeeds on a DC 12 Intelligence (Investigation) check locates a sizable hoard of treasure buried in the silt-strewn morass. Uncovering the treasure also disturbs the silt as described in the **General Features** section, which means those looking for treasure are blinded while immersed in or looking into the soupy water.

Treasure: The buried hoard contains 20 large gold ingots worth 850 gp each, a carved jade statuette of a couatl worth 1,300 gp, a large gold bracelet emblazoned with images of the sun worth 600 gp, a gold lip plate set with bloodstones worth 125 gp, and a small stone coffer containing 12 teardrops carved from jade and obsidian, each worth 350 gp. It also contains a *ring of shooting stars*, a *potion of speed*, a *periapt of wound closure*, and a *macuahuitl of revealing* (see **Appendix C: New Equipment and Magic Items**).

WRAPPING THINGS UP

This section ends if the characters defeat Aaq'eq'. If they slay the dragon and her children and provide proof of their victory (such as by taking trophies of teeth, eggs, or horns), they have the opportunity to earn the assistance of the sea bride as described in **Chapter 2: A Tangled Fate**. If they instead turn Aaq'eq' against the gnolls, she reveals that the individual she believed to have taken her eggs was Metzpil, the fifth son of the tlamacazqui.

At this point, the characters must travel back through the swamp. If they have yet to gather clues from other locations, they can use the canal to revisit or complete any of those sections. If they have enough information to seek out Metzpil, feel free to move on to **Chapter 4: The Secret of the Fallen Son.**

CHAPTER FOUR: THE SECRET OF THE FALLEN SON

This chapter begins when characters decide they want to seek out Metzpil to determine what role, if any, he played in the destruction of Atoyatetl. If they are not sure where to track him down, they may return to his village and ask questions about his whereabouts. The local warriors inform the characters that in their absence one of their hunters captured a Jaguar Cuauhocelotl and is holding him for questioning. Alternately, if the characters do not return to the village, they may encounter the warrior and the captured Jaguar Cuauhocelotl while walking through the woods. Or they may run into a small band of the jaguar warriors themselves and capture one for questioning.

Once captured, it becomes obvious that the warrior is not a real Jaguar Cuauhocelotl. The man (CN male Poqoza half-elf **cult fanatic**), who is disguised as a human, is really a half-elf Poqoza who exhibits more human traits than elf features. His body bears strange ritualistic scars that resemble scales. He is also in very bad shape — crazed, delusional, and badly weakened from some sort of poison.

Characters seeking to determine the details of his condition can either consult with Atoyatetl's storyteller or Nahualipazotic to learn the man is suffering from withdrawal associated with a rare and dangerous hallucinogen known as maht (see **Appendix B**). The psychoactive agent is most closely associated with the fearsome Slaughter Priests who indulge in the psychoactive agent before entering their violent and bloody sacrifice raids. Similarly, a successful DC 20 Wisdom (Medicine) or Intelligence (Religion) check reveals the same information.

Fortunately for the characters, the prisoner's withdrawal symptoms are so intense that he is willing to tell them anything in exchange for maht. He gladly reveals that he serves Metzpil, who boasts that Tlatoani has gifted the Poqoza scion with powerful magic. He prophesies all will bow before Metzpil when he ascends into the Immortal Serpent Emperor. Beyond that information, he refuses to speak until he gets maht.

Maht is quite rare and its fearsome reputation causes most to shy away from it. While the Poqozas readily indulge in most hallucinogenic substances, they greatly fear maht, which is occasionally imported onto the island by Tulita traders from the distant Razor (see **Razor Coast** from **Frog God Games** for more details about this locale), where the grisly Slaughter Priests originate. If the characters ask where they can find the nearest possible source of maht, the reluctant residents tell them to see the tlamatini, an aged and wise Tulita man who serves several of the neighboring villages as a counselor, sage, and medicine man.

The sea bride probably has some as well, but the prisoner would likely die from withdrawals before they could reach her. The tlamatini is much closer and his knowledge of such things is good enough that he could probably procure some of the mystic root. The tlamatini lives in Ipaccanemiliz, Atoyatetl's sister village that languishes along the southern edge of the canal about 3 miles east of the Temetzin River.

IPACCANEMILIZ

The small settlement of Ipaccanemiliz consists of 30 or so mud-brick dwellings along with a few larger structures augmented with broad thatched awnings suspended on wood post frames. The houses center on a great brick fountain connected to a subterranean well where the people get their water. Cooking fires burn in front of many of the homes, while the inhabitants bustle about performing various mundane tasks. A small moat of water piped in from the canal surrounds the village, but the settlement is accessible by four bridges that traverse the water. A statue dedicated to an ancient ancestor stands at the edge of each bridge.

When the characters arrive, the town's warriors (various alignments, male Poqoza half-elf **scout** armed with clubs instead of shortswords) immediately rush to receive them and take the prisoner into custody. The warriors and the townspeople are highly agitated by a terrifying recent event. The warriors seem as eager to interrogate the prisoner as the characters. As soon as the characters ask about the tlamatini or recent events, one of the warriors divulges the following harrowing account:

Metzpil cast a *planar ally* spell and used a fiend to wield a powerful item to steal the tlamatini's soul, which he intends to present as a gift to the Drowned Daughter. She requires the soul for a ritual and prompted Metzpil to collect it for her. The tlamatini is now trapped in a horrific and torturous state between life and death, unable to continue in either direction and forced to confront both simultaneously, even though these realities are in conflict with one other.

If the characters possess magical means of speaking with either dead people (such as a *speak with dead* spell) or some means of communicating with him telepathically, the tlamatini explains his condition to them and reveals that Metzpil commanded a disguised fiend to steal his soul using a powerful item called the *seal of Miquito* that celestials and fiends use to guide souls on their journey to the afterlife. Essentially, his soul has departed on its journey while his consciousness remains in the present. No known human possesses the power to use the item to perform such a task, so therefore Metzpil has either transformed into an otherworldly creature or, more likely, he has a supernatural ally. The tlamatini can confirm with authority that Metzpil is responsible for the recent attacks and has fallen under the corrupt influence of a being he believes to be Tlatoani.

After speaking with the tlamatini, the characters might realize that they cannot acquire maht and may likely conclude that their prisoner is no longer of any use to them. The jaguar warrior has fallen deeper into his withdrawal but he begs the characters to let him go. If they do so, he makes a mad rush for Metzpil's encampment in a desperate bid to momentarily soothe his vicious cravings. At this point, he cares for nothing else and carelessly leads the characters on an easy and direct route to Metzpil who is roughly 20 miles north-northeast of Quizaloa in a locale known as a Nest of Serpents.

Alternately, Ipaccanemiliz's warriors can point the characters in the direction that Metzpil and his allies retreated. They are also willing to help track down their location and suggest that their dogs can easily track the scent now that they have a prisoner.

THE ASSASSIN

Metzpil ordered his agents to keep a careful eye on activities in Ipaccanemiliz. Unless they took precautions to enter the city undetected, his spies observed the characters arrive with their prisoner. Word of such activities piques his interest. His two spies (CE male Poqoza half-elf **spies** armed with daggers and shortbows instead of shortswords and hand crossbows) slip out of the village and report on the characters' activities. If Metzpil hears nothing from them for two days, he assumes the worst, and dispatches a **serpent's kiss assassin** (see **Appendix A: New Monsters**) to kill them. He arrives during the overnight hours under the cover of darkness to quietly sneak into the settlement to slit the characters' throats while they sleep.

Treasure: The serpent's kiss assassin wears *+2 tlahuitztli* (see **Appendix C**) armor, wields a *dagger of venom* and a *+1 longbow*, and has a *wand of enemy detection*.

A Nest of Serpents

Metzpil and his disciples are holed up in the ruins of a forsaken temple compound dedicated to Tlatoani that lies 20 miles north-northeast of Quizaloa. The cataclysm and the hero-gods themselves razed almost all of the structures and monuments to the ground, but a handful of buildings survived the devastation. The early Tozcas attempted to rebuild what they could to no avail. The journey requires a hard trek through 30 miles of festering swampland.

Metzpil's demonic counselor gifted him these ruins as a token of their everlasting friendship. These ruins are approximately 20 miles from the Temple of the Serpent (Quizaloa) where the priestess resides. This locale now serves as a dwelling place for cultists and maht addicts she corrupted to create a living vessel for her father. At present, the ruins consist of three pyramids and a ball-court. All other structures have long since crumbled. Metzpil and his disciples built a small encampment in the center of the ruins. He managed to corrupt 40 **Poqoza warriors** (see **Appendix A: New Monsters**) to his nefarious cause. In addition, he trained 6 **serpent cuauhocelotls** (see **Appendix A: New Monsters**) to serve as his elite commanders. These individuals move freely around the encampment in accordance with their needs or in response to the characters' actions or Metzpil's commands. However, they rarely congregate as a large group and are instead spread out across the ruins with specific numbers listed in areas where characters are most likely to encounter them. Warriors and cuauhocelotls noted in the location descriptions are part of the main group and are not additional enemies. It must also be noted that Metzpil and his disciples regularly indulge in maht and are highly addicted. Assume these individuals always have at least one dose on them at all times.

If given an opportunity, Metzpil and his disciples always attempt to eat maht before entering combat. If they succeed, they suffer from its effects (see **Appendix B**) until they wear off.

After the long journey, the characters reach the accursed region known as a Nest of Serpents. Here, the forest changes and becomes hauntingly quiet and the trees twist at odd angles. Use the strangeness to create tension just before the characters arrive. Once they near the ruins, read or paraphrase the following text box:

A wandering patrol of 8 **Poqoza warriors** (see **Appendix A: New Monsters**) led by a **serpent cuauhocelotl** (see **Appendix A: New Monsters**) walk the perimeter of the encampment to keep a sharp eye out for any intruders. When the characters arrive, determine the patrol's starting location by rolling 1d8 to determine the cardinal direction of their current sector with 1 representing north, 2 representing northeast, and continuing clockwise around the compass culminating at 8 representing northwest. Thereafter, the patrol walks clockwise around the perimeter and explores each section for approximately 30 minutes.

If the warriors or their leader spot intruders, they initially attempt to drive them off. However, if they are unable to force the characters to retreat in four rounds, the warriors send half their numbers back to the encampment to get more reinforcements and to warn Metzpil. Alternately, if the Poqoza warriors and their leader drop to half their number in fewer than four rounds, the entire unit races back to the encampment to warn their allies.

E1: Pyramid of the Lost Moon

The ancients built this temple to honor the moon. They performed monthly rituals for the inanimate satellite during the new moon. It now sits in disrepair, encased in rubble and moss.

Metzpil now uses the temple as a vantage point for his lookouts. During daylight hours, 2 **Poqoza Warriors** (see **Appendix A: New Monsters**) sit high atop the pyramid keeping watch over the surrounding area.

Inside, faded murals portray warriors undergoing several ceremonies that transform them into serpent cuauhocelotls. One mural shows a priest

Who is Metzpil?

Metzpil is the fifth son of the tlamacazqui, which gives him a measure of prestige but no inheritance rights. After his actual father left his mother behind and moved on to the next settlement before Metzpil's birth, the young woman married another man and raised Metzpil in the small trading village. This unpleasant fact coupled with Metzpil's lack of an inheritance has dogged him throughout his life. Metzpil presents himself as a supporter of the common people rather than as a haughty noble. Nonetheless, some villagers secretly wonder if he really is the tlamacazqui's son, though none ever openly expresses this opinion.

Metzpil grew up working trade vessels on the canal. About a year before the current series of events, he stopped in a small village along the canal where a priestess introduced him to a strange new substance that she called maht (see **Appendix B**), a dangerous and highly addictive substance used by ancient warriors to induce battle fury. She knew Metzpil was the tlamacazqui's son and promised him that ritually consuming maht would reveal the young man's true destiny. In his altered state, Metzpil heard the whispers of Tlatoani in the chants of the priestess and experienced a vision where he transformed into a massive serpent and ascended to immortality to take the role of the new god-emperor of Tehuatl. When the maht's influence wore off, the priestess performed a baptismal ceremony upon him and then anointed him the mortal vessel and second coming of the Serpent Who Shall Devour the Gods.

The visions held more truth than Metzpil realized, for the priestess in fact was preparing his body to serve as the new mortal vessel of Tlatoani. What Metzpil does not — and cannot — understand is that Tlatoani needs only his flesh. When the time comes, the banished deity will devour Metzpil's mind and soul in the process of being reborn. Moreover, the priestess is far from what she seems. The demon daughter of the Drowned Serpent, she is orchestrating her father's return by turning Metzpil into a mere puppet, a sacrifice to alter the path of the cosmos.

In the years before their "chance meeting," the priestess seeded Metzpil's jealousy and ego until his disdain for his father and his secondary position in the family hierarchy filled him with greed and envy. Metzpil's arrogant delusions have now sealed his doom, as Tlatoani's haunted whispers slowly consume what remains of his mortal essence.

To his closest allies who act as his violent and murderous agents, Metzpil admits his ancestry and openly denounces his father as nothing more than a despot. He has forsaken Tlatlcolli and sworn himself to new gods who promise a different future that will emerge from the ashes of the old deities.

ritualistically scarring new recruits using obsidian shards and a bag of ash to cover their bodies in a scale-like pattern. Another depicts the warriors leading captured enemies up a giant pyramid topped with a stone serpent's head. Another depicts a man with a snake mask sacrificing a prisoner on a great black altar.

A successful DC 20 Intelligence (History) check recalls that the depiction befits the description of a high temple of Tlatoani.

A primitive calendar set into the middle of the floor is surrounded by a series of circular patterns that represent the moon's phases. Characters can use the calendar to determine the moon's patterns. If the characters have been to the Temple of the Broken Ones, they can use the calendar to make a DC 20 Intelligence (Nature) check to determine that all the events took place on the night of a full moon, probably during an eclipse.

E2: Pyramid of the Broken Ones

Like the other ruins, this temple is speckled with moss and heavily eroded. To enter it, Metzpil excavated several feet of rubble from the main entrance. Inside, he discovered huge murals covering the walls that depicted the prophesy of the return of Tlatoani in mortal form. One panel portrays several priests anointing a man in some sort of oil amid clouds of incense and herbs. The man is naked except for a loincloth, and his body is covered in distinctive serpentine tattoos. A character who examines his panel and succeeds on a DC 15 Intelligence (Religion) check recognizes the body ink as being consistent with serpent rituals that occurred before the hero-gods appeared. Furthermore, anyone studying the murals who succeeds on a DC 15 Intelligence check notices that the events in individual scenes correlate to specific times and dates.

Another shows the same man in the presence of a huge and terrible looking woman with six arms and whose bottom half is that of a great serpent. A series of runes carved below the panel reads "Titechcualtia Ianima," which

A NEST OF SERPENTS
1 Square - 50 Feet
E1
E2
E6
E4
E3
E5
N

is likely the creature's name. A DC 20 Intelligence (Religion) check recalls Titechcualtia Ianima as the name of one of Tlatoani's demonic daughters who was never banished from the world. Legends say she has existed for thousands of years. Every few centuries, she reveals her presence in an attempt to call her father back into the Material World.

The sanctum is never unguarded, as a **serpent cuauhocelotl** (see **Appendix A: New Monsters**) stands guard at the pyramid's entrance alongside 4 **Poqoza warriors** (see **Appendix A: New Monsters**) and 4 **wardogs** (see **Appendix A: New Monsters**).

Metzpil (see **Appendix A: New Monsters**) waits inside this structure, which he uses as his personal sanctum. When the characters meet him, read or paraphrase the following description:

> A proud young man standing before you brandishes a warhammer and shield marked with the yellow and red emblems of a powerful warrior. Tattoos decorate his chest, back, and upper arms, and his braided hair is wrapped with leather thongs and feathers. About his throat he wears a giant gold medallion in the shape of a serpent. A wooden staff shaped into the likeness of an upright serpent dangles behind his back.

When the characters encounter Metzpil, they face off against an obnoxious, spoiled man who bemoans the fact that the circumstances of his birth deprived him of a loftier station in life. He bitterly complains about being passed over for his older siblings, though he now claims to have a greater purpose — one that exceeds any his tlamacazqui father could possibly imagine. With those words, he points to the murals as evidence of his greatness as he demands that the characters bow down and worship him just as every Poqoza and Aztli in Tehuatl soon will do.

Despite his arrogance, Metzpil does not take the intrusion lightly. If he hears the sounds of combat from the entrance, he casts *conjure celestial* to summon a couatl to his aid, an irony that is not lost upon him. He also tosses his staff to the ground to transform it into a giant constrictor snake. The stress of combat also likely causes him to reach for and ingest a dose of maht (see **Appendix B**). Under the psychoactive agent's influence, Metzpil thoroughly and completely believes he is immortal and cannot die. Consumed with this notion, he fights until his mind or body finally give in to reality. If the characters capture him, he gleefully confesses to his crimes and tells the characters that a mighty priestess is preparing to turn him into a god within the confines of her sacred temple. He joyfully leads them to Quizaloa if they ask. If the characters accompany him there or discover the site's location, the journey takes them to **Chapter 5: The Daughter of the Drowned Serpent** of this adventure.

Metzpil ignorantly and mistakenly believes the mural portrays a prophecy that foretells his rise to power. What he has failed to notice or believe is that the panels describe the proper sacrifice of a human vessel. The dates and times coordinate with specific moon phases necessary to perform the ritual. The image resembles Metzpil because the ritual also requires that Tlatoani's vessel be the son of a tlamacazqui.

The interior of the pyramid is sparse, long picked clean of any treasures it once held. Aside from the strange murals, the only other object of possible interest is a basalt coffer inscribed with images of a man being devoured by a giant snake. Metzpil believes he shall be reborn from within and allows no one to touch it. The lid to the coffer is extremely heavy and can be lifted only by a single individual who succeeds on a DC 20 Strength check.

Treasure: Metzpil hides his backup stash of maht (see **Appendix B**) in a large sack within the coffer. He has enough of the psychoactive agent on hand to keep his disciples at bay for three days. Fortunately for him, the Drowned Serpent's Daughter frequently shows up to help him with his transcendence, which means the arrival of more maht. Six smaller pouches contain more ritual components such as coffee beans, dried dog livers, herbs, owl feathers, cacao beans, and some tobacco leaves. A severed mummified human forearm is wrapped in a red cloth.

Metzpil wears a *ring of protection* and *winged boots*. He wields a *+2 ollitetlacotl** carries a *+1 shield*, and wears cipacahuipilli armor*. He carries a *staff of the python* as well. His golden serpent medallion is worth 2,000 gp. A character who examines it and succeeds on a DC 10 Intelligence (Religion) check confirms that the jewelry was commonly worn by the emperor's snake advisors during the hero-gods' rebellion. He carries two doses of maht on his person.* See **Appendix C: New Equipment and Magic Items**

E3: Field of Redemption

The ancient and crumbling remains of what used to be a ballgame court now serve as an arena where Metzpil's disciples train to become serpent cuauhocelotls through ritual combat. During daylight hours, 1d4 + 6 **Poqoza warriors** (see **Appendix A: New Monsters**) spar with each other on the court under the attentive gaze of a **serpent cuauhocelotl** (see **Appendix A: New Monsters**) who oversees the training. When night falls, only 1d4 **Poqoza warriors** practice here. On rare occasions, Metzpil visits to observe their progress.

E4: West Hill

A small hill overlooks the southwest corner of the ruins and offers an opportunistic view to whoever controls it. At all times, a **serpent cuauhocelotl** (see **Appendix A: New Monsters**) and 6 **Poqoza warriors** (see **Appendix A: New Monsters**) keep guard over this location. There is a bonfire here as well, but they do not ignite it unless they need to use it as an emergency signal.

E5: Tower of the Burning Eagle

The largest structure within the ruins is a 500-foot wide, four-tiered tower that blocks off the jungle to the south. At night, Metzpil's disciples illuminate the tower's façade with two large bonfires set on either side of the main entrance.

The ground floor and the first tiers consist of large empty chambers covered with dust and the dried droppings of vermin that use it for shelter. A flight of stairs on the ground floor climbs to the other tiers, eventually reaching the highest level. Metzpil and his serpent cuauhocelotl followers have cleared the top two tiers. On the third tier, a swath of sand covers the center of the floor. Several long sticks are propped against a nearby wall. There are numbers and lines scored in the sand, which on closer inspection seems to be some sort of diagram or map. A successful DC 15 Intelligence (Investigation) check reveals it is a map of the surrounding region. In addition to their current location and markings indicating the general distance and directions to the raided villages, a path pointing south-southwest is marked with a coiled serpent. The pathway leads to Quizaloa and the high temple of Tlatoani, where the daughter of the drowned serpent awaits.

The top tier serves as a sacred space where Metzpil performs the extreme scarification rites and other body modifications that mark his most powerful disciples as serpent cuauhocelotls.

E6: The Encampments

Throughout the field, the vague outlines of weathered mud-brick foundations long buried and overgrown protrude from the ground. The encampment consists of makeshift wooden frame structures with thatched walls and rooftops that are supported by wooden poles pounded into the earth. Metzpil's disciples live here, using the huts for storage and sleeping.

Regardless of the time of day, there are always 2 **serpent cuauhocelotls** (see **Appendix A: New Monsters**) and 1d4 + 4 **Poqoza warriors** (see **Appendix A: New Monsters**) with an equal number of **war dogs** (see **Appendix A: New Monsters**) in this area. Half of them are prone on the ground resting, while the remainder loiter around the fire performing mundane tasks such as caring for their weapons, arguing, gambling, roasting meat on a stick, or taking maht.

Wrapping Things Up

This section of the adventure ends after the characters defeat Metzpil and learn he is being manipulated by a greater evil that lurks in the high temple of Tlatoani. The characters can use the map in **Area E5** as a guide for determining the temple's location. Alternately, they might use magic or spells to find it. The temple is in a dense part of the jungle that marks the edge of the swamp about 20 miles to the south-southwest. It is known as Quizoloa on the regional map.

Chapter Five: The Daughter of the Drowned Serpent

Designated as Quizoloa on the regional map, the site where the temple resides was once a grand city until the hero-gods and the forces of nature and neglect virtually razed it to the ground.

> Dense clusters of trees and vines conceal the ruins of a bygone era. At the center of the tangled mass, a great stepped pyramid climbs skyward at a severe slope to a height of nearly 200 feet. A broad flight of stone stairs runs up the face to the summit where a large stone building carved in the stylized likeness of a gaping-mouthed head of a fierce demonic serpent awaits.

The ominous building atop the temple serves as its only entrance. A number of archways situated around the base and midsections of the temple served as entrances long ago, but they were filled with bricks and mortar and then plastered over with faded frescos of a skull with a coiled serpent emerging from both of its eye sockets. The stairs on the face of the pyramid are not difficult to climb, though the ascent can be tiring. About two-thirds of the way up, the path becomes littered with cacao seeds and spots of blood. Most of the seeds are so old they crumble into dust with a gentle touch. However, a character who examines the seeds and succeeds on a DC 15 Wisdom (Survival) check notices some were left here within the last week. As to the beans' appearance, anyone who succeeds on a DC 20 Intelligence (Religion) check recalls that passing petitioners leave offerings of coffee and cacao beans to the gods on the temple stairs. When the characters reach the summit, the sun passes directly between the great serpent's fangs framing the entrance.

> A large round structure assembled from fitted stones sits near the edge of the open mouth, just between the two fangs where the sunlight spills in. It stands roughly three feet tall, is eight feet in diameter, and has a flat top with a one-foot-wide hole directly in the center almost like a well. A thick shellac of blood coats the entire surface. A series of images carved along the exterior of the stone structure depict humans wearing exotic serpent headdresses plunging daggers into the chests of victims prostrate before them. They tear out their vital organs and hold them aloft. Behind the stone structure, the hollow of the serpent's mouth forms a crude hallway that leads to a set of bronze-plated double doors embossed with a series of swirling patterns.

A successful DC 5 Intelligence (Religion) check correctly identifies the stone as a sacrificial altar. A character attempting to decipher more from the carvings may do so with a successful DC 20 Intelligence (Religion) check. If the character succeeds, they confirm their worst fears, that the scenes are consistent with sacrifices made to Tlatoani, the Immortal Sun. Although it is not immediately apparent, the hole carved in the center of the altar is incredibly deep. If a character drops something into it (such as small stone or a coin), a faint, echoing splash emerges from the depths five seconds later.

A character may inspect the blood covering the stone. If that individual succeeds on a DC 15 Wisdom (Medicine) or Intelligence (Nature) check while doing so, they confirm that most of the bloodstains are ancient, but several are much more recent, perhaps from within the past several days. A DC 15 Wisdom (Perception) check made while searching the stone reveals a small aperture slightly disguised within the grisly carvings that hides two packages, both wrapped in thin pieces of cured leather. The first package contains a lacquered wooden dagger with an obsidian blade wrapped in a piece of leather.

The second package contains a small black pipe carved from black coral. A sticky black residue that reeks of anise coats the bowl.

The double bronze doors frame an archway that is six feet wide and eight feet tall. The swirling etchings carved on the doors are coiled serpents, a fact the characters can determine upon close visual inspection without making a check. The doors are locked, but can be unlocked with a successful DC 15 Dexterity check using thieves' tools or by casting a *knock* spell or similar magic. Alternately, the characters can bash it open with a successful DC 20 Strength check. The heavy doors swing inward to reveal a tunnel-like passage beyond the portal.

S1: Tunnel

Beyond the strange bronze-plated doors is a near-circular tunnel leading into darkness. The walls of the passage are carved from black stones and lined with bronze sconces holding torches consisting of wooden shafts topped with human skulls with the tops shorn off, presumably to hold fuel. The torches are enchanted so that as soon as any humanoid passes through the portal, the first pair of torches ignites. Thereafter, each time the individual continues for another 10 feet, a new set of torches ignites as the previous set goes out.

Angry Torch Trap

The torches are harmless unless a creature attempts to remove one. If a creature tries to pull a torch out of its sconce or otherwise physically manipulate it, the skulls gushes forth a 10-foot cone of magical fire. Each creature in the fire must make a DC 15 Dexterity saving throw, taking 27 (5d10) fire damage on a failure or half as much damage on a success. A character who examines the statues and succeeds on a DC 15 Intelligence (Arcana) check detects the trap. It takes a successful DC 20 Intelligence (Arcana) check to permanently disarm the trap, though each torch operates independently of all the others.

> At the end of the passage, the floor opens to expose a large shaft that drops into black, unknown depths. A curved stone staircase runs along the outer walls of the shaft, descending deeper into the shaft than one might care to guess. The stairs circle around a nauseating ornament: a chain of desiccated corpses preserved with lime that hang just above the shaft.

Anyone who inspects the stairs and succeeds on a DC 14 Intelligence check notices that they have a shallow curve to their surface and angle inward toward the shaft. Every seventh step bears the stylized carving of an ancient serpentine rune that a character associates with Tlatoani by succeeding on a DC 10 Intelligence (Religion) check. The 21st stair bears the mark of the Great Stone and acts as the trigger for a **rolling sphere** trap.

The sphere stops when it reached the bottom of the staircase shaft.

S2: The Serpent's Entrance

About 20 feet above the bottom of the shaft, the spiral stairs pass four secret doors, each of which conceals a passage into chambers in the temple's inner catacombs. Characters searching this location can find each of these doors with a successful DC 15 Intelligence (Investigation) check or Wisdom (Perception) check.

Rolling Sphere Trap

Mechanical trap

When 20 or more pounds of pressure are placed on this trap's pressure plate, a hidden trapdoor in the ceiling opens, releasing a 10-foot-diameter rolling sphere of solid stone.

With a successful DC 15 Wisdom (Perception) check, a character can spot the trapdoor and pressure plate. A search of the floor accompanied by a successful DC 15 Intelligence (Investigation) check reveals variations in the mortar and stone that betray the pressure plate's presence. The same check made while inspecting the ceiling notes variations in the stonework that reveal the trapdoor. Wedging an iron spike or other object under the pressure plate prevents the trap from activating.

Activation of the sphere requires all creatures present to roll initiative. The sphere rolls initiative with a +8 bonus. On its turn, it moves 60 feet in a straight line. The sphere can move through creatures' spaces, and creatures can move through its space, treating it as difficult terrain. Whenever the sphere enters a creature's space or a creature enters its space while it's rolling, that creature must succeed on a DC 15 Dexterity saving throw or take 55 (10d10) bludgeoning damage and be knocked prone.

The sphere stops when it hits a wall or similar barrier. It can't go around corners, but smart dungeon builders incorporate gentle, curving turns into nearby passages that allow the sphere to keep moving.

As an action, a creature within 5 feet of the sphere can attempt to slow it down with a DC 20 Strength check. On a successful check, the sphere's speed is reduced by 15 feet. If the sphere's speed drops to 0, it stops moving and is no longer a threat.

Mosaics and Gemstones

Many of the inlays scattered throughout the temple's mosaics consist of gold and semi-precious stones such as jade, obsidian, and turquoise. If a room's mosaics contain these valuable metals and stones, they appear in the room's Treasure entry. Greedy characters may wish to pry out the stones as treasure. A character with a crowbar or similar tool can remove the inlays from a single mosaic with a successful DC 12 Dexterity (Sleight of Hand) check. Either way, performing the task requires 1d4 minutes. If the character fails, they may make a second attempt taking another 1d4 minutes. A character who fails three times in a row removes the gems, but damages them, reducing their worth by half. If the character uses a dagger or knife to pry out the gems, you may also wish to rule that a failed attempt results in breaking the weapon so that further attempts suffer disadvantage. Each mosaic holds 5d10 assorted small jade, obsidian, and turquoise gemstones worth 5d6 gp.

S3: The Statues of Judgment

The door is locked, though a successful DC 20 Dexterity check made with thieves' tools unlocks the portal. Alternately, if a character pours coffee, a warm cacao drink, or one of the preceding beans on the fresco's tongue, the door unlocks and opens. As a measure of last resort, the characters can also force the door open with a successful DC 20 Strength check. If the characters open the door, read or paraphrase the following description:

The chamber is only 20 feet deep, but twice as wide. Two more alcoves house statues on either side of the entrance. Huge circular, gold-leafed frescoes on each of the far walls show images of various animals in coordination with curious phrases. A successful a DC 12 Intelligence (Investigation) check interprets them as some sort of chronological record of ancient events auspicious to the followers of Tlatoani. Adjacent to the frescoes, wide alcoves open along the south wall. A throne rests in each alcove (see **Areas 3A** and **3B**).

3A: Throne of Awakening

While in power, Tlatoani used this throne to anoint his serpent cuauhocelotls and those priests entrusted to his order. Those pledging their lives to Tlatoani were forced to test their devotion by sitting on this throne to experience death and rebirth into the fold of the great serpent Tlatoani.

A successful DC 10 Wisdom (Survival) check identifies the panoramic mural as undeniably similar to the view from the top of the Serpent Temple.

Throne of Vengeance Trap

The throne emits a magical enchantment aura. A character who searches the throne and succeeds on a DC 25 Intelligence (Arcana) check discovers that the throne is trapped. As the handiwork of a god, the trap can be removed only with a *wish* spell. Any character bold enough to sit upon the throne is stricken with a graphic vision of lying on the altar at the mouth of the temple while a serpent-bodied creature with the torso and head of a human female brandishing several swords in each of her hands rips the character's heart from his or her chest. The character must make a DC 20 Wisdom saving throw or take 27 (5d10) psychic damage and have their palms mysteriously scarred in the likeness of a coiled serpent on a failure. The symbol is that of Tlatoani, which the characters can confirm with a successful DC 10 Intelligence (Religion) check. On a success, the character still experiences the terrifying vision, but takes half as much damage and is not physically scarred in the process.

3B: Throne of Vengeance

Tlatoani used this throne to dishonor those among his chieftains who failed him in some way. In dark ceremonies, he would anoint them for their successes, bestow them an honorary title, and then offer them a seat atop the throne. Anyone who fell for the ruse or is now foolish enough to sit on the Throne of Vengeance quickly discovers it is trapped.

Throne of Vengeance Trap

Any humanoid daring enough to either sit upon the throne or to try to remove its glittering adornments triggers the trap. The throne emits an enchantment aura. A character who examines the throne and succeeds on a DC 25 Intelligence (Arcana) check detects the trap. Like its counterpart, nothing short of a *wish* spell can remove the trap. When triggered, two things occur. First, any individual seated upon the throne experiences a violent vision of serpents being flensed of their skins and flesh as they writhe in agony. The creature must make a DC

TEMPLE OF THE SERPENT
Level 1
S3
S5
T
S4
S2
S7
S6
8b
S9
S
S8
T
8a
S1
Sacrificial Altar
Spiral Stairs
and
Hanging Bodies
Column of
Blood
N
1 Square - 5 Feet

20 Wisdom saving throw or take 14 (4d6) psychic damage from the pain and be stunned on a failure or take half as much damage and not be stunned on a success. At the end of each of its turns, a stunned creature can make another Wisdom saving throw. On a success, the creature is no longer stunned. Second, the throne releases the magical locks on the base plates of every statue in the room, causing them to release 5 **spawn of Tlatoani** (see **Appendix A: New Monsters**). The freed monsters immediately attack.

Treasure: The mosaics on the walls are potentially salvageable. There are 12 mosaics in all (see the **Mosaics and Gemstones** sidebar).

S4: Trapped Corridor

The paintings are barely visible after thousands of years of degradation and neglect. Nothing historically significant is concealed within the artwork, though the displays are not entirely benevolent.

Poison Dart Trap

If a character steps on the space marked as "T" on the map, the character triggers a **poison darts** trap. However, because of the discoloration in the artwork, characters searching the area for traps gain advantage on their checks

---

Poison Darts Trap

Mechanical trap

When a creature steps on a hidden pressure plate, poison-tipped darts shoot from spring-loaded or pressurized tubes cleverly embedded in the surrounding walls. An area might include multiple pressure plates, each one rigged to its own set of darts.

The tiny holes in the walls are obscured by dust and cobwebs, or cleverly hidden amid bas-reliefs, murals, or frescoes that adorn the walls. The DC to spot them is 15. With a successful DC 15 Intelligence (Investigation) check, a character can deduce the presence of the pressure plate from variations in the mortar and stone used to create it, compared to the surrounding floor. Wedging an iron spike or other object under the pressure plate prevents the trap from activating. Stuffing the holes with cloth or wax prevents the darts contained within from launching.

The trap activates when more than 20 pounds of weight is placed on the pressure plate, releasing four darts. Each dart makes a ranged attack with a +8 bonus against a random target within 10 feet of the pressure plate (vision is irrelevant to this attack roll). (If there are no targets in the area, the darts don't hit anything.) A target that is hit takes 2 (1d4) piercing damage and must succeed on a DC 15 Constitution saving throw, taking 11 (2d10) poison damage on a failed save, or half as much damage on a successful one.

S5: Chamber of the Accursed

The door to this chamber is carved with a series of runes. Characters able to read Draconic can easily decipher the ominous warning:

The door is locked, and its perimeter is sealed with wax. It can be opened with a successful DC 15 Dexterity check made with thieves' tools or by

bashing it in with a successful DC 20 Strength check.

Any living creature staying in this chamber for more than one minute attracts the hunger of the undead monstrosities dwelling in the pit. When that time passes, 2 **wraiths** emerge from the slime and attempt to drain the life of any trespassers. Every 1d4 rounds thereafter, another **wraith** emerges from the fleshy morass.

Tlatoani bound the tortured souls of those victims he sacrificed against their wills to this chamber and cursed them to prevent their escape. If the characters leave the room, the wraiths do not pursue them, as the curse prevents them from passing over the threshold. Characters can break the curse by sanctifying the pool of blood in **Area S7**.

Any character slain by a wraith is also bound by the curse and cannot leave the chamber.

S6: The Baths

Anyone inspecting the basin notes a faint white line near the rim. Characters who succeed on a DC 10 Wisdom (Survival) check identify it as some sort of mineral deposit indicating that the basin once held water that left a waterline.

A successful DC 25 Intelligence (Religion) correctly infers that this room once served as a purification room. Priests used the trough to create steam by heating the clay bricks and rapidly placing them in the basin.

The door to **Area S7** is locked and sealed with wax. It can be forced opened with a DC 25 Strength check or unlocked by anyone using a set of thieves' tools who succeeds at a DC 15 Dexterity check.

S7: Blood Column

Investigating more closely, the faces have tiny holes bored into the tear ducts, from which the black tears appear to emanate. A successful DC 5 Wisdom (Medicine) check identifies the tearstains as very old dried blood.

The column lies beneath the sacrificial altar so when the victim's blood spills onto it, it runs down the center of the column and causes the faces to weep. The column is cursed and emits an aura of necromantic magic. The weeping faces bind the spirits trapped in **Area S5**. If the characters sanctify the column with a *remove curse* spell, it breaks the curse binding the wraiths to **Area S5**. Thereafter, the creatures are no longer bound to their chamber.

S8: Portals to the Outer Worlds

The floor of the eastern end of the passage slopes slightly toward the west. Halfway down, the passage branches off to the north and ends in front of a carved stone door that leads to **Area S6.** The far ends of either side of the passage both take sharp turns to the north. The eastern passage connects to **Area S3** while the western passage connects to **Area S8.**

A successful DC 10 Intelligence (Investigation) check identifies the iconography as relating to auspicious dates and times on the calendar associated with aspects of the Immortal Sun during Tlatoani's reign over the southern continent. Tlatoani and his disciples used the alcoves as foci during rituals that allowed them to project their consciousness into other planes of existence.

S8A: The Arrow Cannon

This portion of the chamber contains a trap.

Arrow Cannon Trap

A plaster and clay mosaic in the floor conceals a pressure plate that, when stepped on, ignites an alchemical fuse connected to a long tube packed with explosives and fitted with scores of arrows hidden within the shadows in the back of the portal alcove. Anyone who searches the area for traps and succeeds on a DC 15 Intelligence (Investigation) check notices the pressure plate in the curiously raised arrangement of the mosaic tiles. If more than 20 pounds of pressure is applied to the plate, the fuse ignites. One round later, the charge explodes and catapults the arrows down the corridor with a deafening boom. The arrows fly straight down the hallway, targeting any object in their path. All creatures within 10 feet of the pressure plate must succeed on a DC 15 Constitution saving throw or be deafened for 1d4 rounds. Furthermore, each group of 1d6 arrows makes a ranged attack within a +8 bonus against a random target within 10 feet of the pressure plate. If there are no targets, the arrows strike nothing. A target that is hit takes 4 (1d8) piercing damage for each arrow that strikes it.

S8B: The Secret Door

This portal conceals a secret door located at the back of the alcove. Characters searching the alcove who succeed on a DC 20 Wisdom (Perception) check discover the door and can use it to access **Area S10.** The stairwell beyond leads to the lower catacombs.

S9: The Secret Stairwell

This hallway hides a secret door. A successful DC 10 Intelligence (Investigation) or DC 15 Wisdom (Perception) check spots the outline of the door. Characters who find the door can use it to access the temple's second level.

Chapter Six: Temple of the Serpent (Level 2)

This chapter describes the temple's second level.

S10: The Serpent and the Mothers

Treasure: The mural is crafted mostly from colored clay tiles. However, the serpent's two eyes are set with red garnets. If the characters successfully salvage them, they are worth 200 gp each.

S10A: Sunken Stairs

Approximately one inch of stagnant water covers the corridor floor. A strange door is at the end of the hall.

S10B: The Eclipse Door

The door is locked, sealed with wax, and magically trapped. It takes a successful DC 20 Dexterity check made with thieves' tools to unlock the door. Alternatively, a character can bash the door open with a successful DC 20 Strength check. The door radiates an aura of conjuration magic.

Bog Door Trap

A character who searches the door and succeeds on a DC 20 Intelligence (Arcana) check detects a magical trap that can be dispelled as if it were a 5th-level spell. Anyone attempting to open it triggers the trap. If that occurs, a powerful conjuration spell causes the image of the moon to animate, open its mouth, and vomit forth a **bog creeper** (see **Appendix A: New Monsters**). The mindless plant attacks the nearest living creature in the room and continues fighting until destroyed.

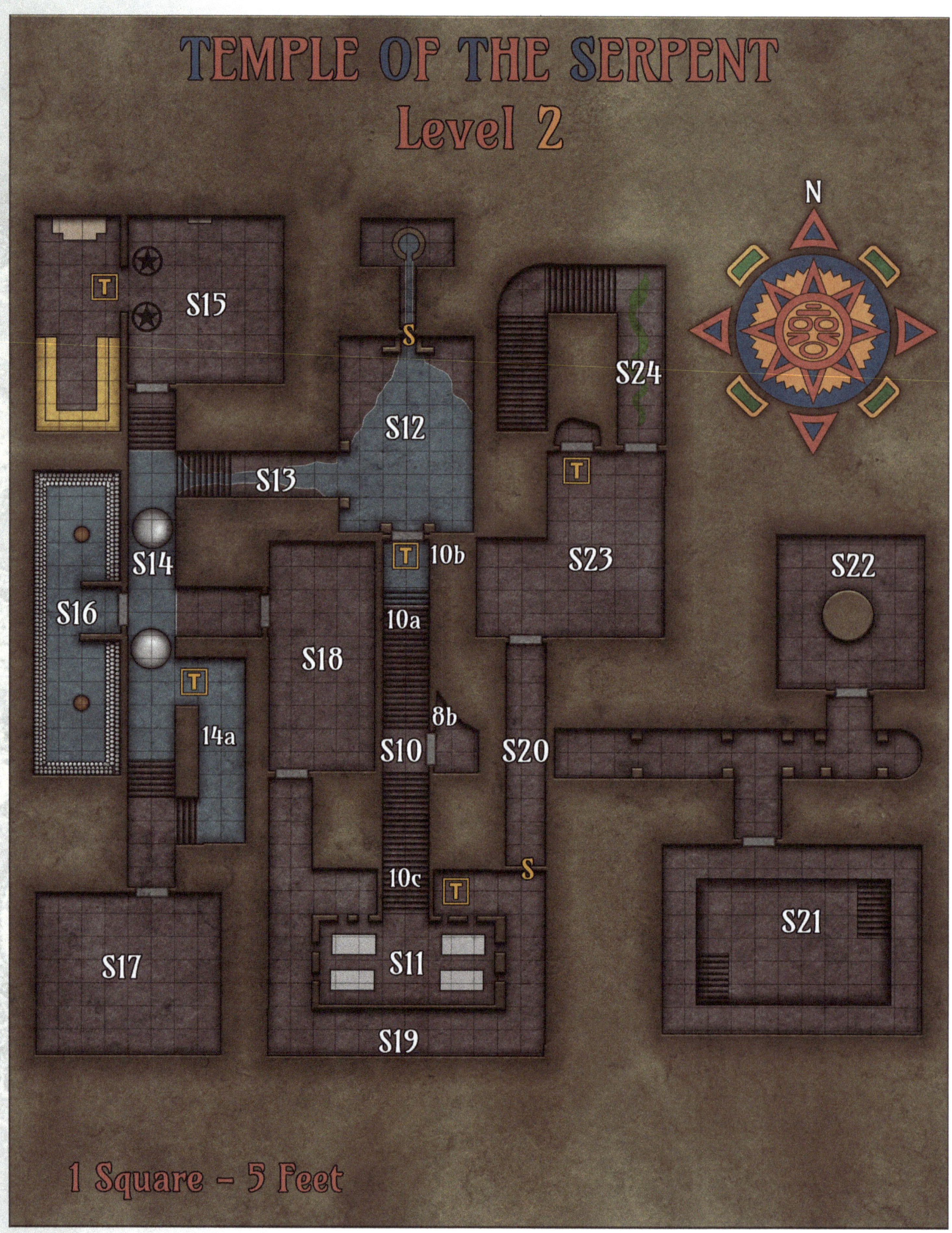

TEMPLE OF THE SERPENT
Level 2
N
S15
S12
S13
S24
S14
S16
10b
10a
S23
S18
S22
8b
S10
S20
14a
10c
S11
S17
S19
S21
1 Square – 5 Feet

S10C: Staircase

This long staircase leads to an archway opening into **Area S11**.

S11: Body Preparation Chamber

Tlatoani's priests used this chamber to prepare the bodies of deceased serpent cuauhocelotls to allow them to continue to serve their master in the afterlife.

A character who succeeds on a DC 8 Wisdom (Perception) check notes several quarter-inch holes bored into the walls at eye level. A character who peers through a hole spots another hallway on the other side of the wall. The peepholes allowed observers in the outer chamber to watch the funerary preparations.

Although there are no exits, the walls are only one-inch thick and fashioned from wood and concrete sealed with lime and plaster. Anyone attempting to break through the wall can do so with a successful DC 20 Strength check.

Treasure: The leather sacks hold different types of precision cutting stones, all made from razor-sharp obsidian. Priests used them to perform intricate cuts needed to prepare the bodies for the afterlife. There are four sets, each worth 150 gp.

If the characters remain in this room for more than a few minutes, they attract the attention of Cihuacoatl, one of the two **spirit nagas** that serve Titechcualtia Ianima. The reptilian creature spies on them through the peepholes long enough to gather basic information about the characters' intent and abilities. When she finishes, she deliberately makes noise to attract their attention while she slithers off toward the west. Then, she silently slinks back east to alert Titechcualtia Ianima, who awaits the characters in **Area S25**. If the characters block her path, she tries to lead them on a wild goose chase until she can slip past them and reach her mistress.

S12: Statue of the Weeping Serpent

Characters investigating the basin quickly determine leaves and other detritus have clogged it for what appears to be many, many years.

Characters searching the fountain who succeed on a DC 15 Intelligence (Investigation) or DC 20 Wisdom (Perception) check determine that it hides a secret door that opens into a narrow crawlspace leading into a small room. In the center of the room rests a two-foot-deep pool filled with rainwater funneled here from a chimney in the ceiling. Four small statuettes of two-headed serpents exquisitely carved from black basalt surround the pool, each poised to strike.

Anyone searching the bottom of the pool easily spots a collection of glittering gold ingots in assorted sizes.

Treasure: The four serpent statuettes are worth 500 gp each, while the 25 gold ingots are worth 3d10 gp each.

S13: The Flooded Corridor

The corridor leads to a short flight of steps. More water pools at the bottom and floods the adjacent hallways. About one foot of water covers the base of the stairwell and the entire lower concourse.

S14: The Long Haul

Characters attempting to traverse the hall soon discover their path blocked by a large round boulder that nearly fills the width and height of the entire passage. The boulder weighs several thousand pounds — easily enough to crush careless characters. A character who succeeds on a DC 15 Strength check can push the spherical stone 2d6 feet forward on each successful check. To successfully navigate a way through the passages, the characters need to push the boulders out of the way. A side passage offers them a convenient place to push the ball out of the way. Unfortunately, just beyond the first boulder, another similar, inconveniently placed boulder blocks the remainder of the passage. A character can simultaneously push both boulders in the same direction with a successful DC 20 Strength check, though a successful check moves the two stones only 1d6 feet.

The secret to navigating around the boulders is to find intersections in the passage that provide the characters an opportunity to slip around the boulders. The best option is to squeeze around the corner at the intersection near **Area S16**, open the door to **Area S16**, and push one or two boulders into that room. While it is possible to push both up the loop at **Area 14a**, the weight of both boulders in that corridor at the same time causes the weakened floor to collapse.

Collapsing Floor Trap

If both boulders are placed in this section of the passage, the characters hear a sudden loud crack. The 40-foot section of passageway marked on the map collapses, plummeting any creature or object in the area 50 feet down into a large natural cavern unless the character succeeds on a DC 20 Dexterity saving throw to leap to safety. A character who fails the Dexterity saving throw takes 17 (5d6) bludgeoning damage from the fall and another 16 (3d10) piercing damage from the sharp stalagmites lining the bottom. If the floor breaks, the water from the chambers above drains into the cavern.

The large natural cavern at the bottom is sealed off from the rest of the temple structure and consists of a small complex of five caverns chained together by water-eroded tunnels. Characters can re-enter the temple by succeeding on a DC 15 Strength (Athletics) check to scale the walls or by using another means to reach the top of the shaft, including flying, levitating, or teleporting. If the characters decide to explore this lower cave complex, they discover a labyrinthine tunnel that leads to an opening in the jungle about one mile west of the temple.

The cavern serves as the home of a clan of trolls. The characters have a 10% chance of encountering 2d4 **trolls** for every 10 minutes they spend in the locale, up to a maximum of 29 trolls.

S15: The Forum

The door to this chamber bears a mosaic of a ring of seven serpents, all biting each other's tails.

The door is jammed shut and sealed with wax. Characters can force it open with a successful DC 15 Strength check.

A character who studies the plates and succeeds on a DC 18 Intelligence (Investigation) check interprets that the symbols appear to describe numerous judgments or sentences imposed for committing various criminal and heretical acts such as stealing, blasphemy, and treason.

If the characters walk past the statues and into the next room, read or paraphrase the following description:

The arch opens into a narrow chamber lined with stone bleachers that form a sort of tiny, makeshift amphitheater facing an altar fashioned from concrete and human bones. On the wall behind it hangs a massive clay tablet bearing a menacing jade statue of a two-headed dragon. Neatly arranged atop the altar rest six obsidian knives, each with a wooden handle carved to resemble a different animal. A colossal carving in the center of the floor depicts a number of creatures and objects located within a large circle or wheel. A dried blackish substance fills the crevices and cracks of the carving.

Tlatoani's seers used this forum to perform and discuss divinations interpreting the stars, auspicious signs, and by performing haruspicy on animal and human sacrifices.

The handles of the knives include the images of a dog, an eagle, an ocelot, a deer, a crocodile, and a snake.

A successful DC 10 Intelligence (Religion) check associates the animals with days, months, and numbers used in divination. A common theme in divination included using ritual knives to draw blood.

A character who succeeds on a DC 15 Intelligence (Religion) check for each animal determines the following information:

The dog represents the 10th day of the first week.

The eagle represents the second day of the second week.

The ocelot represents the first day of the second week.

The deer represents the seventh or eighth day of the first week.

The crocodile represents either the first day of the first week, or the eighth day of the second week.

The snake represents the fifth day of the first week.

Seers used these knives in accordance with their birth signs to draw blood and use it as an offering to Tlatoani before performing their rituals. Anyone using the knife associated with their birth sign to draw 1 hit point of blood as an offering successfully meets the sacrifice conditions for shutting off the magical trap that protects this room.

DEFENDERS OF THE FORUM TRAP

The terracotta statues radiate abjuration magic. Tlatoani enchanted them to protect the secrets of his seers and their secret council. They are firmly affixed to the floor, which requires a successful DC 30 Strength check to rip one from the ground and topple it over, which foils the trap. Likewise, a creature can spend 1d10 minutes bashing one into pieces with the same effect. Detecting the trap requires a successful DC 25 Intelligence (Arcana) check. If a creature approaches within five feet of the arch without paying the proper sacrifice, the statues immediately rotate and swing at the creature. Each statue makes a melee attack with a +10 bonus against a target within five feet of it. A target that is hit takes 28 (8d6) slashing damage. The statues pivot back to their original position after swinging and are poised to swing at the next creature who approaches within five feet of the arch without making the proper sacrifice. The trap does not trigger if the proper sacrifice is made.

Treasure: The two mosaics adorning these walls are salvageable (see the **Mosaics and Gemstones** sidebar).

S16: RACKS OF SKULLS

This door opens into a shallow hall flanked by two larger square rooms. Several racks of human skulls line the exterior walls in a hideous, macabre display. Boreholes cut into the skulls allowed the creators to thread them onto long wooden shafts. The racks run 10 feet from floor to ceiling. A large wicker basket sits in the center of each of the side rooms.

The baskets appear to be filled with bones and ashes; however, if any living creature approaches within five feet of the basket, the contents begin swirling into an angry animated whirlwind of shattered broken bones. The 2 **bone swarms** (see **Appendix A: New Monsters**) are immediately drawn to the presence of life and mercilessly attack the nearest living creatures.

S17: THE FOUNDRY

Several small trenches scar the earthen floor. A basket near the trenches holds a collection of long tubes assembled from animal horn and bone. Three small flat boulders, two dusted with gold powder and one with bluish powder, rest in a wooden bench covered with scorch marks. A collection of granite stones, each about the size of a piece of fruit, sits next to the boulders. A cracked straw basket beneath the bench holds a pile of malachite. Another basket holds rocks threaded with gold veins.

Tlatoani's craftsmen used this room as a primitive foundry and were capable of smelting gold and copper items that were mostly used as jewelry and decorative items. Craftsmen used the granite rocks as hammers to crush malachite and other stones containing gold and copper ore on the large flat boulders. They used the trenches as ovens by filling them with charcoal, covering them, and then using the tubes to blow air over the coals as they used tools to work the extracted ore into jewelry and other items.

Tlatoani's slaves operated his foundry day and night, driven nearly to death daily by the two hulking obsidian creatures he used to enforce his bidding. In the years since, the serpent lord's slaves have died, though the elementals still remain.

The room is still operated and maintained by 2 **large obsidian elementals** (see **Appendix A: New Monsters**) made from the volcanic glass. If living humanoids enter, the elementals express surprise, but their shock quickly wears off as they immediately assign tasks to the new employees. If a character refuses to perform their bidding, the creatures condemn the individuals to death and then enforce their edict.

S18: THE PLUG ROOM

A long bench occupies about half of this chamber's eastern wall. The bench and shelves contain dozens of clay jars filled with powdered pigments and an assortment of bones, thorns, stone hammers, and a stingray spine that are readily identified as tools for scarring, branding, piercing, and tattooing. Above the bench hangs a series of wooden tablets containing images and words that describe the specific rituals for body modifications of the serpent cuauhocelotls, advisors, and priests. Six concrete and wood-slat boxes sit on the bench.

All the boxes are sealed with beeswax and held fast with a latch made from a mummified adder's head. One must break the seal to access the latch, but doing so triggers the trap.

ADDER'S HEAD LATCH TRAP

Opening the latch causes a poison needle to spring out from the adder's fang to deliver a dose of poison. If the trap is triggered, the needle extends three inches straight out of the latch. A creature within range takes 2 (1d4) piercing damage and 16 (3d10) poison damage and must succeed on a DC 20 Constitution saving throw or be poisoned for one hour. A successful DC 20 Intelligence (Investigation) check allows a character to deduce the trap's presence from alterations made to the fang to accommodate the needle. A successful DC 20 Dexterity check using thieves' tools disarms the trap and removes the needle from the fang.

Treasure: Each box contains a small collection of miscellaneous jewelry, including numerous ear and lip plugs, labret plugs, jade plate, gold necklaces and bracelets, earrings, and nose rings. Each collection is worth 3d10 x 10 gp.

S19: THE PEEKING HALL

This curiously shaped hall encircles the body preparation chamber (**Area S11**). Holes set at roughly five-foot intervals along the interior curve of the corridor allow individuals to peek in and observe activities taking place in the other room.

A secret door in the northeast corner provides access to hidden chambers on this level as well as access to the lowest level where the daughter of Tlatoani hides. Characters actively searching the area locate the secret door with a successful DC 20 Intelligence (Investigation) check.

One of the peepholes is trapped with an insidious device that the priests used on unsuspecting temple guests.

PEEPHOLE TRAP

Any character attempting to peer through this peephole is in for a surprise. The moment they attempt to peer through the hole, a pressure plate in the floor releases a store of ground obsidian dust through a hollow within the wall and into the peephole. Anyone within five feet of the hole takes 4 (1d8) piercing damage and must succeed on a DC 20 Constitution saving throw or be blinded by the crystalline shards.

A character who searches the peephole and succeeds on a DC 20 Intelligence (Investigation) check notices irregularities in the stonework that conceal the trap. A character can disable the trap by succeeding on a DC 15 Dexterity check made with thieves' tools.

S20: THE INTERSECTIONS

The hall extends about 80 feet, finally ending before a recessed alcove. About two-thirds of the way down the hall, an exit leads to a door to the south. Near the end of the hall, a second door blocks another exit branching off to the north. All doors that lead from the hallway are locked.

Characters can bash open a door with a successful DC 20 Strength check or unlock a door with a successful DC 15 Dexterity check made with thieves' tools.

Treasure: One of the feather fetishes hanging from the ceiling is a *feather token* (bird).

S21: THE PIT OF SACRIFICE

Anyone making a quick and casual survey of the bottom of the pit spots broken shards of wood and other indicators of the violence and death that occurred here.

Any character who makes a successful DC 15 Intelligence (Religion) check recalls that warriors bound themselves with weighted disks while undergoing ritual sacrifice by combat. They used the weights to make it far more difficult to maneuver and to tire them out quicker.

Tlatoani constructed this chamber to serve as a ritual sacrificial fighting pit. He primarily used it to weed out initiates petitioning to serve as his elite serpent cuauhocelotls. Initiates were taken here, tied with weights, given clubs, and then bound with weighted stones. They would then face off against the pit guardian. Those who survived were granted status. Those who lost offered their deaths as a ritual sacrifice to maintain honor.

A **nalfeshnee demon** (see **Appendix A: New Monsters**) still serves as the pit guardian and waits to test the mettle of anyone who aspires to be a serpent cuauhocelotl. Although it would normally wait at the bottom, thousands of years of boredom prompt the diabolical creature to fly out of the chasm to attack any intruder.

S22: COLUMN OF BLOOD (LEVEL 2)

This room is structurally similar to **Area S7**, which lies directly above it. Like **Area S7**, characters who cast *remove curse* on the altar free the spirits trapped in **Area S5**. The column connects this area to the altar in the serpent's mouth (**Area S7**) at the top of the temple and the blood pool (**Area 25D**) on the level below.

The sleeping beast is a **behir**, an ancient carryover from the age before Tlatoani's arrival. The beast's ancestors occupied the temple's deep caverns for thousands of years, but the current occupant seems content to feed on the fresh blood that recently stained the altar. The creature is currently sleeping, which gives it disadvantage on Wisdom (Perception) checks made to notice the intrusion. However, the instant the beast realizes she has an opportunity for warm meat, she rises and quickly lunges in for the feast.

At this level, the column provides magical sustenance to the children and worshipers of Tlatoani. The column radiates an aura of evil and necromantic magic. The column was created to grant mystical energy to Tlatoani's followers and disciples during their stay within the temple.

Casting a *bless* spell on the column reduces the number of legendary actions a creature native to the temple can take by 1 each turn.

A successful DC 10 Intelligence check determines that each mask represents a different day on Tehuatl's ancient calendar.

CLAY MASKS

These masks carry an ancient enchantment that allows any individual who dons the mask to see and comprehend the nature of magic attuned to the mask. Tlatoani's priests attuned each mask to a specific trap within the temple. If a creature wearing the correct mask gazes upon a trap to which it is attuned, then the wearer senses the trap's presence as if affected by a *find traps* spell. Although they are magical, the seers fashioned them from relatively fragile clay, which can break or crack if subjected to mild pressure.

Lizard: This mask attunes to the trap in **Area S10b**.
Monkey: This mask attunes to the trap in **Area S14**.
Death: This mask attunes to the trap in **Area S15**.
Vulture: This mask attunes to the trap in **Area S19**.
Serpent: This mask attunes to the trap in **Area S23**.

S23: Hall of Sloughed Skins

A collection of eight stretched human skins adorn the walls, each marked with a gold mask decorated with a helmet of snakeskin mixed with feathers. The skins are heavily scarred and tattooed to resemble serpent scales. To the left of each skin hangs a macuahuitl and a round shield. The shields and macuahuitls are finely crafted and decorated with feathers, paintings, and carvings representing the power of their owners.

Two separate stone doors hang upon the north wall. They appear nearly identical, and both are carved with a rising serpent. On both doors, the serpents face inward toward each other.

This chamber served as the covert meeting area for Tlatoani's serpent cuauhocelotls. They convened here to discuss matters of importance, and it is also where they stored their prized weapons and armor.

The two serpent doors are locked. A casual inspection reveals that both doors were also sealed with wax, although the seal to the western door has been broken. The door to the east opens to **Area S24**. The door to the west is a false door. Any creature who breaks its wax seal (either by opening the door or piercing the seal) triggers the trap.

Wax Sealed Door Trap

When the seal to this door is broken, an odorless toxic gas seeps into the room. A creature inside the room for three or more rounds becomes overexposed to deadly levels of the gas. The creature must make a DC 15 Constitution saving throw. On a failure a creature takes 17 (5d6) poison damage and is poisoned and blinded for 10 minutes. On a success, the creature takes half as much damage and is neither poisoned nor blinded. It takes a successful DC 20 Intelligence (Investigation) check to detect the trap on the seal and a successful DC 20 Dexterity check made with thieves' tool to disarm it.

Treasure: The eight gold death masks are worth 300 gp each. There are also eight *+1 macuahuitls**, eight *serpent shields**, seven finely crafted helmets (100 gp), and a *helm of the ebon serpent*.** See **Appendix C: New Equipment and Magic Items**

The monetary and magical treasure in this room consists of items sacred to Tlatoani. Thus, all of them are protected by a curse. Any character removing one or more of the items from the room falls victim to the curse.

Curse of Tlatoani

After leaving the room with one of Tlatoani's sacred items, the cursed character must succeed on a DC 15 Constitution saving throw at the next dawn or gain 1d3 levels of exhaustion. Each dawn thereafter, the creature must make another Constitution saving throw to avoid additional levels of exhaustion until the cursed is lifted by *remove curse* or similar magic or the creature dies.

S24: The Hall of the Descent

This hallway pitches noticeably downward. A large mosaic set into the floor depicts a slithering snake that runs the length of the passage. At the far end of the slope, the hall and arch on the western wall reveals a long, winding flight of stairs that twist and turn their way down into the darkness.

Characters can attempt to remove the gemstones from the large serpent mosaic to gain the treasure. It is big enough that it counts as two mosaics. The descending passage leads to **Level 3**.

Treasure: Players can attempt to salvage either of the two mosaics on these walls (see **Mosaics and Gemstones** sidebar).

Wrapping Things Up

Characters who complete this section of the temple are ready to move on to the final chapter.

When they descend the staircase, read or paraphrase the following description to take them to the adventure's climactic encounter:

Chapter Seven: Temple of the Serpent (Level 3)

One of the Drowned Serpent's most devoted daughters, a **marilith** called Titechcualtia Ianima, assumed dominance over the Serpent Temple and uses the lowest level as her personal sanctum.

This section of the adventure begins when the characters walk down the hall at the bottom of the temple staircase.

S25: The Drowned Serpent's Daughter

The arch opens into a grandiose hall consisting of several levels. Before the arch, a walkway encircles a deep pit filled with crimson blood. The blood flows into the pit via a canal that bisects the middle portion of the hall. Fire pits on either side sprout gouts of red and orange flames. Towering basalt statues carved to resemble striking adders line either side of the chamber, all facing the main entrance. At the far end, a small ziggurat rises, topped by a stone fountain that overflows with blood. The blood overflows from the fountain and spills into the moat that surrounds the ziggurat and flows down the canal. In front of the ziggurat stretches a wide platform, the floor of which bears a huge mosaic of a slithering serpent. Atop the platform rests a huge and hideous creature with the torso and face of a giant, six-armed woman and the lower body of a massive slithering serpent. Gemstones and other objects appear intertwined with her massive tail.

Titechcualtia Ianima, a **marilith demon** armed with macuahuitls (see **Appendix C: New Equipment and Magic Items**) instead of longswords awaits the characters' arrival, hoping to corrupt them to her desires. In addition to the demonic creature, 2 **spirit nagas** (replace *blight* with *time in a bottle* [see **Appendix D: New Spells**]) lurk in the wings ready to fight to the death alongside their mistress.

Titechcualtia Ianima welcomes the characters to her abode. She invites them to share her power, tempting them with the following introduction.

"You have impressed Tlatoani with your cunning and skill, so why waste your abilities on mere mortals? Join with me, join with Tlatoani! You have proven yourselves. Metzpil is a fool whose only use is that of a vessel for the Serpent God's return. The other gods … what have they done for mortals? Tlatoani rose as a great emperor, he conquered Notos, including this miniscule island. He brought peace and order. The others rebelled out of jealousy. They demand sacrifices as well. How are they nobler than the Serpent? What can they offer mighty champions such as yourselves? Come now, we must not fight. We should join, rule the world together, and end this sorrow, end this slavery."

Her speech is merely a ruse to buy time for her allies to use their magic to dominate and charm the characters before she attempts to destroy any mortals brash enough to thwart her plans. When they exhaust their enchantment spells or if the characters resist them, the spirit nagas cast *lightning bolt* and then cast *dimension door* to move about the room, never staying in the same place for long. Likewise, Titechcualtia Ianima teleports out of danger when she can, darting around the chamber to gain an advantageous position in combat, use one of her traps, or drink from the waters in **Area 25C** to regain lost hit points. When engaged in melee combat, she always concentrates her seven attacks against a single target to quickly deplete that foe's hit points or to knock them unconscious. If the characters hold their own against the marilith, you may allow her to summon diabolical reinforcements as an action or have a demon watching her from afar suddenly appear on the scene. Titechcualtia Ianima is an impulsive creature rarely governed by logic and not prone to rigid thinking. If she finds herself in a dire circumstance, she puts her pride on the backburner and calls for aid.

Although she purports that she can resurrect Tlatoani, there is no evidence to support her claims that she truly is Tlatoani's daughter or that she can accomplish her stated goal. Instead, the characters may theorize that she uses this story to entice mortals to accept her diabolical bargain for another dire purpose of her own creation or that of another demon prince, such as Tsathogga who may be seeking to increase his influence in a domain completely surrounded by water and some of his allies. If the characters succeed on a Wisdom (Insight) check contested by her Charisma (Deception) check, the character can neither confirm nor refute her story, though the character senses that the demon conceals or is omitting a crucial detail about her ties to the island's former master or her real motives for her actions, which you are free to create to fit into your plotline.

Treasure: Over the years, the demon and her minions have accumulated a wealth of goods and gear. There are 14 yellow sapphires on the mosaic worth 1,000 gp each as well as a *pamitl of combat coordination**, a *tilmahtli of the owl**, and *xtabentun**.

* See **Appendix C: New Equipment and Magic Items**

25A: The Pool of Life

A pool of partially coagulated blood extracted from centuries of sacrifice rests within a 10-foot recess below the main level of this chamber. The blood helps Tlatoani maintain a connection to the mortal realms. The pool is five feet deep, but the blood in the pool is rank and decayed despite the enchantments of priests and demons to keep it from spoiling. If anyone falls into the pool or drinks from it, the character must succeed on a DC 17 Constitution saving throw or be poisoned for 30 minutes.

25B: Lightning Adder Traps

The statues are enchanted to blast intruders with lightning. They are attuned to Titechcualtia Ianima, and when she touches one of the statues as a bonus action, she can cause that statue to unleash a bolt of lightning that targets any creatures in a 150-foot line directly in front of the adder statues' mouths. A creature in the line must make a DC 20 Dexterity saving throw and take 45 (10d8) lightning damage on a failure or half as much damage on a success. It takes a successful DC 20 Intelligence (Arcana) check to find the trap on the statue and a successful DC 25 Intelligence (Arcana) check to disarm it.

25C: Altar of the Drowned

The mosaic on this platform depicts three serpents encircling a Tehuatl calendar. Tlatoani had multiple aspects and numerous children, at least according to legend. Titechcualtia Ianima claims she is not the only child of the Serpent, though she does not go out of her way to reveal this fact. She would rather die than reveal that she has other siblings. Anyone attempting to decipher the meaning of this mosaic must succeed on a DC 25 Intelligence (Religion) check to correctly infer that Titechcualtia Ianima is not alone in her efforts to resurrect Tlatoani. However, the mosaic, if accurate, provides no clues about the nature, identity, nor whereabouts of her alleged siblings.

25D: The Font of Coagulation

The fountain is fed from above via the Serpent Altar that drains downward through the Column of Blood. An evil creature who uses an action to drink from the fountain regains 22 (4d10) hit points. However, the creature cannot regain hit points again in this manner until the next midnight. A neutral creature gains no benefits but suffers no harm from drinking from the fountain. A good creature who uses an action to drink from the fountain takes 22 (4d10) necrotic damage. Unlike the fountain's beneficial effects, a good creature takes necrotic damage each time it drinks from the fountain.

Conclusion

The adventure ends if the characters defeat Titechcualtia Ianima. The characters can then ransack the rest of the temple or return to any of the villages to offer evidence of her defeat. If they killed Metzpil, they may seek forgiveness from his father, which he readily grants under the circumstances. The priest is curious to learn of the temples and the ruins. He implores the characters to lead him back to these locations so he can consecrate them and destroy any evidence of the rituals that others might use in the future to bring the Drowned Serpent back into this world. If Metzpil lives, allow the characters the opportunity to help him find redemption. His father may send the characters on an expedition to find a cure for his son's addiction or he may ask the characters to take Metzpil to find a cure. If a player's character died, the player may opt to assume Metzpil's role as a character and seek redemption through subsequent quests or expeditions.

If the characters return to either of the villages, the Poqozas offer the characters permanent residence, as well as food and restitution for their services. If they befriended the sea bride, she gratefully gifts them with a magic item of their choice for defeating her "husband's" age-old enemy.

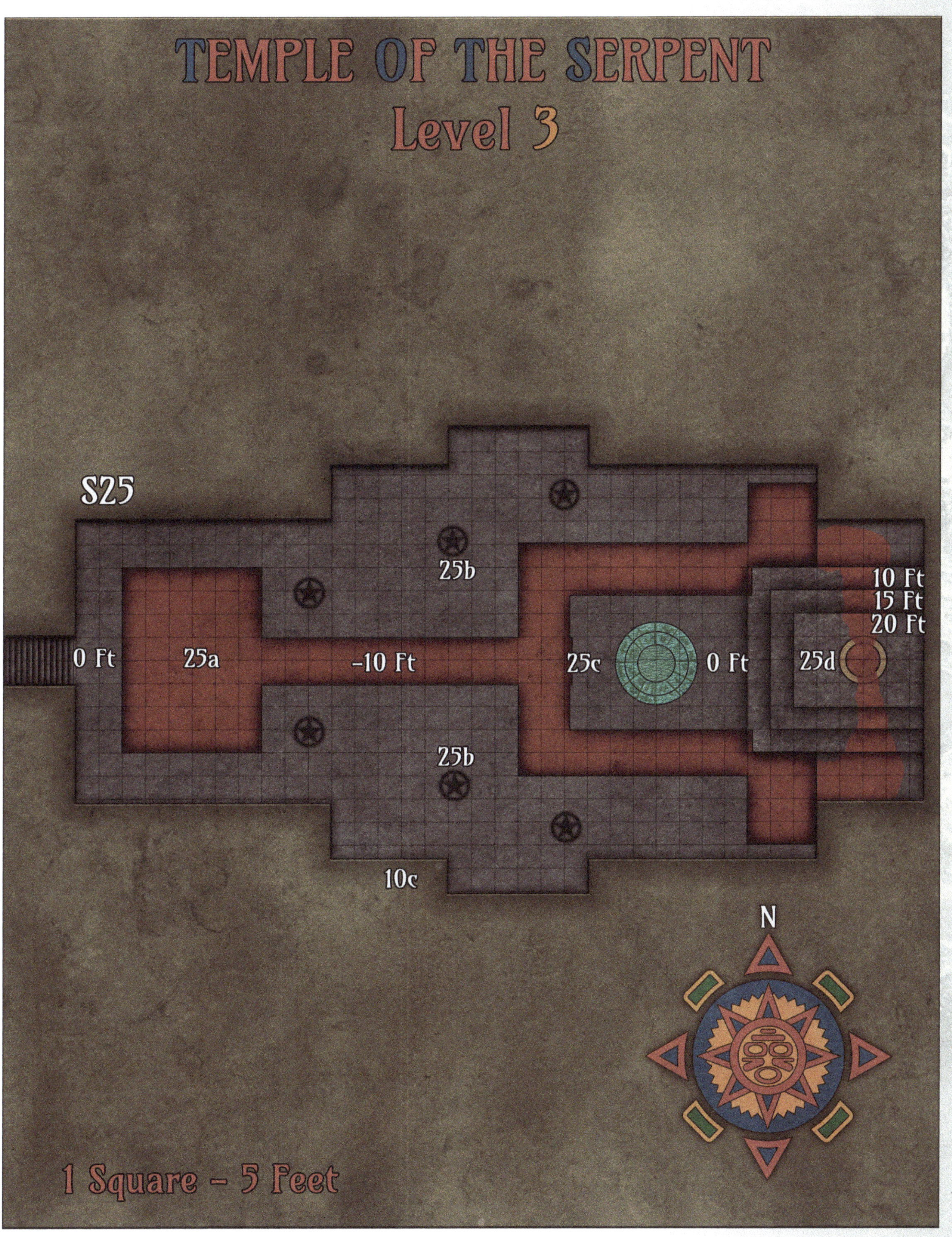

TEMPLE OF THE SERPENT
Level 3
S25
25a
0 Ft
-10 Ft
25b
25b
25c
0 Ft
25d
10 Ft
15 Ft
20 Ft
10c
N
1 Square - 5 Feet

Appendix A: New Monsters

The following new monsters appear in this volume. Other creatures used in the adventures can be found in the Fifth Edition SRD.

Aboleth, Nihileth

Large undead, chaotic evil

Armor Class 17 (natural armor)
Hit Points 135 (18d10 + 36)
Speed 10 ft., swim 40 ft., fly 40 ft. (ethereal only)

STR	DEX	CON	INT	WIS	CHA
21 (+5)	9 (−1)	15 (+2)	18 (+4)	15 (+2)	18 (+4)

Saving Throws Con +6, Int +8, Wis +6
Skills History +12, Perception +10
Damage Resistances acid, fire, lightning, thunder (only when in ethereal form); bludgeoning, piercing and slashing from nonmagical attacks
Damage Immunities cold, necrotic, poison; bludgeoning, piercing and slashing from nonmagical attacks (only when in ethereal form)
Condition Immunities charmed, exhaustion, frightened, grappled, paralyzed, petrified, poisoned, prone, restrained
Senses darkvision 120 ft., passive Perception 20
Languages Deep Speech, telepathy 120 ft.
Challenge 12 (8,400 XP)

Aboleth Traits. Unless noted otherwise or where contradicted below, a nihileth has the same traits as a living aboleth. This includes legendary actions and lair actions.

Undead Nature. A nihileth does not require air, food, drink, or sleep.

Undead Fortitude. If damage reduces the nihileth to 0 hit points, it must make a Constitution saving throw with a DC of 5 + the damage taken, unless the damage is radiant or from a critical hit. On a success, the nihileth drops to 1 hit point instead.

Dual State. A nihileth exists upon the Material Plane in one of two forms and can switch between them at will. In its material form, it has resistance to damage from nonmagical attacks. In its ethereal form, it is immune to damage from nonmagical attacks. The creature's ethereal form appears as a dark purple outline of its material form, with a blackish-purple haze within. A nihileth in ethereal form can move through air as though it were water, with a fly speed of 40 feet.

Void Aura. A nihileth doesn't secrete the mucous cloud of an aboleth. Instead, the undead nihileth is surrounded by a chilling cloud. A living creature that starts its turn within 5 feet of a nihileth must make a successful DC 14 Constitution saving throw or be *slowed* until the start of its next turn. In addition, any creature that has been diseased by a nihileth or a nihilethic zombie takes 7 (2d6) cold damage every time it starts its turn within the aura.

Infecting Telepathy. If a creature communicates telepathically with the nihileth or uses a psychic attack against it, the nihileth can spread its disease to the creature. The creature must succeed on a DC 14 Wisdom save or become infected with the same disease caused by the nihileth's tentacle attack. This ability replaces an aboleth's Probing Telepathy ability.

Actions

Multiattack. The nihileth makes three tentacle attacks or three withering touches, depending on what form it is in.

***Tentacle* (material form only).** *Melee Weapon Attack*: +9 to hit, reach 10 ft., one target. *Hit*: 12 (2d6 + 5) bludgeoning damage. If the target creature is hit, it must succeed on a DC 14 Constitution saving throw or become diseased. The disease has no effect for one minute; during that time, it can be removed by *lesser restoration* or comparable magic. After one minute, the diseased creature's skin becomes translucent and slimy. The creature cannot regain hit points unless it is entirely underwater, and the disease can be removed only by *heal* or comparable magic. Unless the creature is fully submerged or frequently doused with water, it takes 6 (1d12) acid damage every 10 minutes. If a creature dies while diseased, it rises in 1d6 rounds as a nihilethic zombie. This zombie is permanently dominated by the nihileth.

***Withering Touch* (ethereal form only).** *Melee Weapon Attack*: +8 to hit, reach 10 ft., one creature. *Hit*: 14 (3d6 + 4) necrotic damage.

Form Swap. As a bonus action, the nihileth can alter between its material and ethereal forms at will.

Tail Action. *Melee Weapon Attack*: +9 to hit, reach 10 ft. one target. *Hit*: 15 (3d6 + 5) bludgeoning damage.

Enslave (3/day). The aboleth targets one creature it can see within 30 feet of it. The target must succeed on a DC 14 Wisdom saving throw or be magically charmed by the aboleth until the aboleth dies or until it is on a different plane of existence from the target. The charmed target is under the aboleth's control and can't take reactions, and the aboleth and the target can communicate telepathically with each other over any distance. Whenever the charmed target takes damage, the target can repeat the saving throw. On a success, the effect ends. No more than once every 24 hours, the target can also repeat the saving throw when it is at least 1 mile away from the aboleth.

Reactions

Void Body. As a reaction, the nihileth can reduce the damage it takes from a single source to 0. Radiant damage can be reduced only by half.

Legendary Actions

A nihileth may take three legendary actions, choosing from the options below. Only one legendary action option can be used at a time and only at the end of another creature's turn. The nihileth regains spent legendary actions at the start of its turn.

Detect. The aboleth makes a Wisdom (Perception) check.

Tail Swipe. The aboleth makes one tail attack.

Psychic Drain (costs 2 actions). One creature charmed by the aboleth takes 10 (3d6) psychic damage, and the aboleth regains hit points equal to the damage the creature takes.

Lair

While aboleths create their lairs underwater, spending most of their time submerged, a nihileth lair can be encountered out of the water, often in a cave or a ruined, abandoned city.

Lair Actions

On initiative count 20 (losing initiative ties), the nihileth can take a lair action to create one of the magical effects listed below. The nihileth cannot use the same effect two rounds in a row.
The nihileth casts *major image* (no components required) on

any number of creatures it can see within 60 feet of it. While maintaining concentration on this effect, the nihileth can't take other lair actions. If a target succeeds on the saving throw or if the effect ends for it, the target is immune to the nihileth's *major image* lair action for the next 24 hours, although such a creature can choose to be affected.

Pools of water within 90 feet of the nihileth surge outward in a grasping tide. Any creature on the ground within 20 feet of such a pool must succeed on a DC 14 Strength saving throw or be pulled up to 20 feet into the water and knocked prone.

Water in the nihileth's lair magically becomes a conduit for the creature's rage. The nihileth can target any number of creatures it can see in such water within 90 feet of it. A target must succeed on a DC 14 Wisdom saving throw or take 7 (2d6) psychic damage.

A nihileth can pull the lifeforce from those it has converted to nihilethic zombies to replenish its own life. This takes 21 (6d6) hit points from zombies within 30 feet of the nihileth, spread evenly among the zombies, and healing the nihileth. If a zombie reaches 0 hit points from this action, it perishes with no Undead Fortitude saving throw.

Regional Effects

The regional effects of a nihileth's lair are as following:

Underground surfaces within one mile of the nihileth's lair are slimy and wet and are difficult terrain.

As an action, the nihileth can create an illusory image of itself within one mile of the lair. The copy can appear at any location the nihileth has seen before or in any location a creature charmed by the nihileth can currently see. Once created, the image lasts for as long as the nihileth maintains concentration, as if concentrating on a spell. Although the image is intangible, it looks, sounds, and can move like the nihileth. The nihileth can sense, speak, and use telepathy from the image's position as if present at that position. If the image takes any damage, it disappears.

Water sources within one mile of a nihileth's lair are not only supernaturally fouled but can spread the disease of the nihileth. A creature who drinks from such water must make a successful DC 14 Constitution check or become infected.

The aboleth, nihileth can be found in **Tome of Beasts** by **Kobold Press**.

ALLIP

Medium undead, chaotic evil

Armor Class 11
Hit Points 33 (6d8 + 6)
Speed fly 30 ft.

STR	DEX	CON	INT	WIS	CHA
6 (–2)	13 (+1)	13 (+1)	11 (+0)	11 (+0)	16 (+3)

Skills Perception +3, Stealth +3
Senses darkvision 60 ft., passive Perception 13
Languages Common, Deep Speech
Challenge 2 (450 XP)

Babble. The allip incoherently mutters to itself, creating a hypnotic effect. All creatures within 30 feet that aren't incapacitated must succeed on a DC 11 Wisdom saving throw. On a failed save, the creature becomes charmed for the duration. While charmed by this spell, the creature is incapacitated and has a speed of 0. The effect ends for an affected creature if it takes any damage or if someone else uses an action to shake the creature out of its stupor.

Incorporeal Movement. The allip can move through other creatures and objects as if they were difficult terrain. It takes 5 (1d10) force damage if it ends its turn inside an object.

Madness. Anyone targeting an allip with a spell or effect that would make direct contact with its tortured mind must succeed on a DC 11 Wisdom saving throw or take 7 (2d6) psychic damage.

Actions

Touch of Insanity. *Melee Weapon Attack:* +3 to hit, reach 5 ft., one target. *Hit:* 8 (2d6 + 1) psychic damage.

ALUX

The aluxes are made up of several races of proto-humans whom the earliest gods created during the prehistoric ages long before the rise of Tlatoani and the hero-gods. Each of a different era, the aluxes were formed from the remains of the creations that came before them after their worlds were laid waste by cataclysm, war, and other apocalypses that befell the world before the age of man. They span thousands of years of creation and are the precursors to what the world recognizes as human. They walk upright, possess the ability to reason, and are human in appearance, though each age has identifiable traits that are distinctly non-human — some subtle, some hideous, or deformed. The earliest aluxes are more bestial than manlike. They are crude, barbaric, and barely able to speak. Aluxes hold a wide range of dispositions, though most have a chaotic bent. Some are kind and helpful. Others resent humanity, believing they stole the world from them and seek to reclaim it for themselves.

Few aluxes exist today. Those that escaped extinction remain hidden from the world, though they sometimes settle with their own kind. To exist in the realms of the living and the dead, the gods gave the aluxes souls. However, they can remove them when they pass into the land of the dead. For this reason, all aluxes are semi-immortal in that they do not age. Nonetheless, they can be killed by physical violence.

ALUX OF THE FIRST SUN

Large fey (alux), any alignment

Armor Class 13 (natural armor)
Hit Points 84 (8d10 + 40)
Speed 40 ft.

STR	DEX	CON	INT	WIS	CHA
19 (+4)	12 (+1)	20 (+5)	8 (–1)	13 (+1)	7 (–2)

Saving Throws Str +6, Con +7
Damage Vulnerabilities Obsidian
Condition Immunities Frightened
Senses darkvision 60 ft, passive Perception 11
Languages Primordial Notoan (understands but doesn't speak)
Challenge 3 (700 XP)

Keen Hearing and Smell. The alux has advantage on Wisdom (Perception) checks that rely on hearing or smell.

Mountain Camouflage. The alux has advantage on Dexterity (Stealth) checks made to hide in mountain terrain.

Actions

Multiattack. The alux makes two Bash attacks.

Bash. *Melee Weapon Attack:* +6 to hit, reach 5 ft., one target. *Hit:* 15 (2d10 + 4) bludgeoning damage, and the alux can push the target five feet away if the target is Large or smaller.

Block the Path. The alux can use its action to prohibit other creatures from moving past it or escaping its grasp. Until the start of the alux's next turn, attack rolls against the alux have disadvantage. The alux has advantage on opportunity attack rolls, and that attack deals an extra 16 (3d10) bludgeoning damage on a hit. Also, each enemy that tries to move out of the alux's reach without teleporting must succeed on a DC 14 Strength saving throw or have its speed reduced to 0 until the start of the alux's next turn.

Trigger Rockslide (recharge 5–6). The alux begins wildly pounding the surrounding earth and rock to create a rockslide that rushes down the incline atop which the creature stands. The rockslide is 10 feet wide and travels in a straight line down the incline until it reaches the nadir. Each creature within the area of the rockslide must make a DC 13 Dexterity saving throw, taking 18 (4d8) bludgeoning damage on a failed save, or half as much damage on a successful one. A creature that fails this saving throw is also knocked prone.

ALUX OF THE SECOND SUN

Medium fey (alux), any alignment

Armor Class 14
Hit Points 30 (4d8 + 12)
Speed 30 ft.

STR	DEX	CON	INT	WIS	CHA
12 (+1)	19 (+4)	16 (+3)	14 (+2)	13 (+1)	12 (+1)

Saving Throws Dex +6, Wis +3
Skills Acrobatics +6, Athletics +3, Nature +4, Perception +3, Stealth +6, Survival +3
Damage Vulnerabilities obsidian
Damage Resistances necrotic
Senses darkvision 60 ft, passive Perception 13
Languages Primordial Notoan
Challenge 1 (200 XP)

Ambusher. The alux has advantage on attack rolls against any creature it has surprised.

Surprise Attack. If the alux surprises a creature and hits it within an attack before the creature has taken a turn in combat, the target takes an extra 10 (3d6) damage from the attack. The alux can deal this extra damage only once per turn.

Keen Hearing and Smell. The alux has advantage on Wisdom (Perception) checks that rely on hearing or smell.

Mountain Camouflage. The alux has advantage on Dexterity (Stealth) checks made to hide in hilly or mountainous terrain.

Actions

Multiattack. An alux makes one Bite attack and two Slam attacks with its fists.

Bite. *Melee Weapon Attack:* +6 to hit, reach 5 ft., one target. *Hit:* 11 (2d6 + 4) piercing damage.

Slam. *Melee Weapon Attack:* +6 to hit, reach 5 ft., one target. *Hit:* 8 (1d8 + 4) bludgeoning damage.

ALUX OF THE SECOND SUN SNIPER

Medium fey (alux), chaotic neutral

Armor Class 14
Hit Points 45 (6d8 + 18)
Speed 30 ft.

STR	DEX	CON	INT	WIS	CHA
12 (+1)	19 (+4)	16 (+3)	14 (+2)	13 (+1)	12 (+1)

Saving Throws Dex +6, Wis +3
Skills Acrobatics +6, Athletics +3, Nature +4, Perception+3, Stealth +6, Survival +3
Damage Vulnerabilities obsidian
Damage Resistances necrotic
Senses darkvision 60 ft., passive Perception 13
Languages Primordial Notoan
Challenge 2 (450 XP)

Ambusher. The alux has advantage on attack rolls against any creature it has surprised.

Sniper. When using a ranged weapon, once per turn the alux deals an extra 7 (2d6) damage when it hits a target with a ranged weapon attack and has advantage on the attack roll, or when an ally is within five feet of the alux that isn't incapacitated and the alux doesn't have disadvantage on the attack roll.

Surprise Attack. If the alux surprises a creature and hits it before the creature has taken a turn in combat, the target takes an extra 10 (3d6) damage from the attack.

Keen Hearing and Smell. The alux has advantage on Wisdom (Perception) checks that rely on hearing or smell.

Mountain Camouflage. The alux has advantage on Dexterity (Stealth) checks made to hide in mountain terrain.

Actions

Multiattack. An alux sniper makes one Bite attack and two Slam attacks with its fists, or two Longbow attacks.

Bite. *Melee Weapon Attack:* +6 to hit, reach 5 ft., one target. *Hit:* 11 (2d6 + 4) piercing damage.

Slam. *Melee Weapon Attack:* +6 to hit, reach 5 ft., one target. *Hit:* 8 (1d8 + 4) bludgeoning damage.

Longbow. Ranged *Weapon Attack:* +6 to hit, ranged 150/600 ft., one target. *Hit:* 8 (1d8 + 4) piercing damage.

ALUX OF THE THIRD SUN

Medium fey (alux), any

Armor Class 13
Hit Points 19 (3d8+6)
Speed 30 ft.

STR	DEX	CON	INT	WIS	CHA
12 (+1)	16 (+3)	14 (+2)	12 (+1)	13 (+1)	11 (0)

Skills Acrobatics +5, Nature +3 Perception +3, Survival +3, Stealth +5
Damage Vulnerabilities obsidian
Damage Resistance necrotic
Senses darkvision 60 ft; passive Perception 13
Languages Primordial Notoan
Challenge 1/2 (100 XP)

Keen Smell. The alux has advantage on Wisdom (Perception) checks that rely on smell.

Stealthy Traveler. The alux can move stealthily while traveling at a normal pace.

Chom Bonded. If the alux has its soul placed within its chom, and the chom is killed while the alux is on the Material Plane, then the alux also dies. The bonded chom carries the alux's soul only if the alux is currently carrying a departed mortal's soul to the land of the dead.

Summon Bonded Chom. Third sun aluxs are guides and transporters of souls. Each third sun alux is bonded to a specific chom that it can summon as a bonus action. This chom holds the creature's soul, giving its body room to carry a departed mortal soul to the land of the dead.

An alux can summon his bonded chom from any distance on the same plane of existence. If it appears next to an enemy, the chom can make an immediate attack. The chom acts at the start of the alux's initiative.

Actions

Multiattack. The alux makes two Claw attacks.

Claw. *Melee Weapon Attack:* +5 to hit, reach 5 ft., one target. Hit: 5 (1d4 + 3) slashing damage.

ANT, GIANT

Large beast, unaligned

Armor Class 14 (natural armor)
Hit Points 52 (7d10 + 14)
Speed 40 ft.

STR	DEX	CON	INT	WIS	CHA
15 (+2)	13 (+1)	15 (+2)	1 (−5)	9 (−1)	2 (−4)

Senses blindsight 60 ft., passive Perception 9
Languages —
Challenge 2 (450 XP)

Keen Smell. The giant ant has advantage on Wisdom (Perception) checks that rely on smell.

Actions

Multiattack. The giant ant makes one Bite attack and one Sting attack.
Bite. *Melee Weapon Attack:* +4 to hit, reach 5 ft., one target. *Hit:* 6 (1d8 + 2) bludgeoning damage and the target is grappled (escape DC 12). Until this grapple ends, the target is restrained, and the giant ant can't bite a different target.
Sting. *Melee Weapon Attack:* +4 to hit, reach 5 ft., one target. *Hit:* 6 (1d8 + 2) piercing damage plus 22 (4d10) poison damage, or half as much poison damage with a successful DC 12 Constitution saving throw
The giant ant can be found in the ***Tome of Beasts*** by **Kobold Press**.

APE, WOODS

Medium monstrosity, unaligned

Armor Class 11 (16 with *barkskin*)
Hit Points 82 (11d8 + 33)
Speed 30 ft., climb 30 ft.

STR	DEX	CON	INT	WIS	CHA
17 (+3)	13 (+1)	16 (+3)	11 (+0)	18 (+4)	7 (−2)

Skills Nature +6, Perception +7, Stealth +4 (+7 in forested terrain), Survival +10
Damage Immunities poison
Condition Immunities poisoned
Senses darkvision 60 ft., passive Perception 17
Languages Druidic
Challenge 5 (1,800 XP)

Land's Stride. The woods ape can move through nonmagical difficult terrain without using extra movement and can pass through nonmagical plants without being slowed by them and without taking damage if they have thorns, spines, or a similar hazard. In addition, the woods ape has advantage on saving throws against plants that are magically created or manipulated to impede movement.
Innate Spellcasting. The woods ape's innate spellcasting ability is Wisdom (spell save DC 15, +7 to hit with spell attacks). It can cast the following spells, requiring no material components:
At will: *guidance, mending, create or destroy water, detect poison and disease, entangle, speak with animals, speak with plants, tree stride*
3/day each: *animal messenger, barkskin, call lightning, locate animals or plants, pass without trace*
1/day each: *awaken, commune with nature, conjure animals, plant growth*

Actions

Multiattack. The woods ape makes two Claw attacks.
Claw. *Melee Weapon Attack:* +6 to hit, reach 5 ft., one target. *Hit:* 10 (2d6 + 3) slashing damage.

BANC

Medium humanoid (goblinoid), lawful evil

Armor Class 18 (chain mail, shield)
Hit Points 120 (16d8 + 48)
Speed 30 ft.

STR	DEX	CON	INT	WIS	CHA
16 (+3)	13 (+1)	16 (+3)	14 (+2)	16 (+3)	18 (+4)

Saving Throws Wis +7, Cha +8
Skills Deception +8, Persuasion +8, Religion +6
Senses darkvision 60 ft., passive Perception 13
Languages Common, Goblin
Challenge 10 (5,900 XP)

Martial Advantage. Once per turn, Banc can deal an extra 17 (5d6) damage to a creature it hits with a weapon attack if that creature is within five feet of an ally of the hobgoblin that is not incapacitated.
Preach. Banc has advantage on Charisma (Deception) and Charisma (Persuasion) checks that rely on hearing.
***Proselytize* (recharges after a short or long rest).** As a bonus action, Banc weaves a web of lies and honeyed words. All creatures that can see and hear him within 30 feet must succeed on a DC 15 Wisdom saving throw or be charmed for one hour.
Spellcasting. Banc is a 14th-level spellcaster. His spellcasting ability is Wisdom (spell save DC 15, +7 to hit with spell attacks). He has the following spells prepared:
Cantrips (at will): *guidance, mending, resistance, sacred flame, spare the dying*
1st level (4 slots): *bane, command, inflict wounds, shield of faith*
2nd level (3 slots): *augury, enthrall, suggestion*
3rd level (3 slots): *bestow curse, speak with dead, tongues*
4th level (3 slots): *divination, guardian of faith, locate creature*
5th level (2 slots): *geas, scrying*
6th level (1 slot): *harm*
7th level (1 slot): *symbol*
Staff of Charming. Banc has a *staff of charming.*

Actions

Multiattack. Banc can use his Condemning Touch and make two weapon attacks.
Condemning Touch. *Melee Spell Attack:* +7 to hit, reach 5 ft., one target. *Hit:* 17 (4d6 + 3) psychic damage. The target must succeed on a DC 15 Wisdom saving throw or be frightened for one minute. The target can repeat the saving throw at the end of each of its turns, ending the effect on itself on a success.
Longsword. *Melee Weapon Attack:* +7 to hit, reach 5 ft., one target. *Hit:* 7 (1d8 + 3) slashing damage.
Longbow. *Ranged Weapon Attack:* +5 to hit, range 150/600 ft., one target. *Hit:* 5 (1d8 + 1) piercing damage.
Staff of Charming. *Melee Weapon Attack:* +8 to hit, reach 5 ft., one target. *Hit:* 7 (1d6 + 4) bludgeoning damage.

BEAST FROM BELOW THE BLACK

Huge fiend, chaotic evil

Armor Class 16 (natural armor)
Hit Points 94 (9d12 + 36)
Speed 30 ft., swim 50 ft.

STR	DEX	CON	INT	WIS	CHA
22 (+6)	11 (+0)	19 (+4)	2 (−4)	10 (+0)	7 (−2)

Skills Athletics +9, Stealth +3
Damage Resistances cold, piercing
Damage Immunities acid, necrotic

Condition Immunities poisoned
Senses darkvision 60 ft., tremorsense 120 ft. in water only, passive
Perception 10
Languages —
Challenge 8 (3,900 XP)

Hold Breath. The beast can hold its breath for one hour.

Actions

Multiattack. The beast from below the black makes one Bite attack
and one Tail attack.
Bite. Melee Weapon Attack: +9 to hit, reach 5 ft., one target. *Hit*: 28
(4d10 + 6) piercing damage, and the target is grappled (escape DC
17). Until this grapple ends, the target is restrained, and the beast
cannot bite another target.
Tail. Melee Weapon Attack: +9 to hit, reach 10 ft., one target not
grappled by the crocodile. *Hit*: 19 (3d8 + 6) bludgeoning damage. If
the target is a creature, it must succeed on a DC 16 Strength saving
throw or be knocked prone.

Legendary Actions

The beast from below the black can take three Legendary actions,
choosing from the options below. Only one legendary action option
can be used at a time and only at the end of another creature's turn.
The beast regains spent legendary actions at the start of its turn.
Detect. The beast makes a Wisdom (Perception) check. It can use its
tremorsense to make this check when submerged.
Tail Slap. The beast makes a Tail attack.
Breach Hull (costs 3 actions). The beast surfaces beneath the hull
of a waterborne vessel, slamming into the craft and dealing 27 (6d8)
bludgeoning damage. If the vessel is smaller than the beast and
takes more than 60 hit points of damage from a single attack, there
is a 25% chance that the vessel is thrown into the air and capsizes.

Lair and Lair Actions

The beast from below the black lives within the Miquiatoyatl that
leads into the land of the dead. Over the eons, it has adapted to the
environment and perfected several attacks that manipulate the
magic of its foul and necrotic waters.
On initiative count 20 (losing initiative ties), the beast can take a lair
action to cause one of the following magical effects; the beast cannot
use the same effect two rounds in a row.
Tail Splash. The beast can sweep its tail across the surface of
the river, flinging a splash of the toxic waters in the direction of
its opponents. The splash targets all creatures in a 15-foot cone
emanating from the creature's tail. Those caught in the splash must
make a DC 13 Dexterity saving throw, taking 13 (3d8) necrotic
damage on a failure or half as much on a success.

Beast of Itzcuin

Medium beast, neutral evil

Armor Class 13 (natural armor)
Hit Points 22 (4d8 + 4)
Speed 40 ft.

STR	DEX	CON	INT	WIS	CHA
13 (+1)	15 (+2)	12 (+1)	7 (−2)	12 (+1)	8 (−1)

Skills Perception +3
Damage Resistances fire, lightning
Senses darkvision 60 ft., passive Perception 13
Languages Aztli, Common
Challenge 1/2 (100 XP)

Beast of Misfortune. As a bonus action, the beast of Itzcuin can
target one creature it can see within five feet of it. The target must

succeed on a DC 11 Wisdom saving throw against this magic or
suffer disadvantage on attack rolls made against the beast until the
end of the target's next turn.
Keen Hearing and Smell. A beast of Itzcuin has advantage on
Wisdom (Perception) checks that rely on hearing or smell.
Pack Tactics. The beast of Itzcuin has advantage on an attack roll
against a creature if at least one of the beast of Itzcuin's allies is
within five feet of the creature and the ally isn't incapacitated.

Actions

Bite. Melee Weapon Attack: +3 to hit, reach 5 ft., one target. *Hit*: 4 (1d6
+ 1) piercing damage. If the target is a creature, it must succeed on a
DC 11 Constitution saving throw against disease or become poisoned
until the disease is cured. For every 24 hours that elapse, the target
must repeat the saving throw, reducing its hit point maximum by 5
(1d10) on a failure. The disease is cured on a success. The target dies
if the disease reduces its hit point maximum to 0. This reduction to
the target's hit point maximum lasts until the disease is cured.

Black Orc High Priest of Orcus

Medium humanoid (black orc), chaotic evil

Armor Class 16 (scale mail)
Hit Points 127 (15d8 + 60)
Speed 30 ft.

STR	DEX	CON	INT	WIS	CHA
16 (+3)	14 (+2)	18 (+4)	12 (+1)	20 (+5)	14 (+2)

Saving Throws Wis +9, Cha +6
Skills Arcana +5, Deception +6, Insight +9, Intimidation +6,
Perception +9
Senses truesight 120 ft., passive Perception 19
Languages Abyssal, Common, Orc
Challenge 9 (5,000 XP)

Abyssal Blessing. The priest of Orcus gains 10 temporary hit points
when it reduces a hostile creature that is not an undead to 0 hit
points.
Blessing of Orcus. Black orcs have advantage on saving throws
against the spells and effects of undead creatures.
Deadsight. The high priest of Orcus has truesight out to a range of
120 feet.
Spellcasting. The high priest of Orcus is a 10th-level spellcaster. Its
spellcasting ability is Wisdom (spell save DC 17, +9 to hit with spell
attacks). It has the following cleric spells prepared:
Cantrips (at will): *chill touch, guidance, mending, resistance*
1st level (4 slots): *bane, cure wounds, false life, inflict wounds*
2nd level (3 slots): *aid, blindness/deafness, hold person, silence*
3rd level (3 slots): *animate dead, bestow curse, dispel magic, spirit
guardians*
4th level (3 slots): *banishment, death ward, guardian of faith*
5th level (2 slots): *dispel evil and good, insect plague*
Unholy Strike. Once on each of the high priest's turns when it hits a
creature with a weapon attack, the high priest can cause the attack
to deal an extra 18 (4d8) necrotic damage to the target.

Actions

Multiattack. The high priest makes two melee attacks.
Mace. Melee Weapon Attack: +7 to hit, reach 5 ft., one target. *Hit:* 12
(2d8 + 3) bludgeoning damage.
Caress of Orcus (recharge 5–6). Melee Weapon Attack: +7 to hit,
reach 5 ft., one target. *Hit:* 12 (2d8 + 3) necrotic damage, and the
target's Strength score is reduced by 1d4. The target dies if this
reduces its Strength to 0. Otherwise, the reduction lasts until the
target finishes a short or long rest.
If a non-evil humanoid dies from this attack, a shadow rises from the
corpse in 24 hours under the priest's control, unless the humanoid is

restored to life or its body is destroyed. The priest can have no more than three shadows under its control at one time.

BOARFOLK RAGER

Large humanoid (boarfolk), lawful neutral

Armor Class 16 (natural armor)
Hit Points 123 (13d10 + 52)
Speed 40 ft.

STR	DEX	CON	INT	WIS	CHA
20 (+5)	15 (+2)	18 (+4)	9 (−1)	11 (+0)	10 (+0)

Saving Throws Str +9, Dex +6, Con +8
Skills Athletics +9, Intimidation +4
Damage Resistances bludgeoning, piercing, and slashing damage from nonmagical attacks
Senses darkvision 60 ft., passive Perception 10
Languages Boarfolk, Common
Challenge 9 (5,000 XP)

Brute. A melee weapon deals one extra die of its damage when the rager hits with it (included in the attack).
Created Race. The boarfolk rager has advantage on saving throws against spells and effects that would alter its form.
Keen Scent. A boarfolk rager has advantage on Wisdom (Perception) checks based on scent.
Reckless. At the start of its turn, the rager can gain advantage on all melee weapon attack rolls during that turn, but attack rolls against it have advantage until the start of its next turn.

Actions

Multiattack. The boarfolk rager makes three melee attacks.
Tusks. Melee Weapon Attack: +9 to hit, reach 5 ft., one target. *Hit:* 12 (2d6 + 5) piercing damage.
Greatclub. Melee Weapon Attack: +9 to hit, reach 5 ft., one target. *Hit:* 14 (2d8 + 5) bludgeoning damage.

BOG CREEPER

Medium plant, unaligned

Armor Class 12 (natural armor)
Hit Points 104 (11d8 + 55)
Speed 10 ft., swim 20 ft.

STR	DEX	CON	INT	WIS	CHA
18 (+4)	10 (+0)	20 (+5)	3 (−4)	14 (+2)	6 (−2)

Skills Perception +6
Senses tremorsense 60 ft., passive Perception 16
Languages —
Challenge 9 (5,000 XP)

False Appearance. While the bog creeper remains motionless, it is indistinguishable from normal plants.
Marsh Move. A bog creeper doesn't treat marshy, swampy terrain as difficult terrain.

Actions

Multiattack. The bog creeper makes up to four attacks: one with its bite, one slam, and two with its tendrils.
Bite. Melee Weapon Attack: +8 to hit, reach 5 ft., one target. *Hit:* 13 (2d8 + 4) piercing damage.
Slam. Melee Weapon Attack: +8 to hit, reach 5 ft., one target. *Hit:* 15 (2d10 + 4) bludgeoning damage.
Tendrils. Melee Weapon Attack: +8 to hit, reach 10 ft., one target. *Hit:* 11 (2d6 + 4) bludgeoning damage. The target is grappled (escape DC 14) if the bog creeper isn't already grappling a creature, and the target is restrained until the grapple ends. The bog creeper can grapple only one target.
Acid Spray (3/day). The bog creeper sprays stomach acid in a 30-foot cone. Each creature in that area must make a DC 15 Dexterity saving throw, taking 14 (3d8) acid damage on a failed save, or half as much damage on a successful one.

BONE SWARM

Large swarm of tiny undead, chaotic evil

Armor Class 17 (natural armor)
Hit Points 198 (36d10)
Speed 20 ft., fly 60 ft.

STR	DEX	CON	INT	WIS	CHA
22 (+6)	18 (+4)	10 (+0)	9 (−1)	15 (+2)	20 (+5)

Saving Throws Dex +8, Wis +6, Cha +9
Skills Acrobatics +8, Perception +6, Stealth +8
Damage Vulnerabilities bludgeoning
Damage Resistances Piercing and slashing from nonmagical attacks
Damage Immunities poison
Condition Immunities charmed, exhaustion, frightened, paralyzed, poisoned, prone, restrained, stunned
Senses Darkvision 60 ft., passive Perception 16
Languages Common, Void Speech
Challenge 10 (5,900 XP)

Strength of Bone. A bone swarm can choose to deal bludgeoning, piercing, or slashing damage, and adds 1.5 × its Strength bonus on swarm damage rolls as bits and pieces of broken skeletons claw, bite, stab, and slam at the victim.
Swarm. The swarm can occupy another creature's space and vice versa, and the swarm can move through any opening large enough for a human skull. The swarm can't regain hit points or gain temporary hit points.

Actions

Multiattack. The bone swarm can attack every hostile creature in its space with swirling bones.
Swirling Bones. Melee Weapon Attack: +10 to hit, reach 0 ft., one creature in the swarm's space. *Hit:* 31 (5d8 + 9) bludgeoning, piercing, or slashing damage (includes Strength of Bone special ability).
Death's Embrace (recharge 5–6). Melee Weapon Attack: +10 to hit, reach 0 ft., one creature in the swarm's space. *Hit:* the target is grappled (escape DC 16) and enveloped within the swarm's bones. The swarm can force the creature to move at its normal speed wherever the bone swarm wishes. Any non-area attack against the bone swarm has a 50% chance of hitting a creature grappled in Death's Embrace instead.
The bone swarm can be found in *Tome of Beasts* by **Kobold Press**.

CADAVER

Medium undead, chaotic evil

Armor Class 12
Hit Points 22 (4d8 + 4)
Speed 30 ft.

STR	DEX	CON	INT	WIS	CHA
13 (+1)	14 (+2)	13 (+1)	2 (−4)	10 (+0)	10 (+0)

Damage Immunities cold, poison
Condition Immunities exhaustion, poisoned

Reanimation. When reduced to 0 hit points, the cadaver falls inert and begins the process of reanimating. While in this state, the cadaver regenerates 1 hit point at the start of its turn. Hit points lost to magical weapons or radiant damage are not regained. When the creature reaches its full hit point total, less any magical weapon or radiant damage suffered, it rises, ready to fight again.

A fallen cadaver can be prevented from reanimating by salting and burning the bones, casting *gentle repose* on it, or bathing the bones in cleansing *sacred flame*.

Actions

Multiattack. The cadaver makes one Bite attack and two Claw attacks.

Bite. *Melee Weapon Attack*: +4 to hit, reach 5 ft., one target. *Hit*: 5 (1d6 + 2) piercing damage. If the target is a creature, it must succeed on a DC 13 Constitution saving throw against disease or become poisoned until the disease is cured. For every 24 hours that elapse, the target must repeat the saving throw, reducing its hit point maximum by 5 (1d10) on a failure. The disease is cured on a success. The target dies if the disease reduces its hit point maximum to 0. This reduction to the target's hit point maximum lasts until the disease is cured.

Claws. *Melee Weapon Attack*: +4 to hit, reach 5 ft., one target. *Hit*: 6 (1d8 + 2) slashing damage. If the target is a creature, it must succeed on a DC 13 Constitution saving throw against disease or become poisoned until the disease is cured. For every 24 hours that elapse, the target must repeat the saving throw, reducing its hit point maximum by 5 (1d10) on a failure. The disease is cured on a success. The target dies if the disease reduces its hit point maximum to 0. This reduction to the target's hit point maximum lasts until the disease is cured.

CARD SHARK

Tiny fiend (shapechanger), chaotic evil

Armor Class 13
Hit Points 40 (16d4)
Speed 20 ft.

STR	DEX	CON	INT	WIS	CHA
2 (–4)	16 (+3)	10 (+0)	12 (+1)	10 (+0)	16 (+3)

Skills Deception +7, Perception +2, Stealth +7
Condition Immunities prone
Senses darkvision 60 ft., passive Perception 12
Languages Abyssal, Common, telepathy 60 ft.
Challenge 4 (1,100 XP)

Shapechanger. The card shark can use its action to polymorph into an object that weighs 1 pound or less or back into its true form as a tiny, rectangular block of clay with a pair of minute legs and arms. Its statistics are the same in each form. Any equipment it is wearing or carrying isn't transformed. It reverts to its true form if it dies.

Whenever a card shark uses this feature to aid another creature during a game of chance, the participant benefiting from the card shark's interference has advantage on any check made to determine the game's outcome. Using a card shark in this manner may require the target to succeed on a Dexterity (Sleight of Hand) check contested by the opponent's Wisdom (Perception) check to prevent opponents from detecting the ruse, if the opponent is aware of the card shark's presence. If the GM opts to recreate an actual game of chance, a card shark may instead transform into any gaming piece of the player's choice.

Euphoria Drain. A card shark can use an action to establish a telepathic, parasitic link between itself and any humanoid it can see within 30 feet. The target must succeed on a DC 13 Charisma saving throw to thwart the card shark's attempt to create the link and become immune to that card shark's telepathic link for the next 24 hours. When a card shark successfully establishes a telepathic link between itself and its subject, it communicates its intentions to aid the target in games of chance by visually demonstrating its shapechanger feature. Naturally, it omits any details about the price it exacts, though it must succeed on a Charisma (Deception) check contested by the target's Wisdom (Insight) check to allow its omission to go unnoticed. If the subject declines a card shark's offer of assistance after the preceding demonstration or simply ignores the card shark's overtures, the telepathic link is instantly severed, and the same card shark cannot attempt to establish another telepathic link with that same creature for 24 hours. A target who accepts the card shark's offer must voluntarily allow the card shark to absorb a drop of its sweat or any other appropriate bodily fluid that the creature secretes when excited, nervous, or aroused. This act establishes a parasitic link between the pair. A card shark cannot have more than one parasitic link in effect at any time. If a card shark establishes a parasitic link with a new subject, the previous parasitic link immediately ceases and is replaced by the new parasitic link. On the other hand, the host cannot voluntarily sever the parasitic link without a struggle. Each day at dawn, the creature can attempt to sever the parasitic link by succeeding on a Charisma saving throw. The DC starts at 13 and increases by +1 for each day since the card shark established the parasitic link.

A humanoid parasitically linked to the card shark must succeed on a DC 13 Charisma saving throw or take 7 (2d6) psychic damage each time a card shark transforms into a specific object to win a game of chance for the target. A creature who succeeds on the preceding saving throw takes half as much damage. The card shark regains a number of hit points equal to the psychic damage dealt. A creature parasitically linked to the card shark cannot target that particular card shark with an attack or harmful spell. However, it can affect the fiend with area effects. When a card shark takes damage, the parasitically linked creature also suffers damage equal to the damage dealt to the card shark, regardless of its source. When a parasitically linked creature is reduced to 0 hit points, the card shark can attempt to take over the creature's body as though by a *magic jar* spell with the exception that the card shark's transfers its hit points to the new body. The target creature makes a DC 13 Charisma saving throw. On a failure, the subject and the card shark switch places. The card shark's former body becomes a lifeless receptacle that houses the victim's soul. A card shark can use an action to return to its true form, which immediately ends the *magic jar* effect.

***False Appearance* (object form only).** While the card shark remains motionless, it is indistinguishable from an ordinary object.

Actions

Pseudopod. *Melee Weapon Attack*: +5 to hit, reach 5 ft., one target. *Hit*: 1 bludgeoning damage.

***Suicide Kings* (recharge 5–6).** *Ranged Weapon Attack*: +4 to hit, range 20/60 ft., one target, *Hit*: Draw a card from a deck of standard playing cards. Any creature struck by the card takes an amount of damage equal to the card's value. Treat an ace as 1 point and any face card (jack, queen or king) as 10. If the card's suit is diamonds or hearts, the attack deals an extra 7 (2d6) fire damage. If the card's suit is clubs or spades, the attack deals an extra 7 (2d6) necrotic damage.

CHILD OF THE BRIAR

Tiny plant, neutral evil

Armor Class 13
Hit Points 50 (20d4)
Speed 20 ft., climb 10 ft.

STR	DEX	CON	INT	WIS	CHA
6 (–2)	17 (+3)	11 (+0)	13 (+1)	10 (+0)	14 (+2)

Skills Perception +4, Stealth +7
Damage Vulnerabilities fire

Senses darkvision 60 ft., passive Perception 14
Languages Common, Sylvan, +1 additional
Challenge 1 (200 XP)

Fey Blood. Children of the briar count as both plant and fey for any effect related to type.

Thorny Grapple. A child of the briar's long thorny limbs help it grapple creatures up to Medium size. A grappled creature takes 2 (1d4) piercing damage at the end of the child's turn for as long as it remains grappled.

Actions

Multiattack. A child of the briar makes two Claw attacks. If both attacks hit the same target, the target is grappled (escape DC 13) and the child of the briar uses its Thorny Grapple on it.

Claw. *Melee Weapon Attack:* +5 to hit, reach 5 ft., one target. *Hit:* 6 (1d6 + 3) piercing damage.

Spitdart Tongue (recharge 4–6). *Ranged Weapon Attack:* +5 to hit, range 20/60 ft., one target. *Hit:* 6 (1d6 + 3) piercing damage. Every child of the briar can shoot thorns from its mouth.

Entangle. Two children of the briar working together can cast a version of the *entangle* spell with no components, at will. Both creatures must be within 10 feet of each other, and both must use their action to cast the spell. The entangled area must include at least one of the casters but doesn't need to be centered on either caster. Creatures in the area must succeed on a DC 13 Strength saving throw or be restrained. All children of the briar are immune to the spell's effects.

The child of the briar can be found in **Tome of Beasts** by **Kobold Press.**

CHOM

Tiny monstrosity, chaotic neutral,

Armor Class 12
Hit Points 1 (1d4 − 1)
Speed 10 ft., fly 50 ft.

STR	DEX	CON	INT	WIS	CHA
2 (−4)	14 (+2)	8 (−1)	2 (−4)	12 (+1)	6 (−2)

Skills Perception +3
Damage Resistances necrotic
Damage Weaknesses obsidian
Senses darkvision 30 ft., passive Perception 13
Languages Primordial Notoan
Challenge 1/2 (100 XP)

Mimicry. The chom can mimic simple sounds it has heard, such as a person whispering, a baby crying, or an animal chittering. A creature that hears the sounds can tell they are imitations with a successful DC 10 Wisdom (Insight) check.

Actions

Beak. *Melee Weapon Attack:* +3 to hit (reach 5 ft.; one creature). *Hit:* 1 piercing damage

Cast Omen (recharge 5-6). The chom can force a creature it can see within 30 feet to succeed on a DC 12 Charisma saving throw or be afflicted with an omen causing the affected creature to suffer disadvantage on its attack rolls, saving throws, and ability checks until the start of the chom's next turn.

Soul Steal. The chom makes a single beak attack against a target that is asleep or otherwise incapacitated. If the attack hits, the chom can attempt to steal the creature's soul from its body. A successful DC 12 Charisma saving throw prevents the soul from being taken. On a failure, the chom takes its soul and consumes it. The soul resides within the chom, which can carry it about and regurgitate it, typically as a gift to a more powerful entity tied to the Land of

the Dead, that choms often serve. If the chom perishes or the soul is destroyed, the creature to whom the soul belonged also perishes and is forced to exist for all eternity in the level of the Land of the Dead where the chom's servitor entity resides. Similarly, should the individual whose soul has been stolen perish, their soul is forced to the servitor's plane. A being whose soul has been taken cannot be reincarnated, resurrected, or otherwise saved from this fate. A chom can hold only a single soul at a time, including the soul of a bonded alux; thus, it cannot use the soul steal ability if it currently carries a soul.

CHOMTZITZIMITL

Medium fiend, chaotic neutral

Armor Class 14 (natural armor)
Hit Points 67 (9d8 + 27)
Speed 25 ft., fly 40 ft.

STR	DEX	CON	INT	WIS	CHA
17 (+3)	16 (+3)	16 (+3)	10 (+0)	12 (+1)	13 (+1)

Saving Throws Dex +5, Con +5
Skills Acrobatics +5, Athletics +5, Stealth +5
Damage Weaknesses jadeite
Damage Immunities necrotic
Condition Immunities stunned
Senses darkvision 60 ft, passive Perception 11
Languages Primordial Notoan
Challenge 4 (1,100 XP)

Flyby. The chomtzitzimitl doesn't provoke an opportunity attack when it flies out of an enemy's reach.

Keen Sense. The chomtzitzimitl has advantage on Wisdom (Perception) checks.

Sense Living. A chomtzitzimitl can detect the presence of a living creature within 60 feet. If the creature is protected by magic, then the chomtzitzimitl reduces the range of the line of sight to 30 feet.

Actions

Multiattack. The chomtzitzimitl makes two Claw attacks.

Claw. *Melee Weapon Attack:* +5 to hit, reach 5 ft., one target. *Hit:* 10 (2d6 + 3) slashing damage and the creature bleeds profusely. A bleeding creature must succeed on a DC 15 Constitution saving throw at the start of its turn or take 5 (2d4) necrotic damage and continue bleeding. On a successful save, the creature takes no necrotic damage and the effect ends. A creature takes only 5 necrotic damage per turn from this effect no matter how many times it's been clawed, and a single successful saving throw ends all bleeding. Spending an action to make a successful DC 14 Wisdom (Medicine) check or any amount of magical healing also stops the bleeding. Constructs and undead are immune to the bleeding effect.

CIPATENHUA

Medium humanoid (cipatenhua), chaotic neutral

Armor Class 13 (natural armor)
Hit Points 22 (4d8 + 4)
Speed 30 ft., swim 30 ft.

STR	DEX	CON	INT	WIS	CHA
15 (+2)	10 (+0)	13 (+1)	9 (−1)	12 (+1)	9 (−1)

Skills Perception +3, Stealth +2, Survival +3
Senses passive Perception 13
Languages Common, Draconic
Challenge 1/2 (100 XP)

Curse of Itztliteotl. A cipatenhua that is not in contact with standing water, wet earth, or wet stone at the start of its turn takes 3 (1d6) necrotic damage.

Hold Breath. The cipatenhua can hold its breath for 15 minutes.

River Predator. The cipatenhua has advantage on Dexterity (Stealth) checks made to hide in coast and swamp terrain.

Actions

Multiattack. The cipatenhua makes one Bite attack and one Greatclub attack.

Bite. Melee Weapon Attack: +4 to hit, reach 5 ft., one target. *Hit:* 5 (1d6 + 2) piercing damage, and the target is grappled (escape DC 12). The cipatenhua has one bite, which can grapple only one target.

Greatclub. Melee Weapon Attack: +4 to hit, reach 5 ft., one target. *Hit:* 6 (1d8 + 2) bludgeoning damage.

CIPATENHUA DISCIPLE

Medium humanoid (cipatenhua), chaotic evil

Armor Class 14 (natural armor)
Hit Points 44 (8d8 + 8)
Speed 30 ft., swim 30 ft.

STR	DEX	CON	INT	WIS	CHA
15 (+2)	10 (+0)	13 (+1)	10 (+0)	12 (+1)	12 (+1)

Skills Perception +3, Stealth +2, Survival +3
Senses passive Perception 13
Languages Common, Draconic
Challenge 2 (450 XP)

Curse of Itztliteotl. A cipatenhua that is not in contact with standing water, wet earth, or wet stone at the start of its turn takes 3 (1d6) necrotic damage.

Hold Breath. The cipatenhua can hold its breath for 15 minutes.

River Predator. The cipatenhua has advantage on Dexterity (Stealth) checks made to hide in coast and swamp terrain.

Spellcaster (cipatenhua form only). The cipatenhua disciple is a 6th-level spellcaster. Its spellcasting ability is Charisma (spell save DC 11, +3 to hit with spell attacks). The cipatenhua disciple has the following warlock spells prepared.

Cantrips (at will): *chill touch, eldritch blast, poison spray*
Spells (2 slots): *charm person, gaseous form, hellish rebuke, misty step, spider climb, tongues, vampiric touch,*

Actions

Multiattack (cipatenhua form only). The cipatenhua disciple makes one Bite attack and one with Greatclub attack.

Bite. Melee Weapon Attack: +4 to hit, reach 5 ft., one target. *Hit:* 5 (1d6 + 2) piercing damage, and the target is grappled (escape DC 12). The cipatenhua has one bite, which can grapple only one target.

Greatclub (cipatenhua form only). Melee Weapon Attack: +4 to hit, reach 5 ft., one target. *Hit:* 6 (1d8 + 2) bludgeoning damage.

Touch of Madness (recharges after a short or long rest). Melee Weapon Attack: +4 to hit, reach 5 ft., one target. *Hit:* 4 (1d4 + 2) bludgeoning damage plus 10 (3d6) psychic damage. If the target is a creature with an Intelligence score of 5 or greater, it must succeed on a DC 11 Wisdom saving throw or become stunned while babbling incoherently. At the end of each of its turn, and each time it takes damage, the target can make another Wisdom saving throw. The target has advantage on the saving throw if it is triggered by damage. On a success, the babbling ends, and the target is no longer stunned.

Change Shape (recharges after a short or long rest). The cipatenhua disciple magically polymorphs into a giant frog, remaining in that form for up to one hour. It can revert to its true form as a bonus action. Its statistics, other than its size, are the same in each form. Any equipment it is wearing or carrying is not transformed. It reverts to its true form if it dies.

COYOTE WARRIOR

Medium humanoid (human), chaotic evil

Armor Class 13 (hide armor)
Hit Points 60 (8d8 + 24)
Speed 30 ft.

STR	DEX	CON	INT	WIS	CHA
16 (+3)	12 (+1)	16 (+3)	10 (+0)	12 (+1)	12 (+1)

Skills Deception +3, Perception +3
Senses passive Perception 13
Languages Aztli
Challenge 2 (450 XP)

Pack Tactics. The coyote warrior has advantage on attack rolls against a creature if at least one of the coyote warrior's allies is within five feet of the creature and the ally isn't incapacitated.

Sneak Attack. Once per turn, the coyote warrior deals an extra 7 (2d6) damage when it hits a target with a weapon attack and has advantage on the attack roll, or when the target is within five feet of an ally of the coyote warrior that isn't incapacitated, and the coyote warrior does not have disadvantage on the attack roll.

Actions

Club. Melee Weapon Attack: +5 to hit, reach 5 ft., one target. *Hit:* 7 (1d6 + 3) bludgeoning damage.

COYOTL (WERECOYOTE)

Medium humanoid (human, shapechanger), neutral evil

Armor Class 11 in humanoid form, 12 (natural armor) in coyote or hybrid form
Hit Points 117 (18d8 + 36)
Speed 30 ft. (40 ft. in coyote form)

STR	DEX	CON	INT	WIS	CHA
14 (+2)	12 (+1)	14 (+2)	10 (+0)	11 (+0)	12 (+1)

Skills Perception +3, Stealth +4
Damage Immunities bludgeoning piercing, and slashing damage from nonmagical attacks that are not silvered
Senses passive Perception 13
Languages Aztli, Common
Challenge 5 (1,800 XP)

Equipment: Coyotl has a *potion of speed* and a pouch containing eight pearls (worth 100 gp each).

Shapechanger. The werecoyote can use its action to polymorph into a coyote-humanoid hybrid or into a coyote, or back into its true form, which is humanoid. Its statistics, other than its AC and speed, are the same in each form. Any equipment it is wearing or carries does not transform. It reverts to its true form if it dies.

Keen Hearing and Smell. The werecoyote has advantage on Wisdom (Perception) checks that rely on hearing or smell.

Pack Tactics. The werecoyote has advantage on attack rolls against a creature if at least one of the werecoyote's allies is within five feet of the creature and the ally isn't incapacitated.

Sneak Attack (1/turn). The werecoyote deals an extra 14 (4d6) damage when it hits a target with a weapon attack and has advantage on the attack roll, or when the target is within five feet of any ally of the werecoyote that isn't incapacitated, and the werecoyote doesn't have disadvantage on the attack roll.

Spellcasting. A werecoyote is a 4th-level spellcaster. Its spellcasting ability is Charisma (spell save DC 12, +4 to hit with spell attacks). It can cast the following spells.

Cantrips (at will): *eldritch blast, minor illusion, poison spray*

2nd level (2 slots): *expeditious retreat, hellish rebuke, mirror image, misty step, suggestion*

Actions

Multiattack (humanoid or hybrid form only). The werecoyote makes one Bite attack and one with other melee attack.

Bite (coyote or hybrid form only). *Melee Weapon Attack*: +5 to hit, reach 5 ft., one target. *Hit*: 6 (1d8 + 2) piercing damage. If the target is a humanoid, it must succeed on a DC 12 Constitution saving throw or be cursed with werecoyote lycanthropy.

Claws (hybrid form only). *Melee Weapon Attack*: +5 to hit, reach 5 ft. on creature. *Hit*: 7 (2d4 + 2) slashing damage.

Club (humanoid form only). *Melee Weapon Attack*: +5 to hit, reach 5 ft., one creature. *Hit*: 5 (1d6 + 2) bludgeoning damage or 6 (1d8 + 2) bludgeoning damage if used with two hands to make a melee attack.

CUEYATL

Small humanoid, lawful evil

Armor Class 11
Hit Points 21 (6d6)
Speed 30 ft., climb 20 ft., swim 30 ft.

STR	DEX	CON	INT	WIS	CHA
10 (+0)	12 (+1)	11 (+0)	10 (+0)	11 (+0)	10 (+0)

Skills Stealth +3
Senses darkvision 60 ft., passive Perception 10
Languages Cueyatl
Challenge 1/2 (100 XP)

Amphibious. The cueyatl can breathe air and water.
Jungle Camouflage. The cueyatl has advantage on Dexterity (Stealth) checks made to hide in jungle terrain.
Slippery. The cueyatl has advantage on saving throws and ability checks made to escape a grapple.
Standing Leap. The cueyatl's long jump is up to 20 feet and its high jump is up to 10 feet, with or without a running start.

Actions

Spear. *Melee Weapon Attack*: +2 to hit, reach 5 ft. or range 20/60 ft., one target. *Hit*: 3 (1d6) piercing damage plus 7 (2d6) poison damage or 4 (1d8) piercing damage plus 7 (2d6) poison damage if used with two hands to make a melee attack.
The cueyatl can be found in the ***Creature Codex*** by **Kobold Press**.

CUEYATL MOON PRIEST

Small humanoid, lawful evil

Armor Class 13 (studded leather)
Hit Points 81 (18d6 + 18)
Speed 30 ft., climb 20 ft., swim 30 ft.

STR	DEX	CON	INT	WIS	CHA
10 (+0)	12 (+1)	12 (+1)	10 (+0)	16 (+3)	12 (+1)

Saving Throws Con +4
Skills Medicine +6, Perception +6, Religion +3
Senses darkvision 60 ft., passive Perception 16
Languages Common, Cueyatl
Challenge 5 (1,800 XP)

Amphibious. The cueyatl can breathe air and water.
Jungle Camouflage. The cueyatl has advantage on Dexterity (Stealth) checks made to hide in jungle terrain.

Slippery. The cueyatl moon priest has advantage on saving throws and ability checks made to escape a grapple.
Standing Leap. The cueyatl's long jump is up to 20 feet and its high jump is up to 10 feet, with or without a running start.
Spellcasting. The cueyatl moon priest is a 5th-level spellcaster. Its spellcasting ability is Wisdom (spell save DC 14, +6 to hit with spell attacks). It has the following cleric spells prepared:
Cantrips (at will): *guidance, resistance, sacred flame, spare the dying*
1st level (4 slots): *bane, cure wounds, protection from evil and good*
2nd level (3 slots): *hold person, silence, spiritual weapon*
3rd level (2 slots): *bestow curse, spirit guardians*

Actions

Morningstar. *Melee Weapon Attack*: +3 to hit, reach 5 ft., one target. *Hit*: 4 (1d8) piercing damage plus 7 (2d6) poison damage.
Night's Chill (recharge 5–6). The cueyatl moon priest harnesses moonlight, dispelling magical light in a 30-foot radius. In addition, each hostile creature within 30 feet must make a DC 13 Constitution saving throw, taking 16 (3d10) cold damage on a failed save, and half as much damage on a successful one. A creature that has total cover from the moon priest is not affected.
The cueyatl moon priest can be found in the ***Creature Codex*** by **Kobold Press**.

CUEYATL SEA PRIEST

Small humanoid, lawful evil

Armor Class 12 (leather armor)
Hit Points 45 (10d6 + 10)
Speed 30 ft., climb 20 ft., swim 30 ft.

STR	DEX	CON	INT	WIS	CHA
10 (+0)	12 (+1)	12 (+1)	10 (+0)	14 (+2)	10 (+0)

Saving Throws Dex +3
Skills Medicine +4, Religion +2
Senses darkvision 60 ft., passive Perception 12
Languages Cueyatl
Challenge 1 (100 XP)

Amphibious. The cueyatl can breathe air and water.
Jungle Camouflage. The cueyatl has advantage on Dexterity (Stealth) checks made to hide in jungle terrain.
Slippery. The cueyatl has advantage on saving throws and ability checks made to escape a grapple.
Speak with Sea Life. The cueyatl sea priest can communicate with amphibious and water-breathing beasts and monstrosities as if they shared a language.
Spellcasting. The cueyatl sea priest is a 2nd-level spellcaster. Its spellcasting ability is Wisdom (spell save DC 12, +4 to hit with spell attack). It has the following druid spells prepared:
Cantrips (at will): *guidance, poison spray*
1st level (3 slots): *animal friendship, create or destroy water, fog cloud, speak with animals*
Standing Leap. The cueyatl's long jump is up to 20 feet and its high jump is up to 10 feet, with or without a running start.

Actions

Trident. *Melee or Ranged Weapon Attack*: +2 to hit, reach 5 ft. or range 20/60 ft., one target. *Hit*: 3 (1d6) piercing damage plus 7 (2d6) poison damage or 4 (1d8) piercing damage plus 7 (2d6) poison damage if used with two hands to make a melee attack.
The cueyatl sea priest can be found in the ***Creature Codex*** by **Kobold Press**.

Cueyatl Warrior

Small humanoid, lawful evil

Armor Class 13 (leather armor)
Hit Points 36 (8d6 + 8)
Speed 30 ft., climb 20 ft., swim 30 ft.

STR	DEX	CON	INT	WIS	CHA
12 (+1)	14 (+2)	12 (+1)	10 (+0)	11 (+0)	10 (+0)

Saving Throws Str +3
Skills Acrobatics +4, Survival +2
Senses darkvision 60 ft., passive Perception 10
Languages Cueyatl
Challenge 1/2 (100 XP)

Amphibious. The cueyatl can breathe air and water.
Jungle Camouflage. The cueyatl has advantage on Dexterity
(Stealth) checks made to hide in jungle terrain.
Slippery. The cueyatl has advantage on saving throws and ability
checks made to escape a grapple.
Standing Leap. The cueyatl's long jump is up to 20 feet and its high
jump is up to 10 feet, with or without a running start.

Actions

Battleaxe. *Melee Weapon Attack*: +3 to hit, reach 5 ft., one target. *Hit*:
6 (1d8 + 2) slashing damage plus 7 (2d6) poison damage or 7 (1d10
+ 2) piercing damage plus 7 (2d6) poison damage if used with two
hands to make a melee attack.
The cueyatl warrior can be found in the ***Creature Codex*** by **Kobold
Press**.

Daughter of Chalatihuatl

Huge fiend, neutral

Armor Class 20 (natural armor)
Hit Points 210 (20d12 + 80)
Speed 40 ft., fly 60 ft.

STR	DEX	CON	INT	WIS	CHA
18 (+4)	20 (+5)	18 (+4)	19 (+4)	21 (+5)	20 (+5)

Saving Throws Int +9, Cha +10
Skills Insight +10, Perception +10, Persuasion +10, Religion +9
Damage Resistances cold, fire
Damage Immunities necrotic; bludgeoning, piercing, and slashing
from nonmagical attacks.
Condition Immunities charmed, frightened
Senses truesight 120 ft., passive Perception 20
Languages All, telepathy 120 ft.
Challenge 16 (15,000 XP)

Magic weapons. The daughter of Chalatihuatl's weapons are magical.
Spellcasting. The daughter of Chalatihuatl is a 14th-level spellcaster.
Her spellcasting ability is Wisdom (spell save DC 18, +10 to hit with
spell attacks). The daughter of Chalatihuatl has the following cleric
spells prepared:
Cantrips (at will): *chill touch, sacred flame, thaumaturgy*
1st level (4 slots): *bane, detect magic, sanctuary*
2nd level (3 slots): *blindness/deafness, darkness, silence, zone of
truth*
3rd level (3 slots): *bestow curse, clairvoyance, dispel magic, magic
circle*
4th level (3 slots): *banishment, divination, locate creature*
5th level (2 slots): *antilife shell, contagion, scrying*
6th level (1 slots): *create undead, forbiddance*
7th level (1 slots): *resurrection*

Actions

Cry of the Damned. The daughter of Chalatihuatl emits a hideous
screech. All creatures within 120 feet that can hear her voice must
succeed on a DC 18 Wisdom saving throw or be stricken with
confusion as the spell for 2d4 rounds.
Spear. *Melee Weapon Attack:* +9 to hit, reach 15 ft., one target. *Hit*: 17
(3d8 + 4) piercing damage.

Legendary Actions

The daughter of Chalatihuatl can take three legendary actions,
choosing from the options below. Only one legendary action option
can be used at a time and only at the end of another creature's turn.
The daughter of Chalatihuatl regains spent legendary actions at the
start of her turn.
Cantrip. The daughter of Chalatihuatl casts a cantrip.
Spear. The daughter of Chalatihuatl makes a spear attack.
Cry of the Damned (costs 2 actions). The daughter of Chalatihuatl
can use her Cry of the Damned ability.

Demon, Derghodemon
(Cockroach Demon)

Large fiend (demon), neutral evil

Armor Class 18 (natural armor)
Hit Points 147 (14d10 + 70)
Speed 40 ft.

STR	DEX	CON	INT	WIS	CHA
25 (+7)	16 (+3)	21 (+5)	7 (−2)	14 (+2)	16 (+3)

Saving Throws Dex +7, Con +9, Wis +6, Cha +7
Skills Intimidation +7, Perception +6, Stealth +7
Damage Resistances cold, fire, lightning
Damage Immunities poison
Condition Immunities poisoned
Senses truesight 120 ft., passive Perception 16
Languages Abyssal, telepathy 120 ft.
Challenge 9 (5,000 XP)

Magic Resistance. The demon has advantage on saving throws
against spells and other magical effects.
Magic Weapons. The demon's weapon attacks are magical.
Innate Spellcasting. The demon's spellcasting ability is Charisma
(spell save DC 15, +7 to hit with spell attacks). The demon can
innately cast the following spells, requiring no material components:
At will: *darkness, fear, detect magic*
1/day each: *confusion, sleep*
Rend and Tear. The demon has advantage on all melee weapon
attacks against a creature it is grappling.

Actions

Multiattack. The demon makes one Bite attack and two Claws
attacks.
Bite. *Melee Weapon Attack:* +11 to hit, reach 5 ft., one target. *Hit*: 16
(2d8 + 7) piercing damage, and the target is grappled (escape DC
17). Until this grapple ends, the demon can bite only the grappled
creature and has advantage on attack rolls to do so.
Claws. *Melee Weapon Attack:* +11 to hit, reach 10 ft., one target. *Hit*:
21 (4d6 + 7) slashing damage.

DEMON, GERUZOU (SLIME DEMON)

Small fiend (demon), chaotic evil

Armor Class 15 (natural armor)
Hit Points 31 (7d6 + 7)
Speed 30 ft., fly 50 ft.

STR	DEX	CON	INT	WIS	CHA
12 (+1)	15 (+2)	12 (+1)	8 (−1)	8 (−1)	10 (+0)

Skills Perception +1, Stealth +4
Damage Resistances cold, fire, lightning
Damage Immunities poison
Condition Immunities poisoned
Senses darkvision 60 ft., passive Perception 11
Languages Abyssal, Common, telepathy 100 ft.
Challenge 2 (450 XP)

Innate Spellcasting. The demon's spellcasting ability is Charisma (spell save DC 10, +2 to hit with spell attacks). The demon can innately cast the following spells at will, requiring no material components: *darkness, detect evil and good, invisibility* (self only)

Magic Resistance. The demon has advantage on saving throws against spells and other magical effects.

Magic Weapons. The demon's weapon attacks are magical.

Slimy Hide. The demon's hide is extremely slick and oozes with slime. Creatures attempting to grapple the demon do so with disadvantage.

Actions

Multiattack. The demon makes one Bite or one Spit Slime attack and two Claws attacks.

Bite. *Melee Weapon Attack:* +4 to hit, reach 5 ft., one target. Hit: 5 (1d6 + 2) piercing damage.

Claws. *Melee Weapon Attack:* +4 to hit, reach 5 ft., one target. *Hit:* 5 (1d6 + 2) slashing damage.

Spit Slime. *Ranged Weapon Attack:* +4 to hit, range 20/60 ft., one target. *Hit:* 10 (3d6) acid damage and the target must succeed on a DC 13 Constitution saving throw or its speed is reduced by half until the end of the demon's next turn.

DEMON, KISHI

Medium fiend (demon), chaotic evil

Armor Class 18 (natural armor, shield)
Hit Points 119 (14d8 + 56)
Speed 50 ft.

STR	DEX	CON	INT	WIS	CHA
19 (+4)	20 (+5)	19 (+4)	15 (+2)	11 (+0)	22 (+6)

Saving Throws Dex +8, Con +7, Wis +3
Skills Deception +9, Perception +3, Performance +9
Damage Resistances cold, fire, lightning, poison; bludgeoning, piercing, and slashing from nonmagical attacks
Damage Immunities poison
Condition Immunities poisoned
Senses darkvision 120 ft., passive Perception 13
Languages Celestial, Common, Draconic, Infernal, telepathy 120 ft.
Challenge 8 (3,900 XP)

Two Heads. The kishi demon has advantage on Wisdom (Perception) checks and on saving throws against being blinded, charmed, deafened, frightened, stunned, and knocked unconscious.

Innate Spellcasting. The kishi demon's spellcasting ability is Charisma (spell save DC 17). The demon can innately cast the following spells, requiring no material components (when encountered, Charphu only can cast the spells usable at will as the others are spent for the day):

At will: *detect evil and good, detect magic, suggestion*
3/day: *glibness*
1/day: *dominate person*

Magic Resistance. The kishi demon has advantage on saving throws against spells and other magical effects.

Summon Demon (1/day). The kishi demon has a 35 percent chance of summoning one kishi demon. The summoning requires one action.

Trophy Shield. If the kishi demon killed an opponent this turn, as a bonus action, it takes part of the slain creature's essence along with a grisly trophy and mounts it upon its shield. For 24 hours, the Armor Class of the kishi demon becomes 20, and creatures of the same race as the slain creature have disadvantage on attack rolls against it. It tries this ability only if there are multiple characters of the same race.

Actions

Multiattack. The demon makes one Bite attack and three Spear attacks.

Bite. *Melee Weapon Attack:* +8 to hit, reach 5 ft., one creature. *Hit:* 12 (2d6 + 5) piercing damage.

Spear. *Melee or Ranged Weapon Attack:* +7 to hit, reach 5 ft. or range 20/60 ft., one target. *Hit:* 7 (1d6 + 4) piercing damage, or 8 (1d8 + 4) piercing damage if used with two hands to make a melee attack.

The kishi demon can be found in **Tome of Beasts** by **Kobold Press**.

DEMON, PLARESH

Medium swarm of Tiny fiends (demon), chaotic evil

Armor Class 15 (natural armor)
Hit Points 30 (4d8 + 12)
Speed 30 ft., burrow 30 ft., swim 30 ft.

STR	DEX	CON	INT	WIS	CHA
2 (−4)	17 (+3)	16 (+3)	6 (−2)	12 (+1)	3 (−4)

Damage Resistances cold, fire, lightning; bludgeoning, slashing, and piercing
Damage Immunities poison
Condition Immunities charmed, frightened, grappled, paralyzed, petrified, poisoned, prone, restrained, stunned
Senses blindsight 30 ft. (blind beyond this radius), tremorsense 60 ft., passive Perception 11
Languages understands Abyssal but can't speak
Challenge 3 (700 XP)

Grinding Maws. The plaresh demon can burrow through harder substances such as wood, stone, or even metal. While doing so, its burrow speed is reduced to half and it creates a cluster of bore holes that leaves the material porous and weak. The material has −5 to its AC and half the usual hp.

Magic Resistance. The plaresh demon has advantage on saving throws against spells and other magical effects.

Swarm. The plaresh demon can occupy another creature's space and vice versa, and the plaresh demon can move through any opening large enough for a Tiny worm. The plaresh demon can't regain hp or gain temporary hp.

Actions

Bites. *Melee Weapon Attack:* +5 to hit, reach 0 ft., one creature in the swarm's space. *Hit:* 14 (4d6) piercing damage, or 7 (2d6) piercing damage if the swarm has half of its hit points or fewer. The target must make a DC 13 Constitution saving throw, taking 7 (2d6) poison damage on a failure, or half as much on a success. If the target is wearing nonmagical armor, the armor takes a permanent and cumulative −1 penalty to the AC it offers. Armor reduced to an AC of 10 is destroyed.

Infest Corpse (recharges after a long rest). The plaresh demon targets one dead humanoid in its space. The body is destroyed, and a new plaresh demon rises from the corpse. The newly created plaresh is free-willed but usually joins its creator.

The plaresh demon can be found in *Creature Codex* by **Kobold Press**.

DEVIL, SALT

Medium fiend (devil), lawful evil

Armor Class 13 (natural armor)
Hit Points 93 (11d8 + 44)
Speed 30 ft.

STR	DEX	CON	INT	WIS	CHA
18 (+4)	13 (+1)	18 (+4)	13 (+1)	14 (+2)	15 (+2)

Saving Throws Dex +4, Con +7, Cha +5
Skills Perception +5, Stealth +4
Damage Resistances acid, cold; bludgeoning, piercing, and slashing from nonmagical attacks that aren't silvered
Damage Immunities fire, poison
Condition Immunities poisoned
Senses darkvision 120 ft., passive Perception 15
Languages Celestial, Common, Gnoll, Infernal, telepathy 120 ft.
Challenge 6 (2,300 XP)

Devil's Sight. Magical darkness doesn't impede the devil's darkvision.
Magic Resistance. The devil has advantage on saving throws against spells and other magical effects.
Innate Spellcasting. The devil's spellcasting ability is Charisma (spell save DC 13). The devil can innately cast the following spells, requiring no material components:
At will: *darkness*
1/day each: *harm, teleport*

Actions

Multiattack. The devil makes two Scimitar attacks.
Scimitar. *Melee Weapon Attack*: +7 to hit, reach 5 ft., one target. *Hit*: 7 (1d6 + 4) slashing damage. If the target is neither undead nor a construct, it must make a DC 15 Constitution saving throw, taking 5 (1d10) necrotic damage on a failure or half as much on a success. Plants, oozes, and creatures with the Amphibious, Water Breathing, or Water Form traits have disadvantage on this saving throw. If the saving throw fails by 5 or more, the target also gains one level of exhaustion.

The salt devil can be found in the *Tome of Beasts* by **Kobold Press**.

DRAKE, FEY

Small dragon, chaotic neutral

Armor Class 17 (natural armor)
Hit Points 82 (15d6 + 30)
Speed 20 ft., fly 80 ft.

STR	DEX	CON	INT	WIS	CHA
6 (−2)	20 (+5)	15 (+2)	15 (+2)	16 (+3)	18 (+4)

Saving Throws Dexterity +8, Constitution +5, Wisdom +6
Skills Arcana +5, Deception +7, Perception +6, Stealth +8
Senses darkvision 120 ft., passive Perception 16
Languages Common, Draconic, Sylvan, telepathy 120 ft.
Challenge 6 (2,300 XP)

Magic Resistance. The fey drake has advantage on saving throws against spells and other magical effects.
Superior Invisibility. As a bonus action, the fey drake can magically turn invisible until its concentration ends (as if concentrating on a spell). Any equipment the drake wears or carries is invisible with it.

Innate Spellcasting. The fey drake's innate spellcasting ability is Charisma (spell save DC 15, +7 to hit with spell attacks). The fey drake can innately cast the following spells, requiring no material components:
At will: *charm person, color spray, grease*
3/day each: *hypnotic pattern, locate creature, suggestion*
1/day each: *dominate person, polymorph*

Actions

Multiattack. The fey drake makes three Bite attacks.
Bite. *Melee Weapon Attack*: +8 to hit, reach 5 ft., one target. *Hit*: 10 (2d4 + 5) piercing damage, and the target must succeed on a DC 16 Constitution saving throw or be poisoned for 1 hour.
***Bewildering Breath* (recharge 5–6).** The drake breathes a plume of purple gas in a 15-foot cone. Each creature in that area must succeed on a DC 16 Wisdom saving throw or be charmed for 1 minute. While charmed, the creature can't take bonus actions or reactions, and it makes all Intelligence, Wisdom, and Charisma skill checks and saving throws with disadvantage.

The drake, fey can be found in *Creature Codex* by **Kobold Press**.

DROWNED MAIDEN

Medium undead, neutral evil

Armor Class 15 (natural armor)
Hit Points 90 (20d8)
Speed 30 ft., swim 40 ft.

STR	DEX	CON	INT	WIS	CHA
15 (+2)	16 (+3)	10 (+0)	10 (+0)	12 (+1)	18 (+4)

Saving Throws Dex +6, Cha +7
Damage Resistances bludgeoning, piercing, and slashing from nonmagical attacks that aren't silvered
Damage Immunities necrotic, poison
Condition Immunities charmed, exhaustion, frightened, paralyzed, poisoned
Senses darkvision 60 ft., passive Perception 11
Languages Common
Challenge 5 (1,800 XP)

Grasping Hair. The drowned maiden's hair attacks as though it were three separate limbs, each of which can be attacked (AC 19; 15 hit points; immunity to necrotic, poison, and psychic damage; resistance to bludgeoning, piercing, and slashing damage from nonmagical attacks that aren't silvered). A lock of hair can be broken if a creature takes an action and succeeds on a DC 15 Strength check against it.
Innate Spellcasting. The drowned maiden's innate spellcasting ability is Charisma (spell save DC 15). She can innately cast the following spells, requiring no material components:
At will: *disguise self, silence*

Actions

Multiattack. The drowned maiden makes two Claw or Kiss attacks and one Hair or Kiss attack. If she has a creature grappled with her hair, she can replace the Hair attack with a Reel.
Claw. *Melee Weapon Attack:* +6 to hit, reach 5 ft., one target. *Hit*: 6 (1d8 + 3) slashing damage.
Hair. *Melee Weapon Attack:* +6 to hit, reach 20 ft., one target. *Hit*: 14 (2d10 + 3) slashing damage, and the target is grappled (escape DC 16). Three creatures can be grappled at a time.
Kiss. The drowned maiden can kiss one target that is grappled and adjacent to her. The target must succeed on a DC 15 Charisma saving throw or take 1d6 Strength damage.
Reel. The drowned maiden pulls a grappled creature of Large size or smaller up to 15 feet straight toward herself.

The drowned maiden can be found in *Tome of Beasts* by **Kobold Press**.

Dryad, Duskthorn

Medium fey, chaotic

Armor Class 17 (natural armor)
Hit Points 77 (14d8 + 14)
Speed 30 ft.

STR	DEX	CON	INT	WIS	CHA
10 (+0)	20 (+5)	13 (+1)	14 (+2)	15 (+2)	24 (+7)

Saving Throws Con +3, Wis +4
Skills Animal Handling +4, Deception +9, Nature +6, Perception +4, Persuasion +9, Stealth +7
Senses darkvision 60 ft., passive Perception 14
Languages Common, Elvish, Sylvan, Umbral
Challenge 3 (700 XP)

Innate Spellcasting. The dryad's innate spellcasting ability is Charisma (spell save DC 17). She can innately cast the following spells, requiring no material components:
At will: *dancing lights, druidcraft*
3/day each: *charm person, entangle, invisibility, magic missile*
1/day each: *barkskin, counterspell, dispel magic, fog cloud, shillelagh, suggestion, wall of thorns*
Magic Resistance. The dryad has advantage on saving throws against spells and other magical effects.
Speak with Beasts and Plants. The dryad can communicate with beasts and plants as if they shared a language.
Tree Stride. Once on her turn, the dryad can use 10 feet of her movement to step magically into one dead tree within her reach and emerge from a second dead tree within 60 feet of the first tree, appearing in an unoccupied space within five feet of the second tree. Both trees must be Large or bigger.
Tree Dependent. The dryad is mystically bonded to her duskthorn vines and must remain within 300 yards of them or become poisoned. If she remains out of range of her vines for 24 hours, she suffers 1d6 Constitution damage, and another 1d6 points of Constitution damage every day that follows — eventually, this separation kills the dryad. A dryad can bond with new vines by performing a 24-hour ritual.

Actions

Dagger. *Melee or Ranged Weapon Attack*: +7 to hit, reach 5 ft. or range 20/60 ft., one target. *Hit*: 7 (1d4 + 5) piercing damage.

The dryad, duskthorn can be found in *Tome of Beasts* by **Kobold Press**.

Eel Hound

Medium fey, neutral

Armor Class 14 (natural armor)
Hit Points 77 (14d8 + 14)
Speed 30 ft., swim 40 ft.

STR	DEX	CON	INT	WIS	CHA
19 (+4)	16 (+3)	13 (+1)	6 (−2)	13 (+1)	16 (+3)

Skills Perception +3, Stealth +5
Senses darkvision 60 ft., passive Perception 13
Languages Sylvan
Challenge 2 (450 XP)

Amphibious. The eel hound can breathe air and water.
Pack Tactics. The eel hound has advantage on an attack roll against a creature if at least one of the hound's allies is within five feet of the creature and the ally is not incapacitated.
Slick Spittle. By spending two rounds dribbling spittle on an area, an eel hound can cover a five-foot square with its slippery saliva. This area is treated as if under the effects of a *grease* spell, but it lasts for one hour.
Slithering Bite. When an eel hound moves adjacent to an enemy and makes a bite attack, it may immediately move up to five feet, as long as it stays within five feet of the enemy it attacked. If another eel hound already occupies that space, the moving eel hound can keep moving until it reaches an empty space that is still adjacent to that same enemy.

Actions

Bite. *Melee Weapon Attack:* +6 to hit, reach 5 ft., one target. *Hit:* 8 (1d8 + 4) piercing damage, and the target is grappled (escape DC 14).
The eel hound can be found in *Tome of Beasts* from **Kobold Press**.

Elemental, Large Obsidian

Large elemental, neutral

Armor Class 16 (natural armor)
Hit Points 94 (9d10 + 45)
Speed 20 ft.

STR	DEX	CON	INT	WIS	CHA
20 (+5)	8 (−1)	20 (+5)	4 (−3)	11 (+0)	11 (+0)

Damage Resistances cold, fire; bludgeoning, piercing, and slashing damage from nonmagical attacks
Damage Immunities poison
Condition Immunities exhaustion, paralyzed, petrified, poisoned, unconscious
Senses darkvision 60 ft., passive Perception 10
Languages Terran
Challenge 8 (3,900 XP)

Brute. A melee weapon attack deals one extra die of its damage when the obsidian elemental hits with it (included in the attack).
Death Throes. When the obsidian elemental dies, it explodes, and each creature within 30 feet of it must make a DC 16 Dexterity saving throw, taking 21 (6d6) slashing damage and 21 (6d6) fire damage on a failed saving throw, or half as much damage on a successful one.
Molten Glass. A creature that hits the obsidian elemental with a melee attack while within five feet of it takes 7 (2d6) fire damage.

Actions

Multiattack. The obsidian elemental makes two Claw attacks.
Claw. *Melee Weapon Attack:* +8 to hit, reach 5 ft., one target. *Hit:* 18 (3d8 + 5) slashing damage plus 9 (2d8) fire damage.

Elusa Hound

Medium monstrosity, unaligned

Armor Class 12
Hit Points 26 (4d8 + 8)
Speed 50 ft.

STR	DEX	CON	INT	WIS	CHA
15 (+2)	15 (+2)	15 (+2)	6 (−2)	12 (+1)	8 (−1)

Skills Athletics +4, Perception +3, Survival +3
Senses darkvision 60 ft., passive Perception 13
Languages understands Common but can't speak
Challenge 1 (200 XP)

Arcane Sight. Elusa hounds can perceive magical auras from active spells, magical effects, and magic items within a radius of 120 feet.

Once an elusa hound has seen one of the above, it has advantage on Wisdom (Survival) checks to track the origin of the effect for 24 hours.

Keen Hearing and Smell. The elusa hound has advantage on Wisdom (Perception) checks that rely on hearing or smell.

Actions

Bite. *Melee Weapon Attack:* +4 to hit, reach 5 ft., one target. *Hit:* 5 (1d6 + 2) piercing damage. If the target is a creature, it must succeed on a DC 11 Strength saving throw or be knocked prone and grappled on a failure. The elusa hound can only grapple one creature at a time.

Fire Phantom

Medium undead, chaotic neutral

Armor Class 14 (natural armor)
Hit Points 49 (9d8 + 9)
Speed 30 ft.

STR	DEX	CON	INT	WIS	CHA
19 (+4)	14 (+2)	13 (+1)	5 (–3)	12 (+1)	14 (+2)

Damage Vulnerabilities cold
Damage Immunities fire
Condition Immunities charmed, frightened, paralyzed, poisoned, unconscious
Senses darkvision 60 ft., passive Perception 11
Languages Ignan
Challenge 6 (2,300 XP)

Brutal Critical. The fire phantom can roll one additional weapon damage when determining the extra damage for a critical hit with a melee attack.

Death Throes. When the fire phantom dies, it explodes, and each creature within 30 feet of it must make a DC 14 Dexterity saving throw, taking 28 (8d6) fire damage on a failed save, or half as much damage on a successful one. The explosion ignites flammable objects in that area that aren't being worn or carried.

Fire Form. A creature that touches the fire phantom or hits it with a melee attack while within 5 feet of it takes 7 (2d6) fire damage.

Reckless. At the start of its turn, the fire phantom can gain advantage on all melee weapon attack rolls that turn but attack rolls against it have advantage until the start of its next turn.

Actions

Multiattack. The fire phantom makes two Fist of Fire attacks or two Fire Blast attacks.

Fist of Fire. *Melee Weapon Attack:* +7 to hit, reach 5 ft., one target. *Hit:* 11 (2d6 + 4) bludgeoning damage plus 7 (2d6) fire damage.

Fire Blast. *Ranged Weapon Attack:* +7 to hit, range 60 ft., one target. *Hit:* 10 (3d6) fire damage.

Ghoul, Cinder

Large undead, chaotic evil

Armor Class 18 (natural armor)
Hit Points 90 (12d10 + 24)
Speed fly 40 ft. (hover)

STR	DEX	CON	INT	WIS	CHA
16 (+3)	20 (+5)	15 (+2)	4 (–3)	12 (+1)	19 (+4)

Damage Resistances cold; bludgeoning, piercing, and slashing from nonmagical attacks
Damage Immunities fire
Condition Immunities charmed, exhaustion, paralyzed, poisoned, unconscious

Senses darkvision 60 ft., passive Perception 11
Languages —
Challenge 5 (1,800 XP)

Gaseous Form. While in this form, the cinder ghoul can't take any actions, speak, or manipulate objects. It is weightless, has a flying speed of 40 feet, can hover, and can enter a hostile creature's space and stop there. In addition, if air can pass through a space, the mist can do so without squeezing. It cannot pass through water. It has advantage on Strength, Dexterity, and Constitution saving throws, and it is immune to all nonmagical damage.

Magic Resistance. The cinder ghoul has advantage on saving throws against spells and other magical effects.

Actions

Slam. *Melee Weapon Attack:* +8 to hit, reach 5 ft., one target. *Hit:* 14 (2d8 + 5) bludgeoning damage plus 7 (2d6) fire damage.

Smoke Inhalation. One creature that isn't a construct or undead and is in the cinder ghoul's space must make a DC 15 Constitution saving throw. On a failed save, the target takes 10 (3d6) fire damage, and its hit point maximum is reduced by an amount equal to the fire damage taken. The target dies if this reduces its hit point maximum to 0. This reduction of the target's hit point maximum lasts until the target finishes a long rest.

Gnoll Slaver

Medium humanoid (gnoll), chaotic evil

Armor Class 15 (chain shirt)
Hit Points 71 (11d8 + 22)
Speed 30 ft.

STR	DEX	CON	INT	WIS	CHA
18 (+4)	15 (+2)	14 (+2)	12 (+1)	11 (+0)	12 (+1)

Skills Athletics +6, Intimidation +5, Perception +2, Stealth +6
Senses darkvision 60 ft., passive Perception 12
Languages Common, Gnoll
Challenge 3 (700 XP)

Rampage. When the gnoll reduces a creature to 0 hp with a melee attack on its turn, the gnoll can take a bonus action to move up to half its speed and make a bite attack.

Actions

Multiattack. The gnoll makes one Bite attack and two Whip attacks or three Longbow attacks.

Bite. *Melee Weapon Attack:* +6 to hit, reach 5 ft., one target. *Hit:* 7 (1d6 + 4) piercing damage.

Whip. *Melee Weapon Attack:* +6 to hit, reach 10 ft., one target. *Hit:* 6 (1d4 + 4) slashing damage. ***Longbow.*** *Ranged Weapon Attack:* +4 to hit, range 150/600 ft., one target. *Hit:* 6 (1d8 + 2) piercing damage.

The gnoll slaver can be found in ***Creature Codex*** by **Kobold Press**.

Golem, Witch-Doll

Large construct, neutral

Armor Class 17 (natural armor)
Hit Points 94 (9d10 + 45)
Speed 30 ft.

STR	DEX	CON	INT	WIS	CHA
19 (+4)	14 (+2)	21 (+5)	7 (–2)	15 (+2)	11 (+0)

Skills Investigation +2, Perception +10, Survival +10
Damage Immunities poison, psychic; bludgeoning, piercing, and

slashing damage from nonmagical attacks
Condition Immunities charmed, exhaustion, frightened, paralyzed, petrified, poisoned
Senses darkvision 60 ft., passive Perception 20
Languages understands the languages of its creator but can't speak
Challenge 10 (5,900 XP)

Find Target. The witch-doll golem knows the location of a specific target creature, or one creature cursed by its witch-doll curse ability, as long as that creature is within 1,000 feet of it. If the creature is moving, it knows the direction of that creature's movement. If the creature is beyond this distance, the witch-doll golem knows the direction that creature is in.

Immutable Form. The golem is immune to any spell or effect that would alter its form.

Magic Resistance. The golem has advantage on saving throws against spells and other magical effects.

Magic Weapon. The golem's weapon attacks are magical.

Actions

Multiattack. The witch-doll golem makes two Slam attacks or two Needle attacks.

Slam. *Melee Weapon Attack:* +8 to hit, reach 5 ft., one target. *Hit:* 20 (3d10 + 4) bludgeoning damage.

Needle. *Melee or Ranged Weapon Attack:* +8 to hit, reach 5 ft. or range 20/60 ft., one target. *Hit:* 14 (3d6 + 4) piercing damage.

Bonus Actions

Witch-Doll Curse. The witch-doll golem chooses one creature it can see within 60 feet of it. The target must succeed on a DC 17 Wisdom saving throw or be cursed. While cursed, the witch-doll golem deals an additional 13 (3d8) necrotic damage to the target when it hits with a weapon attack, and any damage the witch-doll golem takes from targets other than the cursed target is halved, and the cursed target takes the other half. The witch-doll golem can have only one active curse at a time. The target remains cursed until the golem is destroyed, the golem uses an action to choose a new target, or the target dies; magic such as *remove curse* can end the curse early.

Hobgoblin Acolytes

Medium humanoid (goblinoid), lawful evil

Armor Class 15 (hide armor, shield)
Hit Points 65 (10d8 + 20)
Speed 30 ft.

STR	DEX	CON	INT	WIS	CHA
14 (+2)	12 (+1)	14 (+2)	12 (+1)	16 (+3)	12 (+1)

Saving Throws Wis +6
Skills Religion +4
Senses darkvision 60 ft., passive Perception 13
Languages Common, Goblin
Challenge 5 (1,800 XP)

Martial Advantage. Once per turn, the hobgoblin can deal an extra 17 (5d6) damage to a creature it hits with a weapon attack if that creature is within five feet of an ally of the hobgoblin that is not incapacitated.

Spellcasting. The hobgoblin acolyte is an 8th-level spellcaster. Its spellcasting ability is Wisdom (spell save DC 14, +6 to hit with spell attacks). It has the following cleric spells prepared:
Cantrips (at will): *guidance, light, resistance, sacred flame*
1st level (4 slots): *command, guiding bolt, inflict wounds, purify food and drink*
2nd level (3 slots): *augury, lesser restoration, spiritual weapon*
3rd level (3 slots): *animate dead, speak with dead, spirit guardians*
4th level (2 slots): *death ward, locate creature*

Actions

Multiattack. The hobgoblin acolyte makes two Longsword attacks or two Longbow attacks.

Longsword. *Melee Weapon Attack:* +5 to hit, reach 5 ft., one target. *Hit:* 7 (1d8 + 3) slashing damage.

Longbow. *Ranged Weapon Attack:* +4 to hit, range 150/600 ft., one target. *Hit:* 5 (1d8 + 1) piercing damage.

Bonus Actions

Venomous Hex. The hobgoblin curses one creature for one minute that it can see within 90 feet of it. Until the curse is removed, the hobgoblin deals an extra 7 (2d6) poison damage to the target whenever the hobgoblin hits it with an attack. If the target drops to 0 hit points before the curse ends, the hobgoblin can use a bonus action on a subsequent turn to curse a new creature. A *remove curse* spell ends the curse early.

Reactions

Saw That Coming. The acolyte can use its reaction to partially block a blow when hit by a melee weapon attack. When it does so, the damage it takes from the attack is reduced by 1d8 + 7. It can use this feature three times and regains all expended uses when it finishes a long rest.

Huecuva

Medium undead, chaotic evil

Armor Class 14 (natural armor)
Hit Points 39 (6d8 + 12)
Speed 30 ft.

STR	DEX	CON	INT	WIS	CHA
13 (+1)	16 (+3)	14 (+2)	4 (−3)	12 (+1)	10 (+0)

Skills Perception +3, Stealth +5
Damage Resistances cold, necrotic; bludgeoning, piercing, and slashing from nonmagical attacks that aren't silvered
Damage Immunities poison
Condition Immunities exhaustion, frightened, poisoned
Senses darkvision 60 ft., passive Perception 13
Languages the languages it new in life
Challenge 2 (450 XP)

Shroud of Deception. During daylight hours only, a huecuva is transformed and looks, feels, and sounds like the living creature it once was. A creature that interacts with the huecuva must succeed on a DC 14 Intelligence (Investigation) check to realize the appearance of the huecuva is an illusion. Creatures with the Keen Smell trait automatically pass the check versus the illusion as the scent of the huecuva remains that of the grave.

Actions

Multiattack. The huecuva makes two Claws attacks.

Claws. *Melee Weapon Attack:* +5 to hit, reach 5 ft., one target. *Hit:* 10 (2d6 + 3) slashing damage. If the target is a creature, it must succeed on a DC 12 Constitution saving throw against disease or become poisoned until the disease is cured. Every 24 hours that elapse, the poisoned target must repeat the saving throw, reducing its hit point maximum by 5 (1d10) on a failure. The disease is cured on a success. The target dies if the disease reduces its hit point maximum to 0. This reduction to the target's hit point maximum lasts until the disease is cured.

ICE MAIDEN

Medium fey, lawful evil

Armor Class 16 (natural armor)
Hit Points 84 (13d8 + 26)
Speed 30 ft.

STR	DEX	CON	INT	WIS	CHA
12 (+1)	17 (+3)	15 (+2)	19 (+4)	13 (+1)	23 (+6)

Saving Throws Con +5, Cha +9
Skills Deception +9, Persuasion +9, Stealth +6
Damage Resistances bludgeoning, piercing, and slashing from nonmagical attacks
Damage Immunities cold
Damage Vulnerabilities fire
Senses darkvision 60 ft., passive Perception 11
Languages Common, Giant, Sylvan
Challenge 6 (2,300 XP)

Chilling Presence. Cold air surrounds the ice maiden. Small nonmagical flames are extinguished in her presence, and water begins to freeze. Unprotected characters spending more than 10 minutes within 15 feet of her must succeed on a DC 15 Constitution saving throw or suffer as if exposed to severe cold. Spells that grant protection from cold damage are targeted by an automatic *dispel magic* effect.

Cold Eyes. Ice maidens see perfectly in snowy conditions, including driving blizzards, and are immune to snow blindness.

Ice Walk. Ice maidens move across icy and snowy surfaces without penalty.

Snow Invisibility. In snowy environments, the ice maiden can turn invisible as a bonus action.

Magic Resistance. The ice maiden has advantage on saving throws against spells and other magical effects.

Innate Spellcasting. The ice maiden's innate spellcasting ability is Charisma (spell save DC 17). She can innately cast the following spells:

At will: *chill touch, detect magic, light, mage hand, prestidigitation, resistance*
5/day: *fear, fog cloud, misty step*
3/day: *alter self, protection from energy, sleet storm*
1/day: *ice storm*

Actions

Multiattack. The ice maiden makes two Ice Dagger attacks.

Ice Dagger. *Melee Weapon Attack:* +6 to hit, reach 5 ft., one target. *Hit:* 5 (1d4 + 3) piercing damage plus 3 (1d6) cold damage.

Flurry-Form (1/day). The ice maiden adopts the form of a swirling snow cloud. Her stats are identical to an air elemental that deals cold damage instead of bludgeoning. If brought to 0 hit points, she reverts to her natural form with whatever hit points she had prior to changing.

Icy Entangle. Ice and snow hinder the ice maiden's opponent's movement, as the *entangle* spell (DC 17). The effect lasts for one minute and does not require concentration.

Kiss of the Frozen Heart. An ice maiden may kiss a willing individual, freezing the target's heart. The target falls under the sway of a *dominate* spell, his or her alignment shifts to lawful evil, and he or she gains immunity to cold. The ice maiden can have up to three such servants at once. The effect can be broken by *dispel magic* (DC 17), *greater restoration*, or the kiss of someone who loves the target.

Snowblind Burst. In a snowy environment, the ice maiden attempts to blind all creatures within 30 feet of herself. Creatures in the area must succeed on a DC 17 Charisma saving throw or be blinded for one hour. Targets that are immune to cold damage are also immune to this effect.

The ice maiden can be found in *Tome of Beasts* by **Kobold Press**.

ICHNEUMON

Large monstrosity, unaligned

Armor Class 16 (natural armor)
Hit Points 123 (13d10 + 52)
Speed 50 ft.

STR	DEX	CON	INT	WIS	CHA
22 (+6)	18 (+4)	18 (+4)	6 (−2)	14 (+2)	12 (+1)

Saving Throws Dex +8, Con +8, Wis +6
Skills Acrobatics +8, Athletics +10, Stealth +8, Survival +6
Damage Resistances acid, cold, fire, lightning, poison; bludgeoning, piercing, and slashing from nonmagical attacks
Senses darkvision 120 ft., passive Perception 12
Languages —
Challenge 11 (7,200 XP)

Draconic Predator. The ichneumon is immune to a dragon's Frightful Presence and has advantage on saving throws against the breath weapons of dragons.

Evasion. If the ichneumon is subjected to an effect that allows it to make a Dexterity saving throw to take only half damage, the ichneumon instead takes no damage if it succeeds on the saving throw, and only half damage if it fails.

Keen Hearing and Smell. The ichneumon has advantage on Wisdom (Perception) checks that rely on hearing or smell.

Actions

Multiattack. The ichneumon makes two Bite attacks and one Claws attack.

Bite. *Melee Weapon Attack:* +10 to hit, reach 10 ft., one target. *Hit:* 20 (4d6 + 6) piercing damage and the target is grappled (escape DC 18). Until this grapple ends, the target is restrained, and the ichneumon can't use its bite on another target.

Claws. *Melee Weapon Attack:* +10 to hit, reach 5 ft., one target. *Hit:* 16 (3d6 + 6) slashing damage.

The ichneumon can be found in *Creature Codex* by **Kobold Press**.

JACULUS

Small dragon, neutral evil

Armor Class 18 (natural armor)
Hit Points 65 (10d6 + 30)
Speed 20 ft., climb 20 ft., fly 10 ft.

STR	DEX	CON	INT	WIS	CHA
14 (+2)	18 (+4)	17 (+3)	13 (+1)	13 (+1)	13 (+1)

Saving Throws Str +4, Dex +6, Con +5, Wis +3, Cha +3
Skills Acrobatics +6, Perception +3, Stealth +6
Damage Resistances acid, lightning
Senses blindsight 10 ft., darkvision 60 ft., passive Perception 13
Languages Common, Draconic
Challenge 3 (700 XP)

Spearhead. If the jaculus moves at least 10 feet straight toward a target and hits that target with a Jaws attack on the same turn, the Jaws attack deals an extra 4 (1d8) piercing damage.

Actions

Multiattack. The jaculus makes one Jaws attack and one Claws attack.

Jaws. *Melee Weapon Attack:* +4 to hit, reach 5 ft., one target. *Hit:* 7 (2d4 + 2) piercing damage.

Claws. *Melee Weapon Attack:* +4 to hit, reach 5 ft., one target. *Hit:* 9 (2d6 + 2) slashing damage.

The jaculus can be found in the *Tome of Beasts* by **Kobold Press**.

MARID

Large elemental, chaotic neutral

Armor Class 18 (natural armor)
Hit Points 230 (20d10 + 120)
Speed 30 ft., fly 40 ft., swim 90 ft.

STR	DEX	CON	INT	WIS	CHA
16 (+3)	24 (+7)	22 (+6)	15 (+2)	13 (+1)	19 (+4)

Saving Throws Str +8, Wis +6, Cha +9
Skills Deception +9, History +9, Performance +9, Persuasion +9
Damage Immunities cold, lightning
Senses darkvision 120 ft., passive Perception 11
Languages Aquan
Challenge 13 (10,000 XP)

Amphibious. The marid can breathe air and water.

Elemental Demise. If the marid dies, it disintegrates into a spray of bubbles and water, leaving behind only equipment the marid was wearing or carrying.

Frigid Aura. At the start of each of the marid's turns, each creature within 10 feet of it takes 7 (2d6) cold damage. A creature that touches the marid or hits it with a melee attack while within 10 feet of it takes 7 (2d6) cold damage. A creature must succeed on a DC 17 Constitution saving throw each minute it spends in the aura or gain one level of exhaustion.

Innate Spellcasting. The marid's innate spellcasting ability is Charisma (spell save DC 17, +9 to hit with spell attacks). It can innately cast the following spells, requiring no material components:

At will: *create or destroy water, detect evil and good, detect magic, speak with animals* (water-based creatures only)
3/day each: *control water, tongues, water walk, water breathing*
1/day each: *conjure elemental* (water elemental only), *gaseous form, invisibility, major image, plane shift*

Riptide. If a creature is more than 10 feet away from the marid and it hits the marid with an attack, it must succeed on a DC 17 Strength saving throw or be pulled up to 10 feet closer to the marid.

Actions

Multiattack. The marid makes one Scimitar attack and one Water Whip attack.

Scimitar. *Melee Weapon Attack:* +12 to hit, reach 5 ft., one target. *Hit:* 14 (2d6 + 7) slashing damage plus 10 (3d6) cold damage.

Water Whip. *Melee Weapon Attack:* +12 to hit, reach 25 ft., one target. *Hit:* 12 (2d4 + 7) slashing damage plus 10 (3d6) cold damage, and the target must succeed on a DC 17 Strength saving throw or be pulled up to 20 feet toward the marid.

Whirlpool (recharge 5–6). Water swirls rapidly around the marid. Each creature within 20 feet of the marid must make a DC 17 Dexterity saving throw. On a failure, a creature takes 56 (16d6) cold damage and is knocked prone. On a success, a creature takes half the damage and isn't knocked prone.

METZPIL

Medium humanoid (half-elf), chaotic neutral

Armor Class 17 (cipacahuipilli armor [see **Appendix C**], *+1 shield, ring of pretection*)
Hit Points 156 (24d8 + 48)
Speed 30 ft.

STR	DEX	CON	INT	WIS	CHA
16 (+3)	13 (+1)	14 (+2)	12 (+1)	16 (+3)	15 (+2)

Saving Throws Wis +9, Cha +8 (*ring of protection*)
Skills History +6, Persuasion +7
Damage Immunities poison
Condition Immunities poisoned
Senses darkvision 60 ft., passive Perception 13
Languages Abyssal, Aztli
Challenge 15 (13,000 XP)

Equipment. Metzpil has a *ring of protection, winged boots,* a *+2 ollitetlacotl* (see **Appendix C**), a *+1 shield,* cipacahuipilli armor (see **Appendix C**), and a *staff of the python.*

Dark Devotion. Metzpil has advantage on saving throws against being charmed or frightened.

Mortal Vessel. Metzpil cannot be possessed by another creature.

Servant of the Serpent. As a bonus action, Metzpil can expend a spell slot to cause his melee weapon attacks to magically deal an extra 21 (6d6) necrotic damage to a target on a hit. This benefit lasts until the end of the turn. If Metzpil expends a spell slot of 2nd level or higher, the extra damage increases by 1d6 for each level above 1st.

Spellcaster. Metzpil is a 16th-level spellcaster. His spellcasting ability is Wisdom (spell save DC 16, +8 to hit with spell attacks). He has the following cleric spells prepared:

Cantrips (at will): *guidance, mending, resistance, sacred flame, thaumaturgy*
1st level (4 slots): *bloodbath*, counterattack*, cure wounds, inflict wounds*
2nd level (3 slots): *augury, hold person, spiritual weapon*
3rd level (3 slots): *animate dead, flay skin*, tongues*
4th level (3 slots): *divination, guardian of faith, locate creature*
5th level (2 slots): *dispel evil and good, insect plague*
6th level (1 slot): *planar ally*
7th level (1 slot): *conjure celestial*
8th level (1 slot): *holy aura*
* These spells appear in **Appendix D**.

War Priest. When Metzpil uses the Attack action, he can make one weapon attack as a bonus action.

Actions

+2 Ollitetlacotl (see Appendix C). *Melee Weapon Attack:* +10 to hit, reach 5 ft., one target. *Hit:* 8 (1d6 + 5) bludgeoning damage.

Reactions

Last Second. Metzpil adds 4 to his AC against one melee attack that would hit him. To do so, he must see the attacker and be holding his shield.

MINOTAUR, OBSIDIAN

Large construct, neutral

Armor Class 16 (natural armor)
Hit Points 76 (8d10 + 32)
Speed 30 ft.

STR	DEX	CON	INT	WIS	CHA
21 (+5)	10 (+0)	18 (+4)	3 (–4)	11 (+0)	1 (–5)

Damage Immunities acid, fire, poison, psychic; bludgeoning, piercing, and slashing from nonmagical attacks that aren't adamantine
Condition Immunities charmed, exhaustion, frightened, paralyzed, petrified, poisoned
Senses darkvision 60 ft., passive Perception 10
Languages understands the languages of its creator but can't speak
Challenge 8 (3,900 XP)

Charge. If the obsidian minotaur moves at least 10 feet straight toward a target and then hits it with a Gore attack on the same turn, the target takes an extra 9 (2d8) piercing damage. If the target is a creature, it must succeed on a DC 16 Strength saving throw or be pushed up to 10 feet away and knocked prone.

Immutable Form. The minotaur is immune to any spell or effect that would alter its form.

Magic Resistance. The minotaur has advantage on saving throws against spells and other magic effects.

Magic Weapons. The minotaur's weapon attacks are magical.

Actions

Multiattack. The obsidian minotaur makes one Gore attack and two Claw attacks.

Gore. Melee Weapon Attack: +8 to hit, reach 5 ft., one target. *Hit:* 14 (2d8 + 5) piercing damage plus 7 (2d6) fire damage.

Claw. Melee Weapon Attack: +8 to hit, reach 10 ft., one target. *Hit:* 12 (2d6 + 5) slashing damage plus 7 (2d6) fire damage.

Burning Breath (recharge 5–6). An obsidian minotaur expels a cloud of superheated gas that fills a 10-foot cube adjacent to it. The gas fades after the end of the minotaur's next turn. Creatures who enter the area or start their turn there must make a DC 16 Constitution saving throw. On a failed saving throw, the target takes 31 (9d6) fire damage and is poisoned for one minute. On a successful saving throw, the target takes half the damage and is not poisoned.

MIQUITO ADDER

Tiny fiend, chaotic evil

Armor Class 17
Hit Points 21 (6d4 + 6)
Speed 30 ft., swim 30 ft.

STR	DEX	CON	INT	WIS	CHA
2 (–4)	24 (+7)	13 (+1)	1 (–5)	10 (+0)	3 (–4)

Saving Throws Dex +9
Damage Vulnerabilities thunder
Damage Immunities cold, necrotic
Senses blindsight 10 ft., passive Perception 10
Languages All
Challenge 2 (450 XP)

Actions

Bite. Melee Weapon Attack: +8 to hit, reach 5 ft., one target. *Hit:* 2 (1d4) piercing damage, 7 (2d6) necrotic damage and the target must make a DC 16 Constitution saving throw. On a failure, the target takes 18 (4d8) poison damage, while on a success the target takes half as much damage.

MOBAT

Large monstrosity, neutral

Armor Class 14 (natural armor)
Hit Points 51 (6d10 + 18)
Speed 20 ft., fly 40 ft.

STR	DEX	CON	INT	WIS	CHA
17 (+3)	15 (+2)	16 (+3)	6 (–2)	13 (+1)	6 (–2)

Skills Perception +3
Senses blindsight 60 ft., passive Perception 13
Languages —
Challenge 1 (200 XP)

Echolocation. The mobat cannot use its blindsight while deafened.

Flyby. The mobat does not provoke an opportunity attack when it flies out of an opponent's reach.

Keen Hearing. The mobat has advantage on Wisdom (Perception) checks that rely on hearing.

Actions

Bite. Melee Weapon Attack: +5 to hit, reach 5 ft., one target. *Hit:* 13 (3d6 + 3) piercing damage.

Stunning Screen (recharge 5–6). The mobat emits a piercing screech. All creatures within 30 feet of it that can hear it must succeed on a DC 12 Constitution saving throw or be stunned for one minute. A stunned creature can repeat the saving throw at the end of each of its turns, ending the effect on itself on a success.

MOCAYAHUA

Tiny fey, chaotic neutral

Armor Class 16 (natural armor)
Hit Points 65 (10d6 + 30)
Speed 30 ft., climb 30 ft.

STR	DEX	CON	INT	WIS	CHA
8 (–1)	18 (+4)	17 (+3)	20 (+5)	15 (+2)	17 (+3)

Saving Throws Int +8, Wis +5
Skills Acrobatics +7, Deception +6, History +8, Insight +5, Nature +8, Persuasion +6, Sleight of Hand +7
Damage Immunities cold; bludgeoning, piercing, and slashing from nonmagical attacks
Condition Immunities charmed, frightened
Senses darkvision 60 ft., truesight 30 ft., passive Perception 12
Languages All, Telepathy
Challenge 7 (2,900 XP)

Innate Spellcasting. Mocayahua's innate spellcasting ability is Intelligence (spell save DC 16, spell attack bonus +8). He can innately cast the following spells, requiring no components:
At will: *mage hand, sanctuary, vicious mockery*
3/day each: *confusion, mirror image*
2/day: *teleport* (to the Obsidian Spire or to the Ebon Portal only)

Actions

Staff. Melee Weapon Attack: +2 to hit, reach 5 ft., one target. *Hit:* 3 (1d6 – 1) bludgeoning damage plus 13 (3d8) cold

Reactions

Snatch. Whenever Mocayahua has the ability to take an attack of opportunity, he can instead use *mage hand* to make a Sleight of Hand contested by the target's passive Perception to steal one item from the individual.

MONOLITH FOOTMAN

Large construct, unaligned

Armor Class 14 (natural armor)
Hit Points 60 (8d10 + 16)
Speed 40 ft.

STR	DEX	CON	WIS	INT	CHA
18 (+4)	12 (+1)	14 (+2)	10 (+0)	10 (+0)	10 (+0)

Damage Immunities poison; bludgeoning, piercing, and slashing from nonmagical attacks that aren't adamantine
Condition Immunities charmed, exhaustion, frightened, paralyzed, poisoned
Senses darkvision 60 ft., passive Perception 10
Languages Elvish, Umbral
Challenge 3 (700 XP)

Blatant Dismissal. While in the courts or castles of the fey, a monolith footman that scores a successful hit with its longsword can try to force the substitution of the target with a shadow double. The target must succeed at a DC 10 Charisma saving throw or become invisible, silent, and paralyzed, while an illusory version of itself remains visible and audible — and under the monolith footman's control, shouting for a retreat or the like. The effect lasts for one minute. Outside fey locales, this ability does not function.

Fey Flame. The ritual powering a monolith footman grants it an inner flame that it can use to enhance its weapon or its fists with additional fire or cold damage, depending on the construct's needs.

Simple Construction. Monolith footmen are designed with a delicate fey construction. They burst into pieces and are destroyed when they receive a critical hit.

Actions

Longsword. *Melee Weapon Attack*: +6 to hit, reach 5 ft., one target. *Hit*: 11 (2d6 + 4) slashing damage plus 9 (2d8) cold or fire damage.

Slam. *Melee Weapon Attack*: +6 to hit, reach 5 ft., one target. *Hit*: 8 (1d8 + 4) bludgeoning damage plus 9 (2d8) cold or fire damage.

The monolith footman can be found in ***Tome of Beasts*** by **Kobold Press**.

MUDBOG OOZE

Large ooze, unaligned

Armor Class 5
Hit Points 76 (9d10 + 27)
Speed 10 ft., swim 10 ft.

STR	DEX	CON	INT	WIS	CHA
20 (+5)	8 (–1)	17 (+3)	1 (–5)	10 (+0)	3 (–4)

Skills Stealth +1
Damage Resistances fire
Damage Immunities acid, psychic
Condition Immunities blinded, charmed, deafened, exhaustion, frightened, prone
Senses blindsight 60 ft. (blind beyond this radius), passive Perception 10
Languages —
Challenge 2 (450 XP)

Acid. A mudbog secretes a digestive acid that quickly dissolves organic material, but not metal or stone. A creature that attacks the mudbog takes 3 (1d6) acid damage. Any wood or other organic material that touches the mudbog is pitted. Wooden weapons suffer a cumulative –1 penalty to damage rolls made with it unless it is magical. When this penalty reaches –5, the weapon is destroyed.

Amorphous. The ooze can move through a space as narrow as one inch wide without squeezing.

False Appearance. The mudbog, while not moving, is indistinguishable from a mud puddle.

Actions

Engulf. The mudbog moves up to its speed. While doing so, it can enter Medium or smaller creatures' spaces. Whenever the mudbog enters a creature's space, the creature must make a DC13 Dexterity saving throw. On a failure, the mudbog enters the creature's space, and the creature takes 10 (3d6) acid damage and is engulfed. On a success, the creature can choose to be pushed five feet back or to the side of the mudbog. The engulfed creature can't breathe, is restrained, and takes 21 (6d6) acid damage at the start of each of the ooze's turns. When the mudbog moves, the engulfed creature moves with it. An engulfed creature can try to escape by using an action to make a DC 13 Strength check. On a success, the creature escapes and enters a space of its choice within five feet of the ooze.

ORC SACRIFICIAL PRIEST

Medium humanoid (orc), chaotic evil

Armor Class 15 (hide armor, shield)
Hit Points 30 (4d8 + 12)
Speed 30 ft.

STR	DEX	CON	INT	WIS	CHA
16 (+3)	12 (+1)	16 (+3)	9 (–1)	13 (+1)	12 (+1)

Skills Medicine +3, Religion +1
Senses darkvision 60 ft., passive Perception 11
Languages Common, Orc
Challenge 1 (200 XP)

Sacrificial Dagger. Any attack that hits a charmed, restrained, or stunned creature is a critical hit if the orc is within five feet of the creature.

Spellcasting. The orc is a 2nd-level spellcaster. Its spellcasting ability is Wisdom (spell save DC 11, +3 to hit with spell attacks). The orc has the following cleric spells prepared:
Cantrips (at will): *guidance, resistance, thaumaturgy*
1st level (3 slots): *bane, command, shield of faith.*

Actions

Dagger. *Melee Weapon Attack*: +5 to hit, reach 5 ft., one target. *Hit*: 5 (1d4 + 3) piercing damage.

Bonus Actions

Willing Sacrifice. The orc targets one humanoid it can see within 30 feet of it. The target must succeed on a DC 11 Wisdom saving throw or be charmed by the orc until the end of the orc's next turn. If the target fails the saving throw by 5 or more, it is charmed for one minute instead. A target that succeeds on the saving throw is immune to this orc's Willing Sacrifice for the next 24 hours. A creature immune to being charmed is also immune to this effect.

OZHUMA

Medium humanoid (human), neutral evil

Armor Class 12 (*+1 leather armor*)
Hit Points 65 (10d8 + 20)
Speed 30 ft.

STR	DEX	CON	INT	WIS	CHA
8 (–1)	10 (+0)	14 (+2)	14 (+2)	12 (+1)	16 (+3)

Saving Throws Wis +3, Cha +5
Skills Deception +5, Religion +4
Senses passive Perception 11
Languages Common, Draconic
Challenge 4 (1,100 XP)

Equipment. Ozhuma wears *+1 leather armor* and a *ring of water walking.*

Awakened Mind. Ozhuma can communicate telepathically with any creature he can see within 30 feet of him. He doesn't need to share a language with the creature for it to understand his telepathic utterances, but the creature must be able to understand at least one language.

Beast Speech. Ozhuma can cast *speak with animals* at will, without expending a spell slot.

Eldritch Sight. Ozhuma can cast *detect magic* at will, without expending a spell slot.

***Otherworldly Patron* (the Great Old One).** Ozhuma's alien patron gives him access to *clairvoyance* and *black tentacles.*

Pact of the Chain. Ozhuma knows the *find familiar* spell and can cast it as a ritual. When he casts the spell, he can choose one of the formal forms for his familiar or one of the following special forms: imp, pseudodragon, quasit, or sprite. Additionally, when he takes the Attack action, he can forgo one of his own attacks to allow his familiar to make one attack of its own. When he lets the familiar attack, it does so with its reaction.

Repelling Blast. When Ozhuma hits a creature with *eldritch blast*, he can push the creature up to 10 feet away from him in a straight line.

Spellcasting. Ozhuma is a 7th-level spellcaster. His spellcasting ability is Charisma (spell save DC 13, +5 to hit with spell attacks). Ozhuma has the following warlock spells prepared:

Cantrips (at will): *eldritch blast, friends, poison spray*
Spells (2 slots): *black tentacles, clairvoyance, detect thoughts, find familiar, hideous laughter, invisibility, sending, vampiric touch, witch bolt.*

Voice of the Chain Master. Ozhuma can communicate telepathically with his familiar and perceive through his familiar's senses as long as he is on the same plane of existence. Additionally, while perceiving through his familiar's senses, he can also speak through his familiar in his own voice, even if his familiar is normally incapable of speech.

Actions

Dagger. *Melee Weapon Attack*: +2 to hit, reach 5 ft., one target. *Hit*: 2 (1d4) piercing damage.

Reactions

Entropic Ward. When a creature makes an attack roll against Ozhuma, he can use his reaction to impose disadvantage on that roll. If the attack misses him, his next attack roll against the creature has advantage if he makes it before the end of his next turn. Once he uses this feature, he can't use it again until he finishes a short or long rest.

PHOOKA

Small fey, chaotic neutral

Armor Class 14 (natural armor)
Hit Points 27 (6d6 + 6)
Speed 30 ft.

STR	DEX	CON	INT	WIS	CHA
10 (+0)	17 (+3)	12 (+1)	13 (+1)	15 (+2)	18 (+4)

Skills Perception +6, Stealth +5
Senses passive Perception 16
Languages Common, Sylvan
Challenge 2 (450 XP)

One with Nature. When a phooka is slain through violence, all plants within a 100-foot radius of where it fell die and no new ones grow naturally in that area for one year.

Tree Stride. Once on its turn, the phooka can use 10 feet of its movement to step magically into one living tree within its reach and emerge from a second living tree within 60 feet of the first tree, appearing in an unoccupied space within five feet of the second tree. Both trees must be Large or larger.

Actions

Dagger. *Melee or Ranged Weapon Attack*: +5 to hit, reach 5 ft. or range 20/60 feet, one creature. *Hit*: 5 (1d4 + 3) piercing damage.

POQOZA WARRIOR

Medium humanoid (half-elf), neutral

Armor Class 14 (shield)
Hit Points 52 (8d8 + 16)
Speed 30 ft.

STR	DEX	CON	INT	WIS	CHA
16 (+3)	14 (+2)	15 (+2)	9 (−1)	11 (+0)	9 (−1)

Senses darkvision 60 ft., passive Perception 10
Languages Aztli
Challenge 2 (450 XP)

Blood Sacrifice. At the start of his turn, the Poqoza warrior can use an action to ritually wound himself to gain advantage on his melee attacks. The warrior runs the edges of his macuahuitl across his chest, taking 1d4 slashing damage and gaining advantage to all melee attacks made with his macuahuitl for a number of rounds equal to the damage.

Dog Master. Poqozo warriors often raise war dogs as companions. They gain a bond with one dog that they raise from birth. They can communicate with the dog using simple commands such as "fetch," "heel," "attack," and "track." If the situation calls for an ability check when communicating with his dog, the warrior always has advantage on the check.

Actions

Macuahuitl (see Appendix C). *Melee Weapon Attack:* +5 to hit, reach 5 ft., one target. *Hit*: 7 (1d8 + 3) slashing damage.

PURPLE SLIME

Large ooze, unaligned

Armor Class 7
Hit Points 76 (8d10 + 32)
Speed 20 ft., climb 10 ft., swim 30 ft.

STR	DEX	CON	INT	WIS	CHA
17 (+3)	8 (−1)	18 (+4)	2 (−4)	6 (−2)	1 (−5)

Skills Stealth +1
Damage Immunities acid, cold
Condition Immunities blinded, charmed, deafened, exhaustion, frightened, prone
Senses blindsight 60 ft. (blind beyond this radius), passive Perception 8
Languages —
Challenge 3 (700 XP)

Amorphous. The purple slime can move through a space as narrow as one inch wide without squeezing.

Amphibious. The purple slime can breathe air and water.

Underwater Camouflage. The purple slime has advantage on Dexterity (Stealth) checks made underwater.

Actions

Multiattack. The purple slime makes two Spike attacks.

Spike. *Melee Weapon Attack*: +5 to hit, reach 5 ft., one creature. *Hit*: 6 (1d8 + 2) piercing damage and 10 (3d6) poison damage. In addition, the target must succeed on a DC 14 Constitution saving throw or its Strength score is reduced by 1d4. The target dies if this reduces its Strength to 0. Otherwise, the reduction lasts until the target finishes a short or long rest.

The purple slime can be found in the *Creature Codex* by **Kobold Press**.

RETCH HOUND

Medium monstrosity, neutral evil

Armor Class 15 (natural armor)
Hit Points 45 (7d8 + 14)
Speed 40 ft.

STR	DEX	CON	INT	WIS	CHA
14 (+2)	15 (+2)	15 (+2)	5 (–3)	12 (+1)	4 (–3)

Skills Perception +5
Damage Immunities acid, poison
Condition Immunities poisoned
Senses darkvision 60 ft., passive Perception 15
Languages —
Challenge 3 (700 XP)

Keen Senses. The retch hound has advantage on Wisdom (Perception) checks that rely on hearing, sight, or smell.

Pack Tactics. Retch hounds have advantage on an attack roll against a creature if at least one of the hound's allies is within 5 feet of the creature and the ally isn't incapacitated.

Actions

Bite*.* Melee Weapon Attack: +4 to hit, reach 5 ft., one target. *Hit:* 9 (2d6 + 2) piercing damage plus 7 (2d6) acid damage.

***Retch* (recharge 5–6).** The retch hound exhales acidic bile in a 15-foot cone. Each creature in that area must make a DC 12 Dexterity saving throw, taking 21 (6d6) acid damage on a failure, or half as much on a success.

SERPENT'S KISS ASSASSIN

Medium humanoid (half-elf), neutral evil

Armor Class 16 (tlahuiztli armor [see **Appendix C**])
Hit Points 195 (30d8 + 60)
Speed 30 ft.

STR	DEX	CON	INT	WIS	CHA
12 (+1)	18 (+4)	14 (+2)	13 (+1)	11 (+0)	14 (+2)

Saving Throws Dex +9, Cha +7
Skills Acrobatics +9, Deception +7, Perception +5, Stealth +9, Survival +5
Damage Resistances fire, poison
Condition Immunities charmed, frightened
Senses darkvision 60 ft., passive Perception 15
Languages Common, Abyssal, Thieves' Cant
Challenge 13 (10,000 XP)

Assassinate. During its first turn in combat, the serpent's kiss assassin has advantage on attack rolls against any creature that has not taken a turn. Any hit the serpent's kiss assassin scores against a surprised creature is a critical hit.

***Dagger of Venom* (1/day).** The serpent's kiss assassin uses an action to coat his dagger's blade with poison. The poison remains for 1 minute or until an attack using this weapon hits a creature. That creature must succeed on a DC 15 Constitution saving throw or take 11 (2d10) poison damage and become poisoned for 1 minute.

Evasion. If the assassin is subjected to an effect that allows it to make a Dexterity saving throw to take only half damage, the serpent's kiss assassin instead takes no damage if it succeeds on the saving throw, and only half damage if it fails.

Innate Spellcasting. The serpent's kiss assassin's innate spellcasting ability is Charisma (spell save DC 15, +7 to hit with spell attacks). The serpent's kiss assassin can innately cast the following spells requiring no components:

At will: *disguise self, eldritch blast* (three beams), *false life, poison spray* (3d12 poison damage)
1/day each: *dimension door, contact other plane, scrying*

***Sneak Attack* (1/turn).** The serpent's kiss assassin deals an extra 28 (8d6) damage when it hits a target with a weapon attack and has advantage on the attack roll, or when the target is within five feet of an ally of the serpent's kiss assassin that is not incapacitated and the assassin does not have disadvantage on the attack roll.

Actions

Multiattack. The serpent's kiss assassin makes three Dagger attacks or two Longbow attacks.

Dagger of venom. Melee or Ranged Weapon Attack: +10 to hit, reach 5 ft. or ranged 20/60 ft., one target. *Hit:* 7 (1d4 + 5) piercing damage.

+1 longbow. Ranged Weapon Attack: +10 to hit, ranged 150/600 ft., one target. *Hit:* 9 (1d8 + 5) piercing damage.

SERPENT CUAUHOCELOTL

Medium humanoid (half-elf), neutral evil

Armor Class 13 (shield)
Hit Points 78 (12d8 + 24)
Speed 30 ft.

STR	DEX	CON	INT	WIS	CHA
14 (+2)	12 (+1)	14 (+2)	10 (+0)	12 (+1)	11 (+0)

Saving Throws Str +4 Con +4
Skills Athletics +4 Intimidation +2
Senses darkvision 60 ft., passive Perception 11
Challenge 3 (700 XP)

Bravado. A serpent Cuauhocelotl can use its reaction to lower its guard to an opponent's melee weapon attack against it, granting that opponent advantage on its attack roll. If the opponent's attack does not reduce the Cuauhocelotl to 0 hit points, impose a condition that prevents the Cuauhocelotl from taking an action, or cause the Cuauhocelotl to suffer disadvantage on its attack rolls, the target becomes demoralized. A demoralized creature suffers disadvantage on its attack rolls against the Cuauhocelotl, while the Cuauhocelotl gains advantage on melee attack rolls made against the demoralized foe. At the end of each of its subsequent turns, the target can make a DC 10 Wisdom saving throw. On a success, the target is no longer demoralized. If the opponent's initial melee attack missed the Cuauhocelotl, the demoralized foe suffers disadvantage on its Wisdom saving throw to end the effect. The Cuauhocelotl can use this feature three times and regains all expended uses of it when it finishes a long rest.

Fearless. Serpent Cuauhocelotls undergo a gruesome scarification ritual that transforms them into a fearless soldier. They have advantage on saving throws against being frightened.

Forked Tongue. Serpent Cuauhocelotls have advantage on Charisma (Deception) checks made to tell lies or disguise themselves. Additionally, they have advantage on saving throws against being charmed and against spells and effects where a creature automatically succeeds on its saving throw if it cannot be charmed, such as *compulsion* and *suggestion*.

Actions

Multiattack. The serpent Cuauhocelotl makes two Club attacks.

Club. Melee Weapon Attack +4 to hit, reach 5 ft, one target. Hit: 5 (1d6 + 2) bludgeoning damage.

Javelin. Ranged Weapon Attack +3 to hit, range 40/160 ft., one target. *Hit*: 5 (1d6 + 2) piercing damage.

Shadow, Greater

Medium undead, chaotic evil

Armor Class 13
Hit Points 58 (9d8 + 18)
Speed 40 ft.

STR	DEX	CON	INT	WIS	CHA
10 (+0)	16 (+3)	14 (+2)	11 (+0)	14 (+2)	12 (+1)

Skills Stealth +5
Damage Vulnerabilities radiant
Damage Resistances acid, cold, fire, lightning, thunder; bludgeoning, piercing, and slashing from nonmagical attacks
Damage Immunities necrotic, poison
Condition Immunities exhaustion, frightened, grappled, paralyzed, petrified, poisoned, prone, restrained
Senses darkvision 60 ft., passive Perception 12
Languages —
Challenge 4 (1,100 XP)

Amorphous. The shadow can move through a space as narrow as one-inch wide without squeezing.
Shadow Stealth. While in dim light or darkness, the shadow can take the Hide action as a bonus action.
Sunlight Weakness. While in sunlight, the shadow has disadvantage on attack rolls, ability checks, and saving throws.

Actions

Strength Drain. *Melee Weapon Attack:* +4 to hit, reach 5 ft., one creature. *Hit:* 9 (2d6 + 2) necrotic damage, and the target's Strength score is reduced by 1d4. The target dies if this reduces its Strength to 0. Otherwise, the reduction lasts until the target finishes a short or long rest.
If a non-evil humanoid dies from this attack, a new shadow rises from the corpse 1d4 hours later.

Lair and Lair Actions

On initiative count 20 (losing initiative ties), the greater shadow can take a lair action to cause one of the following magical effects; the shadow can't use the same effect two rounds in a row:
Command Corn: The greater shadow can command a 20-foot-radius section of its cornfield to animate and attack creatures wandering through it. The effect lasts for one minute. For the duration, that area is difficult terrain for all creatures. In addition, any creature the greater shadow chooses in the area must succeed on a DC 14 Strength save or become restrained. A creature can use its action to make a DC 14 Strength check, freeing itself or another entangled creature within reach on a success.
Corn Maze: The greater shadow manipulates the cornstalks within the cornfield to change position, ruining the efforts of anyone attempting to navigate the field. Creatures entering the cornfield immediately lose all sense of direction and make any checks to navigate the cornfields at disadvantage. This effect doesn't affect other shadows.
Obscuring Corn: The shadow can control the corn so that it sways and weaves together, heavily obscuring the vision of any creatures in the fields. This effect doesn't affect other shadows.

Sightless Servant

Medium fiend (human), neutral evil

Armor Class 14 (natural armor)
Hit Points 90 (12d8 + 36)
Speed 30 ft.

STR	DEX	CON	INT	WIS	CHA
17 (+3)	14 (+2)	16 (+3)	12 (+1)	14 (+2)	12 (+1)

Saving Throws Con +5, Wis +4
Skills Athletics +5, Perception +4, Stealth +4
Damage Resistances slashing
Damage Immunities psychic
Condition Immunities blinded
Senses blindsight 30 ft. (blind beyond this radius), passive Perception 14
Languages Undercommon
Challenge 4 (1,100 XP)

Blind Senses. The sightless servant can't use its blindsight while deafened and unable to smell.
Blood Bath (recharge 6). The sightless servant can use an action to lay its hands on a recently slain creature other than an undead or construct to drain its residual life essence and regain 1d4 hit points. The sightless servant must perform the action within five rounds of the creature's death. Once a sightless servant performs this action, the victim is drained and no further energy can be pulled from it.
Keen Hearing and Smell. The sightless servant has advantage on Wisdom (Perception) checks that rely on hearing or smell.

Actions

***Macuahuitl* (see Appendix C).** *Melee Weapon Attack:* +6 to hit, reach 5 ft., one target. *Hit:* 8 (1d8 + 3) slashing damage.

Skeleton, Black

Medium undead, chaotic evil

Armor Class 18 (chain mail)
Hit Points 71 (13d8 + 13)
Speed 40 ft.

STR	DEX	CON	INT	WIS	CHA
11 (+0)	19 (+4)	13 (+1)	13 (+1)	10 (+0)	14 (+2)

Skills Perception +4, Stealth +6
Damage Vulnerabilities bludgeoning, radiant
Damage Resistances cold
Damage Immunities necrotic, poison
Condition Immunities exhaustion, poisoned
Senses darkvision 60 ft., passive Perception 14
Languages the languages it knew in life but cannot speak
Challenge 4 (1,100 XP)

Shortsword Masters. Black skeletons gain defensive bonuses (+2 to AC) and bonuses to attack (+2 to hit) when wielding two shortswords (included in the statistics).

Actions

Multiattack. The black skeleton makes two Claw attacks or two Shortsword attacks.
Claw. *Melee Weapon Attack:* +6 to hit, reach 5 ft., one target. *Hit:* 8 (1d8 + 4) slashing damage, and the target's Strength score is reduced by 1d4. The target dies if this reduces its strength to 0. Otherwise, the reduction lasts until the target finishes a short or long rest.

Shortsword. *Melee Weapon Attack:* +8 to hit, reach 5 ft., one target. *Hit:*
11 (2d6 + 4) piercing damage, and the target's Strength score is reduced
by 1d4. The target dies if this reduces its strength to 0. Otherwise, the
reduction lasts until the target finishes a short or long rest

SKELETON, VINE TROLL
Large plant, unaligned

Armor Class 16 (natural armor)
Hit Points 119 (14d10 + 42)
Speed 30 ft.

STR	DEX	CON	INT	WIS	CHA
20 (+5)	12 (+1)	16 (+3)	6 (–2)	8 (–1)	5 (–3)

Saving Throws Con +7
Damage Resistances bludgeoning, piercing, and slashing damage
from nonmagical attacks
Damage Immunities poison
Condition Immunities deafened, exhaustion, poisoned
Senses darkvision 60 ft., passive Perception 9
Languages —
Challenge 9 (5,000 XP)

Regeneration. The vine troll skeleton regains 5 hit points at the
start of its turn if it is within 10 feet of the duskthorn dryad's vines
and it hasn't taken acid or fire damage since its previous turn. The
skeleton dies only if it starts its turn with 0 hit points and doesn't
regenerate, or if the duskthorn dryad who created it dies, or if the
troll's heart inside the dryad's tree is destroyed.

Actions

Multiattack. The skeleton makes one Bite *attack* and two Claw
attacks.
Bite. *Melee Weapon Attack:* +9 to hit, reach 5 ft., one target. *Hit:* 21
(3d10 + 5) piercing damage.
Claw. *Melee Weapon Attack:* +9 to hit, reach 5 ft., one target. *Hit:* 18
(3d8 + 5) slashing damage.
The skeleton, vine troll can be found in ***Tome of Beasts*** by **Kobold
Press.**

SPAWN OF TLATOANI
Large undead, chaotic evil

Armor Class 16 (natural armor)
Hit Points 65 (10d10 + 10)
Speed 30 ft.

STR	DEX	CON	INT	WIS	CHA
19 (+4)	16 (+3)	12 (+1)	10 (+0)	14 (+2)	10 (+0)

Damage Immunities cold, poison
Condition Immunities charmed, exhaustion, paralyzed, poisoned
Senses darkvision 60 ft., passive Perception 12
Languages —
Challenge 4 (1,100 XP)

Aura of the Grave. Any living creature that starts its turn within five
feet of the spawn of Tlatoani must succeed on a DC 15 Constitution
saving throw or be frightened until the start of the creature's next
turn. On a successful saving throw, the creature is immune to the
spawn of Tlatoani's aura for one hour.

Actions

Bite. *Melee Weapon Attack:* +6 to hit, reach 10 ft., one target. *Hit:* 11
(2d6 + 4) piercing damage plus 10 (3d6) poison damage.

***Barbed Tongue* (recharge 4-6).** *Melee Weapon Attack:* +6 to hit,
reach 30 ft., one target. *Hit:* 18 (4d6 + 4) piercing damage and the
tongue lodges into the target and grapples it (escape DC 14). Until
the grapple ends, the target is restrained and has disadvantage on
Strength checks and Strength saving throws. The spawn cannot
use its bite on another target. As a bonus action, the spawn pulls a
creature grappled by it up to 10 feet straight toward it.

SPÖKVATTEN
Medium fey, neutral evil

Armor Class 14
Hit Points 78 (12d8 + 24)
Speed 30 ft., swim 30 ft.

STR	DEX	CON	INT	WIS	CHA
9 (–1)	18 (+4)	14 (+2)	10 (+0)	16 (+3)	18 (+4)

Skills Deception +10, Insight +6, Nature +3, Perception +9,
Persuasion +10, Stealth +10
Damage Immunities cold
Senses darkvision 60 ft., passive Perception 19
Languages Aquan, Sylvan
Challenge 5 (1,800 XP)

Shapechanger. The spökvatten can use its action to magically
polymorph into a Large cloud of mist, into a beast or humanoid
of challenge rating 2 or lower, or back into its true form (that of a
Medium fey). Anything it is carrying or wearing transforms with it.
It reverts to its true form if it dies.
While in beast or humanoid form, the fey retains its game statistics
and ability to speak, but its AC, movement modes, Strength,
Dexterity, and special senses are replaced by those of the new form,
and it gains any statistics and capabilities (except class features,
legendary actions, and lair actions) that the new form has but that
it lacks.
In mist form, the spökvatten can use only its icy fog ability, and it is
unable to speak or manipulate objects. It is weightless, has a flying
speed of 20 feet, can hover, and can enter a hostile creature's space
and stop there. In addition, if air can pass through a space, the mist
can do so without squeezing, and it can't pass through water. It has
advantage on Strength, Dexterity, and Constitution saving throws,
and it is immune to all nonmagical damage.

Actions

Cold Touch. *Melee Spell Attack:* +7 to hit, reach 5 ft., one target. *Hit:*
26 (4d10 + 4) cold damage. The target must succeed on a DC 15
Constitution saving throw or be paralyzed for 1 minute. The target
can repeat the saving throw at the end of each of its turns, ending
the effect on itself on a success.
***Icy Fog* (recharge 5–6).** The spökvatten exhales a cloud of freezing
mist in a 15-foot cone. Each creature in that area must make a DC
15 Dexterity saving throw, taking 36 (8d8) cold damage on a failed
save, or half as much damage on a successful one.

SWARM OF POISONOUS FROGS
Medium swarm of Tiny beasts, unaligned

Armor Class 13 (natural armor)
Hit Points 59 (17d8 – 17)
Speed 20 ft., swim 20 ft.

STR	DEX	CON	INT	WIS	CHA
1 (–5)	13 (+1)	8 (–1)	1 (–5)	8 (–1)	3 (–4)

Skills Perception +1, Stealth +3
Damage Immunities poison

Condition Immunities poisoned
Senses passive Perception 11
Languages —
Challenge 1 (200 XP)

Amphibious. The swarm can breathe air and water
Keen Smell. The swarm has advantage on Wisdom (Perception) checks that rely on smell.
Standing Leap. The swarm's long jump is up to 10 feet and its high jump is up to 5 feet, with or without a running start.
Swarm. The swarm can occupy another creature's space and vice versa, and the swarm can move through any opening large enough for a poisonous frog. The swarm can't regain hit points or gain temporary hit points.

Actions

Bite. *Melee Weapon Attack:* +3 to hit, reach 0 ft., one target. *Hit:* 11 (3d6 + 1) piercing damage, and the target must succeed on a DC 12 Constitution saving throw or be poisoned for 1 hour.

Troll, Swamp

Large giant, chaotic evil

Armor Class 14 (natural armor)
Hit Points 63 (6d10 + 30)
Speed 30 ft., swim 30 ft.

STR	DEX	CON	INT	WIS	CHA
18 (+4)	14 (+2)	20 (+5)	6 (−2)	9 (−1)	4 (−3)

Skills Athletics +8, Perception +1, Stealth +4 (+6 in swampy terrain)
Senses darkvision 60 ft., passive Perception 11
Languages Giant
Challenge 2 (450 XP)

Keen Smell. The swamp troll has advantage on Wisdom (Perception) checks that rely on smell.
Regeneration. The troll regains 3 hit points at the start of its turn. If the troll takes acid or fire damage, this trait doesn't function at the start of the troll's next turn. The troll dies only if it starts its turn with 0 hit points and doesn't regenerate.
Slimy. The swamp troll is covered in swampy muck. Creatures attempting to grapple a swamp troll have disadvantage.
Swamp Stride. The swamp troll ignores nonmagical difficult terrain caused by swamp water or vegetation.

Actions

Multiattack. The swamp troll makes one Bite attack and two Claw attacks.
Bite. *Melee Weapon Attack:* +6 to hit, reach 10 ft., one target. *Hit:* 14 (3d6 + 4) piercing damage.
Claws. *Melee Weapon Attack:* +6 to hit, reach 10 ft., one target. *Hit:* 11 (2d6 + 4) slashing damage.

T'shann

Small aberration, neutral

Armor Class 8 (natural armor)
Hit Points 32 (5d6 + 15)
Speed 10 ft., burrow 10 ft.

STR	DEX	CON	INT	WIS	CHA
10 (+0)	4 (−3)	16 (+3)	2 (−4)	10 (+0)	12 (+1)

Senses blindsight 60 ft. (blind beyond this radius), passive Perception 10
Languages —
Challenge 1 (200 XP)

Acidic Secretion. A creature who touches the t'shann takes 5 (2d4) acid damage. Any nonmagical weapon made of metal or wood that hits the t'shann corrodes. After dealing damage, the weapon takes a permanent and cumulative −1 penalty to damage rolls. If its penalty drops to −5, the weapon is destroyed. Nonmagical ammunition made of metal or wood that hits the t'shann is destroyed after dealing damage.
In addition, nonmagical armor worn by the target of any of the t'shann's attacks is partly dissolved and takes a permanent and cumulative −1 penalty to the AC it offers. The armor is destroyed if the penalty reduces its AC to 10.
Alien Thoughts. When a creature enters or starts its turn within 30 feet of a t'shann that is not incapacitated, the creature must make a DC 13 Wisdom saving throw. On a failure, the creature can't take reactions until the start of its next turn and rolls 1d8 to determine what it does during that turn. On a 1–4, the creature does nothing. On a 5 or 6, the creature takes no action but uses all its movement to move in a random direction. On a 7 or 8, the creature makes one melee attack against a random creature, or it does nothing if no creature is within reach.

Actions

Slam. *Melee Weapon Attack:* +2 to hit, reach 5 ft., one target. *Hit:* 2 (1d4) bludgeoning damage plus 5 (2d4) acid damage.
Spew Acid. *Ranged Weapon Attack:* +2 to hit, range 10 ft., one target. *Hit:* 5 (2d4) acid damage.

Tukkuru Gargoyle

Tiny elemental, neutral good

Armor Class 13 (natural armor)
Hit Points 27 (6d4 + 12)
Speed 20 ft.

STR	DEX	CON	INT	WIS	CHA
10 (+0)	15 (+2)	15 (+2)	6 (−2)	11 (+0)	7 (−2)

Damage Resistances bludgeoning, piercing, and slashing from nonmagical attacks that are not adamantine.
Damage Immunities poison
Condition Immunities exhaustion, petrified, poisoned
Senses darkvision 60 ft., passive Perception 10
Languages Common, Terran
Challenge 1/2 (100 XP)

False Appearance. While a tukkuru gargoyle remains motionless, it is indistinguishable from an inanimate object.
Swarming Grappler. The tukkuru gargoyle can grapple a creature up to two sizes larger than itself and can move at full speed when dragging a creature it has grappled. Furthermore, a tukkuru gargoyle can grapple a creature already grappled by one or more tukkuru gargoyles. When it does so, the DC to escape the grapple increases by +2 for each gargoyle grappling it beyond the first. A creature that succeeds on an escape check is no longer grappled by any tukkuru gargoyles regardless of how many were grappling it. A tukkuru gargoyle grappling an opponent has advantage on bite attacks against the grappled opponent, but cannot make claw attacks.

Actions

Multiattack. The tukkuru gargoyle makes one Bite attack and one Claws attack.
Bite. *Melee Weapon Attack:* +2 to hit, reach 5 ft., one target. *Hit:* 2 (1d4) piercing damage.
Claws. *Ranged Weapon Attack:* +2 to hit, range 10 ft., one target. *Hit:* 2 (1d4) slashing damage. If the target is a creature of Medium size or smaller, it is grappled (escape DC 10).

Unresurrected Wraith

Medium undead, neutral evil

Armor Class 14
Hit Points 135 (18d8 + 54)
Speed 0 ft., fly 60 ft.

STR	DEX	CON	INT	WIS	CHA
6 (–2)	18 (+4)	16 (+3)	14 (+2)	14 (+2)	17 (+3)

Damage Resistances acid, cold, fire, lightning, thunder; bludgeoning, piercing, and slashing from nonmagical attacks that aren't jadeite.
Damage Immunities necrotic, poison
Condition Immunities charmed, exhaustion, grappled, paralyzed, petrified, poisoned, prone, restrained
Senses Darkvision 60 ft., passive Perception 12
Languages Primordial Notoan
Challenge 11 (7,200 XP)

Incorporeal Movement. The wraith can move through other creatures and objects as if they were difficult terrain. It takes 5 (1d10) force damage if it ends its turn inside an object.

Innate Spellcasting. The wraith's innate spellcasting ability is Charisma (spell save DC 15, +7 to hit with spell attacks). It can innately cast the following spells, requiring no material components:
3/day: *phantasmal killer*
1/day: *finger of death*

Sunlight Sensitivity. While in sunlight, the wraith has disadvantage on attack rolls, as well as on Wisdom (Perception) checks that rely on sight.

Actions

Life Drain. *Melee Weapon Attack:* +8 to hit, reach 5 ft., one creature. *Hit:* 31 (6d8 + 4) necrotic damage. The target must succeed on a DC 17 Constitution saving throw or its hit point maximum is reduced by an amount equal to the damage taken. This reduction lasts until the target finishes a long rest. The target dies if this effect reduces its hit point maximum to 0.

Necrotic Breath **(recharge 5–6).** The wraith exhales a 30-foot line of black shadowy mist. Each creature in that area must make a DC 16 Dexterity saving throw, taking 35 (10d6) necrotic damage on a failed save, or half as much damage on a successful one. A humanoid reduced to 0 hit points by this damage dies and risks becoming the subject of the wraith's Explode the Heart attack.

Reactions

Explode the Heart. The wraith targets a humanoid within 10 feet of it that died violently within the last minute. The wraith can force the target's heart to leap from its chest and explode, showering all creatures within a 15-radius of the victim in a burst of necrotic blood. A creature in the burst takes 15 (6d4) necrotic damage immediately and 7 (3d4) necrotic damage at the end of its next turn.

Wahuapa (Maizefolk)

Medium plant, unaligned

Armor Class 14 (natural armor)
Hit Points 75 (10d8 + 30)
Speed 20 ft.

STR	DEX	CON	INT	WIS	CHA
16 (+3)	10 (+0)	16 (+3)	6 (–2)	10 (+0)	10 (+0)

Skills Perception +2, Stealth +2
Condition Immunities exhaustion, paralyzed
Senses blindsight 60 ft. (blind beyond this radius), passive Perception 12
Languages understands Common but cannot speak
Challenge 3 (700 XP)

Blood Meal. Living creatures hit by the wahuapa's claws must succeed on a DC 10 Constitution saving throw or suffer 1 level of exhaustion. Creatures that succeed are immune to the same wahuapa's blood meal ability for 24 hours. For every level of exhaustion drained, the wahuapa gains 5 temporary hit points.

Innate Spellcasting. The wahuapa's innate spellcasting ability is Wisdom (spell save DC 10, +2 to hit with spell attacks). It can innately cast the following spell, requiring no material components:
3/day each: *entangle*

Maize Camouflage. The wahuapa has advantage on Dexterity (Stealth) checks made to hide among ordinary maize plants.

Actions

Claws. *Melee Weapon Attack:* +5 to hit, reach 5 ft., one target. *Hit:* 10 (2d6 + 3) slashing damage.

War Dog

Medium beast, unaligned

Armor Class 14 (studded leather)
Hit Points 22 (4d8 + 4)
Speed 40 ft.

STR	DEX	CON	INT	WIS	CHA
14 (+2)	14 (+2)	13 (+1)	3 (–4)	12 (+1)	7 (–2)

Skills Perception +3, Stealth +4
Senses darkvision 60 ft., passive Perception 13
Languages none
Challenge 1/2 (100 XP)

Ferocity. When the dog drops to 0 hit points, it immediately makes one attack against a creature within five feet as a reaction before dying.

Scent. The war dog has advantage on Perception checks made involving scent.

Warrior's Best Friend. A single master to whom it shows unwavering loyalty raises a war dog from birth. A war dog's master always has advantage when giving it commands.

Actions

Bite. *Melee Weapon Attack:* +4 to hit, reach 5 ft., one target). *Hit:* 6 (1d8 + 2) piercing damage, and a Medium or smaller creature is grappled (escape DC 12). A grappled creature takes 6 (1d8 + 2) piercing damage at the end of its turn.

The war dog is a modified version of the **dog, medium,** which can be found in *Tome of Blighted Horrors* by **Frog God Games.**

Xoco Tepeyollotl

Large celestial, lawful neutral

Armor Class 17 (natural armor)
Hit Points 136 (16d8 + 64)
Speed 40 ft.

STR	DEX	CON	INT	WIS	CHA
21 (+5)	15 (+2)	19 (+4)	15 (+2)	16 (+3)	19 (+4)

Saving Throws Dex +6, Wis +7
Skills Athletics +9, History +6, Insight +7, Religion +6
Damage Immunities bludgeoning, piercing, and slashing from nonmagical attacks
Damage Immunities charmed, poisoned, stunned

Senses darkvision 60 ft., passive Perception 13
Languages Telepathy, Primordial Notoan
Challenge 10 (5,900 XP)

Innate Spellcasting. The Xoco Tepeyollotl's innate spellcasting
ability is Wisdom (spell save DC 15, +7 to hit with spell attacks).
She can innately cast the following spells, requiring no components:
At will: *blade ward, detect thoughts, sacred flame.*
3/day each: *bane, counterspell, nohpalli*, jaguar spirit**
1/day each: *palpitating heart*, plane shift* (self only)
* see **Appendix D: New Spells**

Actions

Multiattack. The Xoco Tepeyollotl can make one Bite attack and two
Macuahuitl (see **Appendix C**) attacks.
Bite. *Melee Weapon Attack:* +9 to hit, reach 5 ft., one target. Hit: 16
(2d10 + 5) piercing damage.
Macuahuitl (see Appendix C). *Melee Weapon Attack:* +9 to hit,
reach 10 ft., one target. *Hit:* 21 (3d10 + 5) slashing damage plus 4
(2d8) cold damage.
Weird (recharge 6). The Xoco Tepeyollotl draws upon the deepest
fears and regrets of the creatures around it to create illusions visible
only to them. Creatures within 40 feet of the Xoco Tepeyollotl must
succeed on a DC 15 Charisma saving throw or be frightened for 1
minute. A creature can repeat the saving throw at the end of each of
its turns, taking 11 (2d10) psychic damage on a failure or ending the
effect on itself on a success.

Legendary Actions

The Xoco Tepeyollotl can take three legendary actions, choosing from
the options below. Only one legendary action can be used at a time
and only at the end of another creature's turn. The Xoco Tepeyollotl
regains spent Legendary Actions at the start of her turn.
Macuahuitl Attack. The Xoco Tepeyollotl makes a Macuahuitl attack.
Nohpalli (costs 2 actions). The Xoco Tepeyollotl can use the spell
nohpalli (see **Appendix D**) against an opponent's attack.
The Jaguar God's Sacrifice (costs 3 actions). Should a mortal be
reduced to 0 hit points in the presence of the Xoco Tepeyollotl, she
can quickly transport the mortal's soul to her father by moving up to
20 feet and touching the target's chest. Doing so causes its heart to
explode, instantly killing the victim and showering everything in a
20-foot radius in the victim's blood. Any Xoco Tepeyollotl within the
radius of the blood shower regains 3d8 + 4 hit points.

Xotaxtl the Sorcerer-Priest

Medium humanoid (human), neutral

Armor Class 12
Hit Points 33 (6d8 + 6)
Speed 30 ft.

STR	DEX	CON	INT	WIS	CHA
10 (+0)	15 (+2)	12 (+1)	11 (+0)	14 (+2)	18 (+4)

Saving Throws Con +3, Cha +6
Skills History +2, Insight +4, Persuasion +6, Religion +2
Senses passive Perception 12
Languages Primordial Notoan, Common
Challenge 4 (1,100 XP)

Arcane Spellcasting. Xotaxtl is a 6th-level spellcaster. His
spellcasting ability is Charisma (spell save DC 14, +6 to hit with
spell attacks). Xotaxtl has the following wizard and cleric spells
prepared:
Cantrips (at will): *control flames, guidance, light, mending*
1st level (4 slots): *burning hands, comprehend languages, detect magic*
2nd level (3 slots): *darkness, detect thoughts*
3rd level (3 slots): *speak with dead, magic circle*

Actions

Obsidian Dagger. *Melee Weapon Attack:* +4 to hit, reach 5 ft., one
target. *Hit:* 4 (1d4 + 2) piercing damage.
Quarterstaff. *Melee Weapon Attack:* +2 to hit, reach 5 ft., one target.
Hit: 3 (1d6) bludgeoning damage.

Xotaxtl Nitlocati

Large fey (alux), chaotic evil

Armor Class 15 (natural armor)
Hit Points 105 (10d10 + 50)
Speed 40 ft.

STR	DEX	CON	INT	WIS	CHA
19 (+4)	12 (+1)	20 (+5)	12 (+1)	13 (+1)	15 (+2)

Saving Throws Str +7, Con +8
Skills Arcana +4, Athletics +7, Stealth +4, Survival +4
Damage Vulnerabilities obsidian
Condition Immunities frightened
Senses darkvision 60 ft., passive Perception 11
Languages Primordial Notoan
Challenge 5 (1,800 XP)

Innate Spellcasting. Xotaxtl Nitlocati's innate spellcasting ability is
Charisma (spell save DC 13). Xotaxtl Nitlocati can innately cast the
following spells, requiring no material components:
At will: *burning hands, darkness*
3/day each: *conjure animals* (goats only), *scorching ray, spike growth*
2/day: *fear*
1/day: *flesh to maize* (see **Appendix D**)
Keen Hearing and Smell. Xotaxtl Nitlocati has advantage on
Wisdom (Perception) checks that rely on hearing or smell.
Mountain Camouflage. Xotaxtl Nitlocati has advantage on Dexterity
(Stealth) checks made to hide in mountainous terrain.

Actions

Multiattack. Xotaxtl Nitlocati makes two Bash attacks or 2
Macuahuitl attacks.
Bash. *Melee Weapon Attack:* +7 to hit, reach 5 ft., one target. *Hit:* 13
(2d8 + 4) bludgeoning damage, and Xotaxtl Nitlocati can push the
target five feet away if the target is Large or smaller.
Macuahuitl (see Appendix C). *Melee Weapon Attack:* +7 to hit,
reach 10 ft., one target. *Hit:* 17 (3d8 + 4) slashing damage.
Block the Path. The Xotaxtl Nitlocati can use its action to prohibit other
creatures from moving past it or escaping its grasp. Until the start of
Xotaxtl Nitlocati's next turn, attack rolls against him have disadvantage,
it has advantage on the attack roll it makes for an opportunity attack,
and that attack deals an extra 16 (3d10) bludgeoning damage on a hit.
Also, each enemy that tries to move out of Xotaxtl Nitlocati's reach
without teleporting must succeed on a DC 14 Strength saving throw or
have its speed reduced to 0 until the start of his next turn.

Zombie, Nihilethic

Medium undead, neutral evil

Armor Class 9 (natural armor)
Hit Points 22 (3d8 + 9)
Speed 20 ft., swim 30 ft.

STR	DEX	CON	INT	WIS	CHA
13 (+1)	6 (−2)	16 (+3)	3 (−4)	6 (−2)	5 (−3)

Saving Throws Wis +0
Damage Resistances bludgeoning, piercing, and slashing from
nonmagical attacks

Damage Immunities cold, necrotic, poison; bludgeoning, piercing and slashing from nonmagical attacks (only when in ethereal form)
Condition Immunities poisoned
Senses darkvision 60 ft., passive Perception 8
Languages understand Primordial Notoan and the languages it knew in life but can't speak
Challenge 1 (200 XP)

Dual State. Like its nihileth creator, a nihilethic zombie can assume either a material or ethereal form. When in its material form, it has resistance to nonmagical attacks. In its ethereal form, it is immune to nonmagical attacks. Its ethereal form appears as a dark purple outline of its material form, with a blackish-purple haze within. It can change between the two forms as a bonus action.

Zombie Nature. Unless noted otherwise, a nihilethic zombie has the same traits as a zombie, including their Undead Fortitude.

Actions

***Slam* (material form only).** *Melee Weapon Attack:* +3 to hit, reach 5 ft., one target. *Hit:* 4 (1d6 + 1) bludgeoning damage and the target must succeed on a DC 13 Constitution saving throw or become diseased. The disease has little effect for one minute; during that time, it can be removed by *bless, lesser restoration,* or comparable magic. After one minute, the diseased creature's skin becomes translucent and slimy. The creature cannot regain hit points unless it is at least partially underwater, and the disease can be removed only by *heal* or comparable magic. Unless the creature is either fully submerged or frequently doused with water, it takes 6 (1d12) acid damage every 10 minutes. If a creature dies while diseased, it rises in 2d6 rounds as a nihilethic zombie. This zombie is permanently dominated by the nihileth that commands the attacking zombie.

***Withering Touch* (ethereal form).** *Melee Weapon Attack:* +3 to hit, reach 5 ft., one target. *Hit:* 4 (1d6 + 1) necrotic damage.

Reactions

Sacrifice Life. A nihilethic zombie can sacrifice itself to heal a nihileth within 30 feet of it. All of its remaining hit points transfer to the nihileth in the form of healing. The nihilethic zombie is reduced to 0 hit points and it doesn't make an Undead Fortitude saving throw. A nihileth cannot be healed above its maximum hit points in this manner.

Void Body. The nihilethic zombie can reduce the damage it takes from a single source by 1d12 points. This reduction cannot be applied to radiant damage.

The zombie, nihilethic can be found in ***Tome of Beasts*** by **Kobold Press**.

Appendix B: New Plants, Poisons, and Disease

New Psychoactive Plants

Caustic Thistle

This invasive plant species comes from an unknown planet somewhere in the Void. It occasionally hitches a ride to a new home aboard an asteroid, comet, or meteorite. Under normal conditions, caustic thistle cannot take root in Tehuatl. However, it thrives when embedded in foul, gooey, acidic soil, especially mud created by a nihileth aboleth, which naturally leads scholars to speculate that the monster and plant species may share some commonality in the Void. Caustic thistle quickly sprouts into a six-foot-tall stalk surrounded by one-foot-long razor-sharp, serrated leaves. Small nettles grow along the edges of the leaves, which secrete an acidic irritant to protect the base. The flower blooms into a puffy ball about four inches in diameter. The tufts from the flower fly away on the wind and reseed up to one-half mile away. The plant matures in 2d4 hours after being planted, and it can reproduce from seed to fully-formed plant indefinitely — as long as the soil is extremely acidic. Caustic thistle grows in dense patches, with each individual plant only inches apart from its neighbor.

Moving through a caustic thistle patch proves challenging. For every foot a creature moves through the patch, it must spend four feet of movement. Furthermore, the first time a creature enters the patch on a turn or starts its turn there, the creature must succeed on a DC 10 Dexterity saving throw. It takes 3 (1d6) slashing damage and 2 (1d4) acid damage on a failed save, or half as much damage on a successful one.

Chachacomo

Found only at elevations greater than 11,000 feet (3,352 meters) above sea level, this flowering herb can be crushed between the fingers to release its oil, which is then rubbed onto the skin or clothing. When used in this manner, chachacomo emits a sweet, fragrant aroma that most Aztlis find pleasant. An Aztli or Poqoza wearing chachacomo oil has advantage on Charisma checks made while interacting with a potential romantic interest in a relaxed, casual setting. Chachacomo has no effect on humanoids other than Aztlis and Poqozas, and it provides no benefits when used in combat or during any hostile or tense situation. An ounce of the flowering herb produces enough oil to produce four applications that each last four hours before fading away.

Chachacomotzil

The more plentiful poisonous chachacomotzil usually grows in more easily accessible spots. Because the poisonous and non-poisonous species look, smell, and feel almost identical, it takes a trained eye and a successful DC 10 Intelligence (Nature) check to correctly differentiate between the two plants. Merely brushing against the herb has no detrimental effects. However, coming into even brief physical contact with the oil extracted from poisonous chachacomotzil subjects beasts and humanoids to its toxic properties. The beast or humanoid must make a DC 11 Constitution saving throw or take 3 (1d6) poison damage and become poisoned for one round on a failure or take half as much damage and not be poisoned on a success. A poisoned creature develops a line of raised welts within 1d4 minutes after exposure that last for 24 hours before slowly receding over the next 1d4 days.

Although the welts deal no damage, Aztlis and Poqozas publicly ridicule anyone afflicted with them. They consider the bright red marks to be a blight from the gods, who may be laughing at the person's stinginess for not pay the going rate of five cacao beans for one ounce of the nonpoisonous genuine article or for being too stupid or lazy to avoid the poisonous variety.

Maht

Maht is a highly addictive psychoactive plant originally brought to the island of Tehuatl by the slaughter priests known as Maldraht Maht. It is made by drying a thick black root called maht and is frequently smoked in black coral pipes, though it can also be chewed or soaked in alcohol to create tinctures. When smoked, it smells like anise. Maht users experience extreme hallucinations that frequently cause violent and psychotic outbursts, which is why the slaughter priests hold it sacred and use it before embarking on raids. This also made it prized among more fearsome Poqoza warriors dedicated to Tlatlcolli.

Anyone who consumes maht risks such an episode or may willingly succumb to the full experience. After consumption, the user must make a DC 20 Wisdom saving throw or gain the following traits and features for the next 1d4 hours on a failure or gain the following traits and features except for Addled Mind on a success:

Addled Mind. The creature suffers from terrible hallucinations that inhibit its ability to think clearly and differentiate reality from fantasy. It suffers disadvantage on Intelligence and Wisdom ability checks and saving throws, and suffers from vulnerability to psychic damage.

Curse of Maht. A creature that uses maht becomes addicted and cursed. While the addiction can be treated using conventional means, the curse lasts until it can be lifted with a *remove curse* spell or similar magic. Until the curse is lifted, the creature suffers a maddening urge to use more maht beginning 1d4 days after last using maht. When this urge strikes and the creature does not use maht to satisfy its urge, the creature must make a DC 15 Constitution saving throw or suffer 1d3 levels of exhaustion on a failure or no adverse effects on a success. However, regardless of whether the Constitution saving throw succeeded or failed, a creature who feels the urge to use maht must either succumb to the urge or make another Constitution saving throw every day until the curse is lifted.

Reckless. At the start of its turn, the creature can gain advantage on all melee weapon attack rolls during that turn, but attack rolls against it have advantage until the start of its next turn.

Relentless **(Recharges after a Short or Long Rest).** If the creature takes damage equal or less than four times its proficiency bonus, and if that damage would reduce it to 0 hit points, it is reduced to 1 hit point instead.

Uncanny Strength. The creature has advantage on all Strength ability checks.

When the preceding traits and features end, the user suffers one level of exhaustion regardless of whether it succeeded or failed its Wisdom saving throw. While maht improves a creature's combat abilities, a magical curse enhances maht's highly addictive properties and grants the slaughter priests greater control over the warriors under their command.

Maldraht Maht and maht first appeared in *Razor Coast* by **Frog God Games**.

Shori Huasca

These new fungi originally festered in a planar boundary between the Material Plane and an unknown realm in the far reaches of space. Before the rise of humanity, a meteorite carrying thousands of shori huasca spores hurtled across the cosmos and slammed into the land that would ultimately become Tehuatl. The collision's ecological effects were localized, but the meteorite had a secondary effect as the spores and fungi thrived in its new living conditions. The fungi's peripheral contact with a plane of unbridled chaos from the outer reaches of the universe infused the plant with atomic particles charged with chaotic energy.

The cataclysm that later submerged much of Tehuatl beneath the waves wiped away most visual evidence of the crater, but the fungi miraculously survived its prolonged exposure to water. Indeed, some scholars speculate its watery home further empowered its remarkable properties and greatly expanded the cavern complex that would become the Mulla Chanacu. When the Poqozas stumbled upon the site, the network of tunnels and passages garnered their immediate interest, yet further examination revealed the faint trace of an oblong indentation 300 feet wide and 1,200 feet long. In an even stranger development, the original explorers discovered pale orange fungi growing in a bracket formation on the cavern's damp walls. The plants grew into a shelf-like shape with a sweet, dewy, surface that attracted insects that would invariably become trapped in its sticky slime, providing the fungi with its primary source of nourishment. The intrepid souls who first tasted the fungi found it impossible to resist, though they soon learned that ingesting too much of the curious substance came with maddening consequences. Through trial and error, the inquisitive and daring experimented with eating just the right amount to experience enlightening hallucinations without going insane. Healers also found that an oil derived from the fungus could heal sick and injured warriors.

Eventually, the Poqozas of the Caxcalli Grasslands along with smaller numbers from other areas began sending their teenage children to the Mulla Chanacu to embark on a spirit quest that would guide them on their chosen path in life. A community elder or ticitl first speaks with the adolescent over the course of several days to counsel the burgeoning adult about the significance of the visions they are about to see and how they can then use that knowledge to better their lives. However, they also warn the youngster about enjoying the fungus in moderation to avoid getting what they called "mushroom madness." On most occasions, a parent or older sibling escorts the candidate to the edge of the Mulla Chanacu. From there, the individuals are on their own to explore life's endless possibilities. Most teenagers spend roughly three months in the caves indulging their senses in an effort to derive meaning from their visions. A smaller percentage stay up to a year, while a handful succumb to the mushroom madness and never leave.

The fungus lets people see their world through previously unimaginable lenses. Colors take on new hues, while shapes twist and contort without rhyme or reason. Sounds reverberate, echo, fade, or become contaminated with inescapable static. Touch becomes a visceral experience instead of a tactile examination. Temperatures wildly fluctuate. Tastes and aromas intensify and evolve while the user lapses in and out of reality. The person's emotions naturally respond to the plethora of divergent, exhilarating, and sometimes contradictory stimuli. Shori huasca can help some users reach catharsis when coping with a traumatic or tragic event. Others reach a peaceful moment when forgiveness replaces hate and anger. On rare occasions, a person's emotional scars weigh them down too heavily. The fungus fills their minds with dark thoughts that torment their psyches for the rest of their days. For most though, the rite of passage gives them a better understanding of themselves to prepare them for the adult lives. Shori huasca reveals their inner fears, secret desires, grandest ambitions, and hidden talents. Young people who exhibit artistic ability, creativity, or inquisitive minds frequently enjoy the experience more than all others. On the other hand, those whose lives have been dominated by sadness and tragedy have a much greater risk of walking away from Mulla Chanacu with more emotional baggage than they started.

Shori huasca cannot live outside the crater. The fungus dies within 1d3 days after being removed from the Mulla Chanacu's immediate area. Magical efforts to lengthen its efficacy prove to be short-lived. Spells such as *gentle repose* and *purify food and drink* keep the fungus alive only for a few additional days. The Poqozas have perfected a process to create a nonmagical substance duplicating the effects of one dose of *restorative ointment* using an oil extracted from the fungus. However, the elixir known as orihua must be produced onsite rather than in a controlled environment elsewhere. Those able to craft this elixir guard the formula and procedures with their lives. However, the process takes 1d4 days and requires a successful DC 15 Intelligence check to successfully complete, otherwise the effort is lost. (A creature attempting to create orihua without the proper formula and techniques must succeed on a DC 25 Intelligence check after 2d4 days to successfully craft the elixir. The substance loses its potency in 2d4 + 10 days.

When a character ingests shori huasca, the fungus randomly affects one of its abilities as determined by the following table. The creature experiences the effects of the fungus 1d4 minutes after ingestion. The effects last for one hour afterward.

TABLE B-1: ABILITY AFFECTED BY SHORI HUASCA

1d20	Affected Ability
1	Strength
2–3	Dexterity
4–5	Constitution
6–12	Intelligence
13–18	Wisdom
19–20	Charisma

After determining which ability the fungus affects, the creature next determines the strength of the fungus. In this case, the greater the risk, the greater the reward, though it is impossible for a creature to guarantee the strength of a particular piece of fungus before ingesting it.

TABLE B-2: FUNGUS STRENGTH

1d20	Strength	Saving Throw DC
1–6	Weak	5
7–12	Mild	10
13–16	Moderate	15
17–19	Potent	20
20	Intense	25

After determining the affected ability and strength of the fungus, the creature must then succeed on a saving throw corresponding to the affected ability score against the DC corresponding to its strength. Therefore, if a creature ingests a moderate fungus affecting its Strength, it must then succeed on a DC 15 Strength saving throw to benefit from the shori huasca. On a failed saving throw, the creature suffers one of the following detrimental effects found on **Table B-3** for the next hour.

TABLE B-3: DETRIMENTAL FUNGUS EFFECTS

1d20	Detrimental Effect
1	The creature cannot quickly respond to stimuli. It suffers disadvantage on initiative checks.
2	The creature demonstrates no regard for its wellbeing. Opponents have advantage on their attack rolls against the creature.
3	The creature's speed is halved.
4	The creature screams loudly and makes a racket wherever it goes. Opponents have advantage on Wisdom (Perception) checks relying on hearing to notice the creature.
5	At the end of each of its turns, the creature drops any object it is holding.
6	At the end of each of its turns, the creature falls prone.
7	The creature is blinded.
8	The creature can use an action or a bonus action on its turn but not both.
9	The creature is too terrified to touch another creature. It cannot willingly grapple another creature or make a melee spell attack. If another creature touches the target, the target is automatically frightened until the end of the target's next turn.
10	The creature has disadvantage on ranged attack rolls.
11	The creature cannot understand any spoken or written language.
12	The creature passes out and is incapacitated.
13	The creature treats all terrain as difficult terrain.
14	The creature hallucinates that wispy spirits are tightly coiled around it. The creature is restrained.
15	The creature is stunned.
16	The creature incessantly giggles and cannot speak.
17	The creature gets violently ill and is poisoned.
18	The creature grows paranoid. Each turn, it uses its action to make a melee attack against an imaginary enemy.
19	The creature frenetically fidgets, paces, and frets about its current predicament, causing it to suffer 1d3 levels of exhaustion.
20	Unless restrained or unable to act, each turn the creature uses its action to injure itself, automatically causing 1 point of damage to itself with each attack.

A creature affected by shori huasca is not poisoned. However, the harmful effects of a failed saving throw can be reversed by magic or natural healing that ends the poisoned condition, such as *lesser restoration*.

If a creature succeeds on its saving throw, shori huasca raises its awareness to new heights, giving the creature one or more existential dice, a d4, as shown on **Table B-4**. Within the next one hour, the creature can roll one or more existential dice and add the number(s) rolled to one eligible die roll (ability check, saving throw, or attack roll) based upon the efficacy of the fungus as shown in **Table B-4**. The creature can wait until after it rolls the d20 before deciding to use one or more of its existential dice, but it must decide before it knows whether the rolls succeed or fail. The creature can add more than one existential die to a roll, but it cannot roll additional existential dice after making its initial decision on how many dice to apply to the affected die roll.

TABLE B-4: SHORI HUASCA EFFECTS

Fungus Efficacy	Die Roll(s) Affected	Existential Dice
Weak	ability check	1
Mild	ability check or saving throw	1
Moderate	ability check or saving throw	2
Potent	ability check or saving throw	4
Intense	ability check, saving throw, or attack roll[a]	5

[a] Can only be used where the ability affected by the shori huasca is the same ability that adds its ability score modifier to the attack roll, such as a creature adding its Strength ability modifier to a melee attack roll, or its Charisma ability modifier to a sorcerer's spell attack roll.

After ingesting shori huasca, the character cannot safely do so again until the next dawn. If the character ingests the fungus anyway, the creature gains no beneficial effects from the fungus and is automatically poisoned. A character who is poisoned in this manner must succeed on a DC 10 Constitution saving throw to avoid being afflicted with mushroom madness. A creature suffering from mushroom madness becomes addicted to the fungus, causing it to never willingly leave the Mulla Chanacu. Within the next 1d4 days after a creature afflicted with mushroom madness is unwillingly removed from the Mulla Chanacu, that creature must succeed on a DC 15 Constitution saving throw to recover from the ailment and have no desire to return to the Mulla Chanacu. On a failed saving throw, temptation gets the better of the creature, who does everything in its power to return to the caverns and ingest the mushroom again.

NEW POISON

Orange Lotus Blossom (contact). A creature subjected to this poison must make a DC 12 Constitution saving throw or take 21 (6d6) poison damage and become poisoned on a failure or take half as much poison damage on a success and not be poisoned. The poisoned creature is unconscious. The creature wakes if it takes damage. The poisoned creature must repeat the saving throw every 24 hours, taking 7 (2d6) poison damage on a failed save. Until this poisoned condition ends, the damage the poison deals can't be healed by any means. After three successful saving throws, the effect ends, and the creature can heal normally. The price of a dose of orange blossom lotus is 750 gp.

NEW DISEASE
RABIES

When saliva from an infected creature enters a beast or humanoid, the creature must succeed on a DC 15 Constitution saving throw or become infected with the disease. Symptoms manifest 6d6 days after infection and include a sore throat, fever, and nausea. The infected creature gains one level of exhaustion that cannot be removed until the disease is cured.

At the end of each long rest, an infected creature must succeed on a DC 10 Constitution saving throw. On a failed save, the creature suffers one level of exhaustion and exhibits signs of confusion, increased aggression, and dysphagia. The creature cannot swallow, which prevents it from drinking any liquid, including potions. Whenever the infected creature must make a saving throw or an initiative roll, the creature becomes agitated (50% chance) or confused (50% chance) for one minute. While agitated, the creature must take an attack action each round, if possible, against a randomly determined target it can see. It can take no other action while agitated. The creature moves at up to its speed toward the target and even gains a bonus action to move up to its speed toward that target. A confused creature behaves as if under the influence of a *confusion* spell, though it cannot attempt Wisdom saving throws to end the effect.

Left untreated, rabies has a nearly 100% mortality rate. It can be cured only by a *lesser restoration* or similar magical healing.

Appendix C: New Equipment and Magic Items

New Armor

The bulk of the new armor and shields presented in the following section adheres to the principles of providing lightweight defensive options without compromising stealth and mobility.

Light Armor

While wearing this armor, you add your Dexterity modifier to the base number from your armor type to determine your Armor Class.

Ichcahuipilli. This two-inch-thick light armor resembles a vest designed to protect the wearer's torso from the neck to the hips against arrows and sharp blades. It consists of layers of cotton and vegetable fiber stitched together in a network of interconnected diamond-shaped patterns and then soaked in brine or another saline solution to harden the materials.

Tlahuiztli. Made from cotton or linen supplemented by hide or leather, this light armor covers the wearer's arms and legs and is worn over the ichcahuipilli. Unlike the basic undercoat, the tlahuiztli almost always boasts elaborate decorative features such as feathers, dyes, and other ornamental accoutrements. The armor's intricate and beautiful designs flaunt the wearer's wealth and status, giving the wearer advantage on Charisma checks made when interacting with non-hostile Aztlis. The tlahuiztli presented in **Table C-1** incorporates the underlying ichcahuipilli in its cost, weight, and game statistics.

Medium Armor

While wearing this armor, you add your Dexterity modifier, to a maximum of +2, to the base number from your armor type to determine your Armor Class.

Cipacahuipilli. This unusual armor follows the basic schematics for creating ichcahuipilli armor with a few modifications. Surprisingly, this medium armor is thinner than its lighter counterpart, but the flat pieces of hide and bone strategically sewn into the fabric adequately compensate for its lesser thickness. The armor's name comes from the flat sections of crocodile vertebrae and hide stitched into the material at vulnerable spots to improve toughness without adding tremendous weight and bulkiness. Most importantly, the armor's lack of metallic pieces or parts makes it immune to rust and suitable for druids.

Olli. Armor smiths combine latex and the juice from a morning glory vine to create a flexible and resilient material resembling modern rubber. Although typically used to create the tlatchli, clever innovators use the durable substance to protect warriors from injury. The lightweight suit includes a jacket and leggings. An inner and outer lining of breathable linen provides added comfort. While wearing this armor, you reduce any falling damage you take by 5 points, though you cannot reduce the falling damage below 0. Because it is made from plant-based products, druids are permitted to wear olli, and it is immune to rust. Furthermore, you do not have disadvantage on Constitution saving throws against the effects the extreme heat.

Heavy Armor

Heavy armor does not let you add your Dexterity modifier to your Armor Class, but it also does not penalize you if your Dexterity modifier is negative.

Ollixalli. One day, Atoyapaca, an innovative botanist and renowned jeweler, heated olli and combined it with ground quartz to enhance its strength. His bold experiment exceeded his wildest expectations, leading others to follow in his footsteps by adding other silica-based and sulfurous components to the liquified olli mixture. The delicate and laborious process of creating ollixalli is a tightly guarded secret confined to those who have the technical expertise and specialized equipment required to set the ollixalli mold. Unlike conventional heavy armor, a suit of ollixalli consists of a lightweight jacket and pants that protect the torso and limbs. Ollixalli has no metal components, making it suitable for druids and immune to rust. While wearing ollixalli armor, you do not have disadvantage on Constitution saving throws made against the effects of extreme heat. Because of the specialized training and equipment needed to create ollixalli, the armor remains extremely expensive and rare.

New Weapons

Atlatl. This easily made wooden device uses javelins for ammunition. To use this javelin launcher, you must place the javelin's butt into a cup, groove, or spur at the top of the atlatl. With your forearm perpendicular to your arm and the atlatl and javelin both parallel to the ground, you let the javelin rest atop your fingers while you hold the atlatl's base in the palm of your hand. When you are ready to release the javelin, you fling your forearm and wrist forward, which in turn pushes the javelin out of your hand toward the intended target.

Itztopilli. This axe has a wooden haft with a bronze head fitted into a groove built into the haft. The head is long and narrow, and its cutting surface is only slightly wider than the axe's flat back. The itztopilli's versatile design allows you to hack into flesh as well as chop wood with remarkable accuracy and comparable ease. Indeed, most woodworkers incorporate the weapon into a standard set of carpenter's tools. If you are proficient with the itztopilli, and you made an attack roll with the weapon within the last 24 hours, you also gain proficiency with carpenter's tools.

Macuahuitl. Made from hardwood such as oak, this weapon resembles a long, flat paddle with obsidian or flint chips embedded into the weapon's edges. The insertion of these incredibly sharp stones gives the weapon unmatched cutting power at the cost of increased fragility. When you attack a creature with this weapon and roll a 20 on the attack roll, you score a critical hit as normal and deal an extra effect if the attack roll hits the target by 10 or more. The creature struck loses 1d8 hit points at the start of each of its turns due to the blade gouging a deep laceration through the creature's flesh. The damage increases by 1d8 if you inflict another deep laceration during a subsequent attack. Any creature within five feet can take an action to stanch the deep laceration with a successful DC 10 Wisdom (Medicine) check. The deep laceration also closes if the target receives magical healing.

When you attack a creature with this weapon and roll a 1 on the attack roll, you may damage the weapon. If your attack missed by 10 or more, the weapon is damaged. You have disadvantage on your attack roll with a damaged weapon, and you cannot inflict a deep laceration with a damaged macuahuitl. If you damage an already damaged weapon, you break the weapon, rendering

---

Keep it Simple or Realistic?

The following sections present new armor and weapons that share many similarities yet have some noteworthy differences from commonly found armor and weapons. You have two options when dealing with the new armor and weapons presented here. You can choose to keep this section simple by retaining the descriptive entries for the armor and weapons while assigning them the same game statistics and costs as existing armor. Alternatively, you can use the costs, game statistics, and special abilities presented below in their entirety. It is recommended that you adopt a consistent approach to handling the armor and weapons rather than treating some items as currently existing armor and weapon types while incorporating the special rules for other items. If you opt for the simple choice, the equivalent existing item appears as the last entry in **Tables C-1** and **C-2**.

Table C-1: Tehuatl Armor

Armor	Cost	Armor Class (AC)	Strength	Stealth	Weight	Equivalent
Light Armor						
Ichcahuipilli	15 gp	11 + Dex modifier	—	—	4 lbs.	padded
Tlahuiztli	200 gp	12 + Dex modifier	—	—	6 lbs.	studded leather
Medium Armor						
Cipacahuipilli	35 gp	13 + Dex modifier (max 2)	—	Disadvantage	15 lbs.	hide
Olli	75 gp	13+ Dex modifier (max 2)	—	—	12 lbs.	chain shirt
Heavy Armor						
Ollixalli	1,000 gp	16	—	Disadvantage	25 lbs.	chain mail

Table C-2: Tehuatl Weapons

Weapon	Cost	Damage	Weight	Properties	Equivalent
Simple Melee Weapons					
Itztopilli	4 gp	1d6 slashing	2 lbs.	Light, special, thrown (range 20/60)	Handaxe
Tecpatl	2 gp	1d4 piercing	1 lb.	Finesse, light, special	Dagger
Simple Ranged Weapon					
Atlatl	1 sp	—	1 lb.	Ammunition (range 60/240), special	None
Martial Melee Weapons					
Macuahuitl	10 gp	1d8 slashing	2 lbs.	Special, versatile (1d10)	Longsword
Ollitetlacotl	35 gp	1d6 bludgeoning	1 lb.	light	Mace
Tepoztopilli	25 gp	1d10 slashing	6 lbs.	Heavy, reach, special, two-handed	Halberd

it useless. You can repair a damaged but not broken weapon with a successful DC 12 Dexterity check made with carpenter's tools or jeweler's tools. Casting the *mending* cantrip repairs a damaged or broken weapon.

Ollitetlacotl. This hardened rubber club is difficult to manufacture yet greatly valued among Aztli warriors for its lightweight punching power. Because of its unusual components and unique feel, the weapon requires more skill and training to wield than an ordinary club.

Tecpatl. Carved from flint or obsidian, this double-edged knife has a pointed tip and a decorative wooden, stone, or mosaic handle. Although an effective, close-quarters combat weapon, the tecpatl is predominately used in religious rites and revered for its multitude of symbolic roles. When used in battle, it may open a deep laceration in the same manner as described under the **macuahuitl** entry (see above). However, because the knife itself is made entirely of flint or obsidian, the weapon irreparably breaks instead of being damaged when you miss by 10 or more after rolling a 1 on your attack roll with the weapon.

Tepoztopilli. This polearm has two components: a five- to six-foot-long wooden shaft carved from a single piece of wood and an oblong wooden head attached to the end of the shaft. The head ends in a sharp point, and like the macuahuitl, obsidian fragments are glued into grooves cut into the head to increase its deadly cutting power. When used in battle, it may open a deep laceration as described under the **macuahuitl** entry (see above). However, because such a blow requires greater precision than the macuahuitl, you inflict a deep laceration only when you hit by 15 or more when you roll a 20 on your attack roll. Likewise, because the surface area is much smaller than the macuahuitl, you damage the weapon only when you miss by 15 or more when you roll a 1 on your attack roll.

New Codex

Cahuotl's Journal

This nonmagical medical diary written in Aztli describes advanced techniques for diagnosing illness. If you spend 48 hours over a period of six days or fewer memorizing the book's diagrams and following its diagnostic protocols, you may attempt a DC 15 Wisdom (Medicine) check. On a success, you gain advantage on Wisdom (Medicine) checks made to diagnose an illness for one year. On a failed check, you learn nothing from the experience and cannot try to read the book again for one year. When the one-year period lapses, you may reread the book. If you previously succeeded on your Wisdom (Medicine) check to understand the book's contents, you gain advantage on your new Wisdom (Medicine) check. If you previously failed your Wisdom (Medicine) check to absorb the book's information, you suffer disadvantage on your new check. If you have both succeeded and failed on the preceding check in earlier years, you make your Wisdom (Medicine) check normally.

Magic Items

Death Whistle
Wondrous item, uncommon

This item has three charges. You can use an action and expend a charge to emit a horrific sound resembling hundreds of terrified voices screaming in unison in a 20-foot cone that is audible 400 feet away. Each humanoid in the cone must succeed on a DC 12 Wisdom saving throw or take 2d6 psychic damage and become frightened for one minute. On a successful Wisdom saving throw, the creature takes half as much damage, is not frightened, and becomes immune to the effects of this *death whistle* for 24 hours. Deafened creatures and creatures immune to being frightened take no psychic damage and are not frightened. A creature that fails its Wisdom saving throw can repeat it at the end of each of its turns, ending the effect on itself on a success. The *death whistle* regains 1d3 expended charges daily at dawn.

Helm of the Ebon Serpent
Wondrous item, rare (requires attunement)

Fashioned in the shape of a lashing serpent's head, this light helm is crafted from lacquered wicker covered in black snakeskin. The wearer's face is framed by a gaping mouth with fangs in each corner. A crest of ebony colored feathers adorns the top and runs down the neck.

While wearing the helm, you can use an action to spit venom at a creature within 15 feet of you as a ranged attack dealing 4d8 poison damage, and the target must make a successful DC 15 Constitution saving throw or be blinded and poisoned. At the end of each of its turns, the target can attempt another saving throw. If the saving throw succeeds, the target is no longer blinded or poisoned. When you spit venom three times, you cannot do so again until the next dawn.

Lucky Fingers

Wondrous Item, uncommon

These hideous trinkets appear to be a collection of 1d4 dried human finger bones held together only by hard, dry cartilage. They are usually found tied in a bundle hanging from a leather cord or stuffed in a pouch. You may use a bonus action to snap a bone in two, which gives you advantage on your next ability check, saving throw, or attack roll made before the end of your next turn. When snapped, the magic in that digit is released, rendering it worthless.

Macuahuitl of Revealing

Weapon (macuahuitl), very rare

You gain a +2 bonus to attack and damage rolls made with this magic weapon.

When you hit a shapechanger with this weapon, the shapechanger takes an extra 3d6 damage of the weapon type, and it must succeed on a DC 15 Constitution saving throw or revert to its original form. The shapechanger cannot assume a different form for one minute after it fails its Constitution saving throw. Legends claim the hero-gods used these weapons to unmask the emperor's serpent-advisors.

Macuahuitl of Quiahuitl

Weapon (macuahuitl), rare (requires attunement by a cleric or paladin who serves Quiahuitl)

This machuahuitl is carved from heavily lacquered dark wood and set with rows of gleaming obsidian teeth. The flats of the club bear engravings of a serpent coiled around a cornstalk set above a flooded plain. A tightly wrapped snakeskin covers a long wooden handle tipped with a collection of six heron feathers dyed orange and blue that dangle from a woven string.

You gain a +1 bonus to attack and damage rolls made with this magic weapon. As a bonus action, the weapon deals 1d4 necrotic damage to you by siphoning off a portion of your lifeforce as a sacrifice to Quiahuitl. When you do so, the weapon deals an extra 1d6 radiant damage until the end of your turn. You do not deal extra damage if you have resistance or immunity to necrotic damage.

Mask of Quiahuitl

Wondrous Item, rare (requires attunement by a cleric or paladin who serves Quiahuitl)

This stylized mask of lacquered ebon wood has long fangs and wide eyehole carvings that make the wearer appear to have oversized, bulging eyeballs. The mask is topped with an elaborate headdress made from heron feathers. While wearing the mask, you can see through a lightly or heavily obscured area caused by foul weather such as fog, rain, sleet, wind, and other forms of precipitation.

As an action, you can use the mask to gaze at a creature you can see within 30 feet. The target of your gaze must succeed on a DC 12 Wisdom saving throw. On a failed saving throw, the creature is either frightened for one minute or affected by a *command* spell (your choice). After using the mask three times in this manner, you cannot do so again until the next dawn.

Pamitl of Combat Coordination

Wondrous item, rare

Brightly colored feathers adorn the top of this lightweight wooden pole that is strapped to your back. While you carry the pamitl in this manner, you can use a bonus action on your turn to cause its feathers to instantly shift places. Each companion within 60 feet who can see you and has not yet taken a turn in combat may swap their place in the initiative order with another affected companion for the remainder of the combat. For example, if your companions rolled a 17, 13, and 10 on their initiative checks and have not yet taken a turn in combat, you can use this feature to allow them to rearrange which of them acts on initiative count 17, initiative count 13, and initiative count 10. A creature cannot take a turn on more than one initiative count nor take more than one turn in a round. The pamitl cannot be used this way again until the next dawn.

Pumpkin Seed

Wondrous item, uncommon

You can use an action to eat a pumpkin seed. When you do so, your eyes emit a faint, yellowish glow and shed dim light in a 20-foot cone for 10 minutes. An undead or fiend that first enters the cone or starts its turn within the cone must make a DC 12 Wisdom saving throw. On a failure it takes 2d6 radiant damage while on a success, it takes half as much damage. In addition, you can use your action to end the faint, yellowish glow and instead cause your eyes to emit a blinding flash of pure light in a 20-foot cone that lasts until the end of your turn when the seed's effects end. Each creature within the cone must succeed on a DC 12 Constitution saving throw or be blinded. Undead and fiends have disadvantage on their Constitution saving throw against being blinded. At the end of each of its turns, a creature blinded by the preceding effect can make another Constitution saving throw. On a success, the creature is no longer blinded.

Sandals of the Mitote

Wondrous item, uncommon (requires attunement)

These durable sandals are made from maguey fibers and have woven fabric straps that fasten the shoes to your feet. While you wear these sandals, you have advantage on Charisma (Performance) checks made to dance. In addition, you can move through a hostile creature's space regardless of its size, though you still treat the space as difficult terrain, and you cannot willingly end your move in its space. If your movement provokes an opportunity attack, make a Charisma (Performance) check contested by the hostile creature's Strength check. If you win the contest, that creature cannot make an opportunity attack against you for the rest of your turn.

Seal of Miquito

Wondrous item, very rare (requires attunement by a celestial or fiend)

This strange stone vessel is circular shaped, about six inches in diameter and three inches tall. The sides bear thousands of ancient runes, while a grinning skull is carved into the top. The seal separates into two pieces and feels unusually light as it is hollow. As an action, the seal's celestial or fiendish owner can force the soul of any humanoid that it can see within 100 feet of it to depart its body and enter the seal. The target resists being possessed with a successful DC 20 Charisma saving throw, which also prevents the owner from trying to possess the target for 24 hours. On a failed saving throw, the target's soul leaves the body and is trapped within the seal. Once used in this way, the seal cannot be used again for seven days.

The target's body falls into a catatonic state. If the seal is destroyed and the target's body is less than 100 feet away from the seal and is still alive, the soul returns to the body and the target regains consciousness. Otherwise, the target dies. The seal cannot contain more than one soul at any time. If another soul already occupies the seal, the attempt to possess another soul automatically fails. The owner can free a trapped soul from the seal as an action. A celestial uses this magic item to bring a worthy soul to its just rewards in the afterlife. Fiends use the seal to sacrifice unwilling souls to their fiendish masters or a malevolent deity.

Serpent Shield

Armor (shield), uncommon

This small, round shield is crafted from a wicker and wood frame covered with lacquer and serpent's skin and adorned with feathers and various patterns of color to denote the status upon whoever carries it. You gain a +1 bonus to AC while you wield this shield, and you have advantage on Charisma (Intimidation) checks. This bonus is in addition to the shield's normal bonus to AC.

Tilmahtli of the Owl

Wondrous item, very rare (requires attunement)

This dark linen cloak bears the image of an owl with outstretched wings stitched onto the fabric. While wearing it, you can use an action to grip the edges of the cloak with both hands and raise and lower them to simulate an owl in flight. When you do so in an area of bright light or dim light, you cast an ominous shadow in a 20-foot cone. Each creature within the cone must succeed on a DC 15 Wisdom saving throw or take 5d6 psychic damage and be haunted by an intangible, malevolent owl spirit that has no physical form. Creatures with an Intelligence score of 4 or less are not affected. On a successful Wisdom saving throw, the creature takes half as much damage and is not haunted.

A haunted creature senses the owl spirit's presence hovering over its head even though nothing is actually there. Each time the haunted creature takes damage from a source other than this effect, it takes an extra 1d6 psychic damage and it cannot take reactions until the end of its next turn. At the end of each of its turns, a haunted creature can make another Wisdom saving throw. (A haunted creature who took psychic damage since the end of its last turn has disadvantage on this Wisdom saving throw.) On a successful Wisdom saving throw, the creature is no longer haunted. You cannot use the tilmahtli again in this way until the next dawn.

War Paint

Wondrous item, rarity varies

Typically stored in clay jars two inches in diameter, each container holds 1d3 applications of viscous pigments made from dyes and other colorful components. Each jar contains one color of paint, and its contents weigh a half pound. As an action, one dose of war paint can be rubbed onto the skin. The pigment covers roughly six square inches of skin. A creature can wear no more than three different colors of paint at a time, and you cannot simultaneously apply the effects of more than one color of *war paint* to the same creature. Any attempt to apply more than three colors of war paint fails. Each application of paint lasts for 10 minutes regardless of color. The *war paint*'s color determines its effects.

Black (rare): Necromantic energy fills your soul. You can use a bonus action on each of your turns to condemn each creature other than an undead or construct that can see or hear you within 30 feet. Each targeted creature must make a DC 15 Constitution saving throw. On a failed saving throw, the creature takes 3d10 necrotic damage and the creature's hit point maximum is reduced by an amount equal to the necrotic damage it took from this effect. This reduction lasts until the target finishes a long rest. The target dies if this effect reduces its hit point maximum to 0. On a successful saving throw, the target takes half as much necrotic damage and is immune to this *war paint*'s effects for 24 hours.

Blue (uncommon): A frigid chill courses through your body. While your wear this war paint, you can use an action to cause one weapon you are holding to coat itself in frost. The icy coating is harmless to you and the weapon. When you hit with an attack using the frosty weapon, the target takes an extra 1d6 cold damage.

Green (uncommon): Nothing can hold you back. You cannot be restrained or paralyzed. You can use five feet of your movement to automatically escape a grapple.

Xtabentun

Wondrous item, very rare

This fermented beverage made from honey, tree bark, and corn allows the drinker to momentarily defy reality. When found, a vial contains 1d3+1 one-ounce doses of the prized liqueur. You can use an action to drink a dose. The effects last for one minute. The instant you swallow it, you experience a sense of euphoria. You gain 10 temporary hit points and become immune to being frightened. In addition, you can use your reaction to enter a transcendental state until the end of your next turn when *xtabentun*'s effects suddenly end. When you use the magical elixir in this way, you gain resistance to all damage and advantage on all saving throws. Any harmful abilities or magical effects that would affect you while you have resistance do not take effect until the liqueur's magic wears off. If you can counteract the harmful ability or magical effect in the interim, you negate the harmful ability or magical effect in its entirety.

APPENDIX D: NEW SPELLS

BARD SPELLS

WAR CRY

2nd-level enchantment
Casting Time: 1 action
Range: 30 feet
Components: V, S
Duration: 1 round

Your war cry whips your allies into a frenzy. Choose up to three creatures within range. When a target hits with a melee weapon attack using Strength, the target adds your Charisma modifier (minimum of 1) to the damage roll. In addition, each target has resistance to bludgeoning, piercing, and slashing damage.

At Higher Levels. When you cast this spell using a spell slot of 3rd level or higher, you can target one additional creature for each slot level above 2nd.

CLERIC SPELLS

BLOODBATH

1st-level transmutation
Casting Time: 1 action
Range: 30 feet
Components: V, S, M (a drop of your own blood)
Duration: Instantaneous

You create 10 gallons of blood within range in an open container. Alternatively, the blood splashes onto all creatures and objects in a 30-foot cube within range. The blood extinguishes exposed flames in the area and is identical in composition to your own blood. Each creature within the area must succeed on a Wisdom saving throw or drop whatever it is holding and be disgusted. Until the end of your next turn, a disgusted creature cannot willingly move closer to you and averts its eyes from you, preventing it from seeing you. Creatures that cannot be frightened are still doused in blood but are otherwise not affected by this spell.

COUNTERATTACK

1st-level divination
Casting Time: 1 action
Range: Touch
Components: V, S
Duration: 1 minute

You touch a willing creature. Once before the spell ends, the target can use its reaction to make a melee attack against an opponent within reach that missed the target with a melee attack. The target's counterattack must take place during the same turn as the missed melee attack. If one or more of the target's allies are within five feet of the creature the target is attacking with its counterattack, the target has advantage on the attack roll. The spell then ends.

FLAY SKIN

3rd-level transmutation
Casting Time: 1 action
Range: 30 feet
Components: V, S, M (an obsidian chip)
Duration: Instantaneous

Choose a creature other than an undead or construct you can see within range. The target must make a Constitution saving throw. On a failure, it takes 8d6 slashing damage and has portions of its skin flayed from its body. On a successful save, the creature takes half as much damage and its skin is not flayed. Creatures with flayed skin that have natural armor take a –2 penalty to AC. In addition, these creatures become vulnerable to acid, cold, fire, and lightning damage. A creature can take an action to repair the flayed skin with a successful Wisdom (Medicine) check against your spell save DC. The skin also mends itself if the target receives magical healing.

FLORAL BOUQUET

2nd-level conjuration
Casting Time: 1 action
Range: 120 feet
Components: V, S, M (a flower bulb)
Duration: Instantaneous

A flower bulb streaks from your pointing finger to a point you choose within range and then bursts open and releases floral aromas and pungent scents. Each creature in a 20-foot-radius sphere centered on that point must succeed on a Constitution saving throw or be stunned by the sensory overload. A creature that has advantage on Wisdom (Perception) checks that rely on smell, such as the Keen Smell trait, has disadvantage on its Constitution saving throw. At the end of each of its turns, a stunned creature can make another Constitution saving throw. Creatures with the Keen Smell trait still suffer disadvantage on this Constitution saving throw. On a success, the creature is no longer stunned.

JAGUAR SPIRIT

3rd-level evocation
Casting Time: 1 bonus action
Range: 60 feet
Components: V, S, M (a jaguar tooth or claw)
Duration: Concentration, up to 1 minute

You conjure into existence a floating, spectral jaguar that appears within range and lasts for the whole duration. When you cast the spell, you can make a melee spell attack against a creature within five feet of the jaguar. On a hit, the target takes 3d6 force damage and is grappled (escape DC equals your spell save DC). A creature that starts its turn already grappled by the jaguar takes 3d6 force damage.

As a bonus action on your turn, you can move the jaguar up to 20 feet and repeat the attack against a creature within five feet of it. If the jaguar moves at least 20 feet straight toward a creature right before biting it, the target must succeed on a Strength check against your spell save DC or be knocked prone.

At Higher Levels. When you cast this spell using a spell slot of 4th level or higher, the damage increases by 1d6 for every two slot levels above 3rd.

Palpitating Heart

6th-level illusion
Casting Time: 1 action
Range: 60 feet
Components: V, S, M (a mummified animal heart)
Duration: Concentration, up to 1 minute

Choose a creature other than an undead or construct that you can see within range. A spectral hand reaches into that creature's torso and appears to rip out the creature's still beating heart or other vital organ, which then instantly appears in your hand. Blood and other bodily fluids gush out of the creature's chest. The illusion is perceivable only to you and the target. The target must succeed on a Wisdom saving throw. On a failed Wisdom saving throw, the target believes the illusion is real, causing it to be stunned for the duration. At the end of each of the target's turns before the spell ends, the target must succeed on a Wisdom saving throw. When it fails its first Wisdom saving throw at the end of its turn, the target becomes unconscious. When it fails the next Wisdom saving throw at the end of its turn, the target drops to 0 hit points and is dying.

On a successful Wisdom saving throw, the spell ends. Stunned creatures and unconscious creatures are no longer stunned or unconscious. Dying creatures remain in their current state.

Strength in Numbers

2nd-level transmutation
Casting Time: 1 action
Range: Self
Components: V, S, M (a strand of silk from a spider's web)
Duration: 1 round

You draw upon the might of others to empower yourself. When you cast this spell, add the combined Strength modifiers (even if it is 0 or a negative number) of up to three companions that you can see within 10 feet of you to your own Strength modifier until the end of your next turn. If a companion moves more than 10 feet away from you before this spell ends, you immediately lose that creature's Strength modifier for the whole duration.

At Higher Levels. When you cast this spell using a spell slot of 3rd level or higher, you can draw upon the strength of one additional creature for every spell slot above 2nd.

Druid Spells

Flesh to Maize

6th-level transmutation
Casting Time: 1 action
Range: 60 feet
Components: V, S, M (an ear of maize)
Duration: Concentration, up to 1 minute

You attempt to turn one creature that you can see within range into the form of a maize plant, though it retains its creature type throughout the metamorphosis. If the target's body is made of flesh, the creature must succeed on a Constitution saving throw or the target drops everything it is holding and is restrained while its flesh begins to transform into fibrous plant material. Its legs start to turn into roots and a lower stem; its torso into a central stalk; its arms into leaves; and its head into an ear of maize. On a successful save, the creature is not affected. The spell also has no effect on a creature with 0 hit points.

A creature restrained by this spell must make another Constitution saving throw at the end of each of its turns. If it successfully saves against this spell three times, the spell ends. If it fails its saves three times, it is turned into maize for the duration. The successes and failures do not have to be consecutive. You keep track of both until the subject accumulates either three successes or three failures.

A target transformed in this manner has the following traits. The target is incapacitated, and it automatically fails Strength and Dexterity saving throws. Attack rolls against the creature have advantage, and any attack that hits the creature is a critical hit if the attacker is within five feet of the creature. The target is unaware of its surroundings. It continues to age and is wholly dependent upon sunlight and water for nourishment. Its roots burrow into any suitable material beneath it, making the creature immune to the prone condition as well. A creature transformed while atop any solid surface such as wood or stone stands in place, though it may still be knocked prone. The creature's gear melds into its new form, but it cannot activate, use, wield, or otherwise benefit from any of its equipment.

If you maintain your concentration on this spell for the entire possible duration, the creature is turned into maize until the effect is removed. Any spell or effect that ends the petrified condition also removes this effect.

Nohpalli

1st-level evocation
Casting Time: 1 action
Range: 90 feet
Components: V, S, M (a cactus needle)
Duration: Instantaneous

A four-inch-diameter cactus ball with one-inch-long needles streaks toward a target in range. Make a ranged spell attack against the target. On a hit, the target takes 2d8 piercing damage and the ball sticks to the target. The target or another creature within five feet of the target can use an action to remove the cactus ball. Unless removed, the target takes 1d8 piercing damage at the end of each of its next two turns.

At Higher Levels. When you cast this spell using a spell slot of 2nd level or higher, the initial damage increases by 1d8 for each slot level above 1st level, while the secondary damage increases by 1d8 for every two slot levels above 1st.

Sorcerer Spells

Slither

1st-level transmutation
Casting Time: 1 action
Range: Touch
Components: V, S, M (a sloughed snake skin)
Duration: 1 minute

You touch a creature. Crawling does not cost the target an extra foot of movement for each foot traveled, and the target can squeeze through a space that is large enough for a creature two sizes smaller than it. While prone, the target does not have disadvantage on attack rolls, and enemies within five feet of it do not have advantage on their attack rolls against the target.

Wall of Smoke

2nd-level evocation
Casting Time: 1 action
Range: 120 feet
Components: V, S, M (a small piece of copal)
Duration: Concentration, up to 1 minute

You create a wall of thick, black smoke on a solid surface within range. You can make the wall up to 60 feet long, 20 feet high, and five feet thick, or a ringed wall up to 20 feet in diameter, 20 feet high, and five feet thick. The wall is opaque and cannot be dispersed by high winds despite being composed of wispy vapors. It is also difficult terrain.

If the wall cuts through a creature's space when it appears, the creature within its area must make a Constitution saving throw. On a failed Constitution saving throw, a creature takes 2d8 necrotic damage and is blinded by the smoke. The creature takes half as much damage on a successful Constitution saving throw and is not blinded. A creature who enters the wall for the first time on a turn or starts its turn there must make a Constitution saving throw. It takes 2d8 necrotic damage and is blinded by the smoke on a failure. The creature takes half as much damage on a successful Constitution saving throw and is not blinded. At the end of each of its turns, a blinded creature can make another Constitution saving throw. On a success, the creature is no longer blinded.

At Higher Levels. When you cast this spell using a spell slot of 3rd level or higher, the damage increases by 1d8 for each slot level above 2nd.

Wizard Spells

Bumble

Transmutation cantrip
Casting Time: 1 reaction, which you take in response to a creature you can see within 30 feet initially attempting to interact with an object
Range: 30 feet
Components: V, S, M (a drop of oil)
Duration: Instantaneous

A creature of your choice that you can see within range must succeed on a Dexterity saving throw or its initial attempt to interact with an object fails, as if the attempt never happened. If the target used an action to interact with the object, the action is lost. The target cannot attempt to interact with the same object again until the end of your next turn. This spell affects only a creature's first attempt to interact with an object rather than ending an existing interaction. For instance, the spell can prevent the target from drawing a weapon from its sheath or picking a weapon up from the ground, but it cannot cause the target to drop a weapon it is holding in its hand.

The spell prevents the target from interacting with the same object for a longer period of time at higher levels: 2 rounds at 5th level, 3 rounds at 11th level, and 4 rounds at 17th level.

Stumble

Evocation cantrip
Casting Time: 1 action
Range: 30 feet
Components: V, S
Duration: Instantaneous

A creature of your choice that you can see within range must make a Dexterity saving throw. On a failure, it falls prone. On a successful Dexterity saving throw, the target is not affected, and you cannot use this cantrip against it again for 24 hours.

You can target additional creatures when you reach higher levels: two creatures at 5th level, three creatures at 11th level, and four creatures at 17th level.

Time in a Bottle

4th-level transmutation
Casting Time: 1 bonus action
Range: Self
Components: V
Duration: Concentration, up to 1 minute

You save a brief moment of time for future use. Before the spell ends, you can use your reaction to immediately take an extra turn, interrupting the current turn. When you finish your extra turn, the spell ends.

Triplicate

3rd-level illusion
Casting Time: 1 action
Range: 60 feet
Components: V, S
Duration: 1 minute

Three illusory duplicates of yourself, which you can use as the origin point for your spells, appear at unoccupied points you can see within range. Neither you nor the duplicate can occupy the same space. The duplicates last for the duration or until you cast this spell again, cast another spell that creates duplicates of yourself (such as *mirror image*), or use an action to dismiss the illusory duplicates.

The duplicates imitate your actions but remain stationary. As a bonus action on your turn, you can move one of your duplicates up to 20 feet. A duplicate more than 60 feet away from you is immediately destroyed.

Creatures who see you when you cast this spell can track your position unless you conceal your exact location afterward. Otherwise, a creature who examines a duplicate can determine it is a duplicate with a successful Intelligence (Investigation) check against your spell save DC. A duplicate's AC equals 10 + your Dexterity modifier. If an attack hits a duplicate, the duplicate is destroyed. A duplicate can be destroyed only by an attack that hits it. It ignores all other damage and effects. The spell ends when all three duplicates are destroyed.

When you cast a spell, you can designate one of your duplicates as another spell's point of origin, treating it as if it were yourself when determining range, available targets, and its spell attack roll. Weapon attack rolls made by a duplicate automatically miss. You must be able to see the duplicate as well as any targets and areas the other spell affects. If you cannot do so, the other spell fails and is lost.

www.ingramcontent.com/pod-product-compliance
Lightning Source LLC
Chambersburg PA
CBHW042103160726
48295CB00017B/973